Divine Intervention

Terry Wilcock

WOODBRIDGE
PUBLISHERS

Forest House, 3rd Floor 16-20

Clements Road Unit #2048

Ilford, IG1 1BA

Copyright © 2024 Terry Wilcock

ISBN 978-1-917526-23-4

ISBN 978-1-917526-24-1

ISBN 978-1-917526-22-7

All rights reserved

This novel is entirely a work of fiction. The names, characters and incidents portrayed in it are the work of the author's own imagination. Any resemblance to actual persons, living or dead, locations or events is purely coincidental.

No part of this publication may be reproduced, stored in a retrieval system, copied in any form or by any means, electronic, mechanical, photocopying, recording or otherwise transmitted without written permission from the publisher. You must not circulate this book in any format.

Cover Design by Woodbridge Publishers.

Dedicated to a man of honour and extraordinary integrity. Clive Freeman, an innocent man in his 37th year incarcerated for a murder that never was. Please search and support.

FREE CLIVE FREEMAN.

Preface

I was told at a very young age that to escape the concrete jungle you had 3 options:
1: To be sufficiently educated and focused,
2: To be streetwise, shrewd and fearless and,
3: Just lucky.

In the alleyways and street corners, playing cards, and tossing coins, it was inevitably the start of what forced me into the dumb decision of dedicating my life to option two, which would lead me onto a rollercoaster of lows and highs, of joy and misery, of aggression, fear and relief, joys of winning and pain of losing.

Regrets, I have more than a few, but I hope now, in my twilight years, I am making those that matter proud of me.

Read and believe if you want to, it makes for better reading.

God bless.

— *T. Wilcock*

Foreword

Already there are questions about how much of this book is actually real.

What aspects are truth or fiction?

When asked, Mr Wilcock replied, "C'mon, think about it, I've done enough prison time not to write my own death sentence, because that's exactly what it would be, I would die in prison, I'm 62 for Christ's sake. Having said that, All the people and places are real, the time and travel are real. Think of it as you will and let's compromise by calling it Faction."

Arrivals: Luton Airport

2.22 pm, Tuesday
6th November 2000

The Tannoy announced the arrival of flight LT 6228 from Malaga.

"Perfect," mouthed Barry under his breath. He had been anxious that a delay could be on the cards due to bad weather.

It shouldn't be long now, and Jerry will be through. No luggage—that's always a bonus for a fast track.

"Just time to make a call," he decided, walking over to the row of public phones by the exit. He dialled the number. No response.

"Fuck it!" he looked agitated. He would have to compose himself. Jerry doesn't usually miss a trick.

"Here he is now," Barry observed, catching his friend's eye as he walked towards the exit. There was no need for greetings. Jerry would follow him, and that would be sufficient. The black Mercedes 600 SEL was parked by the passenger exit. The driver glanced at Barry, then started the engine.

Seconds later, Jerry sauntered through the tinted glass electric doors, collar up, holding an in-flight magazine over his head with one hand while the other gripped his shoulder bag. He upped his pace to catch up with Barry, who was now nearing the Merc.

"How you doing?" he said, nipping his friend's rump as he came up behind him.

"Good, how was your flight?"

"Fucking lousy. Turbulence! And what with this bleeding weather; Jesus!"

"I know, c'mon, get in. You get in the back," Barry ordered, opening the door. You can talk to Venga."

"I'm saying fuck-all in this car. Has he had it swept?"

"I'm not sure."

"Well, we'll stop somewhere for a coffee, and you can fill me in," said Jerry, greeting Venga, as was customary, with a kiss on each cheek, before sliding through the open door and into the black leather seat.

"How was your flight?" enquired the Turk—all twenty-three stone of him squeezed behind the lowered picnic table. Three phones were laid out on the small mahogany table, each a different colour. Jerry was quick to note a list of what presumably were phone numbers placed in front of the fat man.

"Not the best," he grunted.

"The boys are on the A…" Venga stopped short as Jerry nudged his capacious stomach with his elbow and held his finger to his lips.

"We'll stop for coffee," he said

"Perfect." growled Venga as he pressed a small intercom button on the central console, "M1 South," he instructed the driver through the glass partition. He then pressed another button, which piped out music through unseen speakers.

"What the fuck is this?" said Barry, sitting to the left of Jerry.

"This is my music! You no like?" grinned Venga, glancing sideways past Jerry towards Barry with a smile that showed yellow, decaying teeth. "Without the Village People moustache," murmured Jerry to himself. "They would look even yellower!"

The traffic flowed nicely, "Let's visit the Hatfield Country Inn at Potters Bar," ventured Barry. This wasn't a problem—they had time on their hands. Twenty minutes later, they were all seated round a small table in a quiet corner.

"Alright, let me have it," said Jerry.

"OK, my friend, everything is under control. The boys are on schedule. I spoke to them 2 hours ago, and they were at The Scotch Corner of the A plus one," Jerry smiled at his mistake.

"The A1, not the A plus one," he laughed. "And what time's the meet?"

"5 o'clock."

"Good—what's our position?"

"We are simply there to observe. McFadden may want to speak with us afterward. He is travelling down in a convoy. Our boys are within spitting distance of South Mimms as we speak. They have the merchandise with them—500 Kilos," Venga looked very pleased with himself.

"That's good," said Jerry, leaning back in the comfortable chair as he crossed his legs.

A waitress arrived at the table with a pen and pad ready, "Can I get you gentlemen something to drink?" she purred with a smile.

"Perrier for me," replied Jerry before adding, "and the same for these guys."

"I'll be right back," said the girl as she turned away from them.

"Bernadette," whispered Jerry gently.

"Yes, sir?" The girl turned to reveal a face as red as her hair.

"I noticed your name on the badge," he grinned as he stared at her left breast. "I couldn't help but notice," he went on, "it is very beautiful—the name that is!"

Jerry knew that his smile would look good after Venga's mouthful of plaque and he displayed his set of even, white teeth. The girl smiled back at him, her face even redder than before.

"Could you please see whether any rooms are available for tonight?"

"I'm sure we have some vacancies, Sir. Let me just check. Your name?" she asked, pen already touching the pad.

"Bartholomew," Jerry replied.

Barry stifled a giggle.

"But, please, call me Steven." he smiled. "Oh, and could you check if any tee-times are available for the morning, say, 9:30?"

"Certainly, Sir. Anything else?" she inquired, looking into his eyes. "I suppose a blowjob's out of the question?" he thought to himself.

"No, that will be all," he said, with a broad grin.

He watched her as she turned and walked away, noting her beautiful figure and fine posture. The image of her smart white blouse, black knee-length skirt and pert bottom riding high on four-inch stilettos entranced him.

"Bartholomew!" mocked Barry, as the girls wiggled away. "Where the fuck you pull that one from? You never change, you old bastard!" He laughed, and leant over to slap his friend's thigh.

"Now!" said Jerry, suddenly becoming serious, "What is the return on our investment?"

This question was directed at Venga, who sat opposite with his back to the bar and entrance.

"I have discussed this with Barry…"

"Now I'm asking you to discuss it with me," interjected Jerry, menacingly. "I like to get things directly from the horse's mouth. I don't do second-hand small talk. You should have been told this."

"OK, my friend, you have 50% of the parcel, 250 units, before *alterations,* of course," Venga's shoulder rose up as a knowing smile lit up his round face, showing those ghastly yellow teeth.

"Your investment is £175,000, of which I have received £100,000. You have provided the end user, for which you have given a guarantee. The guarantee will cover anything and everything except a capture and seizure by the authorities. With this understanding, I have agreed to give the full 500 units to your man, McFadden. Negotiations have been underway with myself and Barry." he nodded his head in Barry's direction.

Barry, nodding in approval at all Venga was saying, glanced in Jerry's direction, seeking his endorsement. Jerry's poker face gave nothing away. He leaned back in his chair and crossed his legs in a relaxed manner.

"I have reluctantly agreed to accept £14,000 per unit." continued Venga.

"You shouldn't do anything reluctantly, Mr Venga. If you made an agreement, then you made an agreement. We must make that perfectly clear." said Jerry, stretching his arms above his head.

"Yes! Yes! I did agree, but we all know that this is below market price. I considered the benefits and came to the conclusion that the security that comes with the service is worth the discount. The fact that I am without risk—if, of course, we take away the obvious danger of a police seizure—well, let's just say, it helps me sleep at night."

"Carry on," said Barry.

"Barry has assured me that should any of the merchandise be the subject of a police seizure, then documentation of any arrests will be forwarded to me so I know that it is all genuine…"

"I see…" cut in Jerry, as Bernadette approached with their drinks, "I played it some time ago, it is certainly a little tricky, particularly the dogleg, on the 16th, I seem to remember—ah! Our drinks. Thank you, sweetheart." He stood up to take the drinks.

"No problem, sir, please sit down."

"Thank you."

"Many thanks, young lady." drooled Venga as the girl half-filled each glass from the litre bottle.

"I'm happy to say that the room is not a problem for this tonight, Mr Bartholomew, but I'm afraid the golf is fully booked for non-members. I take it you aren't a member, Sir?" she said sheepishly.

He nodded. "That's fine love, I'll be able to sleep in tomorrow, which means I can have a drink tonight, will you join me?"

"I'm sorry, Sir, I am not allowed to socialise with guests."

"If that's the only reason, I'll book elsewhere."

"I'm sorry, Sir," she smiled and swiftly returned to her duties.

"You never give in, do you?" laughed Barry.

"God loves a tryer," Jerry replied.

"He certainly does," agreed Venga. "Now, back to business. Where were we?"

"You were just telling me how Barry had agreed to guarantee your product and your money." The sarcasm in Jerry's voice was not lost on Barry, who looked sheepishly back at his friend, "and I think you were telling me about the documentation you would receive should something go amiss."

"Yes! Yes, like I was saying," continued Venga, leaning forward in his seat, "the security has been made very clear and it is for this reason that I have agreed to the discounted price. May I say at this point that the product has been diluted in Turkey but there is still room for more cutting agent. But I'll leave this in your hands, this, of course is your prerogative. My concern is that I have 250 units for which you will return me £14,000 per unit. Total £3.5 Million. From this figure, we take the cost of the transport, which is £1000 per unit. We have other expenses for which we have deducted £200 per unit, minor things, handling charges, etc. The total deductions are £300,000. Take this from the £3.5 mill leaves 3.2." He completed his calculations, which to some extent went towards explaining the figures on the picnic table, and, with a wringing of hands and a lop-sided, he tried to fit his bulk back into his chair.

"I would like to collect this money in Holland, which I believe you can arrange for a commission fee of 9%?" He looked at Jerry enquiringly with raised eyebrows.

Jerry nodded, "So you will take the 9% commission from the 3, which will leave a final total, to be collected in Holland, of two million and nine hundred thousand pounds. Whether I choose to take payment in Euros will depend on the exchange rate at the time of transaction. Is that OK?" he concluded smugly, happy with his calculations.

"If everything goes according to plan, I see no problem with this agreement," said Jerry, lifting his glass to accommodate the customary touching of crystal. Venga did not follow suit. Instead, he squeezed as far back into his chair as was humanly possible, his slug-like figure spreading out over the armrests. He examined Jerry with probing eyes that seemed to search within the mind, searching for any signs of disloyalty. Detecting none, he went on, "Barry tells me that McFadden is very proficient and has given me an estimated time for completion of four weeks?" Jerry glanced at Barry over the top of his and saw his nod of agreement.

"The four weeks is something that concerns me slightly," challenged Jerry. "Although, I must admit it is something I have limited knowledge about, I think Barry has been a little ambitious and so I would suggest we leave this. We can confirm the time allocated when we speak with McFadden later. Agreed?"

"So be it!" grunted Venga, struggling to free himself from the chair. He leaned forward to pick up his glass and raised it to both Jerry and Barry, who in turn raised theirs.

"Good health, happiness, success and long life," said Jerry.

Barry smiled while Venga responded with "Good health..." and a chesty cough. Jerry excused himself and headed off to the reception.

"Good afternoon, Sir. Can I help you?"

"Yes, please. Do you have a suite available for tonight?"

"Yes, we do, Sir. Just the one night, is it?"

"Two nights, if that's possible?"

"Certainly, Sir. We have a suite available. That will be £280 per night, including breakfast."

"Lovely. I'll take it. Is cash OK? I'm afraid I've left my cards at home."

"No problem, Sir. Your name?" the receptionist said, not looking up from the keyboard.

"Bartholomew."

"Thank you, Sir. Would you mind filling in this card, please?"

Jerry took the form and filled it in with details from a business card he had lifted from a complementary desk at the airport. This particular one had written on it the details of a certain Mr Steven Bartholomew, Manageing Director.

"Thank you, Sir. Would you like a newspaper in the morning?" enquired the receptionist, relieving Jerry of the completed resident form and handing over a swipe key card.

"No, thank you."

"Very well, Sir, your suite is number 202, which is situated on the second floor. I hope you have a pleasant stay."

"I will. Do you have a public telephone? I'm having difficulty getting reception on my mobile."

"You're not having much luck today, are you, Mr. Bartholomew?" Jerry shot him an enquiring glance. "Well, I mean your cards, at home and now signal?" he smiled.

"Oh! Yes—I mean no, I'm not, am I?" Jerry replied, giving him a mirthless grin.

"You'll find the public phone over by the aquarium, Mr. Bartholomew."

The receptionist pointed towards a gigantic fish tank, situated in the far corner of the foyer.

"Thank you very much," said Jerry as he turned and made his way back to the table. He got the impression of a sudden and dramatic change of conversation as he neared the others.

"I'm going to get a wash and brush up. You guys OK here? Or would do you want to come up?'

"We'll be fine here, Jerry. Just keep an eye on the time," replied Barry.

"15 to 20 minutes, and we'll be on our way," Jerry told them as he picked up his Louis Vuitton hand luggage and strolled over to the public telephone. He dialled the number and heard a familiar Irish voice at the other end of the line.

"Is that you?"

"Yes, one hour, I'll be there."

"Right you are," came the terse reply.

Thirty minutes later, the three men were being driven along the M25 in the rain toward the A1(M) north which should see them at the South Mimms services within 30 minutes.

"The traffic, it is terrible," complained Venga staring out of the tinted window. "I am sick of this weather, where I come from you'll rarely see so much rain like this."

"Why don't you go back home then?" taunted Jerry.

"Why? I tell you why! Because the money's too good, my friend," laughed Venga rapturously before descending into a chesty cough.

"Fucking hell," mouthed Barry under his breath. Jerry smiled.

"Pull over here," instructed Jerry as they approached the slip road to the services.

"Why? What for?" said Venga, firing a concerned look at Jerry. A look of alarm was etched into his face.

"Just do as I say, will you?" snapped Jerry.

"What's going on Jerry?" asked Barry, looking somewhat nervous.

Jerry pressed the button on the centre console and instructed the driver to stop next to a guy standing on the grass verge.

"It's OK," agreed Venga for the benefit of the driver, but still with deep concern on his face.

The car stopped, and Jerry opened the door.

"How are ya? Jayzus, this poxy rain!" said Hutchin, in his broad Irish brogue, clambering into the car. "Shove over, will ya?" he laughed, jabbing Barry playfully in the ribs. The wet from the rain and the heavy rucksack that Hutchin placed at Barry's feet had annoyed him.

"What the fuck is he doing here Jerry?" demanded Barry, showing his obvious distaste for both the man and all his paraphernalia. Jerry and Hutchin both registered his reaction.

"D'ya have a problem wit' me?" asked Hutchin, not looking at Barry but touching the wood of the upturned picnic table in front of him. Barry looked across at his friend for support. Jerry gave none and said nothing.

Venga spotted the black Range Rover and instructed the driver to pull up next to it. The two white Ford Transits, each bearing the same company logo of a mechanical breakdown service, were parked within sight. It was pleasing for all concerned to see that both occupants were going about their business of transferring parts from one vehicle to another, complete with flashing yellow beacons and uniformed personnel.

"Let's wait and take in the scenery," suggested Venga. "How theatrical, look at the motion, like clockwork, how beautiful…"

"Come on, McFadden will be waiting," said Barry leaning across the wet Hutchin to release the door.

"Get out de other side. I'm not movin," Venga opened his door and struggled out into the heavy drizzle, Jerry followed with Barry in tow.

"What the fuck is he doing here, Jerry?" asked Barry again, moodily.

"I have other business to see to with him. I can't go into detail now; we'll talk about it later. There's something in Dublin he wants us to look at. But let's do one thing at a time, shall we? Look," he responded, changing the subject, "the boys are on their way." The trio surreptitiously looked at the company vans leaving the services.

"Lovely!" said Venga, "But what's with the hitchhiker?"

"He's a friend."

"But how the hell did you know he would be hitchhiking there?" Venga asked.

"For fuck's sake! How the fuck have you managed to make so much money?" retorted Barry with sarcasm.

McFadden stood up as the trio entered the concourse area. He had a solitary booth in the corner of the Costa coffee shop. The nearest point to the entrance where a man could sit and observe the comings and goings of the general public. He welcomed the three casually.

Outside, Hutchin sat back in the rear of the plush Mercedes limousine. He cut a dishevelled, incongruous figure amidst the sumptuous surroundings, like a drowned mole on the side of a B road. He was a slight man, weighing in at a measly ten and a half stone, with thinning, wispy yellow hair. He had little style about him and preferred the rustic look of a waxed Barbour jacket, corduroy trousers and leather Tricker boots. He was a little older than his trusted friend and confidant, Jerry Divine. They had met some years before, whilst serving time in prison. He was a loner by nature, preferring the company of animals to humans. Horses were his first love. This was where the connection was made with Jerry. They had discussed racing tactics and antics many times while walking around the exercise yard in Pentonville Prison. Hutchin liked to train them, and Jerry liked to bet on them. Together, they had some memorable tales to tell. Hutchin had many associates within the Paramilitaries of various factions, but his sympathies lay more towards Sinn Fein. The Real IRA was a splinter group of the IRA, disbanded after the Good Friday Agreement, and his contacts within this group were the source of the pair of semi-automatic handguns and three grenades he had stashed in his rucksack. After a quick inspection, he turned his attention to the minimal activity outside, as well as the comings and goings of the general public.

A lifetime of crime had given Hutchin O'Brien a sixth sense that only the truly dedicated criminal can nurture and grow. The driver of this amazing vehicle could neither see nor hear him. The heated leather seats were comforting after standing outside in the rain, and this was as far as this unmaterialistic man's appreciation stretched. He had stood there on the grass verge for almost 40 minutes after hitching a lift on a lorry coming south from Manchester and headed for the channel ferry crossing at Dover. He had seen the convoy of police enter the services as he jumped from the lorry almost an hour previously. "God Bless you, Sir! I'll say a prayer for you!" he said to the driver, before slamming the passenger door of the Skeletal trailer, which, the driver had explained, was on its way to Bordeaux to collect the container of a broken download. For this reason, luckily for Hutchin, as it transpired, there was no obstruction to his view of the rear and side of the trailer when dismounting.

The Passenger of the Dark Vauxhall Vectra had looked into Hutchin's eyes as it eased by, followed slowly by an AA van occupied by two more unmistakable faces of the Filth, and then two more fully loaded cars.

The two breakdown vans had conducted their business without any interference from the convoy, which had driven straight through without stopping for refreshments. Obviously stopping for fuel, surmised Hutchin, who was now relatively dry as he watched Jerry, Barry, and the fat guy exit the service area and make their way towards the Mercedes in the company of another character. He hated these services and was surprised that Jerry would have a meet-in-one. Maybe it was legit, or maybe the fat guy was in control of whatever was going down.

They were now in front of a Range Rover parked next to the Mercedes. Hutchin opened the window barely an inch and listened in while the group said their goodbyes. The unknown man had a Scottish accent. "Drugs?" thought Hutchin to himself, "No, not Jerry. Barry, yes, but not Jerry, surely."

As Hutchin searched his memory banks for the face of the fourth man, he noticed from the corner of his eye the same AA van he had seen earlier drive slowly past. The same two faces. Had Hutchin had not noticed the van earlier? It might have slipped the net. He quickly wound down his window, attracting Jerry's attention, but unnoticed by the others. Hutchin only had to raise his eyebrows and swivel his eyes in the direction of the AA van three metres from them and moving away slowly. Jerry acknowledged with a slight nod and hurriedly ushered the fat man and Barry toward the car.

"It's on top," said Hutchin, as the three men clambered into the Mercedes, "I don't know what the tree of you are up to, but it's on top, and I'm in the focking middle of it."

"Calm down," assured Barry. "The transfer went without a hitch. If it was on top, they would've sprung then and had us bang to rights."

"He's right," said the fat man, with a nervous smile. Hutchin took an instant dislike to him and looked directly into Jerry's eyes.

"Jerry. It's on top!" he repeated, this time with gritted teeth.

"OK," said Jerry. "Let's take this easy. One step at a time. What was it, about the AA van?"

Venga was looking around frantically. First at this little tramp, then at Barry and Jerry.

"About an half hour before you arrived, I saw it pull into the services in convoy wit two or tree other cars full to the focking hilt wit filth. Now you know me, Jerry. I don't make focking mistakes and furdermore I'm sat here loaded up to the high heavens loike Rambo."

He lifted the damp rucksack from the floor and unzipped it, showing the armoury inside.

"Oh Allah!" Venga proclaimed. "We have more from Barry in the boot also."

"Leave those there," dismissed Jerry. He locked his eyes, instead, upon a stash of pistols. "Here, give me one of them."

"Fuck!" grumbled Barry, knowing only too well how dangerous these two could be with loaded guns.

"Just keep cool," reasoned Jerry. "They obviously don't know that we are aware of them. They don't know Hutchin is in the motor with us. Just take it easy. The transaction will be on tape, but that in itself won't be enough. We had no contact with the transfer. Let's play this by ear."

He paused, catching his breath and his thoughts. After a few seconds that felt more like an hour, he turned his head to Venga. "Let's drive."

There was audible panic in Venga's voice now. "The driver has no idea. He is not able to accept a chase."

Jerry gritted his teeth, barely flinching. "Instruct him as normal. Tell him to head north to Hatfield,"

Venga pressed the intercom and relayed what he was told. The car pulled away smoothly, followed by McFadden's Range Rover.

Three lines of parked cars away, the AA van pulled out and waited at the junction for the two vehicles to pass. This was all the proof needed to convince the occupants of the Mercedes that they were, in fact, *'on top.'* Both Jerry and Hutchin checked the clips of their automatics. Hutchin took the three grenades from the bag and inserted one in each pocket of his hunting coat.

The cars entered the slip road with the filling station up ahead and to the right. Immediately, Venga spotted the issue; he mouthed an oath through a worried stare.

To the left on the grass verge was an AA cabin. Alongside it, a car was parked with the bonnet popped, being thoroughly checked by a proper-looking man with a pen and clipboard. Jerry and Hutchin simultaneously realised their situation. Barry buried his head in his hands, a muffled groan escaping his mouth. Venga leaned forward, seemingly deep in prayer.

This was the point of stop and search.

Jerry took charge, grabbing the intercom. "Head for the filling station."

The chauffeur never got the opportunity to move. An abrupt thud bolted the men forward. Venga whipped his head around to see McFadden's Range Rover shunted forward as the AA van rammed itself into the train of vehicles, immediately followed by a scream that was inaudible to the occupants of the sound-absorbent Merc. More audibly, and without warning, was the pinging of gunshots hitting the bullet-proof rear window.

"What the fuck is this? What is happening?" screamed Venga, unaware of the situation.

Jerry and Hutchin knew only too well. They were well aware they would be lucky to get out of this petrol station alive.

Barry had other ideas. "Go! Go! Go!" he hollered, clambering swiftly out of the Merc at the first opportunity and heading for the stationary vehicle in front of the AA cabin. The force of the shunt on the Mercedes had activated the airbags. The Range Rover didn't move again after the demands from the armed police. Jerry looked towards the filling station and noted other armed officers behind two cars parked at the far pumps. He knew immediately what he had to do.

Jerry leaned over Venga—he instinctively turned his nose away as he was hit by the unmistakable stench of urine emanating from his colleague—and rolled down the window. He let off a sharp burst of three shots, not necessarily with a target in mind, but to let the police know they, too, were armed. The message was loud and clear. The police immediately made for cover behind the parked cars, seemingly giving cautious respect to their targets.

Now, Jerry moved forward and smashed the glass partition separating the front of the interior from the rear. What he saw through the windscreen was his old friend Barry, a man whom he considered as close as a brother, running fearlessly through the rain. A blue van was travelling recklessly in the opposite direction from the traffic flow, back up the slip road, and along the hard shoulder at speed. The driver saw Barry and skidded at a right angle, trying desperately to avoid contact. Jerry heard the sickening thump as it hit his friend's side on. Gunshots followed from the police in rapid succession. Barry didn't stand a chance.

The cabin was obviously a base for the operation. Hutchin, who had been eerily quiet, now considered making a dash for it and glanced at Jerry without saying a word. Both of them knew their chances were getting slimmer by the second. They had to act now. The driver was now laid low in the front, Venga was having some kind of seizure, and McFadden was being held at gunpoint in the Range Rover.

Hutchin opened his door, using its armour plate as a makeshift riot shield against the police in front. Jerry leaned across Venga once again, and let rip a sharp burst of gunfire to the rear, giving Hutchin the cover he needed. Hutchin grabbed a grenade and, in one smooth motion, pulled the pin and lobbed the hand bomb in a smooth overarm movement towards the petrol pumps.

Not close enough.

The pumps did not ignite, in spite of the enormous damage. The explosion was deafening, to say the least. Even at the distance, the three men were from the explosion; the pain in their ears was so torturous that they grabbed their ears in synchronicity. Venga could only imagine how loud the noise must have been for the police under the canopy, just the other side of the pumps, as he strained from the agony.

The shop frontage of the retail and checkout area took the brunt of the explosion, with windows shattering in every direction. There were screams from within the shop, amongst the sound of debris and shrapnel falling out everywhere. The cars and a motorbike parked by the far pumps were undamaged; however, Jerry considered making a dash for the bike. He had noted that the slip road up ahead was blocked off by the van that had hit Barry and that there would be no room to escape by car.

His thoughts were interrupted by a bullet ricocheting from the reinforced panel of the rear door. The stray bullet slammed into the lower jaw of Venga and travelled through to lodge in his left shoulder. Venga was suddenly unable to scream but instead produced a sound akin to a gurgle of mouthwash, only liquid that corrupted his voice was much more crimson than any mouthwash he'd ever seen. He made eye contact with Jerry, desperately pleading for help whilst holding his jaw together with both hands. Jerry made a lunge towards him, but before he could reach the injured man, a second bullet entered the car on a similar angle to its predecessor, entered Venga's head through the right temple, and the left side of his head exploded with matter, fluid and brain, splattering all over Jerry and the plush interior of the Mercedes.

"Let another one go!" he screamed at Hutchin as he pushed the dead weight of Venga out of the car and onto the wet tarmac, cursing as he hurriedly slammed the door shut. Hutchin threw a second grenade to the far end of the filling station.

Closer.

This time, a huge explosion threw flames and curdles of smoke high into the sky as the petrol pump ignited. An undercover cop was vaulted up into the air and landed in a jumble of body parts; another ran from the rear of a black Vectra as it burst into flame.

Jerry threw open the door back and dropped to the tarmac, using the lifeless body of the Turk as both a cushion and a cover. More bullets entered the fat torso as Jerry heaved the massive bulk onto its side. At this point, the driver's door of the Mercedes sprung open and the driver tumbled out, losing his feet as he raised his hands above his head. He pleaded with the policemen: "Please don't shoot! Please…-"

The first shot hit him in the right shoulder which sent him half spinning back toward the car, hitting his head sharply against the open door. The next shot entered the nape of his neck, sending a mass of blood, matter and vocal cord back into the newly-decorated interior of his car.

It was Hutchin's turn to scream. He only needed one word: "Fock!" He now found himself beside Jerry. He was panting and out of breath.

"Give me a burst. I'll let the last one go. Oi've got one left. The boike is our only chance. After tree." The two men nodded in agreement, a steely grit in their eyes.

"One. Two. Tree."

Jerry let out a scream as he rose from behind the lifeless figure of Venga, releasing a rapid fire of bullets from the automatic pistol. Hutchin produced the final grenade, aware he had to judge his throw to perfection to give them the best chance of completing their escape. He aimed over the bike and, with every ounce of his energy, launched the cocked bomb long into the centre of the filling station.

Direct hit.

The explosion resounded all through the station, providing the perfect cover for the two as they made a last desperate attempt for life and freedom. Gunfire was now raining down blindly from the rough direction of the port-a-cabin to the left of the two running figures, approximately sixty meters up the slip road towards the motorway. This was the only route of escape for the two fugitives. The blue van that had taken out Barry was still abandoned in the same position. Jerry and Hutchin dived behind it and continued running, using the vehicle for cover from the shooters, who were quickly losing sight of their targets.

The two made it to the blue and white Yamaha R1, surprised that no gunfire had emanated from the AA van, careered into the Range Rover. The armed response officer sat in the passenger seat with his gun pressed to the head of a defeated McFadden. The driver of the AA van was, at that point, alerting Quinn via radio control that the two escapees had straddled a motorbike and would be heading their way within seconds. However, this call was never received among the continuous explosions that rang through the station.

Loud screams of agony from within the garage could occasionally be heard between the intervals of mayhem; an obvious indication that casualties were springing up in different parts of the catastrophe. Jerry found the key still in the ignition and turned it: "Luck's on our side, we're going to make it!" thought Jerry and the bike sprung into life. Funny how such thoughts can enter the mind under extreme adrenalin rush.

The powerful roar of the engine only added to the tension as Hutchin leapt onto the back with a sense of resignation. There was very little either of them could do now. They were in the lap of the Gods.

The bike skidded on the tarmac as the fuel and rain had turned the forecourt into a skidpan. Jerry had to use all his experience to keep it under control, a task made no easier with the cumbersome Hutchin as pillion. The powerful machine raced from the filling station and onto the slip road leading to the motorway. There was filth at the cabin as they passed it at high speed. Jerry could tell that the ambushers were confused. They were unsure who the two on the bike were. Just for a fleeting moment, Jerry allowed his mind to wander.

"This might just work."

He held his head low against the rain and allocated more power through his wrist.

Within seconds, the picture had changed. Senior police officers were trying to restore order and calm. People stood beside parked cars, mouths agape, engines running, and car doors open. There were children hanging through wound-down windows, excited and bewildered by the explosion and mayhem. Curiosity was, understandably, getting the better of the general public. There was total gridlock on the motorway; the explosion and subsequent beacon of flame had caused the steady flow of motorway traffic to come to a standstill. Through the smoke pall, Jerry could just about make out the police team, who had now taken on a different role, as they tried to get the public back into their cars. He was confident there would be no more gunfire, especially from the rear. There were too many people, even though the cops there were the only ones who knew for sure that the motorcyclists were the escaping targets.

The police up ahead soon realised that the rider and pillion were part of the gang as they approached, as neither man wore a helmet, and the bike showed no indication of easing up. The powerful machine swerved around the traffic onto the sloping grass verge, back down the other side and onto the hard shoulder of the motorway. Jerry could not be certain, and was certainly unable to look twice, but he thought he had glimpsed the face of an old adversary.

D.S Wheeler.

A man who certainly wouldn't be seen with arms flying mouthing the words, "Don't shoot!"

Whatever. They were now clear, at least for the time being. The bike weaved and swerved in and out of the stationary traffic until there was movement and continuous flow on the A1 south into London. The motorbike blended almost seamlessly into the crowd.

Shenley Manor Business Suite: South Mimms Services 6 miles

3.48 pm Tuesday.
6 November. 2000

The briefing was more like a recap. Wheeler had no input. His job was done. He could only observe how this specialist team worked. He admired the structure of the operation and the efficiency of how things got to this stage so quickly. If he had a reservation, it was only that certain people were actually going to die this evening.

Yes, he could accept they were scum. Yes, they were responsible for the deaths of many other people. That would be a problem for the British legal system. That was absolutely not his problem at this moment in time.

One of the targets of this evening's operation would, hopefully, see Wheeler's face tonight. Wheeler selfishly hoped it would be as the villain took his last breath. He had no reservations about the death of this particular man, the second priority on the agenda. Wheeler thumbed the pages of his case file with menace. Thirty-four years old, a prolific armed robber, recently moved into the world of drugs.

As far as Wheeler was concerned, this was karmic retribution. What goes around, comes around. He closed the case, all too familiar with the details, and stared at the portrait on the front of the file.

Jerry Divine.

Alongside Divine's lay the file of his trusted friend and confidante, Barry Stone. Similar age, similar history. He was the prime reason Wheeler was invited to join the case. An invitation into a world that all coppers—almost, all coppers—would only see in the movies. He saw people and visited places in the last few weeks that were way beyond his comprehension. Indeed, it was only the evidence accumulated by Wheeler against Stone that had placed him in this position today.

Wheeler prayed that this would, at last, bring him the credit he felt he deserved and reinstate him as a leading contender for the position he had longed to hold for many years: Chief Constable of the Metropolitan Police.

He had been a promising candidate for the prestigious role, having risen through the ranks of the police force with impressive efficiency and angelic diligence. However, Wheeler had been at fault when a critical file went mysteriously astray during a high-profile investigation into an elusive group of robbers, preventing the disbandment and conviction of the group. A group led by Jerry Divine.

His blood boiled at just the thought of the man. God, what he would do to get his hands on Jerry Divine. And what he would do to the little rat when he did…

Wheeler was abruptly snapped out of his thoughts as a loud, booming voice broke the silence in the room.

"Right chaps! Listen in!" growled Superintendent Quinn, the leader of Operation Dispute, "We have covered everything; we have re-enacted every minute detail. The priority is the safety of any civilians. We have closed the fuelling points to minimise the risk to the public. I say minimise, gentlemen, for the risk is still there. Once the culprits enter the slip road, before they reach the refuelling area, the exit will be cordoned off, the result of which will be gridlock. Unfortunately, there will be no escape for vehicular traffic. We have men on the ground and in position. It is dark and drizzly out there. Business is carrying on as normal. We have exchanged the attendants at the pumps for our plain clothed men, and we occupy the AA cabin."

Quinn hesitated, as if unsure how accurate the information presented in front of him really was.

"They will be armed, but the ammo MAY BE doctored. We can't take this as gospel, though."

Another hesitation. Wheeler began to doubt the effectiveness of the plan. He knew what the following words would be, yet his heart sank as they were uttered.

"We shoot to kill—it's them or us. Good luck, everybody. Let's go!"

The team filed out in a numbered sequence, each of the six dressed in navy blue attire complete with Kevlar, armoured dressing and the glinting metal of an automatic assault rifle. They looked a daunting sight, sending a shiver through the spine of Wheeler.

"You stay close to me, Sir," an officer motioned towards Wheeler. "We will be stationed by the exit, just as the slip road joins the A1. The last three cars before the end of the slip road will be ours, blocking the exit for the

Mercedes. We don't have visual contact at the moment, but Target 2 was on schedule, and there is nothing to suggest that the meeting will not take place. Our latest information is that the other two vehicles, a black Range Rover Vogue and a white Transit van, are in convoy. They are now within six junctions of our location."

The officer, whose name Wheeler had not been given, nor positioned on a badge on his breast, looked down at his watch and started walking towards the cabin. Wheeler had no choice but to follow. The officer continued: "With traffic conditions stable along the motorway, this gives us an ETA of 16.50 hours. We will be ready and in position at 16.30."

The two were now standing beside a yellow van, proudly displaying the distinctive logo of the AA Mechanical breakdown services. A gaggle of other vehicles, stationary on the gravel car park to the side of the station, were each accommodated by two occupants who stood beside them in an orderly fashion.

"Gentleman!" Quinn boomed again, his voice grizzly amongst the dire autumnal conditions. "We commence proceedings in the fashion we are accustomed to. Each one of you will now know and understand the duty you have been assigned."

Quinn singled out the driver of a blue Renault van, who was standing holding the handle of a side loading door. "Beckingsdale, you know how vital it is to manoeuvre at the first opportunity into a blind spot to safeguard target 3. He is one of ours—so to speak—the only one wearing a luminous body warmer and will be on foot heading toward the port-a-cabin."

Beckingsdale nodded in acknowledgement as if he had rehearsed this plan a hundred times in his head.

"Everyone else, bear that in mind. The yellow luminous body warmer is NOT a priority, he is NOT a target." Quinn finished, catching the gaze of each special armed response officer individually as though he was speaking directly to that person. Wheeler begrudgingly noted that this was a sign of a good leader.

"Thank you for your service. God bless you all!" Quinn was climbing into the passenger seat of a dark-coloured Vauxhall Vectra. Wheeler's officer gestured for him to follow as the armed police team took to their positions.

Once seated in the rear of the Vectra, Wheeler's heart began to pound. He regretted not taking any lunch. His last cup of black coffee was swirling of its own accord without anything solid to soak it up. He could actually hear it—even feel it splashing around—as the car sped from the car park and into the unknown. As if he could smell the fear in Wheeler's presence, Quinn put his right arm across the back of the driver's seat and turned to face him.

"OK, Wheeler?" he asked.

"Fine. I haven't eaten today, that's all. I'll be fine."

"Look a little pale, that's all," Quinn commented as he turned back to face the direction of travel. Wheeler got the impression Quinn was enjoying his discomfort.

Detective Bill Wheeler had been on numerous operations in which firearms had been employed. The difference between those occasions and this one was clear: the certainty, not a possibility, of many fatalities.

"Talk about a licence to kill!" he grumbled to himself.

He had fought with his conscience and come to a conclusion very quickly that, in this case, the licence was very much justified. Venga was the devil incarnate. The scum of the earth. Divine? He probably had it coming. As for anyone else who should fall? Wheeler very much doubted whether they worried too much about the victims of their crime.

Barry Stone? If the plan works, it works. If not, c'est-la-vie. One thing Wheeler was happy about, but couldn't explain why, was the fact that it was cold and raining with a moderate breeze.

Seventeen minutes later, the police vehicles were in position. The officers were strategically placed. The point of impact was a stretch of road between the commercial/restaurant area and the refuelling service. Positioned midway between the two was the yellow port-a-cabin emblazed with the AA logo. The cabin was the focal point where Barry Stone would make haste to. That was the plan. The blue Renault van, with the side loading door, contained two marksmen with automatic rifles. If Mr Beckingsdale—whose regular job was to train emergency police drivers (along with some stunt work for a local film studio)—did his job correctly, then they were in the best position to intercept. On the opposite side of the spectrum were the plain-clothed officers; two stood by a pump in the filling area, and two behind the counter within the station. Three cars were parked on the slip road twenty metres before it met the A1(M). One of these three vehicles was the Vauxhall Vectra, which seated Quinn, Wheeler and the driver.

In an ideal world, there was no way the movement of the general public would be disrupted. This would only give rise to suspicion. Divine, in particular, was an expert in anti-surveillance techniques—the type of guy who could automatically sense anything untoward in a desert. The only thing that may prevent an influx of the public is to shut down as many of the pumps as possible. Quinn had decided the magic number was three of the nine pumps.

Surveillance reported that the black Range Rover and white Transit van, which travelled down from Scotland, were now in position: stationary in the car park of South Mimms Services. The occupant was seen to leave the Range Rover and enter the service area. The van driver remained in the van. There would be no interference from the police in the transfer of the drugs from one van to the other. This transaction will be videoed for evidence and any subsequent trial. Arrests would be made later in the day. The priority of this operation was to eliminate Targets 1 and 2. Venga. Divine. That was the plan.

A plan which suddenly spiralled out of all control.

Gunfire. The radio Quinn was holding came alive with screams of "Attack! Attack!." Quinn went into a panic.

"Are they live? I repeat, are they live? Is the ammunition live? Priority to all parties… The general public—I repeat, the safety of the public is priority!"

He turned to look at Wheeler—all the colour draining from his unshaven face.

"Fuck!"

The redness around his eyes from the lack of sleep gave him an almost ghost-like appearance.

"Where the fuck has the live ammo come from? Your man assured me they were safe. Fuck! Get those bastards back in their cars!" The superintendent struggled to keep his self-control, pointing frantically to the curious onlookers standing beside their gridlocked vehicles. At that moment, the first explosion was heard—then seen—as a pillow of smoke erupted from the overhead position of the filling station.

"What the fuck was that?" exploded Quinn. The blue van driven by the specialist stunt driver had already reversed up the hard shoulder in the direction of the port-a-cabin, and shots could be heard coming from that direction. Quin and Wheeler could not see, and they weren't expecting to see it until the commotion had ceased. They did not see the return fire from the targets or know that two were already dead and another was being held at gunpoint.

Further gunshots were heard, followed by another large explosion, this time resulting in a tower of flame and billowing smoke. Screams of terror and agony escaped from the carnage. Panic was rife. Push had come to shove.

Wheeler knew that now was the time to call a ceasefire, before the general public got caught up in the fight. Quinn had the same thought and picked up the radio to order his men to stop firing. They were both taken aback by the third explosion, which was far greater and louder than the previous two. Flames shot high above the station. Smoke mushroomed, thick and heavy. Chunks of the structure had been catapulted high into the sky; the public was in grave danger if the explosions couldn't be controlled. Car horns sounded continuously from the traffic, now parked on the motorway, and screams poured out from this direction.

A motorbike carrying two people roared out of the debris. It accelerated towards Quinn and Wheeler. Wheeler peered out of the window and caustically enquired of Quinn what he made of the situation. Quinn was caught in a dilemma. He was frantically deciding what to do. His hand instinctively grasped for his revolver. The high-powered bike mounted the grass verge thirty metres in front of them. They had no idea whether the rider or the pillion were the intended targets or just frightened public members caught up in the devastation. Wheeler knew the time to act was now. They needed to take the shot, or the targets would get away.

He glanced at Quinn.

"What are we going to do?"

Quinn hesitated. "We can't take the risk," he croaked with a wavering voice.

The bike roared past. Wheeler's heart sank. He looked straight into the unmistakable eyes of his nemesis, Jerry Divine.

"Job's fucked," Quinn muttered, shaking his head.

He sounded quieter, resigned.
"We're in deep shit," agreed Wheeler reluctantly.

Book One

Chapter One

Six Years Later
Day One

Jerry Divine stood in the power shower, letting the blast of the water from every direction hit him hard, washing away all the luck—bad luck, that was, because if it wasn't for bad luck, he would have no luck at all. Things had to change; no losing streak—or winning streak for that matter—can last forever. Unfortunately for Jerry, it was the former. Yet again, he resigned himself to the fact that it could be worse. He had lost before, many times, and on occasion, the stakes had been much higher. What Jerry had to do now was to concentrate. Put things into perspective. A clean sheet. Blank canvas. Forget about the losses of days gone by. Wash them down the drain with the water cascading from his body.

Jerry had just celebrated his fortieth birthday. He had always told himself that he would retire at forty. But, as he exited the luxurious shower room, through the dressing area and into the plush, spacious surroundings of his bedroom, he stopped to look at himself in the mirror. If truth be told, he was pleased with what he saw. Six foot two inches, two hundred pounds (give or take) with an athletic physique; the regular squash games and outdoor tennis, the swimming in the Mediterranean sun (not to mention the plethora of females he regularly entertained) had given him a chiselled body with a notably bronzed hue, alongside a full head of black hair which he usually wore slicked back, with the help of some Vidal Sassoon's estimable products—yes, he was more than happy with his appearance.

The appreciation of his reflection was suddenly disturbed by the sound of a car horn, and Irish Tom's voice brought the realisation that he was without wheels. He walked back to the bathroom and looked out of the open window towards the street—or calle as the Spanish call it.

"Won't be long. You must have brought me home last night?" Jerry queried, giving the newly acquired Mercedes 500 SL AMG the once over.

"Fuck's sake, don't you remember? There were four of us in this thing, I couldn't get the roof up last night, so it was parked outside mine all night like this; some jealous dickhead could have shat in it. How d'you get the lid back up?"

"Let me dry off; I'll be down shortly," said Jerry, shaking his head in disgust. There was little need to towel dry; by the time he had walked back into the bedroom and out through the French doors onto the veranda overlooking the stunning Oriental garden he kept in pristine condition, he was bone dry. Indeed, the heat from the midday sun would soon dampen him again with perspiration.

Looking down, Jerry savoured the scene. It was pleasant to behold. The garden had matured over the last three years, and with the additional features he had invested in, it had come together: the enclosed bar and barbeque had seen little use since its construction at a cost that most people would spend on building a house; the gazebo was a place he liked to sit in the evening time and watch the girls enjoy the pool.

His thoughts again were disturbed by the sound of the damned horn.

"Is that for you?" Kathy glared, covering her eyes from the sun with one hand as she squinted towards the balcony from her Lilo floating in the pool.

"It's always for him, Mummy," replied Julie, the younger of his two daughters, who had suddenly stopped chasing Bonito around the vast garden. Bonito was a miniature poodle, and the only dog anyone had seen that climbed trees. Jerry had chased him one day with the sprinkler, and cornered him by the gigantic urn at the bottom of the lawn, when he suddenly ran up the 800-year-old olive tree. Jerry and the girls had often since tried to get him to repeat the feat while they captured it on film, but the little bugger seemed to know what he was after, as if he was unspeakably camera-shy, so his party trick had been hidden from the family ever since.

"Where's Jasmine, Kath?"

"Gone shopping. Don't forget we have a barbie tonight. Demitra and Jezzie are coming down.""

"Oh fuck, I forgot."

"Do you have to swear in front of Jules?"

"Sorry darling!"

Jerry caught Julie's eye and mimed to her to bomb into the pool next to Kathy. The little girl crept up to the side of the pool, nervously anticipating the forthcoming screams. Bonito seemed to know exactly what was about to happen and scampered off to the tree. In a flash, he had scaled the bottom half of the tree, turning proudly to his owners to display his climbing skills once again.

Typical!

The splash startled Kathy before the water hit her. Julie squealed in delight as Kathy screamed, struggling to keep her balance on the bed. Jerry allowed a small laugh to escape as he went back through to the dressing area, until he heard the horn blast for the third time.

"Impatient Irish bastard," thought Jerry.

"I'll be down in a minute," he hollered. Just then, he heard the grand front door slam. A teenage girl shouted up to him.

"Dad, Irish Tom's waiting for you."

"I know Jaz, I'll be right down," he sighed, as he buttoned up the baggy black silk shirt that he wore over cream light linen slacks. Both items were premium Versace, giving the man the look of a retired sports star with a sponsorship deal. He loved to wear baggy clothes, especially in July and August when the temperatures often reached the late nineties on the Costa del Sol.

"Hi, love," Jerry called out affectionately as he skipped down the arched staircase. Jasmine, the elder of his two daughters, was surrounded by shopping bags. Jerry winced at the brand names, knowing his hypocrisy was demonstrable to his daughter. He kissed Jasmine quickly on the cheek.

"Switch the water feature on, darling." He was proud of the recent addition to the vestibule: it added character and sound. He enjoyed the calming sound of water and the coolness of the shade, which gave the antechamber a Thai theme. Jerry had a particular fascination for Thailand, having been there on vacation a couple of years earlier. He was scheduled for a repeat visit in the near future—more business than pleasure this time— and not a particularly profitable business at that. A close friend, a throwback to the first few drug trades that Jerry enjoyed, had taken his greed a step too far: mixing with the wrong people who decided to double-cross the guy and hand him over to the Thai judicial authorities on some trumped-up minimal drugs charge which had landed him in the Bangkok Hilton for a term of seven years. Resentful as he was, Jerry felt it his duty to help out with his assets and any other problems a situation like that could induce. Not to mention taking care of the 'source' of the matter.

"Dad, you said you'd take me and my friend to Gibraltar this weekend!" Jasmine begged from the lounge to his right.

"We'll see, love."

"Dad, you promised!"

"I promise we'll talk about it tonight."

"Urgh, alright. Oh, and Mum said, Bring some fish, bread and wine back."

"Jesus, sounds like the last supper."

"It will be if you forget, so don't be late," Kath instructed, striding through the lounge and into the kitchen to confront her husband. Bonito, fresh from a dip in the pool, came charging in with Julie in hot pursuit. "Or drunk."

"I'll call you if I get stuck."

"Dad!"

"Get that dog out of here; it's wet through!" demanded Kath, over the sound of the damned car horn. Jerry saw his chance, and burst out of the door and through the gate. Kath shouted desperately at him as he hopped over the passenger door of the convertible, pressed the automatic start button and instructed Tom to floor it.

"Go, go, go!"

There was no hesitation from the driver, his close mate.

"The last time I heard that was after taking an unauthorised loan from a bank in Limerick," laughed the Irishman, as he accelerated from 0 to 60 in what must have been under four seconds. The two of them laughed as the sleek black Mercedes joined the coastal road. Over the roar of the merc's engine, Jerry did not pick up the steady *'chug, chug, chug* of rotor blades in the sky as a distant helicopter hovered behind the car.

The Mercedes headed south toward La Linea with the sound of an old reggae tune *"as sure as the sun will shine, one an all..."* blaring out and deflecting the sound of the breeze. Jimmy Cliff. Jerry grinned.

"What happened last night then?" he enquired.

"Are you sure you wanna know?"

Jerry thought for a second. "Not anymore." He leaned back in the leather seat, resting his feet upon the immaculate dashboard. "Just drive. We need to get to Gib ASAP"

"You're the boss."

Chapter Two

He could not relax. He was unsettled. He played with his Gucci sliders out of frustration. He looked at Tom. He looked back at the road. He grumbled nothings to himself.

Something's wrong; he could sense danger.

Something that Tom had said about an unauthorised loan in Limerick had struck a chord within him.

Jerry made his money these days in gambling, and from time to time, he won big. He thought back to what he had built up over the last twelve years or so; his wonderful family that he loved so dearly. The last thing Jerry ever wanted to do was put his girls in danger.

He knew that if he carried on gambling, he, too, would be calling for a loan. Jerry was not foolish. He had to find a reliable way of earning sooner rather than later for Kath and her sanity.

Jerry believed that most things in life—in fact, life itself—were a gamble. His problem was that gambling was a vice, and he was partial to most vices. Each one was as potentially damaging as the other, and all were expensive. They could all have a profound impact on the mind, body and soul—that is, if the heart stood up to the battering. Jerry often looked into the mirror and wondered how he looked and felt as good as he did. The only time he ever remembers seeing a doctor was last year when he was in the capital, Madrid. And that was for vital circumstances—Preservation of genitals. He was unwell quite often, but that was mainly self-inflicted (usually after one of his many sessions of over-indulgence).

"Put yer feet down, you'll ruin the vinyl," muttered Tom, catching a glimpse of Jerry's restlessness. It didn't help Jerry's mood.

"Vinyl! Fucking vinyl, you silly twat. They don't put vinyl in a motor like this!"

Tom gave a snigger as he fixed his eyes back to the road. He knew better than to mess with his mate when something was on his mind.

Jerry was not expecting too much. He'd had offers within the last few years, and he'd approached them with caution. He preferred jobs of his construction, like his previous six operations: he was in total control, and his security was paramount. All he knew about today's meeting was that he was meeting someone in Gibraltar who was privy to some inside information about the transport of a significant cash transit. He had little more to go on; the call he took a month ago this very day was not the most detailed:

"Be in Gib at noon 1st August. It's your old profession."

Jerry knew vaguely what this would entail and where it was going.

It had been quite some time since he and the original team, minus one, had relaxed operations: five years to the very day, to be precise, following the botched jewellery heist in O'Connell Street, Dublin. There had been unfortunate loss of life on that fateful day: one in the form of death by a Garda bullet; two others which resulted in a lengthy trial, a conviction and a 22-year prison sentence. The same words that echoed through Jerry's head now.

"*Go! Go! Go! Go! Go! Go!*"

Jerry knew that Tom was full of bullshit. If there was ever a blag in Limerick—of which no doubt there will have been many—there was no way Tom was responsible for any of them. You could bet your last few quid on that one.

"*There he goes, gambling again.*"

Looking across at him, Jerry sometimes worried if he let Tom see and hear too much. He noted the rugged looks of a broken face—the fractured nose, scarred lips, the twitch of the left eye. Tom's excuse for his messed-up features was many years of semi-professional Gaelic football. Jerry gave him the benefit of the doubt.

"How old are you, exactly?" he asked, looking straight ahead.

"What the fock brought that on?" replied Tom, momentarily losing focus on the road. There was a long, awkward pause as Jerry declined to respond. "I'm fifty noine and a half. I know, I don't look it. C'mon why'd you ask?"

"No reason," Jerry continued to watch the road more than Tom. "If you were to describe yourself, what would you say?"

"Well Oi'd say I was a yootful 59 year-old bachelor, a professional chauffer to a renowned celebrity, which I do solely because I enjoy the perks…"

"Seriously," interrupted Jerry, "Imagine you're posting an ad in the 'lonely hearts' column. Come on. What would you say?"

"Now you're socking diesel," Tom laughed. "I'd probably say I was a retoired gentleman, 59 years of age, recently bereaved, enjoys squash, dining out, and going to the teatre."

"You lying dirtbag," Jerry scoffed.

"Well, Jaysus, if I were to tell the truth, only the brass and bold would reply. Could you imagine? Irishman living on the Costa-del-crime, driver come bodyguard, specialist…"

"Fucking bodyguard!" Jerry retorted.

"You haven't put me to the test, Jeez. I'd die for you. You don't really know me."

Jerry nodded in appreciation, a sly grin playing on his lips.

"Where was I? Teatre, yes, loves the teatre. Now, a description. Let me see." He angled his face towards the rear-view mirror, flicking his eyes between the road and his reflection, concentrating hard on his flattery. One hand rubbed the stubble on his chin, the forefinger crossing his bottom lip; the other clenched and relaxed upon the steering wheel.

"Should Oi tell the trut' here or a little whoite lie?"

"I think you need to be telling some whoppers you ugly mug."

"Aroight, aroight. Let's see," responded Tom, trying to avoid the hurt showing on his face.

"This is only an exercise," Jerry reminded him, giving him a gentle dig in the ribs.

"I know, I know, but this is me future we're talking about here. I may only get one crack at this. A young 59 with an atletic build from years of semi-pro football. I won't say Gaelic, that's like saying rugby. I'd go on to say, looking for someone- "

"Finish off the description," Jerry butted in, holding back a snigger.

"Is that not enough?"

A dismissive shake of the head told Tom all he needed.

"Right, Athletic build, 59, full head of hair, black, no greys," he perused for a second before adding, "Top and bottom, broad shoulders, with a Shergar resemblance from the waist down. There, how's that?"

"Depends what type of girl you want to attract," Jerry laughed.

"I'd like the type with a big hairy minge and a few quid," responded Tom, his laughter drowning Jerry's.

"A hairy minge?"

"Yea, fanny, a hairy fanny, like in the 70's… "

"I know what a… what you mean by… my point is you can't say that, for fuck's sake," Jerry taunted with a chuckle. "I suppose the Shergar bit might help," he conceded, starting to think seriously about this guy. No one had ever gotten this close to Jerry without knowing him for many years (or by introduction with a guarantee). He argued with himself that Tom was only a driver and that if he did see Jerry with anyone, he was not privy to any conversations that were important or incriminating.

They had met in a local gambling club where Jerry had an account and would regularly call in for drinks. Wagers were placed by the run-of-the-mill customers, like Tom and those who played for high stakes, like Jerry. On this particular occasion, Jerry had had a good day and stayed after hours for drinks with the owners. The food and beverages were complimentary, and some personal, moderately-cut cocaine was on offer. Day turned into night, and the crew ventured to the port for late-night entertainment. Jerry had recently taken delivery of an S600 Mercedes, and Tom had volunteered to leave off the booze and do the driving. By the time midnight struck, Jerry was in a Jacuzzi in the middle of God-knows-where with two Russian hookers. As the sun rose over the sea, Tom diligently drove him home. Having seen Jerry safely in the front door, the considerate Irishman had then taken himself home in the S600, returning later that day with the car freshly cleaned and polished. Unsurprisingly, Jerry had forgotten that he'd asked Tom to pick him up from home at 6 pm as he was collecting someone from the airport at 7, so he was mightily impressed when, on the very dot, Tom was there with the car freshly cleaned. Tom had volunteered to drive to the airport after seeing Jerry was in no fit state, and the rest was, as they say, history.

Jerry had to admit he was pleased with Tom, who, if anything, tried to please too much. Sometimes, Jerry thought it was an act; others, he was glad of the assistance, and that was of much more importance to him. Nine months had now passed, and Tom was still happily employed—he must be doing something right. Intuition automatically told Jerry how much Tom should know about his life, when and where he was required and who and what he should see or hear. Sometimes, even a one-sided telephone conversation can be too much, and that is the extremity of seriousness to which Jerry took his security.

"Park in the underground. I'll walk over," Jerry suggested as they approached La Linea.

"Why don't we park at the fish restaurant? I can get a boite to eat if you're gone too long."

"We parked there last time. We're going underground." Jerry barked, annoyed at the interference with his concentration. Tom said nothing. He'd got the message. The car veered left towards the car park. As Tom slowed to take the time card from the attendant, Jerry was out the door without saying a word.

"Do you have your passport, phone and other bits?" Tom called after him, resembling a mother sending her child off to school for the first time. No reply. "Oi'll take that as a 'yes.," then," mumbled Tom at Jerry's retreating back.

He wondered, then, what was so important. For the last fifteen minutes of the journey, they had travelled in silence. He knew not to question Jerry's affairs. There must be an important meeting. He would give the car a once over, polish the windows and go for a walk. It could be a long day. Tom would generally wait for a call, although Jerry had a habit of just appearing from nowhere within seconds of Tom checking his surroundings. Tom thought it spooky at times.

Just then, the phone in the car rung.

"Tom."

"Jerry. You forgot something? You'd forget your balls if they weren't in a bag."

"No mate, any tips?" Jerry replied, laughing.

"Yes, leave off the brass."

"Are you going to answer the fucking question or what? Did you speak with the Indian?"

"Yes, there's a cert at the 3.45 McCoy's on it. The Indian was speaking to Hutchin. He said to put your granny on it."

"Is he on it?" Jerry enquired.

"Who, the Indian or Hutchin?"

"The Indian."

"What isn't he on?"

"Find out how much and half that for me" said Jerry

"How am I supposed to find out? I certainly don't have the authority to ask him that," replied Tom, fear in his voice.

"Call Macrony, and tell him I asked. If he doesn't tell you, call the Indian himself. Tell him I'm chasing, so this fucker'd better be nailed on."

"OK," said Tom, hanging up. "Fuck!" he grumbled, replacing the handset. He started to get the uncomfortable feeling that this job was probably too much for a fifty-nine-year-old.

Chapter Three

Jerry hung up the receiver and immediately regretted making the call. "I'm going to have to knock this gambling on the head," he told himself as he stepped out of the phone booth. He'd done it all his life—it was a big chunk of his character.

"That's who I am," he mused. "Life's a gamble, but boy, does it interfere with business. Fuck it!"

He pondered the idea of making a second call from the public phone when the mobile in his small leather man gab started to ring. He swiftly walked toward the terminal and didn't answer until he was 30 metres from the phone box. How many times had he seen idiots stand at a public phone talking into a mobile, a typical stereotype out here, shoulder bag and Prada? You could tell them a mile away, your average numpties, just waiting to be nicked.

If he'd been taking notice, as alert and observant as he was in his heyday, he might have looked up and seen the chopper hovering in the sky, just out of earshot.

He looked like everyone else in the queue at passport control, blending in well with tourists and residents alike entering Gibraltar. The UK. He still struggled to get his head around the fact that within minutes, he would be leaving Spain for England. He often found it amusing asking a police officer for directions and getting them in Spanish from a cozzer in English uniform. He recognised the passport inspector as the same as the last time he'd been through the terminal, only this time, he had a female trainee with him trying to look severe and stern. It didn't suit her. Jerry could think of better positions to have her in wearing that uniform.

"Pasaporte Senor," lisped the inspector without the hint of a smile.

"And a very buenos dias to you, too."

Jerry handed over his documents to the trainee. He could feel her superior's eyes boring into him. He gave the man a glare—same greasy moustache, same beaded, sweaty skin, same thick 70s spectacles that narrowed his eyes. Jerry threw the female officer a knowing smile which she accepted with a blush as she returned his passport

"Have a nice day," Jerry wished the girl playfully, ignoring the oily male.

"Gracias, senor." she smiled, displaying pure white, even teeth; whose brightness was enhanced by her rose blush.

A plane had just taken off, leaving the smell of aviation fuel in the hot, humid air. Jerry had used this airport recently to fly to Paris-Charles De Gaulle and found it much more convenient. He made a mental note to check out flights to Dublin on his way back through.

Mere minutes later, he was sitting in the back of a taxi.

"The Rock Hotel," he instructed the driver, passing him a 10 Euro note. "Keep the change." He knew as well as anyone how the taxi cabs love to rip off tourists.

Out of habit, Jerry sat to the right of the driver, which obscured him from the rearview mirror but still enabled him to use the right-hand side wing reflector to check behind.

Had the car been fitted with a glass sunroof, he may also have seen the helicopter in the clear sky, a mere three thousand feet above him.

He was second-guessing what to expect from this meeting and secretly hoping that a big number was on offer. The last six operations had been hugely successful regarding value, but once the jewellery had been broken up, the re-saleable value was greatly diminished. The most expensive items were so recognisable and hot, that, for security reasons, the only sensible option was to put them away for a considerable length of time, and that didn't help Jerry's lifestyle, which was in dire need of regular and large cash flow.

Although Jerry Divine looked like a figure of success in his appearance and demeanor, he loved to remind himself of a phrase an old timer had once told him:

'It's not a sin to be skint, but it is one to look it."

While an average person would consider financial worry as struggling to meet the everyday living, Jerry believed that anything under realisable cash to the tune of a million was a major concern. Of course, there were investments and ongoing building projects—not to mention the expensive jewels, stashed far away from anyone's eyes, and the mortgage-free bricks and mortar. However, it was his nature, his very core, to look for more. He could have achieved financial stability right now were to sell up and retire, but he had to admit that he actually loved the buzz. Everything the job entailed: the initial idea, the planning, the meetings, every detail which had to be scrutinised to assure that nothing should go wrong.

These thoughts remained with him as he left the cab, made his way through the grandiose foyer of the upmarket Rock Hotel, and headed to the lounge. He positioned himself on a tall stool at the bar with his back to the entrance and reception area but with the benefit of highly polished mirrors behind the bar, which gave him a full view of the open area. The barmaid placed some sparkling water with lemon and a complimentary bowl of nuts in front of him, along with the tab and a smile to die for. Jerry acknowledged her casually with a raised glass and an approving smile.

Having taken the precaution of removing both battery and SIM card from his mobile phone before entering Gibraltar, he opened his bag. He started sifting through the notes and scraps of paper he had accumulated over the previous week: reminders of things he had to do, people he needed to see, and business cards he had recently been given. Some of these would be useful, such as the rast he tore into shreds and deposited in the ashtray in front of him. Occasionally, he glanced up at the pretty girl behind the bar and, on a couple of occasions, was pleasantly surprised to catch her looking his way before blushing and frantically wiping the already immaculate bar. He raised his empty glass, his excuse for wandering his eyes in her direction, and she obligingly refilled it.

"Gracias"

"You're most welcome," she purred with a broad smile. Jerry guessed her age at roughly 22 and felt almost guilty for looking at someone so young and beautiful. Thoughts of what he would like to do to her flooded his pornographic male brain. She gave him a cheeky wink as though to say, 'us youngsters grow up quickly nowadays." As well as being beautiful, she possessed a figure to die for.

"A figure to die for? Come on, Jerry!"

He was on the verge of asking if there was a presidential or marital suite available to rent when he heard the swish of the revolving door and looked in the direction of the disturbance. Jerry did a quick double-take.

Then he stared, eyes boggling, at *a ghost*.

"It can't be, it must be a delayed hangover" he told himself. He grabbed on to the polished brass rail that surrounded the mahogany bar and gripped it tight to stop himself from being sucked into a black hole. The pressure in his lungs was increasing, fresh air failing to fill them up.

"What the fuck's going on? You're supposed to be dead!"

Jerry stared at the drink in front of him and thought for a second it might have been spiked. The girl was looking at him, with concern written across her face. He dared himself to look again in the mirror, hoping, dreading, to see who he had seen, and yet knowing it wasn't possible.

But it was. The figure was only eight metres from him, in the flesh. This was no ghost because the consignor was now talking to him, beckoning him in the direction of the lounge bar.

"What's happening? What the fuck is going on? How can this be?" Jerry's head was swimming. He felt the blood drain from his body. He felt weak and wet with perspiration, trying to work out how this…

"Are you alright, Sir? Sir, are you OK?"

The voice came from a distance but had a familiarity about it. Jerry relaxed slightly as the barmaid swam into view, but she sounded a million miles away. Jerry fished for some ice from the bucket on the bar and held the cold block to his brow. The scenario took only seconds, but he felt everything happening in stop-motion, like on a video recorder. He pulled himself together like the professional he was, determined to show this was no crisis. The girl was now handing him a serviette like the professional *she* was, and he took it with a forced smile, wiping the melted water from his brow,

"Gracias senorita," he gasped.

"De nada," she responded, no longer concerned. She was busy greeting the newest member of the bar.

"I was under the impression you knew all along, Jerry, but by the look on your face, you look like you've seen a ghost,"

Barry Stone pulled up a stool and sat down next to his friend. "Don't get up on my behalf," he grinned mischievously.

"Get up? I'm turned to fucking stone! What in God's name is going on Barry?" The colour was slowly returning to Jerry's face. He was experiencing the twin emotions of fear and anger simultaneously. The former was a rarity in itself.

"Relax, Jerry. I've booked us a table in the San Roque for dinner. I'll explain everything there once you've recovered your initial shock."

"Shock!" croaked Jerry, "It's more like a fucking 10 on the Richter scale."

"I know, Jerry, I know," soothed Barry, as he placed a reassuring hand on his friend's shoulder. He really wanted to give him a big man-hug, but felt this was probably not the right moment.

"I wanted to do the preliminaries here. I understand how hard this must be for you, but I couldn't see another way of breaking the ice. Please try to pull yourself together. This evening, I'll tell you everything you need to know, but keep an open mind; it won't be pleasant. It will soon become apparent why I did what I did. You will understand. You may not agree, but you will understand. Are you OK?" Barry removed his hand, surprised at the slight tremor he felt from the muscular shoulder.

"What time?" asked Jerry, looking squarely into the other man's eyes.

"Nine." replied Barry, standing up slowly in the hope his friend would do the same and embrace him. As Jerry didn't move, Barry walked slowly out of the bar and through the revolving doors. Jerry looked in the mirror and saw a black road racer stop. The rider handed Barry a helmet and invited him onto the back of the bike. Jerry noted the long black hair underneath the driver's helmet. Female.

And then they were gone.

Jerry sat, shaking his head. He considered another drink. Deciding against it, he slowly rose off the stool. He hobbled to the reception and booked a room. He needed to rest and clear his head. He moved towards the elevator. He paused. He turned. He picked up the public phone. He called Tom.

"Don't ask any questions," he instructed, "and don't interrupt."

"OK, boss."

"Bring the car through and call at Gino's on Main Street. Get me a suit off the peg with all the trimmings. Do you have sterling?"

"No."

"Put it on a tab, get me a pair of shoes to suit, then come up to The Rock Hotel and hand the parcel to the *conserje* along with the car keys, and say they're for Mr. DuPont. I'll call you later, Oh, and call Kath. Tell her I'll be home at 10.30."

"Consider it done." A pause. "How do I get home?"

But Jerry had hung up.

The bed looked inviting. Jerry kicked off his shoes and jumped on it, fully clothed. Sleep was not an option; he lay face down for a moment or two before turning to face the ceiling. This was going to take some time, some time to absorb the shock, let it slowly sink in.

"Breathe slowly Jerry, deep, deep and slowly, very slowly."

Barry had made some attempts to alter his features. There was the obvious—new nose, different hair colour, the Botox. Together it would have convinced most people, but Jerry was not most people. He had immediately seen the confident skip in his walk, the way he carried those broad shoulders, the cheeky smile—he and Jerry, they were certainly a breed unto themselves.

Loyalty is valued highly by Jerry's type of villain, unlike today's fly-by-night crooks, and certainly not like the majority of those down on the Costa. Gone were the days when a man's word was his bond. In the past, their loyalty was as valuable as life itself. Each one's life belonged to the other and would be given as a last resort.

This was unquestionably the case with Jerry and Barry. Way back when... Before Barry was hit side-on by a van and gunned down six years ago. Jerry had barely escaped with his life alongside Hutchin O'Brien, the only two from the party who had survived the holocaust at South Mimms Services. Riat Venga wasn't so lucky. He and two others had gone down in a hail of police bullets. Three others had been arrested and eventually sentenced to 28 years each. The police had hailed it as the most important and successful crackdown operation to combat the importation and distribution of heroin throughout the United Kingdom and Southern Ireland. The drugs seized with 'Operation Dispute' were three tonnes of almost pure heroin.

Jerry had returned to the cordoned area of the services three days later. He couldn't explain the urge to return, especially when he was a wanted man from the situation. To return to the scene of a crime, when it had gone wrong went against all his instincts, but something that he could not put his finger on told him to do just that, like some kind of sixth sense. He had to go back.

There was nothing to see that wasn't to be expected: officers protecting the area, which was still cordoned off with yellow police tape, the chalked outlines of the bodies of the fallen, nothing left but the sawdust, stained a dark crimson as the blood had mixed with oil. The remains of his closest friend, Barry, had been scraped, cleared away. Jerry shuddered as he recalled the last living moments of his greatest ally. He found himself returning to the same pump, only the last time there had been a matter of urgency, a matter of life or death. Hutchin, wisely, had decided that death was a better option than capture and was on the heels of Jerry. They roared from the service area on the top of the R1, smiling maniacally at the cops who sat and watched, open-mouthed.

Jerry was re-living this as he refilled the tank of the Range Rover at the pump. The motor was intentionally left low on fuel before returning to the scene, giving him more time to look and think, surveying everything and storing it in his memory bank. The temporary port-a-cabin used by the police as a base for the investigation; it crossed Jerry's mind to return and sabotage it late in the evening, but he dismissed the notion.

"Why did I come back here today?"

Maybe today, here, in Gibraltar, he would discover the reason.

Laying in silence, looking at the ceiling, Jerry's mind returned to that fateful day. The sound of screeching vehicles, the demands of the police, Barry shouting.

"Go! Go! Go!"

The panic and adrenalin, the thump of the unmarked police van as it careered sideways into Barry, the sound of gunshots and the agonising scream as his friend was hit would forever be imprinted in his mind, regardless of the afternoon's encounter.

A knock on the door sprang Jerry to life. He glanced at his watch as he moved across to open the door; he was shocked to see that he had laid on the bed for three hours.

"Your clothing delivery, Senor," said a young bellboy, sweeping past him gaily to hang the fresh suit upon the clothing rail.

"My God, how camp!" thought Jerry, amused.

"On the bed is fine." Jerry motioned limply towards the bed, not that the bellboy obeyed. "Any car keys?"

"Si. Your friend requested a mini valet. The keys are waiting for you in reception."

"Perfecto," said Jerry.

'Tom's learning fast," he thought.

The bellboy stood looking at Jerry like a panting dog. Jerry pulled an open wad from his pocket, peeled off a 10 Euro note and passed it to him.

"Gracias, Senor," said the boy as Jerry locked the door behind him. He walked back to the bed, stripping off his clothes as he did and leaving them on the floor where they fell. After giving the suit the once over, he turned to look in the mirror. He ached for a cold beer from the mini bar but eventually decided against it and settled for the faithful Toblerone as he strode into the shower. He soaped down in the shower with his mouth full of chocolate, realising only then that it was the first thing he'd eaten all day.

Jerry had to admit that he was utterly baffled. What kind of answers was he going to hear tonight? How was Barry going to explain himself? What about his wife, Jane? And the children? Surely they weren't wrapped up in this?

No, he had overheard Kath speaking to her on the phone on many occasions. Jerry swallowed another triangle and turned the temperature of the water to cold, and crouched into a squat, letting the water bounce off his back. He remained in this position until his legs went numb, then rose and walked from the shower into the suite, hitting the air con as he went. He laid out on the bed as if to drip dry. For the first time that afternoon, he felt composed.

Once dry and with a deep sigh of resignation, Jerry climbed off the bed and dressed. He plastered himself in the hotel's cologne. The cream double-breasted suit fitted like a glove, and the brown shirt with gold tie complemented the whole outfit. He slipped on the brown suede shoes and transferred the wad from his discarded trousers to the new ones. Jerry was never complete without the old faithful roll of readies. He returned to the bathroom and used a little shampoo and a lot of gel to slick back his black curls. He was once again satisfied with his appearance.

He collected his clothing from the floor and dumped them ceremoniously into the complementary plastic laundry bag. Double-checking that he had not left anything, he consulted his watch and saw it was time to go. He decided to use the stairs to avoid sweating up in the confines of the lift. Once in the open, air-conditioned reception, he glanced toward the bar, only to be disappointed to see a young man on duty. Not that it mattered. But he was disappointed, nonetheless.

The *conserje* greeted him with a smile and Jerry shook his hand warmly, transferring a twenty as he did so. He stepped out of the coolness of the building into the humidity of the outside world. The car was ready, roof down. Jerry eased slowly from the car park with a mixture of feelings he couldn't describe. He tried to identify the ones he could individually. Apprehension. Anxiousness. Annoyance. Anger. Anticipation.

He felt a wave of guilt at the last one.

Chapter Four

Driving down the incline of the rock, Jerry was now, for the first time, in control. He was not the guilty party here. He was not the one who had some serious explaining to do—he chose some sixties ballads to listen to. On the approach to the vehicular exit from Gib, Jerry was pleased to see the queue was small and moving at a steady pace. He glanced at the entrance to the airport with a rye smile, thinking the flights to Dublin would have to wait; life was a funny thing, for sure; you could never envisage what was around the corner. The customs officers randomly asked drivers to open the boots of their cars, no doubt checking for duty-free cigarettes. When it was Jerry's turn, he was not surprised to be asked to stop and open his boot, too. He didn't leave the car but pressed the button to put the roof up, opening the boot to enable the roof to come out. The officer, complete with greasy olive skin, a large belly and thick moustache slapped the roof once it was in position and waved Jerry on. *Fucking cunt*, Jerry mouthed through the wing mirror with a smile.

Within minutes, he was racing up the hills to The San Roque Golf and Leisure Resort, a five-star complex of exquisite facilities to pamper the rich and famous, one of many oases that had sprung up along the Coast in recent times due to the property and investment escalation. The 310-day-a-year sunshine never fails to attract. This was one of the places Jerry and the girls liked to frequent, usually for Sunday lunch. As he entered the complex, he wondered if it was purely coincidental that Barry had chosen this location or whether he knew this and had done it purposely to make Jerry feel at ease. The attendant smiled and welcomed him as he opened the car door.

"Buenos notches, Senor Jerry. May I park your car for you?"

"Yes, in the shade, please," replied Jerry, looking up to see the sun was still on show. He handed the attendant a small note for the service provided.

"Good evening, Mr. Jerry! Do you have a reservation? I'm sorry I don't have you listed." said Marie in the form of an apologetic greeting while scouring a large red register placed on a wooden plinth.

"Hello Marie, I am meeting an old friend. I am actually a little early. I'll take a drink on the terrace, thank you." not answering the question,

Marie raised her hand without taking her beautiful eyes from Jerry's and like magic, a young assistant was at hand to see Jerry to a table.

"The terrace," Marie instructed the young boy, still holding Jerry's gaze. Her smile broadened. "I'll see you later," she said

"God willing," replied Jerry, letting her see him inspect her bodily form.

The terrace was busy, but Jerry saw a position that suited him and walked directly to it. The table had the benefit of views to the golf course, plus the restaurant entrance, with the added attraction of easy exit. His escort and waiter had the chair from under the table before Jerry even reached it, so was the efficiency this place demanded,

"What can I get you to drink, sir?"

"Agua sin gas con Limon por-favour"

"Si." Said the waiter, easing the chair comfortably so Jerry could be seated.

"I didn't know you spoke the lingo," said a familiar voice.

"Fuck me, where did you spring from?" said Jerry standing to greet Barry. They embraced briefly, as is customary in these parts, and Jerry would have laughed had the circumstances been different—the fact that Barry stood there wearing the exact same suit was not humorous at this point.

"I thought I had all the angles covered," said Jerry reclaiming his chair.

"You did. I was in the toilet," replied Barry

"Fuck! You startled me."

"Sorry," Barry said, taking the only other seat at the table. The waiter placed Jerry's glass and half filled it with cold water from a bottle, put some olives and nuts on the table and looked at Barry with a smile,

"The same, please," said Barry, who turned to look at his old friend with a face etched with apprehension.

"I could do a brandy," said Jerry. To ease the situation, he crossed one leg over the other, stuck a cocktail stick through three olives and leaned back in his chair. He loosened his tie slightly to give an appearance of relaxation, which he was far from, but he could feel the anxiety flooding from the man opposite him,

"Let me have it, Barry," he said, brushing his thigh with the back of his hand ever so slightly removing some imaginary debris. He sometimes amazed himself with where these motivational gimmicks came from. He certainly succeeded in making Barry feel at ease.

"Brandy sounds like a good idea," said Barry

"There'll be time enough for brandy when the dealings are done," said Jerry with just a hint of impatience.

"I'm not sure you will have one with me after I've told you everything. I'm taking a gamble here, Jerry."

"Let me be the judge of that. Give it to me, Barry. Do I call you Barry?" asked Jerry, growing more impatient by the second.

"For now, yes," he replied, taking the glass and bottle from the waiter

"Thank you," he said, filling his glass and emptying it in one go.

"Sit back and relax, Barry. Nothing will happen to you here. Take a deep breath and start at the beginning."

Barry looked at the man facing him, the man he loved like a brother. He gave an audible sigh, loosened his tie and leaned forward with elbows on his knees.

"I know how difficult this must be for you, Jerry. Believe me, you can multiply it by one hundred, and you still would not know how difficult it is for me, but I have to do this."

"I know, go on," said Jerry, completely composed on the outside.

"Please try not to interrupt until I have finished. I will tell you how it was, why it was, and what it is, after which you can digest what you have heard, take some time to mull it over and decide if I did the right thing. You can decide whether you would've acted the same way had you been in my position. I hope you will realise I had very little option, and I want you to ask yourself what you would've done. I am here to ask for your understanding and forgiveness, Jerry. If I receive that, I have a proposition for you which is on your doorstep, but let me begin by telling you how it was for me."

"Go on," said Jerry, almost exhausted. He could see the desperation seeping into the eyes of a man he adored all his life and now felt a surge of compassion for.

Barry took a deep breath and began.

"Do you remember the safety deposit place we looked at in Mayfair?" he asked. Jerry gave a slight nod of his head.

"The information I received was from a source." he continued, "Jefri, the brother of the Sultan of Brunei, had taken 20% of the boxes, 100 in total. You refused to be involved because I would not declare the source. I had been sworn to secrecy. When you refused to participate, I asked for your blessing. Unfortunately, you gave it." he looked down, rather sheepishly, before inhaling loudly and continuing, "I will start from the beginning as I see it." he looked up and into the eyes of his friend, "The opposition was on to us from the moment the evidence file relating to the cash depot disappeared in February 99. Wheeler was in the frame from his peers, and some heads had to roll. Not only that, but Wheeler's go-between told me that the money Wheeler received was later stolen from him. It seems, or at least he believes, there was a tracking device sewn into the lining of the attaché case. So basically, the service provided by him was of no benefit, to him that is. He believes that the missing papers cost him his promotion, and for that reason alone, he was out to get us, fuck us up big style! I believe that Wheeler indirectly provided the information for the Mayfair job. It now transpires that before the initial introduction to the inside man, Wheeler had been assigned to provide security for Jelfri and secure reputable safekeeping for his jewels. Your intuition paid off again." said Barry, looking down at the drip mat he was nervously folding. At the same time, Jerry looked up from the one he was holding tightly. Their eyes did not meet in crossing. If they had, two would have seen the anger from the two looking with fear.

"Wheeler regained his reputation, but not his promotion after contributing to Operation Dispute," Jerry looked directly at Barry at the mere mention of this operation. His mind was racing. The frown lines on his forehead creasing, for the first time, showing signs of age and confusion mixed with anticipation and realisation. For a split second, he considered getting up and leaving before he heard anymore. He knew what he would have to do should he hear this guy say what he was now expecting him to say. He didn't know if he was capable of doing that to him.

"Please hear me out," continued Barry, sensing the situation to be in a delicate position. He knew that this was a crucial time and had to move quickly to complete this hurdle.

"You tell me, what choice I had? I was set up from the very start Jerry, they knew we were talking to the Turks. They had surveillance footage of our clandestine meetings with Venga. They knew everything, about me, you, our move into that shit. But the saving grace was it was no longer us who were the prime targets. Having said that, they had enough on us to secure a conspiracy conviction. Believe me Jerry, they had us by the short and curlies! And me for the Blags! That's without the evidence relating to Mayfair, but even still, I was going to take it. But you, Jerry, were going with me. So be it… I know you; you would've taken it, that's the way you are, the way you've always been. But then there was the deciding factor. I had to weigh up the pros and cons. Number one was your safekeeping; they knew full well you wouldn't give up without a fight, and I had to make sure there were no firearms at South Mimms. And if there had to be, I would supply them, assuring the bullets were blanks. I made one stipulation, and that was that you had to go, you had to escape. The bike Jerry, the fucking bike was there all the time; it was there for you, Hutchin was a bonus. I had no idea he was going to turn up." Barry was now leaning forward, one hand gripping the table edge; he could see the realisation etched on his friend's face and felt the same emotion at the pit of his stomach. He was connecting.

"The driver of the fucking van was some stunt driver from the latest James Bond movie or something. The van hit me side-on, there was a door that opened, and I was dragged in; you were already gone, and the vest I gave you was an extra precaution. Hutchin was lucky to stay with you, knowing you wouldn't leave him anyway. I did nothing wrong as far as you were concerned, mate." Barry pleaded, now putting his hand on Jerry's thigh and squeezing it hard. Jerry looked down as the blood circulation stopped with the grip, and Barry released his hold, knowing he was pushing his luck. All the time, Jerry said nothing, taking it all in and assessing the importance and relevance; every word said was banked. This was not going to be an easy feat, that was for sure.

Barry knew full well he was taking a risk here. Jerry was old school, as staunch as they come. It was them against the opposition, the opposition was the police and "them" was anybody who wasn't.

"As I was saying, Jerry, the information for the Mayfair job was supplied by the manager who, as it transpires, was instructed by Wheeler. How Wheeler got to him, I don't know, but it was ingenious on his part; he must have thought this through long and hard. He was hurting and he was angry. Then Wheeler was called upstairs, for obvious reasons; he was an encyclopaedia of information on us and our activities, no one knew us in the Metro like him, he'd seen us grow, knew our history, the very nature of our being and what we were about. Anyway, it seems the Turks had been bringing a large amount of that shit in for a long time before we got involved. Our problem was that at the time of our introduction to it, there was a consignment of contaminated stuff on the ground. Venga knew full well that it was bad merchandise and let it run and hit the streets. There were many people in a bad way, we didn't know, we don't live in that world. These things are not reported. It's not good for the government, and the elections were around the corner. The problem was that there were many fatalities down to the same shit, which, again, nobody would be any the wiser had one of these fatalities not been a certain nineteen-year-old Law student from Edinburgh University who also happened to have royal blood running through her pretty veins along with the poison. It now became high on the agenda for Venga's head to roll, but he was cute, as you know, Jerry. Venga was really cute. What you have to understand at this point is that we were up there with him. For fuck sake, Jerry, look at what I had to sacrifice,"

"Go on," said Jerry, showing no emotion now. The anger was still there but had now moved down to the pit of his stomach, and he could feel it working its way up in the form of vile. He was now beginning to perspire. The world was moving too fast. Events of that whole episode from his life were rewinding and fast-forwarding like a tape in his mind. He was now using all his energy and experience to remain seated. He had to hear this. This was real life, not some movie with a prologue, main body and epilogue. These were things that had actually happened in this life, not some figment of some author's imagination. The waiter approached the table,

"Mr Jerry, will you be dining with us this evening?"

"No, Fredo," replied Jerry without looking at Barry sitting opposite him.

"More drinks then, perhaps?"

"Yes, the same, please," annoyance now in his reply. "As you were. Carry on," he said, looking at the man facing him. He stood as he said this and removed his coat. The boy was there to take hold of it before he fully removed it. *Fucking amazing,* thought Jerry, his shirt now damp with sweat. *I wouldn't be surprised if the kid didn't return with a fucking tumble dryer.* He thought.

Barry now looked at the waiter as he returned and placed the drinks on the table. He also replaced the shredded drip mats and wiped the table. All this time, Barry held his breath, waiting for the boy to be out of earshot before commencing. He was gaining momentum and had a sense of urgency in his speech. Was he getting there? Could he swing this? He desperately needed Jerry's forgiveness and understanding. He felt the urge to hold his friend. He wanted to say please but knew weakness was not the way into this man's world. After all, he, too, was his own man.

"I want you to put yourself in my position, Jerry. First of all, I was looking at 25 to 30. They had me at the manager's house. They had me at the school of his children. They had surveillance footage of me at a convention he was attending in the Midlands and had me talking to him in the Hyatt in Birmingham. All this was on tape, Jerry, and then, to cap it off, they produced plans for the safety deposit box house with my dabs on. I knew I was fucked and resigned myself to the fact. Then Wheeler enters the cell and tells me we are going for a ride. I see an opportunity, but he assures me we will have plenty of company. I wonder what the fuck this is, but as it was, I thought I had nothing to lose; I'll go along with the flow. I was intrigued. Wheeler knew full well he was barking up the wrong tree for dealing anyone away. He may as well have been talking to you, so I agree to go."

Jerry was now anticipating the worst. He looked around the room; the lounge bar was busy, and the overflow of patrons had filled out onto the terrace to see the sun go down. Any other occasion would have been a pleasure to be seated here. As it was, there was tension in this place, with harmony less than two metres away on the other tables—*different worlds to say the least*.

"We head up north," Barry continued, "I'm in a car, not a sweat box, we have escorts front and rear and a chopper above. I am now beginning to wonder, what the fuck is all this about? Wheeler tries to make small talk in the car. I say fuck all, I assume the car's bugged. We stop for petrol, a guy comes with sandwiches and drinks, which we have in the services car park. I'm allowed to piss. I say I want a shit, so we have to detour to a nick. Believe me, Jerry at this stage, I'm baffled." Jerry nodded his head slightly. Barry drew comfort from this.

"Anyway, we eventually arrive at this country estate near Edinburgh, a place called Musselburgh. The escorts in the front stop at the gates, which open automatically. There is a small sentry box just inside, and a guy walks over with a walkie fucking talkie; now I'm waiting for Blowfield to show up," a slight hint of a smile from Jerry, *great* thought Barry,

"The escorts front and rear remain outside the gates, but the helicopter remains above. I can hear it but can't see it, for the trees line the approach. It has to be half a mile long. Now we're met at the door of a stately home, more like a palace, by a fucking butler complete with a black suit, white gloves and a fucking tea towel draped over his right arm," now a laugh from Jerry, not a belly laugh but a laugh and a "*fuck me*," which will do. Jerry leans forward with a smile on his face. This is the Jerry Barry was praying for.

"My cuffs are taken off, and we are escorted through the hallway with high ceilings, oak panels, stuffed bears, lions, deer and suits of armour. I'm led into a library with enough antique books to retire on. I'm telling you, Jerry, we did a few gaffs on the way up, but one or two like this, and we could have retired long ago. Anyway, I'm seated at a table the size of this terrace, not as wide, but definitely as long. Wheeler's looking at me all the time, but I show no sign that I am impressed or intrigued, but I am wondering *what the fuck is going on?* The butler arrives with a silver tray like someone out of the fucking Adams family. I'm telling you, the cunt looked like he'd never seen a minge in his lifetime, he probably only had one fuck in him, and it was holding him together."

That was it; both Barry and Jerry laughed out loud. *Fucking brilliant,* thought Barry, relieved, to say the least. The table next to them turned to look at what was so amusing and laughed along with them after another outburst came when Barry added, "I asked him for a brandy and a King Edward, the cunt only returned with them." more laughter, this time from Jerry alone. This is what Barry wanted. This was how it used to be. Maybe this was how it could be again.

"This is how bizarre it was, mate, I'm telling you. But, now it gets serious. The door opens, and there's three of them. One was the man of the house; old cunt, wispy grey hair, frayed green velvet dinner jacket and a pair of checked slippers with holes in. The other two are MI5 or 6. I don't know, does it go any higher? MI-fucking-100 whatever. Anyway, there is no introductions, and the old cunt is looking at me like the bear in the hallway has shit all over me, and the fucking lion is licking it off. Believe me, I felt like I needed to be wearing that suit of armour, but you know me, I'm not letting them see my inferior complex. I'm sitting there with my Brandy and the King Edward thinking, *What the fuck in this world is coming next.*

"What comes next, Jerry, is one of these fucking secret agents throws a file on the table in front of me, leans over my shoulder and opens it. Who the fuck is looking at me?"

"Me?" asked Jerry with dread.

"No. Venga!"

"Thank fuck for that," Jerry said, relieved.

"Yes, Venga. I see then, other pictures, terrible pictures of youths, boys, girls, dead! All of them, some as young as Jasmine. Believe me, Jerry, it was not a pleasant sight."

"Where is this going, Barry?"

"Venga was responsible for the deaths of these kids. The faces stare back at me, and then Steptoe gasps when a particular face looks up at me. A young girl, pretty as they come, but a grey-blue in colour. I look toward the gasp, and the old man has tears running down his face. I now begin to understand." Barry knew he was treading on delicate ground here, Jerry being a father and all.

"Now everyone takes a seat, and one of the suits turns on a projector directed at the only wall not worth a fortune. He starts clicking, and the story unfolds with the help of some narration," There was a pause from Barry. Jerry was quick to detect that this was for impact, so he took advantage of this to make himself more comfortable. Sitting back in his cozy chair, he crossed his legs, put his elbows on the armrest and made a church and steeple with his hands caressing his steepled fingers to his dry lips.

"And?" He coached enquiringly, now very much, the old Jerry. Composed and confident.

"Then we move on to more familiar territory, faces were looking at me from the wall, some I had seen before, some I hadn't. Venga and others. To cut a very long story short, Jerry, The world we were moving into had now overstepped the mark. It transpires that a consignment had moved from Afghanistan to Turkey, destination: the United Kingdom. We know there is nothing unusual about this, it happens all the time, that shit is a commodity, that's how we looked at it when we decided to hold talks with Venga. If it wasn't us, it was someone else. And with the heat after the cash depot scenario, we agreed that it was a sensible move for us. The payment took care of the evidence; we were lucky to walk but had to look at other avenues. The fact that I introduced Venga still haunts me to this day, but that's water under the bridge that has now evaporated." Barry now took a drink, a deep breath and continued. Jerry was quickly getting the picture.

"Back to the shipment, this shit lands in the UK undetected, to the delight of Venga, who has it tested for cutting purposes. His chemist, who looks back at me from the library wall, custody number intact, his name is Akrim; he is the one who told Venga the stuff is contaminated with some lethal agent. Poison if you like. The stuff had some name, I couldn't even begin to pronounce with a list of fucking E numbers after it. Anyway, Venga gets hold of Akrim and swears him to secrecy. The stuff then is transported to Glasgow, 500 fucking kilos of the shit. When injected, the unlucky ones would be blinded, and the nervous system would be attacked over a short period of time, leaving the poor cunt in agony before comfort is drawn from paralysis. The lucky ones would convulse like they were on a fast spin and die shortly after. A terrible death Jerry and the cunt knew the implication. This was terrorist-linked, without a doubt. When the casualties began to show similarities, the officials were put on alert, and then, when the deaths were related, the police were getting it from all angles. Some of the bulk was seized, and the word spread quickly on the street. An amnesty was declared, and the scum informants were coming out from under every stone. In all, there were 44 deaths and over 500 fucked cases; there were nearly 2000+ needing medical treatment. Obviously, the more the shit was cut, the less dangerous it became." Barry now took his drink and sipped it; Jerry noted he was more relaxed, he himself was starting to get the complete picture. Barry continued.

"The one not using the projector made it clear that they knew we were not involved in this poison; he was the good cop out of the good cop, bad cop duo. The break in the case, for them, was the chemist, and of course, we had never met him… Now Polanski, the film producer, turns off the machine, and the old man pulls a cord beside a fire surround big enough to walk into. Lurch appears and takes the orders, I took a black coffee; I don't think another brandy would have been a good idea. Anyway, when Lurch fucks off, the show commences; the old man is now fast asleep with his cat, and the machine is noisy enough to overwhelm the purrs and snores. The next feature is more familiar. This is where the case against me is put forward. Like the opening of the crown's case in court, the evidence is overwhelming. I wouldn't stand a fucking chance; they had it all, mate: the meetings, the tapes, the voice recognition, telephone records, the business; there was no way I was going to beat this one, Jerry and certainly no one to pay." Barry now took off his tie and unloosened the top two buttons of his shirt, his forehead, nose and area surrounding his top lip had little beads of sweat clearly visible. He continued.

"Moving along swiftly. You are introduced. A full frontal of you and Venga on the golf course. Obviously, at the Belfry in the Midlands. They have us at the Metropole, the Hilton on Park Lane and lots of other places. But these are just surveillance pictures; I know they mean fuck all, but then, good cop plays some telephone conversation which in itself would not be enough. I mean, you don't mention fuck all, really, a jury wouldn't make heads nor tails of it, but you know how corrupt and dishonest these prosecutors are, not to mention what the cunts are allowed to get away with. The top and bottom of it was, I was not prepared to take the risk."

"Isn't that for me to decide?" Interrupted Jerry

"Please! Let me finish. I'm nearly there." responded Barry, a little annoyance creeping in.

"The character of Venga then became the topic of conversation, although the conversation was totally one-sided." he paused slightly for impact. The pace was now quickening, and Barry leaned forward in his seat, almost desperate to keep up the momentum.

"In all this time, I had not spoken. They now go on to tell me what they knew about Venga. Totally slating him. I know this could have been propaganda; I'm not that naïve, but I want you to listen, Jerry and I also want you to think back. Think back to our second meet with Venga and then to other times after that. What these suits were telling me is that amongst his other illegal activities were ones that were not for finance, but purely sexual. And when I say sexual, I mean the man is a fucking animal. Worse than an animal. There was plenty of evidence, as far as I could see. A few photos of him in the company of minors in some African country, other pictures depicting sexual torture if you like, fuck knows what you'd call it but the scenes were despicable; there was one…"

"Spare me the details." Interrupted Jerry.

"OK." said Barry, relieved that the message was received. He didn't go on to tell how other pictures were shown, and he was asked if he recognised one individual, in particular, sitting in the background of a photograph taken in a cellar, a child having despicable things done to him for the sexual pleasure of the adult perverts watching on. It was unlikely that the child could have survived such abuse and lived to tell the tale.

"Now, Jerry. Think back to the times we have met Venga. Think about the interest he showed toward little Barry. Remember the first meeting? You suggested the golf course for security. The vast open space. No listening devices, etc. Where did he opt for? The fucking swimming baths. You gave him credit for that. Remember? But think now Jerry, think back and try to remember how he acted in the changing rooms, how unusual he became. At the time, we put it down to this religion shit, but the fact of the matter is he was fucking noncing even then. Take it from me, mate; the man was worse than shit, and he deserved every fucking thing he got. If I could have done the deal with those cunts to put a bullet in Venga's head myself, I would have been more than happy to do it, but not before cutting the cunts balls off first and making him eat them."

"How do you feel about the fact that you introduced this piece of shit into our lives?" asked Jerry, now looking older than his years again for a split second.

"I'm sorry"

"You're sorry?"

"What more can I say?"

"Have you finished?"

"Wheeler wanted you, Jerry," urged Barry, agitated now in his deliverance. "It was personal with him. He wanted you as much as the other cunts wanted Venga." He now wiped his brow with the cuff of his sleeve. Desperation now clearly heard in the tone of his voice.

"I stayed awake all night. I was taken to the nearest nick and bedded down. The next morning, first thing, in walks Wheeler with some cunt who doesn't have the decency to introduce himself. Obviously, it's some big wig. Anyway, I decline their offer to participate unless I have the assurance of your liberty. Wheeler was seething the cunt. Anyway, away they go. Presumably, leaving me to sweat. I'll be truthful: I was. Sweating, I mean. Not long after, they return. They agree. This had to be done in a way that you didn't look like the one who had put them in. It was agreed that I would be taken out. I suppose they were thinking once they had me, I could be useful again in the future. Who knows what they were thinking? Anyway, the rest is history." Barry was now looking for any sign of accomplishment on Jerry's face. There was none. He tried with one last desperate attempt to gain the support and understanding of his lifelong friend.

"I was a goner, whichever way you looked at it, Jerry. And so were you. It was just a matter of time. There was no way I was leaving that nick other than in a box or many years later. As far as I was concerned, I was dead. To Jane and the kids, I was dead." As a last act of desperation, Barry leaned over and grabbed Jerry's forearm. Jerry shook him off with a look of resignation.

"I need time to digest this." He said, leaning further back into his chair. He beckoned Fredo over.

"Yes, Mr. Jerry. What can I get for you?"

"Another tonic, please," a pause. "with a large gin." He raised his eyebrows in Barry's direction.

"Not for me, thanks. I'm exhausted. I feel like I've done 10 rounds with Tyson. I'm staying here anyway. I must go lie down. I have aromatherapy booked for 7 am, Mr. Viceroy, if you want to leave a message, Jerry. I leave for Thailand in two days." Jerry raised his eyebrow. *What's this cunt up to?*

Jerry stood as Fredo arrived with his drink. He took it from the tray and drank it in one gulp without adding the tonic. "Put this on Mr. Viceroy's room." he looked at Barry with screwed-up features against the Gin.

"308." Said Barry with a grin. The two embraced. Barry had the stronger grip. Jerry got the feeling his friend was reluctant to let go.

"I'll be in touch," said Jerry as he swung on his heels and walked toward the exit. Barry looked at him, walking away before turning to the waiter. He apologised for making such a mess with the drip mat. How he needed that rubdown!

Chapter Five

Jerry left the Club House and drove only a short distance before stopping the car in a lay-by on the mountain edge. He got out of the car leaving the door open as music poured out. It was "A Change Is Gonna Come" by Sam Cooke.

The view was breathtaking and the cool breeze was more than welcome as he stood to look at the moon lighting up the sea until the lights of Gibraltar took over.

He rested one hand on the exposed windscreen and the other on the open door as he looked from the moon to follow the flight path of a Jet more than six miles up and travelling at over 500 miles an hour, who where they and where were they going? Did they have a care? They were the victors of the world. How he envied the regular folk.

He inhaled deeply and looked out over the Med to Gib and beyond, the blue black of the water glittering to the coastline of Africa and its nearest point Morocco, he had plans to be in Morocco tomorrow. This may have to change depending on a very difficult decision. He stayed here looking out over the sea for some time, contemplating his decision. He slowly ran tonight's events through his mind and meticulously scrutinised the important aspects as he saw them.

Jerry eventually made his mind up but decided not to contact room 308 tonight. He turned towards the car and thought about a massage of a different kind. He was stepping into the Merc when he heard the helicopter before he looked up to see it. He subconsciously realised that this was the fourth time in two days that he had seen it. Not that unusual. Unless, of course, one was active.

Damn! The realization began to hit him. The barbeque!

"Fuck!" he mouthed looking at his watch. "9.54?! Fuck it!"

There was a new club recently opened in Algeciras. He needed to relax.

Chapter Six

Detective Inspector Wheeler

Bill Wheeler was thirty-seven years into a career that he would be relieved, with a tinge of disappointment, to see the end of. He had climbed the ladder the hard way, he kept reminding himself. He had earned his position and rank and was not opposed to voicing his disappointment with and opinions about those who had gone before him. As far as Wheeler was concerned, there were two breeds within the force: the ones who were pushed up the ladder with the assistance of qualifications and the might of a pen; and there were the *Wheeler type*, the type who actually fought and gained respect from the former through some damn good detective work in the field.

Granted, Wheeler had some unorthodox ways of achieving some results, often at the expense to others. Many had lost their liberty due to the determination of Wheeler and his sidekick, Smith. It didn't matter to him if they were guilty of the crime or not. If they were in his sights, they were probably guilty of something. Just as long as they get put away. Did it really matter what for? *C'est la vie.*

His wife always reminded him that he deserved more than he had got for the years of hard work and the sacrifices he had made. Just like the kids of the villain, the children of the hero detective might as well have grown up without a father. The only difference is that the successful villain's children reap the rewards of their ill-gotten gains: private education, holidays in exotic places, the latest technology, gimmicks and a sweet sixteen birthday complete with car keys and alcohol. He hated the lot of them.

Approaching his sixtieth birthday, he was looking at a second bite of a very ripe cherry; the 'Grand Finale' to complete his journey full circle. He knew he would regain the respect and adulation he duly deserved. As far as most were concerned, he was very much still the scapegoat for the catastrophe of Operation Dispute.

Wheeler had been drafted into Operation Dispute - a major drugs operation—through his involvement with its targets stemming back to the nineties, when there had been a number of successful armed robberies stretching the length and breadth of the U.K and Southern Ireland. Wheeler was proud to say he was the man who uncovered the link.

Although geographically, these crimes were widespread and varied. there weren't that many of them. The connection was the same modus operandi: The team committing the robberies would take time to befriend the manager of a bank, supermarket, jewellery shop, manufacturer or wholesaler and, on one occasion, a failed attempt at a money security depot. The managers, in most cases, would be married with children; if not, their parents would suffice. These immediate family members would then be used as tools to instil fear into the manager, blackmailing him into giving away security details of the intended target. Fortunately for the victims, there was rarely violence, but they were left traumatised and mentally scarred. In each case, the manager was put under constant surveillance by the robbers, who would watch their every move for months on end before each attack. Contact would be made after this time. The locations depended on the lifestyle of the victim; A hotel bar, sports centre, golf club, even a flying club.

This was the extent to which the crooks were prepared to go to structure their crime. If the opportunity arose, a female was used to lure the victim into a relationship: an added attraction and bargaining ploy for the team. If all went to plan, the manager would be the only victim; the honey trap would eliminate his family.

Sometimes, though, there would be no choice but to involve the family. To do this, a member of the team would be dispatched to the home of the target, usually when the children had been dropped off at school. The wife would be given instructions in a note to be relayed to the husband, who, by this time, would be hard at work. The notes would be destroyed: burnt or flushed down the drain. Random hair and cigarette butts would always be left at the scene to reveal innocent parties who had recently used a hairdresser, thereby giving the villains the benefit of time and confusion within the investigation. But, it also told the officers dealing with the crime that this was one team operating in the same way. All it required was a lead.

One thing the robbers did not account for was the sheer determination of the officer assigned to bring the team down. Wheeler had started his career as most did, treading the streets of South East London. The monotonous 'day in, day out' of walking mile after mile. He was of the opinion that the more he nicked, the faster he would climb the ladder. He had a mean reputation amongst the local delinquents, two of which would grow to be Wheeler's adversaries and a constant thorn in his side throughout his career: Jerry Divine and Barry Stone.

He gradually rose through the ranks, entering the more demanding—yet thoroughly interesting—world of the burglary division, and given a senior partner: the well-respected JJ Fields, a man with over forty years of experience who was heading towards retirement. After discovering Fields helping himself to some of the proceeds left at a crime scene, Wheeler turned him in, for which he received another promotion to the robbery department. This gave him more scope to expand his obsession for recognition and promotion, working relentlessly with little interest in anything else. His wife, having only recently given birth to the second of their two kids, would nag him constantly to spend more time with his family. That only added to the frustration Wheeler felt towards the enemy and his ambition to put them away.

Almost forty years later, here he was, sitting in the departure lounge at Stanstead Airport, deep in thought. Divine, Stone and their team were eventually brought down by Wheeler and Smith, only to walk away on a technicality and the mysterious disappearance of some damning CPS documents. Documents which would have secured their conviction and heavy prison sentences.

That was before Wheeler got the call, which started the negotiations and the deal that he constantly regretted getting involved with. And for what? To be beaten at the last hurdle?

No. Not him. Never again.

Not to mention his ageing parents. For them to be attacked in such a way in what should have been the safety of their own home, was unforgivable. He was relishing that justice may finally be seen to be done for everyone concerned. He was brought back to the present by the loudspeaker, informing him that the 21.48 flight ESY 2020 to Malaga was ready for boarding. He heaved his one hundred and thirty-kilo frame from the low seating and swept his hand through his sparse silvery grey hair. He struggled to balance the strap of his shoulder bag on his sagging body, so he settled for carrying it limply by his side. The sweat from his unfit body left wet stains seeping through his shirt and jacket to leave dark patches under his arms and at the top of his back. Struggling with his light luggage, which also consisted of a cheap brown briefcase, he made his way to the departure gate for boarding.

Before stepping onto the plane, he took his mobile phone from his pocket to check for messages. There were two: one from his boss which read: *Contact made. An appointment has been arranged for you to attend Central Police Station, Malaga, tomorrow @ 1300. Ask for Angelo Perelta.* The second was from his wife, which he deleted without reading.

The plane landed at 23.52 local time, 15 minutes ahead of schedule thanks to a tail wind. This made little difference to Wheeler, who had drunk three vodka and cokes in rapid succession before lapsing into a coma for almost the complete journey, much to the annoyance of a young Spanish in the seat next to him who was returning from her student exchange experience in Colchester and trying to write a philosophy essay amid the loud snores and sweaty aroma that invaded her personal space.

Wheeler had insisted that he was not met at the airport and that he would make his own way to the meeting the next day. He and his wife Maud had landed here once before on a package holiday that he had hoped would take him down to the affluent area of Marbella, but that instead had removed him to the more commercialised Torremolinos. He had demanded the representative to either change their hotel or fly them home. This was before seeing some guys frolicking, and then more than frolicking, in the pool late one evening. Having looked around the hotel the following morning, Wheeler realised the resort was the preferred holiday destination to hundreds of gay men and women. Too late he discovered they were in the gay capital of Spain. But that was then and this was now. Homosexuals were the last thing on Wheeler's mind. He knew that this time around he would at last be seeing Marbella.

Chapter Seven

Day Two

Barry was alarmed into reality by the bedside bleeps set for 6.30 am. He rolled over, wishing he had put the time for six; he felt like he needed another hour to come round and prepare for his rub-down.

The night hadn't been kind. It had been the total opposite: restlessness, anxiety, memories, frustration, consequences and hope, a combination of everything he associated with weakness. He accepted he was no longer the man he used to know but was determined to become the man he used to be. A man with morals and dignity. A man of his word. A man with honour and respect.

Like Jerry. It was always 'like Jerry." Jerry had it all. He always did have, ever since they were children. Barry had always looked up to him, but he was never comfortable with it. He was constantly searching for that specific something that Jerry had that made people look up to him and respect him. Barry preferred to look at Jerry and not up to him. He was on his level.

Wasn't he?

There was so much more he could have said last night, even despite the endless monologue he eventually delivered, but he was confident he had covered the main points in the short time they had. He doubted whether he would regain his main man's respect, at least in the immediate future. But that would come with time.

He rolled from the bed, damp with sweat; Barry was not used to living in such heat. He turned on the T.V and the air-conditioning and made his way to the bathroom. He examined himself closely in the mirror. He looked older than his forty years; his hair was simultaneously thinning and receding, his eyes were sunken, making the surgery on his nose and lips look even more prominent. The shoulders were still broad but without the muscular shape. His barrel chest had sunk to his midriff.

Something gotta change.

Something certainly had to change, especially if Jerry was to consider his proposal.

The proposal! He got a shiver through his spine to the lower abdomen just thinking about it. A sensation he liked. It brought back fond memories of the times gone by. Times he wanted back: He and Jerry working together again, with the boys, Winston, Hutchin, O'Rourke and McNess, back together again as a team!

Barry stuck his head under the cold water tap before towel-drying. He took the complimentary robe from behind the bathroom door and popped on a pair of pristine white slippers. Checking the safe was locked, he grabbed a towel before turning off the T.V, which was reporting some major crackdown within the local government office, something to do with corruption and planning authorities. For once, it was nothing that concerned him.

"Welcome Señor, your name please?" asked a friendly girl in the spa reception. She was full of life, with a smile that could wake any well-mannered person. Unfortunately, Barry showed little interest today.

"Good morning, Mademoiselle. Viceroy, Mr Viceroy. 7 o'clock massage."

"Yes, Señor. Please come this way," she grinned, amused by his dire attempt to speak her language. The indifference was mapped on Barry's face. He followed her through to the treatment area, which was relatively quiet considering the facilities on offer.

"Please make yourself comfortable. Lie face down on the bed. Your masseur will be with you shortly." Barry did as he was told, to the beautiful sound of music reminding him of remote beaches and birds of a feathered kind.

"Oh, could you check, there aren't any messages for me? Room 308."

"No problem, Señor. I will let the masseur know if you have some."

Barry had drifted back to sleep when the masseur entered the room. He didn't consider the fact that he was letting his guard down by doing this. If Jerry had an issue, he'd raise it face to face. If anyone else had found him, they were bloody good at their job.

There were no messages, as he would have been woken. The following words he heard were from the deep voice of the male masseur asking him quietly to turn over. Barry did with his first smile of the day.

Chapter Eight

Jerry woke from a restless night at 6 am and was now sitting on the terrace, contemplating the direction to take. It was only a preliminary meeting arranged in Morocco, nothing that couldn't be postponed without any inconvenience, not on his part anyway. He could forget he had ever seen Barry. That was an option. He had to question if he actually had. He would give it an hour or two before considering the validity of his decision.

"You're up, bright and early," Kath said quietly as she came up behind him and gently massaged his temples. She had a knack for knowing when he was deep in thought. He reached back, and she put one hand in his, whilst continuing with her free hand to comb his hair back with her fingers.

"Fresh orange juice?" she whispered, bending to kiss his neck.

"Yes, love, with some dry black toast, please."

"You and your dry toast!"

"I love the smell. It reminds me of my childhood," he said, quietly.

"Why?!" Kath laughed.

"Because that's all we bleeding got!" Jerry thought back to his childhood briefly. The black toast and black coffee, both of which tasted like dirt, but a reassuring taste that childhood memories often bring back: the scrapheap of a house he grew up in, just outside Brixton; the tiny black piano that he and Barry stole from outside the music shop down the road; this reminded him that he HAD to visit the piano shop in Malaga.

"Remember, I always told you," he called just loud enough for her to hear without disturbing the kids, who were probably still sleeping, "one of my dreams was to one day own a white Grand Piano?"

"Many times."

"Well, I thought we may as well have one here as opposed to the UK. After all, we very rarely go back these days. What do you think?"

Kath reappeared in the doorway, holding a plate of toast in one hand and a glass of orange juice in the other. "It's nice that you want to ask me, but you have obviously decided anyway." She placed the breakfast on the table beside Jerry and clambered over him into bed.

"Jezzie left some documents for you last night. They must be important because he asked me to put them in the safe. He wasn't a happy bunny…

Now, what's this obsession with a baby Grand Piano anyway?" She wrapped her arms around his neck like a lover, not a killer.

"Firstly! It's not a baby Grand. It's a Grand."

"I bet it's more than that."

"Does that matter?"

"Just tell me," she smirked.

"When I was a kid at school," Jerry began, "my favourite lesson was music, the one I enjoyed the most. Actually, there were two: Drama and music. I mean, you always said I would have made a terrific actor," he said laughing. "Anyway, music and drama. The drama…" he tailed off, looking puzzled. "Well! I don't know. I didn't think I was very good at it. I wanted to be like Cagney or Bogart."

Kath laughed, playfully rubbing his hair. "See," she said, "you're acting now."

"Or even Rock Hudson, he was another favourite of mine, but look what he turned out to be. A bleeding shirt lifter."

"No!"

"I'm telling you. As queer as they come. He died of AIDS. Didn't you know that? Everyone knows that."

Kath stiffened. "Don't call them that, alright? You say it like there's something wrong with it." She paused, hoping her pep talk had inspired him. "He was beautiful, though, wasn't he?' she added as an afterthought.

"Not when he died, he wasn't. Did you see the state of him?"

"Carry on with the blinking story," she said, growing impatient and playfully digging him in the ribs.

"Right," he laughed. "This is the serious part. The music lessons were my favourite. I can still remember how excited I used to get when the trolley was wheeled in once a week. I think on a Wednesday afternoon. I mean, I even remember the day. That's how much of an impact it must have had on me. Anyway, Mr. Bruno. Another, umm, one of those, you know, Hudsons, as it turned out. He used to play this piano. Not a Grand, obviously, but this upright thing. A normal, everyday piano."

"Yes. A bleeding piano!" Kath butted in, laughing.

"Right, don't interrupt. This is hard for me, talking about my youth."

"OK, no more interruptions."

"Right. In comes the trolley, and the instruments are handed out. I'm like a dog on heat. There's this small music box thing, what's the name of it? You know?" He was now moving his hands around Kath's waist, to the front and back again.

"An accordion?"

"That's it, a miniature accordion. Then, there were the drums, the ca-clappers, like they have here."

"Castanets?"

"That's the one," he corrected himself, laughing with Kath. "Guess who always got the music box?"

"You?"

"I wish!"

Kath laughed again: "What did you get?"

"The bleeding Triangle. And I had to go stand in the far corner."

"Why?"

"For effect." He said, laughing even harder now.

"Stop," giggled Kath, "I can just see you now."

"Barry used to get the frigging accordion. The twat. He had that pouf wrapped around his little… "

He stopped abruptly, as he saw Kath had stopped laughing and was, instead, glaring at him. He realised his mistake.

"Ahem, yeah. I used to be seething. I wanted that damn accordion. Anyway, one night me, Barry and Winston burgled the school and made for the music room. We destroyed the lot. I put the drum over Winston's head. I got the Triangle, straightened it and stuck it straight through a bean bag. Beans every-bleeding-where. I took the accordion, amongst other stuff, and later, I was nicked by the truant officer for slamming off school. I only did a deal with him to let me go in return for it."

"No!" said Kath, in genuine disbelief. She was continually fascinated by the constant trail of breadcrumbs her husband's past kept dropping.

"No word of a lie, I'm telling you. I dealt him up for the accordion… Right! back to the grand. I always promised myself one." He was more serious now, and paused in thought. "To replace the triangle."

Kath giggled some more but then showed sympathy by wrapping her arms around Jerry and kissing his neck. She then stood and let the gown drop from her shoulders.

"Fancy a dip?"

Jerry admired her beautiful body. She turned and walked to the pool's edge, carefully dipping a toe in to feel the temperature. As he watched her graceful movement, he asked himself what it was about this woman that made him feel the way he did whenever he looked at her; the way that all the problems he encountered could vanish for that brief moment. She was the one who could always steer his emotions. If there was anything in this world that he was truly grateful for, it was the fact that she was in his life... Yes, with Kath and his children, he was truly blessed.

Now, as she walked to the deep end of the pool, putting her hair up in a bunch as she moved, his feelings were steered sexually. He wanted her now, which was evident as he, too, stood and dropped his robe to the floor.

"You!" She said, before diving into the cool water. She surfaced somewhere in the middle, surprised to see him. He now stood with his back to the Villa and a prominent bulge in the front of his boxer shorts. She splashed water in his direction.

"Get in here before the girls see you; you're like a dog on heat." She giggled.

"You asked!" he said and jumped high, gathering his knees to his chest as he rose above the water, hitting the water with a loud splash beside her.

"'Jerry! The girls." She screamed, then laughed, and splashed water in his direction. He didn't see or hear her. He was already heading towards her way under the water. Her legs moved rapidly in anticipation.

"Ah!" she cried out and giggled as he wrapped his strong arms around her thighs and nibbled her bikini line. She pulled at his ears, laughing out loud, then began to push his head down. He forced his way up, lifting her at the same time. She screamed again, much to the annoyance of the two girls who looked down from the veranda with sleep in their eyes. "You two are like kids sometimes," said Jasmine sternly.

"Duck him, mummy," said Julie, who was struggling to control Bonito, yapping excitedly at all the commotion.

"Come and help me, Julie," Jerry called in mock desperation. She didn't need to ask twice. She was on her way within seconds, Bonito barking at her heels. Jasmine, on the other hand, did not see the funny side of the situation as she slammed the French doors and returned to her beauty sleep.

Little Julie was now beside the pool, waiting for an opportunity to help Mum avenge her dad and overpower him with the element of surprise.

"Hold him, mummy!" she called excitedly, as Bonito yapped in support at her heels. "Here I come," she warned as she leapt above the two adults who shielded themselves from the mock bombardment.

"That's enough! That's enough. I give in." laughed Jerry; the two brave females overpowered the monster. He scrambled to the side.

"Mum!" cried Jasmine, "This is not funny, I'm part way through my exams. I need to sleep!"

"It's time to get up anyway, love," called her father, who by this time was under the poolside shower. Jasmine didn't answer. She returned to her room and slammed the door.

"How's she doing at school, Kath?" Jerry enquired as he dried himself beside the pool.

"She's doing great. Her business studies are very interesting, you should spend a little time discussing with her sometime."

"Yes, I know. I will," he answered sheepishly. Kath watched him as he did some light stretching under the shade of the gazebo.

"He looks good," she thought, as he flexed his muscles. Yes, he did certainly; tall, dark and handsome. His defined muscular shape was still a pleasure to see and hold. Sometimes, her friends commented on how it would be nice if their partners took the same pride in their appearance as Jerry did. She was happy that he belonged to her. She was also thankful for what she was blessed with: him, the girls, nice family and friends, what the two of them had achieved together, each of them coming from broken homes to what they have now. Material goods were not the be-all and end-all, but she appreciated nice things and enjoyed the houses, cars and jewellery. The lifestyle, although it could get a little monotonous, was amazing at times. The people they met and the places they went to really helped with the charity work Kath was involved with. She had set up Breast Mate Foundation with Debra, a close friend. She first met her when she and Jerry started holidaying in Marbella in the early nineties. They had booked for a week in the only five-star Hotel in Marbella at that time: The El Feuete. Jasmine was a toddler then and played each evening with little Sara, who was three or four years older. Kath and Debs had stayed in touch after the holiday and talked on the phone daily. One day, Debs dropped the bombshell that she had been diagnosed with breast cancer and that the doctors had given her twelve months to live. Kath, who had never been away alone, had begged Jerry to travel with her to Dublin. Jerry, for reasons still unknown to Kath, had refused because of commitments in the U.K. She never dared to ask what was so important that he could not support her when her friend needed her.

Kath flew out to Dublin the next day, intending to stay for three days. As it turned out, she was there for three weeks, and when she returned, it was with Debs and young Sara. Sara, who was nine at the time, stayed with her surrogate parents when Debs returned for her treatment of radio- and chemotherapy. In the short time leading up to the treatment, she said the thing she dreaded most was losing her hair. The weakness and the fatigue, the nausea and incontinence—all things she was told to expect—she felt she could live with, but losing her hair was intolerable. Kath tried to comfort her and tell her that the wigs they have today are so realistic that *"You yourself wouldn't know the difference."* While Kath was in Dublin, the two had gone shopping and tried on some wigs. It was one of the funniest times in their lives, especially when Sara had tried on an afro, while Kath sported a blonde one, complete with pigtails and ribbons. They were eventually asked to leave the premises for causing too much disruption.

Kath cried each night on the phone to Jerry, who listened patiently to his wife pouring out her heart to him about her friend. He was very apologetic about being unable to be there, and suggested that Debs and Sara return to the UK with Kath.

Now, as she watched him doing his Yoga, she was very proud of him. She was proud of the things he had done to help Debs. Both of them knew that if it wasn't for this man, *"This fine figure of a man"* as Debs would say to him, tugging his cheek with finger and thumb, she wouldn't be here today.

When all else had failed, the doctors confirmed there was nothing else that could be done, and they generously gave her three months to live. Debs and Kath refused to take this defeatist attitude and scoured the internet for alternative treatments: new trials, different opinions, old-time remedies, China, new discoveries, anything! Please help. Just as she was reaching the point of exhaustion, Kath discovered some literature and brochures about euthanasia at The Swiss Dignitas Clinic.

"How could you even contemplate such a thing?" demanded Kath, angrily, "Don't you owe it to Sara to keep trying right up until your last breath?"

The two of them had collapsed in each other's arms as Jerry had entered the room. He, too, was overcome with emotion, and the three of them bonded together from that moment on. Kath has often said that she genuinely believed that someone had looked down at that very instant and given Debs a new lease of life because the following page on the computer screen showed the details of a new innovation in treating all types of cancer, but primarily breast cancer. The clinic was in Washington D.C, and the only entry criteria was that you suffered from the illness—Oh! Plus the starting fee of one hundred and ten thousand pounds. Debs didn't believe she had the energy, or the time, to do all the charity events it would take to raise this type of money. She certainly had never seen such an amount. She was comfortable enough with her own hairdressing business and all. But being a single parent—her husband had been killed by the IRA when she was pregnant with Sara—she could only dream of such wealth. This is where Jerry had become the fine figure of a man he was. The very next day, Jerry had handed over the money in a small attaché case. Again, the three had a joint hug, which lasted for some time, without either one of them speaking—words could not explain what emotions were flowing within the combined space.

Thanks to that act, Debs survived. But, things did not turn out the same for *not-so-little* Sara. On her sixteenth birthday, she, too, was diagnosed with the same illness. But, because she had said nothing to anyone for months after discovering her first lump, the disease had progressed so that when it was diagnosed, she was already in hospital receiving treatment for pneumonia. The results of the Biopsy came back the same day she died in St. Luke's Hospital in December 2003. It was because of this tragedy that both Debs and Kath worked constantly to raise money for the prevention and treatment of breast cancer.

"Kath! Kath—the girls, shall I take them or will you?"

"Sorry, love, I was in a daze," she said, shaking her head to dismiss the daydream, "It's OK, I'll take them." She looked at the tips of her fingers and saw they were crimpled with the water. She looked at her watch and realised she had been standing in the pool for twenty minutes. She must give

Debs a call; she hadn't spoken to her for all of three days. She took another look over to the gazebo to see Jerry, who had completed his daily Yoga and was now looking at her.

"Are you ok? You haven't said a word for ages."

"Yes, I'm fine, love. I was just thinking."

"You—thinking!" He mocked, as he walked toward the poolside shower. Again, she looked at her handsome man. Suddenly, she was overcome with a sense of dread. This was not unusual. She had had the same feeling many times over the years. It scared her, but she had learned to live with it. It started with a tingling sensation in her legs and moved up to her stomach like hunger pain, then up to her throat, where she had to swallow the bile that came into her mouth. She never mentioned it to Jerry, principally because he was the cause.

Every time it happened was when everything was rosy, and she was looking at him. She worked out for herself that it was fear. Fear of losing everything, everything dear to her. Not the material things, but Jerry and the girls. She knew that if she lost him, her world would fall apart, and she didn't think she could cope. She wasn't sure if she could live without him. Whether it was a sixth sense, or a woman's intuition—call it what you want—she knew when things weren't right and that something was about to happen. It was a bad feeling.

Bonito broke her thoughts as she scampered around the pool and garden at an alarming rate, yapping excitedly, almost hysterically, at the helicopter flying surprisingly low overhead.

"Bonito!" She called out as she walked up the pool steps, where Jerry was waiting with a large bath towel in his outstretched arms. "Make yourself comfortable love. I'll make you some nice poached egg on toast."

"You spoil me."

"You're worth it." He said, kissing her and meaning every word. He, too, had heard the helicopter but did not look up. He assumed it was the same one he had seen recently, and if so, it was the Policia. *Was it a coincidence?* He didn't believe in them. He had seen the chopper many times patrolling the coast, usually along the 340, but recently it had been inland. Even as far as Ronda. He assumed that it was there to help combat the ever-increasing drug importation from Morocco. The lack of marine facilities to compete with the super-fast boats and ribs used by the smugglers these days called for something more extreme, and those boats were certainly no competition for the chopper. So, why inland? And why was Jerry seeing it so frequently? He had also seen it above him some weeks ago in Portugal. It couldn't have been—he had gone there quickly. Surely, the Spanish would need a court order to follow someone using another country's airspace? Even more alarming was last night after leaving Barry. Jerry felt a shiver run down his spine, as he placed his wife's breakfast in front of her, and she plaited her youngest daughter's hair. "There you go love, go rinse yourself by the poolside, and try not to get your hair wet. Then go up to your room and get yourself ready. I'll be up shortly."

"Kath," said Jerry, seriously enough for her to stop eating and look up at him. "How's Jane?" He asked.

"Jane?" Kath enquired.

"Yes, you know, Barry's Jane," he replied, pouring fresh orange juice from a jug into two glasses. As he passed her a glass, he avoided eye contact, something not lost on Kath.

"Do you know, I've been meaning to call her. I'm not sure; I mean, I'm sure she'll be fine. I'll call her later. Why? Why do you ask?' She eyed him curiously.

"No reason," he said, casually.

"Come on, Jerry. You never mention Jane. Or the kids for that matter. I know you leave the envelope religiously with her name on it, but you never ask about her. Not in these six years, anyway."

"I know love. It's just that I see our two and how they are growing up, and I do often wonder how they are coping."

"Well, I do know that they are fine. She has issues with my friendship with Debs. She always has and always will. Jealousy, I suppose. It's a shame, but these things are sent to try us. Having said all that, she herself is happy in another relationship. No doubt you know about that?" Jerry didn't respond so she continued, "It started almost immediately after Barry got killed. I've always assumed that was the reason you never asked about her. I presumed you were disappointed."

Again, Jerry made no response. "Anyway, it wasn't just a fling. The two of them eventually got married. Well, I don't know… Is that the term? A civil wedding anyway. The children have accepted it. They had some tough times in the beginning. At school and so on. You know how cruel children can be. Jane still tells me it wasn't going on when Barry was here. Some say different. Some even say it was— and that Barry knew—you knew my feelings about Barry. I always thought he could be a little peculiar. But answering your question, the last time we spoke, all three were in good health. I'm happy she's happy. Maybe it helped that she is what she is, and if it was going on while Barry was alive…Who knows. Maybe that helped, too. Barry was no angel!"

"Kath! The man's dead," said Jerry, looking at his wife for any sign. Nothing would surprise him. Not after last night. But no. Not Kath. Jane? Who knows?

"Ask them over, love. For a holiday. All four of them." Said Jerry, again avoiding eye contact.

"Are you sure? That would be great! Thank you, darling. I'll get right onto it today. Maybe we can arrange it for August. That way, they can join us at the Breast Mate event."

"Fine by me," said Jerry.

"Mum! We're about ready," called Jasmine.

"Good God! Look at the time. I better rush. Don't forget those papers Jezzie left. They are in the Barbi floor safe."

Chapter Nine

Wheeler was also awake at 6 a.m. For some unknown reason, the time and place of today's meeting had been changed, and he was notified about this by text in the early hours. The time, he could live with. Very inconsiderate, but he could live with it. What got him thinking was the place had changed to the airport.

"Sorry! Time and place change. 7 am Malaga airport -Domestic." the message had read. He was showered and shaved within minutes and left his room the way he found it—dark damp, and rancid. He would book it down for €170, which was about £110, and keep the difference from the €60 it had actually cost. Stepping out of the grey building, situated in the red-light district of the city, he managed to flag down a taxi. The overweight girl who stepped out of the car thought she had one last punter to kick off a new day. He declined her offer with a brisk gesture and *"Me no understand."* He hurriedly instructed the driver to take him to the airport. After the short journey in the cramped car with no air-conditioning, he was actually pleased to be stepping out into the early morning sun. He paid the driver €10 and made a note in his little black book for €20.

Why was he suited in this weather? The tie could come off. He was removing it with one hand, his briefcase in the other and his small but bulging luggage bag on the floor between his legs, when a young girl dressed in a blue pinstriped suit, complete with clipboard and name tag, addressed him.

"Good Morning, Sir. You are Mr. Wheeler?" Wheeler had the impression she knew bloody well who he was, and grudgingly respected his boss for his descriptive skills.

"Please, come this way, Sir." She held her hand in the direction of the Domestic Flights terminal. Wheeler noticed this was the light aircraft and helicopter division. There was no passport or luggage control and the girl asked if he wanted to leave his heavier bag in a safe-keeping locker. Wheeler agreed and, having stowed his overnight bag, he was led out onto the tarmac, across a narrow runway and over to a chopper emblazed with blue and white colours and signs stating *Policia*.

The blades were already rotating, and Wheeler was surprised at how noisy these machines were when you got up close to them. He automatically lowered his head as he approached the aircraft and the door was opened for him by its occupant.

"Good Morning, Señor Wheeler," shouted Angelo Perelta, holding out his hand to help the big, heavy Englishman aboard. The girl was agile enough to step in without any assistance.

"What's all this about?" asked Wheeler, as the girl helped him fasten his seatbelt. There was a mixture of anger and annoyance in his voice, which disguised his fear of flying in such a flimsy machine. "There has been no briefing Mr.—What's your name again?" he asked sarcastically.

"Perelta, Señor Wheeler," the man replied coldly, and passed over a set of headphones.

The girl sat opposite him, and behind her were the two pilots. Perelta settled in beside and gave the thumbs up to the pilot, who began talking into his mouthpiece. The girl gave Wheeler a reassuring smile as the chopper lifted from the ground with a sudden jerk. Almost immediately, they were 20…30…50..100 metres in the air and moving forward quickly. The chopper's nose was slightly dipped, so the view was of the tarmac, unless one lifted one's head, which Wheeler did and almost vomited over the pretty girl.

"Can someone tell me what the fuck is going on, Mr. Pirelli?"

"If you don't mind, the girl Mr. Wheeler, she too is wearing earphones. And it's Perelta!"

"I'm sorry. I'm a little nervous. I've never been in one of these things before," he apologised, adding. "I do like to know what is happening—What, When, Where and Why."

"We have to move fast, Señor Wheeler. The first contact has been made, and keeping surveillance on your Divine has not been so easy." Perelta handed Wheeler a slim file that had 'Operation Canary' stamped across the front of it.

The girl leaned forward towards Wheeler, "Please brief yourself, Señor. We have twenty minutes to our first port of call." Wheeler liked her. Not just because her skirt had risen slightly above perfect knees but mostly because she was matter-of-fact and straight to the point. She was young but had an air of authority about her.

"A great fuck!" he grinned to himself. "Behave!" he chastised himself. He cleared his throat, sat upright and smiled at her. She blushed and turned to look out of the window.

Chapter Ten

Wheeler removed his reading glasses from his top pocket and opened the file. Yes! This was his territory. He was comfortable now. He got a shiver in his lower abdomen; a warm sensation. Someone had certainly been busy, and geographically so. There were six locations shown, each one a capital except Barcelona and Malaga. The others were Madrid, Dublin, Lisbon and Paris. Top brand names in the Jewellery industry were listed: Cartier in Paris, Harry Winston in Madrid, Bulgari in Lisbon, and Chopard in Dublin. The stores in Barcelona and Malaga were not exclusive to one famous brand, but were agents for top of the range expensive watchmakers, some of whom Wheeler was familiar with and others he had never heard of: Patek Philippe, Bruget, Audemar Paquet, Vacheron Constantin, Rolex and Frank Muller. Yes, our Mr. Divine had some very nice touches. Wheeler turned the page to see transcripts of telephone dialogue. This was in English but was obviously translated, as some of the conversations made little sense, and there was no mention—from what Wheeler could make out—of anything that would incriminate the speakers.

What was interesting were copies of travel bookings made by Divine to each of the destinations. But that alone would not secure a conviction. Whether most of this telephone intercept evidence would be allowed in any subsequent trial, he wasn't sure. As it stood, Wheeler was uncertain if and where there would be a trial at all. Looking at this flimsy file, he very much doubted it. What he did know was that Interpol had requested his assistance in Spain, but he didn't know exactly why. Interpol were not brilliant at law enforcement, but they were a significant force in the intelligence of suspects. Wheeler himself had considered compiling a file on Divine, with a view to bringing him back to answer for his past deeds in the UK, but was frustrated because all the evidence he acquired had a habit of getting bogged down in the complexity of international law. So, he had been elated to be given this assignment and was only too happy to oblige. He glanced sideways to Perelta, who beckoned with the palm of his hand in the direction of the folder. Wheeler's reluctance to return the file was increased by the fact that Perelta had asked him to. Perelta looked in no better shape than he was and probably no higher up the police ladder. He appeared similar in age, weight and shape. Wheeler thought the only difference between them was that he didn't get to go up in these machines, and Smith, his sidekick, certainly didn't look like the little beauty facing him.

Page three in the file showed mug shots of the associates and suspected accomplices involved in the robberies. Two of them were known to Wheeler, and three weren't. One of those three was declared deceased by a crude red inscription *'muerto'* scrawled through the picture. Two others were in prison. Which just left the two with whom Wheeler was familiar. Divine and O'Rourke. A brief biography of each followed.

"You could fit that on the back of a postage stamp," thought Wheeler, contemptuously. "Maybe that's why I'm here."

Chapter Eleven

"Hey, Kath!" Jerry called up the stairs. "Would you like me to do the school run this morning?"

"No thanks, love, I'll do it. I've arranged to meet Demitra at Puerto Sotogrande for a coffee," she replied, much to his relief. "Do you have a message for Jezzie?" she asked. "I know he was upset you didn't make the Barbie last night."

"Yes. Tell him sorry and that you left me reading the documents this morning and that I'll call him later."

"Ok. Come and see the girls off."

Jerry stood by the door, as the girls descended the spiral staircase carrying their books and satchels slung over their shoulders.

"Come here," he said, and hugged and kissed them both. He was their provider and protector, and he loved every bone in their fragile bodies. "Be good."

He pressed the button to release the electric gates, and Kath slowly reversed the Range Rover out of the garage."Come on girls, we'll be late," she called.

"I'm in the front, mummy," cried Julie, running around the front of the 4x4.

"Those bleedin' T.Vs were a waste of money!" complained Jerry, "Love you." he waved and blew kisses at the departing car. Once it was out of sight, he closed the gates.

Jerry returned to the back of the house and entered the barbeque enclosure. He retrieved the safe key from the false air vent and pulled out the small wheeled fridge from behind the bar. He took the papers from the safe, feeling relieved that there weren't that many, and went to sit in the shade of the gazebo.

Jezzie's message, stuck to the first page, read:

'Jerry. What was so important that you could not attend this evening's gathering, as agreed. It has prevented me from explaining our predicament in person and at the earliest opportunity. Please look at these documents. Some are in Spanish, so I will have to explain. The others are in English

with notes added by me. They should be self-explanatory. In a nutshell, Jerry, we are fucked—to use your phrase. Unless, of course, we come up with further funding. And a good lawyer!'

"What the fuck!" Jerry exclaimed aggressively, throwing back his chair and grabbing the phone from its holder on the stone pillar. He frantically dialled Jezzie's number. "Fuck, fuck, fuck!" he mumbled into the handset before it was answered by Demitra.

"Hi, love. It's Jerry here. Could I speak to Jezzie, please?" he said, pleasantly. She didn't reply, instead, Jezzie's voice came on the line.

"Jerry, my friend, where were you last night? We need to talk. How about I come down to Sotogrande with Demitra, and we can talk over breakfast?"

"Shut up and listen!" Jerry commanded. "Yes and No. Yes, we meet in Soto, and no, we don't talk over breakfast. One, I've already eaten and two, you know I don't discuss business when the girls are around." He said this with undisguised annoyance. Jezzie, detecting the tone responded in a similar vein.

"May I remind you, it wasn't me who didn't turn up last night."

"I know. And I'm sorry Jez. We can walk the Jetties. Look at some boats. Ok? That way we can get the privacy I prefer."

"Yes, all right, my friend. Forty minutes." He hung up the phone.

"Fuck! Fuck!" Screeched Jerry. A twat like Jezzie, talking to him like that.

"Fuck!" He slammed the phone heavily into its cradle, snapping the whole thing off the pillar and onto the floor. He let the dressing gown fall from his shoulders, walked over to the pool, and dived in without a pause. He stayed underwater as long as his lungs would allow. He surfaced, inhaling loudly, drawing the air in. He walked up the pool steps and rinsed off in the shower. He didn't dry himself but walked around the garden's perimeter, giving him time to compose himself.

"Money?" he muttered to himself, "or *funding* as Jezzie calls it. Fucking money! Hard-earned cash, hard earned! And Jezzie was asking for more. Well, we'll see about that. Alright. Let's see. Ten minutes to dress. Twenty minutes to Soto. I'll take the bike. Just quickly call the Arab to cancel Morocco. Then, I'll meet this twat and see what all this is about.

Fucking BBQ! I wasn't there because I was somewhere else, cheeky bastard! What does he know? Fuck all. I'll tell him what was so fucking important…I was speaking to a fucking ghost, for fucks sake!" The heavy dose of expletives had helped to calm him down a tad.

Not needing the whole ten minutes he had allocated himself, Jerry was dressed and ready to go with four minutes to spare. He stood in front of the mirror and admired his reflection. "It's not a sin to be skint." He combed back his gelled hair with his fingers. The shadow of a two day growth gave a stark contrast to the brilliant white shirt, worn baggy over his loose-fitting, cream cotton trousers. He chose a heavy Breitling watch from a rotating case holding eight different mechanical timepieces. After one final inspection, he told himself to keep calm under pressure. He knew how important Jezzie was to him and how much money was invested in various projects. He slipped into some comfortable slip-ons and stepped out the door just as the cleaner was coming in.

"Hola Señor, Jerry!"

"Hi, Cleo. Kath had guests last evening. Could you please sort out the barbeque area?" He didn't wait for a reply, but ran back upstairs to retrieve his brown leather shoulder bag. Checking if his phone was fully charged and counting his money, he headed for the garage.

The MV Agusta 1200 was specially modified to give maximum speed and performance. It had been custom-painted by the previous owner, who was a motorcycle fanatic.

He straddled the machine and pressed the electric start. The roar of the engine and the blast of the dual exhaust were enough to deafen him in the confines of the garage. Jerry felt the vibration of his phone and fished it from the bag resting between his legs.

"Hello," he shouted into the mouthpiece and switched off the engine.

"Bloody hell, Jerry! Can you hear me?"

"Yeah. Is that you Jez?"

"It is. Please bring the file with you."

"Sure. I'm on my way. Are you there?"

"I will be, shortly. I just wanted to remind you to bring the file."

"Don't worry, I've got it here," Jerry lied. He dismounted and returned to the gazebo for the documents. As he walked back to the garage, he called Cleo.

"See you, take care of Bonito, please."

"No hay problema, Señor."

Jerry folded the documents in half, long ways, and pushed them down the back of his trousers at the small of his back. He eased the motorbike out of the garage and onto the drive. The sun was already high in the sky, and the temperature was in the mid-seventies; it was going to be another hot one. Within minutes, he was high up along the new road that bypassed the small towns dotted along the coast road from Malaga to Algeciras. The freedom of the fresh air and open road should have made him feel good, so why was he feeling so very apprehensive?

Chapter Twelve

"Sr. Wheeler! Sr. Wheeler. Please look down to your right. See the large house painted terracotta? The one with the black Mercedes on the drive? That is the residence of Señor Divine. We have visual contact at the moment but limited audio. The Mercedes has recently been fitted with a tracking device and a voice monitor, which is only effective while the vehicle is stationary. If the car is in motion, we only have partial reception, and even then, only if the roof is closed."

"I am very surprised."

"What about?"

"That you managed to have a device fitted."

"Why is this a surprise?" Perelta couldn't see the relevance of the point.

"Well, unless Jerry Divine has suddenly decided that his anti-surveillance techniques are no longer a security requirement, I would assume that if he hasn't found the device yet, he will do shortly. When and where was it fitted?"

"We had a technician fit it two nights ago at the home of his driver."

"O.K. So, it wasn't fitted while the car was in the garage or anything? Like for a service? A mechanical fault or anything like that?"

"No, like I said, the car was parked outside his driver's home. A certain Thomas Callahan. Fortunately for us, the roof was left down all night which gave us instant access to fit the vocal device, and the tracking system is simply attached magnetically to the wheel arch."

"O.K," said Wheeler, evaluating the situation. "We must remove the tracker and make do with the vocals for now. If Divine was to find these devices it could jeopardise any investigation you, or I, or both of us might conduct."

"I see, I see," replied Perelta, a hint of concern in his voice.

"Can evidence from a listening device be used as evidence in this country?"

"We have ways," laughed Perelta, happy to move on.

"Good," said Wheeler. "But retrieve the tracker, pronto! That's important."

"I will see to it!" said Perelta sheepishly. He looked over to the girl who was already writing the reminder in her notepad.

"Now, please, Señor Wheeler." It was the girl who spoke. She placed her pad into an elasticised holder on the side of her seat and removed another file from her smart briefcase. "Up ahead, you will shortly see a development site. Please take this file and familiarise yourself with it." The girl passed over the folder just as the chopper hit an air pocket.

"What the fuck was that?" exclaimed Wheeler. His shirt was by now even damper, verging on saturated. The grey wisp of hair had now fallen over his forehead, and sweat was dripping from his nose as he adjusted his seating. He looked for reassurance first from Perelta, then the girl.

"Don't worry, it is only an air pocket caused by dry humid air rising to meet the colder climate. It happens from time to time," said the girl with a smile. Wheeler now began to wonder. "Is she an air hostess-cum-copper or vice-versa?" He looked at the name emblazed across the front of the binder containing the documents: *Operation Escatura.* He made a mental note to ask what it meant. He opened the file. On the first page were thirteen passport-size pictures of faces in a spider's web formation. Wheeler recognised only one. Divine looked back at him from the third line, which obviously indicated he was not the central figure. Not the primary one, but still an important piece in the jigsaw. "Jigsaw. That's exactly what this is, a jigsaw. Only we've got no pretty picture to help us solve it!"

In each photograph, the sitter was well-dressed. It reminded Wheeler slightly of those catalogues of faces you see in American graduation books. He had only ever seen them in the movies. This whole escapade was getting like that. So surreal. Just like the movies.

The second page didn't contain pictures. It was a list of names, dates of birth and nationalities. Spanish, English, Irish, Russian and French. The majority were Spanish. Wheeler turned over to the third page, which was an Ordnance Survey map. The following page was similar, as were the next thirty. "Somebody's got to explain all this to me," he mused. "Who the fuck takes a bloke up in a chopper, gives them a file, and frightens them half to fucking death—all without a briefing?" He was on the verge of venting his frustration when Perelta spoke.

"Please look down, Sr Wheeler. You see that new construction development site?" Reluctantly, Wheeler looked down. The helicopter was hovering above what looked like an oasis of green turf and water features covering about 100 Hectares.

"You will observe," continued Perelta, "that work on this particular site has ceased as of this morning. See the people dressed in orange?" Wheeler nodded. "They are officers who have been assigned by our jurisdiction, with power of attorney from the Central Court in Madrid, to implement an embargo on this and many other sites along the Costa Del Sol. Other departments are doing exactly the same right across Spain as we speak."

"What has this got to do with me?" asked Wheeler, who was, by now, feeling quite out of his depth.

"Your friend, Señor Divine, is an investor of black money into our economy. He, along with many others, has seized the opportunity to invest their ill-gotten gains into our infrastructure. To do this, he has bribed and corrupted our local officials. Greed, Señor Wheeler, is a disease. Like jealousy, it festers and spreads like ivy. It is poison and has no boundaries. Unfortunately for those who have been caught in the web, the dragonfly has pounced."

"Look now, Señor! Please, to your right," interrupted the girl. Wheeler looked down at the area below. Yes, Divine had been busy. And, looking at the development, successful too.

"Do you see the area up ahead and to the left?" said Perelta, taking over. He leaned across Wheeler slightly and pointed to the left with his pencil.

"Yes," replied Wheeler, trying desperately not to breathe in the body odour coming from his neighbour.

"This is a recently built 9-hole golf course. The area with the limestone markings shows where the houses will be built. Each plot, and there are four hundred in total, has a licence officially granted and approved by the Town Hall of Estepona. The Mayor of Estepona is the son of the Mayor of Marbella. We have no evidence that Emilio Sanchez Junior—they share the same name—has any involvement with taking black money for the building permits. Having said that, there are some who believe that he has contacts in the underworld, especially in the Russian sector. We are looking into this. Believe me, Señor Wheeler, there will be no stone unturned. We will fish them out. There will be more for you to digest later. We have a briefing tomorrow at 8 pm. Then, you can fill us in with Señor Divine's history. But, before we head back to Malaga, we have three smaller sites to show you. After that, you can relax and settle into your accommodation. How is it?"

"What?"

"Your accommodation."

"Oh, I see! Sorry. It's fine. A little noisy, I shall probably have to find someplace else," he lied. It didn't matter to him that it was scruffy, dry and humid. What mattered was that it was cheap.

Forty minutes later, the chopper touched down at Malaga Airport, to Wheeler's great relief.

"We can take you back to your hotel," said the girl.

"No, thank you. If you could take me to a shopping centre, one of those indoor ones. I need to buy a suit for the conference tomorrow."

"No problem. We can drop you at El Corte Ingles. It is central, and you can buy almost anything there. It has many stores so you can browse at your leisure."

"Thank you," replied Wheeler, who had already decided to spend most of the day there.

Chapter Thirteen

The open road was a welcome release valve for Jerry. Heading inland from the coast and up the winding road, he had opened up the throttle and taken some of the hairpin bends at a speed many might consider life-threatening. Once he was on a straight run on the wide Carretera, which cut through the mountains, he relaxed his wrist and cruised along at a steady 100 kilometres per hour. The warm air hitting him through the open visor had a soothing effect. He was relaxed. Composed.

He stopped at the *peaje* and paid the €3 fee. Although only a relatively short span of road, the Carretera had the benefit of getting you to a destination in a fraction of the time it took on the old road. He wondered, professionally, how many lots of €3 were handed over on a good day.

Jerry entered Puerto Sotogrande and rode to the left of the security barrier, which provided a thoroughfare for pedestrians. This was one of the benefits of coming by bike, especially during the summer months when traffic on the coast road was horrendous and parking even more so.

The traffic was relatively quiet. The time of day was an obvious advantage. The sun was high in the sky, and the morning heat promised an even hotter afternoon. He saw the girls before they noticed him. In fact, he had parked the bike within a metre of them, and they were about to complain about the exhaust fumes, when Jerry relieved himself of his helmet.

"Couldn't you park any closer?" asked Demitra, laughing.

"Those bleeding fumes. Enough to give you lung cancer," Kath taunted.

"Sorry, girls." Jerry grinned, placing his helmet under the table.

"Look at the state of those papers!" complained Kath as she removed them from the back of his trousers while he bent over.

"Straighten them out for me, there's a good girl." he bent over to kiss, first his wife and then her friend Demitra. "I need a swill, won't be a mo."

"Do you want coffee, love?"

"No thanks, darling, just fresh orange for me."

Jerry washed his hands and face and slicked his hair with water before returning to the girls. "I didn't realise it was you on the bike," laughed Kath.

"That's why I like it!"

"You're never too far behind," said Kath, smiling.

"I like to keep my beady eye on you," he teased. He turned to Demitra. "Is Jez going to be long?"

"I don't know, love. I wasn't aware he was coming."

"Here he is now," said Kath, and waved madly at him.

"I'll order him some eggs. He likes the eggs here." Demitra put in.

Jezzie strolled over at a pace that showed how much he struggled on his pins. He reached the table as the waiter put down drinks and food for the girls.

"One more fresh orange, please, and some poached eggs—I know how much you like the eggs here, love," she added to Jezzie.

"No, not for me, love. I'm fine," Jezzie answered. He looked agitated. Jerry was immediately on his wavelength and stood up. He downed his orange juice in one gulp and picked up the file. "Let's take a walk." He put his arm around Jezzie's shoulders and guided him toward the jetty.

"What we have here, Jerry, is a total fuck-up!" began Jez, once they were out of earshot.

"Tell me all about it." They strolled down the first Jetty.

"Where to begin?" Jez mumbled softly, his eyes cast skyward. "OK, let me start at what—after careful consideration—I see to be the beginning of our problems." He paused. "Do you remember when I told you I was approached by the architect for the Russian, Kristos? I told you he had offered to sell us his shares in the Casares Development?"

"Yes, At the Don Carlos Hotel."

"That's right. We were there to see the model of the Selwo development. Well, I believe that should have been a warning to us that something was amiss. I mean, why would Kristos want to sell? Of course, we don't know everything or everybody. Where the money comes from, or what they do. But what we do know is that the profit margins on that particular development are astronomical. So, for him to want to sell out at such an early stage should have sent us a message. Maybe we were blinded by the hype, I don't know."

"What exactly are you trying to tell me, Jez? I don't give a fuck about no Russian. Or where he gets his money. Or what the fuck he does with it!"

"I know, Jerry, I know. Keep calm. The girls can see us." Jezzie was now not only looking concerned, but sounding it too.

"All I am trying to say is that when he wanted to sell, we should have asked ourselves, why? Been more vigilant. We should have looked closely at the structure of the development and our investment, because shortly after the Russian offered to sell, do you remember? Banco Santander pulled the plug. Why? There was sufficient funding. It had to be something else. The bank's excuse was that they wanted more finance injecting. Which, as you know, we as a consortium, were able to provide. You yourself committed another €1.4 million."

"Jez," exclaimed Jerry, now very annoyed at his friend's prevarication. "You still haven't told me what the fucking problem is yet!"

"O.K." Jez had detected the anger in Jerry's voice. "Why don't we go and find a seat that will make it easier for me to review my notes with you?" He obviously wanted to seek the sanctuary of the girls.

"No! We keep walking! But get to the fucking point, Jezzie. I am beginning to get impatient. Anyway, I like looking at the boats. I may get one of these big ones someday. That's what you've always told me, isn't it?" The sarcasm wasn't lost on Jezzie.

"Please, lets walk for a while, Jerry. I need to compose myself. Just give me a few minutes, and please stay calm."

Jerry looked at the man walking slowly beside him, and under normal circumstances, he would have had sympathy for him. He could see no advantage in getting irate. He needed the full story, and to have Jezzie scared could result in getting only half a tale. He ran the contents of Jezzie's note through his mind.

Jerry. What was so important you could not attend this evening's gathering - as agreed - This has prevented me from explaining our predicament in person and at the earliest opportunity. Please look at the documents. Some are in Spanish, so I will have to explain. The others are in English with notes added by me. These should be self-explanatory. In a nutshell, Jerry, we are fucked - to use your phrase - unless, of course, we come up with further funding. And a good lawyer!

Chapter Fourteen

He looked at Jezzie. This was a man whose advice and instructions he had taken over the last five years. Yes, some small projects had shown a healthy profit from the investment. And yes, it was a good opportunity to clean some money. The joint account was sitting comfortably, which is more than most could say in today's climate. But Jerry had been promised more, and he expected just that from someone who was now considered a close friend as well as a business partner.

Jez had introduced a member of the Council of Casares to Jerry at a charity gala in aid of breast cancer. The charity *Breast Mate* was set up some time prior by Kath and her friend Debs in memory of Debs' daughter Sara, who had died of the disease. It was an annual event and is now firmly established in the high society calendar.

Jerry had arranged for a number of friends to attend with their spouses, an arrangement welcomed by Kath and Debs as Jerry's associates were usually the highest bidders at the charity auction. That particular year coincided with the opening of a new five-star hotel, The Kepinsky, in Estepona. Jerry had pre-booked twelve rooms to accommodate his friends.

The evening had got off to a great start. The cars and limousines arrived as early as 6 pm. The guests, all dressed beautifully in designer gowns and dinner suits, were greeted on a red carpet. Jewellery sparkled under the camera flashes. Debs and Kath were proud to have worked so hard to establish this yearly spectacle. Some local news reports likened it to a *mini Oscars*.

The special guest on this occasion was a British chart-topper from the 1980s. He was scheduled to come on and sing a few of his hits from yesteryear. Unfortunately for him and the guests, he had refused to leave his dressing room without some Dutch-courage in the form of white powder. Kath had ushered Jerry into a corner and explained the dilemma. Jerry had laughed so hard he nearly blew a gasket. "What the fuck is going on here?" he had demanded as he entered the celebrity's dressing room.

"The guy's a bleeding nervous wreck," stated Verne O'Rourke, a close friend and one of the guests Jerry had invited over from the U.K.

"I get stage fright," replied the has-been, "I ain't got the voice no more! I know it!"

"Fucking Hell!" exclaimed Jerry, laughing. "I've seen it all now."

"What shall we do?" asked Verne, "Do you have a bit of stuff?"

"Do I fuck!" retorted Jerry, looking at Kath. "Go on out, love. Take care of the guests. I'll take care of this." He gently ushered her through the door and closed it behind her. Turning around, he gave O'Rourke a look to let him know he spoke out of school. Verne got the message and relayed a meek apology. With that, Jerry turned to the other guest in the room before speaking.

"OK, my friend," he said, as the man of reason. "First of all, let me make something clear." He looked directly at the deflated singer. "You are going out there. Even if you have to mime, you're going out there. You can fucking mime can't you?'

"Yes. No. I mean yes, I can lip-sync."

"What?"

"I have, before I mean, but I'm not very good at it. And the band?"

"Now, what's this lips – lips *thing*?' said Jerry, confused.

"Lip-sync," said Verne. "It's another word for mime. The same thing."

"So why not say fucking mime," said Jerry, now getting annoyed. Just then, the door opened, and Jezzie entered in with the wannabe from the local government.

"Good evening, gentlemen. May I say how dapper you all look? Jerry, I'd like you to meet Augustine Gonzales. Second only to the Mayor of this province."

"Good evening Señor," said Jerry, holding out his hand to the politician. "We appear to have a small problem here."

"Anything I can do to help?" asked the politician, showing concern. Jerry looked at Jezzie, then at the others present, before turning back to the singer. "It seems our friend here, whom may I add, has agreed a contract, is unable to perform his duty, due to a slight nervous disposition. He is lacking a little bottle, and requires a little dandruff of the devil's kind." Again, Jerry turned to look at the celebrity.

"Devil's dandruff?" said the politician, looking confused and bemused.

"Cocaine," explained O'Rourke.

Divine Intervention

"Then why don't you give him some?" The local councillor pulled a small plastic bag from his waistcoat pocket. The singer's eyes lit up with delight.

"Fuck me! I've seen it all now!" laughed Jerry as he took the bag from the councillor's hand without invitation. He threw it on the table in front of Verne and the singer.

"Put one out," ordered Jerry, "for each of us."

"Not for me, Jerry, thank you," said Jezzie, "I don't use the stuff."

"Tonight, you do." countered Jerry, "Just the one."

Verne chopped the white powder with a card supplied by the politician. Once he had finished, Jerry took the credit card and handed it back to Gonzales, checking the details swiftly as he did so.

There were nine men present in the tiny dressing room, all of whom were known to Jerry, with the exception of the singer and the politician. The musician took two lines, so another had to be cut. Jezzie was the last to snort the powder and was relieved that no one noticed him blow down the rolled-up bank note.

"We must talk later," the politician said to Jerry, placing a hand on Jerry's shoulder as they filed from the room. Jerry never liked or trusted someone who got too familiar too soon. He glanced at Jezzie, who nodded in agreement.

"Not tonight," corrected Jerry, who never conducted business under the influence. "Tonight, we enjoy the function."

"Certainly," agreed Jezzie, "As long as the introductions are out of the way…" Jerry had the impression that this councillor was a greedy, fat bastard. He knew full well why Jezzie was introducing him. But this was not the night.

"Very well, gentlemen, have a truly wonderful evening. I believe we are seated at the same table. I look forward to your company." He held out his hand to Jezzie, before placing it in his pocket and then offering the same hand to Augustine Gonzales.

"Do you have my package?" questioned the councillor, before he suddenly realized he was holding it. Jerry was right—a greedy, fat bastard.

Chapter Fifteen

"Alright, Jerry. Let me continue," Jez looked composed. It seemed to Jerry that he had been contemplating how much to tell Jerry, *how* to tell him. Jerry decided to give him a little advice.

"Can I make a suggestion? Actually, I'm going to make a suggestion Jez, and I strongly advise that you follow it. Tell it to me how it is. Leave nothing to my imagination. Just tell me the truth."

"O.K. But you must understand that what has happened is beyond my control."

"I know that."

"The High Court in Madrid has imposed a restraint order on the development at Casares. Frozen solid. The grounds for the enforcement are corruption. I have tried calling Manuel in Benahavis, but all I get is his answer phone. I spoke to his wife, who said he left for work this morning as usual, so we can safely assume the same has happened there. I had a call from one of the suppliers at Selwo, who told me that the kitchen delivery was seized by some government officials on site. They confiscated the truck, and the driver was only free to leave after giving suppliers' details to the officer in charge."

"Tell me I am not hearing this, Jez."

"I'm sorry, Jerry. I have tried to call Augustine. No reply. Same from Emilio Sanchez, the Mayor." The two stopped walking and stood at the end of the Jetty. The heat from the sun was intense for the time of day. The only sounds were the smooth lapping of the water, the straining of rope, the occasional bump of fibreglass on wood and the calls of water birds. Jerry was thinking hard. He was not in control and didn't like the feeling. Neither spoke for some time until Jerry broke the silence.

"So, what the fuck exactly are you telling me?" He turned to face Jez. "Have there been any arrests? Am I likely to get a visit? Have we lost our money? Correction, have you lost our money? Because as I remember it, this was a risk-free investment. Wasn't that how you sold it to me? And that fat twat Gonzales! Where's he? Get him on the phone and get him here now!"

"He's been arrested, Jerry." replied Jez as he stared at a text on his mobile.

"For fuck's sake! Will he talk?"

"I don't know."

"He'd better not, for your sake!" growled Jerry sternly. He looked directly into Jezzie's eyes, which were starting to cloud with tears and fear. Jezzie looked over towards the girls as if seeking comfort. His wife smiled back and beckoned over, indicating that his eggs were getting cold. How wanted to swap places with Demitra.

"Take it easy, Jerry!"

"Take it easy? Are you fucking mad? You twat! I'm telling you now, if I lose my money, you'll be sucking the fucking barnacles from the bottom of those boats. If I get nicked, them other two bastards, Sanchez and Gonzales, Mayor or not, will be joining you—take it from me!"

"Jerry, please, the girls!" pleaded Jez. Jerry turned and smiled at the spouses who were waving for the two to join them.

Jezzie had never seen this side of Jerry. How could he change so swiftly, like a psychopath? Jez was nervous and scared.

"I promise you, Jerry. I'll find out everything in the next twenty-four hours."

"Make sure you do, Jez. Now, we are walking over there, and you're eating your fucking eggs as though nothing has happened."

Jerry switched on a smile as the two men walked back towards the girls. Still smiling, Jerry continued, "After that, my friend, you are going to get on the telephone and find out which lawyer is representing the fat bastard and get a message to him. You tell him that we are holding the fort. Make some excuse to go in and see him. Try not to say too much on the phone. Always remember you are talking to a third party. Once you get in to see him, get all the information you can. Have the lawyer use his dictaphone and get the machine back to me without rewinding it, just as it's turned off. O.K.?"

"Yes."

"Don't fuck up, Jez."

"I won't, Jerry."

"I'm going to see some people. See what I can find out. I'll see you this evening at the Dame la Noche."

"Dame la Noche?"

"The nine-hole opposite Banus. It has a small clubhouse. I have to meet someone in the port at 8.30, so shall we say 7.30? Yes, 7.30. Be there!" Jerry finished. Jez had no more options.

"I'll be there, Jerry."

"C'mon, darling! I've ordered fresh coffee," called Demitra as the boys neared the terrace bar. The waiter erected an umbrella to shelter them from the sun, showering hot rays in the mid-morning. Jerry looked at his watch. 10:22. Demitra rearranged her man's knife and fork and placed a napkin on his lap as he sat beside her. Once the waiter returned with the fresh coffee, she poured him a cup and added one sugar lump. Jez looked up at Jerry with embarrassment. Jerry looked back at him as he took his seat and wondered how the hell he had placed so much responsibility on this child-like figure. He turned to look at Kath. She seemed to be reading his mind. She had a knack of doing that. He smiled at her and hoped she wasn't reading the truth of the predicament. Jerry stood up suddenly. Jezzie nearly had a heart attack and choked on his soldiers. Demitra quickly slapped him between his shoulder blades and rubbed the small of his back.

"There! There!" she soothed.

"Sorry, love, got to go." Jerry bent down and wrapped his arm around his wife's shoulders. He kissed her cheek.

"I have to shoot. Something's come up. I'll call you later." What he really wanted to say was, "I've got to get away from this man before I throttle him!" He moved round the table and kissed Demitra. "Have a nice day love," he said, before moving on to his business partner and friend. He leaned over and gripped him firmly by the nape of his neck. He leaned forward so that his lips were just a centimetre or two from Jezzie's ear. "Get to work, son," he whispered. He patted his head playfully and slid the file in front of him.

Picking up his helmet, Jerry parted without saying another word.

Three minutes later, he was cruising along the coast road. The tarmac was sticky from the heat, and the sound of the tyres could be heard as the grip released the road. The shops and cafés that lined the route were getting busy. Through the intermittent gaps between the buildings, he could see fishing boats hard at work and people on the shore relaxing or water skiing. The beaches looked deserted, and the cool air on his face had a soothing effect on him. Any other time, Jerry would thank God for the life he had. He decided to travel as far as the following entry to the new bypass and join it there. He had no idea where he was going. Perhaps he would just open the machine up and head to Malaga and back—give himself some time to think. He had just decided to take the next fork in the road and head up to the pay road when he felt his phone vibrate in the bag resting between his legs. He drew the bike to a standstill just as the vibration stopped. He fished the phone from the bag to see whose call he had missed. It was Tom. He pressed redial.

"Hello! You good ting ya!" yelled the Irishman, cheerfully.

"Glad to know someone's happy."

"It's a grand day!"

"What's so grand about it?" Jerry knew what the reply would be but doubted if the weather news would have any positive impact on his day.

"De horse come in at 9/2!"

"And?"

"You had twenty grand on it. I was shitting myself. C'mon, tell me you love me! Where are you anyway? I'm outside your house."

"I'm on my way to Malaga to buy a piano!" replied Jerry, and pressed the red button. With that, he started the engine and opened the throttle. He joined the new road, and within 6 seconds, he hit the 200 km/h mark.

Chapter Sixteen

Stopping at the first *peaje*, he fished some change from his bag. He heard it before he saw it—a black Porsche 933 turbo. It stopped at the next kiosk. Jerry looked across and was pleased to see that the girl driving it was looking back at him. He was even more pleased to notice how beautiful she was. Her dark hair was tied up at the back with a black ribbon to complement the black strapless top she was wearing. Jerry raised his dark visor to show his appreciation with a smile. She smiled back, her smile illuminating the oval-shaped face with its high cheekbones. "This girl has style!" thought Jerry as he opened up the throttle, sending an enormous roar from the tailpipes. She responded with a blast on the accelerator, and the race was on.

This is what Jerry needed. Both the bike and car were touching the 250 mark within seconds. The next pay station was high above Marbella, approximately 48 kilometres away. Eleven minutes later, they were both paying again. This time, Jerry could hear the music coming from the open window of the sports car—Marvin Gaye's *Sexual Healing*.

This was too much.

"What's your name?" He inquired, removing his helmet.

"Victoria," she replied with a smile.

"English?'"

"Yes"

"Whereabouts?" asked Jerry, smiling broadly

"London," she replied. Her smile showed even, white baby teeth.

"Fucking gorgeous." thought Jerry. He noted the car was on Spanish plates and registered in Madrid.

"You live here?" He asked.

"Yes, Madrid, but I may be moving down here. I'm here looking at a property." She placed her hands on the steering wheel. Jerry guessed this manoeuvre was designed to show the absence of a wedding ring, but it gave him a clear view of an emerald cut, 5 or 6-carat solitaire diamond. The ring, coupled with the white gold Chopard with happy diamonds dancing on the face, gave Jerry the answer to the question he already knew. It was blatantly obvious that this girl was either part and parcel of some lucky wealthy guy or had been born into wealth. Jerry hoped it was the latter, as the former can produce complications.

"Can I buy you a drink? It sure is a one hot today."

"I'm not sure." the girl answered hesitantly. "I was always told not to talk to strangers!"

"We're not strangers," he pressed on, confidently, "we met at the last *peaje*."

"I'll think about it," she said with a cute giggle, then pressed down hard on the accelerator. There was a screeching of tarmac, a little smoke from the burning rubber and she was gone, with Jerry in hot pursuit.

Within a few moments, Jerry was within 3 metres of the Porsche. The automatic spoiler had risen from the rear end within four seconds, showing 0 to 60 at the same time. Both machines cruised along at a moderate 90 kph. Jerry could see the smiling green eyes looking back at him from the rear-view mirror. He imagined Marvin now telling her to *get it on*. It was less than 10 minutes to the next *peaje* at Benalmadena, high up on the new road, with terrific views of the sea.

Jerry was more than pleased when, this time, it was she who spoke first. He had pulled up beside her, sharing the same *peaje deesk*. He lifted the visor on his helmet as she said, "I'm on my way to the airport. I have a flight at 1.40."

"Great!" replied Jerry, "That gives us plenty of time. At least 2 hours. How about a light lunch? There's a lovely new complex called the Plaza less than a couple of miles from the airport. Do you like Mexican? I get withdrawal symptoms if I don't eat tacos for more than a day." he said with a short laugh.

"I'm not sure," she said, apprehensively.

"C'mon! please. You'll enjoy them." He paused. "You're like bleeding Speedy Gonzales anyway!" he laughed.

"OK," she giggled, "Thanks. I'll follow you."

"Perfect!" Jerry felt a quiver in the pit of his stomach. It wasn't often he spent time with a straight girl. More often than not he found them time-consuming. Somehow, he felt more guilty about winning and dining a girl than paying for a brass. The brasses were cold. He accepted that. Some were better actors than others, but they all provided a service. A release valve. *A luxury wank* is what an Estonian friend used to call them. "That's how I look at them, my friend, a luxury wank," he had said. "You can give them no part of your heart."

"The most expensive wank I ever had," Jerry had retorted, "I've just given her €300!" The Estonian had laughed. But he was right. Jerry could never give another any part of him but his manhood. Victoria could have more, though. He could certainly give her more, which is exactly why he chose to have brass. Because everything he was, belonged to Kath. There was nothing within him he could share with another. He enjoyed sex like the next man and had recently discovered that sex could be an addiction. That explained everything. He was suffering from an illness. He was unsure if he would welcome a cure. He liked the illness. It was expensive, but he liked it.

"Stay with me," he said, forcing himself back to the present. "The road down to the coast is very windy. I'll take it easy O.K.?"

"Yeah, sure. Thanks"

Chapter Seventeen

Leaving the Carretera at the next exit, Jerry slowed down. Moving slowly down the steep mountainside, he was happy to see the Porsche behind him. Victoria could have quite easily had second thoughts at the exit and carried on to the airport.

Moving now onto the old road leading into Malaga, Jerry kept within the legal speed limit. Three kilometres before the airport, he pulled into the newly constructed commercial complex, complete with Cinemax, bowling alley, shopping centre and communal square accommodating restaurants serving almost every national cuisine.

He parked the bike in a space nearest to the entrance that had a space adjacent to it. Jerry thought, "The only thing that can go wrong now is that she's bottom-heavy."

The car door opened next to him. He hung his helmet on the handlebars, then held out his hand. Victoria took it and stepped from the low sports car.

"Hi," he said once she was upright. He kissed the back of her hand lightly. "My name's James, and I'm very happy you decided to come."

"Thank you," she replied, taking back her hand. Jerry was more than happy. Victoria stood around 5ft 9 without heels, which she held in her right hand. A multicoloured Fendi clutch bag was draped from her left. Her hair was the colour of coal and unusually natural for such darkness. The strapless boob tube stopped short of her belly button which housed a diamond stud. Her skin was deeply tanned from lazy days in the sun. A tight-fitting denim skirt enhanced her curves and stopped just above her knees. Her legs were the most beautifully shaped that Jerry had seen on a woman for a long time.

"You are truly beautiful." was all he could think of to say, and he regretted it immediately. He blushed slightly, as he looked into her green eyes, which dilated—she blushed too.

"Why! Thank you, kind sir," she smiled, "shall we eat?" she bent down to put on her flat shoes.

"Yes. I'm starving," said Jerry, unable to resist taking in her rearview as she did so. "Let's go!" The girl straightened up and hooked her arm into his.

"I'll have you know, I don't usually accept lunch invitations so quickly."

"Well, to be perfectly honest, Victoria, this is the first time I have done this. I don't know why I asked you to lunch. I'm glad I did though. I've had a bad day, I suppose that may have something to do with it."

"A bad day? It's only 11:20 am!"

"I know. Well, a bad morning then."

"Work?" she asked with a concerned look on her face.

"Yeah, but let's forget it. My day has certainly brightened up now. C'mon, let's enjoy!"

To an outsider, the couple looked just that—a couple like any other—comfortable in each other's company. At the door of the Mexican restaurant, they were met by a pretty young girl wearing a multicoloured poncho and straw sombrero.

"Welcome! For two persons," she welcomed, smiling, "Please follow me."

"Could we have a booth, please?" enquired Jerry.

"I am very sorry, señor, the booths are for 6 persons." she apologised.

"We have others joining us."

"Oh! I am sorry. Certainly, señor, come this way. You have a preference?"

"Yes, in the corner. This one will do nicely." He stood aside to let Victoria sit down and then sat opposite her.

"Agua sin gas for me, please." He looked at Victoria

"The same. Thank you." This she said with a smile that Jerry was having difficulty taking his eyes away from.

"Do you always get what you want?" she asked him, once the waitress was out of earshot.

"The place is not exactly busy, is it?" He smiled back at her.

"You're mad!" she laughed and took the napkin from the polished glass and placed it somewhat nervously on her lap.

"You think so? Why?"

"You just are," she answered, like a young girl.

The girl who took the order was not the girl who brought the drinks. Jerry noticed the first girl had now returned to her original position.

"A very good day to yous. Here is you drinks," she said in very bad, broken English. "Must I now taken you order." she continued to their amusement.

"You may. And I will make it easy for you," said Jerry. "Tacos, two, dos, por favour," he said, holding up two fingers in a reverse v sign.

"Si, perfecto." said the girl, blushing slightly. She turned and walked away, still writing on the order pad.

"I think this complex was built primarily to cater to the natives," said Jerry with humour but with hidden knowledge of the fact.

They sat in awkward silence for a few moments, each thinking of something to say. "So!" Jerry ejaculated, making her jump slightly. They both laughed. "This is very unusual."

"What is?"

"An extremely beautiful girl, brimming with confidence." She raised her eyebrows. "In a very expensive car, looking for a property in a very expensive location. Tell me more."

"Well, I thank you for the compliment," she said. "And yes, I am driving an expensive car, but it does not belong to me, unfortunately. The property I am interested in is a one-bedroom apartment on the water, in the port of Sotogrande, which I liked, but again, unfortunately, I am not in a position to buy. I will be renting it—should I take it—I've yet to make up my mind. I have been for a job interview, which was the main reason for coming down here in the first place. The Porsche belongs to a friend of my father's, and the apartment is €600 per month. There you have it!" she finished, matter-of-factly.

"And the ring?" he pursued, "Which, I may tell you, nearly blinded me in the sun. Not to mention the watch." She blushed slightly, and Jerry regretted moving too fast. Both were thankful when the girl returned with the tacos. "I'm sorry. Would you like me to change the subject?"

"Not at all," she smiled reassuringly, "I can see that curiosity is getting the better of you." She paused a moment before going on. "You see, my father is in the entertainment business." Once again, she paused, thinking what to say next. "He is actually a famous movie star. One you'll be familiar with. A household name. Do you want to guess?"

"I'm sure I will get it in one," replied Jerry confidently.

"I doubt that," she said, laughing, "there are loads of movie stars, and I somehow don't like to think that I resemble my ageing father!" Now, it was Jerry's turn to laugh.

"Forgive me," he said apologetically, "I didn't mean it like that. It's just that there are only a couple of prominent English movie stars, stroke celebrities." said Jerry, using that two-finger gesture he hated so much, "who have a connection—that we the public know of—with Spain."

"Who said he was English?" she taunted.

"What's the difference?" said Jerry, giving her a way out, "I didn't invite your Papa for lunch. I invited you." He raised his glass and held it over to her. She clinked it with hers, which concluded the matter.

"To good tacos!"

"To good tacos!" she repeated.

"So, this job then?" said Jerry, scooping up some chilli mince with the crispy wafer. "What and where is it?"

"Teaching," she replied, "at Sotogrande school." Jerry coughed up his mouthful of food and dabbed his mouth with a napkin. Victoria quickly passed him his glass of water as he struggled to cough the food from his lungs.

"I'm so sorry," he gasped, "It went down the wrong hole!"

"Here," she said, offering him a clean serviette, "Wipe your eyes. Dear God. Are you O.K.? You look like you might explode," she added, laughing as the gasps became less strained.

"I'll be fine." coughed Jerry, taking a drink of his water. "What the fuck!" he thought. "First Barry. Then Jezzie. Then this. My daughters' school! This is too fucking much."

Chapter Eighteen

He knew he could have her. She was certainly sending out all the right signals. But there would be repercussions. Imagine Parents' Day, etc. Fuck that. Too close to home.

"So, will you be taking the job? I'm sure your interview was a success." he ventured.

"The interview did go well, yes, but I am unsure whether I will be taking the job though. Which will disappoint my friend."

"Oh?" Jerry tried to look disappointed.

"Yes, Richard, a friend from University, works there. He's my best friend actually, and before you ask, he's gay! Well, he wants me to take it, but I'm unsure."

"Why is that?" he asked, with an air of innocence, hoping she would turn it down and leave the field free for him to oblige her—and himself—with the inevitable.

"If you have come all this way from Madrid, surely you must be seriously considering it? I presume it's a teaching job?"

"Yes, that's just it. I am a drama teacher and, like Richard, I have a real passion for theatre and it is the only subject I am qualified to teach. The trouble is that the position requires me to teach other activities. Like a stand-in. I did explain to the Head that I don't have the qualifications to do it, he assured me I would be fine. I think at one point the word *babysit* was mentioned!" she said, exasperated. "Well! I mean, what was I to think? The Head said that part of my duties would be to stand in for Maths or English or any other subject if the teacher was ill or anything like that. *'Drama is not a priority,'* he said." Jerry got the message.

"I understand," sympathised Jerry, "That's all fine until the Science teacher gets a puncture!"

"Exactly," she said laughing, "I couldn't have put it better. Anyway, that's enough about me, tell me about you." she said, changing the subject.

"Me? Oh! Nothing exciting," he responded, caught slightly off guard. "Real estate, construction, that sort of thing, you know?"

"No, I don't, tell me. Sales? Rental? Large? Small?"

"We invest in land. Land without a licence to build. The hard work starts by convincing the powers-that-be that developing a certain site is necessary, good for the economy and so on. It's very time-consuming and frequently very frustrating. It can be expensive, and it's not unusual to get all the way through the planning process only for some local bigwig to pull the plug on you. So, the parcel that is not successful will then be added to the growing land bank. That's when it becomes expensive." he concluded with a shrug of his shoulders, picked up a fresh napkin and rearranged it on his lap. "It's a gamble, I suppose. But hey! life's a gamble!" He looked up from his napkin arrangement and made his first move towards the inevitable. "Large or small?" he said, "I like to think, large."

Victoria looked over the top of the glass she was holding up to her mouth. Her eyes were smiling but she said nothing, indicating she was on the same wavelength. She put down her half-empty glass, picked up the bottle and added fresh water to Jerry's glass and then to her own. She set the bottle down on the table, and, using both hands, wiped the condensation from its spout. She slid her left hand to the base and held it with a firm grip. The forefinger of her right hand remained on the spout, slowly circling it. The entire time, she looked mischievously into Jerry's eyes. He started to blush and smiled back. She gripped the top of the bottle with her right hand and slowly moved down the length of it, causing the drips of moisture to soak her left hand, which still gripped the base.

"Fuck me!" thought Jerry, "This one is good." They looked deeply into each other's eyes. Slowly and huskily, she whispered, "Maybe you could show me exactly how large, James."

"All in good time," said Jerry, who could feel a stirring in his loins and the beginnings of an erection.

"How are the tacos?" he asked, trying to avert his thoughts. He wanted to piss, but was unable to stand as his penis grew in length and girth with every heartbeat. This was the problem with loose-fitting slacks. They were great in the heat, but in a situation like this, they were impossible.

"Lovely," she purred back, licking her lips and sucking some sauce from her fingers, "Truly scrumptious," she added, grinning. "Stop!" thought Jerry.

"Excuse me, I must use the bathroom," he said. She stuck her fingers in the sauce, then licked it off each finger, one by one. Jerry had thought the bottle trick was good, but this licking job was something else. He stood up and used his napkin to disguise the bulge in his trousers which was growing by the second. It didn't go unnoticed as Victoria blatantly looked in that direction.

"I won't be long."

The cold water from the tap helped to cool him down, and his erection was now at the semi stage. He looked at himself in the mirror. "How the fuck do you get yourself into these positions. You twat!" he said to his reflection before moving to the hand dryer and pushing the button. The blast of air was cool and noisy and helped to reduce the swelling in his trousers. He turned the air direction to his face and ran his fingers through his hair.

As he walked back to the table, he could see her long, bare legs under it. She crossed them from right to left and back again, a la Sharon Stone. He couldn't tell if she was wearing any knickers, but that only added an extra thrill.

"Sorry about that, love," he said, taking his seat.

No problem," she replied, "I'll have to leave shortly, so if you will excuse me, I must powder my nose." Jerry stood up with her as she bent over to pick up her small bag from the floor and in doing so gave him a terrific view of her cleavage. He watched as she walked elegantly to the ladies.

"She is one hot babe," thought Jerry, "A fucking sports car and no more than 40 minutes to play with. Bollocks!" He contemplated following her to the bathroom. After all, the place was relatively quiet. But what if he was wrong? How embarrassing would that be? He laughed to himself as he imagined her chasing him out and hitting him over the head with the Fendi bag! As this vision passed through his mind, she came back.

"You look stunning," he said, as he stood to pull back her chair. The smell of recently applied perfume added to the attraction.

"Why, thank you, kind sir. Do you mind if we leave now?" she asked, bending her head coquettishly to one side.

"Not at all," replied Jerry, beckoning the waitress. Victoria took her keys from her handbag, rubbed the side of her nose and sniffed.

"Have you got a cold or is that a touch of Columbian 'flu?" he inquired, smiling. He peeled some notes from a wad big enough to choke a donkey and threw them on the table.

"It's been a long day." she smiled, "I need a little help."

"Well, don't be shy. Is it any good?"

"I think so. Would you like to try some?"

"Sure, but in the car though," said Jerry. The waitress picked up the money and started counting it. "Keep the change, pet."

"Gracias, señor. Was everything O.K.?"

"Everything was absolutely amazing!"

Once seated in the confines of the relatively compact Porsche, Jerry asked Victoria to drive to a vacant spot at the rear of the car park. He commended her choice of music.

"I'm glad you like it. I aim to please," she said, not looking at him. "All that modern drum and bass crap—it's not for me."

"Me neither," said Jerry, unable for once to think up a witty retort. He was happy that the music stayed on when she turned off the engine. He didn't need any awkward silence.

Jerry watched her as she put her left hand down the side of her seat, and it began to move back smoothly. He copied the action as she leaned over the centre console and removed a CD case from the glove compartment. She placed her right hand on his upper thigh as she did so. She put the case where her hand had been and removed a small homemade envelope from her bag.

"Nice bag." he remarked and immediately regretted it. He was not in control, and that made him uncomfortable. She didn't respond, as if she hadn't heard him.

"Do you like them large or small?" she asked.

"Medium," he replied, feeling a slight tremor in his outstretched leg. "This is surprisingly spacious for a sports car, isn't it?" he said, and once again regretted opening his mouth. Still, she didn't respond, but instead, started chopping the flakes into four white powdered lines.

Jerry was now feeling a recurrence of the sensation in his loins. Each throb of his heart sent the blood flowing into his nether regions. This time, he made no attempt to stop it. The chopping motion and the sight of her hand moving in a swift rhythm added to the thrill of the situation.

"Look what you are doing to me," he complained as the bulge in his slacks grew.

"I hadn't noticed." she lied with a girlish giggle. She proceeded to roll up a five hundred euro note.

"It had to be a fucking Bin Laden!" thought Jerry, referring to the rarity of the note in question, "class!"

She leaned further over him, brushing her breast on his left knee as she took two lines of the coke in quick succession, one up each nostril. After that, she sat upright and gripped her nose before releasing it to the sound of her breathing in sharply through it. Passing the note to Jerry, she said with a smile, "Your turn." he took the proffered note. He then took hold of one of the curly locks that had released itself from the black ribbon and tucked it behind her ear.

"You are truly beautiful." He lifted the case to his face and snorted the remaining two lines.

"I know." she replied and burst out laughing.

Jerry used his forefinger to clear the remaining specks from Marvin Gaye's face and rubbed it into his gums. He again wiped the CD case, but this time he offered the finger to Victoria, who took hold of his wrist with both hands and slowly began to lick and then suck ever so slightly, first one, then each finger in turn, her eyes continually focused on Jerry's.

He hesitantly put his left hand on her right knee and began to move it in a circular motion. She continued to look at him with eyes that were, by now, showing the influence of the cocaine. Jerry was also feeling the effects of the drug as the first wave of adrenalin rushed through his body and tried to explode from the endpoints, his cock included. He now ventured upwards toward the hem of her denim skirt, risen up and revealing the v of her black lace panties. With his right hand, he unzipped his trousers and freed his throbbing organ, which felt at bursting point.

"Let me." she whispered. She expertly released the button on the waistband of his trousers, which gave him some much needed breathing space. She kissed him full on the lips, and Jerry opened his mouth to let her venture in search of his tongue. His response was to seek out hers, and the war of the tongues commenced, both searching and exploring.

As one tongue now danced with the other, Jerry put his left arm around the back of her neck and massaged her shoulders before moving down over the insubstantial material to the back of her lower waist. The top of her panties was easily accessible, and he slid his fingers inside them and caressed her rump. She felt and smelled as good as she looked. Now Jerry moved his remaining, free, right hand to the back of her neck and, with controlled urgency, moved her head down to his neck and upper chest.

She kissed his upper chest and released the remaining buttons of his loose-fitting shirt, leaving his middle torso fully exposed. Victoria nibbled the hair on his chest before moving to his right nipple and taking it in her mouth.

Jerry felt a strong need to please her. He had never been a selfish lover—brasses excluded—but in the confined space, he knew it would be impossible to make love to her properly. With increasing intensity, they pleasured each other until their mutual passions were sated, and they lay slumped, exhausted in their seats.

"Turn on the engine. We need some air in here." said Jerry.

"That was amazing." he sighed.

"Awesome," she murmured, eyes tightly closed. Jerry laughed.

"What's so funny?" she asked, opening her eyes and looking up at him.

"Awesome, Amazing, I hate those words."

"Why?" she asked, sitting upright in the driver's seat. She smiled at him and began to rearrange her clothing.

"I don't know. Maybe they remind me of those god-awful judges you see on TV, you know, the talent show ones. It seems they describe 90% of the acts as *amazing or awesome*. What's that bloke's name? Cowell, is it?"

"Simon Cowell?" she stopped to look at him in disbelief. "What the hell has he got to do with what we just did?" There was humour in her question, which made Jerry laugh even more.

"Nothing," he said defensively, "Like I said, they just use them words a lot, that's all. Forget it." he said, leaning over to kiss her cheek. "Listen," he said, "Do I get a number? I would like to see you again."

"I bet you say that to all the girls!"

"Ha ha! No! Seriously, that was awesome, amazing, it really was." They burst out laughing. She fished in her bag for a business card.

"I was wrong." said Jerry, reading the name on the card.

"I don't use my father's surname, for obvious reasons." she said, "I want no favouritism." She passed him her passport.

"I was right." he said

"Hardly a difficult assumption, I'd say."

"True," conceded Jerry, "I'd love to meet him. I've always been a fan."

"Maybe, baby." she laughed, and took back the passport. "I'm really sorry James, I have to rush. Please give me a call. I'm undecided about the job, maybe I'll look at another school. There are one or two good international ones down here on the coast. Do you have children, James?" she asked, applying the finishing touches to her makeup.

"No." Jerry said this too quickly. She looked at him suspiciously.

"If you lie to me, James, you will never get to meet Papa." she teased him with a mocking smile.

"I have one, a boy," he lied, "Well, he's a young man now. He's in the U.K. A law student. I'll call you. Maybe I'll look you up the next time I'm in Madrid."

"That would be amazing."

"Awesome!" he corrected. He adjusted his clothing. Before opening the door, he leaned over and offered his cheek. She made to kiss it, and he turned to meet her lips. She laughed. She really liked this guy.

Jerry walked the 100 metres back to his bike and heard the blare of the Porsche's horn as it passed behind him. He didn't look back but lifted his hand to wave.

Chapter Nineteen

Once seated in the confines of the relatively compact Porsche, Jerry asked Victoria to drive over to a vacant spot at the rear of the car park. As she did, he commented on her choice of music.

"I'm glad you like it. I aim to please," she said without looking at him. "All that base of today. It's not for me."

"Me neither," said Jerry, not thinking of a more constructive response. He was happy that her music remained on when she turned off the engine. He could do without any awkward silence.

Jerry watched as she put her left hand down the side of her seat, and began to move back smoothly. He repeated the action with his seat as she leaned over the centre console and removed a C.D. case from the glove compartment, resting her right hand on his upper thigh as she did so. She placed the case where her hand had been and removed a small self-made envelope from her bag.

"Nice bag," commented Jerry, immediately regretting it. He was not totally in control and felt slightly uncomfortable. She didn't respond, as if she hadn't heard him.

"Do you like them large or small?" she asked.

"Medium," he replied, feeling a slight tremor in his outstretched leg.

"The legroom is surprisingly spacious for a sports car, isn't it?" he said again, immediately regretting opening his mouth. As before, she didn't respond but commenced to chop the flakes into four white powdered lines.

Jerry was now feeling the same sensation in his loins. The throb of his heart sending the blood flowing into his manhood. This time, he did not attempt to restrict it, and the chopping motion and the sight of her hand moving in a swift rhythm only added to the attraction.

"Look what you are doing to me," he said as the length and girth grew in his loose-fitting slacks.

"I hadn't noticed," she said with a slight giggle. She was now performing the second act which involved the rolling up of a five hundred euro bank note.

"It had to be a fucking Bin Laden!" thought Jerry, a term commonly used for the rarity of these bills. Class!

She leaned further over toward him brushing her breast on his left knee as she took two lines of the coke in quick succession, one up each nostril, after which she sat upright and gripped her nose before releasing it to the sound of her breathing in sharply through it.

Passing the note to Jerry, she said with a smile, "Your turn."

He took the note and took hold of one of the two curly locks of hair that had released itself from the black ribbon and secured it behind her ear.

"You are truly beautiful," he said as he lifted the case to his face and snorted the remaining two lines.

"I know," she said confidently.

Wiping the remaining residue with his finger from the face of Marvin Gaye, Jerry commence to rub his upper gum with it, then once more as if to delete any evidence he did the same, only this time offering his finger to Victoria who took hold of his wrist with both hands and slowly began to lick and then suck ever so slightly, first one, then each finger in turn, as she did this her eyes where continually focused on Jerry's.

He, hesitantly put his left hand on her right knee and began to move it in a circular motion. She continued to look at him with eyes that were, by now, certainly under the influence. Jerry too was now feeling the effects of the drug as the first wave of adrenalin rushed through his body and tried to explode from the end points, his cock included. He now ventured upwards towards the hem of her denim skirt which had risen up to show the v of her black lace panties. With his right hand, he began to unzip his trousers and take out his cock, which was now at bursting point.

"Let me," she said, leaning over and slowly taking his hand from his large penis. She released the button on the waistband of his trousers, which gave Jerry some breathing space. He raised his backside from the seat, and she gave the material a slight tug as far as his knees.

By now, Jerry's cock was fully exposed, and to Victoria's delight, it was long, thick and hard. She now eased her body weight over in his direction and supported herself by placing her left hand on his right shoulder. Her right hand, now holding his cock, moved down the stem of it with a firmer grip so as to pull the remaining foreskin back and reveal the full head. She kissed him full on the lips, and Jerry opened his mouth to let her venture in search of his tongue. His response was to seek out hers, and the war of the tongues commenced, both searching and exploring, the sound of the wetness not felt due to the numbness caused by the cocaine.

As one tongue now danced with the other, Jerry put his left arm around the back of her neck and massaged her shoulders before moving down over the brief material to the back of her lower waist. The top of her black panties were easy accessible and he slid his fingers into them and caressed her upper rump. She felt and smelled as good as she looked.

Now Jerry moved his remaining, free, right hand to the back of her neck and with controlled urgency moved her head down to his neck and upper chest.

She kissed his upper chest at the same time as Jerry released the remaining buttons of his loose fitting shirt, leaving his middle torso fully exposed. Victoria nibbled the hair on his chest before moving to his right nipple and taking it in her mouth, all the time moving in even stokes up and down his cock with a firm grip of her left hand.

Jerry felt a strong need to please her. He had never been a selfish lover—brass excluded—but in the confined space, he knew it would be awkward to fuck her. He moved his left hand lower and traced the crease of her bottom to the moist area of her cunt. The warm, wet area told him she was more than excited and the groan released from her after his finger tips entered her slit confirmed this.

Almost immediately, she lowered her head within an inch of his cock, and he could feel the heat of her breath on the tip of it. He wanted her to take him in her mouth and suck for all the breath in her, but he had remained calm up to now, and this was too good to rush. Gently now, she began to lick around the perimeter of the shiny purple head of his rod.

"Yes," he said. "That's good," as if to let her know his appreciation. At the same time, he moved even further into her wet hole.

Unable to respond verbally as she had now taken him within her mouth, she acknowledged his comment by letting out a moan from within. Jerry swapped his forefinger for his two middle fingers and moved his forefinger to the part of her womanhood housing her clitoris. As soon as he made contact with this sensitive area, her head and mouth reacted in a dramatic change of pace which in turn had Jerry moving his fingers in and out of her wet cunt at a faster pace.

"Suck harder," said Jerry through clenched teeth as he stretched out his tensed legs. He grabbed a handful of her hair complete with the black bow and helped to set the motion and speed he preferred. She, on the other hand, had now become a little more adventurous, releasing the grip on his cock and cupping his balls in her hand, firmly massaging them and, at the same time, now taking almost the full length of his cock in her mouth and down her throat, occasionally gypping as she took him too far.

She momentarily left the sack containing his swollen balls and moved her hand below his arse and teasingly caressed the crack of his cheeks. Jerry raised his hips giving her easy access to briefly tickle his rectum with her finger tips. This was now becoming too much for Jerry to handle and he knew full well that it was only seconds away before he explodes. His movements became more erratic as he now thrust his hips up to meet her at her own pace. She too was moving faster to join him in a frantic race to come. All movements were in sequence and the wetness of her cunt told Jerry that the time was near. Both were being pleasured by the other in the confines of the small space.

Jerry decided the time was right. He had little choice as her speed and rhythm were accelerated, more from the fact that she too was wanting to come first. As if in a race to the finish line, both athletes were to the maximum. She felt the jerk and the shudder from his hips as she automatically released him from her mouth and continued to wank his throbbing cock at an even faster pace. She remained looking at his manhood as he screamed, "Yes! Oh yes! I'm coming."

"Come," she urged. "Come on, spunk. I want to see it, I want to taste it." With that, the first squirt hit her above the left eye and the second was erupting as she took him in her mouth again.

"Aahh! Yes! Yes, fuck," said Jerry as he drained into her. She took his fluid, at the same time moving her arse in an upward motion helping him to delve deeper into her with three fingers now.

"Faster," she screamed as she came up for air.

"Oh yes, yes, faster!" she repeated bucking up to meet his thrust. The squelching sound of her wetness could now be heard above Marvin as the come started to flood from her, running from her like a river drenching his hand.

"Oh my god, I'm coming!" she screamed out loud as she jerked back and forth. "Yes! Yes, oh yes, I've come," she said, going limp.

"Jesus, that was wonderful," she now whispered, resting her head on his abdomen. His cock was now going limp in her relaxed hand as the two regained their composure.

"Turn on the engine. We need some air in here," said Jerry.

Chapter Twenty

"That was amazing," said Jerry.

"Awesome," was her response. Jerry had to laugh.

"What?" she asked looking up at him.

"Awesome, amazing, I hate those words."

"Why?" she asked, now sitting upright in the driver's seat. Smiling, she began to rearrange her clothing.

"I don't know. Maybe they remind me of those judges you see today on TV, the talent show ones. It seems they describe 90% of the acts as amazing and awesome. What's his name? Cowell, is it?"

"Simon Cowell?" she stopped to look at him in disbelief. "What the hell has he got to do with what we just did?" There was humour in her question which made Jerry laugh a little more.

"Nothing," he said defensively. "Like I said, they just use them words a lot, that's all. Forget it," he said, leaning over to kiss her cheek. "Listen. Do I get a number? I would like to see you again."

"I bet you say that to all the girls."

"No! Seriously. That was awesome, amazing. It really was." The two burst out laughing as she fished out a business card from her small bag.

"I was wrong," said Jerry, looking at the name on the card.

"I don't use my father's surname for obvious reasons," she said. "I want no favouritism," she concluded. This time, passing him her passport.

"I was right," he said.

"Hardly a difficult assumption, I'd say."

"I know," said Jerry. "I'd love to meet him, I've been a fan for a long time."

"Maybe baby," she said, taking the passport from him and returning it to her bag. "I'm sorry, James, I have to rush. Please give me a call. I'm undecided about the job, maybe I'll look at another school. There are one or two good international ones down here on the coast. Do you have children, James?" she asked whilst applying a little makeup.

"No," Jerry said too quickly. She looked at him suspiciously.

"If you lie to me, James, you will never get to meet Papa," she teased with a smile of mockery.

"I have one. A boy, well, a young man now. He's in the U.K. A law student," he lied. "I'll call you. Maybe I'll look you up the next time I grace Madrid."

"That will be amazing," she said.

"Awesome," he replied while correcting his clothing.

Opening the door, he leaned over before stepping out. He offered his cheek. She made to kiss it and he turned to meet her lips. She laughed. She really liked this guy.

Jerry walked the 100 metres back to his bike and heard the blow of the horn from the Porsche as it passed behind him. He didn't look back but lifted his hand to wave.

Chapter Twenty-One

Again, there was no passport control. Wheeler wondered if it was the same for all domestic flights or just the helicopters. He was impressed with the authority Perelta seemed to relay within the airport and got comfort from the fact that he was in a little better shape than himself, physically, that is.

"My bag." Wheeler said as the trio made for the exit.

"Your bag is in the car." Volunteered the girl as they left the comfort of the air-conditioned building. Fortunately for Wheeler—who wasn't happy with the heat—a large air-conditioned Lexus was waiting for them directly in front of the exit. The door was opened for them as they approached. This told Wheeler that within his division, this Perelta fellow must have a little more influence than he had at the Met. He was already beginning to dislike himself even more.

Moving smoothly away from the airport, the driver commented that the traffic was slow due to three commercial arrivals before the chopper landing. But even so, it should be no more than thirty minutes from central Malaga.

The girl sat in the front, commencing to fill in her report of today's events. Lucky cunt, this man beside him. He, Wheeler, had to do all his own paperwork.

The driver suddenly braked sharply.

"Imbecile." he muttered. "Loco Diablo!" he shouted to the screen. The girl looked up from the logbook. The driver apologised. The two of them looked at the motorbike which had crossed the road directly in front of them.

"I hate motor bikes," said Wheeler.

"They are a death trap for sure," responded Perelta. "Here in Spain, there are very few right-of-way ways to cut across the road. But you can bet the man on the bike, he is a tourist. They never abide by the law of the road. We have totally different laws of the road."

Chapter Twenty-Two

The traffic was very heavy in the Capital of the South. The noise, combined with the heat of the city and his surplus body weight had Wheeler feeling very agitated as he climbed out of the car.

"What's with the car horns?" he asked.

"We Spanish," answered the girl, "we talk with our hands, so do we drive with our horns." she replied.

"Please, take my card," she continued as she now walked back from the rear of the large saloon. "Your bag is relatively light, Mr Wheeler. Do you have more luggage?" she asked, handing him his leather holdall with one hand and holding a business card in the other.

"No, I like to travel light, and besides that, I only intended to stay overnight. It doesn't matter. Like I said, I will buy a suit for tomorrow today."

"Perfecto," she said smiling.

"Have a pleasant day Mr Wheeler. We will be in touch" called Perelta from the comfort of the car. 'I will, a lazy cunt," thought Wheeler. Why didn't he get out and help with the luggage?

"I will," he called, bending over slightly to look into the rear of the car. He looked at the name on the card. Angelica. He liked that. Turning to look at her, she was standing there smiling at him. He thought he detected sympathy in her eyes. He smiled back at the same time, glimpsing himself in the large window of the store. He could see why she sympathised. He certainly did look a sight for sore eyes.

"Good buy, Mr Wheeler. Have a good day," she smiled.

"Please hurry, Angelica," called Perelta from the open door. She turned and took the place of Wheeler in the rear. With that, the car rejoined the slow-moving traffic, leaving Wheeler standing alone but for the heat of the day. He certainly looked a sorry sight with his briefcase between his feet, his leather holdall in one hand, and his jacket in the other. An internet coffee shop. That's what he needs, to pass an hour or two, see if there's anything on Divine and this Operation. Perelta did say the warrants were enforced today. Last minute dot com, for cheap rooms too.

Chapter Twenty-Three

"I shall leave you here to relax, sir," said the masseur into the ear of a very content Barry. "Please, in your own time. There is a clean towel and robe by the door. The service has been charged to your room account. Thank you, sir."

"Thank you. That was beautiful," said Barry drowsily. "I may need the same tomorrow. Are you on duty?"

"Yes, sir, it would be my pleasure."

"That makes two of us," said Barry as the door silently closed. He didn't stir for almost another thirty minutes before making his way back up to room 308.

Once the door was closed behind him, Barry immediately called reception. "Hello, yes hello, good morning, any messages for Mr Viceroy? room 308."

"Yes, sir. Just the one. No name, I'm afraid. Just an enquiry, let me see."

"How long you will be staying with us," she read, "and what room number you are staying, something we don't give the information about, but I believe it was for the flowers, sir. Did you receive the flowers?"

"Yes, thank you," Barry lied, looking around the room. It had undoubtedly been attended. Fresh linen and towels were replaced. Fresh flowers had replaced yesterday's arrangement but weren't a special delivery. Jerry? No, he had given him the room number and told him when he would be leaving. Jerry would have banked that information. He checked the safe. Removing the papers and DVD, he made for the air vent and removed its cover, securing the small package within the confines, and replaced the plastic grill. He now picked up his mobile and called Beatrice, "Hi darling, did our friend arrive on time?"

"Yes, 6:30 this morning. He is in the room sleeping," she replied with her strong East African accent. "Your friend, he collect the bike."

"Lovely. Did you mention where I was staying?"

"No."

"Ok, love. Have you called home? Did you tell anyone back home where we were?"

"I called my Mama, I tell her we are in Spain. I did not mention Gibraltar or where you were staying, my lovely. Is there something the matter?"

Barry did not answer the question, but asked the question. "Did you use your mobile or the phone in the hotel?"

"I use de mobile."

"OK, petal, I'll call you shortly. Don't call me, wait for me to call you. You understand love?"

"Yes, my love, I understand."

'Fucking imbecile," thought Barry pressing delete with venom.

Who made the call? How did anyone know where he was staying? It was obvious to Barry that it could only be the same people who had tried to kill him in Gambia. Who or why was still a mystery. But, what was no mystery to Barry was the determination these people had. The lengths they were prepared to go to see him dead. The resources they had to find him, out there in West Africa of all places, and even more impressive to the north of the capital Bengal to a small village called Maya. This remote place, containing nothing more than two thousand locals, the majority farming the dry land, two small hotels, four shack-come-bars where the entertainment went as far as a TV with sky, a market selling livestock and tools visited fortnightly by an average of twelve hundred people from surrounding areas. Granted, Barry stood out like a sore thumb amidst the local gentry. It had suited him to invest in one of the two hotels, and the footings for a third one were dug out just weeks prior to the failed attempt at his life. But how did they find him there? And who and where were they now?

Picking up the hotel phone, he dialled 9 for the reception.

"Hello, Mr Viceroy. Good morning. How may I help you, please?"

"Good morning," replied Barry, looking at his watch and realising there wasn't much of it left. 11:55. "I would like to extend my stay, please, for three more days. Is that possible?"

"Let me check for you." a pause. "Certainly, sir. So, you will be leaving us on the Friday. Consider that done, Mr Viceroy. Will there be anything else?"

"Yes. Could I book the aromatherapy tomorrow at the same time?"

"I will connect you to the health spa, sir. Just hold the line."

'Come on, come on," thought Barry impatiently, continually looking at the door.

"Buenos dais. How may I help you, please."

"Yes. Could I book aromatherapy for tomorrow morning 7 o'clock?"

"Momento por fa vor."

'Fucking hell," thought Barry looking nervously at the door but then realising with reason that it had to be the call made by Beatrice to her mother.

"No problem, senor. We will see you tomorrow, in the morning, at 7 o'clock."

'Thank you," he replied, hanging up.

Dressing quickly, he retrieved the package from the vent and replaced it with a note. He disarranged the bedding, hurriedly packed his luggage and was out the door for the last time. He made his way to the reception and paid the balance for the three days he had just booked. It wasn't much of a deterrent, but it was something, and it could buy him a little time. He was sure the pursuers would realise what he had done quick enough, but to Barry, something was better than nothing.

Now, in a taxi on his way to La Linea, his mind was racing. He had done some bad things in his life, things he wasn't proud of. He and Jerry had upset a lot of people throughout their careers as professional criminals, but it was nothing to die for. No. This was something Barry had done with others, others who had no connection to Jerry. If it were, it would be a comfort to Barry to know that he had the protection of his old friend. But he had to defend himself in this instance. The problem was, defend himself against who? Who were they?

He accepted that, for what he was, what he had become or had been involved with, and who he had conspired with, did, in fact, deserve nothing less than his life. He had an illness, an illness that had no cure and one that could not be talked about, especially to Jerry.

Chapter Twenty-Four

Once in Gibraltar, Barry walked the short distance to the communal square. The restaurants and bars surrounding the perimeter were busy with the lunchtime trade. Tourists from a regular cruise were filtering into the popular square from the main street. A band was playing in the centre, and the sound gave the whole scene an even more English feel. The heat of the sun reminded him that, geographically, he was obviously still in Spain. The dominant factor seemed to concentrate its rays in the confines of the square and reflected in all directions off the brass instruments.

Beatrice was waiting for him at the entrance to the square and rushed to embrace him.

"My darling, you been away too long," she said, her bottom lip looking even more prominent as she sulked mockingly.

"I'm here now, my sweetness." he was in no mood for pleasantries, "Stuli, where is he?"

"In the hotel. I say we call him once you arrive, and he will come to us by taxi."

"OK baby, call him now. Ask him to make for the square. The Lord Admiral, OK love. And please use the public telephone. Give me your phone." he held out his hand, and she gave it to him. She was concerned but knew better than to question the request. Once she had walked away, he removed the SIM card, broke it in half, dismantled the phone and dropped it down the drain by his feet. Almost immediately, he felt a sense of relief.

Chapter Twenty-Five

Stuli Bressla was still sleeping when the phone beside the bed woke him. He did not pick up the receiver but leaned from the bed and washed each hand with water from the bucket left conveniently placed the night before.

Right, left. Right, left. Right, left. After the last cup was poured, he wet his brow with his damp hands and was ready for the day.

Evolving from a Hasidic ancestry, he could trace his family tree, originating in Yemen for almost twelve hundred years. Nearly all of his ancestors would turn in their graves if they could see what he had become.

He fought with his demons as many times a day as he prayed. His son Toli, who was just out of Yeshiva, was his priority. Toli was the last in the bloodline of the Bressla's. Stuli's brother Abi was without a child and left the Motherland for Europe as a young man. Now, the two were more like strangers as the only connection the two had was young Toli.

How Stuli found himself running a hotel in West Africa is another story, a story which he had never told anyone. He would rather die. But it was at the same hotel, The Rafter, where he had begged for the service of a permanent resident, Vincent Viceroy.

It was no secret that the hotel was used by predominately male tourists who preferred the sexual services of minors. Stuli had seen and heard some despicable sights and sounds, but to him, despicable sights and sounds were nothing new. He had lived and breathed them all his life, some real life and physical, but the worst ones were in his mind.

The night he called on Vincent for help was one he sometimes wished he would not have to see anymore. He seriously considered taking his own life, but Toli needed him. Toli, who called his father daily from Israel, where he lived with a grandparent, was all Stuli lived for. One day, he would return back to his son, but first, he had to seek redemption would take time. He no longer had the urge to feel the flesh of a youth of the same sex, and living with it all around him proved that it was only a matter of time before he could return without temptation.

Forcing his legs from the bed, he sat looking at the phone. He could only imagine what would have become of him if Vincent hadn't helped dispose of the two bodies from room 12 on that fateful night. Stuli feels sure he could have prevented the deaths if he had intervened when he took the call of complaint from room 11 just after midnight. He had stood outside the room where the T.V had its volume turned up to the maximum. Even so, he had heard the scream and the child's muffled plea as the two Americans had lived their fantasy. Too scared to knock on the door for fear of being reprimanded himself and an even greater fear of losing custom, he had knocked on room 11 to assure them the noise would not be for too much longer. He had returned to the reception area and called room 12. When he received no reply, he went back to stand and listened at the door. Thankfully, the noise was at an acceptable level. Good job, because this time he would have had to let them know. Anyway, it wasn't necessary.

Again, he returned to his place behind the counter of the reception area.

Shortly after, the first of the two yanks had come down looking flustered and asked for some cleaning material. No request was denied, and no questions were asked at The Rafter. Stuli's offer of assistance was refused, and within minutes, the remaining yank came looking for his friend.

Concern was etched on Stuli's face as the two almost emptied the cleaning store. He watched as the two tried to keep calm and hurry back up to room 12 with almost a month's stock. Stuli looked down at the register as if not to notice the two in panic mode. He looked at the names of the two guests: Cagney and Lacey. No doubt they were fictitious. It was a hotel policy not to request a copy of their passport, and this is why they kept returning. The guest received total anonymity at The Rafter.

Forty minutes later, the call had come to reception from room 12. Taxi please to Banjul. When the two had left without the boys, fear and curiosity had got the better of Stuli, who took his six-foot, 140-kilogram frame back up to room 12, fearing the worst.

The room was clean but had a smell Stuli had smelt before, a long time ago back in his homeland. It was the unmistakable smell of recently slaughtered flesh. Death. The T.V was on, but there was no picture. The bed was made, and the en-suite bathroom was in order but full of condensation. Stuli picked up a bucket containing cleaning material and was disappointed with the weight. There was no sign of the two young boys, which came as a relief to Stuli; they had obviously left by the fire escape. This wasn't unusual; in fact, some even entered the same way.

Stuli went to turn off the TV and noticed there was a disc on the DVD machine. He instinctively pressed the play button and immediately recognised one of the two youths tied to a chair. The same chair was now holding Stuli's weight. He gasped as the camera then, showing the other youth lying face down on the bed with his hands and legs bound with rope and secured to the four corner posts. The taller of the two Yanks came into view as he moved onto the bed. He was naked except for a gas mask and a studded collar. In his hand, he was holding an enormous dildo, which he was showing to the camera in a seductive manner, then pointing the sex tool to the youth, who seemed to be whimpering on the bed. The camera then did a manoeuvre to the other boy, who was crying without sound as he was gagged.

Stuli was getting aroused as he continued to watch the film. He wanted to turn it off but was unable to. He moved his hand down to his rising penis and rubbed the cloth concealing the bulge. He knew he was relapsing from all the progress he had made, but he couldn't help himself. Just as fast as the arousal appeared, so it was diminished as from nowhere, as if like magic, emerged from behind the youth in the chair, a cut-throat razor. The blade was obviously held by the one who was controlling the camera, doing the filming, as the camera was focused directly in front of the one tied to the chair, the eyes were bulging from the boy, not yet a teenager.

The first cut was made just below the left breast and continued over to the right one. It was not made to kill, only for the impact of fear. The cut was not deep, as only a little blood was produced from it. The noise from the TV with the volume turned up to the max gave the whole aspect a sense of disbelief. It's nothing less than a real-life horror movie. The sound of children playing could clearly be siphoned, and yet, in reality, there were two being molested and tortured.

The footage was now concentrated on the face of the one tied to the bed. The tall Yank had straddled the small figure and had twisted his head around to view the spectacle. Pulling a rag from the child's mouth, the scream that came from him without sound was probably the same scream that resulted in Stuli receiving the complaint from room 11 less than an hour ago. Stuli could imagine the terror. The man now kept the youth's head in the same position as he converted his straddle position to one of completely covering the small, defensive child with his long, pale body. The pain was evident for whoever watched the film as the man entered the anus of the child with his shaft. The giggles of the children on the TV were too much of a contrast for Stuli to handle, and he was moving toward the stop button when suddenly the vision changed back to the boy in the chair.

With one hand holding the camera steady enough to convince all that this was not new to the filmmaker, the other hand, which had once held the cutthroat blade, was now holding a large gold vibrator. The tool was turned on because as it made contact with the wound, there were splashes of blood going in every direction. Then, with the camera still filming, the Yank, taking the terrible scenes, walked over to the two on the bed and commenced to push the blood-soaked toy into the mouth of the child. The eyes of this youth were almost leaving their sockets as the first beast rammed home with such force the bed buckled under the impact.

Stuli pressed the fast forward, which speeded up the act of the one raping the youth on the bed. He stood up and took the camera from the other. The focus was now on the shorter of the two, who were also wearing rubber masks. He, too, was naked other than a strap-on cock. From beneath the strap-on, it was clearly visible that this one was not sexually aroused, as his small penis was limp. The guy was much shorter than the other and much heavier.

Stuli reset the machine to normal play and watched as the short, fat one now took his turn on the bed. There was little movement now from the boy as the second beast now mounted him for the benefit of the camera. As the yank forced his way with the strap-on into the boy, he also pushed the small head of the victim into the bed, and after a number of strokes that took the breath out of the adult beast, it also took the final breath out of the child. And, with this realisation, Stuli alarmingly looked around the room and then back to the box. What he saw next almost sent him into panic mode. As if in fast motion, the short, fat one removed himself from the bed and made for the blade, now on the floor beside the boy tied to the chair. The boy was crying and struggling uncontrollably. He was bleeding from the vessels in his eyes, which were now bulging from the sockets. He had just seen his friend killed for the pleasure of the vilest of paedophiles and for the benefit of others who would pay to watch. He hoped that he would die soon.

He did. As the blade sliced his lower abdomen from left to right, he looked down in disbelief. He then looked up as if to plead with the butcher to finish the job. The camera then returned to the wound, as slowly as if in slow motion, and the intestines began to show themselves like creatures seeing a new world for the first time.

Stuli cried as the boy died on film.

Chapter Twenty-Six

After the ordeal in Gambia, Stuli wondered if it was only a pipe dream that he would one day return to his homeland. As these thoughts entered his mind, he was startled into reality by the phone ringing.

"Hallo, this is Stuli."

"Hello, Mr Stuli," said Beatrice. "Could you please order a taxi and ask that the driver, he bring you to de square in Gibraltar? We are waiting for you there, in de Lord Admiral bar and restaurant. Please come immediately. Thank you." She hung up the phone before Stuli could respond. That was the way it was. Vincent gave the orders, and Stuli jumped.

He called reception and conveyed the request, after which he combed his beard, placed his hat on his head and combed the hair that remained visible. There was no need to dress as he had slept fully clothed. Within a couple of minutes, he was making his way down to the reception.

"Your room is taken care of, sir. I have you booked in to stay with us till Friday."

"Perfect, Miss."

"Your taxi is waiting. Have a pleasant day, sir."

"Thank you very much, Miss," said Stuli, making his way out to the cab.

"The square, please," he said. Wondering how the hell he was in this position and what he was about to do. *God forgive me.*

Chapter Twenty-Seven

In the back of the taxi, Stuli's thoughts returned to that dreadful night.

The bodies of the two boys were rolled up in a rug under the bed. He hadn't pulled them from under the bed. He just knew. Having got down on his hands and knees, he had looked and seen what was only obvious. Sitting back on the edge of the bed, his mind and thoughts raced. It would be highly unlikely that the boys would be reported missing; the majority of the youth in this region had little parental guidance, not many had the benefit of education, and if they weren't begging on the streets, they took the easy option of selling their bodies to wealthy tourist. Now, with his eyes darting from the rolled-up rug to the blank TV screen and then to the door, Stuli's mind was in turmoil. He had time on his hands. He needed help. *Who?*

Vincent was the one who immediately sprung to mind. Together, they had spent many hours pouring out each other's issues and dramas. They had confided in each other and told things to one another that they would never tell anyone else. They had connected. In fact, it had been Stuli who had introduced young Bert to Vincent, and it had been he who had organised the sex change. Bert had become Beatrice after a number of operations over a period of 5 years, and most of this was due to the fact that Stuli had the contacts.

He had knocked on Vincent's door in the early hours of the morning. Beatrice had answered and ushered Stuli in. The suite was rented long-term to Vincent before he bought shares in the hotel from Stuli during one of the couple's regular drinking sessions. It seemed that after each of these booze-ups, Stuli was less land-rich and a little cash-richer.

"Please, Beatrice, I need to speak to Vincent alone." he said, sitting down on the first chair he made contact with. Barry walked in from one of the three bedrooms adjacent to the main room.

"Bee. Coffee pet." he said, fastening his thigh-length silk gown. "What's wrong, S?" he enquired. "You're not looking for a booze up, are you?'

"No, Vincent. Please, I need to speak with you alone." he answered, pleading with his eyes, sitting with his cap in hand.

"Darling, go to bed." said Barry, turning on the radio. Once Beatrice was out of earshot, he turned to Stuli.

"What's wrong, partner?" he said, concerned. "Look at you, you look like you've seen a ghost."

"Worse, my friend." said the fat Jew, breaking down, sobbing like a baby. He was unable to get the words out, so he stood up and waved for Barry to follow him. Down the hall, he descended two flights of stairs before walking up the dim corridor to stop at room 12. Opening the door with shaking hands, he beckoned Barry to follow him in. Once inside the room, Stuli pointed to the bed. Barry looked at the bed and then back at Stuli, who was sobbing now and unable to speak a word. He directed Barry with his hand to look under the bed. Bending over, Barry looked under the bed and again back at the fat Jew. Stuli then walked over to the TV and pressed the play button on the DVD. Immediately, the upsetting scene had Stuli sobbing even more; he again looked at Barry and pointed under the bed.

"Fucking Hell!" said Barry, as the realisation hit him. "What the fuck have you done, Stuli?"

'Not I. No, not I. It was the Americans, they clean up the mess, but they leave the bodies, and the disc in the machine," now perspiring profoundly, Stuli pleaded, "I need your help, Vincent, to dispose of the bodies. If the police find the boy's here, they will kill me."

"OK, Keep calm. Let's think. OK, the boys will not be missed, at least for a few days. We can take them up to the hills and bury them. You must drive the bodies up to the base of the mountain with a pick and two spades. I will follow you up on my bike. OK, keep calm Stuli," said Barry reassuringly, "I can pay the commander. It may cost a few thousand US dollars, but it will assure your liberty should we be discovered."

"Can we not pay this only if and when we are discovered?" asked the typical Jew.

"We pay this not to be discovered, you fool." said Barry, already counting the dollars. "And you owe me one for this."

"OK, OK, let's do it." with that, the two of them spent the remainder of the early morning until the sun rose, digging and concealing the bodies of the two young boys. Stuli worried about capture while Barry was scheming how to subtract the information he required from the source.

"Euros or Stirling?" asked the driver, stopping at the taxi rank. "Sir! Will that be Euros or Stirling?"

"Oh! I'm sorry, so sorry." replied Stuli, coming out of a trans-like state. "How much?" now fumbling in his pockets.

"How you pay?"

"Cash." replied the dim-wit.

"Yes, I understand, but with Euro or with Stirling?"

"Please forgive me. Euro."

"Twelve Euro." The knock on the window startled Stuli as he searched for change. Beatrice now beckoned the driver to put down his window. She handed him a ten euro note, and he accepted it reluctantly.

"Come Stuli. Vincent is waiting. I'm afraid his friend cannot make it, so we are making alternative arrangements, but don't worry, we will talk before Friday. Maybe tomorrow."

Chapter Twenty-Eight

Jerry rode the bike steadily along the road leading to the airport. His helmet was securely fasted to his seat behind him. It was too hot to wear. Should he be pulled over by the Guardia, he would be very unlucky if the officer didn't take the fifty Euro note on the cover of his passport.

When the perspiration had dried from the cool air flow, he pulled over and put on the helmet. No point in drawing attention.

The Porsche was now out of sight as he rejoined the flow of traffic. Turning off at the landmark, the San Miguel brewery, Jerry looked at his watch. 1:10. The Paligamo would close as most do in Spain at 2 pm for siesta. The traffic leaving the airport was busy, so Jerry waited for a gap before cutting across the oncoming. He hesitated for just a fraction too long, as did the driver of the black Lexus. Both accelerated at the same time, thinking that one and the other were giving way. Jerry carried on whilst the Lexus braked hard and sounded his horn.

"Fuck you!" screamed Jerry as he mounted the curb. He rode over the grass verge and joined the secondary road, which ran parallel to the main one he had abruptly left. He was more than relieved to dismount and remove the helmet. He looked at the traffic moving at a snail's pace and noted the Lexus was but a dozen motors away. He considered running up to it and giving the driver a slap but thought better of it.

"No parking! No parking!" called the Chinese salesman from within the spacious unit. The front of the shop was the width of four large double-high patio doors, all of which had one-half open.

"I buy piano," called Jerry. "Me buy." now slapping the bulge in his pocket.

"Oh! I see. Come come," said the little chink beckoning him into the showroom with his arm outstretched. "This way. You like? Hables Espanola?"

"Pocito." replied Jerry, holing up thumb and forefinger. "Me Inglaterra." he said, pointing to his chest

"Vewy goo, wha I can do for yoou."

"I would like to buy a chandelier."

"Oh! No can do. Only piano, I have only piano." disappointment now etched on the tiny yellow face, followed by realisation as Jerry smiled. The little china man gave a squeaky giggle, bending over and holding his stomach. *It wasn't that funny,* Jerry laughed.

"Come on, you show me piano," he said, walking into the cool showroom from the heat of the midday sun.

"This one," he said, placing a hand on the first one he came into contact with. "How much?" the piano was upright, and Jerry had no interest in it, but he wanted to see what he was up against. The small calculator was in the chinks hand like magic, and the speed of his hand put Victoria's to shame. Jerry gave a rye smile at his inner comparison. "Leave me to browse, please," he asked, looking around the large area.

From deep within the store, the beautiful sound of someone playing could be heard but not seen. He wondered if the music started as he entered the showroom. There were roughly about thirty to forty pianos to choose from. All different shapes, sizes, colours and styles. Jerry could make out the Grand pianos immediately as most of them had their lids in the upright position.

He could sense the little man at his heels, even though he had requested that he leave him to browse. Jerry turned suddenly and caught the little man off guard. Startled, the chink looked down at his adding machine. Jerry guessed it very rarely subtracted.

"Where's the music coming from?" he asked.

"Plea, this way," he replied, going ahead of Jerry at a million miles an hour. Jerry liked the little tryer, with his floral oversized shirt hanging over shorts with the same pattern. The little legs carrying the delicate frame were like matchsticks. He looked back at Jerry, smiling, and pointed to the source.

Jerry had heard the music before. *Some movie? Maybe. Love story? A star is born?* He couldn't put his finger on it, but it was being played beautifully. He stopped at a blind spot so as not to distract the musician.

The top of the White Grand was in the upright position, and Jerry and the little man stood to the right of the slowly rotating platform. Very slowly, the piano turned. All the pianos on the show were given a theme. Some were placed on marble, with the walls depicting pictures reflecting the era. Others were complemented with flowers and candelabras. Each base and flooring was changed to accommodate the different styles. Some were placed on carpet or parquet flooring, while others were standing on different coloured marble.

Slowly now, the pianist came into view. The flowers from the free-standing Jardinière were the only thing concealing her face. Jerry could see the intricate feminine hands producing the sound and could only imagine the face being as beautiful as the symphony they were making.

He sensed the salesman was about to speak, so he instinctively held up his hand to stop him in his tracks. Very slowly, he held a finger to his lips without looking at the little man who had gotten the message.

The girl playing for anyone who would listen—in this instance for Jerry alone—was more pretty than he had imagined. She was sitting bolt upright on the stool with a posture only the dedicated could perfect. She was attached to the instrument—part of it. Her hair was as black as the piano was white; shiny and straight, it stopped approximately four inches from the floor. Jerry estimated it would fall below her backside, if she were to stand. The brows of her brown eyes were without contrast to her hair, and her olive skin gave her a certain Mediterranean look. *Spanish?* She was lost in the music, as though absorbed within the theme, almost watching the scene from the movie. She could have been in film because everything about her should be seen and not touched. The respectable cheesecloth loose-fitting dress she was wearing covered her legs and left the feet on the piano peddles on view. The unpainted nails were natural. There were no gimmicks.

She instinctively knew she had an audience, and she acknowledged this with a nod of her head and a smile, almost embarrassed, if not shy.

"Beautiful," whispered Jerry ever so silently that he was surprised she mouthed,

"Thank you." 'She speaks English," thought Jerry. Her smile broadened as if she had read his mind. Her cheeks gave a tint of red. Trying not to embarrass the girl any further, he turned to the little chink.

"I like this one."

"Yes. Yes, this one vewy goo. You lie? Steinway, vewy goo," said the salesman. Jerry placed one hand on the piano and moved at a snail's pace with the rotating platform.

"You lie pri?" continued the little man urgently. "I give you pri."

"Yes. Goo pri?" Jerry mimicked, still moving. Still looking. He could hear the calculator being punished frantically. The music stopped. Jerry clapped at the same pace he was moving, slow and deliberate.

"Bravo! Bravo."

"Thank you very much, sir." she replied, looking down.

"That was awesome, truly amazing," he smiled. The chink was now becoming a pest as he tried to come between the two. Jerry spoke as if he wasn't there.

"Your English is good. Where did you learn to speak such good English?"

"My Mother is Canadian and my father a Gibraltarian. And you, you are English?"

"Half Irish, half English. My mother's a Dub."

"A Dub?"

"Dublin."

"Oh, I see."

"Why are you playing this particular piano?"

"I play all the pianos. But I must confess, this is my favourite. It is a Steinway. Circa 1860. I believe it was salvaged after the revolution and restored in Burgos. Some say it was housed in the residence of Franco for some time, but this providence is only hearsay. I'd say it was always owned by someone with culture or at least someone who understands music. At the very least, someone who had nothing better to spend their money on. It is truly a wonderful work of art."

"Sounds like you will be sorry to see it leave."

"You could say that," she laughed. "although the commission will alleviate any pain. I do get a small bonus if the one I am playing sells at the time." she explained without looking at him.

"Twenty-four thousand," butted in the irritation, "Tha is goo pri."

"Take off the four thousand, and I'll take it."

"No possible! No can do."

"No problem," said Jerry, making to leave.

"Twenty-two thousand. Final pri, goo pri."

"Nineteen thousand, this better pri."

"You already offer twenty."

"Eighteen and a half."

"OK. Twenty thousand," said the little chink urgently. "We deliver, where you lie? You leave ten percent. Where you lie?" he touched Jerry and urged him over to the nearest piano with the lid down. From the back pocket of his shorts, he produced a small receipt book and, with a pen released from behind his ear, began to scribble frantically. "Mr?"

"Mrs," said Jerry. The chink looked at him confused. "It's a present for my wife." he said just audible enough for his ears.

"Vewy goo, vewy goo, Shush." he said seriously, holding a finger to his mouth.

"Where you lie?"

"Today."

"Where you lie?"

"Oh!" replied Jerry, a little confused. "Marbella."

"Marbella vewy ni!" he smiled, showing teeth as yellow as his skin. *Greedy little cunt!* Jerry thought.

"You lie today? No possible today. Tomorrow me can do."

"Today." said Jerry, rolling up a fifty and replacing it where the pencil had sat behind the little man's ear.

"No problem." said the ferret, handing Jerry the notepad and pencil. "Please, you write address. 9 'o clock, OK?"

"Perfecto," said Jerry, handing back the pad. He looked at the girl who was smiling, bemused. Giving the chink four rolled up Bin Laden's, he moved back over to the rotating platform.

"Do you know any Beetles?"

"Of course." she smiled.

"Would you play one for me?"

"Sure, it would be my pleasure. Which one would you like?"

"Hey Jude, I love that song."

"Can you sing?" she asked.

"I'm afraid not," he answered seriously. She began to play. "Please," he said. "play it slow and light. I would like to talk to you."

"What would you like to talk about?"

"You." said Jerry.

"I'd rather not if you didn't mind. I'm not really used to that kind of thing. You know?" this was more like a statement. "talking about myself. I mean, there isn't much to talk about."

"Please let me be the judge of that." he said reassuringly. "Could I at least start by asking you your name?"

"Yes," she said, slightly embarrassed. "My name is Ebony."

"Ebony. Ebony," Jerry rolled the name from his tongue. She played his choice. He closed his eyes and listened.

Chapter Twenty-Nine

The choice of the suit wasn't a problem; if it fits, it will do. The problem was finding a salesperson who could speak English.

"A fucking nightmare," thought Wheeler as he moved from one department to another. All the known brands were available: Armani, Versace, Ralph Lauren, he couldn't give a fuck, they were too dear anyway. He knew if he was struggling here, it would be even worse elsewhere. He knew those little boutiques outside in the centre would be impossible.

Moving to the next one, a Spanish brand he couldn't pronounce, he was tired, hot and exhausted.

"English? You speak English?" He asked, already looking at the next department.

"Yes, sure, step in, Sir," replied the young man smartly dressed in the same brand. "What can I do for you?"

"A chair first, son," replied Wheeler, seating himself on a low bench with a shoe-fitting stand attached. "I'm so glad I found you, kid. Why does no one speak English around here?"

The boy laughed, "We are in Spain, sir," he said apologetically. "I'm sure back in London, the salespeople at Harvey Nicks don't all speak Spanish."

"I know, son. I know. I'm too old for this."

He placed the bag over his shoulder on the floor to the side of the seat and the briefcase on the shoe-fitting stand in front of him.

"Help me take this coat off, son," he said, struggling to peel the jacket off in his sitting position.

"It's wet with the heat," said the boy, accommodating. "Here, let me hang it for you, sir. Would you like a drink of water?"

"No. I'll be fine. Just give me a second."

Forty minutes later, Wheeler was suited and booted. It transpired that the salesman was a student, travelling Europe on his gap year. How he ended up here, in a gents' clothes store in Malaga, was a long story that involved a young lady who had the beauty and influence to change his life and disappoint his parents.

But "Hey! That's life" was his philosophy.

Now standing at the counter of a backstreet coffee/internet shop, Wheeler ordered the obligatory espresso. When the girl placed the miniature cup in front of him with a token to sit at keyboard 9, he looked first at the girl serving him, then at the ridiculously small thimble of tar, then to the guy beside him receiving his large Cappuccino. He picked up the small cup and made to down it in one before scolding his lips and spitting the boiling liquid into the saucer.

"What the fa-- is that?" he asked, looking at the girl, his face screwed up in disgust.

"This is what you ordered, sir. This is espresso."

"I thought this was coffee. A normal coffee."

"Would you like something else?" asked the girl, wiping up the mess.

"Yes, one of those," replied Wheeler, pointing to the Cappuccino in the guy's hand next to him.

"Please take a seat, number nine. I will bring over your coffee, sir."

"Thank you, and sorry," replied Wheeler, looking sheepishly at the spillage.

Operation Escatura. He typed the name into the tobacco-stained keyboard 9. The screen was barely visible through the small space's smoke-filled confines. There was no privacy, either way, as his policeman's instinct had him viewing the screen of the occupant sitting next to him.

He coughed to let the hippy know he didn't appreciate him sharing his cigarette. The hippy didn't care. Wheeler looked back at the monitor. Nothing.

"Too early," he imagined. The warrant was enforced only this morning.

"This morning! God!" It had seemed such a long time ago.

Government corruption. Spain. There was plenty to look at, but there was nothing relating to Operation Escatura as far as he could see.

Costa Del Crime. Plenty.

Divine. Jerry Divine. Plenty but very little to do with Our Divine Income tax investigation over 10 years ago, nothing else.

"Fuck it. Let it rest." He would wait and see what tomorrow's conference would bring. He punched in the keyboard with one finger. Last minute rooms dot com. Malaga. Spain. For the next fifty minutes, he browsed the bargains. The cheaper he got, the more profit he earned.

Chapter Thirty

"We have to get this right the first time," said Barry anxiously, looking into Stuli's nervous eyes. They were now seated in the busy Lord Admiral. The large portion of steak and kidney pie an hour into digestion mode.

"What you must understand, S, is that this man takes no shit. We have to convince him that the diamonds are there. My friend, there is absolutely no margin for error here. We need him to accept this project, and he will want to hear that the information you provided is direct source material. Do you understand?"

"Yes, certainly, my friend. I will tell him what I know and more like we agreed. I fully understand what I have to do."

"Perfect. Go through it one more time as though you were talking to my friend. I am he. Call him Jimmy."

"O.K. Hello, Jimmy," commenced Stuli, looking deep into Barry's eyes. As serious as it was, Barry had to restrain himself from laughing back at the big fat Jew.

"The information I am about to tell you is from one who knows. It is from me, who has seen," he paused a fraction too long, as if for effect, before continuing, "My brother, Abi, is the owner of a company which employs over one hundred diamond cutters."

"Why are you smiling? Don't smile," said Barry.

"Sorry, I think maybe Jimmy is impressed."

"Don't try to impress. He will see right through you," urged Barry, now looking concerned. "Just tell it how it is."

"I am sorry."

"Stop fucking apologising."

"OK, sorry. Please let me continue, my friend, and you are making me nervous."

"Here, have some water," said Barry, handing the fat man his glass.

"As I was saying… The diamond-cutting business is predominantly Jewish, although many Asian companies are paramount, particularly in India. But my brother has one of the main distributors in Africa. He has shares in a mine and is involved with some black movements in Sierra Leon.

The information I receive comes directly from another family member who has regular contact with my brother."

"He may want to know who?"

"It is my son, Vincent. I cannot involve him."

"If he asks, you must."

"Well, we'll come to that if we have to, and if I have no choice in the matter…" A look of dread now on the face of Stuli.

He continued, "The other source of the information is a mutual friend of the two of us. His name is Malkit Sandu, an Indian Sikh. He lives in Antwerp, where the cutting factory is, and he travels to Gambia two or three times a year and stays with me at my hotel."

"Good," interrupted Barry. "That's good. You've told him where you live without being asked. He will take note of this. He may then ask you later where you live. He will always be one step ahead of you, so always remember what you say because he will spring something on you during the conversation."

"Malkit likes to talk. He tells me everything. Things I am not even interested in. I was never interested in my brother's business. Not until Vincent asked me to find out what I could."

"Why would you tell Bar—Vincent," Barry corrected himself, "about your brother's business interest. In fact, for that matter, why would you even consider setting your brother's company up to be robbed?" asked Barry as a possible question.

Stuli understood he was playing a part here.

"Mr Jimmy, there is no love lost between my brother and I. You see, the company was founded way beyond our first breath, and Abi, the elder of the two, inherited the company. On the other hand, I was left to find my own way in this world, so I have always felt hard done by. I hope you understand; I am being very honest with you. I am extremely bitter."

Stuli was not about to divulge the fact that he was captured by his older brother molesting a child from the next village.

"O.K, and why Vincent?"

"Vincent and I have been friends now for almost six years. It was not an easy decision, but I trust him, and during our long hours speaking together, I took him into my confidence, as he did I. I truly believe that I can trust this man one hundred percent."

"Good. I like that bit. Good, but don't overdo it. Remember what I said; he will ask you certain things."

"Is that enough?"

"Yes, I think so," replied Barry. "Let him ask the questions. He will obviously go on to ask where, when, how, numbers, times, amounts, value, etc. Make sure you have answers, and if you don't, lie, but remember the answers."

With that, Barry stood to leave the table.

"Stay here. S. B. should be back shortly, and I will be too. I just need to make a call."

He left and walked over to the crowded square to call the San Roque Hotel.

Chapter Thirty-One

"These bikes are alright, but a full day on the cunts can certainly make the balls ache," thought Jerry as he now parked it in the garage.

He had stopped at a filling station on the way back from Malaga to use the public phone. The hotel receptionist had put him through to room 308, which had rung out, automatically diverting back to the front desk. The girl had told Jerry that Mr Viceroy had extended his stay to Friday. Jerry had hung up. He would call later or maybe drive down. He would listen to what was on offer. He had decided to take what Barry had told him at face value.

"What choice did he have? He couldn't prove otherwise, but he would take it with extreme caution. He was certainly intrigued by what was on offer."

Kath and Julie sat on the terrace looking at some pictures that had recently been developed. Jasmine was under the gazebo studying.

"Hi, babe," he said, kissing his wife on the cheek.

"Where's mine?" said little Julie, offering her cheek. He leaned over to kiss it when she turned to meet his lips.

"Got yer!" she laughed.

"That's my trick," he said, ruffling her hair.

"Hi, love," he called over to his eldest daughter.

"Hi, Dad, can you help me with this?"

"I'm shattered, love. I need to rest."

"Please!" she asked as he walked over. The sun was slowly moving down behind the mountains. This was his favourite time of the day. Peace and quiet, only the sound of the water pump and crickets.

"What is it, love?" he asked.

"Business studies. Market research and advertising. I have to do a mock advertisement. I can't think," she said, sitting back and tapping the pencil on the table.

"What do you mean, an advertisement?"

"I don't know," she answered frustratingly. "Like, you know, how would I advertise something."

"You mean like a washing machine?" he asked seriously. Jasmine laughed.

"A washing machine?" she looked at her dad with distaste.

"Why not? Everyone has one," he said defensively.

"I suppose," she conceded.

"Or what about Jeans? Levi's. They could do with a comeback. All these fancy names. These Beckom's and such the likes. What about the founder? The original? The real McCoy?"

"Yes, that's fine, but what can I say? What can I do?"

"Well! A good idea is to write the name first and see what can be done with the letters, like a corundum."

"A what?" asked Kath, who was listening, bemused.

"Like on Countdown," he answered.

"What are you on about, Dad?" called Julie. The two walked over to join her under the gazebo. Jerry took hold of the pen.

"Come here," he said, sliding the book over. He wrote the name LEVI'S in bold capital letters.

"Right! Come, get your thinking caps on," he said.

"Elv…" said Kath enthusiastically.

"Elv," retorted Jerry.

"Elf, Mum," laughed Jasmine mockingly.

"That's an Irish midget. Even I know that, silly," said little Julie. "E.L.F", she spelt out.

Jerry laughed, too.

"It's a little fellow, but not Irish. You're thinking of a Leprechaun, but she's halfway there. Look! Elvis. E.L.V.I.S the King of Rock 'n' Roll. He could be the ambassador."

"He's dead, Dad," said Jasmine mockingly.

"There's many who believe he isn't," corrected Kath.

"L.I.V.E. Live," said Jerry, studying hard.

"Lives!" exclaimed Kath.

Jasmine laughed.

"Well done, Mum," said Julie, hugging her.

"Elvis lives in Levi's," said Jerry in a low voice. "The King of Rock n Roll. Play around with that love. It's inventive, and it shows imagination." He stood up, "Now let me get a cold one. Just something light for me, love," he said, rubbing his belly. "I have to see Jezzie at seven-thirty," he looked at his watch.

"Look at the time," he said, realising he only had less than an hour to prepare.

"Don't worry, love, I'll eat out." He removed his shirt, shoes and trousers before diving into the pool and resurfacing at the shallow end. Walking up steps from the water, he took the cold beer from little Julie and made it for the poolside shower.

"What time did Tom take the car?" he asked as he towel-dried on the terrace.

"I'm not sure, love. Do you want me to call him? I don't want you taking mine." she said.

Jerry had a habit of leaving his car parked anywhere and everywhere if he was in no state to drive home, and Kath needed hers for the school run.

"Yes," he answered to her relief. "Oh! By the way, we have a delivery tonight at nine o'clock."

"What is it, Dad?" said little Julie, who never missed a trick.

"You'll see, baby," he replied, smiling at Kath.

Now, in the dressing area of the bedroom, Jerry asked his wife to lay something nice on the bed while he finished shaving. She had a better dress sense than him.

"You just seeing Jez?" she called as she looked at the clothes hanging.

"No, I have a business meeting at the port. I'll be dining out later," he said, standing next to her. She raised her arms to lift a salmon-coloured light flannel suit from its hanger. Jerry looked down to see the silk wrap-a-round lift up to show she was naked under it.

"You not wearing any? You cheeky little thing," he teased, moving behind her and enveloping her with his strong arms. He leaned down slightly and put his head on her shoulder with his lips just below her ear lobe.

"Do you want some?" he whispered. She didn't reply but kept her arms raised, leaning back, and moved them backwards to grasp the back of his head with her hands.

"Em. Yes, yes, please," she said, forcing her backside into his crouch.

Jerry now moved his hands around the front of her body and continued to feel the heat of her flesh beneath the silk cloth. He clasped one breast in each hand and moulded them with a firm grip to the shape of the smaller grip. Kath winced at the firmness of his grip and was immediately soothed by the response as he eased his hold and ran the forefinger of both hands over the erect nipple of each breast.

"That's good," she whispered as Jerry now kissed her lightly around her right ear and upper neck.

"Sorry, love, I'm short on time; I just want to have you," he said gruffly.

"Take me," she responded urgently as his right hand had now lowered to her damp crutch.

"Have me, Jerry." she moaned as his long middle finger rubbed urgently at her clitoris before joining the forefinger of the same hand that had already entered her wet fanny.

Jerry now moved down to her waist area with his left arm and lifted her up. Holding her above his raised erect penis, he expertly lowered her down and slowly entered her from the rear.

Moving slowly to the right, Jerry positioned the two of them directly in front of the dressing mirror. Kath placed her feet on the glass top and opened her legs while Jerry's large penis was still inside her. He now put each hand on either cheek of her bottom and started to move in a controlled rhythm. The sight of his manhood pushing in and out of her only enhanced the already heated passion between them. A purely sexual urge that was to have no boundaries. She forced herself up from his manhood before letting the weight of her body do the rest. She landed hard back down, taking the full length of the penis.

"Oh! Jeez, yes!" she called as Jerry now took her weight in his arms and, keeping his member inside her, he turned and walked over to the bed. Now bending his knees, he remained within her as he lowered her face down on the bed with him on top of her. He speeded up the action as his thrusts became more erratic, shoving his full length into her as she bucked up to meet him. He raised himself up and rested on straight arms.

Looking down, he could see his hard wet cock going in and out, making squelching noises as the fluid dripped from the saturated area.

"Yes!" she called. "Harder, Jerry! Slow and hard."

Jerry now gritted his teeth and pushed home for what he knew was to be the last few strokes before he ejaculated. The urgency was shown within the pace as the speed intensified, and he declared with urgency that he was about to come.

"I'm coming," he said through his locked jaw. "I'm coming now!"

"Come!" replied Kath. "Come, come, yes! Come!" Jerry's knees buckled at the first explosion, and he rested his inner thighs on the outer thighs of his wife. He leaned over and placed both hands on the bed on either side of her head, as the second release soon followed the first.

"More!" called Kath as she raised her backside to meet his thrust. She, too, was reaching the climax and let Jerry know as she reached back and grabbed for flesh. She found it in the form of his tensed buttocks. Now pulling him in, deep inside her, she released the first of a quick succession of an uncontrollable flood of euphoria. She came to join him, and the two of them enjoyed the moment of ecstasy.

"That was wonderful," said Jerry, lifting his dead weight from Kath and rolling over to lie face up.

"Do you have to go?" asked Kath, turning and placing one arm and one leg over his body.

"Sorry love, needs must," he said, turning to kiss her forehead. He stood feeling quite guilty and walked into the bathroom.

"These bidets were made for this, weren't they?" he called.

"Yes."

Standing in the doorway smiling, Kath said, "Hurry up, my turn."

Jerry stood, his cock still erect. Swapping places with his wife, he kissed her tenderly before moving back into the bedroom and dressing.

The sound of the car horn had him leaving through the front door, calling his goodbyes as the door slammed behind him.

"Dame La Notches," he instructed Tom.

Kath heard the car take off as she stepped into the cool surroundings of the large marble shower area. She turned the water to moderate flow and the temperature down to low.

Gently now, she began to soap her hair and body. The feeling returned. The deep feeling of dread started at the pit of her flat stomach, soothingly massageing and rising up to compress her chest. She held on to the chrome safety rail attached to the inner wall and took several deep breaths. She didn't see or hear Little Julie come and join her in the large cubicle, and she only realised she was sharing the shower with her when the little one turned on the music. Looking down at her young daughter, she smiled, thankful that the water disguised her tears.

Chapter Thirty-Two

"Pull over here in the shade," directed Jerry, pointing to the far corner of the car park.

"Da yer tink dis place will do any good? It's only a nine-hole, and I can't imagine the boys ud want to play golf late at night!" said Tom, trying to make conversation.

Not a word had been spoken by his boss during the fifteen-minute journey. Jerry didn't respond; instead, he stepped out of the car and checked his watch.

"What do you want me to do? Wait here or what?" Tom called from the open car.

"Yes. And put the roof up." Tom watched his boss walk over the loose gravel car park. He envied him at times and, to be perfectly frank, hated him too. He looked at the bollocks he had to give him that fucking pink suit, black polo shirt, and shoes to match.

The watch he was wearing would probably pay for a house good enough for Tom to live in. If he hadn't talked to him the way he did at times, he knew he wouldn't have felt this way now.

So fucking inferior.

I suppose he must have something major on his mind. This could be a late night.

He turned the music on.

The Rolling Stones.

The cunt didn't even mention the ninety grand he won on the horse.

The clubhouse was small, more like a giant greenhouse with air-con. Jerry was disappointed that Jez was not there waiting for him. He took a seat at one of the six tables. Only one other table was occupied by an older man with a younger girl.

Jerry sussed him out immediately. Sixty-five to seventy, all the toys and his clubs had little use, but she had plenty. She didn't want to be here, but the money was good. She lifted her glass of orange and looked over the top of it in his direction, quickly looking down when Jerry smiled ever so lightly. She was embarrassed. Jerry had seen her before, around the port. She was definitely brass and, without a doubt, would be more comfortable sitting in a bar on the front row than sitting here eating a club sandwich and listening to this old cunt boring her with tales of his wealth, half of it lies, both she and Jerry guessed. Again, she looked at Jerry with a look of resignation, and Jerry nodded for her eyes only. They were communicating without words, and the old chap didn't have a clue.

The barman walked from behind the counter with his pad in one hand and a bowl of complementary olives in the other. Placing the olives on the table, he took a small pencil from his top pocket, which housed a badge informing Jerry that his name was Pedro. How many of these lost souls are called fucking Pedro mused Jerry.

"Just water for me, please." He couldn't be bothered making the effort with the lingo. Too much on his mind.

"Certainly, sir. I'll be right back," Jerry smiled.

He spoke much better English than he spoke Spanish.

"Make that two," he called as he saw Jezzie heading up the path to join him.

"Hi," said Jez, taking a seat. "What is this? No greeting?"

"I'm in no mood for pleasantries, Jez. How've you gone on?"

"Augustine Gonzalez has been moved from the police station in Estepona to Alhaurin de la Torre Prison near Malaga. The Abadagos acting for him are based in Marbella. One…" He looked down at the papers he had placed on the table before him. "Azzorio Manzella has been assigned by the company Ottellimes. They are the best. I can assure you of this."

"O.K. and?"

"Well. O.K Senor Manzella is going into the prison tomorrow at two o'clock. He has an assistant whom I have spoken to in private. Her name is Brogonia. She has given me her word that she will use her own Dictaphone machine and will see me tomorrow evening to pass the recording to me."

"The machine," said Jerry, looking sternly at Jez. "…as it leaves the prison? Not even re-winded?"

"Yes, yes, Jerry. As you requested. Don't worry."

"That's good. What else?"

"Emilio Sanchez Junior is in his office as we speak. He will not speak with me or anyone else for that matter, and he is more concerned for the welfare of his father, who was arrested this morning and is currently being held in the central Policia station in Marbella. The papers should tell us more tomorrow. At present, we must make do with the radio bulletins, which keep us informed of the same thing every hour. This was said with resignation and a shrug of some tired, weary shoulders.

Jez looked at Jerry before accepting the cold drink from the waiter. Jerry waited until the waiter had left the table. He looked hard at Jez before very deliberately saying, "You haven't told me fuck all I don't already know."

"I've told you as much as I can, Jerry. We will know more tomorrow. Please be patient for one night only."

"Augustine—fat, greedy cunt—Gonzales. Have you spoken to anyone other than this Brogonia? Who, by the way, seems to me to be the bottom of the bleeding ladder."

"She is Jerry, but she is also the mistress of the lawyer, Azzorio Manzella. She will keep us well informed. The tape recording, for instance! Come on, Jerry. A little credit, my friend."

"How did you get to her?"

"She is an ex-girlfriend of my son, David and would do most things to be back in that position."

"O.K. Alright, Jez, good work, keep it up. I'm going to relax tonight, but you're not. I want you to keep working, Jez, keep thinking and if there is anything you can dig up, no matter how small or inappropriate you may think it is, do it. I expect a lot more tomorrow. What time are you seeing this girl?"

"7 o'clock."

"Where?"

"Benalmadena Port, she lives there."

"Good. I'll see you at the Torracabrada Hotel when you are finished. I'll be in the casino."

"Perfecto," said Jez, now a little uncomfortable. He had hoped to have a social drink with Jerry once the formalities were over and had dressed with this in mind. This was obviously not to be as Jerry now stood. Peeling a Ten-euro note from a wad, he dropped it on the table and walked from the melting igloo without saying another word.

Jerry was a little more confident than he had been. He liked the fact that they had inside help, even though it was in the form of a mere secretary. It was better than nothing, he thought.

"That was quick," said Tom. "Where to boss?"

"The port."

"Which one?"

"Stop being cute, you cunt. The nearest one." Jerry smiled at Tom's attempt to lighten the mood.

"I could do with a drink myself. Will I be joining you?"

"For the first drink or two, but when the guy comes, you'll have to leave us be, but it could be a long night, and if you fancy a drink, I'll make my own way home," said Jerry before adding, "don't be driving this fucking car under the influence."

"I won't, boss."

"And cut the fucking boss out."

"O.K, mate," said Tom, smiling.

Vehicular traffic was permitted only to patrons with either a business interest or mooring holders.

"Pull up to the barrier," instructed Jerry, indicating the entrance for vehicular permit holders

"Since when did we have a card?" asked Tom, looking surprised. He stopped the car at the barrier.

"Here," said Jerry, passing Tom a bank card. "Put this in the slot and keep hold of it."

Tom did as he was told.

"Pull it back out."

Again, he did as he was told.

"Now press the intercom," instructed Jerry.

Tom pressed the speaker button.

Jerry leaned over to the driver's side. "No functional," he called. The speaker crackled into life, and the controller activated the barrier to lift.

"Fucking hell!" said Tom moving the car forward. "But how do we get out?"

"How do you get out?" Jerry corrected.

"Well, how do I get out with your car?" he reminded Jerry.

"I told you to stop being cute… simple. Just stay up the arse of the car in front."

Puerto Banus was the brainchild of Jose Banus a local property developer and friend of Francisco Franco. He was approached by an architect, Nildi Schreck, who in turn had been approached by Prince Alfonso de Hohenlohe in 1966, who asked him to work on the Hotel Marbella Club. Together, they came up with the idea to build the port to accommodate the rich and famous who preferred this microclimate, which resulted from the protection of its northern parts by the coast mountain range of Cordillera Penibetica.

A marina was located in the area of Nueva Andalucia, just a few kilometres to the southwest of Marbella. Constructed in 1970, it now attracts over 5 million annual visitors, mostly tourists from northern Europe (especially the United Kingdom) and Arabs (especially Kuwait and Saudi Arabia), along with Spanish tourists. The focal point of Puerto Banus is the marina. It has berths for 915 boats, including those of the King of Saudi Arabia and several international celebrities. Its streets are lined with expensive luxury boutiques, such as Christian Dior, Gucci, Bvlgari, Versace, Dolce & Gabbana, and others. Leading Hotels of the World surround the port, The Marbella Club being the forerunner, followed by The Hotel Puente Romano and The Hotel Gvadalpin Banus.

The port was coming to life with evening drinkers and diners. Although at this time of the evening, the place was relatively quiet. The flow of human traffic was leaning more toward the outbound. Young families who had merely come to sightsee a few coach parties on an excursion from the package holiday destinations along the coast. The holidaymakers look with wonder at the magnificent boats lining the concrete Jetties. The A-line was easily accessible to the tourist. They would look for hours at the larger boats and yachts lining the first row and then turn to view the immaculate open-fronted bars and restaurants. The menus positioned on placards or displayed in windows would be an attraction in themselves as the general public would stand and wonder how people could spend on one meal what would pay for food for a week in their lives. Looking at how the other half lived would soon get the better of their imagination, and as mealtime arrived, it was inevitable that they had spent enough time browsing.

As evening became night, the lights would become neon, and the music would sound from only a few bars, which cater to drinkers only. The main focal point was the first corner by the entrance, which was an ideal position to stand with a drink and watch the flash cars and the flashier occupants cruise the perimeter of the port. For such a small area, the number of top cars on the show would be hard to find in many more European hotspots. Lamborghinis, Ferraris, Austin Martin, Porsche and Bentleys are bumper to tail, some looking for parking while others are a free show for those wanting to admire or ridicule.

"Park on the second row," instructed Jerry. "We'll walk around."

"I prefer that anyway," Tom lied.

Jerry looked at him sideways.

"I do!" said Tom unconvincingly.

"Whatever. Just park here, let me out, you park," said Tom, opening the door. "I'll be in Sinatra's."

"Get me a beer," said Tom as Jerry slammed the door.

The small bar was already full, and the seating was occupied, so Jerry ordered a couple of beers and stood on the opposite side of the road. Looking down between the first boat and the twelve-inch wall he was now standing on, he watched the fish in the water three metres below, dropping some nuts he had grabbed from a bowl on the bar. He was surprised how many came to the surface to fight for them. He also wondered if these were the same fish sold on the menus. Turning to look back at the bar, he was beckoned over by the barman who had placed the cold beers still bottled in the bar.

"Tab?" asked the barman.

"Si," answered Jerry. He turned to see some local gangster cruise by slowly in an open-topped Bentley Assure, and both he and they acknowledged each other with a slight nod. The next car stopped to let Jerry cross, he looked to see some rich chick, way past her sell-by driving a one-owner 1970s Mercedes SL. She smiled at him; through courtesy alone, he was obliged to return the compliment. Once back on the opposite side of the road—which was only the width of the one-way traffic—he regained his position.

"The girls are out in force this evening," said Tom as he re-joined his friend and gaffer.

"You can say that again," replied Jerry, passing one bottle to Tom and raising the other with a smile to a supermodel complete with Chihuahua in a Channel bag.

"What time you seeing the guy?"

"Eight-thirty."

"It's nearly that now."

Jerry looked at his watch and then scanned the road and the bar next to Sinatra's, which had under-shade seating.

"Yes, he won't be long."

"Do you want me to leave as soon as he arrives?"

"No, finish your drink first."

"Good. Here! Look at the fucking shape of them," Jerry turned to see two striking blonds still in swim ware with the briefest of covers from matching silk wrap-around, complete with beach bags. They had obviously finished a day soaking up the sun.

"Hello, girls. How are ya?" called the Irishman. Jerry cringed with embarrassment.

"Hello, girls. How are you?" he mocked. "What the fuck was that?"

"What do you mean?" said Tom.

"No talk, no fuck. You always tell me that," he added defensively.

"There's a fucking million people around. And you shout, Hello, girls, how are you?"

"What's wrong with that?"

"I'll tell you what's wrong with that. Are they talking back?"

"No. they've gone."

"Exactly."

"What would you have said to them?"

"Nothing," said Jerry. "Leave it."

"Two fucking lesbians, that what they were," said Tom spitting some beer from his mouth into the water to see the fish gather.

"Hello, my good friend!" said Abdul. "If Mohamed will not come to the mountain…" his arms were open and reaching up to hold the shoulders of Jerry, who now stood down from the security ledge. Jerry placed his hands on the elbows of the short spiral of a man and bending slightly, they kissed one another's cheeks. Behind Abdul stood a taller version who said nothing but nodded his head without the same enthusiasm as was, without question, his more superior brother or some other relative.

"Your friend?" asked Abdul, looking in Tom's direction.

"My driver," replied Jerry. "Drinks? What would you like?"

"Water I have, my friend," said Abdul. "My brother, Memhet! He is fine. He does not drink too much. He like a camel."

Tom looked at the bottle in Jerry's hand and seeing it was half empty, he made it to the bar.

"You hungry?" Jerry asked the two Arabs.

"Very," replied Abdul. "I could eat a horse," he laughed, showing a small fortune's worth of implants too large for his face.

"My stomach feels like the throat is cut," he continued rubbing his flat stomach. Memhet didn't respond but continued to look straight ahead. A personality to die for, thought Jerry.

"That ignorant eediot wouldn't bring over the drinks," complained Tom, holding two beers and one water.

"I thought you had somewhere to go," Jerry reminded him

"Oh yer," sulked Tom. "Do yer mind if I finish this?" he asked, indicating the remaining bottle he was holding.

"Please yourself, but you don't want to be late for the guy," Jerry advised. Tom took the hint and quickly finished off the beer.

"Call me if you need me."

"O.K, good luck," said Jerry.

"Nice to meet you, my friend," Abdul said, holding out his hand. Tom took it.

"You too," he said and looked at the tall version, who simply nodded his head, leaving Tom to retrieve his outstretched hand.

"So!" said Jerry, easing a slightly awkward silence. "What culinary delights would you like to consume this evening?"

"You have a wonderful way with words, my friend. My mouth is watering at the thought. I think maybe we can try the Indian."

"Perfect, my favourite. There are two in the port. Khans on the back or Mumtaz on the front there, down by the big boats."

"Which do you prefer, Jerry?"

"For the food, I like Khans, but for the ambiance and the service, the Mumtaz takes some beating."

"We toss a coin because both are important to me," said Abdul, searching his pockets for change. He looked to Memhet, who had one ready. Abdul took it from him. Looking at it, he handed it back to him. "We are tossing the coin to see where we eat, not for the price of hashish," Memhet embarrassingly swapped the double-headed coin for a mint-produced one.

Thirty minutes and two beers later, the trio were seated in the plush surrounds of the Indian restaurant. Once the preliminary orders were made and the three were seated alone, Abdul was the first to open the subject of business.

"I know, Jerry, that you are a busy man," he said seriously, "and there must be matters that take priority, but I have to tell you that we, too, are very busy people and what may not be a priority to you, could be one to me." He paused slightly for a response but got none other than Jerry glancing from one to the other and back again.

"We have an amazing opportunity, my friend, to do some business. Business that will see us make good money," pushed Abdul.

Jerry gave a slight nod of his head.

Abdul continued, "If you would rather not give me an explanation why you did not come to Morocco today, that is fine," he raised his shoulders, dipped his head sideways and held his hands out before bringing them together and rubbing one with the other.

"The fact that I am here, Jerry, tells us all that the business is serious."

Again, Jerry acknowledged this with a nod of his head. Once he realised there was nothing more coming from the little guy and it was time for him to speak, he said, carefully choosing his words, "First of all, I am sorry that I was unable to come over to see you. Something very important and unexpectedly came up at very short notice. And I'm afraid it had to take precedence above all other matters."

"Could I ask what?" asked Abdul, looking concerned. "A death in the family? I hope not."

"No. No, nothing like that, Abdul. You could say the opposite." The two looked back at Jerry, confused. The first sign of emotion from the tall one. "I can't go into the detail, it is far too confusing."

You'd think I was lying or completely gone off my fucking head if the truth be known, thought Jerry.

"But nothing to do with the law?"

"I'm not sure at this stage, but it is certainly nothing to do with my scheduled trip to Morocco. You can rest assured," said Jerry.

Abdul didn't look too rest assured. In fact, he looked quite concerned.

"Listen," said Jerry. "Maybe it is for the better that the business, which hasn't been started anyway, should be put on the back burner for now. As a matter of fact, if you have someone else in mind, it might be a good idea for you to consider talking to them instead," Jerry completed reluctantly.

"I take it back burner is an English phrase," said Abdul before he added, "I like you, Jerry. I like the fact that you don't jump in. You take things very seriously, and you would not jeopardise our operation for the sake of finance. The fact that we have not discussed our intended operation with you at this stage gives us some movement, but having said that, my friend. We didn't choose you lightly. You came very highly recommended, and as with all our new partners, we did our homework. Homework, do you say?"

"Yes," replied Jerry. "And I really do appreciate the opportunity, but at this time, it is not good for me and it could bring some uninvited attention to you through me." Jerry knew what he was saying would be taken very seriously. After all, he was not gaining anything by refusing the offer to get into bed with these guys. On the contrary, he could be losing out. Big time. But security was security and the time to look at a big project was not now.

Fucking hell! Memhet does speak, albeit in his native tongue. The two were speaking in rapid succession, almost at the same time. But the action and movement of the two looked to be what Jerry was hoping for. Understanding and agreement.

"O.K, my friend," said Abdul as he placed the intricate embroiled napkin on his lap. After a pause for thought, he continued, "Jerry. It seems without going into detail that you have something that, if you were to commence business with us, could, in fact, jeopardise our operations."

A trolley was wheeled to the table with the food spitting and sizzling on hot cast platters. This was to the annoyance of Abdul, who stopped speaking. The two waiters politely placed the assortment of starters in the centre of the table before leaving the three in peace.

"Before we decide if we talk to someone else. Would it not be sensible to give you some time to see which way the difficulties you are experiencing at the moment go? At this time, we could finalise some of the loose ends we have."

This was an option Jerry was secretly hoping for. Nobody looks a gift horse in the mouth.

"I appreciate the confidence you show, Abdul. It is touching that you would give me the option to stay in tune, and for this, I am truly grateful. And yes, I will know more tomorrow and even more next week. Next month, I will be in a position where I will be able to let you know if we can move forward together. But I have to be straight and to the point here. Although it is quite obvious what the proposition involves, I am unsure what my intended part in the operation will be, and yes, I can guess, but if I'm wrong, how do I know I am able to do what you want me to do?"

"Like I have said, Jerry, we have done our research, and you are quite capable of doing what is required… So, shall we leave it at that for now and enjoy our food? Just one other thing, Jerry. If we do move forward, one month from today you will come and see us in Morocco, yes? We will show you what we have and what we do."

"Yes, I will. It will be very interesting, I'm sure," finalised Jerry placing his napkin between the button holes in his shirt.

The evening turned into night and the night into early morning as the three ventured from bar to club and club to an exclusive brass house. Jerry was a great host to one who enjoyed the sights and sounds and the other who was indifferent to the delights on offer. Once in the trendy nightclub Olivier Valeré, frequently used by celebrities from across Europe, the three were joined by three beautiful ladies of the night. Jerry mused that the evening had a ring of familiarity, having started off at The Dame la Notches.

His thoughts were continually venturing off in the direction of Barry, and on more than one occasion, Abdul had to remind him to enjoy himself, but Jerry was having difficulty in doing so. The VIP area where they were seated consisted of six booths cordoned off with red rope hanging from brass poles. The drink was on overflow and at €240 per bottle for the Don Perignon, which only allowed the seven seated around the table. Abdul opted for two girls, one glass each, and Jerry could see this was going to be an expensive evening.

"More champagne!" said Abdul, draining bottle number six and holding it mid-air for the waiter's attention.

"You are very quiet, James," said the girl sitting next to Jerry.

"Yes, I know, I'm sorry, I have something on my mind," he replied, placing a reassuring hand on her slender olive thigh.

"Maybe I can help," she responded, placing hers on his, higher up.

"Here," said Jerry, handing her a small parcel. "Go and powder your nose. Take your friends."

"Certainly. Thank you."

When the four girls left the table, Jerry told the two they should be making tracks.

"But the girl, Jerry, she is beautiful. No?"

"Yes, they all are. But if we are going to My Lady's. The place is full of them, so what's the point?"

"I am in love with my two," said Abdul with a mock plea.

"Well, if you would rather stay with these, and we could get a suite someplace?"

"No," replied Abdul, "we don't want complaints from unappreciative neighbours."

"Well, let's move while the girls are preoccupied," said Jerry, standing and raising a hand slightly for the attention of the waiter.

The people were still queuing, waiting to come into the club as the trio was leaving. Now standing at the entrance, the doorman whistled for a taxi to collect them. Just then, a Cadillac Escalade stopped close by, and the rear doors opened. Kristos, the Russian with two other Eastern Europeans, stepped from the club on wheels along with three of the most stunning girls on show tonight. Jerry had to give it to this guy. He certainly had some style, but he knew it. Jerry wasn't sure if he liked him or not. He didn't quite know if he took him seriously or found him comical. He knew the guy certainly didn't give a fuck. That was written all over him. Now, as Kristos looked at him and then at the two standing with him, Jerry could see his mind working overtime. This triggered Jerry's to do the same.

Do you recall when I told you I was approached by the architect for the Russian Kristos?... Jerry composed. Well, I believe that that should have been a warning to us that something was a-miss… He could see Jezzie in his mind's eye. Why would Kristos want to sell? Maybe all will be revealed.

Kristos was laughing. He was ushering the girls to the entrance, bypassing the queue to the annoyance of the people waiting. He, like Jerry, would have a large bill for the privilege. The two now looked at one and another, each one knowing the other, but neither had ever spoken. They shook hands as Kristos offered his first before each went their separate ways. Jerry heard the Russian laugh out loud as the door closed behind him and his entourage.

Chapter Thirty-Three

The large villa situated on the Golden Mile was an impressive structure. Standing alone with a six-foot high wall surrounding the perimeter. The combination is lit up by multicoloured spotlights against the night and so enhancing the magnolia-coloured building broken only with intervals housing windows embraced by Juliet balconies. The grand structure, which showed a stark contrast to the terracotta roof tiles, gave the whole building a vision of a miniature palace.

The idea was a terrific business concept for the consortium of entrepreneurs, and one Jerry sometimes wished he was a part of. It would certainly have saved him a few quid, he often thought. The concept was not rocket science. You didn't have to be Einstein. Where's the money? The cash was relatively new and easy. What's the oldest vice in the world? What product has virtually no age barrier? Never goes out of fashion. Is it re-saleable, quick, and expensive, and does it have a good shelf life? Sex. We'll aim for the rich and famous. The investors were already based on the Costa Del Sol. Where was it better to be? The Golden Mile. A stretch of road leading from central Marbella to the playground of the rich and famous. Puerto Banus. We'll call it My Lady's Palace. And if walls could speak… The rest is history.

"Good evening, gentlemen! Welcome. Please, come this way, make yourself comfortable," said the middle-aged stereotype, complete with red lips and beehive hairdo. "May I take your coats? Thank you. Please go on through." They moved from the entrance into the large lounge, which is complete with a splendid bar. The girls were very welcoming and professional.

A mixture of delights was dressed in evening wear, showing just enough flesh to entice the imagination. It was customary in this place to let the customer make the first move, not like most places of ill repute where the girls fall over each other for custom, so the boys sat comfortably on the plush sofas. The décor was splendid, with French ormolu furniture complete with original works of art, both free-standing and hanging from the walls. The night was mild enough for the French doors to be left open, leading out to a large terrace with seating overlooking an immaculately pruned garden area with an illuminated pool.

"Come. Let us sit outside," suggested Abdul, standing, "the night air will do us good."

Jerry stood. He was actually wishing he was home in his own bed but felt obliged to see the night out. Maybe the fresh air will revive him. A line of Charlie would, but again, he wasn't in the mood. He decided there and then that once the boys had ventured up for release, he would hit the high road.

Seated comfortably on the terrace, Jerry thought for a moment that he should feel like he was in heaven. Three of the girls soon followed them outside and, as an added attraction, had changed into swimwear. Another two brought the drinks to the table. Jerry recognised one of them as being the girl who looked after him the last time he was there. Placing the tray on the table, she deliberately revealed the cleavage to a breast Jerry remembered well. She looked directly into his eyes and smiled beautifully.

"Hello, sir. How are you?"

"I'm good. And you?"

"Fine, thank you."

"Your English is better," commented Jerry.

"Thank you. I am trying," she said, pouring a generous vodka into his glass and water into the remaining two.

"And me," said Abdul. "I am fine, too."

She blushed slightly as she stood, replacing a long curl of blonde-coloured hair behind her ear.

"Can we get you anything else?" asked her friend, who was much shorter but every bit as gorgeous.

"You can join us if you like," said Abdul.

"That would be nice. Thank you."

"What would you like to drink'

"Oh, for me, water, please," said the first girl. Jerry remembered she was from Argentina.

"And for me also," said her friend, who looked Eastern European to Jerry.

"Come, sit here," said Abdul, looking at girl number two and patting his lap. Being the professional she was, she made it look like a privilege and took the position she was invited to.

The tall girl took the chair next to Jerry and enquired whether another girl should be beckoned to accommodate Memhet. Jerry looked at Memhet, who declined the offer, with an abrupt shaking of his head.

"He never do this," commented Abdul. "Sometimes, I worry for him."

Jerry let the comment go over his head, not wanting to embarrass his guest. He could see that the effects of the champagne they had consumed earlier and the fresh air were taking effect on Abdul as he seemed to be getting a little loud.

"We have some bubbly. Is that what you say, my friend? Bubbly?" he asked Jerry.

"Yes. Sure."

"We have Cristal," offered the madam, who seemed to appear like magic at the mere mention of the word.

"Why not? Cristal, it is," said Abdul, slapping his own thigh.

It was going to be a long one and the sensible option for Jerry, if he was to leave without offending, was to take his lady friend upstairs. Once that was done, everyman did it for himself. He decided to make a move.

"Abdul," he said, standing up. "It has been a pleasure spending time with the two of you this evening. Please excuse me, I am going to retire for an hour or two with my lady friend." He held his hand out, and the tall Argentinean stood to accept it gracefully.

"But Jerry, the night is young."

"The morning is very young," corrected Jerry, looking at his watch. "It is almost 2 a.m."

"As you wish, my friend," conceded the little man, standing up and walking around the low table to embrace Jerry.

"Please call me and keep me informed. I pray for you, my friend." Releasing his grip, he looked to his comrade, brother?—Jerry was still unsure—to do the same.

On leaving the group, Jerry had absolutely no intention of having sex with the girl, who reminded him her name was Sapphire.

"Like my eyes," she said, flickering her long eyelashes to show amazing deep blue-coloured contacts.

"They are truly beautiful," said Jerry lightly touching her eyelids with the tip of his fingers. "Fill the Jacuzzi," he said once they were in the plush surroundings of the room he had booked for €400 an hour. It had a view looking over the Med, and on a night like this, it was too good to miss.

As Sapphire filled the large bath, Jerry opened the large French doors leading out to a private balcony large enough to hold a small party. Thankfully he could hear but not see Abdul and the group below. Instead, what he could see was the vast blue-black swell of the sea, like a giant silk sheet moving softly in the glimmer of a breeze. He turned to see Sapphire sitting on the edge of the raised bath looking at him. She smiled. He looked. She crossed one long leg over the other, intentionally letting the long purple crush velvet cocktail dress split at the desired position to reveal her long legs and the hint of some exquisite La Perla. She took her Champagne glass from the edge of the bath and raised it.

"To someone deep in thought," she said.

"Yes, I know. I'm sorry."

"That's fine. It makes a pleasant change, usually the guest, they are too quick, too urgent. Is this the word?"

"Probably watching the clock," Jerry said. "especially at these prices," he added under his breath.

"The clock? You have a watch." she misunderstood "It is almost 2.30." she said. Jerry smiled.

"Do you know what I would like?" he said, walking back into the room

"I can guess," she replied

"You would be wrong," he said placing his drink on the bedside cabinet and removing his top over his head.

"Please let me," she said standing.

"No. Please, undress we will share a Jacuzzi and then I want you to give me a relaxing massage. How's that?"

"I am here for your service," she said releasing a small bow behind her neck. The dress dropped smoothly to the carpeted floor and Jerry stopped removing his trousers to watch her turn and make for the bathroom. He could truly understand why some punters would be too quick, too urgent. The exquisite two piece white lace gave the bronze colour of her skin an almost magical appearance and the curvature of her body was one of natures finest without the brushstrokes. On returning to the room she had removed the underwear and let her hair down.

Jerry had also taken of his trousers and now stood there looking at the girl as she turned off the water and tested the temperature with her toe. Grimacing slightly, she turned on the cold water at speed, which in turn produced the Pyrenees in foam form. Now sitting on the edge, she again tested the water, this time using her hand before closing the tap. He walked over slowly and sat down beside her; he, too, feeling the water. She removed her hand from the bath and put the foam she had cupped within it onto Jerry's nose. He drew her to him and kissed her full on the lips. She responded without hesitation and kissed him back with sincerity. Releasing his grip from the back of her neck he now swung his legs over the edge of the bath and turned to take her in his arms. He lifted her and slowly lowered her onto the top tear then placed himself beside her.

Sapphire now pressed the on switch which produced even more foam but felt good against his body he didn't complain that she was out of view for a few seconds. She laughed as she rose from the suds to receive the glass Jerry was holding for her. "Cheers," he said, clinking it with the one he was carrying.

"This is very beautiful," she said looking directly into Jerry's eyes.

"You don't know how much I need this." He replied

"Tell me."

"I just do."

"You like Cocaina?" she asked.

"Not tonight, Josephine", he answered, lowering himself deeper into the hot water.

"Josephine?" she asked sitting up bolt right like a scorned wife.

"It's a joke." said Jerry without explanation

"Tell me the Joke. I am not laughing."

"Relax. Come here." he said holding his arms open. She moved over and he wrapped them around her, carefully placing his glass on the baths edge behind her head.

They stayed in this position for some time before Jerry realised his watch was showing over one hour had passed. "Come." he said easing her head from his shoulder.

"I am sorry James. I was sleeping."

"Does that entitle me to a refund?" he joked standing up. She didn't respond but stood to join him as he made his way to the four poster without drying. He laid spread eagle face down and she sat on his lower back and firmly massaged his neck and shoulders. He could feel the heat from her as she gradually moved herself lower down his body. Her legs were wider apart as she straddled his splayed legs and continued to put pressure on his lower back.

"That's good" he responded as she now, lightly rubbed his buttocks in a circular motion.

"You like?" she whispered as she lowered her body onto his and kissed the nape of his neck before slowly delving round to nibble his left ear. "You want to make love to me James?"

"You want me to?" He counter asked without turning.

"Yes." she breathed into his ear. Jerry knew this would be a struggle. He had told himself, not tonight, but who could refuse such an offer? Especially when one had paid. It would be a crime. He eased up slightly, which had Sapphire extend to her knees before Jerry turned. She looked down to see his cock had hardened to it's capacity before kissing him firmly on the mouth and lowering her hand to grasp his shaft. Jerry was not about to make love. He never did. He fucked but he didn't make love. Unless of course it was Kath.

He took a firm hold of her hair and smoothly put enough pressure to ease her down stopping only when her mouth surrounded the top of his manhood. She had little time to lick or kiss as he eased up to meet her open mouth filling it with as much as she would allow. He looked down to see the top of her head move in an frantic way as if she understood this guy just wanted to release. His arms were now out to his side with her hands pushing his into the Egyptian Silk. She managed to raise her body into a kneeling position with her legs now between his, which he raised on bended knee. The curve of her back, dipped to show the perfect round shape of her bottom in the air. Looking back to her head, Jerry gave a final grunt as he raised his hips to meet her one final time before releasing his fluid into her mouth. He didn't cry out or make a sound as he held the tensed cheeks of his arse off the bed. She continued to suck his cock and consume the cum as she now released his hands and cupped and squeezed his balls as if to drain him of every last drop of juice. Finally, Jerry cupped his arms under her arms and raised her up his body to lay her head on his chest. Now he just wanted to be out of here. He wanted to be home, in his bed, with Kath. He was terrible and he knew it, but he was sick, he needed treatment. That was how he could forgive himself.

The Madam was waiting in the foyer, which housed an elegant French Ormolu desk. Seated behind it, looking busy, she could have won an Oscar for imitating surprise.

"Oh, hello. How was everything? Sapphire is very good, No?" she asked. Jerry didn't answer but asked.

"My friends?"

"The one is still by the pool. And the other, he is upstairs."

"O.K." said Jerry, removing a wad from his pocket. Peeling of six €500 notes he handed them to her. "This should cover everything," he said "If it's any more, I'll settle up next time."

"No Pasanada," she said smiling broadly, showing as much lipstick on her teeth as her lips. "It has been a pleasure senor. Please. Anytime. Would you like a taxi?"

"No." He said, walking out into the mild air.

Jerry walked along the golden mile for as long as its name sake before flagging a taxi. As soon as he sat in the rear and gave instructions to the driver, he wished he hadn't bothered. The walk was good. His mind was clear. He had made some decisions he was content with. And now, seated in the taxi, the fumes from the chain-smoking driver was enough to give anyone cancer of the lungs. He opened a window and extended his arm from it to direct the flow of cool air into his face. 'At least the tobacco will disguise Sapphire', he thought. He looked at his watch 5.15 am. The sun was rising.

Chapter Thirty-Four

Day Three

Barry had slept only a little. He imagined Stuli had slept even less. The auditions had gone on for almost three hours, continually repeating the same thing over and over again, until Barry was confident that Stuli had mastered the craft. He knew that after the shock of seeing Barry again—in the flesh—that Jerry would be very reluctant to consider this operation. He had to win back his confidence.

First things first. Nobody knew how Jerry's mind worked better than Barry. Jerry would have to listen to what was on offer. Once his old friend had contacted the hotel, his antlers would go up. One way or another, Barry was confident Jerry would find his way to the air vent in room 308. The two of them had used this practice on more than one occasion over the years. All he had to do now was wait.

Throwing the duvet from the bed, he suddenly realised that Beatrice was not laying beside him. The feeling of panic turned to dread as he remembered how he had stayed in the hotel bar until the early hours. Back in the room, he had had Beatrice perform for him. Now, putting his hand down to his genital area, he could feel the dried blood matted in his pubic hair. He looked down and scrapped some of the flake from his abdomen. There wasn't much, not as much as previous occasions, anyway. Thank God! He rose and made his way to the en-suite, knowing what he would find behind the closed door and already working out an apology.

The door wasn't locked but was jammed. Barry pushed hard with his shoulder. The door opened enough for him to put his head through the gap and look down to the floor.

"B," he called softly, but there was no response. "B, wake up darling."

"Leave me alone." She responded quietly.

"Look at me."

"No. I'm hurting Barry. You do it again." she complained.

"I'm sorry, baby. I promise I'll get help. Please look at me, baby." Beatrice raised her head slowly, revealing last night's delights to the instigator.

"Oh, B. I'm so sorry. Move over. Let me in," he gently pushed some more on the door. At the same time, Beatrice released her weight and eased her bruised body into a kneeling position on the tiled floor. Barry dropped beside her and held her close. He cupped her chin in his hand and eased her swollen face into view. Her right eye was closed and bruised, there was a lump the size of an egg protruding from her forehead, blood drops had dried around the nose and mouth, and her lips were swollen even more than her breeding accounted for. She was naked but for a studded dog collar with a lead attached. Her hands were tied behind her back, and the skin on her knees was missing, showing crimson welts of clear fluid.

"Oh! Baby, what have I done?" The animal couldn't remember. Or so he said.

Why? Thought Beatrice. *What have I done to deserve this? How much more can I take? How long before I am killed at the hands of this man, whom I love so much?* Barry held her tight. Tears rolled down his cheeks onto hers, bringing the blood back to life.

"I cannot take much more, my love. I am hurting so much. Why you do this to me?"

"You must stay in the room," replied Barry, already arranging to hide his handy work. "Jerry cannot see you like this," *or Stuli, for that matter,* he was thinking. "You stay in the room, sweetness. Get yourself cleaned up, O.K.?" He kissed the top of her head and soothed with his hand the back of her neck. He realised he was getting aroused, more so, because he was now in charge. He was the protector. He loosened the leather strap holding her hand together and released the knot. Holding her wrist, he gently massaged the swollen welts before slowly placing one of her free hands onto his semi-erect cock.

"No. Please," she said, looking up with her watering eyes, pleading.

"Do it," he said, wrapping her hand around his now stiff member. She reluctantly began to move in an altered motion, too weak to refuse.

Chapter Thirty-Five

Wheeler made a cup of coffee. He checked his watch. 10.15. He had slept well, considering. The room was 40% cheaper than it's normal cost. The hippy who sat next to him in the shop was kind enough to help him book it online with his credit card. The hotel had three stars, which probably meant you got the coffee-making facilities and a fan because apart from it being cleaner, there was little difference from the room he had stayed in the previous night. Anyway, it didn't accommodate all the prostitutes. That was a bonus. Not to be accosted. He might get tempted; it had been a long time. What was another bonus was the room tariff card on the reception desk showing the room prices without the discount. Lovely for his expenses account.

He stood by the window and pulled the recently bleached netted curtain to one side, just enough to give him a view of the road below. Placing his cup on the polished mahogany table, he gripped the window at its base with two hands and lifted up. The noise from the traffic and the heat from the humid air gave him a wave of energy, and for a moment, he felt 10 years younger. Releasing the window, it stayed in the upright position, he did the same and stretched his arms up in the air. He breathed in and held it a few seconds before exhaling. This is the life, he thought. He could see a result after this. Either nicking or, at the very least, seeing the nicking of Jerry Divine. The weather, the place, getting paid (with inflation), the sights and sounds, Angelica, and no Maud in sight. Fucking Heaven!

Sitting back down, he picked up the remote and switched on the television. Flicking through the channels, he stopped at one showing some people getting arrested. The footage changed from location to location. A building site, offices in the city, a bank, a town hall, businessmen, politicians? It suddenly dawned on him. This was Operation Escatura, without a doubt. He turned up the volume. Fucking Spanish. He looked closely, trying to identify anything: the people, the building site, it could be the same one, or at least one of them; things looked so different from the sky. Perelta! He was being interviewed, three microphones centimetres from his mouth. Questions. He was giving the answers. In fucking Spanish. Wheeler moved closer to the box as if being closer would help him understand. Flashing bulbs. Photographers. Press conferences. This looked bigger than Wheeler thought. And Divine was in the mix. Wheeler moved backward, feeling for the chair without taking his eyes from the screen mounted on the wall. He sat, picked up his phone and read the text. 8 pm The Grande Palace Hotel. The Conference and Business Suite. 1st floor. Angelica.

He took the briefcase from the floor and opened it on the bed. He had some idea what he could contribute to the investigation. It was obvious now, to Wheeler, that Divine was one of many, and it was more than likely that the investors and the ones parting with the bungs would be the last to be arrested. The first would be the receivers. The white collars. The ones most likely to talk. Yes, this was big. And now, looking at the flimsy material contained in the case, Wheeler suddenly felt out of his depth. If the case had been solely confined to Operation Canary he would be more at home. As it transpired, the operations combined, gave Wheeler the smaller part to play. Does it matter? So long as Divine gets his just. The answer was Yes. It did matter. He wanted to play a major part in bringing the Divine down. It wasn't enough for him, just to be a cog in the wheel. He wanted more. Divine should have paid him for what he did.

Chapter Thirty-Six

"Stop here," said Jerry, indicating with his hand and eyes through the driver's rearview mirror.

"Si. Senor," responded the driver pulling over. "Diez Euro por-av-or."

"Grasias," said Jerry, handing him a twenty. "Keep the change." his Spanish wouldn't run to that. He was surprised the driver thanked him in English.

He often stopped the taxi, or anyone else driving him home for that matter—unless of course, he was familiar with them—a distance before the house, out of habit as opposed to any other reason. Now, walking slowly, the two hundred metres left to travel, his mind began to wonder, as it had in recent times. What was it all about? What was it all for? Why had his life always entailed risk? And more importantly. Where would it end? He often thought about his brother Victor. Two years older than he and two worlds apart. Victor was married with two children—like jerry—but that was where the similarities ended, his brother worked as a counsellor for people with drug and alcohol addiction, as much as he disagreed with Jerry's way of life, he still gave him a certain amount of respect. Jerry believed that this was down to the fact that he was never involved with the illegal drug trade—at least that was how Jerry saw it. Victor only got to know what Jerry wanted him to know. He sometimes wished he could change lives with his siblings. Not to have a care in the world. Bliss. But then he had to remind himself, that it was odd he only ever thought about, and wished this, when things were not going to plan.

He put his key into the lock and eased the gate open slowly. Ascending the steps to the large oak door, he repeated the action, not wanting to disturb Kath and the girl. He was doing well until Bonito detected him and yelped excitedly. She had to be forgiven for not knowing the time.

"Shush, Bonito," whispered Jerry. The little dog scurried down the stairs to race around and jump up to meet Jerry's outstretched arms. She licked his face, whimpering and panting. "Shush baby," said Jerry, kissing the little mutt. "You'll get me shot."

"Is that you?" called Kath.

"Yes," answered Jerry walking into the bedroom. He looked down at his wife and was glad to be home. He placed the dog on the bed and walked to the bathroom, undressing as he did. Stepping into the shower he washed all traces of Sapphire from his person.

"You're late," said Kath, as he got into bed and snuggled up beside her.

"I know. I couldn't get away. Go back to sleep baby," he said, holding her close to him.

Approximately five hours later, Kath shook him until he stirred.

"What time is it?" he asked.

"11 o'clock," she answered. "Jez is on the phone. It sounds important." Jerry reached for the cordless without opening his eyes. Kath took it from the bedside cabinet, pressed the receiver and placed it in his hand without speaking.

"Thanks, love," he said. Then "Hello" into the phone.

"Jerry, turn on the T.V." instructed Jez. Jerry opened his eyes and was wide awake within a second. "Remote," he said quickly to his wife. Kath walked quickly over to the dressing area and fetched the remote back to Jerry, pressing the on switch as she did.

"The news channel," said Jez. Jerry scrolled through the channels until he found what he was looking for.

"Fucking Spanish!" said Jerry.

"I'll explain everything later," said Jez

"Shall I call Cleo?" said Kath, looking concerned. Jerry had to check himself.

"No, it's fine love, sorry, I'm still half asleep. Do me some burnt toast please, and some black coffee. I'll be down shortly." he sat on the end of the bed and hung up the phone without saying anything else to Jez. Kath did as asked. She knew when she was being told. Jerry was troubled.

Jerry washed and shaved before selecting a black Louis Vuitton suit, black Polo shirt and suede shoes the same colour with silver buckle. He took a platinum Rolex Masterpiece with a meteorite face and checked himself in the mirror. He was in a sombre mood as he walked into the spacious living room. The piano was positioned exactly where he would have wanted it.

"How did you know where to place it?" He asked as Kath walked from the kitchen.

"I didn't," she answered. "But I thought about moving the dining table for some time now, and I suppose the new arrival gave me an excuse."

"It looks lovely, Kath. We'll have to look for someone to teach the girls."

"Julie seems keen, but Jasmine just laughed. She said, 'You wouldn't see me playing that thing.' Thinks it's old fashion, she does."

"She might come around," said Jerry, now sitting on the stool, and pressing some keys, and playing some notes which Bonito didn't appreciate. She howled. Kath and Jerry laughed.

"Your toast," said Kath.

"Yes, two minutes," he said, walking out to the garage. He took a boxed mobile phone from a bag containing two more and some credit receipts. Once he had opened it, he inserted a new SIM card and entered the credit code. He called the San Roque. When he was told there was no reply from room 308 and no one had seen Mr Viceroy, he became slightly confused and hung up. Once he was disconnected, he pressed redial.

"Hello, could I speak to Marie, please?"

"Certainly, Sir. I will put you through. One moment please."

"Hello, this is Marie. How may I help you?"

"Hello, Marie. This is Mr Jerry"

"Oh, Mr Jerry. How are you?" she said reservedly

"I'm fine, thank you. My friend, Mr Viceroy. Have you seen him, Marie?"

"Nobody here has seen Mr Viceroy. He did call by phone to check of messages, that is all, but we have a problem, Mr Jerry. His room he is staying was broken into."

"Marie, Please. Can I see you in private?"

"In private, Mr Jerry?" she was concerned. Jerry had to move quickly here.

"It's nothing to worry about, Marie. You might be able to help me." he added as calmly as he could.

"O.K. Mr Jerry, but I am working."

"That's ok. What time do you get off duty? Maybe we could meet in Duquesa, in the port?"

"Very well," she said cautiously. "I finish my work at 2 o'clock. But I have to go to Estepona. It will be better for me if I can see you in Estepona port."

"That's fine," he said, relieved. "2.30, shall we say? In Renaldo's on the corner."

"No problem. I'll be there."

Jerry's mind was racing. What was going on? Was it a coincidence? There was a lot of wealth within the walls of the San Roque, and the recent wave of Eastern Europeans has seen a large increase in crime on the Coast. Especially burglaries, where the method used was to insert gas into the air-conditioning unit, usually placed on the outside wall. It sent the occupant into a temporary coma, giving the burglars a free run over the place. But this was normally done in the large villas. Maybe the five-star hotels were just as profitable to these professional thieves.

Placing the phone back into the bag, he called Jez on his personal.

"Hi, Jez. We need to talk before you see the girl this evening. Meet me in Duquesa in 40 minutes."

"Where in Duquesa?"

"In the Tapas bar. The one in the filling station, by the roundabout. Don't be late, Jez. I'm on a tight schedule."

"I'm on my way, Jerry."

Chapter Thirty-Seven

Jez was already there finishing his second espresso when Jerry arrived. He saw his friend stop at the petrol pump in his Merc and give the attendant some euros and his car keys. He stood to greet his business partner as he entered the small service area.

"Hi, Jerry. What can I get you? Did you eat?"

"Yes, I'm fine, Jez. A fresh orange will do. It's so hot out there."

"Certainly." said a slightly nervous Jez. He held his hand up apologetically for attention. The waiter looked over.

"Sumo Naranja Por-fav-or," he called "Dos," he added as an afterthought, holding up two fingers.

"I am on it, Jerry," he said before Jerry spoke. "I haven't slept all night. I can assure you, my friend, this has my full attention."

"Good," said Jerry, accepting his glass of freshly squeezed juice and downing it in one. "I needed that," he added, grimacing. "O.K, let's take this nice and easy and logically." he took a seat opposite Jez and made himself comfortable. "Let us assume that the authorities are cleaning up their act. Someone somewhere is upset, and they didn't get a slice of a very large cake, and for that reason, they have exposed someone who has. Because that is what all this is about, is it not?" He looked directly at Jez, who was more than relieved that Jerry was composed and thinking within reason. Jerry didn't wait for Jez to answer but continued.

"From what I can gather, having the limited communication skills I have, and from what I can make of the box. This looks like a major exposure operation by the Government and their planning policies."

"You're quite right, Jerry."

"I know... But let us assume that the powers that be rollover. Because that is the likelihood, knowing what I know, and from what I have seen of the slimy, no, good cunts." Jez could now see the change coming.

"Carry on with your theory, Jerry." he urged, preferring the diplomatic tone.

"Well. As I see it. From where I stand as the developer and, of course, the land owner, I have done nothing untoward. Obviously, someone somewhere thinks otherwise, or the sites wouldn't have been closed. I understand that. Who and why will come later, but for now, we have to look at the evidence, or in this case, the lack of it."

"Jerry, let me but in here for just a moment, my friend. I understand where you are coming from, and I understand your line of thought, but when the operation was unfolding, and more information was disclosed to the media, it transpires that a large amount of cash was recovered from the homes and business premises of various council members. One of which was yours truly, Gonzalez. Over three hundred thousand euros, to be precise. Now he has to answer where them euros came from. Due to the fact that he'd be lucky to clear 10% of that per year."

"Em…" Jerry was thinking hard. "I have never personally handed Gonzalez any money," he said, thinking out loud.

"I know." comforted Jez before adding almost reluctantly. "But you have handled it. Of course, it depends on how far the authorities are prepared to obtain evidence. At this stage, we don't know what they have." He paused before continuing, "Phone taps?" this asked as a question. "We know if they have been investigating the local gentry, they will have photographic evidence. I mean, Gonzalez attends all the functions Kath and Debra put on."

Jerry held up his hand to stop Jez in his tracks. Jezzie was now starting to perspire as he beckoned over the waiter.

"Could we have two more of these, please?" he held up his empty glass.

"O.K.," said Jerry after just a moment. "I see where you are coming from, but we may be jumping the gun. I'm all for preparing for the worst, but let us see what this evening's meeting with the secretary brings. Is it a good idea to visit this lawyer directly? Or would you wait a couple of days to see what else transpires?" Jez considered the question before concluding and confirming the second part of it with a positive. There was no need to show their hand at this stage of the game, although it was far from a game. Jerry raised his eyebrows at the mere mention of a game. Jez looked down sheepishly.

Jerry accepted his fresh orange and was thinking overtime. He hadn't actually manhandled the money passed to Jez to give to Gonzalez—although Jez didn't know this—Jerry knew only too well how incriminating fingerprints could be. The money had always been placed in either an envelope or a larger brown paper parcel secure with string, which had, on every occasion, been taken from a briefcase or a holdall by Jerry before handing it to Jez. The envelope between two fingers or the parcel by the string. So, Jerry was okay with that, but he didn't enlighten Jez about it. The photographs... He was sure he could explain that away.

"I told you. I never liked that fat cunt," he suddenly said, startling Jez.

"I know," replied the weaker man sheepishly.

"The fat bastard bought that two-seater sports car with three kids! I knew then what the cunt was. And his wife, poor girl, in that old Chrysler. Does she still drive that thing?"

"Yes," said Jez rather delicately as though he was partly to blame.

"He'll talk," Jerry said, standing, his chair scraping on the tiled floor. He peeled off a note from a large wad. "And when he does, we will have to..." he stopped short before adding, "I'll see you tonight, you know where," He turned to leave before looking back

"This Brogonia, is she pretty?"

"Very."

"How old?"

"Twenty-eight/nine," he said smiling "right up your street." Jerry smiled back, lightening the mood somewhat. There was a method in his madness. Jez was confused as he watched Jerry walk to his car.

Jerry walked across the forecourt to where his car was parked. Suddenly, he got a feeling he was being watched. By whom? He was unsure, but he had experienced this before. The garage attendant was polishing the screen as Jerry started the engine.

"Gracias," he called as he drove slowly from the station. Intuition told him to circle the roundabout twice and park at the first opportunity to record at least the next six vehicles that overtook him. He did this before turning around and travelling in the opposite direction. Once he had crossed the roundabout opposite the filling station where he had met Jez, he again parked his car on the side of the road. Checking the vehicles as they passed, he did note that one of these matched one of the six earlier. The motor was a black Lexus saloon and contained four people. The rear windows were tinted, which gave Jerry the shadows, so he was unable to see if they were male or female. The Toyota was not a typical surveillance car. In fact, back in the UK, it would be the last thing they would use. But who knew how this team worked over here?

He watched as the Lexus stopped approximately 200 yards up ahead, confirming his suspicion. Jerry was curious, not to the extent of pulling up beside them and asking for directions, which he had done on other occasions, but more so as to determine why he was being followed. He decided to carry on past the parked car and loose it up ahead, and then once the Lexus had passed him, he could about turn and revert back to his original direction and head for Estepona.

Now, as he drove along and occasionally checked his rearview mirror, he actually hoped that the people in the dark saloon were connected to this latest scandal. He agreed with himself that it could only be that. Not admitting to himself that this is what he secretly hoped. It was either that or the UK. It couldn't be anything to do with his last job in Madrid. That had gone without a hitch. Yes, the jewellery and watches were identifiable, but he knew who had bought the bulk of it, and as far as he knew, nobody had been arrested. He still had some of the more intricate pieces, which were too good to break, but they were securely hidden. The other jobs prior to Madrid were spread over various countries, and the time between each one was usually a year or thereabout, so as far a pattern goes... he wasn't worried.

The UK South Mimms. That was different. Jerry had always expected to have his collar felt for that one. Why it had never come, he didn't know. He was actually baffled. It was almost six years. He knew there was a shoot-to-kill policy, but that evening, the other side didn't know the occupants of the Mercedes were armed. Even Jerry didn't think he was going to be until Hutchin joined them. Fucking good job he did, thought Jerry. He now realised he was approaching Estepona from the north side. He looked at his watch. 1.30. The port was 5 minutes away. The Kempinski Hotel had him pulling in and parking to the rear. Taking his sunglasses from above the visor, he picked up the car phone and called Tom.

"Fucking hell, that was quick," he said as Tom answered after the first ring.

"I know I'm sat here bored to fuck. I thought you'd never call. Where are ya?"

"Down the road," said Jerry, changing the subject "What's happening? Any tips?"

"Yea leave of the brass," he replied. Then, as an after thought, "Unless I'm wit ya." He laughed. "Listen, can you come and get me."

"No, I'm busy. I'll call you later. See what the Indian's on."

"O.K. boss," he said, hanging up.

Hanging up the phone, he checked himself in the vanity mirror before stepping from the car into the heat of the midday sun. He took off his suit jacket and hung it from the centre door pillar before closing the door and walking to the side entrance. Once in the comfortable confines of the air-conditioned hotel, he made for the lounge bar. He took a table in the corner and picked up a Spanish paper from the seat.

"Sorry, sir. I did not see the paper. May I take it from you?"

"No, that's fine. Could I have a café con leche, please?"

"Immediately, sir," he replied, walking away briskly.

Jerry sat back and looked at the pictures on the front page. From what he could make out, the Mayor of Marbella and Estepona were arrested as part of Operation Escatura. Operation Escatura. How original, thought, Jerry, and obvious for that matter. Escatura is Spanish for deeds, as in property deeds. He turned over the page but could make little sense of the Spanish. He called Jez and got the answer phone. He left a message asking him to get the same paper and read it before they meet tonight. Anyone listening could fuck themselves. His construction sites were on hold because of this. It was common knowledge by now.

"Your coffee, sir." said the waiter, placing a silver tray on the table.

"Thank you," said Jerry, putting the paper down. Once the waiter had left, he took the cup from the tray, added one lump of sugar, dunked one of the fancy biscuits and sat back to continue pondering from where he'd left off when parking the car. He had at least 45 minutes.

Yes, South Mimms…His mind wondered. What exactly was that all about? Riat Venga! There was a character. Larger than life. Not so much of it left when they parted company. Jerry could half understand the explanation given by Barry, but there was more. How much more, he was unsure, but he knew that Barry was only giving half a tale. And this cunt in the stately home. Who the fuck was he? Obviously, the father or grandfather of one of the victims who succumbed to the poison Venga distributed, but who the fuck has the power to give those kind of orders… Shoot-to-kill in motorway services, for fuck sake. And then he, Jerry, did not have a visit after all this time. There was more to come from Barry, that's for sure. But where was Barry? Jerry had to gain access to room 308. He had received no further call from the original source—the cash in transit—which means no one knows what had happened to him. Jerry knew if he, Barry, was safe and well, he would have left a message for him. First, he had to convince Marie. He checked his watch. Fuck! Where has the time gone? He had been sitting here for all of 40 minutes. He picked up the coffee. Cold. He put it back down with a 10 euro note.

Chapter Thirty-Eight

The large Mercedes drove down the slope to the security barrier at the port entrance.

"Buenos Tardes." said the guard from the sentry box.

"Buenos Dias," replied Jerry. "Mucho callo."

"Yes, very hot senor. You have permit?" Jerry handed him a small note.

"Gracias," he said, raising the pole.

Estepona port was quiet in comparison to Banus, which was 17 kilometres further north, up the coast towards Malaga. It didn't have the fancy boats or the same class of restaurants and shops as its neighbor, but what it did have was fewer prying eyes. It was certainly more relaxed, quiet and a better meeting place to have a talk.

Marie was sitting outside Renaldo's in the sun. She stood and waved as Jerry drove by slowly.

"Two seconds, baby, I'll just park," called Jerry through the open window. There was a place directly in front of the bar which he took advantage of. She smiled as he walked over. "Nice car."

"Thank you," he said as she stood again, this time to greet him. He kissed her on both cheeks. She smelled gorgeous. He told her so as he took his seat. She blushed slightly as she took hers. Sitting back, she crossed her legs. Jerry looked, and she blushed even more. She uncrossed them and smiled at Jerry.

"This is very unusual," she said

"What?"

"Meeting a customer, of course! Out of working hours." she raised her Dior sunglasses from smiling eyes to look at him.

"Do you mind?" asked Jerry

"I'm intrigued."

"I'm sorry."

"Don't be sorry," she said. "I am also flattered."

"Well, thank you, I'm honoured."

"So tell me."

"Well, I wish it was pleasure," he responded. "but I'm afraid it isn't. I need your help, Marie."

"Explain, Mr Jerry. Now I am even more intrigued."

"It's my friend," he said, looking at Marie.

"Can I get you some drinks, people?" asked the waiter, wiping the table.

"Yes, Agua for me."

"Si." said Marie, smiling up at Pedro. *Unbelievable,* thought Jerry.

"What are you smiling at?" she asked.

"Nothing," said Jerry. "anyway, let me explain." he continued, leaning over the table slightly. "My friend, his name is Brian, by the way, he has been having trouble with the brother of his wife. He and his wife are going through a hard time. She has found out about his mistress." he paused a little for reaction, and got none, so he continued. "Now, Brian hasn't been in touch with anyone since yesterday, and his daughter called me this morning," he lied. "She was distraught, to say the least." Jerry now sat back in his chair.

"What have you heard, Marie? You mentioned that the room he was staying in was broken into?" Marie now took off her sunglasses and placed them on the table. Looking directly at Jerry, she picked up her glass, took a drink from it before telling Jerry what she had seen and heard from other employees. It transpired that Mr Viceroy had extended his stay and was last seen leaving the hotel yesterday, around noon. Later, there was a message to pass on, so the bellhop took it up to room 308. He was about to slip the envelope under the door when it had opened. Two men were startled when they saw him and made haste for their departure. The bellhop had entered the room and reported to the reception that it was in disarray. The duty manager had gone up to inspect and was surprised that nothing one could associate with the room being occupied. No toiletries, a change of clothing, no documents, the safe was open, Nothing! The security DVD footage showed Mr Viceroy leaving with some luggage, and shortly after, the two leaving the room so hastily are seen entering the hotel and making for the elevator.

"That is as much as I can tell you, Mr Jerry."

"Please, just Jerry."

"Sure, Jerry. I don't know if I can be of any more assistance. I hope your friend is alright. But the two men leaving the room?"

"I'm not sure. You said the room was broken into?"

"Yes, they had forced the door, but there was very little damage; a sprained lock is all."

"The DVD footage, could I see it?"

"I'm not sure. The management did not inform the police. I suppose they didn't want to alert the other guests, so I imagine the disc will still be in the machine. I don't think I will be able to take you into the office, but I may be able to go get the disc. I have a friend who works in administration where the machine is located."

"I would appreciate it, Marie," said Jerry, looking concerned. "I am beginning to worry for his safety."

"I will see what I can do."

"Lovely. Can I get you another drink?"

"No, I'm fine, thank you Jerry. Another time, maybe."

"I hope so," said Jerry, standing. She stood, too, and he raised his hand to assist her movement around the low table.

"Are you driving?" he asked

"No, I took a cab."

"Can I drop you anywhere?"

"No, thank you. I have to go back to work now, and it would raise eyebrows if I were to be seen with a hotel customer."

"There is one other thing you could do for me, Marie," She looked at him as she clipped her hair up to the top of her head with a grip, causing her white blouse to rise, revealing a small diamond stud secured within her belly button.

"Tell me," she said, now bending to retrieve her glasses and some things bought from the pharmacy, Jerry noted.

"I would like access to room 308," he said before adding, "today."

"If you booked a room, you could ask for that one specifically."

"The lock?" he reminded her.

"Yes. I see."

"Do you think you could help?"

"I'm sure I could get the key for you, but now you are starting to worry me. Is there more I should know, Jerry?"

"No, not at all, Marie. I believe my friend may have left something for me, that is all."

"But the room has been cleaned."

"He would have left it in a special place for me," he said as a matter-of-fact, trying to play down the importance.

"Well, in that case, I will accept your offer of a lift, but you can drop me at the rear entrance. That way, I am less likely to be observed. You can then enter the hotel from the front and make your way directly to room 308, where I will be waiting for you."

"That sounds good to me," He paid the tab and placed his hand on the small of her back as the two walked the short distance to his car.

"The room is as it should be." Marie said as Jerry entered, "There doesn't seem to be anything in here that shouldn't be." *What about us?* thought Jerry, as he made directly for the en-suite. She didn't see it, but she heard him remove the condensation panel from the vent. Placing the small package in his pocket, he replaced the plastic grid, and stepped down from the bath's edge. He turned to see Marie standing in the doorway, looking at him curiously.

"I told you," he said, smiling.

"What is it?" She asked.

"I'm not sure, but I can guess it holds a forwarding address and a telephone number."

"So it's not a suicide note?"

"I hope not," he replied. "He owes me." he laughed, trying to lighten the scenario. "By the way, you suit your hair down."

"I'll remember that," she replied as he brushed past her in the narrow doorway.

"Thank you, Marie." he placed his two hands on her upper arms and kissed her lightly on each cheek.

"You're welcome, Jerry," she replied. Jerry got the impression she preferred Jerry without the mister. He made his way back to the car and opened the package. Just as he thought. A simple note. Mr Maine. The Rock Hotel. Gib. And a telephone number. There was also a small envelope containing a singular key. A small note explained this to be the key to a rented secure box at a service centre in Malaga. He would call the telephone number before checking out the box.

Driving home, Jerry called Kath from his car phone. She was home and would prepare something light to eat. He hung up and then stopped at the local Super-macardo to pick up a bottle of wine. Carol explained that the girls were staying back at school to practice for the upcoming sports day.

Paying for the vino, Jerry asked at the check-out for some coins. He used these to make several calls from the payphone by the exit, one of which was to the Rock Hotel. He was transferred to Mr Maine's room, and Barry answered after the second ring. Arrangements were made to meet in the hotel bar the next day at noon. Jerry made the last call to Harold, a Gibraltarian antique dealer and trusted ally.

Kath wanted more of Jerry's time this evening. Cleo picked up the girls at 8 o'clock, which gave them some time to relax and talk. Jerry explained he had an important meeting and added lemonade to the two glasses of wine.

Chapter Thirty-Nine

Barry was elated to receive the call from his old friend. He knew Jerry was astute enough to gain access to his vacated room at the San Roque. They had used the vent scenario on more than one occasion over the years, yet again, it had reaped rewards. At least, that is what Barry was hoping. There was nothing to say Jerry would be interested in what was on the table. For all Barry knew, Jerry could be retired. He may well have used the money he had earned over the years and gone legit, but at least contact was made, which meant there was hope. Hope for the future. His future, because that was all he was concerned about. He knew Jerry could look after himself. He, on the other hand, often wondered if he was able to. He called Stuli.

"Meet me in the bar downstairs. Me and you are going to get well and truly plastered." He hung up and looked at Beatrice, who didn't like what she had just heard.

Chapter Forty

Wheeler had spent most of the day in the same internet café. This time, some information relating to Operation Escatura was available. From what he could tell, several politicians, solicitors, police and currency exchange companies had been arrested in connection with the operation, which primarily centred on corruption within the government. This part deals with the issuing of licences for building permits. It seemed to Wheeler that the core of the conspiracy was centred in the Malaga region, and the majority of the arrests were made in Marbella. The television and newspaper pictures depicted the same operation, and it is evident to Wheeler that the topic of conversation among the natives was the same.

It was mid-afternoon, and Wheeler was already wearing his new suit. If anything, it seemed a little tighter than when he had tried it on prior to buying it. Sitting back in the computer chair, which the designers failed to give any consideration to his bulk, he ordered his sixth espresso—he had noticed how popular the drink was with the locals so he had given it another try—and welcomed the boost in energy but was embarrassed by the wind.

Now standing and stretching to his full 6 foot 4 inches, he felt the button securing the waistband of his trousers burst. He took the tatty belt from his holdall and fastened it around his waist. He had found an even cheaper hotel for this evening so he made a mental note to buy a new belt from one of those black guys selling fake goods on the street. He looked at his watch. The damn battery had gone. Looking at the clock on the wall, he could just about make out through the smoke that it showed 6.15. He decided to make a move to the Grande Palace. He had nothing better to do, no doubt the conference suite would have air-con. Moving to the counter he paid his tab of €12. Pocketing the receipt, he walked over to the dingy toilet, which was more like a sauna. He washed his face and combed some water through his thin hair with the palm of his hand. Giving himself the once over, he was in no doubt that he was doing his best to represent the police department of his country, at the same time reclaiming his dignity.

"La Grand Palace?" he asked, showing the text on his mobile to the mother with the child strapped to her chest.

"Si, total directo." she replied, pointing straight down what looked like the main street, not unlike any other main thoroughfare through a major city with its tall buildings and noise from the traffic. The people scurrying about like mice in a cage didn't seem to let the day's heat bother them. *I suppose they are used to it,* thought Wheeler. They must be like dried leather in the desert, the cunts, he imagined as he made his way. He would walk 100 yards, then ask again. His luggage was heavy now. Good job he kept the same shoes. A newspaper shop to his left had him walking into it; it looked dark and cool. He bought a bottle of Lucozade, hoping it would quench his thirst and give him some energy.

The next person he stopped spoke a little English, not that it was required because the hotel was directly opposite on the other side of the road. *Thank fuck*, breathed Wheeler. The pedestrian smiled. Wheeler licked the sweat from his top lip as though he had found an oasis.

The large stone building with its mahogany glass and brass frontage gave Wheeler goose bumps. He waited for a gap in the traffic large enough not to embarrass him with the sound of car horns and made a dash for it. The tall porter, complete with a long coat and flat hat, came to meet him by the sidewalk. He took hold of Wheeler's holdall and briefcase, for which Wheeler genuinely thanked him.

"You're a diamond son. Thank you. Thank you!" he repeated as the guy put his luggage on a chrome trolley with wheels.

"You are a guest in the hotel, senor?"

"Yes, I have a conference at 8 pm in the Conference and Business Suite," he said, fishing for his mobile telephone.

"No problem. This way, sir. Do you have a room? Are you staying in the hotel this evening?"

"I'm not sure. That depends." It hadn't dawned on Wheeler that a room may be included. He certainly hoped so, but then again, there would be no benefit to him financially.

"I will put your luggage on hold for you, sir."

"Great. Just give me the case," said Wheeler, bending to take his briefcase. A girl at the luggage department gave him the receipt, and he made his way to the reception.

"Do you have a reservation, sir?"

"I'm not sure if I have a room booked. My name is Wheeler, Detective Wheeler. I'm here for the conference this evening."

"Yes, we have you booked in for one night only." said the receptionist, pressing the keyboard and checking the monitor. "Could I have your passport, please? Do you have any luggage?" she smiled.

"Yes." replied Wheeler, handing her the receipt

"I will have this delivered to your room. You are on the third floor, room 362. Here is your card."

"Thank you." He said, feeling like a weight had been lifted from his shoulders.

The room was elegant but basic. Not the suite he suddenly realised he was entitled to but a vast improvement from the previous two nights. The temperature was good, nice and cool. He placed his case on the bed and started to undress when there was a knock on the door.

"Who is it?"

"You're luggage, sir."

Opening the door, he took the bags from the youth, thanked him and dropped them on the floor. The TV screen welcomed him and hoped he had a pleasant stay. He curiously checked the cupboards and discovered one of them held an assortment of cold drinks and snip bits. Opening a beer, he sat on the bed and pressed the remote to turn on the TV. Scrolling through the channels, he stopped once he had found what he was looking for. He looked at the faces of the people on the screen. Newsmen, police, men in suits being arrested from offices, men in casual wear being taken from their homes with distraught family members within a shot. He was trying to memorise as many as he could. Perelta was on again, but it was the footage Wheeler had seen earlier. Although the commentary was in Spanish, Wheeler thought he had the gist of it. The remote had a small clock emblem; he pressed the button and a digital time was relayed on the screen. 7.15. Just time for a quick shower. Stripping off in front of the full-length mirror, he realised he hadn't bought any new underwear.

Chapter Forty-One

"Ladies and gentlemen. Thank you. Thank you to you all for coming here this evening." The guy speaking was standing behind a head table situated along the wall opposite the entrance to a room that was larger than it appeared due to a temporary partition.

"My name is Louise Suarez," he looked around the 20 to 25 people in the room. "Please, could those of you standing, please take a seat? You will see there are name tags on each table, please look for the one with your name on it, you will see some information in your own language for those of you who neither speak Spanish or English."

There were whispered conversations. This was an obvious indication that those who didn't speak the lingo had interpreters. Wheeler found the table with his name on it. He sat down and poured himself a glass of water. The guy continued.

"We still have a few minutes before we start our discussions, and there are one or two still to join us, so relax and familiarise yourselves with the literature before you."

"Hello, Mr Wheeler," Wheeler looked around to see Perelta standing there with Angelica. He was about to stand when Perelta placed a hand on his shoulder.

"Please, stay seated. I will be sitting at the front."

He sat down on the only other chair at the table.

He began. "Listen to what is said this evening. You will then begin to better understand what the investigation is about. Your man Divine will feature someway along the proceedings, at which time you will be asked to rise and give a profile. We already know some things about him, but not much about the person. There are representatives from other countries who are here for the exact same reason as you. We have to know what we are dealing with. Some, if not all, of the subjects will be arrested in the very near future," He paused now to fill a glass with water, turning to look at Angelica. She shook her head and smiled at Wheeler. Perelta continued.

"A lot of important people were taken into custody yesterday, some very important and influential people may I add. You may have seen this on the news, most of the papers have it as the main story, and the public is talking about little else. Work has been denied on many construction sites along the coast and the whiplash from such an order is going to have a major impact on a lot of legitimate investors from a number of countries." He took a drink and some air before continuing.

"We are only interested in the corruption that has been taking place for some time now, and of course, the large amounts of black money which have been changing hands, the majority of which we believe to be drug and arms-related," he turned to look at Angelica who now placed a briefcase on the table in front of the two detectives. Opening it, Perelta took from it a photograph of Jerry Divine shaking hands with another man outside what looked like a restaurant or nightclub.

"This guy here," he said, pointing to the other man, "is Kristos Koiduste. You will hear more about him, in particular, as the day goes by. We know that he had an investment in one of the sites for the most part, owned by your man," he said this as he circled the face of Divine with a pencil.

"And the other two?" asked Wheeler, pointing to Abdul and Memhet.

"We are not sure at this stage, but we are working on it," he replied, putting the picture back in the case.

"Please, gentleman, and ladies of course," said a different speaker, looking at Angelica and one other female. "Let us start," he bent his lanky frame to rearrange some documents. The taller-than-average guy looked young for the position to speak at such an important event. Wheeler had him down for one of the lucky ones, a silver spoon. A fucking pen pusher.

The top table looked similar to any other conference Wheeler had attended. A typical news conference. Six people in all, seven when Perelta took his place next to the speaker, who introduced himself as Pierre Le-Blaque from Lyon in France. Wheeler guessed he was from Interpol as Lyon was where Interpol headquarters was. Unlike the others seated, he is all mature in years, all male, and all but one overweight. Each one had a look of determination—a look that could not be mistaken for any other profession than that of detecting criminals. The speaker was standing while the others sat tapping pencils and rearranging paperwork. All but the speaker was wearing a suit.

"I am a director with Interpol, and as you know, we are not responsible for enforcing the law but are solely concerned with gathering international intelligence. What we have done to date is compile what we have and structure some kind of plan which is relatively easy for us to grasp as a group," he paused to take a drink and lift a remote and notepad. He now walked to the rear corner of the room and stood behind a small desk. Once behind it, he remained standing and pointed the remote to the ceiling, which in return showed a light on the wall behind the head table. The people seated at this table turned to share the view.

"We will start by looking at the people who were taken into custody yesterday morning. These persons will be in order of importance as we see them within the government. We will move down the ladder and then move on to who, we believe, are the ones who have paid for the licences. The licences that have been issued for cash will coincide with the land in question, again we will look at these. We have a number of nationalities involved in this operation, and for those who have not been arrested yet," he paused to look at the people seated either side of him, and continued with confidence.

"We have colleges from various countries. You know who you are and why you are here. Each of you has knowledge of our intended targets. But first, we will look closer to home. Mr Suarez will bring us up to date with the people who are already in custody. Most of these are local people… but please, Mr Suarez?" He smiled down at his Spanish counterpart, who in turn rose to take his stand and deliver his speech.

Wheeler listened intently as he and then others took their turn to stand and relay various aspects of the operation related to them, both specifically and for the attention of the group as a whole. Angelica sat beside him, taking notes and filling him in with information relayed in a different language. He was impressed when the language was changed from speaker to speaker, which had little effect on the service she provided.

He understood perfectly now why he was here. It transpired that the long-running investigation involved various nationalities with international criminal connections who had infiltrated the Spanish government and secured land and government funding for large development sites. Some of the people involved had purchased the land and greased the palms of some scrupulous powers in office. Received the building permit and gone on the sell for a hefty profit. Others, like Divine, had gone the whole nine yards and further invested in the actual construction. This way, finance obtained by any means had been cleaned.

Various banks had been involved in the conspiracy, along with solicitors, accountants, and government officials, some holding the title of Mayor for a particular region. The Operation was spread across Spain, and it was disclosed that other conferences were taking place across the country.

Once the official site of the schedule was over, the ladder was reduced to the investors, the ones who had purchased the land, paid for the permits, and introduced the black money into the system. The scale of the operation was brought home to Wheeler when the amount of cash disclosed was hundreds of millions of Euros. Wheeler was preparing himself. It was getting close. The picture on the wall at the moment was the guy Wheeler had seen in the picture earlier, shaking hands with Divine.

"Mr Wheeler," said Angelica, moving closer to him. "This man you see here is one who goes by the name Kristos Koiduste." she listened now to a tall, blonde-headed guy talking in Russian. Wheeler was more than impressed with Perelta's sidekick and became deflated about Smith for a split second.

"He is part of the Russian mafia. Drug trafficking. People trafficking." Angelica was listening intently. Russian didn't seem to be a language she was too familiar with.

"Prostitution," she translated, "And the latest information received from Europol is that he is suspected of selling plutonium to North Korea. He has no idea that we are privy to this information, and for obvious reasons. This is our intention to keep it this way," she looked at Wheeler before adding cautiously something that was not a translation. "Mr Perelta has had talks with Koiduste, discreetly, you understand?"

Wheeler did, but still…"A nasty piece of work." he commented.

"Very." agreed Angelica. "Please, prepare yourself, Mr Wheeler," she added. "I believe your Mr Divine will be coming on the screen very shortly."

Wheeler looked at the relatively small file he had on Divine. He could only give them what he had. It did cross his mind to beef it up a bit, but then he thought better of it. After all, Divine himself was a nasty piece of work.

"Ladies and gentlemen," said Louise Suarez, who was taking over from Pierre Le-Blaque. He took a drink before turning to look at the projected features of Jerry Divine.

"Another complicated figure, and one we know very little about, is this person." he turned back from looking at the image to turn over a page of a large file placed before him on the table.

"This individual, it has come to our attention, used to visit Marbella throughout the nineties for pleasure only. We have nothing filed within our system that he was involved with any business—legal or otherwise—in our country, or region, before 2003. He was issued an NIF number in July of that year and applied for residencia in August of the same. We know he has travelled to various countries." he looked closely at a list within the file.

"France, Ireland, Italy and Holland. Mr Le-Blaque has given us some information on why Divine may have travelled to these destinations. We have evidence, but I must say, this is circumstantial." He looked closely at the papers contained in the file as though to decipher what was applicable. "This evidence has been compiled by Interpol and has resulted in Operation Canary, which remains live and has been handed over to our colleagues from the UK." He looked up in the direction of Wheeler.

"Please, Mr…" again, he looked down at the file in front of him. "Mr Wheeler. Could you please give us some history, and anything else relating to Divine which, you think, may assist our operation."

Wheeler looked at Angelica, who smiled encouragingly back at him. He stood and pushed the shirt back into his trouser waistband. Clearing his throat, he took a drink and wiped his brow with his shirt cuff.

"Good evening, Gentlemen." he coughed. "Excuse me," looking down, he smiled nervously at Angelica. She nodded encourageingly.

"I need no file," he said, picking up the flimsy bundle Perelta had set before him. "I have our man Gerard Divine engrained here." he pointed to his temple.

"I know everything there is to know about this…" he thought carefully, but only for a split second. "This dangerous, ruthless, manipulative, professional criminal. We have heard details of some scrupulous, devious individuals this evening, and the common denominator between them is greed. I have heard the term *circumstantial* used on more than one occasion. It is interesting to learn that we may be on the verge of bringing a number of international criminals to justice for something they may have considered one of their less risky escapades, shall we say?" he paused slightly. He was gaining more confidence by the second.

"I know Divine will revel in the easy nature of making the astronomical amounts of money I have heard tonight." He held two fingers up, "Without a gun!" he paused now to let the different tongues catch up. He took his glass and smiled at Angelica. He looked at Perelta and winked. Perelta was surprised at the sudden confidence Wheeler was showing.

"Because, Gentlemen." he raised his voice "The Gun! This is where Divine natured his craft. Jerry Divine is an armed robber, a thief who uses violence, and a villain with determination who will stop at nothing, even murder, to complete the deed. We know, but unfortunately cannot prove, - we have only, circumstantial," he raised two fingers in a cliché, "within our Judicial system that he is responsible for no less than four gangland murders. The closest we ever got for a conviction of any substance was a number of robberies with violence and intimidation throughout the nineties. Unfortunately, for us, we were unable to secure a conviction due to our CPS, I wouldn't say, *misplacing* some vital evidence documentation into the wrong hands." he thought carefully now about choosing his words, and decided to throw caution to the wind.

"What would you say?" called someone from the rear.

"I would go so far as to say *placing* some vital evidence documents into the right hands, as far as Divine was concerned," Wheeler looked around at the faces of the detectives and decided to leave it at that. He now considered telling them about Operation Dispute but opted not to, recalling how he was told during the aftermath not to discuss this Operation with anyone other than Quinn or Phelps, his Commander-in-Chief. Now Quinn was dead, and he had no reason to speak with Phelps. Quinn had died in a fishing accident in Loch Lomond. Wheeler was happy to let the facts of Operation Dispute die with him. The room was now silent as the interpreters brought the conversion up the date. Wheeler finalised his stint with a small recap.

"So, you see, gentlemen." again, he looked at Angelica apologetically. "We have a major criminal. A very dangerous criminal who has evaded capture for a very long time. We are aware of his co-conspirators from his previous life, and I will be looking at these people when I return to the UK. The monies invested in these property deals by our man Divine is, I must stress, the proceeds of crime."

"Thank you, Mr Wheeler," said Suarez, now standing. "Now Gentlemen, We have with us now…" he looked down at his papers "a Mr

Ochoa from Argentina. South America, and he is here to tell us more about this guy." Again, he looked at his documents before pressing the remote and producing the face of another conspirator.

Wheeler excused himself and manoeuvred his bulk around the tables and out onto the corridor. He had seen and heard enough. He walked to the toilet and washed his face with cold water. He turned on the hand dryer and put his head under it before standing upright and using the same to dry the perspiration from his damp shirt. When he returned, the room was emptying out into the corridor. Perelta walked up to Wheeler as they neared the group.

"A break, Mr Wheeler, for those who wish to have a cigarette, and a hot drink, perhaps." he shrugged his shoulders and curled his bottom lip like the Spanish do.

"I see," acknowledged Wheeler. "How did I do?"

"You did very well, my friend. You gave us some insight into one of the culprits. Come, let us walk outside and get some fresh air." he said, placing a hand on the shoulder of the large man. The two of them walked slowly along the corridor like old friends.

"There is little point in you returning to the conference," said Perelta. "If you prefer, you could go back to your room and rest. I will see you tomorrow and fill you in with the remainder of what is said today."

"That sounds good to me."

"What I am about to tell you now will not be discussed this evening," said Perelta as the two walked across the large concourse area towards the main entrance. Wheeler was entranced but did not let this show as Perelta held open the manual door beside the large brass and glass rotating one. Now stepping out into the cool night air, Perelta continued without urgency.

"There will be a number of arrests in the early hours of Friday morning."

"Friday," said Wheeler. "I was hoping to leave for home tomorrow. Do I have to be here?"

"No, no, not at all," he gave Wheeler an encourageing pat on the back as the two strolled slowly along the busy street, "not unless you want to, of course. Come, let me buy you a cold beer, it"s too noisy out here," he said, ushering Wheeler into the dimly lit, smoky bar.

The small café/bar was empty, but a couple sat in the corner. The two detectives took a table in the opposite corner and ordered two small beers from the guy behind the counter.

"We have 30 minutes before I have to return," said Perelta, leaning closer to Wheeler. "Shall we make that two?"

"Why not?" replied Wheeler, almost finishing the first beer in one gulp. "The measures are short here anyway."

"Dos mass Por-fav-or." Perelta instructed the waiter.

"The arrest," said the Spanish detective leaning close to Wheeler, "they will be in conjunction with each other at exactly the same time. 5.30 on the morning of Friday. There will be thirty-three in all. Armed units will be deployed to carry out the operation, and among those arrested will be Divine, his driver Thomas Callahan and Jerry Divine's partner Jezard Dupree. I will be the interviewing officer. From what you have said today, I don't expect to get too much from Divine, but I hope we will break both Dupree and Callahan." He looked at Wheeler for a response. Wheeler looked back at Perelta and told him he would be wasting his time completely to expect anything but a negative response, if any, from Divine. He said it was highly unlikely that Callahan would have any information if he were only a driver.

"Dupree? I don't know," said Wheeler. "This will depend how much he knows about his partner's past." *God help him.* "What's this Dupree's history? Does he have previous?"

"Previous? What is this?"

"I'm sorry," apologised Wheeler. "Thank you," he said taking the second beer from the waiter. "Previous convictions," he explained.

"I see. No, he has nothing," replied Perelta, passing the two empties and receiving his beer. He waited until the waiter had left the table before telling Wheeler what the authorities knew about Dupree. There wasn't much to tell. He was an architect who ventured into the property market after the boom of the early eighties. He has full residencia, he originates from Portugal—even though the name sounds French—where he still has an interest in a popular golf course. He is married, with one boy, a young man actually.

"We know nothing about how or where his relationship with Divine transpired. We know they are friends outside of business and our recent surveillance shows he and his wife socialising with Divine and his wife. We know Dupree is a patron of Mrs Divine's charity, Breast Mate. And my friend that is about all we know about Mr Dupree."

"And Callahan?"

"Callahan," said Perelta, shrugging his shoulders and curling his Spanish lip, which told Wheeler all he needed to know.

"There are a million Callahan's on the coast. He is nothing. A driver, nothing more."

"He is Divine's driver." reminded Wheeler.

"Yes, I know." acknowledged Perelta. "So, maybe he is different in that respect, but we find nothing. Divorced, he landed here two years ago, he worked the bars, a little construction work, we have arrested him for drunken behaviour. I think maybe he just got lucky, meeting our Mr Divine, I mean." he concluded.

"I don't know about lucky," said Wheeler "but there is one thing for sure."

"What is this?" asked Perelta.

"He could be our weak link," replied Wheeler.

"I am sorry, my friend, look at the time." cut in Perelta and standing.

"Sure, sure," said Wheeler, standing, "I think I will stay here and enjoy my own company for a while."

"Yes, certainly, you do that. We will meet for breakfast tomorrow, and I can bring you up to date with any developments."

"Thank you, and good night," said Wheeler, holding out his hand. "I'm sorry," he added sheepishly. "Could you get the tab? I'm afraid I didn't bring any money with me. Maybe a little extra too, I could do with a couple more of these." he added, finishing the last dregs from the bottom of his glass. Perelta took a €20 and placed it on the table. Wheeler looked at the barman and ordered one more beer before walking to the door with Perelta.

The two shook hands again as Perelta held the door open, the noise of the evening traffic filtering through.

"Just one other thing," he said, taking a photograph from his inside pocket. "This is a still from the security camera situated on the terrace of a hotel and leisure centre. It is recent, only a few days, in fact. It shows Divine with another guy. Do you recognise the other man?" he handed Wheeler the picture. Wheeler took it and studied it intently. He could hear Perelta speaking in the distance as if from another dimension. "We run his picture through our database and haven't come up with a match. I meant to give it to Suarez, but it slipped my mind."

It certainly looked like Stone thought Wheeler. *There was a striking similarity, that's for sure.*

"I'm not sure." said Wheeler hesitantly "The quality is not very good."

"I should run a further copy and give it to Le-Braque," said Perelta, taking the picture back from Wheeler.

"I wouldn't do that just yet, Mr Perelta," advised Wheeler.

"Oh? And why is that."

"I cannot be certain just yet. Could you have the picture super imposed and let me have a second look? Because if that is who I think it is, we may be playing in a different ballpark."

"I think at this stage, Mr Wheeler, you will have to be a little more specific."

"I'm sorry, Mr Perelta. I can't, not at least until I can confirm my suspicions."

"O.K. you have me intrigued. Angelica will take care of it and I will have a copy at breakfast tomorrow."

"Before anyone else sees it?"

"Sure," said Perelta with resignation. "7.30 is good for breakfast?"

"Perfecto," replied Wheeler attempting to smile.

"Your Spanish is good." laughed Perelta.

"I am trying, maybe you could get me a book? I could revise on the plane."

"I will see you in the morning, Mr Wheeler. Buenos Notches."

"Benis nochess."

The two detectives parted company. Perelta went back to the conference, and Wheeler stepped back into the bar.

"Do you have a public telephone? he asked the waiter.

"No comprehend."

"Telephonio." said Wheeler, putting his thumb to his ear and little finger to his mouth, he realised that by adding an O to the end of every word would get him understood in Spain.

"Ah! si, si." said the man, taking a portable phone from under the counter. He handed it to Wheeler reluctantly. Wheeler noticed this and assured him the call was local. He dialled the number.

"Hello. Smith, is that you? It's Bill here."

"Where the fuck are you, Gov? I thought you'd be back by now."

"No, not yet. Listen, we may have a problem."

"Anything I can do, Bill? What is it."

"Fucking Stone."

"Stone? Barry Stone?"

"Yes, hear me out, Kid," he said impatiently, "the slimy bastard has just turned up here, in Spain. With Divine. I nearly had a fucking heart attack. The guy I am working with just sprung a photo of the two of them on me. They don't know who Stone is yet, and for our sakes, they don't need to know."

"Where is he, Bill? Down there with you?"

"I don't know, Son. Some hotel and leisure centre by all accounts. I'll know more tomorrow. In the meantime, I want you to check with the witness protection. Find out where his last known whereabouts were and who his handler was, or is."

"Will do Bill. What you gonna do?"

"I don't know… I was fucking dreading this day."

"Relax Bill. There's absolutely no evidence. At the worst, there's only circumstantial. Stone's never going to put us in. I still say it's that cunt who stole the money anyway."

"No way, Kid. That was Divine, anyway enough, said Son. Be discreet, O.K?"

"Don't worry, Bill."

"I am worried." He hung up the phone, feeling somewhat relieved he had shared the burden.

Chapter Forty-Two

Jerry played no music on the drive to Benalmádena, instead, he kept the roof up, the windows closed and kept the airflow temperature on cool. He took the new road and kept the speed on the clock hovering around 100 kilometres per hour. He parked the car in the hotel car park fifty minutes after leaving his home address at 7 pm.

Closing the car door, he stood and looked out to the med for few minutes before making his way to the hotel and casino entrance. He had dressed smartly this evening as the dress code did not allow casual wear into the casino. He was apprehensive but, for some reason, felt lucky. He had placed €20,000 in crispy new Bin-Ladens in the inside pocket of his black dinner suit as he had left the house.

"Be lucky." Kath had said sarcastically, as she kissed him at the gate.

"I have to get the piano money back from somewhere." he'd smiled.

Now he made his way to the casino bank and exchanged the new notes for 40 mother of pearl €500 plates in a small, clear plastic case. Looking around the gaming area, he saw an empty table and thought he would try his luck at blackjack.

"Good evening, Mr Divine. Would you like a privacy table?" asked the floor manager, holding out his hand. Jerry took it with his free hand and declined the offer.

"I'm keeping small this evening, Nicholas." offered Jerry. "Maybe a glass of champagne."

"Very well," said Nicholas, snapping his fingers. "What's your preference?" he smiled at Jerry as the girl in evening wear made her way over.

"L&P pink will be fine. Thank you." The manager relayed the order into the ear of the tall waitress, who smiled back at Jerry and briskly walked away. Jerry looked at the girl leaving with her long, black, topless cocktail dress.

"Very nice," he said.

"Very," confirmed Nicholas. "Good luck this evening, Mr Divine." Jerry took his seat and confirmed that he would operate two boxes because he was the only person at the table. He placed one plaque on each and broke the golden rule of asking for a card on 16 and 17. Both hands bust and lost, as did the next seven hands, which had Jerry losing €4500 in less than two minutes and before the bubbly was placed on a portable table in a bucket beside him.

"Two glasses, please."

"Certainly, sir."

"This is good timing," said Jerry as Jezzie joined him. "Did you smell the champers?"

Jez didn't respond.

Jerry got the message. It was bad news.

"Take a seat over there," he instructed his friend "I'll be with you shortly." Turning now to the girl, he asked that she transfer the drinks to a small table over in a quiet corner. The pit-boss asked if he should take care of the remaining plaques. Jerry confirmed he should, he thanked him and followed Jez.

"It's not good, is it?"

"I'm afraid not," replied Jez, the colour already drained from his dark complexion. "Not for me anyway," he confirmed. "This is big, Jerry. Bigger than we imagined. The fucking Mayor of Marbella is being charged with corruption, taking bribes and money laundering. The son is being released tonight but is on house arrest. His father is being transferred to a prison in Madrid tomorrow. Our man Gonzalez has a bail application being heard tomorrow. Brogonia is confident we can get him out but there will be sureties required. He is of previous good character, which eases the situation somewhat, but even so, Jerry, they will be asking that we put up a sizable amount."

"We?" cut in Jerry.

"Jerry, I don't have it."

"How much are we talking?"

"Your champagne, Gentlemen."

"Yes. Thank you," said Jerry rather abruptly.

"That's not like you, my friend," said Jez.

"Shut the fuck up. How much?"

The girl scurried away.

"Brogonia…"

"Fuck Brogonia. How much are we talking Jez?"

"€250,000."

"Where's the Dictaphone?"

"It's here Jerry. Just like I said it would be." Jez was fumbling through his suit jacket. He placed the machine on the table. Jerry picked it up and untwined the wire with an earpiece attached to it. He placed the plug in his ear and switched on the tape.

"Have you listened to this?" asked Jerry rather loudly. Jez shook his head. He had no idea how he was about to tell Jerry that both their arrests were imminent. He looked at him now, hoping to get a sign, a reaction, anything that may relay a clue. He had not dared listen to the tape. Instead, he had followed the instructions to bring it directly to Jerry, just as it had left the prison visit. He looked again at the man he was beginning to fear. Jerry was engrossed. He was listening intently. Jez took his glass and emptied the flute in one gulp. He topped it up and looked at Jerry, raising the bottle to fill his half-empty glass. Jerry shook his head. Jez refilled his own and replaced the bottle. Fifteen more excruciating minutes passed. Jez had completed the remainder of the champagne. The girl had noticed and delivered a new bottle. Jerry hadn't touched his glass. He was absorbed in the audio. Jez noted his friend's movements. He was agitated, to say the least. Jerry was now leaning forward in his seat, his hand clasped together as if wringing the perspiration from them. He was sitting back in the chair, touching each earpiece with the forefinger's of each hand. Now, almost 55 minutes later he pulled the plugs from their position with a yank of the wire hanging down his front to the machine resting on the table. He pressed the off switch, rewrapped the cable and passed the machine back to Jez.

"We're fucked." he concluded, lifting his glass.

"Tell me, Jerry. What did he say?"

"He has told them everything. About you. Me. Every-fucking-thing. And you're right. We do need him out on bail."

"Jerry, you're not saying what I think you mean! Surely."

"I didn't say anything. Now, what else did this Brogonia have to say?"

"Not a lot, really. She did say that most of the stuff that was relevant would be self-explanatory on the tape. But I haven't listened to the tape, Jerry. Like you said, I brought it direct to you. What do you mean Jerry, *He has told them everything?*"

"Listen to the tape."

"O.K. I will. There is one other thing, Jerry." he said hesitantly. "Brogonia, did say it might be an idea if we took a little holiday. She said that we will be arrested in the very near future."

"I gathered that," replied Jerry, looking at the small tape recorder. "but I don't think it will be tonight or tomorrow. I have to go to Portugal," Jerry lied. "But I will be gone only for a day or two. What about you? Where will you go?"

"I don't know Jerry. This is not my kind of life. I don't know how to run."

"Maybe you should have thought about that before you entered into this conspiracy."

"I didn't see it as a conspiracy, Jerry. Just a way of getting rich quick. Not unlike you, Jerry," he attempted to remind his partner. "None of us had the remotest idea it would come to this." he reasoned.

He underestimated Jerry. Jerry now looked at his friend and felt the first pang of sympathy for the one who had done all the negotiations and money transfers. Jerry was far too astute not to take precautions from the very beginning. This whole scenario could end up being nothing more than a financial loss and huge inconvenience.

"You're on your own, Jez. Call my house tomorrow at 5 pm and collect the bail money. Listen carefully to the Dictaphone and prepare yourself. Get a good lawyer." Jerry now stood up to leave. "Are you alright?" he looked down at Jez who was still seated, too deflated to stand.

"I'll be fine, Jerry. Will you call me?"

"I'll be in touch." He made his way to the bank and opted for a cheque made out to Kathryn Divine, as opposed to cash, before leaving the casino and walking outside and down through the car park to the water's edge.

Chapter Forty-Three

"This whiskey is fine stuff," said Barry holding up his glass of Green Label Jonnie Walkers to the light. "Only the Scottish know how to brew this stuff," he said looking through the glass. Stuli was not comfortable seated next to him on the high buffet. The two of them were the only customers at the bar in the Rock Hotel.

"I was in Scotland only once you know," he held up his forefinger as he pulled his stool closer to his fat friend. "not through choice, I have to add."

His fat friend was a good listener and now looked at his rather drunk companion enquiringly.

"Yes, it's true!" Barry continued. The alcohol was taking the effect of loosening his tongue. The two had been drinking for almost two hours, not long after Barry had taken the call from Jerry.

"I was under armed escort. A very important meeting, to say the least," he said, nodding his head and moving even closer to put his arm around the wide shoulders of the fat man who was now wondering whether he really wanted to hear this tale.

"One day I will tell you the story." he completed to the relief of Stuli.

"What you say, you and I venture up the Torremolinos?" He asked, already making his mind up.

"I think I would rather retire early, Vincent. Don't forget we are seeing your friend tomorrow. What time will that be?"

"Not while later in the day. Midday, to be precise. Relax, the night is young. Plus, I'm as randy as a rampant mule." he slapped the thigh of Stuli and grasped a handful of lard. He squeezed it tightly making the fat man wince with the sudden pain.

"O.K. my friend. Do you think we should freshen up first?" asked Stuli, removing Barry's hand.

"Of course!" answered Barry. "I'll see you back down here in 40 minutes."

Exiting the lift, Barry walked slowly along the corridor to his room. He would enter the room silently, hoping to find Beatrice sleeping. He and Stuli hadn't spoken in the lift. Barry only had one thing on his mind. He would surprise Beatrice by silently letting himself into the room and pouncing on her as she slept. She would have little chance of defending herself because he would have the benefit of surprise on his side. He would turn her face down and throttle her from behind. Just as she was to loose oblivion due to the lack of oxygen, he would enter her through malicious force. He liked it that way. She didn't, but what right did she have to like anything? He was the one who had saved her, who had got her out of that menial existence. Selling his little male arse to disgusting foreigners, almost begging to suck cock for a pittance. Look at him now! A full-blown woman, with him! Barry, a real man, flying around the world and staying in fine hotels. She has to pay.

Opening the door quietly, Barry was disappointed to see Beatrice sitting at the dressing table applying make-up.

"Hi, Darling. Look, the bruising is almost gone. I mean, the powder has disguised it." she said nervously as the disappointment showed on the face of her man.

"What are you doing?" he asked.

"I taught I would make an effort, my love and come and join you in de bar." she hoped and looked at Barry, almost pleading for the *nice* Barry

"I didn't ask you to come and join us," he said, moving to stand behind her.

"I wanted to surprise you, my lovely," she said quietly.

He soothed the top of her head with his two hands as she spoke. She looked back at him through the reflection of the mirror. She smiled apologetically. He moved his two hands down and slowly massaged her slender black shoulders, gradually moving inward to surround her small neck. She looked back at him worriedly. She was right to worry. Suddenly he intensified his grip with one hand while the other grabbed the hair at the top of her head. He yanked it back with such force that if it weren't for the music playing lightly to invite the mood of love, he would have heard the breath being sucked from her lungs. She froze with fear as he leaned down and kissed her lips with such force he may as well have punched her in the mouth. Forcing her lips open with his tongue, he sucked hers into his mouth and pitted it. She rose as if to take her body in the same direction, almost feeling that if she were to resist, he would bite the tongue from her. He became more erratic as soon as he tasted the blood from her mouth and released his bite to force her by the neck in the direction of the immaculate bed. Pushing her face down, he lifted the robe she was wearing up and wrapped it around her head. She was naked under the robe, so he took little time entering her. The lack of any lubrication made the entry painful for both. Barry welcomed the pain. As for Beatrice, she was numb with fear.

Forty minutes later, he rejoined Stuli at the bar and ordered a taxi to take them to the border.

Beatrice stayed alone in the room. She tended to her wounds and wondered if she was not better off before she had met her new man. She was so alone. Why had he taken her phone? If only she could talk to mum. Again, she cried herself to sleep with nightmare visions of Barry's return.

Chapter Forty-Four

Jerry's mind had worked overtime on the journey back home. He was deflated, like his world was crumbling around him. He wasn't so much concerned about a conviction. The inconvenience could be significant. Some time spent in prison on remand? *Maybe.* He was unsure how the Judicial system worked over here. What he did know was that there was more scope for bribery. He had some lawyer details, which a close friend gave him some time back. *First things first.* He would leave tomorrow for Gibraltar and maybe fly out from there? Where to? That was the question. One option was to contact Abdul and visit Morocco? He decided to first see what Barry had on the table. He had checked the two phones for missed calls and noticed a text from Marie, which read *Jerry, Please call me.* He would call tomorrow.

His attempts to enter the house without disturbing anyone were foiled by Bonito, who came scurrying down the stairs excitedly.

"Shush, baby. Come here," he whispered as he bent to scoop her in his arms. She welcomed the embrace and showed her gratification by licking Jerry's face rapidly. He walked quietly into little Julie's room and placed the dog on the bed. Thankfully, his youngest baby didn't stir.

"You're early," said Kath as he walked into the master bedroom. He was happy to see that his wife was still up. She was reading with the bedside lamp on.

"Yes, I know darling. I'm glad you're still awake. I need to talk to you."

"Oh... that's unusual. Nothing too serious, I hope."

"No, love," said Jerry, playing the issue down. "We have a few problems with one or two of our investors." he paused slightly, wondering for a split-second how much he should disclose and how much of a lie he should make of it. "You will see in the next day or two, some activity relating to a couple of our development sites. There have been some arrests, and there may be more," he now sat beside Kath and loosened his bow tie.

"Some government people have been taking backhanders and pushed through some building permits. Nothing for us to worry about." Kath put her book down and looked at her husband. Jerry could see the concern etched across her face. He didn't want to worry her; he always tried to protect her, her feelings were just as important to him as was her well-being.

"Don't worry, love. If they do come, it will only be to question me..." he let this sink in before adding, delicately, "I have decided to go away for a day or two. Give myself an advantage, some time, you know? To see how the grass lies. I should imagine that, at the very worst, this could cost me a lot of money, but nothing more than that love, I promise."

"And Jezzie?" said Kath, looking directly into her husband's eyes, for any sign of deceit.

"I've told him to do the same, but I somehow think he will stay. I don't think Demitra will let him go," he said, holding Kath's hand. He now released it and stood to take off his jacket.

"Anyway, it might be good if he stays, that way, I'll know more. If he's nicked, you can go see him with Demitra. When I get back, you can fill me in."

"And the girls?" asked Kath.

"Kath, they'll be fine. Don't mention it to them, I've gone on another business trip. I'll be back in a day or two O.K?" he now removed the only clothes remaining, which were his silk socks, and climbed in the bed beside Kath.

"Now turn off the light and come here you."

The two of them made love for two hours before Jerry lapsed into a coma in Kath's arms. She, on the other hand, did not sleep but lay until the sun rose. Periodically, throughout the long hours, the feeling of dread returned.

Chapter Forty-Five

Day Four

"Buenos Matins, Mr Wheeler. How was the remainder of your evening?"

"It was fine, thank you. Please remain seated." He held out his hand to Perelta first and then Angelica, who stood anyway, removing the starched towel from her lap.

"Good morning, Angelica." he took her hand and kissed the back of it; he was getting used to this, and he liked it. She curtsied with a smile and blushed ever so slightly. Wheeler attempted to squeeze into the chair with arms before giving up and changing for one without from the next table.

"I think I need to lose a little weight," he commented. "That's better," he added as he made himself comfortable.

"Angelica," said her superior. She opened a leather-bound folder and took from it an A4-sized photograph.

"Thank you," said Wheeler, holding out his hand to retrieve it. The eager act not gone unnoticed by Perelta and Angelica. They looked at one another with acknowledgement as Wheeler scrutinized the picture.

"When was this picture taken?" he asked, not taking his eyes from it.

"Two days ago," replied Perelta

"Where?" again, Wheeler did not take his eyes from the image

"On the terrace of The San Roque Hotel and golf resort."

"Which is?"

"Two kilometres inland from the coast and approximately one hundred kilometres south from here," answered Angelica this time.

"I see," said Wheeler. "The man with Divine is Barry Stone, an old friend and partner of his and an old adversary of ours. The two are lifelong friends. I am shocked that Stone has resurfaced. He was killed 6 years ago in a shoot-out with the police in the South of England." The two Spanish detectives looked at each other as if they were both hearing things.

"I know! I know," said Wheeler, holding up his hand, "Please, let me get some breakfast and…" he made to stand before Perelta asked him to sit back down.

The Spanish detective held up a hand, and a waiter was with them immediately. Wheeler guessed that the same waiter asked him what he would like to eat in Spanish. Perelta explained to the waiter that his companion was English. He then asked Wheeler what he would like to eat and drink. The overweight English man ordered a full English breakfast with extra bacon and two eggs. Perelta relayed the order and asked for croissants with jam for two. All three ordered coffee and fruit juice.

"I thought I had heard everything in a very long and active career," said Perelta.

"I'm sure you have," said Wheeler, looking across the table. "I am not sure… let me rephrase that." he sat back in his chair, which gave the other two a view of the full width of his girth. He rested his hand on the swell.

"I am uncomfortable with this, but I feel if I am to gain your respect and cooperation with my request, then you are entitled to the truth."

"I am sure that I speak for the two of us, Mr Wheeler, when I say that I thank you for your honesty in what you are about to disclose, but to be quite frank, there is never any other way."

"Of course. Well, let me begin."

"I would say, under any other circumstances, shall we at least wait for the food?" said Perelta butting in, "but you have me at the tip of the iceberg. Is this how you say?"

"Yes," said Wheeler, starting with the story. "Barry Stone was arrested almost 7 years ago for conspiracy to rob a safety deposit box depot. The evidence against him was overwhelming, for this and various other crimes. He was looking at a long stretch in prison, 25 to 30 years. The problem for us was we didn't have Divine. Divine played no part in this particular conspiracy. We had the two of them within our grasp prior to this but were unable to pursue the investigation due to a clerical error, which had wider implication. This matter is too complicated to explain, and it is not relevant to my request so we'll leave it at that. What is relevant is that, if at all possible, we must bring Stone in. If he is on Spanish soil, I must ask that you help me to bring him in. I need to speak with him. You see, Mr Perelta, Stone is a unique case, he is presumed dead by all his previous life and the associates within it. He sacrificed his past life and even his immediate family to trade his liberty for obscurity."

"The full breakfast." said the waiter placing the large plate of greased delights in front of Wheeler. "And the croissants." he smiled at the more familiar faces.

"Thank you." said Wheeler, placing his napkin between his shirt buttons. He didn't look up at the waiter but continued speaking.

"Both he and Divine were involved with a large-scale, class A drug importation with Venga." The two Spanish detectives looked at each other with the mere mention of such a high-profile criminal. Angelica took a notebook and pencil from her pocket and commenced to scribble frantically.

"Alba or Riat?" she asked.

"Alba?"

"Yes, the younger brother to Riat, he is here now, somewhere in Spain, he flew into Madrid 4 days ago from Banjul, West Africa."

"Venga, of course," said Wheeler. "Didn't you hear? He was killed, it's public knowledge, 6 years ago in a service area on a motorway in the UK. Our Barry Stone…"

"We heard, of course, but we hear so much, one can never be sure. Anyway, we had no reason to follow it up, he was chased out of our pastures a long time ago. I think the last we heard he was arrested in Lisbon." Wheeler was taking little notice, his indifference was beginning to annoy the slightly embarrassed Spanish detective, who looked at his English counterpart now tapping the face on the picture with his fork.

Wheeler continued as if Perelta hadn't spoken at all, "…was instrumental in the orchestration of this successful for some, and failure for others, operation. He too," he stopped talking and stuck the same fork into a thin pink sausage, "was killed, or so it seemed to everyone, other than a select few. Divine not being one of them. Which leads me to think, that something very big is going down. If these two have re-established a working relationship, it is not likely to be run of the mill. Believe me, Mr Perelta, this will be something above the norm, and it is likely to be on your patch. You need to be one step ahead." he paused to insert the full sausage into his mouth and washed it down with some pale tea.

"How do you know Stone will talk?" asked Angelica.

"We have something on Mr Stone which he likes to keep very much a secret, miss," he replied before turning back to Perelta.

"We have photographic evidence which places Stone in a room with other Paedophiles, Venga included. Barry Stone is a paedophile. The still pictures were produced from a tape recording of what we call in the UK, a snuff film. It shows a boy, no more than 10 or 12 years old, being tortured, sexually tortured, some of the most depraved acts of barbarism I have ever seen after almost 40 years in the business, our business." he looked at the two detectives with moist eyes.

"Stone was made aware that we were in possession of this material prior to the events of Operation Dispute coming to the dramatic end that it did, with, of course, the cooperation of Stone. I have to say that I myself have not seen the film footage, only the stills from it, and I have to add, I have no evidence that the child was killed. I can only assume, I didn't ask." he paused before saying in a quieter voice, "I suppose I didn't want to hear the answer."

"But this was the turning point!" he now continued in his usual tone "and the evidence which had Stone talking. We recruited him into Operation Dispute from that instance. You see, it wasn't just the fact that we had the evidence on the heists, we needed more. Venga was our priority. Divine was number two, then Stone, followed by others. We could sacrifice Stone if we had the other two."

"The other two being Venga and Divine," said Angelica.

"But Divine is still with us." queried Perelta.

"Divine was lucky, it pains me to say." continued Wheeler. "The shoot-to-kill policy was sanctioned from above. I can't go into detail in that respect, but you can take it from me, it doesn't get any higher, it went way beyond the government. I'll have to leave it to your imagination. But the whole point of the matter is that Stone was instrumental in bringing a whole professional organisation down."

Wheeler now refilled his mouth with some streaky bacon and egg yolk as if to refuel his body to give and supply energy to carry on. The yolk dripped and missed the napkin staining his white shirt. He didn't notice, and the two were not about to interrupt him, so they stayed silent and waited for him to continue.

"We know that without the paedophile evidence, Stone would not have talked. You could say, it pains me to say, that we were fortunate that Venga was involved in paedophilia and lucky, for want of a better word, that Stone was wrapped up with him. Otherwise, we might never have got our man. We had our trap! Our inside man." He pushed the half-eaten breakfast away and wiped the dribble from his chin. He noticed the stain from the yolk and wiped it with the towel, adding more staining from the tomato mopped from his chin. He threw the cloth on the plate and continued. The two Spanish detectives were completely absorbed.

"Stone was killed," he did the two-finger manoeuvre "in the same shoot out that Venga met his maker. Divine, on the other hand, escaped. We have to live with that. Target one, Venga, was eliminated, that was a success as far as the instigators were concerned. Divine was my priority, but I was in the minority, I'm afraid. I wasn't given the resources to track him down. He took a Lear jet from Exeter and landed in Bordeaux. The next I heard was when my commanding officer gave me this assignment." He now lifted his cup and drained the cold tea from it without taking his eyes off his Spanish counterpart.

"Now!" he said, lifting the saucer from the table and pouring the dregs into the cup. He deliberately took his time to empty the cup, all the while looking directly into Perelta's eyes. His mobile vibrated. He took it from his pocket and read the text.

"Gambia West Africa. No name of handler, still working on it, I'll be in touch as soon as. Smithy."

"What we have, Mr Perelta," he said, finally replacing the phone casually, "is a mutual dilemma which will not go away, unless, my friend, we find a way of bringing Barry Stone in. He will have to explain to us how and why he has made contact with Divine. I can only assume it is for one thing only, and that has to be something big."

"Is it wise, Mr Wheeler, at this stage, to show our hand? I mean, are you confident that Stone will talk?"

"Oh, yes. Being a nonce in the circles where Stone came from under his stone—pardon the pun—is more than a taboo."

"Nonce? What is this?" asked Angelica.

"A beast, Angelica. Scum, kiddy fiddler, Paedo. If there is one thing that is not accepted in the world in which Divine lives and Stone lived, it is a Paedophile. Actually, there are two or three things as far as Divine is concerned, two of which we can attribute to Stone. A grass and a nonce.

Believe me, Barry Stone would do almost anything to keep this information from his friend Jerry Divine."

"I see," said Angelica, now replacing the photograph. "Will you need a copy?" she asked.

"No, thank you, Angelica. Mr Perelta," he said, turning to look at the Spanish detective, "we need to bring Barry Stone in for questioning."

"Yes, yes, Mr Wheeler, but we need something to bring him in for." he replied, thinking, studying. "there may be something," he said, looking directly at Wheeler.

"Your Mr Stone is, or was, staying in the Hotel San Roque. For some reason—which I am now beginning to see the picture—he left the hotel, having extended his stay to Friday. Shortly after, I mean almost immediately, he left the hotel and has not been seen since, and, to make matters even more suspicious, his room was broken into. You see, this is the reason we were contacted by the hotel. Not an issue at the time, you see Mr Wheeler, but it became one after your Mr Divine was under observation entering the same hotel the previous evening. We had already asked that we see the security DVD footage, and it transpires that he meets with your Mr Stone? Did you say Stone, Mr Wheeler?" Bill Wheeler nodded. He moved his bulk forward, listening carefully to this new information.

"Because our information tells us that this man is going under a different name." Perelta now looked at Angelica, who took some papers from the same binder which housed the photograph.

"Mr Viceroy." she offered

"Does the name Viceroy mean anything to you?" asked Perelta.

"No, but it is not unusual for this type of criminal to use aliases. My God, I imagine Divine will have many, and Stone, especially Stone, in his situation. I have some of my people looking into his current whereabouts, I mean, where he should be, or at least, his last known whereabouts. You see, he is registered on the witness protection program. I mean, he was instrumental in bringing some big boys down! Which brings me back to something you said." he looked from Wheeler to Angelica, knowing she would be the one to answer the next question.

"Do we know why, or who broke into his room?" Perelta, too, looked at his rock.

"I'm afraid not. We have pictures," she said, fishing them from the binder. "they are not the best, I'm afraid." she explained, handing them over.

Wheeler looked at them. *Eastern European? certainly not Turks. Police? Could be. Wait a minute!* Wheeler looked closer. There was something. Something about the two tall figures, he couldn't quite put a finger on it, but it was there. He composed himself, not wanting to alert the two Spanish detectives looking on. Wheeler guessed they were waiting for a reaction. He gave them none.

"These are the two men who entered the room forcefully."

"Can we have something done with these? Enlarged? Maybe have an expert assess the probable nationality of these guys."

"Yes, we have someone working with them now."

"Good," said Wheeler. "Was anything taken from the room?" this was directed to Perelta.

"The room was empty."

"Empty?"

"Yes. Mr Stone had vacated the room completely."

"Like he knew they were coming."

"Exactly."

"So that's it," said Wheeler. "We bring him in for that. We let him know that we are aware he had paid for an extended stay, emptied the room, vacated the hotel and all the time, aware that his room was a target. We let him know that he is not under caution, he is helping us with our enquiries, after all, there has been a crime committed. No?"

"Yes. I suppose this is plausible." Perelta looked at his partner, who in turn agreed with a nod of her head and a note added to her little black book.

"Mission control, we have a problem," added Perelta.

"You are going to tell me you don't know where Stone is?" said Wheeler.

"Correct. Stone, Viceroy, whatever his name is. This will make things difficult."

"I will check with the recent departures. I will wire an image to air and ferry ports."

"Do the same with the toll roads." Perelta included.

"Yes," said Angelica. "Would you like me to visit the San Roque? I should look at the registration documents. To see if he added a vehicle to his details." she asked Perelta. Wheeler acknowledged her efficiency with a polite smile.

"Yes, call them now, make sure there will be someone there to assist with our enquiries. In fact, ask them to look at his registration details immediately, this will save time, if there is a number we can get it out there now," said Perelta.

"Don't worry, Mr Wheeler. We will find him," she assured him, dialling a number on her mobile and asking to be connected to the San Roque Hotel Costa del Sol.

"Do we know where Divine is?"

"We have eased our surveillance slightly. We took your advice. The tracking device was removed, and we are getting very little from the voice activation. Mr Divine says very little in the car and the little he does say is far from incriminating."

"I could have told you this."

"I know Mr Wheeler, but at the time, we thought it was for the better."

"Yes, I know, please excuse my criticism. Divine can get under your skin after a while. It's frustration, that is all."

"Well, you can rest assured, we are batting for the same team, Mr Wheeler. If you want to stick around, I can tell you, off the record, that the thorn in your side will be arrested at dawn tomorrow."

Chapter Forty-Six

"My God, look at the time!" cried Kath.

"Leave it, love."

"Never mind, Leave it, Jerry, they're late already," she said, swinging her legs from the bed. Jerry leaned over and playfully wrapped his arm around her waist, pulling her back onto the bed.

"Jerry, don't!" she laughed as he tickled her. "Stop!"

He took little notice as he got up on all fours to straddle her. Bending over, he muzzled around her neck with his lips and teeth, gently nibbling her neck and tickling her midriff with his hands.

"Please, Jerry, stop." she laughed, until he fell on her, covering her with his body.

"Mum, what's happening?" called Julie through the locked door.

"Nothing, baby. Give me two minutes."

"We're late for school."

"I know, love." called Kath "Stop it, Jerry!"

"You can have the morning off, pet," called Jerry.

"Fantastic Dad!"

"Jerry. You just can't do that."

"Why? I'm going away for a couple of days. We can have a long breakfast together."

"I suppose." conceded Kath. "Let your sister know, baby," she called to her youngest.

"Whoopee! C'mon Bonito." cried Little Julie.

"Come here, you," said Jerry, gruffly. "Round two," he said, kissing her tenderly.

Chapter Forty-Seven

Barry opened his eyes and looked at his watch.

"Fucking hell!" he said, realising he had less than two hours to get up, find Stuli and hit the road for Gibraltar. He looked around him at the scruffy room. The smell reminded him of a damp cell. There was no window, and the low-watt bulb hanging without a shade from the centre of the ceiling had remained on all night. It was surprisingly cold for this time of year. He guessed he was in a basement. He kicked the damp duvet from his legs and almost jumped from the bed with it. Curled up in the bottom left-hand corner was the slight figure of a youth. Touching the pale blue cold skin with his toe, Barry knew immediately that the boy was dead. He tried to remember the night before but couldn't. Panic soon set in. Where was he? Where's Stuli? The first question was half answered with the fact that he knew he was in Torremolinos. He touched the body again, this time pushing steadily with his foot. The body moved easily but stayed in the same position. He realised the boy must have died some hours before as rigour mortis had already set. He pushed even more, and the frail figure fell from the bed. Barry now looked down for any signs of blood. There was none. He looked at his hands for any damage. None. His own body had no marks to show he had been involved in a struggle. He was almost disappointed. Nothing. Now he began to wonder if he had actually killed this boy? He had every intention of killing someone or, at the very least, mutilating a victim. This was to celebrate the call he had received from Jerry. Beatrice was lucky. He leaned over from the bed to look again at the body, to see if there were any clues as to the course of death. Nothing. Had the kid died of natural causes? Maybe he had died from his own vomit? He didn't even consider trying to revive the poor soul; he was too busy planning how to clean up and get out of there.

He made to rise from the bed and fell back, holding his head. The drink and drugs had left him with a terrible hangover. He laid flat on the bed and again looked around the room. A small sink was positioned on the far wall with a bucket underneath to catch the leaking water. A stained toilet was the only other convenience, and Barry forced himself from the bed to use it. Sitting on the crapper, he further surveyed the room. A chest of drawers, most of them open, with clothing hanging over the edges. A wardrobe with a mirror attached to the handless door. The carpet didn't fit the floor, and the piss stains were the probable cause of the rancid smell. The walls were painted white but had turned creamy yellow with the smoke from many cigarettes and burning foil. It was only now that Barry again looked at the corpse. Realisation hit him. The boy's features triggered the memory. Although the youth's face was discoloured due to death, it was clearly visible as that of the boy he had met in the gay club the night before. He was the one who had supplied Barry with the Ketamine. Barry had asked for some ecstasy or a little coke when he had been approached by the kid in the toilets. He had given him €50 and told him to join him at the bar once he had got the drug.

He remembered now. His name was Jesepi. He had returned with the drug in powder form and had told Barry it was the new thing.

"Better than an E. A horse tranquilliser. Great for sex."

"Will you show me?" Barry had asked.

"Sure, for a price. You can come back to mine."

"You have your own place? How old are you kid?"

"Eighteen." he had lied, strutting his stuff.

Barry didn't mind, he looked at the boy dancing, selling his wares. The music was loud.

"Is it far? your place?" He called into the boy's ear.

"Less than 100 metres." Replied the kid, lighting a cigarette.

"Good. You leave first, I'll follow."

"Sure. Now?"

"Yes, Now," said Barry. This was going to be easy. He liked Torremolinos. The boy walked slowly from the club, looking back only once. Barry nodded. He poured the powder into his drink, swirled the contents and downed it in one. He looked around the dimly lit club until he saw Stuli dancing on the floor with a transvestite. He walked up behind him and told him to keep his phone on.

The rest was a blur. Try as he might, he couldn't recall. He noticed some Vodka bottles on the floor beside the bed, no glasses indicated this was taken neat. Some scorched silver foil at his feet, obvious signs of drug abuse. Standing now, he looked for some paper. There was none, so he walked with trousers around his ankles to the small sink. Turning on the tap, there was nothing, and then suddenly, the spout coughed and gave two short bursts, releasing some brown water.

"Fuck," he muttered, then the water cleared, giving a slow dribble of clean water.

"Thank fuck." he said, turning around and placing his rear end in the sink. After washing himself, he pulled up his trousers and swilled his face and neck. There was no towel to dry himself with, so he pulled some of the strewn clothing from the drawers and dabbed himself dry. He noticed a small package in an ashtray beside the bed and walked over to investigate. It was what he thought it would be: 4 wraps of brown powder and 3 more of white. He searched the drawers and found what he was looking for. Taking the syringe from its wrapping, he walked back over to the toilet and extracted some fluid from his waste so that the syringe was a quarter full. He then emptied all the powders from the wraps into an aluminium takeaway container and used a lighter he found in the trousers of the youth to burn the mixture into a fluid. Now filling the remainder of the syringe, he walked over to the lifeless boy and searched for a vein in his stiff arm. Having difficulty finding one, he looked elsewhere on the body. The eyes looked back up at him as he turned the boy over effortlessly. *Nothing*. He put some pressure around his neck, being careful not to leave any marks. *Nothing*. He considered injecting it directly into both pupils but was unsure whether this would give the desired effect. *The cock. They usually have a good one*. The boy's knees were curled up in the foetus position which made looking in this area difficult. He attempted to straighten them and was surprised at how difficult this was. Eventually, he used the weight of his own knees and body to straighten the corpse out. Now holding the penis of the boy in his left hand, he squeezed the end of it and bent it in two at the same time. Seeing what he was searching for, he injected the concoction directly into it. As an afterthought, he took one of the half-empty bottles of Vodka and poured the spirit down the throat of what was once, not so long ago, somebody's son.

He considered torching the gaff before realising there were obviously others in the same building. He looked at his watch. *'Fucking hell'* he took some clothing from the drawers, wet them quickly and wiped all the surfaces in the room.

Fifteen minutes later, he was standing in a penny arcade by the seafront, waiting for Stuli to join him.

"Where the fuck have you been?" Asked Barry as Stuli walked into the small café that housed the kiddie's ballpark.

"Don't ask." the fat man replied.

"Let's go," Barry said, standing and finishing off his cold drink.

"I need a drink, my friend. I am as dry as a donkey carrying a heavy load," he complained.

"You sound like a donkey too, c'mon, we haven't time," said Barry, walking out into what promised to be a not-so-welcome, hot day.

Eighty minutes later, the two were dropped by taxi at the entrance to the border at Gibraltar.

Chapter Forty-Eight

Jerry used the same phone from the bag in the garage, which he had called the San Roque last time.

"Hello Marie," he said cheerfully. "You left a message that I should call you."

"Yes, Mr Jer… Jerry. Something has transpired. I thought maybe you should know."

"Oh?"

"Yes, the Policia, they came to the hotel, the management called me into the office, and the Policia asked me some questions."

"And?"

"They have a picture of you with Mr Viceroy taken from the security camera situated on the restaurant terrace. This is why I was called to the office. I was asked if Mr Viceroy had been in the restaurant before with you."

"What did you tell them, Marie?"

"Of course, Jerry, I tell them the truth; I said no."

"Good Marie." he paused. "Very good. Will you contact me if they come again, Marie?"

"Yes, of course."

"I owe you one, Marie. I won't forget." *definitely not,* he thought.

"One other thing," said Marie.

"Yes, tell me."

"They checked with the taxi company, the one which caters for the hotel. I don't know what information was given to the policia, but you can assume they were given the destination."

"Thank you, Maria, I'll be in touch."

"Buenos Dias, Jerry."

Jerry now took a new phone from the plastic bag and placed it in his shoulder bag. He pressed the remote, closed the garage door and returned to the late breakfast Kath had prepared for the four of them.

"I'm sorry, love. I'll have to cut this short," he said.

"I'll get your bag," she replied, leaving the three still seated.

"I'll be gone for just a day or two girls, so be good for your mother, OK?"

"We will Dad," said Jasmine.

"We will Daddy," added Julie. "Will you bring me a present back?"

"I will, baby," he promised.

"Is Tom driving you to the Airport?" asked Kath, returning with two medium-sized cases.

"No, and I won't be calling him, so tell him I'll leave the key on the back wheel and the ticket on the sun visor. It will be in the usual place in La-Linea. He may ask you to take him for it. If he does, that's fine by me, but don't offer." he advised, standing now to kiss each of them. Kath was the last. He whispered into her ear not to worry.

"One other thing, love, Jez will be calling at 5 o' clock, there's a brief case, in the far corner under the desk, in the garage, give it to him." He kissed her now and assured her he would call tonight.

Chapter Forty-Nine

He checked the time on his Vacherōn against the clock in the car and added more pressure on the accelerator to take the Speedometer up to 170kph. Thirty-five minutes later, he parked the Mercedes in the exact same spot in the underground car park as he and Tom had just a few days before. *Three days? It seems so long ago. So much had happened.*

He placed the exit ticket above the sun visor and got out of the car before he inserted the SIM card into the new phone and dialled a number he knew by heart. It rang only once before the familiar voice answered.

"Yes. Who's calling?" asked Harold.

"You're on the ball. Do you have this thing stuck to your lobe?" said Jerry without answering the question. The voice recognition would be enough.

"How the fuck are you, my friend?" asked the old man sounding pleasantly surprised.

"I'm fine, old chap. How are you?"

"As good as can be expected, the job's hard, though, can't earn a fucking shilling."

"You're always crying the poor tale," said Jerry, laughing.

"I'm telling you, mate, the job's absolutely fucked!"

"Good thing you've got plenty then, init? You can live off the fat."

"I wish I was a quid behind you. I'd be OK."

"Listen, mate, I'll be with you shortly."

"I look forward to seeing you," Harold said, ending the call.

Jerry took the SIM card from the phone, broke it in two and placed it with the phone in his trouser pocket.

Now standing in the queue at passport control, having discarded the phone and SIM card, he felt agitated and uncomfortable; agitated from the slow pace the customary procedure was taking and uncomfortable with the way he was dressed in the heat. The two cases weren't heavy, but they didn't help either. He had an idea and decided to try his luck in the airport which was less than 30 metres from the border entry into Gib. Once he was through passport control, he walked into the small building, which was more like a mini bus terminal. He checked the departure listings before making his way to the information desk.

"Hello, Miss," he smiled, placing the cases on the floor. He reached into his inside coat pocket and took out some papers. Holding them in his hands, he explained to the assistant that he was booked on the 18.56 to Brussels. He was early because he had to vacate his hotel room at Valderarma.

"Us golfers get little priority nowadays. Is there anywhere I could leave my luggage while I take a stroll around Gib? Maybe go see the monkeys?" he laughed. She had agreed reluctantly and let him place them in a room behind her desk.

Now feeling quite happy with himself, Jerry joined the relatively short queue at the taxi rank outside. He checked his watch. *12 minutes past 11. Perfect.*

"The far side of Main Street," he instructed the driver, "by the fishing dock."

He let the taxi travel 100 metres past the small antique shop before he asked the driver to pull over. Once he paid and stepped out of the car, he waited till it was out of sight before he doubled back to the shop, which looked from the outside exactly what it said on the tin: the paint on the door and the shop front was flaking, the windows were dirty, the pine dresser displayed for the benefit of the shopper, was more of a deterrent. The whole picture was very Victorian, and this could have been a marketing ploy but Jerry very much doubted that. He opened the door to the ring of a bell, which made him smile. The dry smell of the timber and cobwebs gave the feel of a studio set. He almost expected Ebenezer Scrooge to come from the back room.

"I'll be with you in a sec, Jerry," called Harold.

"How do you know it's me?" he shouted back.

"I have you in the mirror."

Jerry looked toward the rear of the shop and noticed a mirror giving him a view of the back. He saw his old friend looking back at him and smiled.

Harold walked through to greet Jerry. He finished drying his hand before he threw the table cloth onto the antlers of a stag's head resting on a chair.

"Come here, you!" he said holding out his arms to hug his friend.

"It's good to see you, Harold." Jerry said, embracing the old man.

"You too. It's good that you called first. You never know with these cunts, although I must say lately, they give me little of their time."

"You're retired, Harold!"

"Me? Retired. I don't think so, son. What do I owe the pleasure? Shall we go for a walk? We could go upstairs. I had the place swept two days ago. Fuck it, let's walk and talk, then we can come back for coffee or something a little stronger if you prefer. I have a good Louise X111."

"Slow down, Harold, you're going to give yourself a heart attack."

"I'm sorry, Jerry. I'm just happy to see you."

"I know," smiled Jerry. "C'mon, let's go, I'm pushed for time, I have an appointment at midday."

Harold looked at a Vienna wall clock mounted on the wall.

"It's night at 11.30 now. That doesn't give us much time."

"I know. I don't like to, but maybe I should make a call and give us some breathing space."

"Do that if you can, Jerry. We don't want to be hasty. Let me get my keys."

Jerry watched the old timer walk through the back. This man was one of the very few that Jerry trusted impeccably. They had shared a cell in Pentenville in 99 and had seen the millennium end together with some late-night breakfast cereal and a gallon of Hooch.

Harold had opened up to Jerry that night. It could be said that it was the result of the hooch, but Jerry preferred to think it was because they had developed a true bond throughout the previous 9 months, and they had been locked up together for 23 of the 24 hours each day. They had laughed and cried throughout this period, played backgammon, chess and scrabble until they had become almost professional. If Jerry had learned anything from his time spent with this man, who had become more like the father he never had, it was that whatever you put your mind to, whatever you do in life, you do it to the very best of your ability and do it while trusting no one.

Harold had told Jerry about how he had lost his wife and two children in a terrible fishing trip tragedy. They had set off with six others on an ordinary fishing excursion from Gibraltar one beautiful sunny morning. It had been a birthday treat for the youngest of his two boys, Jerry —a total coincidence — It was 1977, Jerry was 6 and Jake 9. The sky had turned black within seconds, and the storm followed shortly after with little warning. The captain had drunk too much during the day, and his mate panicked when the mini tornado almost capsized the revamped 1930's Smack. Harold had shed a tear as he relived the ordeal within the confines of the prison cell. It was difficult for him to tell Jerry how he was unable to help his family after he had sustained a knock on his head by a broken mass. He was still riddled with guilt, even that day, more than twenty years after the event, even though he was knocked out. Vera was his childhood sweetheart; the two were married in Gibraltar, and the day was special to them but remembered by most as the same time and place as that of the wedding of John Lennon and Yoko Ono.

Jerry listened intently and was amazed to hear that Lennon took time out to have photo's taken with Harold and his bride.

"Did you ever have them valued?" asked Jerry. "I recently seen some undiscovered photos of the Beatles making a nice few quid in Sotheby's."

"No, these very personal, Son." he had responded with glazed eyes. "I probably would have considered it if my Vera weren't on them, but she is. I will show you them one day, Jerry. Did you like Lennon?"

"Yes, I did, I still do, as a matter of fact. He stood up for what he truly believed in—that's what I liked about him, Harold, plus his music, of course, he was a great lyricist."

"He was that."

"What was the record he sang about his marriage in Gibraltar?" Jerry had asked.

"The Ballard of John and Yoko," replied Harold. "It reminds me so much of that beautiful day."

"I'll bet. Will you be extradited back to Gib, Harold?" Jerry had asked, changing the subject completely.

"I think so, Son. Once these cunts have raped the living daylights from me."

"What they after?"

"The cigarettes were valued at 4.2 million. They have them, and the cunts want the same again. Trouble is, Kid, they have it already. They have put restraining orders on a couple of accounts, plus a few properties I have an interest in both, here and in Gibraltar and Spain. So I have a fight on my hands, which I might add are tied."

"I'm sorry, Harold."

"Enough about me, Jerry. I'll be fine. I have my health, and I suppose health is wealth, we can always get money. My family have been smugglers for generations, we are in high demand, Kid, we always will be."

"I'm sure you know what you're doing, Harold. My case. Well, it's looking good, Mate. I spoke to the brief this morning, Barry too, they brought him up from SEG, looked a fucking mess he did, anyway, the latest is that the Crown prosecution service may well be offering no evidence."

"Oh," said Harold with a mixture of surprise and suspicion. "And why's that?"

"Listen, Harold," Jerry had detected the suspicion. "I have got to know you pretty well during the last 8 or 9 months, and I like you. I like you a lot. You remind me of a father I never had. That may sound odd, let's say, like a father I wish I had had."

"I'm sorry, Jerry. But you told me about your case, and…" Harold was cut short by Jerry, wanting to get his point across.

"The CPS have lost some vital documents, Harold. How or why is immaterial, the fact of the matter is they have disappeared." Jerry nipped the lobe of his left ear, swept the cell with his eyes and winked at Harold.

"Come on!" said the older man, getting the message. "Let's play some scrabble."

Jerry took the board game from under the bed, placed it on the bottom bunk and arranged some pieces spelling out the message **Three Hundred Grand.** The two chuckled for the benefit of anyone listening, and Jerry refilled the two plastic mugs with foul hooch.

"Fucking hell, Harold. You getting married again?" said Jerry as his old friend reappeared dressed in a tweed suit, silk shirt and cravat. The stick he was holding had a handle resembling a silver fox; the highly polished wood complimented his Tricker brogues.

"It's not a sin to be skint Jerry…"

"But it is to look it." the two finished in unison.

"You need to make a call, buy us some time." said the older man.

"Yes, come, we'll stop at a box," said Jerry opening the door; the sound of the door bell, the brightness of the sun, the noise of the seagulls and the heat of the day giving some rest bite from the musty, dusty shop.

"I like it here, Jerry." Harold stated as the two walked along the water's edge. "I like to watch the boats come in. I look out at the sea, I hear the gulls, and I talk to the skyline, which connects to the water. Way off in the distance. When no one is looking, of course." he added.

Jerry stayed silent. He knew full well what his friend was thinking. Harold continued.

"I ask for advice. For guidance. I listen, and I imagine I can hear something coming back. Who knows, maybe it's wishful thinking, but it helps Jerry. It helps to ease the pain." he stopped walking and turned to look at Jerry.

"Make your call, Son, there's a call box over there." Jerry smiled sincerely and walked alone over to the telephone. He called the hotel and was put through to Mr Maine's room.

"Jerry," answered Barry. "How are you mate? I'll be down in to minutes. You in the bar?"

"No, as a matter of fact, I'm running a little late," replied Jerry to the relief of Barry.

"That's fine, Jerry, I'm here ready and waiting for you. How long you thinking, mate?"

"I'm not sure," said Jerry looking over at Harold. "Maybe an hour, is that OK?"

"Yea, that's fine. Everything alright?"

"Yes, everything is good. Anything over an hour, I'll call you again."

"I look forward to seeing you, pal." said Barry, hanging up the phone.

"Right, Harold, where were we?" he said, returning to stand beside him.

"You tell me, Jerry. I'm all ears."

"I don't know where to begin," he said as the two looked out to sea.

"Not like you, son. You usually have everything in order. How about starting with the reason you are here? What is it that brought you here, Jerry?" He turned to look at the younger man. "Shall we walk." this was said more of a statement as he casually commenced strolling, the tip of his stick tapping on the cobbles beside him.

"I have to get away for a few days," began Jerry "My arrest by the Spanish police is imminent. You may have seen it on the TV. It's in all the papers." he looked sideways at Harold, who was nodding his head. This shrewd fox had already put two and two together.

"The property licence scam."

"I wouldn't call it a scam, Harold but be as it may, they have little evidence on me. I know that, even before I get on my toes, the reason I'm fucking off is purely for breathing space. There will be other arrests, many of them, no doubt. I have the benefit of getting to know you before the event, so why not take advantage of it?"

"Yes, that makes sense," said Harold "But why do I get the feeling there is something else on your mind?" he asked this without breaking the slow pace and without turning to look at Jerry.

"You're right, Harold, there is something else, one or two things actually, but first, let me explain what I believe could be a problem."

"Go on, sorry for interrupting."

"One of the guys who has already been arrested has direct contact with me. He is a councillor in local government, he's one of those who have been taking the bungs. I don't think he is the sole recipient of the money, I think this has been shared by a few, the Mayor of Estepona being one." Harold raised his eyebrows, and Jerry nodded his head.

"Yes." continued Jerry. "His Father, the Mayor, I mean, is the Mayor of Marbella, by all accounts, with the information I have, the Marbella Mayor is fucked, he's been dipping into the coffers for years. I have no connection to him and none with his Son. We have met a few times, the son and I, charity galas, for instance, but nothing that can't be explained." He paused now before deciding to tell all.

"This other cunt is different, his name's Gonzalez, Augustine Gonzalez. You heard of him?" he asked, looking for an answer. Harold shook his head.

"I've heard of the Mayor, Sanchez, is it?"

"Yes, Emilio Sanchez, father and son, they share the same Christian name."

"Yes, I have dealt with the father. A long time ago, we were bringing tobacco into Spain from Gib, then by road up to Valencia. He supplied a licence all the way. A real fat greedy cunt he was."

"Aren't they all. Anyway, this Gonzales is up for bail today, I have a man talking to his lawyer, my partner in the land deals."

"Jez, Jessie? Yes, I met him one time I think."

"That's right, Harold you did, I forgot. Anyway, he's not like us, I don't know how he'll hold up. You see he is the one who handled the money, you know, gave it to this Gonzales fellow."

"I see."

"You always do Harold, anyway, he's been told the councillor will be granted bail tomorrow, around about the two-fifty mark."

"And who's putting this up?" asked Harold. already guessing the answer. Jerry didn't have to reply before the wise owl gave the realisation.

"Which will make it expensive to eliminate the problem."

"Yes."

"Surely this Gonzales has been working with others? Why is it you are the one putting up the bail money?"

"I don't know Harold. I can't very well start a kitty, can I?"

"No, I suppose not. What you can do, in Spain, is apply for the surety back after a period of time, and then take care of business, but will the authorities have accumulated too much by this time?" He did not wait for an answer. He already had it. "I see the dilemma," he said, thinking now for only a few moments before saying what Jerry didn't want to hear. "It seems to me that the problem here is Jez."

Jerry didn't respond. He was deep in thought. This really was a dilemma.

"Which means you could leave the councillor where he is." reasoned Harold.

Jerry's mind was working overtime. Could he kill Jez? Could he bring himself to do such a thing? Yes, he had killed before, on more than one occasion, but there were valid reasons for those acts of violence. What had Jezzie done? Jerry would be killing him to save his own hide, which was half plausible in some respects. But Jez was a friend as well as a business partner. This was too much. He needed time to digest this. He had till 5 pm, that was when Jez would collect the bail money. *Move on Jerry!*

"Do you want to move on, Jerry?" asked Harold, as if reading his mind.

"I think so." he replied "This next scenario, number two, is a little more complex."

"I find that somewhat hard to believe," said Harold.

"Wait till you hear me out. I think even you will be amazed with this one."

"Shall we get a coffee? There's a lovely delicatessen just opened by the port and an even lovelier girl who runs it." he smiled.

"Why not?" said Jerry. "That's a fine stick you have there, Harold," he added, taking it from his friend as the two walked towards the commercial port.

Chapter Fifty

"I am very happy you have decided to stay with us, Mr Wheeler," said Perelta. "Did you have any difficulty convincing your superiors?"

"Yes and No," was Wheeler's reply. The two were now sitting in Perelta's office at The Central Headquarters in Malaga.

"Yes and no?" queried the Spanish detective.

"Yes, I have a number of cases which need my attention back home. My undergraduate is pulling his hair out and basically, what the chaps upstairs are saying is *I was only over here to give a profile. How long does it take?*"

"I see. Would you like me to speak with someone?"

"No. I told them I was staying, I also said that Divine would always be a problem to us in the UK. I hinted at an operation from days gone by which automatically gave me carte blanche."

"Very good, and how long will you be staying with us?"

"Until tomorrow evening, certainly. How many arrests will there be in the morning?"

"In our jurisdiction, eleven. Why do you ask this question, Mr Wheeler?"

"No reason in particular. I would like to attend the raid on Divine's residence if that is at all possible."

"I don't see why not. Would you like to be present when he is interviewed?"

"Yes, I would," said Wheeler before adding, "Would I be able to speak with him alone?"

"You mean just him and you?" asked Perelta, looking somewhat confused.

"Yes," replied Wheeler, disguising his anxiousness.

"I'm not sure, let us talk later. First, we have to catch the rabbit."

"The Fox would be more fitting."

"The Fox." said Perelta "I like that. Come!" he said, standing abruptly, almost giving Wheeler a heart attack. "We are meeting Angelica for lunch. Look at the time, it's almost 2 pm."

Chapter Fifty-One

Stone was fresh and relaxed. He had taken the call from Jerry which allowed him enough time to visit the Spa and take a sauna. He had called Stuli and told him to freshen up and relax for an hour, that the meeting had been delayed, and to brush up on his rehearsals, albeit alone.

He had given Beatrice some time alone. For some reason—which he was having difficulty understanding—he had felt a little sympathy for her. Again, she had made an effort to disguise the marks and bruising with cheap makeup. He wondered why because she would not be leaving the room until he was good and ready to check out.

He checked the time on the TV against his Stainless Daytona Rolex. 1.15 am.

"Baby, I'm going down to the bar."

"You drinking already, Honey? she asked cautiously. Barry was annoyed with the question but decided to let it ride.

"No," he said. "I need some air, this room is claustrophobic. If the phone rings you ask that they divert the call to the bar OK. Give it 30 minutes and call Stuli, tell him to join me in the bar."

"I will, my love," she answered as the door closed behind him, to her relief.

Chapter Fifty-Two

"And, obviously, it is this chap Barry you are late to meet?" asked Harold, taking hold of a rose gold Albert chain attached to his waistcoat buttonhole, he pulled it gently to reveal a Bruget half-hunter, he pressed the winder, which opened the case for him to see the time was almost 1.30 pm. Jerry smiled. The old man had listened to what the younger one had had to say, only once interrupting the one-sided conversation to order fresh coffee.

"Nice little touch, Harold," said Jerry, admiring the timepiece.

"The watch? Yes," he said, pressing a small button and leaning towards his friend. He smiled as the chimes rang out.

"Unbelievable," said Jerry. "very nice and yes, It is Barry." He looked at the porcelain dial. "Actually, I'm late," he added, getting to his feet.

"We need to talk some more, Jerry. By all means, go and see your resurrected friend. It costs nothing to listen. Don't commit yourself, kid. No hasty decisions, eh? I know your predicament requires action, but action comes in many forms nowadays, there are opportunities out there for making money. Remember, liberty is paramount. Come back and see me, Jerry. We still need to talk about the first dilemma."

"I know," said Jerry "What a fucking mess. I'll be needing papers, Harold. I have a feeling I may be heading out of here tonight."

"I will have them ready for you, my friend. Don't call, just come back to the shop, I'll wait in for you. There will be answers, opinions, advice, it's up to you if you take it." He stood now to shake Jerry's hand. Jerry thanked him, walked from the coffee shop and out into a day that he was struggling to get his head around. He was not surprised to feel like some of the burden was lifted from him after having spoken to his friend and mentor.

Chapter Fifty-Three

Jerry took a taxi to The Rock Hotel. His mind was racing, undecided, in turmoil, but he had to compose himself as he walked through the rotating doors and into the Hotel. He could see Barry seated at the bar with a fat guy. Jerry swept the foyer, reception and the remainder of the bar with his eyes as he walked casually over to join the two sitting on the bar stools. Barry smiled through the mirrors and swivelled around to greet his friend. The two shook hands warmly before Jerry was introduced to Stuli.

"Shall we take a table?" asked Barry. "Have you eaten Jerry? A salad, maybe?"

"No, I'm fine, thank you. I'm sorry about the delay, something cropped up."

"No problem, Jerry," said Barry. "What can I get you to drink?"

"Just a water for me, please. Listen. Barry. I don't want to be rude," he said, looking first at his friend and then smiling at Stuli, who was now looking at Barry in confusion. Jerry continued, "but can we cut to the chase here, I really do have to be making tracks as soon as possible."

"Yeah, sure, Jerry. Come, let's sit in the corner, it's so much cooler inside." He turned to the barman. "Three more waters, please. Could you bring them over to the table?"

"Certainly, Sir."

"So!" said Barry placing a hand on Jerry's shoulder as they began to stroll over to a table in the quiet corner. "What have you been up to then?"

Jerry didn't answer, instead he nodded towards Stuli, who was struggling to release himself from the barstool. Barry smiled apologetically, turned and held out his hand, which Stuli took and pulled himself free.

"Your water, gentlemen." said the waiter placing three glasses topped with ice and lemon on the low table. "Can I get you anything else?" he asked, putting a large jug of water in the middle.

"No, thank you." said Barry. The waiter left, and Stuli filled the glasses from the jug. The tremor of the Jew's hand was duly noted by Jerry.

"Are you OK, Jerry?" asked Barry. "You seem preoccupied."

"I'm fine, Barry. Why am I here?"

"OK," said Barry, leaning over and looking directly at his friend. "I have two operations to talk with you about. Number One involves Stuli here." he said, looking at the fat man and placing a hand firmly on his thigh. Jerry looked at the fat Jew, who was sweating profusely. Barry continued.

"We can tell you about number one. If you are interested, Stuli here can leave us, and I can give you the preliminaries on number two. Number two is the big one, Jerry, but we need to look at the first one to finance number two. Don't get me wrong, Jerry, number one is alright, there's plenty in it for all of us, but number two is going to cost a nice few quid to set up and unless we get an earner, no one's going to put any hands in pockets to finance the big one."

"Yes, I see," said Jerry, listening to reason.

"So!" said Barry, sitting back in his chair. "Stuli here has a brother in the diamond business based in Antwerp."

Jerry listened to the information given with complete authority. Stuli did a good job and both Jerry and Barry were impressed. A plan was drawn from memory by Stuli in Jerry's direction. Barry could see how Jerry's mind was working. There were enthuses on the waterways. Stuli was having difficulty here but assured the two that the factory was surrounded by the canal system. Jerry asked Barry the usual and familiar questions. The manager? Number of administration staff? Cutters? Layout of internal structure. Times in and out. Alarm systems, positions of panic buttons (if any). Deliveries of merchandise. Cut off points to meet orders, etc. There was little point in robbing the place and leaving with the majority of stones uncut.

Toli, Abi. Malkit Sandu, they were all mentioned and vetted, details were given reluctantly, again this was detected by Jerry. The domestic circumstances of his brother were discussed and much, much more.

Jerry was satisfied that the source material was genuine. He was happy with the basics but was not in a position to give the green light at this initial stage. He thanked Stuli and asked him to leave him and Barry to discuss other business. Stuli looked relieved to be leaving the table. He picked his weight up from the comfortable chair with agility Barry hadn't seen from him before. The briefing had taken only thirty-five minutes, and the minimal notes taken were lodged in Jerry's head. Even when Jerry had effortlessly turned the conversation into a social aspect, Barry knew he was still hard at work. He retrieved from Stuli information on a domestic level, but this was still as vital to Jerry as the water surrounding the factory. Barry was more than impressed with Jerry's professionalism; he certainly hadn't lost his touch.

Now, with Stuli absent from the table, Barry asked Jerry what he thought about what he had just heard. Jerry picked up the paper Stuli had drawn the plan on and tore it into small pieces, which he discarded in the ashtray. He told Barry he liked it and to move on. Barry was more than willing to move on. He wasn't perturbed by Jerry checking his watch regularly. He was keen, eager and thrilled.

"Depending on how you would like to tackle Antwerp will decide who we call into play." he started. He moved forward in his chair and rested his elbows on his knees.

"I know you were interested in the water, Jerry, which leads me to believe you were thinking of… Jet Skis? Small boat, maybe? We looked at Holland before, do you remember? The kidnap?" Jerry nodded.

Barry continued,"I have no problem with Winston, we will need him for the mechanics, O'Rourke and McNess too, but Hutchins out Jerry. You know what I think of him? He's too unpredictable, compulsive. He's dangerous, Jerry. Plus the South Mimms thing, fuck knows how he'll respond to me springing up."

"Let's leave that in abeyance for now, Barry. Nothing's set in stone here; give me the second job."

"OK, Jerry." Barry lifted his glass to his lips and looked at his old friend over the top of it as he took a large gulp. There was a hint of consideration and hesitation, which, again, was not lost on Jerry.

"Play the ace, Barry. You've come this far."

"I know Jerry. Alright, here it is, mate." Again, there was a slight pause. "It's here," he said, leaning back now in the comfort of the chair, each arm overlapping the rests and his hands pointing down to the floor. He smiled knowingly, as though he was the one to solve the puzzle.

"Here?" asked Jerry. "In this hotel?"

"Here! In Gibraltar, Jerry. September. I have inside knowledge direct from the source of the largest movement of cash that this Island has ever seen!"

"I'm not with you, Barry, tell me more." It was Jerry's turn to move his body forward.

"Every week, the majority of the money generated on the Rock, from a whole spectrum of businesses, different concerns, from tourism to sales, you name it, all the money banked on this relatively small Island is transferred by road to Madrid. A multiple of currency, the dollar, sterling, yen, euro, of course, and everything else, but monopoly. Those cruise ships, Jerry, come from all over the place. The Banco-de-change alone. These people don't change their hard-earned cash on the boat, do they fuck? They do it here, on the island, for a pittance of a better rate and believe me, it's not just the steak pie and beer they spend it on. The gold, diamonds, tax-free this, that and the other, it's big money, Jerry, and that's every week, by road. But that's not it, Jerry." Jerry was now the one getting excited. He took a drink from his glass without once taking his eyes from Barry. Barry, too, was now leaning forward on the edge of his seat, making the two conspirators look exactly that. Jerry raised his eyebrows. Barry continued.

"In September, starting on the 1st and finishing on the 30th, there will be a convention. A massive convention. Here. In Gib. All the Spanish are coming down from Madrid. Talks are going on with regard to this fucking place, there has been for years. Who owns it? Do the Spanish want it back from British rule? Anyway, fuck that, who gives a fuck, what matters to us is the fact that throughout September, there will be no movement—that's vehicular—no commercial movement by truck coming in or out of Gibraltar. This is solely for security reasons. There's talk of the King of Spain coming down, British politicians, too, taking part in the talks. You can imagine the security. But, the boats, they stay the same Jerry. The cruise ships still come. All the provisions will be brought in by boat. I do know, Jerry, that on the first Saturday, after the convention, rallies, whatever, that the money will be moved from the Island by air."

"Helicopter?"

"Plane. Too much for a helicopter, Jerry. The bulk, used notes, you'd need half a dozen of the cunts."

"Fucking hell, Barry. How solid is this information?"

"As solid as the rock we're sitting on, my old friend."

"If I go for this, you're going to have to give me more, Barry."

"I'm ready when you are Jerry."

"How long do I have?"

"Before you make a decision?"

"Yes."

"It needs to be quick, Jerry, two, three days."

"Alright. Leave it with me. You staying here till then?"

"Yes."

"I'll be in touch." Jerry said, standing to leave. Barry looked disappointed.

"I thought maybe we could have a drink," he said, also standing. "You know? catch up? It would be great to talk with you, Jerry." he looked sheepishly at his more confident, ex-partner in crime. "Kath, the girls, my team. Do you see them, Jerry? Jane and my two?"

Jerry didn't answer. He wanted to tell his friend he should have thought of them before he chose to do the deal. He looked at him; he seemed to be pleading with those eyes that couldn't change. The desperation was so evident in them.

"Another time," said Jerry. "I'll be in touch. Say goodbye to your friend for me…what's his name again?"

"Jerry, you're talking to me," said Barry seriously.

"I'll be in touch. If it's a positive Hutchins in…" Jerry could see the disappointment on his friend's face.

"You're the boss," said Barry under his breath as Jerry stood abruptly and turned to leave.

"Just one more thing," Jerry said, turning back.

"Go on." offered Barry

"What's the estimate?"

"Minimum, Thirty Mil."

"Thirty Mil?" he wanted to make sure he had heard Barry correctly.

"Sounds more when you say it twice, doesn't it? That's a minimum." Barry assured him. "Could be more. All used notes, mate; untraceable."

"Keep that phone on," instructed Jerry before adding. "I'll want an in-depth on this one."

"I know, Jerry. I have it."

"Later!" said Jerry as he walked confidently away.

"Later." repeated Barry to the departing figure.

Chapter Fifty-Four

Jerry took a handkerchief from his pocket and cleaned a small section of the window, enough for him to peep through and see Harold wearing a brown smock coat and cleaning the brass face of a grandfather clock. He tapped lightly on the window and startled the old man. Jerry laughed and entered the shop.

"Fuck me, Jerry, you nearly gave me an heart attack." It was only then, at that moment, that Jerry imagined what a great loss that would be.

"I'm sure you've had bigger shocks than that."

"Yea, I suppose you're right, but I'm not getting any younger, son. I can't ride them like I used to."

"What, the girls?"

"I wish! Can't remember the last time."

"Why don't you get to one of those clubs, Harold, and empty the balls now and again?"

"No, not me, kid. I'd sooner polish one of these old clocks, something worthwhile. Besides, there's only one fuck in me, and it's holding me together. Come on, let's go up stairs." he said, smiling as he reached for a key hidden in the mechanism of the works behind the clock face.

"Did you bring yours?" he asked. Jerry confirmed he did by taking it from his pocket and holding it up.

Harold removed the dusty overalls as the two walked through the maze of furniture to the back room, filled with more stock.

"Do you ever sell much of this junk?"

"Junk! Junk!" he responded, throwing the dusty cloth at a wall-mounted fox. "I'll have you know there's a right few quid in here."

"Yea, and a load of dust and shit. I always feel like I want a good bath when I've been here," said Jerry brushing down his trousers.

"You remember the number?" asked Harold as he pressed the combination on the security pad to gain access to the living quarters upstairs.

"7224. Your old prison number." Jerry answered. Harold laughed.

"Correct. You're the only one who has it, Jerry, and believe me, you'd need it to gain entry, this place is like fort-fucking-knox. If anything should happen to me up here and you weren't about, they'd have to come in through the roof." The two of them laughed as they mounted the stairs.

If there was ever a contrast, it was here now, in this place. The difference from downstairs to up was so extreme, one had to take a moment to compose oneself. Harold clapped his hands lightly, and the room automatically lit up, showing a lounge which was spotlessly clean with all the mod cons, a black and chrome leather settee was fixed to the far wall and extended halfway into the centre of the room in an arc shape, dark glass and chrome fittings rising above a white marble floor gave the whole room a futuristic theme, Bang and Olufson music and cinematic equipment adorned the place. Harold pressed a digital pad on the wall, which produced some piped music. He walked over to a bar situated in the far corner, which must have been above the boarded-up shop two doors away from the dusty windows of the antique shop, and poured the two of them a large brandy.

"Use this sink," said Harold, indicating the one behind the bar.

"Where's the tap?" asked Jerry, moving in behind the smaller man.

"No taps, son, they're only to clean. Just pop your hands in the sink, the water comes on automatically."

"You don't mind cleaning old clocks but no taps, eh Harold?"

The old man laughed and passed the Waterford-cut brandy glass to Jerry. "Cheers!" he said as the two checked the crystal which left a ring hanging in the air above the low-sounding music.

"Cheers," said Jerry. "This place Harold, it's so clinical, like a hospital, so clean. Do you stay here much?"

"Not really, Jerry. If I'm tired, I get my head down, I very rarely sleep in the bed, just doss out on the couch there. Do you fancy a massage? Come on, sit down here next to me."

The two of them took their positions on the suite, and Harold selected an easy orthopaedic massage.

"To be honest with you, Jerry, I struggle to get a good night's sleep anywhere but the old house." He took a larger-than-small gulp of brandy, which made him grimace before he continued. "Do you know, I don't know if I've told you this, but when I came back from doing that bit of bird with you, I had very little left. The old man was astute enough to have the big house in a trust which prevented the cunts from taking it, but there you go!" he finished by draining the remainder of the warm liquid. "That's it for me now." he said, taking his glass behind the bar. He washed it and dried it before replacing it on the glass shelf.

"One glass a day does me. Any more, and I start forgetting things." He leaned on the bar and looked over at Jerry, who was still seated on the comfortable settee, with his head pressed into the kid's hide and his eyes closed.

"Nice, eh Jerry?"

"Fucking glorious, Harold. How much was this?"

"I had it made, a nice few quid, I can tell ya."

"I'll bet. My team would love this."

"Right, Jerry fuck the suite, save your money, if anything should happen to me, you can take it."

"Can I have that in writing?" laughed Jerry, now with open eyes and looking at Harold.

"Back to business, Jerry. We can either go out for a walk again, or we can talk here. What would you like to do? Before you answer, may I remind you that I had the place swept professionally only last week, I have a machine here also," he lifted a small black box with LEC lights attached, plugged it into a socket and waited till the green light illuminated.

"You see the green light?" he asked. Jerry acknowledged that he did. "This prevents any frequency or radio, including phones, activating within 50 metres." he laughed as he recalled. "Before I bought the three shops adjacent to this one, I used to cause so much disruption when I used this machine," he said, tapping the box.

"All the mobiles and landlines would go down." he chuckled "The amount of time I saw the maintenance appear. Look," he said, now returning to sit next to Jerry. He showed him his mobile, which had no signal on it.

"Yes, that's fine," said Jerry. "We'll stay here."

"Right," said Harold, looking straight ahead. "I've been giving this some serious thought. That's what it needs," he added, looking now at Jerry sitting next to him.

"I have one or two options, none without reason, may I add, but they are suggestions, Jerry, for you to consider. Now let's look at the first scenario. I haven't given the second one much thought, to be honest. What has been discussed at your most recent meeting can stay with you. I'm sure you know what you are doing, and I have faith in your judgement. Just be careful, Jerry. Your friend did a deal, for whatever reason, he did a deal, and for that reason alone, you can never fully, one hundred per cent trust him. I know you know this." he finished by tapping Jerry on his thigh.

"Now then," he paused slightly, remembering, choosing his words carefully, he continued, "Scenario one, this, I see to be more of an issue, unlike scenario two, where you have a choice, this one you don't. You are in, and you have to get out. To get out, I mean to eliminate any obstacle which sees you prosecuted, remember, liberty is paramount. By not being prosecuted, you retain your assets, assets I may add that you have risked your life to gain." Again, the old man paused, this time a little longer.

"We know where the politician is?" He looked at Jerry, who confirmed with a nod. Harold knew how and what to say. He also knew that although the apartment they were now talking in had been electronically swept, with the addition of the mechanism he had produced himself, Jerry would still be reluctant to talk.

"We let your friend, J, run for now," Harold knew this was what his friend wanted to hear. "Without the 250, may I add." he looked at Jerry, who raised his eyebrows. "Instead, we…" he made a cut-throat motion with his forefinger across his own throat. "The politician."

"How?" asked Jerry

"I have some Columbian friends who have people in there, some of which have little prospect of seeing daylight. They have families back home who are hungry." he again looked at Jerry. "Need I say more?"

Jerry shook his head.

"What about the consequences?" he said as an afterthought.

"For you?" asked the wise old man. "You're in a no-win situation, my friend. Only you can decide. I can only give the options and advice. The only other possibility is your friend."

Jerry stayed silent. Harold asked the question. "Do you want to know what I would do?"

Jerry didn't answer but instead looked at the old man. Harold didn't have to think about the answer.

"I would take the politician." he said.

Jerry stayed focused on Harold and nodded in agreement.

"I'll take care of it. You need to go away. Tonight." he added. "Do you have business elsewhere?"

"Yes." Jerry answered before asking the question. "Do they have flights to Liverpool from Gib?"

"No." said Harold. "Manchester, I could make a call, check the times."

"Good. I have luggage already there."

"Where? In Gib, How? Were you flying out anyway?"

"I knew there would be a more than average chance, I blagged the girl on the information desk earlier."

"I like your style, Jerry." said Harold, standing up. "What did I do with that handset?"

"I seen one behind the bar." answered Jerry.

"Do you know, I'd forget my balls if they weren't in a bag. Ah! Here it is." he said, retrieving the phone and dialling the number.

"8.30 pm." he repeated from the handset. "Arriving in Manchester at 10.15." Jerry nodded in an agreement. Harold thanked the girl by name and hung up. "Give me two minutes. I'll get my coat. We have our keys, so we can go to the box. Do we need to go to the box? I have your papers here."

"No. I have enough money. Do you have credit cards with the papers?"

"Yes."

"Well, we can leave the box. I'll keep my key with me, though, in fact," he said as an afterthought. "I'll take the London box key from you."

"OK. let me get your papers."

"This case is x-ray proof, carbon paper lined." said Harold, opening the small Hermes leopard skin case. "You see this?" he said, taking a credit card from his own wallet, pushing it into one of the six allocated slits in the silk lining and pressing it down firmly. The interior lining gave way with a click to reveal a secret compartment with two passports and matching driver's licences. Other documentation was there to support the identification, medical papers, national security numbers, etc.

"You leave Mr Divine here, Jerry. He is about to become red hot in the not-to-distant future. It may be an idea to leave me your key? I'll make sure everything goes in the box." Jerry gave him the key without question this time, and Harold gave him one back that he had retrieved from some undisclosed hiding place.

"You kick on Jerry, call me in 7 days. Are you sure you have enough money?"

"Yes, I'll be fine. I'll be looking up some old friends, if I run out, they'll take care of me; besides, I have some nice pieces put away with Martin McNess; if I have to, I can always pull something out and knock it in. Come here, you!" he added, opening his arms and moving close to his friend. He took the small frame in his arms and squeezed just enough to let him know he cared.

"What you going to do now? You have a few hours to kill."

"I don't know. Maybe go for a walk or take a tourist cab up to see the monkeys, time to think, you know?"

"Yes, good idea. Do you want me to check in on Kath and the girls while you're away? Maybe have someone watch the house?" asked Harold.

"No, thank you. I'll have my driver look in on them should it be necessary."

"OK, Jerry. Goodbye, and good luck. Let yourself out, you know the number. Try not to worry. Oh! One other thing,"

"Yes."

"Those bits you have put away, anything nice for me?"

Jerry smiled.

"Goodbye, Harold. Three or four days, I'll call you." he looked back before the door closed behind him and was a little surprised to see Harold pouring himself another brandy. Odd; maybe there's one or two things Harold would like to forget…

Chapter Fifty-Five

Wheeler was content with the 2 o'clock luncheon meeting. The same day, arrangements were made for him to make his own way to the Central Policia Station at 4 am. He would be briefed and supplied with a bulletproof vest first and foremost before other safety and precautionary measures would be considered. It was too late in the day to make the formal application for Wheeler to be issued with a firearm, but he agreed with Angelica. It would make more sense to attend the meeting that preceded the raid on Divine's villa. Though he was disappointed about not being issued with a firearm. This could have been an opportunity missed. Any chance of eliminating Divine would make his life a little less complicated. As long as Divine and Stone were around there was always the risk that the truth could come out in regards to the missing documents.

The next best thing was the fact that Perelta had provisionally agreed to let Wheeler speak with Divine alone. *But what about Stone? Where was he? And why was he meeting Divine?*

Wheeler spent the rest of the day sitting in the hotel foyer, looking at the newspapers and ordering coffee. Wheeler was only too aware that, out of the two, he would get more sense from Stone. He was still holding the photographic evidence that Stone would pay dividends to keep them hidden away. With a bit of luck, the Spanish authorities will discover his whereabouts.

"You staying here tonight, Mr Wheeler?" asked Angelica. "May I join you?" she said, taking a seat opposite him.

"That would be a pleasure," said Wheeler, after she had already seated.

"You not finished work yet?" he asked.

"When do we ever." she smiled.

"Yes you're right; a detectives work is never complete." he studied her features for a second and thought before throwing caution to the wind.

"You know, when I first met you, at the airport, I thought you were a stewardess. I honestly didn't have you down for a detective." Before she could answer he added, "Now that's meant to be a compliment because where I come from, we don't make female police officers like you." As soon as he had said it, he wished that he hadn't, and he could now feel the blood rushing to his face with embarrassment. *Did it sound cheap? What a fucking idiot!*

As if she hadn't heard him, or as good as she was with detection, she answered, only, the part before the cheap compliment, as though it was never delivered in the first place.

"You have only to look at the papers" she said "they are full of crime. You see this one, Mr Wheeler?" she asked, referring to a young boy pictured on the front page of the local sheet.

"Yes," he said, rearranging the paper to look at the report again. "Sixteen years of age," he reflected, "I have grandchildren the same age."

"You do? Maybe you feel the impact," she said, looking sombre. She touched the face of the victim. "I have a brother this age, he too is called Jesepi, he lives with my father." she paused for a split second, as if to consider something more. Wheeler smiled considerately, he didn't push. "My parents are separated," she concluded.

"I'm sorry."

"No need, Mr Wheeler. They are alive, and there is harmony. It works."

Wheeler looked again at the photo fit of the murder suspect accompanying the story. He couldn't help but feel some connection. For some odd but demur moment, the crude picture looked familiar. Stupid, he knew, but, nevertheless, the intuition was there.

Chapter Fifty-Six

Jerry walked back to the coffee shop. He and Harold had left earlier, and ordered himself a black coffee with a touch of brandy. There were two stainless steel tables with chairs placed on the pavement by the entrance. He asked the girl to bring the drink outside, where he positioned himself with his back to the window. It was a sun trap, to say the least, but it was nice to see the people walking by without a care in the world. He envied them sometimes. Victor came to mind, and Jerry gave a rye smile as he reminded himself how things weren't going to plan.

Almost an hour passed, but it wasn't wasted as Jerry's mind had worked overtime. It didn't matter where he went. What mattered was that he made himself scarce for a few days, at the very least. After careful deliberation, he decided to call Abdul. Sitting there for the last hour had confirmed there was no unwelcome attention, so it might be an idea to catch the shuttle helicopter—the one Abdul had mentioned—from Malaga to Ceuta, then fly from Morocco directly into the UK. He still had over 3 hours to go before the flight to Manchester was due to leave. He could call in and apologise to the nice girl at the desk. She may be required another time.

He asked the waitress if he could use the telephone, and she was kind enough to oblige. Jerry let the phone ring for quite some time before Abdul answered. He knew only too well how these Arabs liked to sleep through the day.

"Hello, Gringo,"

"Ah! Hello, my friend. How is you?"

"I'm good," said Jerry carefully, as was Abdul; he, too, did not address one and other by name.

"And with what do I owe the pleasure of this call."

"There has been a slight change of plan. Nothing for you to worry about. I have decided to come and see you after all, sooner rather than later. As a matter of fact, as soon as this evening, if the shuttle service is available that is."

"Shuttle, my friend?"

"Yes, the flight shuttle, there is a reason I have decided to come this route," he replied, having already thought about how this route might come in handy one day.

"Whichever way this pleases you, my friend. Please call me, and I will be waiting for you. You will walk through the border. Ignore anyone offering you assistance. They will rob you as soon as they look at you, my friend. Push the taxi away, they will make a terrible nuisance. It is advisable to give the customs man a little Dinar, three or four euros worth; that is all, my friend. This will speed up your entrance. Shalom al a cum amigo."

Jerry listened to the advice and assured Abdul he would take and use it and call him later. He handed the waitress back the telephone, paid his bill with a generous tip and asked her to call a cab. Twenty minutes later, he was at the same desk where he had left his luggage earlier. The girl was kind enough to call Malaga airport and check on the helicopter flight times to Morocco.

"20.45, Sir. I can book it for you now?" she asked, holding her hand over the mouthpiece and looking at Jerry for an answer. "There are only two seats available, and they are likely to go."

"Yes, please. That's so kind." smiled Jerry.

"No problem. What name is it, please?"

Damn! realised Jerry. He hadn't taken one of the new passports from secret compartment. He looked at his watch.

"I'm sorry love, I may have to make a quick call before I confirm. Could you ask if they will hold a seat for 5, maybe 10 minutes at the most please?"

The girl spoke in Spanish before telling Jerry that they would, but 10 minutes was the maximum. He moved quickly to the public phone booth and called Kath. He suddenly remembered the case with the money left in the garage. He had to tell her not to give it to Jez when he called at 5 this evening. There was no reply at home. He called her mobile. No reply. He left a message with the instruction before squatting down and opening the briefcase. Once he had retrieved one of the passports, he quickly noted the name and made his way back to the girl who was waiting for him.

"I'm sorry pet. Yes," he said, "Could you book it for me please?"

"Yes sure" she smiled "What name is it?"

"Vine, D Vine"

"D?"

"Daniel."

"Thank you, sir."

Very clever Harold, thought Jerry, as he picked up his luggage.

"You won't need a passport, Sir, because your flight is internal, but you may be asked to show your identification before boarding."

"Thank you very much pet, you've been an absolute diamond."

He offered her 20 euros as she handed him his departure time confirmation; she refused the offer but thanked him, gracefully. He made his way back through Gibraltar customs and walked a short distance to the underground car park. He made one last call to Abdul from a phone booth and relayed the landing schedule before flooring the Mercedes accelerator all the way to Malaga. Again he called Kath from the car phone. This time she answered, she was out shopping with the girls and was unhappy with the instruction—especially if Jez was expecting to collect something—she agreed with Jerry to stay out and Miss Jezzie's call. That done, Jerry relaxed a little, turned up the music and pushed even further down on the gas.

He parked the car in the short-stay, as near to the entrance as possible and was about to do the same with the ticket and keys as he had done in La Linea when his personal phone rung.

"Jesus, Jerry, the car, it's gone! Did anyone see you put the keys on the wheel? These little scallywags down here have had it away Jerry, what the fuck will I do? Will I call the police? Did you have anything in it? I am in the right place, aren't I? You should have let me drive you down here. Why didn't you call me?"

"Shut the fuck up!" called Jerry. "And calm down. I'm in the car."

"Tank fuck. Where are yer? Do you need me for any ting?"

"Yes. Same situation, Malaga short-stay."

"Where you going? Macrony wants to talk to you. What'll I tell him?"

"I'm away for a few days. You don't know where and I'll call him in a day or two." With that Jerry hung up the phone, removed the battery and SIM card, swapped it for a new one from the glove compartment and made his way toward the domestic flights and heliport.

He didn't call Macrony, or anyone else for that matter. He could do without any distractions. He did consider calling Harold to ask him to collect the money from Kath but decided against it. He would call him tomorrow; it would be at least another day or two before any raids and so long as the money was picked up before lunch tomorrow… that would be fine. No distractions. He had his plan set out. Morocco tonight, straight down to business, talks into the early hours even; any visits, any meetings could take place all day tomorrow. Get as much wrapped up as possible and be out of there late evening or, at the very latest, early the next day.

Chapter Fifty-Seven

Barry had spent the remainder of the day sitting at the bar brooding. He was happy in some respects but unhappy in others. Yes, he had established old ties, which had been, surprisingly, relatively easy. He had pulled it off and regained Jerry's confidence, to a degree, anyway. Barry was not stupid; he understood better than anyone how Jerry Divine's mind worked. What Barry had beef with was the fact that Jerry was, and always has been, the one calling the shots.

He was feeling level-headed, regretting drinking more brandy than water—bored more than anything, but still level-headed. Stuli had retired by the pool some hours previously, leaving Barry alone to study. Now, as he finished eating his second club sandwich in as many hours, he checked the time, 10 minutes past 7. His mind wandered back to last night's events. The boy. Barry was disappointed, disappointed that he had no recollection of what actually happened in the room. How the boy died? Was it an overdose? Maybe some drug contamination? Barry was certainly aware of the consequences of dirty shit. Or had it been him? If so, how?

Remembering the kid, Barry had seen no evidence of foul play. Suffocation? A good possibility. Barry had had every intention of killing the kid, that was for sure. Sitting here now in the luxury surrounds of the hotel he felt no remorse, no pity for the kid. This world was a million miles away from the squalid conditions he had left the boy in, and yet Barry so much wanted to be back there. He knew he was sick. Not evil, he wasn't evil, he was ill—warped maybe but he liked it. He made his mind up, right there and then, to venture back up to Torremolinos tonight and get himself another victim. Only this time, he would drink less alcohol and take no drugs. He would be in control. Savour every moment. He would take Stuli. It didn't matter what Stuli might witness. He had Stuli well and truly where he wanted him, by the short and curlies.

Chapter Fifty-Eight

Jezzie made one more attempt to call Kath on her mobile phone. He had been calling Jerry for most of the day and had given up trying. Now, as of the last six attempts, Kath's phone went straight to voicemail. Either she had it turned off, or she, too, was avoiding him. He hoped it was the former as he left yet another message on the voicemail.

"Kath, it's Jez. I'm outside yours. I was supposed to collect something from Jerry. I've called him but no joy, maybe he's gone away. Has he left a message for me? Please call me Kath. I'm at my wit's end here, call me Kath!"

Kath took the phone, yet again, from her handbag and turned it on. There were six more voicemails and two text messages from Jezzie. She blushed with embarrassment; this was not her, not her way of doing things. She would undoubtedly be having words with Jerry.

"Can we go home, mum?" cried little Julie.

"Yes love, give it another 10 minutes, and we can go home."

"What is it, mum?" asked Jasmine, looking at her mother with concern as opposed to anger or frustration. She could see her mum was in a dilemma and was reluctant to add to it.

"Your father's put me in a predicament. That's all love. Jez is at home waiting for us, he has come to collect some documents that daddy's decided not to give him, that's all."

"Let's go, mum, please!" cried Julie.

"Can't you just tell him daddy hasn't left them?" asked Jasmine.

"Come on then, girls," said Kath, resigning to the fact she has to go home sometime. Surely Jez should take the hint, she thought angrily.

Jezzie saw the Range Rover and breathed a massive sigh of relief. He knew better than to show his anger and frustration, so stepped from the car with a strained smile. He was annoyed that the welcome was not returned and more so when the Jeep hardly stopped to let the gates fully open before driving into the entrance and directly through the garage door that opened automatically. He made his way to the gates and slipped through before they shut him out.

"Let me help you with those bags."

"It's fine Jez, we can manage," she replied, looking nervously toward the desk positioned in the far corner at the rear of the garage.

"I insist," he said, relieving Kath of the heavy load.

"I've come to collect something." he said as the two of them walked across the yard and entered the house. Kath put down the shopping and tapped the security code into the alarm.

"I'm sorry Jezzie, I have no instruction to give you anything." she replied. Jez could see she was unhappy with the situation but had to press the issue.

"Can you call Jerry, please?" he asked, following her into the kitchen, where she emptied the bags and placed the shopping into the cupboards. There was an uneasy silence. Kath didn't reply. She was angry, not with Jezzie so much, but the situation—she wasn't used to this. She decided to come clean.

"Jez, I don't know what it is you were supposed to collect, but I have been told to give you nothing. I'm sorry, Jezzie; you will have to take this up with Jerry when he comes back."

"You don't underst…"

"I don't want to understand!" she screamed, slamming the cupboard door.

"Mum!" cried Julie, standing in the doorway holding Bonito.

"Kath! Please! Calm down, love." said Jez, moving closer to embrace her. "There, What is it, pet?"

"I'm sorry, Jez." she wept.

"It's alright, Kath. What's wrong, love?"

"Nothing, Jez, just leave us, eh? I'm sorry, Jez, things have just been a little hectic."

"That's alright, love," he said gingerly, handing her a paper towel.

"Ask Jerry to call me. And you call Demitra if you need anything, ok?"

"I will Jez. I'm sorry, Julie. Let Jez out, please." Kath just knew there was something seriously amiss in their perfect life and that something was brimming to the boil.

Jez left the Villa, got into his car and made a call to Brogonia, the solicitors clerk. When he received no reply, he called Demitra, again he received no response so he left a message for her to call him back.

He stayed stationary outside the large villa, almost seeking sanctuary from the high wall surrounding it. There was very little traffic that used this road; the villas along it were few, each having the benefit of space between them. How he wished Jerry would come home. He was reluctant to call him because other than asking him for the money—the money which Jerry had decided to hold on to—there was very little else to say. He looked at his watch, he looked again to check, yes, he had been seated outside Jerry's home for almost 4 hours, 3 before Kath arrived and 1 after leaving her in such a state. Again he called Demitra, again, no reply, *damn!*

He had listened to the interview tape, three times, and it was true what Jerry had said; it would be a good idea to leave, get away for a day or two. He had asked Demitra, but she flatly refused, so there was no way he could go anywhere without her. Maybe David would fancy a trip fishing? He could call him in Madrid and tell him to leave the venture he had allocated to him? Just two days ago, Jez had sent David to look at a property deal—how things could change in such a short period of time. He dialled his son's number, realising this was, out of desperation.

"Dad?"

"Hello, Son. How is things going up there?"

"Not too good, I'm afraid, Dad. There are some preservation issues with the building. I don't think we will get the permission to demolish." *They say it comes in threes.*

"Come home, David."

"No way Dad, not yet, I have a meeting in two days time, I'm trying to resolve the problem. Is everything ok, dad?" Jezzie didn't answer. "Dad, hello, Dad, Are you there?"

"I'm here, David." replied Jez quietly, "I love you, Son."

"I love you too, Dad."

Jezzie waited till the line went dead then let the phone drop between his legs.

Why did he feel so alone? He looked into the rear-view mirror and wiped away the tears which were now forming and threatening to run down his cheeks. He wasn't stupid! He told himself this in the red eyes that looked back at him. He was the one who handed over the money. He was the one who did the negotiations with Gonzales. The interviewing officers seemed to make this point clear when interrogating the councillor. *Yes, Jerry was the clever one, alright.*

10.45 pm. Where was Demitra? Surely, the police hadn't been to his home already. He couldn't go home. Not until he had spoken to Dem. He had driven away from Jerry's house less than 30 minutes when he stopped the car at a filling station, filled the tank and bought a bottle of whiskey. The cashier asked him in Spanish if he was alright. He thanked her, held the bottle up, smiled and told her he wasn't.

Driving up the narrow mountain road toward home, almost 3000 feet above sea level, he drove through a gateless entrance to a partially built Finca. The workmen would be here around 8 am; that was the norm, and he didn't want to be alone for too long. He was still unsure, after subconsciously making up his mind, whether he could go through with this and asked again for God's help. He knew there was no-way he could ever do a prison sentence. He parked the car off the makeshift drive and around the back of the windowless house. A sea view. He wound down the two front car windows and let the breeze come through. The only sounds were the crickets and some night birds. It was so peaceful. Would it soon be like this forever?

Taking the top from the whiskey bottle, he took a large gulp and let the warm liquid slowly enter his body. He grimaced at the strength and again looked at himself in the mirror, again, there were tears; this time, he let them find their own way down his face to rest on the collar of his shirt. *What have I done?* He turned on the stereo. Matt Monroe, the bus driver, his favourite crooner. He smiled, *life, Was it so wonderful?*

The bottle was empty, he was drunk, he was determined. Getting out of the car, he stumbled to the trunk and sorted through the tools and junk until he found what he was looking for. He had already placed the hosepipe in the dirt beside his feet and the grey electrical tape in his trouser pocket, now, with three cable ties secured by his teeth, he stumbled and bent down to unravel a few metres from the hose. Taking a small rock in his hand, he placed the hose on a larger rock and beat it several times with the stone in his hand, almost taking his thumb off in his attempts, to divide the pipe.

He inserted the damaged end of the hose into the exhaust and secured it with the tape, moving around to the rear door furthest away from the driving seat. He fed the pipe through the window and taped up the gap left by the tube. He stood unsteadily on his alcohol-infused legs and surveyed the operation up to scratch, *tape the doors*, yes, he stuck a strip of the tape down the exterior gap between the front and rear doors of the passenger side and then along the top and bottom, he decided to leave the drivers side as he was more than sure that having filled the tank with petrol there would be more than enough time and carbon monoxide to gain the result he was craving.

He searched the glove box for a pen, having taken a scrap of paper from his pocket, mumbling and fidgeting; he didn't find one, so he scribbled with his finger on the dusty bonnet that he was sorry and that he would wait for Demitra and David.

The tears were dry but the sobs commenced as he started the engine and turned up the music. He moved the seat back as far as the mechanics would allow and bent forward to secure his feet together with one of the three ties. Once they were secure, he put one of the other two ties loosely around the steering wheel and then placed one of his hands to the wheel. Closing the driver's door, he did the final act which would prevent any escape; it would prevent him from either reopening the door or window and so would secure his intentions. He placed his free hand into the prepared loop and took the end of the cable tie into the grip of his teeth and pulled back.

Jezzie did have a change of heart, which he knew full well he probably would have, but he was in an impossible position. He struggled and kicked back. He tried to raise his legs to push with his feet at the windows, but it was impossible. Exhausted, he resigned himself to his fate and said his last prayer out loud. His final thoughts were, *would Jerry do the right thing for his wife and son?*

Chapter Fifty-Nine

Barry Stone was dressed to kill. He was wearing a tight, silk, white shirt, opened to the navel, with black leather trousers tucked into shin high. Laced leather boots and the studded belt holding up the trousers matched the cap and the metal studded neck collar he hung on the rearview mirror. Stuli was wearing the same scrunched up suit he had for the previous two days and was now seated beside him in the small economy hire car. They had moved through passport control quickly. Barry liked Gibraltar; customs were relatively slack, all they cared about was a bit of duty evasion, which seemed to be the highlight of the day if an old dear had more than her fair share of cigarettes. "Good," thought Barry, "whatever keeps the cunts busy."

"Why don't we try Marbella? I should imagine there to be some nice bars and restaurants there?"

"No," replied Barry. "Torro's the place. There's more of what we're looking for there."

"A drink is a drink, no? And food is food. I think fish will be good tonight, Vincent. Do I call you Vincent or Barry?" asked Stuli, keeping his face looking straight ahead.

"Vincent and don't you ever mention the name Barry again, you hear me?"

"I hear you," replied Stuli, quietly. He began to wonder, even more, what the hell he had gotten himself into? A little kiddie fiddling, that was the extent of his wrong doing, although he sometimes wondered what was wrong with that anyway, he was successfully fighting the problem, and certainly never hurt anyone.

Now, as he looked at the man beside him, he got the deepest feeling of dread. Barry could sense the fat Jew looking at him and knew exactly what he was thinking. He felt a surge of pleasure from this man's discomfort. He smiled.

"What is so funny?"

"You, Stuli. You worry too much, relax! Put your seat back, your belly, look at it, it's touching the dashboard. You need to loose some weight." Barry placed his hand down beside Stuli's seat and released the catch, securing the seat's position and pressing the brakes for a split second at the same time. The seat surged forward before Stuli regained control, at which time it slid back with such force it nearly ran from the tracks. Stuli screamed as his feet left the floor, and his hand automatically came up to guard his face.

"Oy Vay! My God!" yelled Stuli. "What is this?"

"Fucking hell, Stuli." laughed Barry. He banged the steering wheel with his right hand as he continued to laugh. He looked at Stuli, who was not amused and was sweating profoundly. The state of him made Barry laugh even more. Still, Stuli could not see the funny side of the action. He remained unamused.

"What the fucks wrong with you?" asked Barry, between bursts of laughter. "Can't you take a joke, for fucks sake," he said, stifling another outburst.

"I would like to go back to the hotel, please," responded Stuli.

"Shut the fuck up, you're going nowhere." The odd couple continued the remainder of the journey in silence, one thinking about being home alone and the other relishing in the thought of someone's misfortune tonight.

Chapter Sixty

There were ten of them, including the two pilots, comfortably seated in the Jet Ranger. Most of the eight passengers looked, as Jerry did, like businessmen. Only one of the passengers was female, and Jerry was struggling to work her out. Seventy, looking fifty, a definite throw-back from the '30s, bleached blonde hair scraped back tightly into a bun with a small, black, square hat securing it. Her cheekbones were high and protruding due to too much cosmetic surgery. Her lips were full and purple with gloss. The fox fur attached to the collar of her black pencil suit still contained the head, which seemed to smile at Jerry. The brooch fastened to her lapel, secured with the help of a safety chain, told Jerry the large diamond in it was genuine. Jerry didn't linger there; instead, he clicked his tongue and leaned over to stroke the little Chihuahua protruding from an early-model Vuitton bag. The little mutt snarled and went to bite Jerry's finger. Jerry was quick; the dog missed. The lady tapped the dog's nose, gave it a verbal warning in a language Jerry didn't recognise but guessed was German, and apologised to Jerry.

"Thank you," said Jerry, "but the apology is mine to give. I should have asked."

She smiled, showing larger teeth than necessary for such a small face. She liked this man. Out of the other six passengers, she was happy that he was the one who sat directly opposite her and even more so for the fact that he had now struck up a conversation. She also imagined that, with his confidence and good looks, he was quite used to chatting up the ladies.

"Do you use this service much?" he asked.

"Once, every month."

"Oh?" enquired Jerry without specifically asking.

"Yes." She smiled.

Wise old cunt, thought Jerry.

"The girl said approximately 40 minutes. That's a good service."

"It's a very good service."

"Beats the ferry, eh? The drive down to meet the boat would take much longer, wouldn't it?"

"Yes, that's quite right."

One or two of the other passengers, who weren't wearing earmuffs, acknowledged with their heads.

Jerry mused. *Is everyone going over to Morocco so reserved?* He, too, was usually reserved, especially with the lack of female company, but he was slightly intrigued, especially with the old dear. He checked his watch—roughly 30 minutes to go. He was determined.

"Is it business?" *Can't be pleasure, that's for sure. Having said that, who knows?*

"It's actually a pleasure," she hesitated slightly before adding, "and to observe."

"The pleasure I hope you enjoy," said Jerry, "but I'm intrigued. Observe?"

"Yes, it is a pleasure to enjoy the flight, and I feel it is my duty to observe. You see, I will not be leaving the craft in Ceuta. In fact, I will return once we have loaded with our return passengers."

Jerry was now even more puzzled. He looked at the other passengers who were within earshot. One or two were privy to the conversation; others were either reading, listening to music, or looking out and down from the windows. The guy seated next to the madam gave Jerry a knowing smile. Jerry immediately assumed he was a companion. He smiled at Jerry; the old lady spoke to the man, who, Jerry noted, agreed with what she had said to him.

"Madam Schwineshtieger," he said. Jerry congratulated himself on recognising the lingo. The name Skowinctega, or whatever, had to be Kraut. The companion was still talking. "She is the owner of the company which operates this service."

Jerry was impressed and raised his eyebrows in appreciation.

"I see! And you like to keep tabs?"

"Tabs?" The lady looked at the man doing the speaking for her. He explained in German. The lady smiled.

"We have three helicopters operating from Malaga and two from Madrid. Mr Schwineshtieger, who is no longer with us"—he placed a comforting hand on the old dear's; she smiled at Jerry—"was a pilot for Air France. He was a captain in charge of Concorde from the '70s until its demise recently. His passion was flying. And we! We like to think that we carry on with his legacy."

"That is very interesting, thank you very much for sharing your story with me." Jerry's mind was working overtime. *This could be very useful information.*

"It is a pleasure," replied the pleasant man. The lady agreed, again with a smile.

"Do you charter the helicopters out on a private basis?"

"Yes, of course, but not the ones already doing a service. We have two others; they do go out quite regularly. The horse racing in France is a frequent arrangement we have with customers of ours. Do you think maybe you might one time in the future require one of these machines?"

"One never knows," said Jerry, smiling and looking out at the coastline. "Is that Gibraltar?" he asked, changing the subject and looking down through the window. "It is so difficult to recognise places from up above, especially when night falls."

"Yes, it is, and beyond, to the right, is Ceuta, where we will be landing in 17 minutes." The chap looked at his watch. Jerry recognised the quality of the IWC.

"Do you have a business card?" asked Jerry, looking at his own watch. The guy took a silver and tortoiseshell case from his inside pocket and gave Jerry an embossed card from it.

Franz Schwineshtieger.

Jerry was able to grab a taxi within minutes of saying his goodbyes to the old lady and who he presumed to be her son. It's funny how things can fall into place from the most unusual events. Already, he was planning ahead; it would help to have some knowledge of the company and, of course, the owner if and when he chartered a helicopter. Those lessons taken by McNess, what seemed a lifetime ago, may come in handy yet!

Taking his luggage from the driver of the taxi, he paid him for the short journey and walked through customs and into Morocco. It was that easy—a few minutes leaving, but entering was the total opposite. Jerry couldn't tell the difference between the customs and the officials; it seemed the customs were unable to ask for money, but the officials were.

"I carry your bag? Taxi, you like taxi?" A screech of a whistle. "Good hotel, mister?"

"Everything is good," said Jerry, letting the guy in the worn, faded, dusty blue uniform take his two suitcases.

"This way, sir. Taxi!" he called, holding up a grubby hand.

"No taxi. I have friend."

"Manchester United," he said back to Jerry, giving him a gum smile. "Beckham!"

"What the fuck are you talking about?"

The guide didn't understand. Thank fuck Abdul was meeting him here; he didn't know how much of this he could take. Thank God the sun was down and the moon was up because he could only imagine how difficult this would be in the heat of the day. There was hustle and bustle, hustlers and buskers, beggars and thieves—there were hundreds of them—slowly walking away from the customs area, back into the night. The ground rose on either side of the muck road, bankings of dried earth and dust. This was Morocco. The people! Like a biblical scene in their long robes, some with sheep—fucking sheep—leather sandals, babies crying, dogs scavenging, and wrecks of cars as opposed to camels, moving away into the town, city, coast. Jerry had no idea why, but he didn't like it. It was not what he was expecting, but, he supposed, you have to take the rough with the smooth. He clasped the briefcase close to his chest, only to quickly lower it beside him in a not-too-conspicuous position. He was nervous, he had to admit, and a little scared. These people had very little—nothing, in fact. The sound of a continuous car horn and a familiar voice calling his name had Jerry looking for Abdul. He eventually saw him, standing on the sill of a jeep, holding onto the top of the open door. He was laughing, and Jerry knew why. He must have looked a sorry state.

"My friend," Jerry shouted over the noise. He tapped the shoulder of the guide and pointed in the direction of Abdul. The chap looked disappointed, obviously missing out on the taxi commission. Jerry waved at his contact and made his way through the crowd, walking in the same direction, making sure the guy carrying his luggage was slightly ahead of him.

"This is bleeding surreal, Abdul," he called. "How are you?"

"I am very good, my friend. How are you?"

"Yes, good. Can we go somewhere quiet? I want to get straight down to business, if that's alright with you."

"This is music to my ears. Let us go," he said, taking the luggage from the guide and giving him some notes that were well past their sell-by date.

"Food, Jerry. Are you hungry? You try some lamb with us; this is good. The women, they prepare for us. Come, let us go." He held open the door for Jerry to step in and take a seat in the rear. The Toyota Land Cruiser was relatively new, especially compared with all the other vehicles on the dirt road, but it was still dry and dusty. The leather interior was coarse from the heat of the sun, but the air-conditioning was heaven.

"We go to Tetouan. Memhet is waiting there for us. It is his home where we will go, and it is there that tonight you will lay your head."

"Lovely. How long is the journey?"

"One hour, one hour twenty, maybe," he turned from the front seat to look at Jerry. "You in a hurry, my friend?"

"Yes, I am hoping we can get what you have to say wrapped up tonight, and I can leave tomorrow."

Abdul looked disappointed.

"I had planned to take you up to the Rif Mountains tomorrow, and the day after, we would go to Rabat, the capital. There are some very important people I would like for you to meet."

"No can do, Abdul. I'm very sorry; I have things to attend to in the UK. This is why I have come to see you now. I think maybe what you want to talk to me about may have some connection to the UK, no?"

"Yes, it does, my friend, but it cannot be agreed over dinner. There are many things for you to consider. There is a lot at stake here, and if you agree to the contract, you will have responsibilities—responsibilities which require your full attention, Jerry." Abdul's face was serious. Jerry got the impression that he was underestimating Jerry's commitment. He was annoyed but tried not to show it as he looked back at the Arab and said,

"I take all my responsibilities seriously, Abdul. I have come here this evening for the basics only. You don't have to give me the full rundown, just the preliminaries. That will be enough for me to make a provisional decision. When I return from the UK, I will give you a definite answer, and if it is positive, then we can do the sightseeing."

"Alright, Jerry, I understand." He turned around to look straight ahead through the dusty windscreen.

"This is for the better, Abdul. For both of us."

"As you wish, Jerry."

The bumpy ride took a little over one hour but felt more like two to Jerry. There was little conversation, if any, since the last brief discussion. Abdul spoke first.

"You see the lights straight ahead?" He didn't wait for an answer. "This is my brother's village. We are not from here, but he stays here because the family of his wife number two are from here."

"Wife number two?"

"Yes, he has three."

"Lucky Memhet!"

They entered the residential area as if by magic from the dark, rough terrain, with only the headlights giving assistance to the street lights, which hardly lit up the muck roads. Memhet's house was illuminated, as though it was a lighthouse giving sanctuary to a vessel in distress—at least, that was how Jerry imagined it.

The 4x4 turned sharp right, down a steep slope, and directly into a garage positioned under the house. There were two sheep tied in one corner and two young girls hand-washing some clothing in the opposite one. The boy who had signalled the jeep into the garage followed the motor down the slope and shut the door behind them. The driver lit a cigarette and left the engine running until Memhet came through an internal door and shouted at him. He greeted his brother with a kiss on each cheek and did the same to Jerry as he stepped from the vehicle and into the smoke-fume-filled garage. Jerry felt sorry for the children who had to work at this hour and in these conditions. He needn't have bothered because each one of them was smiling broadly at the westerner.

"Welcome, welcome to my home. You are very welcome to my home," said Memhet, taking hold of Jerry's luggage.

"Thank you, Memhet, your English is very good!"

"No good, no very good," he looked at his brother for help.

"Memhet has been learning all day, for almost six hours. Ever since he learned you were coming to his home, he has been learning this."

Jerry was humbled and smiled at Memhet.

"Thank you, Memhet." The tall Arab said something to Abdul in his native tongue. Abdul turned to Jerry.

"You are most welcome, and may your God bless you." He put a hand on Jerry's shoulder. "Come, my friend, we have a lot to talk about. This way," he said, leading the way up some stairs into the main living quarters.

The room was square and basic, with a white tiled floor and mosaic-tiled seating, which was fastened to the wall and completely wrapped around the room. Red velvet padding made to fit was resting on the top for comfort. There was a large, low-to-the-floor, carved wooden table in the middle of the room with miniature bean bags scattered around it. One of the most beautiful girls Jerry had ever seen in his life entered the room and placed a tray containing a tarnished silver teapot and six small red glasses on the table. She left the room as silently as she entered, only this time she put her hands together, bowed her head, and smiled with embarrassment at Jerry.

"Your wife?" Jerry asked Memhet as she scurried from the room. He looked at Abdul for an answer.

"His wife's sister. She is very beautiful, yes? There are nine of them; she is the oldest, which is why she brings the tea." He lifted the pot and held it high above the glasses before tilting it with precision to let the mint tea flow into the ornate glass. He smiled at Jerry without faltering in the art. "The younger ones will bring the food. We have some business associates coming to join us." Again, he spoke Arabic to Memhet. "Fifteen minutes, they will be here."

"And you want to wait? Until they arrive, I mean, before we talk?"

"This is true."

"Can I use the bathroom to wash?" Jerry asked, standing.

"Yes, Memhet will show you to your room. This will only take a little time, then our friends will be here. Please take your tea with you; it is not the same when it goes cold." Jerry took the glass and followed Abdul's brother.

The room was on the top floor of the three-storey house. It was large and airy with a fan attached to the singular light fitting in the centre of the ceiling. It was minimal, with nothing but a single bed and a chest of drawers. A large bowl with a jug of water and a fluffy white towel were resting on a wooden chair by the door. Memhet placed the two cases by the bed, and Jerry put the briefcase on it. Memhet smiled at Jerry and reversed from the room, closing the door behind him. Jerry placed the hot drink down and

Divine Intervention

took a mobile phone from the case. He placed a new SIM card in it, the phone bleeped and automatically set itself to some Arabic cell site. He pressed a credit card into the allotted slot, retrieved a list containing four numbers, and texted a message to the first one: *Will be in touch. Keep yourself available for the next 2 to 3 days.* He knew Hutchin would check for messages at least once every other day.

"Come in, please meet my friends," said Abdul as Jerry returned to the room downstairs. The three men who had arrived while Jerry was upstairs now stood to shake hands with him. No names were exchanged. Jerry understood this; there was no point in full introductions at this stage, especially when it was still uncertain whether there would be any business.

"Now!" said Abdul, "Please, gentlemen, take a seat." He clapped his hands once. Jerry almost laughed; for a split second, he imagined some exotic belly dancers prancing into the room. Instead, the girls filed in, four of them, with trays of food. Jerry was famished, and it was unusual for him to give priority to culinary delights over the female species.

"My friends," said Abdul, "we have with us tonight, each who has a very important part to play in what we are about to discuss. We have a senior member of our customs," he offered his hand with his palm up in the direction of a short, fat man sitting opposite Jerry. The guy didn't smile but looked at Jerry and nodded his head.

"This one to the left is a government official. He is a landowner who gives much of his land to be worked by the hashish barons." This guy, Jerry noted, had nervous, shifty eyes. He was tall and thin, immaculately dressed, and surprised Jerry when he spoke with a good English accent.

"It is very nice to meet you. I hope that we can entice you to consider our proposition with confidence." Jerry gave the guy a respectful nod of his head.

"Which leaves us with the last one," said Abdul, slapping the third person on the back. He was seated between Abdul and Jerry, he was overweight with close-cut thick black hair, eyebrows like caterpillars, and an untrained bushy moustache. His eyes were slits in the chubby face but had a glint which sparkled and gave him a friendly feel.

"Unfortunately, this one speaks no English but has told me to tell you, if you decide to do the business and we are successful, 'he is prepared to learn.'" With this, the others laughed, even Memhet and the fat man himself.

"You didn't tell me his role," said Jerry.

"He is the baron who produces from the plant, and my partner in this venture." Again Abdul slapped the back of this man, who by this time must be getting annoyed. He smiled again, which automatically told Jerry that Abdul must have more than enough respect around these parts.

"So! Would you like to tell me what all this is about, Abdul, and where I fit in?"

"Yes," said Abdul, taking a half chicken in two hands and ripping a large chunk from it with his teeth. He washed this down with some water and, without rushing, he cleared his mouth and his throat and thought clearly before speaking. He began.

"My friend here," he said, indicating the baron, "has been dealing with some Englishmen based on the Costa del Sol. Names are not necessary," he said flippantly, "you will know… knew," he corrected, "them, or knew of them at least. Things were good, good for a long time, until someone got greedy and others got brave." Jerry listened intently. He had a feeling he knew what was coming. He looked at the fat man sat beside him. The fat man could not understand but knew what was being said. The friendly int had gone from the hazel eyes, which had turned dark brown. Abdul continued. "You are aware of the recent shootings? On the coast, in Spain, Tarifa?" Jerry acknowledged with his head.

"There were two groups, both customers of our friend here," Abdul smiled at the Baron, who did not return the gesture. "Mainly rib work," Abdul continued, "by water. The amounts were not large, a tonne, fifteen hundred kilos max, but it was regular, sometimes two times a week, to both parties, totally separate. What happened was a coincidence with bad consequences. Two ribs, they take 500 kilos each to the beach 20 kilometres north of Tarifa, towards the coast of Portugal. At the same time, a small fishing boat meets three more ribs out in the water. The people who were waiting for the two ribs saw the activity with the fishing boat and the three ribs; they followed it, at a distance, with a Jet Ski and a satellite phone. The Jet Ski was relaying the location to their accomplices on the coast who made preparations to take the boat and steal the merchandise. It wasn't long before each party was aware of the circumstances leading up to the actions, especially when the stuff, with the same markings, was offered for sale to one of the people who should have been receiving it in the first instance, anyway... You know the rest..." he tailed off, letting Jerry put all the pieces together.

"You seem to have resolved the situation. There was certainly enough blood spilt, but where do I come into this?"

"We, that is my friend and I," said Abdul, placing a hand on the fat man's shoulder. Jerry couldn't help but notice the grease stain when he removed his hand to lift a skewer filled with meat, peppers, and onions. "We are already working with our friend here," Abdul added, indicating the man in the long suit crouched opposite Jerry, slightly to the left. He took his cue and explained.

"It was my idea to come into Spain by road. This is already an option, of course, and the controls on our side are not so stringent as they are on the Spanish side. We in the government do not see hashish as the purge that the Europeans do; on the contrary, we have benefited from the profits in certain sectors, although we would never admit to this fact. The transportation by road will always be there and has been for many years for anyone who is prepared to take the risk, but our customs officers are poor people. They look to find, and now, with the scanning machines and the dogs on the Spanish side, there is very little that escapes them." He smiled at the customs man sitting beside him, who took this as his turn to talk.

"We don't take risks, especially when they are not calculated. The customs workers, my friend, they earn very little money, and it hurts them to see others making some. It's the, what you say? The green-eyed monster." Jerry understood what the man was saying but wished he'd get to the point. This was more than interesting, and he was beginning to feel excited.

"We know, from our sources," interjected Abdul, "that you have some political people on the payroll. We also know that they all have a price." He looked closely at Jerry for a reaction. Jerry was a little disheartened at the thought of Gonzalez. He didn't show his hand and made no reply, even though Abdul was waiting for something. Abdul continued, "We would like you to make some enquiries of your own and guarantee us a passage into Spain with security as far as Madrid and Barcelona."

"I see," said Jerry, "and if I do?"

"We divide the parcel."

"Is that it?"

"No, my friend," Abdul laughed, and the others followed suit out of politeness. "Of course not, there is more. We need you to take control of the merchandise once it reaches the destination."

"Which is the UK," said Jerry.

"And the Republic of Ireland. You see!" exclaimed Abdul, looking proudly at the others. "I tell you, this one is clever."

"To the point, Abdul," said Jerry, looking seriously annoyed at the little Arab. Abdul detected the attitude and relented.

"You have to excuse me, my friend. It is my duty to produce someone with authority and power. The truck will be carrying a full load, with the cover. This will allow for eighteen tonnes of our product."

Jerry was impressed and a little apprehensive. He raised his eyebrows in admiration. Abdul continued.

"As you can appreciate, this is quite a responsibility."

"A responsibility which may take a little time for me to consider."

"We anticipated this. How long do you need?"

"I am away for a few days. This will also give me the opportunity to speak with some people. I think seven days will be enough."

The four Arabs spoke among themselves. Memhet said nothing; he sat and watched Jerry as he periodically delved into the snippets. It was obvious to Jerry, as he observed the four speaking, that they were in agreement with the outcome from their body language.

"Will we see you back here in seven days' time?" asked the tall one with a smile. Jerry was unsure about this one. Out of the five present, this one gave Jerry the jitters.

"Yes, certainly," he replied. "Now, gentlemen," he added, standing, "if it's alright with you, I would like to retire. It's been a long day."

The group stood, some more agile than others. Jerry offered the drug baron a hand, which the fat man accepted gratefully.

"May I speak with you in private, Abdul?" Jerry asked as he wiped his hands and discarded the lace cloth.

"Of course, my friend. I will see you to your room."

Jerry made a brief enquiry about accommodating an unauthorised helicopter landing sometime in the not-too-distant future. He didn't go into detail, suffice it to say that the chopper would be holding something which would have to be dispatched quickly and safe-housed for a period until the heat died down.

Abdul all-too-readily agreed for Jerry's liking, but it was a positive and something that could be discussed in more detail in the near future.

The night was long for Jerry, with very little sleep.

Chapter Sixty-One

The music was loud, ridiculously loud. Barry made his way to the bar with Stuli shuffling close behind him.

"Hold on to my waistband." Barry turned his head whilst still moving through the crowd to shout over his shoulder. Stuli didn't hear the instruction over the mayhem but felt Barry's hand grasp his and guide it to the thick leather belt around his protector's waist. A massive hooray was escalated with a surge to the dance floor, the crowd cheering and moving to an obvious club anthem. The place was unusually cool considering the number of people cramped into the relatively small confines, and the lights of the bar were Barry's intended destination. Eventually, they got there and ordered two large measures of whiskey each.

"Is there a VIP area?" Barry asked the tall transvestite who placed the drinks on the bar. The lips parted to speak, Barry heard nothing but followed the direction in which the lady/guy pointed.

A taller-than-tall muscle-bound hunk stood by the entrance to the cordoned-off area, which preceded two glass doors. He wore black lycra shorts, which left nothing to the imagination, a criss-cross studded leather belt overlapped each broad shoulder, and this was matched by boots of a similar design. He didn't speak but stood guard by the doors and shook his head at the approaching odd couple. Barry took a fifty Euro note from his pocket and grasped the doorman's hand. The guy said nothing but moved sideways to allow Barry and Stuli to gain access.

"This is much better," said a relieved Stuli.

"Much," agreed Barry, looking around the spacious VIP lounge as the doors closed behind them. There weren't many customers in this section, and as Barry took a seat and looked at the menu laid flat on the glass table, it became apparent why.

"Look at the price of the drinks," he said, sliding the plastic sheet across to Stuli.

"It is worth it for the breathing space alone, yes?" commented Stuli, removing his jacket and wiping the sweat from his face with the sleeve of it.

"Get a serviette, you scruffy cunt, or go to the toilet and have a wash," slammed Barry, who was already looking around the room for a potential victim. Stuli noticed his friend was very agitated, like a dog on heat. This made him nervous, very nervous.

"L'chaim!" he said, holding his drink up in Barry's direction. Maybe a few quick ones would lighten the mood.

"Cheers," said Barry, meeting the fat Jew's glass with his.

There were only a few other tables occupied and a couple of secluded booths where talk and giggles could be heard. Barry imagined that anything goes in this room. There was no bar, but a couple of bunny waiters stood unobtrusively in a dark corner. Barry finished off his second glass and held it up for service. Bunny number one hopped over immediately and took his order for another large whiskey and a bottle of water for Stuli. When Stuli objected to water, Barry told him he would be driving back to Gib, unless, of course, they got lucky.

The rest of the evening and late into the night was spent in the same room, at the same table, with the two of them talking the same idle bullshit. Barry's tongue was getting looser by the glass and louder by the hour. Eventually, talk turned to their passion and one of the only things the two had in common: Stuli's brother and young boys.

It was public knowledge that a youth from the Torremolinos gay scene had been taken from a club two nights ago and had been killed before being sodomised. The murderer had tried to make the crime look like a drug overdose, but witnesses had seen and heard the guy arguing with the youth outside the last place the boy was seen alive.

The bunny boy was not sure he heard the Englishman correctly when he was speaking to the big fat man, but he was sure he heard a comment referring to the dead boy. The reaction of the fat Jew was enough for one bunny to mention it to the other. Between the two of them, they decided to speak with the manager who, in turn, went to the office and looked at the photo-fit picture in the local newspaper. It was enough for him to call the police and report his suspicions.

Stuli asked Barry to keep his voice down. Although there was enough room between tables to hold a conversation in private, the fact that Barry was getting loud with the drink and the moderate volume of music in the VIP area had Stuli realising what his friend was, in fact, implying. Stuli was unsure if he was getting the message correctly, but it seemed to him that Barry had done something terrible the last time the two of them were here in Torremolinos.

The only other door in the room, other than the one the two had used to enter the VIP lounge, was the one where the bunnies brought the drinks from. This door opened, and two men came in and walked over to the back wall, which housed the three booths. Almost immediately, the people sat in the booths stood and left through the same door. This left only four tables occupied, including the one where Barry and Stuli were seated.

"One more!" called Barry, holding up his empty glass. The service did not arrive. Stuli could sense something amiss. One of the two guys who had left with the people seated in the booth returned to the room and sat with an elderly couple seated at the table furthest away from them. Like the others before them, they, too, stood and left through the door. Barry banged his glass hard on the table. The people sat at the two remaining occupied tables looked over at the commotion.

"More drink here!" called Barry.

"Please, come this way," said the second man, instructing the occupants of the last two tables to leave through the back door with him. With this, the doorman wearing the lycra shorts turned from looking into the club and stood facing, through the glass doors, into the VIP lounge.

"What the fuck's he looking at?" growled Barry.

"I'm not sure, Vincent, but something is not right."

"What do you mean something ain't right?" he asked, looking around. His speech was slurred and his vision hazy. He stood awkwardly and made for the doors leading into the music venue. The doorman did not move, and when Barry attempted to open the door, he discovered it was locked. The guy looked straight through him, so Barry turned unsteadily to look at Stuli enquiringly and saw for the first time that things were not how they should be. He looked over to the corner where the two bunny boys had been. When he couldn't see them, he looked to the empty booths, then around the room at the empty tables and realised for the first time that it was on top. He couldn't grasp for what, but it was without a doubt, on top.

He moved quickly, his senses returning immediately. Like a trapped animal, his instincts for survival were sharp and aggressive. He moved past the table where Stuli was sitting and towards the only other door. As he reached out to push the handless panel, it swung open to meet him head-on. He didn't see or hear anything for a few seconds after the full force of the panel momentarily stunned him. Going down on one knee, he used his hands to break his fall. He raised up as quick as he fell, with the full force of his body carrying his head into the chin of the first person to manhandle him. The sound of bone breaking with the powerful contact and the scream of pain had the second undercover reaching for his weapon, a third bulk was moving in swiftly behind him. Barry saw the movement and the glint from the gun. He reached to push the two hands holding it upwards as the first charge was released. The loud bang was enough to draw Mr. Universe in his lycra shorts from his position at the entrance to charge in a rugby tackle and hit Stone from behind in the lower region. Barry buckled with the impact and received a blow to the left temple from the butt of the gun to help him on his way to the floor and oblivion. A dark void with a passage to hide, darkness and sleep, the softness of the carpeted floor. Police? He hoped so. It was almost welcome.

Book Two

Chapter Sixty-Two

Day Five

Unusually for Wheeler, he was fresh for the time of day, 03:45 hours. He was standing on the stone steps at the entrance to the central Policia station, a cigarette in one hand and a polystyrene cup of black coffee in the other. The roads were quiet, and the eerie silence was broken occasionally by the vacuum of a road sweeper. The pavements were littered with the dregs of late-night drinkers stumbling home. Wheeler took the odd glance at the semi-naked female revellers over the top of his hot coffee cup. The sun was still slowly making its way above the tall buildings. He felt good within himself until he looked down at his midriff. *If it wasn't for his age and shape, this would be one of the best days of his life.* How he was relishing the thought of watching Divine being dragged from his slumber. *The early bird catches the worm.*

He was summoned back inside. There were between fifty to sixty officers standing silently in the room. Wheeler was surprised to see 30% of these were female, although he had to look carefully to decipher. *99% of the 30% dykes,* he calculated. Having said that, Angelica was rigged out in combat gear too.

There were no suits and ties now. Wheeler guessed most of the outside help had returned to their respective homelands. It was only Wheeler and one or two others who had stayed. He wondered how many would be dispatched to Senor Divine's residence. All the instructions were given in Spanish. His unasked question was soon answered when Perelta asked him and a further twelve officers, including Angelica, to follow him to the small arms supply. He was asked to sign a document and was given a 9mm semi-automatic Glock in return.

Fifteen minutes later, he was seated in the back of a Mazda people carrier on his way to Divine's home address. Perelta leaned over from the front passenger seat and spoke in Spanish to the other eight special unit officers travelling with Wheeler. When he finished saying what he had to say, he looked at Wheeler.

"We go in last. You stay with me, Bill, OK?"

"Got yer." replied Wheeler. He was surprised, and happy, to be called by his Christian name for a change.

Wheeler turned back to look at the Lexus travelling in convoy. Angelica was seated in the front passenger seat. She saw him look at her and gave him a wave without a smile. Wheeler got the first twinge of apprehension mixed with a little excitement and a lump of fear.

The roads were deserted off the main 340. Wheeler did not recognise anything he had seen from the helicopter, but he knew they were nearing the target as the talking had gone from discussion to the odd comment, to a whisper, and then to complete silence.

The area was affluent, to say the least. The roads were tree-lined, and the street lights, which topped ornate poles painted black and gold, were switching off automatically as the sun rose, giving the vista an almost chocolate-box effect. The walls surrounding the properties were thick and high. All the houses were accessible through large gates, some steel, but most, Wheeler noted, were wood. Some were carved and splendid with names as opposed to numbers; others were plain and highly polished with black and brass fittings. Those gates, which were wrought iron, gave some idea of what lay beyond. Wheeler could see some long drives, tree-lined, others with arched driveways preceding large painted houses. Some of the cars which he caught a glimpse of were all top of the range. *Yes, Divine had done very well for himself,* it pained Wheeler to admit.

The Mazda and Lexus were met by two more familiar types at the beginning of a short road, which Wheeler guessed must be the target street. Each of the green Guardia municipal Nissan patrols had four officers seated in them. As the Mazda and the Lexus stopped behind the two Jeeps, the eight Guardia got out. Perelta wound the window down and spoke to the obvious leader. Agreements were made, and Perelta spoke in Spanish. When he finished speaking, all the occupants of the Mazda, including Wheeler, left the vehicle in silence.

Battering rams were taken from the rear of the Mazda and given to the largest members of the crew. Others secured their helmets and began walking the short distance to the target in a uniform manner, Wheeler and Perelta bringing up the rear.

There was no sound, not even a cricket. The smell was what got Wheeler; it was beautiful. The vision and aroma of red and blue flowers which sprouted out of the ground and smothered the wall reminded him of an artist and his works he had studied at school—Monet. *If it wasn't Divine on the other side of this high wall, it would almost be a shame to shatter and disturb the whole picture.*

Small collapsible aluminium ladders were produced from a black nylon bag. One of the guys placed them quietly against the wall and secured the bottom with his booted foot as each of the party climbed over. Wheeler made for the ladder when there were only three of them remaining streetside. Perelta stopped him by placing his hand on his arm.

"Wait here, Bill. The gate will be opened for you, me, and Angelica," he whispered. Wheeler didn't have time to respond before the loud bang sent alarms ringing from the box fastened to the exterior wall high above the front door. The barging of the ram and the crack of splintered wood was followed immediately by screams and demands from the team entering the property. A small dog barking for protection was not long, followed by yelping of fear as it scurried for shelter. A small girl screaming and an older one shouting for her mum was nothing Wheeler hadn't heard a thousand times before. The gate clicked open, and Perelta was the first in, followed by Angelica. Wheeler was sweating profusely in his safety helmet. He took it off and threw it on the grass verge before walking briskly through the gate. Only seconds had passed since the first heavy-duty baton thud. He now entered the house, which was in uproar. The orders from the officers were loud and clear, both in Spanish and broken English, orders to lie face down on the floor. The children were screaming louder now, the sound coming from different rooms in the house. Without warning and to Wheeler's surprise, a small white dog came racing down the stairs and brushed past him. He kicked out automatically and caught the mutt on the back end. It yelped more from fright than pain. A young girl, Wheeler guessed no more than 10 years old, screamed at the sight of Wheeler kicking out at her pet. She chased down the stairs after the dog. Wheeler turned and grabbed for her as she ran past him. Perelta called from the balcony for someone to secure her. The dog ran through the lounge, under the legs of a grand piano, and straight out through the open French doors, which were secured by wrought iron security gates. Wheeler chased after the little girl, who was now screaming the dog's name. The girl was stopped short by the gates, which were locked, and Wheeler took hold of her around the waist and picked her up. She kicked and screamed, crying out loud as Wheeler covered her mouth with his hand.

"Calm down, girl," he said. "Look there, the officer will get the dog." He assured her, now releasing his hold on her small mouth. The two of them watched as the dark-clad officer chased the small dog, which skidded along the dew-damp tiles surrounding the pool. The pet could not hold its grip and slipped along the floor and into the water. The little girl kicked with her heels violently at Wheeler's upper thighs. The officer tried to grab hold of the dog, but the weight of its wet fur drew it away from him and nearer to the vacuum skimmer pump. Perelta screamed from an upstairs terrace in Spanish. Wheeler assumed it was to leave the dog and get back onto the operation. The guy left the dog in the water and ran quickly to the bottom of the garden. He crouched down with one other in a commando position, gun in hand. The dog was struggling to escape the water, the level too low from the edge to give it any chance of a firm hold, its back end all the time being sucked into the vacuum. Wheeler turned with the girl, who was hysterical by now. She was kicking back at him and struggling viciously for a girl of her age.

"Bonito! Please, my dog," she cried. "Bonito, Mummy!"

"My fucking child!" Wheeler heard a female voice from above. He listened now for a second. No male voice of protest, no Divine. Again, a female voice of dissent.

"Where's my baby?"

"Mummy!" a girl from another upstairs room.

"Jasmine!" the mother's voice.

Still, no Divine. *They had missed Jerry Divine.* He guessed only two minutes had passed. He gave the child to a female officer who promised the girl everything would be fine. Another female officer joined them, and they took her into the kitchen. Two more officers came from the downstairs guest room. Nothing. They shook their heads. Others came from upstairs, guns down by their sides. Another one carefully placed a miniature pistol, held with a pencil through the trigger guard, into a plastic evidence bag. But no Divine. Divine's wife, Kathryn, was frog-marched down the wide spiral staircase, dressed in a silk lilac dressing gown and with her hands in cuffs—the result of the weapon find. A teenage girl called out to her as she, too, was marched from a room with her arms held behind her back.

"Will somebody tell me where my fucking child is?" the mother said through gritted teeth. The small girl called from the kitchen that she was being held there.

"Bonito's in the pool, Mum!" she cried. "Mum, please!"

"My God, what have you done!"

"Where is your husband?" asked Perelta.

"Where's the bleeding dog?" she screamed.

Perelta spoke to someone, no one in particular, to bring the dog. Wheeler walked into the hallway through the broken door.

"They are going to get the dog now, Kath."

"You! What the hell are you doing in my home?"

"Where's Jerry, Kathryn? We need to speak with him."

"I want a lawyer," she said, shaking free from the grip. She stood there defiantly and demanded that her youngest daughter be brought from the kitchen to her.

"You will see a lawyer at the police station," said Wheeler.

"The police station? I have done nothing wrong. Take these bloody handcuffs off me."

"Not until you calm down."

"Calm down? Calm dow—"

One of the officers who had searched the garage came into the hallway behind Wheeler and placed the case containing the euros onto the floor, and opened it. Behind him came a Guardia Civil dressed in green. He didn't speak. The white ball of wet fluff was clearly visible against the dark uniform. There was no movement from Bonito, which clearly showed the dog was not alive.

"You bastards!" screamed Kath, raising her arms to hit out at the nearest impostor.

"Mum!" cried Jasmine. "Don't let Julie see Bonito like that."

"Bonito!" called little Julie.

Perelta told the Guardia holding the dog to take it away quickly and discreetly.

"You are under arrest, Mrs Divine. You will have to explain the possession of the firearm and the source of such a large amount of cash discovered at this property. If you raise your hands again to one of my officers, you will be charged with assault. Do you understand? Now, you are entitled to legal assistance, and this will be taken care of at the police station. You will be taken from here to Malaga. How old is the girl?" he asked, indicating Jasmine.

"She's sixteen," Kath lied in a quiet tone.

"Alright, she is permitted to be guardian. Would you like to make a call now?"

"No," she whispered.

"Where's Dad, Mum?" asked Jasmine.

"He will call you later, love. Tell him what has happe—" Perelta didn't let her finish but forced her through the door and placed her in the back of a Policia car.

The two girls were brought into the lounge and seated at the large oval table.

"Where's my dog?" whimpered little Julie. Her sister embraced her and cried. How could she tell her?

The search of the property commenced and took all of two hours before various documents, some jewellery, and more cash were seized. A document was produced and signed by Jasmine. She was asked if there was some relative or family friend she could call and that a liaison officer would stay with the two girls until someone arrived. Jasmine answered yes and called Demitra.

The phone didn't even ring out before it was picked up at the other end by a distraught Demitra.

"Hello Jezard?" Jasmine had never heard the name before. She wondered for a second if she had dialled the correct number.

"Hello, is that you, Demitra?"

"Yes, it is. Who is this?"

"It's Jasmine," she sobbed, now, the result of brief salvation.

"Jasmine, tell me, baby, what is it? What's wrong? Why are you crying? Where's your father?"

"He's away," she cried. "Mum's been taken by the police. They've killed Bonito, Dem!" This was said as a whisper to protect the statement from being overheard by her little sister.

"Oh, baby. How? I'm so sorry, love. I will try and contact your father. Why have the police taken Mummy? Is there an officer there now?"

"Yes, there is," she answered, looking at the female officer who was listening to the conversation.

"Bonito drowned in the pool. The security gates were locked; they wouldn't let anyone out to save her. I don't know why they've taken Mum." She broke down uncontrollably. This time it was the younger sister comforting the elder one.

"Okay, baby. Put an officer on the telephone," said a determined Demitra.

When the female Policia officer took the receiver from Jasmine, she wrapped her arms around little Julie and laid her face on the top of her head. She was about to soothe her with some comforting words when the little one spoke softly. Releasing the grip her older sister had on her, the younger one looked up with wet eyes and whispered to her that she had heard and understood what Jasmine had told Demitra. The two girls embraced and cried uncontrollably.

Jezzie had never stayed out all night, not in the 30 years the two had been married. Demitra had no need to call the Policia as the sun rose above the high mountainous range where they lived. In fact, she too had been crudely and rudely awoken by the Policia breaking down the door. She had gone into panic mode immediately, her initial thought was that the earth was quaking and the mountainside on which the house sat had collapsed. Like a trapped animal with her knees drawn up under her chin, she remained laid on the bed with only the duvet for protection. When the raid on her home had been explained to her, she had gained some composure, and when asked about the whereabouts of her husband, she explained that she was about to call the Policia with the same question. They had conducted the search on the strength of a warrant offered without acceptance. The house had been searched thoroughly before the Policia had taken the computers and some documents from Jezzie's office and asked Demitra to sign for the confiscation.

Now, as the disruption had subsided to a degree and the only officers left at the property were now concentrating on the outbuildings, Demitra tried to assure Jasmine that she would try to contact her father and take care of things.

The female officer who had stayed behind took the phone from Jasmine and spoke to Demitra in Spanish. When she had finished talking and replaced the receiver, she looked at the two girls before leaving the room and going in search of the officer who had discovered the dead dog. Unable to find either him or it, she returned to the lounge shortly after and told Jasmine quietly that the other officers must have taken it away. Jasmine, with gritted teeth, demanded that the pet be brought back home so that she and her sister could bury Bonito in the garden. The officer was in agreement as Cleo rushed through the lounge and hugged the two girls to her bosom.

Chapter Sixty-Three

Augustine Gonzalez had been awake since 5 a.m. He was excited about the prospect of being released on bail today. Azzorio Manzella had assured him that Jezzie had secured the finance to cover the surety, and he would agree to submit his passport and abide by any other conditions the judge wished to impose. Just to get out of this kiln, to be home with his loved ones. How he missed them. How he took them for granted. He would never leave them again, never put himself in this position, ever. He had and would cooperate further with the authorities, tell them everything. The Policia had found and confiscated most of the money. There was more, secured in an offshore account. He would give them the details of this and any other relevant information they required, about him, or anyone else for that matter. *He was not cut out for this.* He was the one who had pushed in favour of building more of these prisons and filling them. He didn't agree with bail—not until today, anyway. *Tonight, he would take his family out to dinner, tell them the truth about his involvement, and apologise from the bottom of his heart. He would make it up to them, he would promise them everything a husband and father should give and be. Love, and protection, loyalty, and comfort.*

He moved quietly around the cell, more from fear than respect. He had no respect for the guy who was sleeping on the top bunk. As a matter of fact, he had little respect for any one of these criminals languishing in the penal system. Augustine was all for throwing the common criminal behind bars. He had been told that others would be arrested today, this morning, about now, in fact. He checked his watch again. 5:15. He realised he had looked at the time every 5 minutes. The cell doors were expected to open at 6 a.m. for those inmates who were scheduled to appear in court. Augustine moved quietly toward the TV and turned it on, quickly turning the volume down low. He moved his chair up close to it.

The news report said he, by name, the Mayor of Marbella Emilio Sanchez, his son, who carries the same name, and others would be attending the central Malaga court today. Other people suspected of being involved in the operation had been arrested at dawn and would be questioned at length. The operation was widespread and in-depth. It was estimated to take a number of years and to cost many millions of Euros before its conclusion. Long custodial sentences were inevitable for those who would eventually be convicted.

Augustine looked around the cell, which measured no more than the box room his children kept their toys in at home. He could hear and smell the guy sleeping. The two had not exchanged names; they hadn't said one word to each other. Augustine had tried. On entering the cell, he had said hello and held his hand out. The guy had looked right through him as if it was he who was the vermin, and then he had scoffed at his hand as if there was vermin in it.

The cell was dirty, hot, and cluttered. The toilet in the corner was, thankfully, relatively clean compared to the remainder of the room. There was graffiti on the walls and dried excrement from a previous dirty protest.

"Long custodial sentences were inevitable for those who would eventually be convicted."

He checked his watch. 5:30. *Thirty minutes to go.* He reminded himself, yet again, that he had been told the cell would be opened at 6 a.m. for production process. He could breathe again.

The convict stirred. He released wind loudly from his rear end. The smell was rancid. The sheets rustled as the brute, who had barely spoken, kicked out. More wind, more stench. Augustine stayed silent, hoping the guy would not wake and he could slip out of the cell and out of this man's sorry life.

"Turn off TV," he grunted in English with a heavy, Spanish, broken accent and a deep, coarse voice. Gonzalez wondered why, but didn't question the demand.

"Sorry," he apologised, quietly doing as he was told.

He could hear some movement directly outside the cell door, then it was gone. He stood and moved closer, putting his ear to the door. Down the landing, maybe three or four cells away, he could hear a door being opened. Voices whispering, shuffling, obviously moving silently so as not to disturb the other prisoners still sleeping. These were, no doubt, others going to court. Keys now, coming closer again, thank God, one being inserted into the door lock, very slowly. He stepped back, not actually clearing the way before the door swung open violently. The guard remained at the entrance as the two prisoners came rushing in. The door closed. The sock containing the heavy battery struck Augustine Gonzalez in the temple, sending him sideways. He protested loudly. The volume of the TV was turned up to disguise the assault. The guy, whose name he never did get, pushed him away from the bed which supported his fall. He tried to scream for help, but no sound came from his mouth. The decibels were frozen with fear at the pit of his stomach. He turned to look where the push had come from, high up on the top bunk. The excuse of a man turned away to face the cell wall as though nothing was happening. The next swing of the self-made weapon struck Augustine on the back of the head, buckling him at the knees. As he dropped to the littered floor, he made to scurry beneath the lower bunk. This time, the scream was released but weak.

"Please! Please," he whimpered. "What have I done? Please don't hurt me anymore. I'm sorry, I'm so sorry."

The muscular man knelt down beside him and took hold of him by the hair. He yanked him from beneath the bed and dragged him to the centre of the cluttered cell, where he straddled him, making it impossible for Gonzalez to move. The aggressor's accomplice took the pillow from the bed and smothered the frozen, stiff, dazed man's face with it. The two brutes put enough pressure on the pillow to suffocate a bear, so it was not surprising to hear the bone crack as his neck was broken. Augustine's life flashed before him in the dizzy few seconds it took for him to die. *How could he see so much in such a short space of time? His school days, graduation, marriage, children, happy times, Emilio Sanchez, Jerry Divine.*

Chapter Sixty-Four

Barry Stone turned over. His head was banging. The smell of urine and his face sticking to the rubber mattress told him he was not in his hotel room. He forced his eyes open to look at the grey woollen blanket he was holding up to his face. Pushing the itchy cloth down, he studied the tight, white fibre jumpsuit he was wearing. His gaze was automatically diverted to the ceiling from the horizontal position on the scarred wooden bench of a bed. A low-watt bulb set behind a glass panel secured in the far corner gave the room some life; the remainder was bare, except for the graffiti in Spanish. He forced himself up to sit with his legs dangling to the floor. He remembered for the first time some of last night's events. He bent forward and put his head into his hands, running his fingers through his thinning hair. He winced with the pain as he made contact with the wound. He searched for the gash and pulled slightly at the hair surrounding it. Bringing his hand into view, it was covered with blood and matted hair. *Bastards!* He had a flashback of the arrest. *Murder? Was it murder?* He wasn't sure. *Stuli, where was he? Stuli knew nothing about the boy. Evidence? There was none. He had wiped the place clean. Even if they find a print... What the fuck was that? Witnesses? Maybe, but not to the kid dying. For fuck's sake, even he couldn't tell anyone how the boy had died. Autopsy? Let's see,* he thought. *Keep stum for now.*

Standing unsteadily, he walked over to the stainless steel WC. He held his breath and his nose with one hand while he used the other to release the thing that got him into this shit in the first place and pissed through it. He pressed the wall-mounted flush with his elbow and gasped for breath as he made his way back to the bench. Looking toward the door, he noticed a red bell-push beside it. After thinking hard for the next few minutes, he walked over and pushed it, smiling briefly at the arsehole someone had creatively drawn around it. *Smiling. How the fuck could he smile?*

The keys jangled and echoed down the corridor. The guard called out in Spanish. Barry imagined it was a warning that this had better be good. *Most jailers were lazy cunts. He could see no reason why they should be any different in Spain.* The hatch dropped down with a bang, which did little to help Stone's aching head.

"Digame."

"Digame! What the fuck's that? No Spanish, Gringo," tried Barry. "English," he said, pointing to his chest. He walked closer to the door. The guard raised his voice and said something Barry assumed was to step back. The hatch slammed shut.

"Fuck!" called Barry. He started to pace the floor, looking at the graffiti, searching for something English to pass the time. There was nothing. He needed a drink but thought twice about pressing the bell. *Fuck it,* he pressed it, this time holding his finger on it, pressing hard in defiance. He heard the steps but no keys. The hatch opened, and he was quite surprised to see a female.

"I need a drink," he said, mimicking the action. "Drink," he repeated.

"Tea or coffee?"

"Thank fuck! Coffee and water, please," he tried. "Why am I here?"

"Someone will speak with you soon. Be patient."

"Where's my friend?"

"Someone will speak with you soon."

"But I—"

The hatch was returned to its upright position, without a clatter this time.

Two cells away, Stuli was listening to the activity. He waited for the footsteps to disappear before calling out to Barry. Barry knew from experience that there would be an echo of Stuli's voice within the Jew's cell, so he waited a few moments before responding.

"Count to six," he instructed, "and then reply. You got that?" He waited and silently counted to six himself.

"Yes."

"1-2-3-4-5-6," he mimed. Perfect. "Have you spoken to anyone yet?" he called. After six seconds, the reply came from Stuli that he hadn't and the question, "What is going on?" Barry advised him to stay silent and not to answer any questions until he had taken legal advice. Barry also knew that this conversation was being listened to, so he was careful not to say anything that might incriminate him.

Footsteps and the sound of a trolley, other hatches being opened. Barry could hear talking before they were slammed shut. He heard Stuli.

"Yes please, coffee please. No thank you, I'm not hungry. What is happening to me? Could you ask someone to come and speak to me? I need to get out of here. I have done nothing wrong!" *Fucking hell!* thought Barry, *he'd be alright getting interrogated about something he knew about. He would have to look seriously at him after Antwerp. Antwerp! There will be no fucking Antwerp if Jerry gets to hear about this!*

"You like tea, coffee, cereal?"

"Just coffee, black, and water if you have it. My mouth's like the flaps of a whore's crutch," answered Barry, releasing a gush of breath through the hatch.

Chapter Sixty-Five

It was 08:30 a.m. Angelica was back in the Malaga office, which she shared with Perelta. She was making enquiries about Barry Stone/Vincent Viceroy. The taxi company used by the San Roque Hotel and Leisure Centre had replied positively to her question; they had taken the fare and dropped him at the border to Gibraltar. Customs had checked passport control; there was no record of an entry by either name entering Gibraltar on or about this time. Angelica had used her training initiative and wired through a copy of the still taken from the security camera at the San Roque. This was compared by customs with the stills of entrants on the security tapes at the relevant time. Yes! They had a match but no name; the traveller had not had his passport scanned.

The Gib police had been very accommodating. Angelica dealt with Susan Sharp, an acquaintance she had met at a number of police seminars. She, too, had received a copy of the picture, only this time Angelica had included Divine. Susan had assured her she would do all she could to help and had responded within the hour. Good news on one of the subjects: the heavier of the two with the lighter thinning hair.

Susan had called a number of hotels on the island and intended to call more when she was cut short and called back from The Rock Hotel. She had advised the manager that she would be called back by a detective from Malaga and had forwarded the details to Angelica.

"Yes," the female manager of The Rock Hotel had answered, they had a guest who matched the photograph they had received. The guest's name was Maine, Barry Maine. "Yes," he was still a guest and had recently extended his intended stay for a further six days; he would be leaving on Wednesday. "No," he was not in residence just now; in fact, there is no record of him returning to the hotel last night. The manager checked the ledger and entries made by the night porter. Arrangements had been made for a hire car to be delivered to the hotel in the early evening, and Mr. Maine and another guest, Stuli Bressla, had left the hotel just after and had not yet returned. This is not unusual. There is another person staying with Mr. Maine. Would the detective like the hotel to make further inquiries? Angelica had answered "No" to any further assistance but did ask the manager to confirm that these enquiries be kept between the two of them. As an afterthought, and one she was a little annoyed with herself for almost forgetting, she asked the manager to wire a copy of the guests' passports through. The manager refused, so Angelica called Susan Sharp again. Angelica received the copies fifteen minutes later.

One final check now, before she would pass on the results of her enquiry to Perelta. She fed the details of the passports into the computer and was almost immediately taken aback by the results.

Unbelievable! Both persons were in custody! In Torremolinos! She quickly grabbed for the telephone and called the station.

Angelica asked to be put through immediately to the custody officer in charge, who informed her that the two men were arrested last night in a gay bar. Both were held on suspicion of murder. The evidence was minimal, but even still, it was something he was not prepared to discuss over the telephone. What he could tell her was that one of those arrested had an uncanny resemblance to the last person seen talking to the victim. His passport photo was compared to the security camera footage taken at the time and place of the last sighting of the victim in a club. The comparison was not 100%, but enough to arrest. DNA samples were on the agenda, and the two would be interviewed later in the day. This was all.

The custody officer assured Angelica that the interviewing officer would be informed that she and Angelo Perelta had an unrelated interest in the prisoners and would be asked to call Malaga ASAP.

She called Perelta, who was conducting an interview with Kath Divine. He would call her back. She considered telling Wheeler but decided against this until she had spoken with Perelta. Something told her that things were about to get very interesting.

Chapter Sixty-Six

There was no direct flight to the UK from Ceuta, only a connecting one from Madrid. 12:45 p.m. out of Ceuta, arriving in Madrid at 1:38 p.m. The connection was not until early evening, 6:22 p.m., landing in Manchester at 7:40 p.m. British time. Abdul agreed it would be better to travel into town and use the hotel facilities to make the booking. Jerry asked if it was safe to go for a walk alone before the trio made for the town. Abdul laughed and assured him it was. It was a little after 6 a.m., and Jerry agreed to take no more than an hour. Abdul gave him a handful of coins and told him, when asked, that there was a public phone situated in the convenience store less than 1 kilometre away and pointed him in the right direction.

It surprised Jerry, while he was walking, that the kids were out playing so early, and then he realised that most of them looked like they probably had no homes to go to. If this was a good area, he dreaded the thought of a bad one. Memhet's house was definitely the best on the block; the further he walked from it, the more dilapidated the other houses became. The tarmac covering the road outside Memhet's home had turned to gravel and dust within 50 metres. There were no sidewalks or pavement, just earth leading up to the heat-cracked wooden doors and boarded-up windows of a row of unused shops. Scores of dogs roamed the area looking for food. The opened tins, scattered with other debris, were licked dry to the hot steel. A woman holding a toddler in her arms and an infant strapped to her back looked up at Jerry as he passed. Her eyes were transparent, like a glass marble without the coloured centre. She held out her hand made of leather as opposed to skin, begging to Jerry. He needed the coins; he would get her on his return but had no idea how to tell her this. The baby looked dead. A dog ran from the side of an alley adjacent to a second-hand tyre shed and nipped at Jerry's feet. He kicked out, and his stomach turned with fright. *This little cunt could be riddled with rabies. Fucking Abdul! He had asked him if it was safe.*

He could see the convenience store up ahead. He looked back to the house and decided the shop was the nearest. He continued. The store was more like a storage warehouse. All the goods were still boxed except for a singular item placed on the top of each to display what was on offer. These boxes were stacked and shelved to completely fill the small industrial unit. Convenience? The answer depended on how one would interpret convenient. There were more flies than one would see in a cow field on a hot day, making more noise than the electrical fans, which only helped the breeding process. Jerry ordered a bottle of water from the old guy who looked like he was welded to the wrought iron chair behind a low counter with a high-security cage. It was obvious the phone was for the benefit of the paying customer. Maybe this was "The Convenience."

He called Harold. No reply. *Too early.* He considered calling Kath but decided to call her from Madrid instead. *Jezzie? No. The less telephone contact with him, the better, at least until after the politician was taken care of.* There was someone else, but he couldn't quite put a name to it. *Madrid. Yes!* he remembered. He took a number of business cards from his wallet and fished through them until he found the one he was looking for and dialled the number. The phone rang out before the answer phone message brought a smile to Jerry's mouth.

Hi, this is Victoria. Please leave a message and a number, and I will get back to you. Have a nice day, byee!

"Hello, Victoria, this is James speaking. Just to let you know, I will be passing through Madrid this afternoon. I will be there for just a few hours, and thought maybe I could buy you lunch. I will call you again later this morning to see if this is a date. Bye, darling." He blushed as he replaced the dirty receiver and looked around until he saw a door leading to the washroom.

Chapter Sixty-Seven

Peralta called Bill Wheeler and told him to meet him at Central. Wheeler rolled over in the comfortable bed and cursed. He was having such a lovely dream.

He was the co-pilot in the same helicopter, Peralta was the pilot, and Angelica was sitting in the rear, looking out of the open door. The wind was gushing in, and the documents from the briefcase were swirling around in the tight confines. Angelica was calling; no sound could be heard above the rush of the air, but her mouth was clearly instructing Peralta to climb higher. She would look down and then back at Wheeler.

"Higher!"

Wheeler would shout the same to Peralta, who would raise the machine higher.

"Is he still holding on?" Wheeler was asking.

"Higher," she called back. "He can't hold on much longer."

That was when the phone rang. Divine was saved by the bell.

What could be so important? He checked his watch. 9:40 a.m. He had been back at the hotel for 90 minutes and sleeping for one hour. He wasn't sure if he should leave the hotel today—nobody had told him to, so he would stay. He wasn't happy with the way the raid went; it was far too abrupt. Divine wasn't home. The money—€250,000 in a case—funny that, he had seen something similar, in sterling, a long time ago. That money, too, had originated from Divine. The gun? He was unsure about the laws in Spain.

He supposed the Spanish had no choice but to arrest Kath Divine; possession of a firearm and a money laundering charge were certainly enough to hold her. She would no doubt say both the gun and money belonged to Jerry. Jerry would want her to say this. Of course, he would have to explain where this money came from, and could well lose it if his account was without legitimate foundation.

Wheeler knew Divine well enough to know that he would be absolutely fuming when he got the news that his wife was in custody. The dog? Well, that too, but these things happened. He had asked Peralta on the way back to Malaga what had happened to the dog and had been told it would go off to be incinerated. Yes, Divine's face—what a picture that would be. This could be a good day.

Angelica came down to meet Wheeler in the reception at Policia headquarters.

"We have good news, Mr. Wheeler."

"Please, Angelica, call me Bill."

"Very well, Bill."

Wheeler noticed she didn't smile. How good is the news?

"Hello again, Mr. Wheeler," greeted Peralta, not looking up from his desk as the two entered the room.

"Twice already. Bill, please."

"Yes, Bill, Bill," said Peralta, not holding out his hand. *This was business for sure,* thought Wheeler.

"We have Vincent Viceroy in custody," he advised, again, without looking up from the documents he was studying.

"Vincent Viceroy?" repeated Wheeler as a question. He was getting annoyed with the lack of respect.

"Yes, Vincent Viceroy, Barry Stone, one and the same, no?"

"Yes, where?"

"In Torremolinos. Going under the alias Maine this time. I have spoken to the officer in charge—good for us, he is a friend of mine."

"And?"

"He is speaking with him this morning, now, as we speak. Stone—you prefer Stone, yes?" the Spanish detective looked at Wheeler for the first time since entering the room.

"To avoid confusion, yes."

"Very good. He has been detained for questioning in relation to a murder inquiry. This is all I know at this time. The detective has told me that it is unlikely that, with the evidence they have at the moment, they will be able to hold him for more than twenty-four hours."

"When was he arrested?"

"01:30 hours this morning."

"Murder?"

"Yes. The investigating officer has agreed to bring him to Malaga when he has finished with him. That way we can speak with him here, and if he is to be released, we can do this also."

"What about Kathryn Divine?"

"She is still here. She has refused to answer any questions in relation to the money discovered in the garage at her home. The gun? She says it is licensed. She is more concerned about the dog and the children, obviously. She has also asked, repeatedly, for legal representation; we have delayed this right somewhat."

Wheeler ignored the last remark.

"We can't have her seeing Barry Stone; this could jeopardize the whole operation," he urged in slight panic.

The telephone on Peralta's desk rang, and Perelta spoke Spanish into it. He looked at the visibly tired British detective as the colour drained from his own face. He clicked his fingers and pointed to a desk positioned in the corner at the opposite side of the room. Angelica walked over briskly and picked up the extension. She, too, looked physically exhausted by what was being said. She took a seat without taking her gaze from Perelta. Perelta now looked at Wheeler with a venom he had only seen from the opposition. Wheeler looked over at Angelica, who shifted her gaze to the floor. This was serious. Peralta spoke slowly and deliberately; again, he was silent for a few moments. The two Spanish detectives replaced the receivers together, neither of them spoke.

"Is something wrong?" asked Wheeler, not wanting to hear the answer. He looked from one to the other and back again. Still, neither spoke. Wheeler stayed silent. Angelica said something in Spanish before leaving the room. When the door was closed behind her, Peralta said something in Spanish to Wheeler before realizing his mistake. He apologized and asked Wheeler a question he wasn't quite prepared for.

"How much influence has your man Divine got?"

"I don't understand the question."

"I want to know more about this man."

"I will tell you all you need to know, as much as I am able to anyway."

"What are we dealing with here?"

"Divine is a serious criminal. I told you and your colleagues this at the conference."

"We hear this all the time, Bill!" he rebuked. "They come down here with their ill-gotten gains, driving the flashy cars, living on the best side of town, high up in their posh apartments, enjoying the sun," Wheeler noticed

Peralta was going redder in the face, "splash their money around until it runs out, and then they commit more crime. We catch them, take their cars and the fancy watches, take off them everything else that we can, put them in prison at our expense until such time as we can send them home. Some stay away, find different pastures to pillage and rape, some come back." Perelta reclined in his leather chair, took a cigarette and lighter from a wooden box, lit it, inhaled deeply, and asked the same question before exhaling the smoke and fumes.

The British detective didn't answer the question but instead pushed with his own.

"What is it? Tell me," he urged, trying to emulate Peralta's composure. It didn't work, and beads of sweat were now forming on his forehead.

"Augustine Gonzalez was killed in prison today. This morning, before he was brought to court."

"Who is Augustine Gonzalez?"

"The contact of Divine and Jezard Dupree."

"My God!" responded the British detective. He took hold of the chair opposite his Spanish counterpart and sat on it without taking his gaze from him.

"Yes, sorry, excuse me, please," said Peralta, holding out his hand in the direction of the chair.

"It's ok."

"Again, I ask you, how much influence has your man Divine got?"

"Divine is certainly a man of means with a lot of influence and respect amongst his contemporaries."

"A man of means with a lot of respect," Perelta echoed, his face now turning purple.

"He is someone who has contacts, people in many places, some of them high, as we've discovered. He is someone who will provide a service and could call upon a favour if the need should arise."

"Do you think he is capable of calling on such a service as murder in a Spanish prison?"

"If you were to ask the same question and have the same situation in a British jail, I would have to say yes, but I would have to say it with hesitation if the target was indeed a politician."

"Sí, sí," he responded, stubbing out the cigarette. Again, he sat back in the chair. Wheeler was about to speak, but Perelta cut him off by holding up the palm of his hand.

"We know that Gonzalez was prepared to cooperate and testify. The trouble is, Divine was not the one who did the deal with him. Dupree was the one who did the negotiation, a mediator no doubt, acting on the instructions of Divine. Like Divine, Dupree was not at home when the warrant was enforced this morning." He stopped short and made a note with a stub of a pencil. "We know that this man, Jezard Dupree, he is not a criminal, he is without a criminal history, of previous good character, you understand? We have his passport and, unlike Divine, we are sure we will apprehend him today. We will need him to testify in return for leniency." Perelta now put his two hands up to his face and gently massaged his temples with his manicured fingers. "Let us see."

"All is not lost. We still have Stone; maybe he can give us something on Divine."

"And why would he do that? Especially if this Divine is the man you say he is."

"Leave that to me," he replied confidently. He studied for a while, thinking carefully before choosing his words. Perelta stayed silent, watching the British detective at work. *What was going through this old-timer's mind?* Between the two of them, there must be sixty years of criminal detection. Very rarely had Perelta taken his profession to a personal level with a suspect the way Bill Wheeler had with this Divine. *What was it that drove him so hard to bring this man down?*

"I have it!" said Wheeler, sitting bolt upright in his chair. Perelta wasn't expecting the sudden outburst. It actually startled him.

"I'm sorry," apologized Wheeler before thinking aloud. "You said the evidence against Stone may not be enough to charge him, right?"

"This is what I am being told, yes."

"Alright, can we speak with the officer in charge before he either releases him or brings him to Malaga? You said he was going to bring him to Malaga, right?"

"Yes."

"Okay, we speak with the detective. We ask him to play up the evidence—not to lie but to exaggerate. If he can leave Stone sweating, this helps. This is only going to work if there is insufficient evidence; it's only hypothetical, you understand?" Perelta didn't answer but asked Wheeler to continue.

"This is where I come in. I tell Stone I can get him off the hook in return for information that will lead to the arrest and conviction of Divine, both for the murder of your man in prison and for whatever it is that Divine is planning with Stone."

"Will he go for it?"

"Would you?"

"I am asking you, Bill."

"I'm sure he will. Who wants to spend the rest of their life in a Spanish jail? We know what has happened to Gonzalez. Stone would be under no illusion that the same could happen to him, especially with the fact that it is always a danger that the photographs could fall into the wrong hands."

"Photographs? Oh yes, I remember. Yes, yes, I see." Wheeler could detect a slight hesitation; maybe the Spanish judicial system was not adept at gaining results the easy way. He knew he had to push.

"If we want results, we have to be as devious as these criminals, Mr. Peralta. We have to go by any means. I don't have to remind you we are dealing with killers here, kidnappers and thieves. God knows what they are planning next, here, on your soil. You can prevent this; we have to be one step ahead. Do you understand, Mr. Perelta?"

The Spanish detective looked directly at Wheeler for some time before he spoke.

"But first, we have to talk to my friend in Torremolinos. Of course, I cannot speak for him, you understand?"

"Sure, of course, this goes without saying. Can you call him?"

"Yes, right away," he said with a little more enthusiasm as he grabbed the phone to make the call.

Peralta replaced the receiver after what could have been 10 minutes but felt more like 30 to Wheeler.

In those 10 minutes, Peralta had hardly spoken, just listened with only the occasional question in Spanish. He had scribbled some notes on the large blotting square, nervously looking in Wheeler's direction when something of interest caused him to light up yet another cigarette.

Angelica returned to the office. She placed some documents on her partner's desk and made an exit again as requested.

"Coffee?" she asked without the usual smile.

"No, thank you." *This was no time for coffee or distractions of any kind,* thought Wheeler.

Peralta waited for Angelica to leave the room and close the door before he spoke.

"A preliminary report suggests that the victim was not murdered. It is a young man, a boy actually, just sixteen years old, homosexual, seen leaving a music venue only a minute before Stone. Witnesses say the boy sold drugs to Stone, who, it is presumed, followed the boy from the club and stayed the night with him." He looked down at the jotted notes. "Witnesses also say that the boy sold drugs but was not a user. This claim is backed up by a medical examination of the corpse. There were no drugs in the system." Perelta lit the stub of the cigarette he had extinguished when Angelica had entered the room. He took a large drag, released the smoke upwards as he reclined in the leather chair.

Something in the back of Wheeler's mind was niggling him; there was something there he just couldn't put his finger on. He was brought back to the moment as Peralta continued.

"Stone, it seemed, panicked. This, I tell you now, has to be confirmed, but as it transpires, the boy died in his sleep, choked on his own vomit—natural causes, who knows, the medical term will follow. The death was made to look like the result of a drug overdose, but you see, the administrator of the drugs knew nothing about how the body works—or does not work, in this case—after death. The heroin was administered post-mortem." Again, he paused, this time to extinguish the cigarette for good. Wheeler wished he would cut it out and get on with it.

"So there was no murder?"

"No murder," he confirmed. "Why someone would want to make the death look like a suicide, only he knows."

"Will the detective play ball?"

"He will transfer the responsibility and let me release the suspect. What I tell them is my choice."

"Will I be able to see Stone?"

"I will allow this."

"How soon?"

"Soon. He will be questioned about the false details on the passport; once that is done, he will be transported to Malaga, when I, too, will have to make inquiries regarding the forgeries. I think this can happen after lunch, which is good, because that will give you time to buy it for me."

Wheeler preferred not to hear the last part and was quick to stay on track.

"And the other guy, Bressla, was it?"

"Yes, I know nothing of him, suffice it to say he has done nothing wrong. He will have to be released from Torremolinos."

"I see," said Wheeler, thinking hard now. Who was this Bressla, and what part did he play in all this? Where was Divine? Kathryn Divine! What about her? He asked the question.

"She will be charged with money laundering and released. She has refused to cooperate, but there is little point in holding her."

"Remand in custody?" tried Wheeler.

"Even we are not that cold," answered Peralta.

"But the gun?"

"It transpires there is a license issued to that address."

"Okay, so we wait for Stone. This is going to be very interesting, to say the least."

"I'm sure," replied Peralta, seeing the steely determination on the face of this British detective, followed by what looked like realization.

"Could you have one of your men take me to Torremolinos?"

"Could I ask why?"

"Yes, of course, I'm so sorry. I would like to speak with this Mr. Bressla, pick him up as soon as he is released."

"And Viceroy, Stone, whatever his name is?"

"Let him stew a little. I could speak with Bressla and still be back here in a couple of hours. No?"

"Yes."

"Could you assure your friend keeps hold of Bressla until I get there?"

"Yes, I will call him now," said Peralta.

Wheeler again sat back in his chair. As Peralta picked up the telephone, he looked across the table and could see the realization again on Wheeler's face. It was either the fact that there would be no lunch expense—the fact that he had not put his hand in his pocket once was not lost on the Spanish detective—or it could be something else.

Angelica...

"You have only to look at the papers."

"The boy!" said Wheeler quietly.

"You said something?"

"It's nothing."

"They are full of crime. You see this one, Mr. Wheeler?"

"Sixteen years of age."

"I have grandchildren the same age."

"I have a brother this age. He lives with my father."

The photo fit of the suspect in the newspaper. It was him. Stone!

Chapter Sixty-Eight

The builders had discovered the black BMW coupe parked at the rear of the construction site and had, at first, mistaken it for lovers, drained after a night of passion. One had pushed the other forward hesitantly; giggling like schoolchildren, they had attempted to get a glimpse of flesh through the window. The engine was running, and the windows were steamed. Approaching from the side of the car, they were unable to see the hose attached to the exhaust. Moving slowly now, one tapped the other and directed him to move to the rear of the vehicle. It was only then that the realization hit them—that what they were witnessing was someone's determination to end a life. Quickly now, the elder of the two called back to the other builders who were watching from the windowless shell of the three-quarter villa. All who were brave enough scampered down, while the others that remained elevated stayed put and watched from the safety of a distance.

As soon as the driver's side door was yanked open, a cloud of smoke gushed out into the open air and engulfed the morning dew-covered car. After seconds, the lone figure of a man was visible. There was no hope for the victim who had meant to do the business; it was obvious that much time had elapsed since the start of the ritual. The man's face and upper chest were blue-black, his lips parted with thick fluid still dripping from his open mouth, and his chin was resting on his chest. His hands, which had also turned blue, were locked onto the steering wheel, and it was only when the builder attempted to drag the dead man out by his loose shirt that he realized the man was secured to the wheel with plastic ties. He called for something sharp and, at the same time, turned off the car engine. A knife was passed to him, and he proceeded to cut the ties. The victim fell sideways, making it relatively easy for the builder to drag the dead weight from the car and lay it on the damp earth. The smell was rancid, and the men gagged as the bodily fluids were released from the bound trouser bottoms. The same builder cut the ties securing the corpse's feet. There was no attempt to resuscitate the dead man. The witnesses stood back and looked at the sad figure, some wondering what could bring a man to such a state as to take his own life, others feeling *there but for the grace of God go I*. One of the workmen noticed the writing on the dirty bonnet, and taking a pencil from behind his ear, he used it to scribble the words onto the inside of a torn-open cigarette packet: *Please forgive me Demi, I am so sorry. David, I love you. I will wait for you both. Try not to cry, I am with you always.*

Chapter Sixty-Nine

Stone had called out to Stuli a number of times without getting a response. He thought he heard him talking to a guard in the corridor over an hour ago. He gave the cell door another try. The Spanish jailers were a lot more tolerant than the English. Eventually, one came and unlocked the door.

"Come this way, Señor."

He was taken to a small interview room containing nothing more than a table and three chairs. The door was closed behind him, so he took the seat facing back towards the door. He looked around and noticed a camera looking back at him from above the door. There was a speaker box housed within the casing, and he assumed this to be the recording device for the interview.

Almost 30 minutes went by before a lone detective came through the door, closed it, and placed a file on the table. Taking one of the chairs opposite Stone, he scraped it across the floor, making a loud noise within the tiny confines.

"Your name?"

"You get me a lawyer, I'll tell you my name," answered Stone.

"You need a lawyer?"

"Correct."

"Okay, this may take some time—maybe one, two, three, maybe even four hours."

"No problem," said Stone, now the one scraping back on his chair. He pushed back with his body weight so that the chair rested on its hind legs. He leaned back until his shoulders were resting on the wall behind him and put his feet on the desk to keep his balance.

"Please sit in the correct position, Mr. Maine. Or is it Mr. Viceroy? How about Mr. Stone? Maybe we go back to the original name, shall we?" he said this with confidence as he opened the file, showing a brief history of the Englishman sitting opposite him.

"Where's my legal representative," said Barry, just as confidently as the Spanish detective. "I have rights."

"You will be moved from here to Malaga to be questioned about the death of..." He looked again at a paper lying in the same file. "Jesepi Hernandez."

Stone didn't flinch at the prospect of being interviewed about the death of another, which confirmed to the detective that this was no ordinary civilian seated opposite him. He knew from experience that this would be one hard cookie to crumble, but he wasn't so much worried about that—it would be the problem of his comrade Peralta. What this detective was more concerned about was the fact that this man was travelling on false documents. And now, having started the interview, he decided to let Peralta deal with that too. He stood and left the room without saying another word to Stone. This unsettled Barry Stone, who was just about to kick up a fuss when the door opened and he was escorted back to his holding cell. He checked the names on the two other closed doors along the way and noticed that both had the names of Spanish prisoners written in chalk beside the doors. Stuli had been released.

Chapter Seventy

Stuli closed his eyes against the glare of the midday sun. He rested his hand on the car parked directly outside the station doors and quickly removed it from the heat. The noise from the traffic was horrendous, especially in contrast to the silence inside. His suit was crumpled, and the hat that disguised his unkempt hair was misshapen from sleeping on it. He checked the plastic bag with the property taken from him in the early hours and transferred the passport and money from it into his jacket pocket. His mobile phone was kept back, along with certain other documents the police said they would like to hold onto. He didn't object, mind, or even understand; he was just happy to be out in the fresh air. Fresh air? If one could call it that—the police station was beside the buildings where the fishing boats deposited their catch every day. The smell was overwhelming, but it was free, like he was.

Stuli waited for a gap in the traffic and was just about to make a dash for the bus station opposite when a car stopped, halting his run. The rear window was open, and he was surprised to hear and see a friendly face call him by name.

Placing his hands on the roof of the car, which was somewhat cooler than the last, he leaned closer. Wheeler turned his face away from the rancid smell coming from this odd-looking man's mouth.

"How do you know my name?"

"I am a police officer, Mr. Bressla," said Wheeler, opening the door and then sliding over to make room for this fat man. "Get in the car, please."

Stuli hesitated and stopped short. He leaned into the car and asked Wheeler for some identification. Wheeler produced his card, which Stuli scrutinized before taking a seat beside the man, who was identical in size, and closing the door.

"What is your business with the man you were arrested within the early hours of this morning, Mr. Bressla?"

"Mr. Viceroy? Why do you ask, Detective?"

"Please just answer the question, sir."

"Am I under arrest?"

"No, but this can be arranged."

Fearing the worst and enjoying his newfound freedom, Stuli decided to tread with caution.

"Mr. Viceroy has an interest in my hotel. We are looking to expand our operation, and he wanted to introduce a friend of his who has connections with the property sector here in Spain."

"Does this friend have a name?"

"He does, but I am afraid I don't know. I was introduced to him once, but the name, I cannot recall."

Wheeler knew this fat Jew was lying. He also knew full well that he couldn't hold him much longer and didn't want to jeopardize the operation by doing something silly that might come back to haunt him in any future investigation and subsequent trial.

"Can we drop you anywhere, Mr. Stuli?"

Stuli was tempted but knew exactly what the detective was after.

"No. I will be fine."

"Where are you staying?"

"I'm not sure now. Maybe my plans have changed. Maybe I take a flight back home."

"Which is?"

"The Gambia, West Africa."

At least there was some truth in his story. The text received from Smith confirmed this.

"The hotel, does it have a name?"

"Again I ask the question: Am I under arrest?"

Wheeler leaned over the fat man and released the door handle.

"Get out," he said. The fat man struggled to release himself from the car, and Wheeler was glad to see the back of him. No sooner had he straightened himself up on the causeway when he heard Wheeler call out.

"Just one other thing, Mr. Bressla." Stuli turned to look down at the fat man reaching for the handle of the open car door.

"Yes," he said, straightening his clothes.

"Stone. Barry Stone. Does the name mean anything to you?"

The overweight Jew didn't respond, but Wheeler knew from the change of expression and the way his short steps had him hurriedly scurrying across the busy road that he had hit a nerve. He didn't see any harm in trying, and any further opportunity would call for some simple surveillance. As it was, he had to get back to Malaga and prepare to see Stone.

Chapter Seventy-One

Jerry and Abdul had embraced at the border. Now back on Spanish soil in Ceuta but still divided by water from the mainland, he settled down with a coffee 20 minutes before loading and 45 minutes before departure. He could see the plane on the tarmac refuelling—it was one of the smaller, 24-seater propeller types. *Focher, Facker, Little Fuckers—that's what they were.* He didn't like the small propeller type. He looked at the other passengers sitting within the group, mostly businessmen, again, he guessed. The television, with the volume turned up way too loud, was bracketed to the wall. *Operation Escatura yet again.* There were more arrests being displayed, and the reporter was talking seriously, fast and furious into a microphone. Pictures of faces with titles below—important people. A prison with reporters gathering at the main gates. Camera crews. *It can't be! Not so quick.* An ambulance. *It must be.* His face. Taking the full screen. Augustine Gonzalez. Dead. Murdered this morning. The ambulance leaving at 7:10 a.m. The commentary in Spanish. Other faces, two—typical mug shots, the killers. Jerry was sure some of his fellow passengers could translate; he decided against this request. He also decided to keep his ticket—*his mind was racing*—he may have to, one day, account for his whereabouts. His stomach churned with excitement. He needed the toilet.

The plane landed on time in Madrid. Jerry was advised by the stewardess to remain within the departure lounge due to the fact that his travel plan was a crossover. She explained to him that his luggage would be transferred within the process, so there would be no requirement to check either in or out. There were plenty of facilities within the airport, so the time should pass quickly, she smiled. He wasn't worried about this, just disappointed about not being able to follow through with his intended meeting with Victoria. *Another time. Maybe on the way back.* He decided against calling her. Instead, he called home.

"Hello," he said. The connection was made, but there was no one speaking at the other end of the line.

"Hello," he repeated. He could hear his daughter sobbing.

"Jasmine. What is it, baby? Tell me, honey, it's Dad here. What's the matter, honey?" The sobs became uncontrollable, and Jerry quickly assumed the worst, within reason.

"Has somebody been to the house, pet?" he coaxed.

"Yes, Daddy," *sob* "the police," *sob* "they've took Mummy, Dad."

"Jesus! What for, love? Why did they take Mummy?"

"I'm not sure; they came early, Dad, broke down the door, we were sleeping, Bon…"

Uncontrollable sobs now were all Jerry was getting from his daughter. He didn't want to push her and changed tactics.

"It's alright, baby, I can sort it out. I will call a lawyer now, he'll have her home in no time. Where's Julie, baby?"

"She's here beside me," a little composed now. "Bonito's dead, they've killed Bonito, Dad." More sobs, more than before. Jerry bit the knuckles of his free hand and almost drew blood. He took his hand from the bite and brushed back his hair with it.

"How, baby?"

"She drowned, they wouldn't let us save her, Da…" Again, more sobs. *This was too much for Jerry to take.*

"Listen, Jasmine. I need to make this call. Your mummy will be home soon. What have they done with Bonito, pet? Where is she now?"

"They took her away, come home, Dad, we need you home." This was said silently, and the sound of little Julie crying in the background was more than Jerry could handle at the moment. He knew that returning home at this stage was completely out of the question. The priority at this time was to get Kath home, *but why have they taken her? The money! The fucking money*, he realized. *He should have called Harold back. A mistake, a costly one.*

"Darling, sweetheart," he said. "Please listen to me. Who's there with you now?"

"Just Cleo. There was one police lady, but she has gone now. We did call Demitra."

"Is Demitra on her way?"

"I'm not sure."

"OK, listen, honey, sit tight. I'll call you back. Wait by the phone. I love you."

"I love you too." The phone went dead. Jerry looked at the one in his hand and wanted to crush it. He quickly dialed a number.

"Hello!" Demitra answered eagerly after just one ring.

"Hello, Demitra, it's Jerry here."

"Is Jezard with you?" Had the situation not been too serious, Jerry would have laughed at the name Jezzie had been christened with.

"No, he's not, Dem. Why are you not on your way to ours?"

"Jezzie didn't come home last night, Jerry. I assumed he was with you. What's going on, Jerry?"

"I'm not sure, I—"

"There's something wrong, I know there's something wrong, Jerry." Jerry could detect she was losing it. "Tell me what the hell is going on here, Jerry!"

"Keep calm, Demitra. I want you to go to ours, and I want you to sit with the girls until Kath comes home, alright?"

"The Policia broke into our home, Jerry, looking for Jez. You have to tell me what the fuck is happening, Jerry." This was the first time Jerry had heard language of this nature from Demitra, who would usually frown at any cuss word above "bloody hell." It took Jerry off guard. "I'll sort it, Dem. The quicker you do as I say, the quicker I can get off this phone and make some moves. Do you understand, Dem? Now compose yourself and do as I say, honey, it's for the best. Let me get to work, love, okay?"

"Okay."

"That's a good girl. I'll call you at mine in one hour. Promise me, Dem, you're on your way."

"I'm on my way."

"Promise me, Demitra?"

"Yes, Jerry," she said with resignation. "I'm leaving now."

"Good girl," said a slightly relieved Jerry before finalizing the conversation with a definite, "One hour, Dem."

Once again, he delayed pressing the end button. Instead, he remained standing with his briefcase between his feet, oblivious to the other travellers passing either side of him. He looked around and saw what he was searching for up ahead. Placing the mobile phone in his pocket, he made his way to the bank of public telephones. It was only when he reached the phones and picked up the receiver that he realized he was without change. Slamming the phone down in disgust, he walked briskly to the newspaper stand, picked up a packet of mints from the counter, and quickly handed a twenty to the girl, asking that the change be all in coins.

"Cambio, por favour," the attendant handed him a fistful of loose change. Now, walking briskly back to the public telephones, he was more than annoyed to see all three were in use. *This was no time for pussyfooting around.* He picked up the suitcase resting against the leg of the young man using the middle phone of the three. The other two were engaged with females. The chap made to object and reached to retrieve his luggage. At the same time, Jerry swiftly snatched the receiver from the guy's hand and pressed the lever to disconnect the call. One steely look from Jerry had the young chap scampering away with his heavy case. Jerry dialed a number; Harold answered after the second ring.

"Is that you?"

"Yes, what's wrong?" asked the old-timer.

"Everything."

"Tell me."

"They came sooner than expected."

"The money?"

"They have it."

"Fuck!"

"I know."

"Anything I can do?"

"Yes, I need the lawyer."

"Why, she gone?"

"Yes."

"Leave it with me."

Already, Jerry was relieved somewhat. He called Jezzie from the call box. He wondered why the sixth sense was kicking in. *No reply.* He got a feeling of dread and then realized the worst could work in his advantage— *two for the price of one.* Sometimes he wondered how he could be so callous. The telephone beside him became vacant; he moved over, lifted the receiver, and dialled a number he knew from memory.

"Hi, who's this?" asked Hutchin.

"It's me."

"*Jaysus, holy Mary, mother a God, how are ya? I got ya message. What's the crack?*"

"Can you see me in Manchester tonight?"

"Is it that important?"

"Yes, I wouldn't put it on you otherwise."

"I know, leave it wit me. I'll check the flights into the other place. If you don't hear from me, I'm on me way. Same place?"

"Yes."

"God bless." The Irishman hung up.

Jerry took a business card from his wallet. On the back of it were three telephone numbers; he called one of them. *No reply,* shame, things were moving swiftly. He looked across to a Costa coffee house, checked his watch, considered making another call, decided against it, and made his way over for a quick coffee. *Hutchin would be landing in Liverpool.* Jerry knew Hutchin had a phobia with Manchester Airport; he never did ask him what it was.

Chapter Seventy-Two

Abogado Francis Alexandro Cordeso took the call from Harold and immediately made a call to a corrupt detective based in Marbella. Within 15 minutes, Cordeso was armed with the information required. Kathryn Divine was in custody in Malaga. Charge? Money laundering. Release? Imminent. Bail conditions? None. Representation? Thankfully, as far as Cordeso was concerned, none. He called Harold back and explained he had had to pull a few strings, call in a favour—*not a problem*—and to get her to come into the office tomorrow. Harold thanked him and waited for Jerry to call back. He took a high stool at the bar, poured himself a stiff brandy, and picked up the photograph he had been looking at before he was interrupted by the call from Jerry.

Little Jerry, Harold's other son Adam, and the one and only love of his life were smiling back at him as if from yesterday. He could recall vividly taking the picture—it was the morning of the tragedy. *The last picture he had taken of the three of them before they were killed that very day. How cruel life was. Funny how Little Jerry shared the same name. In fact, his son would be the same age now as Jerry Divine, had he lived.* Harold could feel himself welling up. He kissed the picture three times and placed it back under the bar, telling himself for the hundred thousandth time that he would have it enlarged and put in a frame.

This Cordeso fellow was good, very efficient—but what the fuck was Jerry leaving that kind of money at home for? He would have to have a serious chat with him. *Maybe Jerry was getting too complacent, and that is certainly one thing that should be avoided in this industry.* The politician job had gone according to plan. Harold thought Jerry had made the wrong decision; he would have eliminated the other one—*what was his name? Jes? Jez?*—something like that. It seems he is the only concrete connection to Jerry. *Anyway, that can be taken care of later should the need arise. Whatever it took, he would be there for Jerry.* He took a sip of the warm brandy, then stood with it to walk across the room and look out of the window to the street below. The holidaymakers were taking a stroll. He liked to look for the families, the ones with two sons. He would watch them until they walked out of view. If he was outside, walking himself, he would usually follow them. *He had actually walked into a restaurant and taken a table beside some of them before today, listening to the conversation, trying to remember a time and place when that was him, with his family. How lucky these people were.*

He was startled back into reality by the ringing of the phone. Scurrying in his slippers back across the highly polished parquet floor, he caught it on the last ring.

"It's me, any joy?"

"Yes, phone home in one hour."

"Thanks." The line went dead.

"You're welcome..." he said, placing the handset back on the bar. He finished his brandy and made up his mind. *He would go for a walk by the sea and ask for guidance.*

Chapter Seventy-Three

Jerry drained the last of the strong coffee, grimaced, picked up his case, and walked back over to the bank of phones. He called Jezzie—no reply. He called home, and thankfully, Demitra answered. He assured her that Kath was on her way home and asked that she stay with the children until she arrived. Demitra asked about Jezzie, and he told her he would do all he could to find out where he was. She asked if he would like to speak with the girls; when she told him they were in their room, he decided against it. Once he had told her to tell Kath he would call back tonight, he hung up and looked at the phone resting on its cradle.

He needed to think. Again, he took the small card from his wallet and dialled the top number. This time, a familiar voice answered.

"How the fuck are you, lad?"

"I'm good, mate, and you?" replied Jerry.

"All the better for hearing your voice, mate."

"I'll be on your side tonight, you about?"

"Yeah, sure. You landing at mine?"

"No, the next one up."

"Where d'ya want me?"

"In the Painter's."

"What time?"

"Nine o'clock, that all right with you?"

"I look forward to seeing you, mate."

"Me too, it's been a long time."

"Too long." Jamie O'Rourke pressed the end button. "Yes!" he hollered with a clenched fist.

Jerry, too, was happy to hear his old friend's voice and was excited about what lay ahead. With recent occurrences, it was becoming more and more inevitable that the two robberies would go ahead. He decided against calling the other two numbers until he landed in the UK tonight. He knew Hutchin would be flying into Liverpool but decided against asking Jamie to collect the Irishman, preferring each accomplice to make their own way, thus avoiding cross-contamination. He looked around the busy concourse and decided to venture into the welcoming Irish bar for a long, cool pint of Guinness.

Chapter Seventy-Four

James O'Rourke—Jamie to his friends—had waited a long time for this call, nearly seven years to be precise, and it couldn't have come at a more-needed time. Things had not been good for Jamie, especially since his club had lost its license and the police had closed it down. He had tried to sell the building, but the family who had lost their son as a result of a stabbing in the club had filed a civil suit against the company owned by Jamie. The legal team acting for the bereaved family had successfully gained a high court restraint order preventing Jamie from selling the building. *The police had something to do with this,* he knew. The fact that there was no conviction got right up their noses. It had been a lengthy process; in fact, Jamie had spent over twelve months on remand. It was only the fact that his team had managed to remove the DVD footage from the security system that had allowed Jamie to beat the rap. *It had been coming for some time—if it hadn't been the other guy, it would have certainly been him.* The opposition had tried to muscle in. A few skirmishes had taken place, and this had been going on for almost six months before the fatality. The Keenans were trying to expand their operation into Liverpool from over the Mersey in Bootle. It was expected to come to a head either by someone getting shot or else some from either side getting a bit of bird. Although Jamie was a bit of a force, he had been trying for a long time to show himself as the total opposite. He had been told, under no uncertain terms, by Jerry, to keep his head down and his nose clean.

After the job that went drastically wrong in Ireland, he had done exactly what Jerry had instructed. It hadn't been easy, but he had done it. Things weren't that bad—he was single, living with his mother, and his overheads were low. Yes, he drove a nice car, and the birds cost a few quid, but it was okay. He was worried about the lawsuit; it could cost a bit, and since the club shut, very little was coming in. So yes, he was happy and excited. *It must be something reasonably big for Jerry Divine to call.* He walked in from the garden, where he had taken the call, and kissed his mum on the forehead. She smiled and rubbed his hand, which he had placed on her shoulder. She was about to stand from her Shackleton before he put a little tender pressure on her shoulder.

"Relax, Ma, I'll make you a nice cuppa tea."

"You okay, love?"

"Great, ab-so-fucking-lutely. You want a nice chocolate biscuit?" he called from the kitchen.

"Yes, pet, two, please."

He smiled. *Tonight was going to be a good night.*

Chapter Seventy-Five

Barry Stone was placed in a van with blacked-out windows and driven in convoy to the Central Policia Station in Malaga. The murder detective dealing with the case was all but finished with the suspect. Stone had been cleared of any involvement in the death of the young male prostitute. A full autopsy report had confirmed that the youth had died as a result of inhaling and choking on his own vomit. Blood samples taken from the liver had shown positive results for hepatitis B and C; the kid was HIV positive, which could, if justice prevails, see this beast contracting the disease. Stone was being transported to Malaga under such conditions at the request of Capitan Perelta. It made little difference to this detective—he would deliver him and be done with the piece of shit.

The van stopped at the entrance and was allowed through the automated gates after a few seconds.

Stone looked through the window of the sweatbox before the door holding him in the confined space was loudly opened onto a secure chain. He was asked to feed his cuffed hands through the gap and was double-cuffed to a burly officer before the door was released entirely, and he was taken into the station. There was little difference from any other nick in the UK he had been processed in. The waiting area attached to the garage entrance had four prisoners before him who were left sitting there as he was walked through as a priority. The desk was quite high—chest height. Stone assumed the guy, equivalent to a British desk sergeant, who was looking down at him, was assessing him, reading him. *Fuck him,* thought Barry. *So what if I do look like a big poof, who gives a fuck.* He looked up at the guy and smiled. The officer looked away and took the file from the guard still cuffed to Barry and opened it. Again, he looked at Barry, then at the file, and again at Barry, obviously comparing a photograph.

"It's me, alright," he said sarcastically.

The sergeant didn't acknowledge the comment. He nodded in the direction of the cuffs, and the guy chained to him released the bracelet from Stone's wrist. Another Policia stepped down from the desk and took hold of Barry by the arm. Barry shrugged him off.

"This way, señor, please," he said, indicating the door leading to the custody suite. Stone followed him and almost bumped into a female officer coming through from the opposite direction. The middle-aged woman with the officer apologized as she brushed up against the man wearing the tight leather trousers and open-neck shirt. She looked once and then again at Barry as he immediately tried to compose himself. *He wasn't sure if Kath Divine recognized him.*

Chapter Seventy-Six

Demitra rushed toward the door as the bell rang, calling up to the girls who were also racing down the stairs. The only thing missing from the scene was little Bonito. Little Julie was the first to reach the intercom beside the door, and she pressed the speaker button.

"Mummy?"

"Yes, darling," answered Kath eagerly.

Jasmine pressed the button to release the gate outside, and Demitra opened the door. The sun immediately lit up the entrance as the wide door let in the light, followed by Kath, who embraced her two daughters. Demitra stood back, allowing the three a moment to comfort each other. Eventually, the girls released their mother, who stood to her full height and stifled some tears.

"It's going to be all right, everything is going to be fine," she attempted to put on an air of authority. Demitra took her cue.

"OK, girls, come on, let your mother through. Jas, you put the kettle on. Julie, you go on up and pour your mummy a nice hot bath." Kath smiled at her friend and nodded toward her youngest daughter.

"Bonito's gone, Mummy," cried Julie. Kath couldn't hold it any longer. She held out her arms to little Julie, who again came into them sobbing.

"I'm so sorry, baby, I'm so, so sorry," she said soothingly as she picked up her daughter and looked over the girl's shoulder at Demitra.

"I'll run the bath," said her friend, walking up the stairs. Kath carried little Julie into the kitchen, where Jasmine was pouring hot water from a kettle into a teapot. Kath noted how composed and brave Jasmine was, just like her father. *She wondered how composed he would be when she let loose.* And that guy in the police station—*he looked so familiar.* What was it about him that had her continually retracing the brief, chance encounter?

Chapter Seventy-Seven

Jezard Dupree was identified almost immediately. The evidence was there, in the car—everything to make it a formality. Abogado details, business information, passport, home address, wife's details—it looked like a cut-and-dry suicide. Simple. Or so it seemed until the officer assigned to the case was called into the office of his superior. He was asked to bring the file up to date and then return to his duties, pre-discovery of the deceased. The package was then couriered to Malaga and was on Peralta's desk by 6 p.m.

It was open and shut. There was very little Peralta could do or say. As far as Divine was concerned, there was little point in pursuing the matter. He would arrange to see Kristos Koiduste later in the day; he had already agreed with him—*off the record*—that he would be allowed bail with conditions. For that reason, the officer in charge was entitled to a little something in return. He could always use the threat of pulling the rug. Detective Wheeler, on the other hand, would have to be a little more open with Peralta, especially regarding his deep-rooted personal vendetta against this Divine fellow. *There was obviously some aggressive cancer eating into the flesh of the British detective,* and Perelta saw no reason why he should breach protocol and put his own reputation on the line to find a cure. *He had no problem giving a little morphine, but not to the extent of jeopardizing his position.* He decided to call Wheeler from the interview, where he had left him with the prisoner almost an hour earlier.

Chapter Seventy-Eight

Bill Wheeler had been escorted by Angelica to the custody suite. The route was cold and claustrophobic, with long corridors painted pale blue, and there were no doors along the way. Wheeler guessed the two of them were walking under the busy roads of Malaga, probably toward the criminal courts. A red strip of plastic integrated within a mould ran the entire length of the long whitewashed walls of the walkway—an attack alarm. This stopped abruptly at a grey steel door. Angelica pressed the intercom button beside it and spoke into a speaker; a response directed her to show her identification to the lens, looking at the two from the corner above. A sound indicated the security release, and she pushed the steel door, which echoed loudly back along the tunnel.

"Please walk straight ahead. Captain Peralta will be waiting for you at the other end. When you have finished, you will be escorted back as far as this door, where I will return to collect you." She didn't smile or shake his hand. Wheeler tried to smile and was about to hold out his hand before she turned and walked away. He watched her leaving and wondered what had brought about the change in attitude. The speaker cracked into life, and Wheeler guessed he was being told to release the door.

He joined Peralta to look through the one-sided glass at Stone, and if the situation weren't so serious, he would have laughed. *What the fuck was this cunt wearing? And what was with the change? The bleached hair and big lips.* He had to scrutinize the man sitting back on the hind legs of the wooden chair. It was him, alright—the same cocky, confident brute. He was rocking slightly with his feet against the side of the table, his arms held high with his hands resting on the top of his head. He looked at the glass, obviously admiring the reflection, and smiled. *He smiled—could he see him?* Wheeler looked questioningly at Perelta standing beside him. The Spanish detective guessed the question and shook his head without Wheeler asking it.

"You confident fuck," he muttered under his breath. "What the fuck are you up to?" An officer standing with the two policemen and holding the keys to the room looked at this big Englishman and smiled. Wheeler nodded his head and looked at the door; the officer opened it and ushered him in.

Divine Intervention

Peralta stopped and took hold of Wheeler by the arm, stopping him in his tracks. He indicated that he had a message received on his beeper. He read the message and told Wheeler to carry on without him.

Barry Stone tried hard not to show his surprise. He took his feet from the table and let the chair fall hard under his weight to its correct position, placing his elbows on the table. Wheeler noticed and remembered how he had threaded his fingers in a tight grip before, the whites of his knuckles the only sign of duress. Wheeler took a seat opposite and looked straight into the eyes of Stone. Neither of the only two present spoke. Barry looked at the glass and back into the eyes of Wheeler.

"What the fuck are you doing here?"

"You tell me, Barry. What are you doing in Spain with Divine? You better seriously think before you answer that question, Barry, because let me tell you, son, you are in deep shit here. Your overdose gimmick isn't going to save you—not this time, kid. The boy was already dead." Now, it was Wheeler's turn to push back his chair. He dared not push his luck for the two-legged position, but he did lift his feet up and cross them onto the desk, resting his podgy hands on his podgier stomach.

"You're not under caution, Barry. There is no one listening. Think carefully, Barry—I want to know what's going on. Everything!"

Barry didn't respond, his mind working overtime. Wheeler could see this all too clearly. Although one and the same, he and Jerry Divine, Stone could never hide the way he was thinking—not like Divine, who was difficult to read. Stone was not as self-disciplined as his superior and partner in crime.

"How did you get here so quick?"

"Spain? I was already here."

"For me?"

"For Jerry."

"For what?"

"Doesn't concern you."

"Then why are we talking?"

"Because I'm the only one in this world that can help your sorry hide."

"And why would you want to do that, Mr. Wheeler? You'll have to tell me more."

"Barry, son. Don't get too comfortable asking the questions here. I'm the one holding the key." Wheeler replied, taking his feet from the table and replacing them with his elbows. "I don't have to tell you fuck all. You're the one who's up the creek without a paddle. You're the one who is going to spend the rest of his life in the oven these grease balls call prison. I've told you once, and I'll tell you again, Barry—think very carefully and give me an answer. I'm not playing cat and mouse here. I helped you once, and I can help you again, but you must give me what I want. I want Jerry Divine, so don't fuck with me, Barry. Do not fuck with me!"

"You can get me off this one? The kid thing?"

"That's up to you, son. The ball, as they say, is in your court."

"I don't know," replied Stone hesitantly. "I'm not sure."

"You're not sure? You're not sure what? What you're doing, why you're here? What? What are you not sure about? I'm warning you, I've told you—do not fuck with me."

"Why I'm here? I got a message from Jerry. I came," he said, raising his shoulders matter-of-factly.

Wheeler knew he was lying. *Why didn't he mention the hotel? Unless this Bressla chap was lying.* He decided to give him a little rope.

"This Bressla fellow, Stuli—I've spoken to him. He seems to know a little more than you about why you're here. Now, I'm going to give you one more opportunity to come clean before I walk out of this room and from your decrepit life forever." Again, he relaxed back in his chair. He studied the face of the man opposite him. *He wanted to ask about the change in appearance, what he was wearing, etc. He knew this man was a beast—a despicable child molester—but he had to admit he hated Divine more.* Once he had Jerry Divine where he wanted him, he could do the same with this scumbag. First things first. Again, he looked directly into the eyes of Stone. They were scared. *The eyes never lied—not like the straightened nose or pouched lips.* The beads of sweat in the air-conditioned room told Wheeler Stone was ready, almost there. *It was coming.*

Stone, on the other hand, was thinking about what he could tell this man to keep him happy for now. There was no way he was giving away the project. *Divine could go; he didn't give a fuck about him—but not yet. He needed the money just as much as he needed his liberty.* He was desperate for time, and he knew it showed—he couldn't retain his composure.

"I can..." The door opened—to his relief—and Peralta looked in without entering. He held a file up and beckoned Wheeler to leave the room. Stone looked from one to the other and then at Wheeler's back as he left the room and closed the door.

"This had better be important," said an annoyed Bill Wheeler. "I had him—he was just about to open up. What is it, Mr. Peralta?"

"You can use the interruption to your advantage. Tell him we have more evidence, evidence that implicates him in another murder. Tell him anything. There is no recording. This is important—for me, for you, and for Divine. Mr. Jerry Divine, who, it seems, without even trying, is winning the case against him."

"What do you mean?" asked Wheeler, looking from the detective back to the closed door and back again.

"Jezard Dupree is dead."

"Dead? How?"

"Suicide. Unlike the little gay boy, this one is genuine."

"Fuck!" screamed Wheeler, slapping the wall with the flat of his hand. He looked intently at Stone through the glass. "You come back in there with me, hold the file under your arm, and say nothing."

"I will not be entering the room, Mr. Wheeler, unless, of course, we place the prisoner under caution." Wheeler looked at Peralta. *He could feel Divine slipping away.* Again, he looked through the glass.

"Okay," he said, taking a deep breath.

"May I also remind you, Bill, I am doing this only as a favour to you." Peralta joined Wheeler to look at the prisoner. The two overweight detectives, with the same aim, one perspiring more than the other, between them took the full width of the large two-way mirror. The Spanish one was the first to break the silence, except for the heavy breathing. "I will have to release him soon. All I have to do is speak with him in relation to the fake identification, retain the forgeries, and release him. I can, of course, impose conditions."

Conditions! Conditions mean fuck all! thought Wheeler. *This man would be on his toes at the drop of a hat.* He had one last hope, and that was to drill in the seriousness of the kid's murder. He knew that Stone would be no use to Divine with a murder rap. Divine would run a mile, and what would he say if he knew that it was a kid, a poof?

"How long do I have?" he asked Peralta as he mopped his brow of sweat despite the cold air blowing from the unit.

"Thirty minutes at the most."

Detective Bill Wheeler didn't respond but walked directly into the room.

"Right! This is getting very interesting. The pathologist's report says the cause of death is asphyxiation—smothered. Buggered and smothered, Barry. We could add rape; there was damage to the rectum, obvious indications of force. Samples of deposits taken from this area already indicate a DNA match to you." Wheeler bluffed, retaking his position opposite the now not-so-confident Stone. Wheeler was already feeling much better. "You're fucked, Barry. Just like the boy, but in a much tighter position. Whichever way you look at it, you're as fucked as the young stiff. Whether I let you go and tell Jerry, or you go back to the oven and I tell him, it's all the same—you're snookered. Do you know he had a man killed in prison this morning? Eh? Do you know this? A politician, no less. What would he do to you, Barry? What is it, you know? What would the two of you like to keep secret?" Again, Wheeler moved forward in his chair, the creak of wood reminding him not to get too excited. "Come on, Barry, save yourself."

"Do you trust me, Mr. Wheeler?" Barry Stone asked quietly, surprisingly controlled. His head was bowed, but his eyes were focused on the ageing, overweight detective he couldn't stand the sight of.

"Should I?"

"Did I let you down the last time?"

"I didn't get my man."

"You will this time if you trust me."

"Why? Why should I, Barry?" Wheeler moved even closer; he could smell the stale breath of someone who had slept off a night of drinking in the confines of a windowless cell.

"I need time."

"For what?"

"I only have half a story."

"Tell me that half, and I'll take the other half for final settlement."

"One is no good without the other. It could jeopardize the job."

Wheeler had to concede he had little choice but was not about to declare this.

"Tell me something, Barry. Is it a robbery? Is it here? In Spain? Give me something." He decided to ask a question that would tell him something of the calibre of this man. "Where have you been for the last few years, Barry?"

"Africa. The Gambia."

"Did you abscond from the protection system?"

"Yes."

"Who was your handler?"

"I don't remember; I had very little contact."

"I see."

This was at least something—something of truth. Maybe, just maybe, he could work with this. What choice did he have?

"OK, listen," said a cautious Wheeler. "You're going to have to bear with me. If I can swing this—and I haven't decided yet—you'll have to answer some questions in relation to some false documents. The dead boy won't get a mention, but I warn you, Barry, you have to go all the way with me on this one." Wheeler looked deep into the eyes of the man he had watched grow up in the shadow of Divine, never far behind. Barry Stone acknowledged and nodded back in agreement, this time a broken man with tears. Wheeler gave an audible sigh of relief; he was content he had done enough. One more subtle push.

"It is, isn't it, son? A robbery?" This was asked quietly as the detective walked around the table to stand behind Stone. He rested his hands on the shoulders of the broken man and watched the head nod slowly, again, in agreement. Wheeler's heart skipped a beat. *Yes!*

"Where are you staying?" he coaxed.

"Gibraltar."

"How long?"

"How long have I been there, or how long do I intend to stay?"

"Both."

"A week and a week, at the most."

"Where's Divine?"

"I'm not sure."

"Is it armed?" Quick, tactical.

"Armed?"

"The robbery."

"Please, Mr. Wheeler…"

"Don't fuck with me, Barry!" Wheeler screamed. He moved forward, his full weight and girth almost knocking Stone from his chair as he slammed the palm of his hand on the graffiti-laden table. This more than startled the seasoned villain, who cowered slightly under the unexpected verbal onslaught.

"I'm not, for fuck's sake! You've got to let me work this my way, Mr. Wheeler. Jerry's back in a few days; this is all I know. You know him—he's up to all sorts. He has business every fucking where."

"Do not fuck with me, Stone. Which hotel are you in?" Change, fast, furious. All the training, experience, concentrating on the target. The answers were fluent. Wheeler was content.

"The Rock."

This is good. Wheeler knew this—Angelica had told him earlier. He was happy.

"Mr. Maine?"

"Yes."

"I'll call you." Wheeler was more than pleased with the way his scheme had gone to plan so smoothly. He picked up the nondescript papers from the desk, placed them securely under his arm, opened the door, and turned to look one more time at the not-so-confident-now Barry Stone. He smiled at the sorry state and closed the door quietly behind him.

When he left the room, he was surprised to see Peralta still waiting outside. He had been watching the whole affair through the two-way glass. It was obvious from the actions that Wheeler had made progress, and if Perelta hadn't received the information about Dupree, he would have congratulated him. As it was, he could see the case, as far as Divine and Operation Escatura were concerned, slipping through his fingers. Peralta himself now entered the room and took the seat that Wheeler had occupied and left somewhat damp. This time, it was Wheeler's turn to watch as Stone was placed under caution and questioned briefly in regard to the false papers. He watched Barry Stone sign a declaration admitting to using the documents. He was then bailed to reappear at a later date.

Wheeler checked his phone for messages. *Call me ASAP—Smithy.* He was about to make the call when he realized there was no signal, and the door to the interview room opened. Stone was placed in the safekeeping of the young custody officer, and Wheeler followed Peralta back through the underpass to join Angelica in the office.

Once the three were sitting comfortably, Wheeler waited until the time felt right before he opened the line of inquiry with the oldest phrase in criminal investigation. He imagined it was universal—and it was. In answer to his question, *Where do we go from here?* Peralta looked at Angelica, who shrugged her shoulders.

"As far as Jerry Divine is concerned, we have nowhere to go—back to the drawing board. We must not lose sight of the fact that we have others to focus on," Perelta smiled at his junior colleague.

"This is true. There are indeed other fish to fry."

"Can the Russian help?" she asked.

"Maybe. I will see him tonight. You go home now, dear; it has been a long day."

"The driver, Callahan, is it?" asked Wheeler.

"Yes, Thomas. Thomas Callahan. I spoke to him myself," she offered. "Not much to report, I'm afraid—he knows very little, and I believe him. I also believe that if he did know things, he would indeed be a good ally. He cried like a baby! Is that the phrase, Bill?"

"It is. Do we still have him?"

"No, but we issued him a phone. He has agreed to maintain contact."

"To work with us? Do you trust him—not to tell Divine, I mean?"

"We spoke to a division in Limerick, Ireland. He has been arrested in the past on a number of occasions—nothing serious, but he has acted as an agent provocateur. I let him know we were aware of this, and he agreed it would be more advantageous to do the same for us."

Angelica stood. Wheeler looked at her, then at Peralta, who smiled broadly. Wheeler was happy with the way things were going but was aware, only too well, that there were, in fact, two operations running parallel here, and the way things were going, his might well be the forerunner in respect to Jerry Divine. He was pleased that Angelica had referred to him by his first name—his chest puffed up slightly at the mention of it from her pretty lips. She did look tired. He smiled; she smiled back as she gathered some paperwork. *Fucking amazing,* thought Wheeler. *Smithy!* He was disheartened for a brief moment with the comparison.

"Excuse me, I must make a call," he said, scrolling through his contacts and calling his sidekick.

"Boss, that you?" said a voice that felt distant, even though it had only been less than five days.

"What's up, Smithy?"

"They want you back, Bill."

"Fuck! Who? Why?"

"Phelps. Says you've had long enough."

"Tell him you're having difficulty getting hold of me."

"He's not going to buy that, Boss."

"Just do it. I'm onto something here, Smithy—something big. Keep them off my back, son. There's a good lad."

"I'll do my best, Gov."

"I'll call you at home from now on. Keep sending me the texts to show you're trying."

"Will do. Good luck."

"See ya, kid." *Fuck!* "Sorry, Angelica," he blushed.

"Your superiors want you to return?" asked Peralta.

"I'm afraid so."

"Adios, gentlemen."

"Goodbye, Angelica. Please excuse my language."

"By now, I am becoming accustomed to it." She smiled—a smile that warmed his heart.

The two Spanish detectives spoke in their native tongue before she left the two men alone in the room.

"Do you like to have a drink, Bill?"

"Of?"

"Whatever you like," said Peralta, opening a large mahogany drinks cabinet.

"A whiskey, neat, for me, please, Mr. Perelta."

"Please, you may call me Angelo."

"Angelo..." mused Wheeler. "Angelo and Angelica—nice ring to it."

"She is named after her father," said Peralta, handing Wheeler his drink. Wheeler was flabbergasted but very pleasantly surprised. He was immediately envious of this shrewd detective.

"I would have never guessed. Congratulations!" he said, holding up his glass.

"Thank you, Bill."

"Cheers, my Hispanic friend."

"To our good health," smiled Angelo Peralta.

Chapter Seventy-Nine

Demitra was sitting on a poolside lounger. She couldn't hold back much longer; she had to let it out. Surely Kath knew what was going on. The girls were now in their rooms, and her friend had showered and was now across the pool in the enclosed bar area, pouring the two of them a large gin and tonic. Demitra looked up at the sun, which was as red as she had seen it in a long time, trying to make sense of the way it lowered itself behind the mountain. She almost wished she, too, could disappear. She looked over to see Kath watching her through the glass partition. Something was seriously wrong, and she was beginning to feel like she was the only one in the dark.

"There you go, darling," said Kath, avoiding eye contact and placing the tall glass on the low table beside her. "Get that down you, pet, it'll do you good."

"Thank you, babe."

"What are you thinking, honey?"

Demitra picked up the cold drink, took a large mouthful, and pressed the glass against her cheek. The cold drops of water were soothing against her skin. What was she thinking? She wanted to tell Kath exactly what she was thinking! How she blamed Jerry for this, whatever it was, she blamed Jerry. And where was he? Where was he now? When the doors were kicked off, when her husband was missing, when the girls were heartbroken about their pet dog. Where was he? Surely Kath was feeling the same way? She had to let her know.

"I'm going to make one more attempt to ring my husband, Kath, and then I'll tell you what I'm thinking, honey!"

Kath truly understood how her friend was feeling, and for this reason, she let the sarcastic remark pass. She, too, was angry, very angry, more than annoyed with Jerry. She said nothing as Demitra made the call; instead, she looked towards the sea and watched the large moon rising above it. It seemed to be looking down at the two of them, almost mocking them. Kath tried to imagine what it saw: the two of them in distress, sorry states to say the least, lost souls. She knew that without Jerry, she was nothing; without him, she was halved automatically, but she also knew that she was on the brink. The girls were now old enough to understand. It was different before they were born and even when they were young, but now they understood. They understood between right and wrong; they were being affected. Kath had serious reservations about her future with Jerry. She was deep in thought when Demitra spoke to someone on the mobile phone.

"That was the Policia," she said, looking straight ahead as if in a daze.

"And?"

"I don't know," she said vacantly. "They wouldn't say."

"Were they in your home?"

"No, they answered Jezzie's mobile."

"Maybe they have him in the police station."

"I'm not sure, Kath." She now looked at her friend. All feelings of hostility towards her were gone. She needed her, like she had come to give support to her and the children. Now, it was she who needed her.

"What did they say exactly?"

"They asked me who I was, where I was, if I could come to the Policia station in Estepona, and if I could bring someone with me for support. Weren't you listening, Kath? I'm scared, Kath! Something is seriously wrong." She was losing it; Kath could see this. She moved closer to her and took her in her arms. Demitra let it out. It wasn't what she had planned to let out. She had every intention of giving Kath a piece of her mind. Now it was different. She needed her.

"I'm frightened, Kath."

"Try to hold yourself together, love. Maybe Jez has been involved in an accident or something. Let's not jump to hasty conclusions, hey, pet? C'mon, I'll come with you. Come on, babe, I'm with you."

"Thanks, Kath."

Chapter Eighty

Jerry had drunk more than he had intended to. The Guinness had given him some escape—he wasn't a man to hide behind the bottle, far from it; he liked to face a challenge head-on. *"Drink was never a cure, that's for sure,"* Hutchin liked to say, but the dark beer was soothing, and the few whiskey chasers had seen the time disappear. He checked his watch. *Fuck!* Less than one hour to boarding. He called home—no reply. On the third attempt, Jasmine answered. Mummy wasn't in; she had gone out with Demitra ages ago. Demitra was upset. Three pints later, Jerry had to compose himself before joining the other passengers at the gate.

He slept on the plane for the complete journey and was gently shaken on the shoulder by the stewardess to wake up and disembark at Manchester. Jerry had predicted the likelihood of problems, and it was for this reason that he had asked Kath to pack two medium cases. Once these were collected from the carousel, he made his way out into the mild evening air and flagged the first taxi available.

"The Lowry Hotel, please."

"Very nice, sir. Business?"

"You could say that." When the driver didn't respond, Jerry spoke again, "Sorry, pal, I had one too many on the plane—my head's banging."

"I get it, mate. Some like to talk, some don't—you don't, and I understand completely."

"Thanks."

The Lowry Hotel was approximately ten miles from the airport, which gave Jerry enough time to compose himself. He wound down the window and let the cool breeze deflect off his extended arm and brush across his face. Twenty-three minutes later, he could see the lights of the bold contemporary architectural achievement with its dramatic, curved, glass-fronted façade overlooking the banks of the River Irwell.

The concierge remembered Jerry from his last stay; he recognised him immediately and urged the bellhop to relieve him of his luggage. Jerry explained to the Frenchman that he would not be staying, that he was meeting friends for drinks, and asked if he could check flights for that evening to Exeter. He gave the chap a folded note, for which the hired help returned and gave him a ticket for his luggage.erry looked at the concierge's name badge and pushed his luck—he asked if there was somewhere he could freshen up. Vincent Distel looked somewhat perturbed until Jerry made a motion to the same pocket the banknote had come from just a moment before.

"Maybe we can help, sir." He took the small bag from Jerry's hand and made for the reception area. He said something quietly to the girl behind the desk, who passed him a key.

"Please! The bathroom only."

"Sure, thank you," said Jerry, looking at the key fob and making for the lift.

Chapter Eighty-One

Jamie O'Rourke was a little early. It would be a sin to be late, especially after such a long time. He looked at his watch—seventeen minutes to nine. He checked it against the time illuminated on the console of his Range Rover Vogue: 8:43 p.m. He parked directly outside the doors to the Lowry Hotel and waited for the valet to approach. He disconnected his mobile phone from the charger, checked it for messages—there were none—switched it off, and placed it securely in the glove compartment. Stepping from the motor, he gave the young man his keys and a £10 note and made his way leisurely into the lounge bar. He knew he shouldn't, but he ordered a large vodka and tonic to calm himself down.

He had just ordered his second vodka when Jerry joined him. O'Rourke checked his watch; Jerry did the same and smiled. It was exactly 9:00 p.m. when the two embraced.

Chapter Eighty-Two

Hutchin O'Brien

Hutchin had given strict instructions to the head stable hand. There was one special mare in particular that needed to be prepared for Saturday's meeting at The Curragh. Today was Thursday; hopefully, this evening's meeting with Jerry would not develop into a two-day event, which should, hopefully, see him back in Ireland tomorrow night at the latest.

He had been preparing this horse for a long time now, holding it back in all the right meetings. Most of the punters had completely lost faith in her, given her failure to meet expectations, especially when one scrutinised the bloodline. The faith had withered, and the money wagered on her—because of the great expectations in the early days—had now dried up. Suckaterri would be coming out of the gates at no less than thirty-three to one at 2:35 on Saturday. He made a call to the Indian in Spain to confirm that the plan was to go ahead, that Suckaterri was *"a sure ting,"* and to get as much on the nose as possible.

Hutchin O'Brien lived alone on the highly regarded stud farm situated on the edge of Galway on the west coast of Ireland. His home was a recently constructed, sectional, wooden two-bedroom affair delivered by mail order from Canada. No planning permission was required because it was under the required footprint in size, and it was all manufactured from wood, which blended in nicely with the stables. To anyone visiting the stud farm, Hutchin looked like any other employee who gained just enough respect from the toffee-noses. He would give some potential buyers of fine breeding the grand tour with advice for investment; they would listen intently to his reasoning, gained from many years of *"hands-on"* experience and knowledge. He would go on to convince the rich to leave their newly acquired live toy in the safe hands of Manor Heath Stud Farm, where the filly would receive special treatment—he would see to that.

The profile he portrayed was exactly the one he enjoyed, the life he chose. Only the boss living in the grand house knew that, if Hutchin decided, it would be he in the hut and Hutchin in the house. The others employed there had absolutely no idea that each and every one of them was on the payroll of Hutchin O'Brien.

The Ryanair flight touched down at John Lennon Airport almost thirty-five minutes late, at 18:38 on a wet evening. Hutchin stood as soon as the plane came to a standstill and the sound indicated the release of the seatbelts. He took his hand luggage from the overhead locker and, as he did, he quickly scanned the faces of the other passengers for the second time. The first had been when he was the third person to board the one-hour flight from Dublin. Mr O'Brien had requested a front exit seat, which gave Hutchin the opportunity to check out all the other passengers as they entered the plane. He was more than happy, and even more so when he was the first one, after the two cabin crew, through departures without a hitch.

His photographic memory of the relatives and friends waiting to greet the travellers showed nobody he recognised. He pulled the corduroy collar of his waxed jacket together with one hand and raised the other, which was holding his small holdall, to lift the peak of his deerstalker. He was half expecting James O'Rourke to tap him on the shoulder as he climbed into a taxi; he didn't, so he asked the driver to deposit him at Lime Street train station, where he sat in the cafeteria drinking coffee and people-watching for almost forty minutes before buying a ticket to Manchester.

The slight drizzle in Dublin had turned into a mild, dry night in Manchester. It was 9:20 p.m. when Hutchin stood in the doorway of the Lowry Hotel and removed his jacket and hat. He placed these under the arm, holding his bag, and flattened his hair with his free hand. He quickly ran each foot down the back of the opposite leg, then walked confidently through the door into the reception area. He was out of his comfort zone in these places; he preferred the outdoors, the sticks, with nothing but the creatures of the night to observe, but this was where Jerry wanted to see him, so here he was.

"Can I help you, sir?" asked the bellhop.

"No, I'm grand."

"Take your coat, maybe?"

"No, thank you," said Hutchin, looking towards the bar.

"Have a pleasant night, sir."

"Yeah," he answered.

Divine Intervention

Hutchin smiled as he made his way to join his friends in the far corner. Jerry was on his feet before he reached the table, and Jamie stood as he approached. The three shook hands, and Hutchin took a seat next to Jerry, facing the entrance.

"Drink?" asked Jerry, placing a hand on the Irishman's knee.

"Coffee, please," answered Hutchin, tapping the back of his friend's hand. Jerry released the comforting grip and held up his hand for the attention of the waiter.

"Coffee, please, and..." He looked at Jamie O'Rourke, who held up his glass. "Vodka and tonic, and more water for me, please."

When the waiter was out of earshot, Jerry placed a hand on Hutchin's shoulder. At the same time, he moved forward, bringing the Irishman with him to rest closer to the table. Both Hutchin and Jamie were eager to hear what was coming next. The three friends looked like any others, catching up on old times—nothing too clandestine but enough to keep what was about to be discussed private.

"I have two projects coming up, both nice, but the second is a little more complicated."

"Complications," said Hutchin, raising his eyebrows. "The tings I thrive on."

The Irishman smiled knowingly, and Jamie laughed. Jerry remained serious; the other two got the message and straightened their faces.

"OK, this is it. What we have"—he looked from one to the other—"is a blag in Belgium, a nice little touch: diamonds, cut and uncut. We take what we can in the time allowed."

"Value?" asked O'Rourke.

"I'm not sure exactly, but in a way, it's immaterial. It's enough—enough for a wage, but more importantly, enough to finance the second number."

"Which is?" asked Hutchin.

"Cash. Thirty big ones." He looked at his friends, each in turn, and then back to Hutchin. He could see the glint in the green Irish eyes.

"Thirty mil... cash?" he asked, the glint almost watery.

"Minimum," stressed the boss.

"Fucking hell!" said O'Rourke under his breath, moving his body slightly closer. The three professionals knew that there were plenty of thirty-mill lumps in the cities—fifty, a hundred million—but it was the knowledge, the inside information, which was hard to acquire. The two criminals looking at Jerry knew full well that this information was in the bag. If Jerry Divine had called it on, it was a fact: the thirty big ones were accessible. What were the complications? That was the question.

"Whereabouts is this babysitting?" asked Hutchin.

Jerry didn't answer immediately. He noted first and then waited until the waiter arrived and placed the drinks on the table. He thanked him and waited until he was, again, out of earshot.

"The diamonds are in Belgium, Antwerp. The money…" He sat back in his chair with his glass of water. "I want to hold this back for now, but I can tell you it will be ours during the first week of October."

"Does that give us enough time to prepare? We have the first one to organise," said O'Rourke, he too, reclining comfortably in his chair.

"I'm on with it," answered Jerry. "I fly to Exeter tonight." He looked at his watch. "In fact, I should be making tracks shortly. What I wanted to make sure of is, number one, if you were available, and number two, whether you're up for it, and of course, the obvious—is there any heat about?" He looked at both for a brief moment. Neither responded to the latter, which was what Jerry was hoping for.

"Who's in?" asked Hutchin.

"You, me, Jamie, Martin, and Winston." He left Barry Stone out of the equation for obvious reasons; he still hadn't worked out how he was going to approach this issue. After all, these were not men to be taken lightly—they were all individuals in their own right. Jamie O'Rourke smiled; he was excited at the prospect of working with the old team, not to mention the great opportunity for some welcome finance.

"I'm in," he said, draining the vodka from his glass.

"Count me in," added Hutchin.

"Good," said Jerry, raising his glass of water. His Irish friend raised his coffee cup, and Jamie joined them with his empty glass in a toast.

"Good health, happiness…" The three of them finished the toast, "…success and long life!"

"And here's to Suckaterri in the 3:45 at the Curragh on Saturday," added the Irishman with a twinkle in his eye. Jerry put his glass down and smiled. O'Rourke shook his head. Jerry asked how sure the trainer was.

Hutchin assured him it was a good ting. Jerry completed the toast, "To Suckaterri." O'Rourke refused to lift his empty glass for this occasion.

Chapter Eighty-Three

Winston La-Bhatt

Winston La-Bhatt didn't know how or why he was taken from his native Nigeria and ended up living in Great Britain. He attended a predominantly white school—the same junior school as Jerry Divine—in Leeds, West Yorkshire. When Jerry had moved down south for a few years in his early teens, the two had stayed in touch by letter and in person when Jerry returned up north during the school holidays. Winston was exactly the same age as Jerry and Barry Stone, who made up the terrible trio.

It wasn't easy in those days, being so tall for his age, black as coal, with a funny accent. The guardians who looked after him were white, above middle class, and both doctors. Everything was fine in his new home when he was young, up until the age of eleven or twelve. Then things began to change; he realised the novelty was wearing off for his carers, and at times, he believed his adopted parents were embarrassed by him. The kids at school didn't make things any easier, especially as the older he got, the taller he became. At the age of eleven, he was up there with the teachers—not in intelligence, but in size. It wasn't funny when all the other boys used to take the piss, until Jerry came along with his sidekick, Barry Stone, and saved his hide from what could have been a severe beating. One of the school bullies had taken it upon himself to enhance his status by challenging the *Zulu* to a straightener behind the bike shed after school. Winston knew he couldn't win—if he did, he would get it from the bully's gang anyway. The worst part about it was that Jane would see it all. Winston liked Jane, and he got the feeling she liked him too—just the way she looked at him. He felt a connection, either that or she felt sorry for him. Maybe it was wishful thinking; it must have been because she ended up with Barry Stone, and he was totally different to him. Barry was okay, but he was taken away and put into a community school for two years. That, and the sudden departure of his friend Jerry, left Winston feeling alone and very vulnerable. Winston was hoping this would lead to an opportunity to get a little closer to Jane, but no, it didn't happen. Barry had some kind of hold over her; Winston could never get his head around it. He always had him down as a little weird

Divine Intervention

but okay. He never told anyone how he felt about Barry, or anyone else for that matter. Anyway, all that was a lifetime ago. What was not so long ago—last night, in fact—was when a stranger had called to the Fish Inn where Winston had lodgings. He had asked the landlady about her guest and his whereabouts, and the old dear had freely passed on the information. Winston didn't use the bar, but the landlady, a sweet widow, had told him over breakfast this morning. She had described Jerry Divine to a tee; it couldn't be anyone else. Jerry was the only one to whom Winston had told where he was staying.

A remote, small, coastal fishing town in North Devon was where he chose to lie low almost seven years ago. He was the one most unlikely to get a visit from the police because he was not on the job in Ireland—he had merely supplied the vehicles. It was from the advice—or as Jerry termed it, *instruction* is what it really was—that he found himself in this little place. Mortehoe was as good a place as any, and he was familiar with it, having spent some happy times here in his youth. Dr La-Bhatt and his doctor wife had holidayed in this small piece of heaven on earth— as they used to say—since as far back as the 1950s. The old dear who rented Winston a room was a close friend of the La-Bhatts. Winston had originally intended to stay for one year at most but had bought a little fishing boat and now ran a steady business through the summer months with the holidaymakers, taking them out on half-day excursions. The rest of the time he spent fixing other boat engines for his neighbours—that was his forte. He was a wizard around anything mechanical; he could alter almost anything that used fuel to run. Barry Stone used to call him *Turbo,* ever since they were young men stealing cars, the three of them. Winston had certainly saved their hides on more than one occasion—he was an expert behind the wheel, and he could hold his own.

He wasn't a people person; he preferred his own company. He had his dog, which lived on the boat, a golden Labrador. She was enough for him—females were complicated. He had adopted the bitch after his blind friend Albert had died. They had wanted to take her away and give her to another blind person, but Winston had promised his friend that, should anything happen to him, he would take Betsy and look after her.

It was now 6:30 a.m., the sun was rising steadily halfway, making its journey to the top of the sky. It was going to be a beautiful mid-June day.

The two of them, man and best friend, were now on the fishing boat, the dog sleeping, and Winston fixing some nets. Suddenly the boat rocked slightly to the weight of someone creeping aboard. There was no sound, but Winston had spent too many days and nights on this thing to not recognise the creak and the added weight. He didn't look up but carried on with his chore, his head staying in the downward position as he looked above his glasses at the dog, who was now in the upright position with her ears pricked high.

"It's been too long, man," said Winston.

"How the hell did you know I was here, and who I was?" replied Jerry. Winston dropped the rope and stood to his full height. The dog whimpered as the slim, tall, black beanpole of a man turned to greet his friend, who was now looking up at his lifelong pal. He held his arms open and moved forward. Winston bent slightly to embrace his one and only true friend in the world. His glasses slipped down his nose, revealing tears in his eyes. He was very happy. Jerry smiled.

"Come here, mate, it's great to see you." The two comrades held each other briefly, both tapping one another on the back. To anyone watching—other than the seagulls circling above—it was a true show of camaraderie, full of warmth and sincerity.

Breaking the embrace and holding the tall black man at arm's length, Jerry looked at his friend. Winston was the one who now stood back, sliding his hands down Jerry's arms without losing contact, and grasping the well-trained muscles through the cloth. The two scrutinised each other.

"You feel strong, Jerry, still working out?"

"Never stop, mate. And you? What's all this about?" he asked, turning to look around at the boat docked among many others.

"I love it. Come here, look at this." Winston walked to the back of the boat and lifted a large fibreglass lid that extended the full width of the vessel. "That's a Perkins," he said, looking down as if for the first time. Jerry guessed it was probably the thousandth. "Twin turbo, eight-cylinder. This truly is the bollocks, Jerry. I've had thirty, thirty-five knots out of it." Jerry didn't want to upset his friend, piss on his fire, or rock the boat, so to speak, but he really couldn't give a fuck about the oily engine. He looked down into the hole; to be fair, as he looked at the lump, he was impressed. He could see not one drop of oil.

Divine Intervention

"Beautiful, Winston. Is there someplace we can get a cuppa?"

"Aye, sure, there's a nice little café over there by the arcade. Let me put these nets away," he said, closing the lid, securing it with a padlock, and moving over to push the nets he had been working on under a table, covering them with a rubber mat.

"They steal things, even out here," he said, securing the ropes out of view. "Come on, Bess." He clicked his tongue, and the dog rushed to his master's side, its tail wagging furiously.

The two old chums took a small table by the window overlooking the moorings. The dog took its usual position under the table, and the Greek owner came over with a bowl of water for it and took their order.

"The guy allows the dog?"

"Yes, he knew the previous owner. Everyone knows everyone in a place like this, Jerry."

"I'm sure they do. Is that a good thing?" he replied, unimpressed.

"I'm clean, Jerry. Just a guy earning an honest living, totally."

"That's good, Winston. I'm sorry it's been so long."

"Things are meant to be, Jerry. What will be will be, you know this."

"How long have you two been partners?"

"The dog? Just a year. The owner—he died," said Winston, bending now to pat the Labrador's head as though the canine understood. The dog looked up at him, thankfully. "He was a regular here, blind. That's the only reason the dog's allowed."

"I see."

"What's happening, Jerry? Why are you here?"

"What's wrong? Can I not come and see my old pal?"

"Of course you can, Jerry," said Winston, hurting now and a little embarrassed. "But I know you. Is something wrong, Jerry? Do you need to lie low?"

"No, no, I'm fine," he said, patting the hand of his friend. The Greek, complete with apron and curly moustache, placed the hot tea and croissants on the table. Jerry waited until the café owner was out of earshot before he continued.

"I have something going down shortly. We're going to need some bits."

"Motors?"

"Yes," said Jerry, moving slightly closer to his friend, "and a couple of those." Winston followed the direction in which Jerry was looking.

"Boats?"

"The smaller ones."

Winston looked again and saw about six Seadoo Jetskis chained together on a dry dock floating below the jetty.

"There's plenty of those along the coast. Anything else?"

"Two motorbikes."

"Performance?"

"Initially, yes, but then I thought about it and decided motor scooters will be more fitting for this one."

"Not a problem. How soon?"

"I want to move fast, Winston—within the next three to four weeks, max."

"Ok."

"There is one other thing."

"Go on, Jerry."

"The job's in Belgium."

"Ok." Winston studied for a few seconds. "It will be safer to get the cars there—I can take care of that. Better to get the other bits here. I can transport them over in a box van. Anything else, Jerry, tell me now."

"No. The van, that's fine; this is for you to decide. But I want you on to this, Winston—the four weeks is a maximum."

"Am I in on the action?"

"Yes, if you really want in, you're in. I don't know what's in it for us—the plan is to finance a big one after this one."

"McNess?" asked Winston, not questioning the plan of action.

"I'll know tomorrow. Can you take me to Taunton this evening? I have a train to catch."

"Yes, of course, Jerry. Who else?"

"O'Rourke, Hutchin O'Brien, and one other. I'll tell you in Belgium about the third person."

"We looked at one in Holland one time. Is this anything to do with that?"

"No," Jerry answered. "That was computer chips, if you remember. This is diamonds." He picked up his croissant, took a bite, and swilled it down with a large mouthful of hot tea. "Fucking gorgeous, this," he said, looking at the remainder of the roll and taking another generous bite. Winston smiled; he was excited and happy to see his old friend. He pushed his bread roll over. Jerry noticed him looking at the clock on the wall.

"What's up?"

"No, nothing, Jerry."

"The clock, Winston—you've looked at it three times in as many minutes."

Winston smiled.

"You never miss a trick, Jerry."

"It pays to be observant."

"It certainly does. I have a party of six in one hour, but I'll be back by lunchtime. You hanging around, Jerry? Of course, you want me to take you to Taunton."

"Hang around? I'm fucking coming along for the ride, son!" he said, standing. "C'mon, let's go—I haven't been fishing since I was a nipper."

Winston's smile brightened the day. He was happy and proud to have a friend like Jerry Divine.

Two hours later, the fishing boat was anchored out at sea with the coastline barely visible. The party was positioned around the bow with the rods silently baiting the fish, the slight chop in the water giving the only sound from the break in the wave and the creak of the ageing wood. Jerry watched Winston take a six-pack from the cooler box and pass the drinks to his customers, the golden Labrador brushing up against his long legs as he walked carefully around the tackle scattered on the lower deck. The black man turned to look up at Jerry, who was seated comfortably on the upper deck. Jerry smiled back at his friend from behind the large spindled wheel. There were two things going through Jerry's mind: one, would he feel comfortable risking Winston losing this simple life? And two, would this boat be more beneficial to a new venture from Morocco?

Chapter Eighty-Four

Martin McNess

Martin McNess had recently had cause for double merriment: his 35th birthday and the fact that he could enjoy it as a free man. McNess had only recently been found not guilty after a trial which, if he had his way, could have embarrassed a number of the city's high society, had the reporting restrictions been lifted. The fact that some of the victims chose not to give evidence at the trial helped McNess to leave the Old Bailey for the dual celebrations. A career criminal who preferred to work his trade alone, he admired the Victorian criminal character of Raffles and liked to model himself on the thief's antics. He would never consider working with anyone other than himself unless, of course, Jerry Divine was available. The two of them had seen through a number of successful jobs, and it was with these thoughts that Martin McNess was anticipating what was to come next as he increased the speed to maximum for the last 60 seconds on the treadmill. He had completed thirteen kilometres in one hour—*not bad*, he thought as he picked up the 10-kilo dumbbell weights to complete the circuit. The small gymnasium, which had recently been converted from a spare bedroom, gave the penthouse the finishing touch to be what it was intended to be: an exclusive bachelor pad. The full-length mirrors, which he watched himself through as he trained, gave him the extra push, the determination to carry on and work hard to retain the perfect physique. There was no way his business would allow him to slacken off with his fitness regime; that day may come when he hung up his bit and brace.

He let the weights fall to the rubber mat and spent the next fifteen minutes stretching out. Exhausted now, he stood under the open shower to rinse before entering the domestic sauna. Sitting naked, he listened to the piped music and laughed out loud as he pictured Jerry's face this evening when he told him about his recent trial and a job he had just pulled off.

Jerry looked at his watch; it showed 8:47 p.m. He was standing by the rattler door as the train came to a halt at King's Cross, Camden, London. He stepped from the first-class carriage and was immediately engulfed by the cooling sound of the engine noise, gusts of wind, the scream of whistles, and the ringing of tannoys, the machine-like voice giving the arrival and departure times. All this, and the surge of people moving frantically in the same direction, gave him a surreal feeling. He did like to travel by train; he felt safe in a crowd, especially when he was commuting between towns and cities. He had considered using a hire car, but with this new vehicle recognition system, he decided against it, at least until he had finished with the reunions.

He had called Martin McNess before boarding the train at Taunton. Martin, like all the others, had been pleasantly surprised but retained his professionalism. The two had said very little; after the formalities, they had arranged to meet in the same restaurant they had eaten at the last time they ventured into Chinatown, Soho. Now moving along, as though on a conveyor belt, Jerry made his way outside and joined the queue at the taxi rank. He guessed he had saved at least a dozen places by exiting the train hastily. He carried only his briefcase and one suitcase, having left one with Winston to dispose of.

"Chinatown, please."

"Anywhere in particular?"

"No."

"A night on the tiles?"

Jerry didn't answer.

"The weather's changed this evening, a little cold, wouldn't you say?"

Again, Jerry made no reply. The driver got the message, and Jerry spent the remainder of the journey in deep thought.

Martin was different from the others and more like Jerry in many ways. He, too, was more of a leader, his own man who answered to no one. Jerry was the only one, in this world the two lived in, who could chip into the hard exterior of Martin McNess. He was the one who Jerry had kept in contact with and the one who had joined him on a number of jobs after the Irish travesty. There was no way Martin would wait for Jerry, or any other man for that matter, if a job was on offer. He would look at it. Should the opportunity arise for him to pull one off himself, then he would. He was a natural, an out-and-out thief; he couldn't help it, and he loved it. He had spent some time on remand and got himself a not-guilty verdict recently. This was Jerry's only concern: Was he too hot? He was the best to have by your side on a big score—nerves of steel and would never leave your side.

He would stay with you no matter what the consequences. A real, loyal partner to have, and besides that, he was the one who could fly a helicopter.

Jerry paid the taxi driver and apologised for the lack of communication. The driver accepted the money and the apology after Jerry told him to keep the change. Now, leaving the suitcase with the maitre d', he smiled over at Martin sitting in the far corner, looking back at him. As he approached the table, his friend stood to greet him. The two embraced, and Martin kept his eye on the door.

"What's happening, Jerry? Something going down?"

"Fucking hell, Mart, let me sit down," laughed Jerry.

"We're not getting any younger."

"Relax."

"You hungry, Jerry?"

"Fucking starving, but those ducks hanging in the window don't help."

"Freshness, son, freshness!" He inhaled deeply through his nose. "You can't beat it. You want a cold beer? Tiger's good."

"Why not."

Martin clicked his fingers, and the smiling waiter came running over with his pad and pencil. Once the food and drinks were ordered and the two businessmen were left to conduct just that, Jerry asked his friend what he had been up to recently.

"Well, you know about the *not guilty*?" Jerry said he had heard. "I was expecting you over—we had a fucking party and a half, I'll tell you, mate, a right fucking knees-up."

"I was happy for you, Mart, but those celebrations are not for me, you know this—they only get the other cunts back up."

"Fuck 'em, Jerry. What do they want me to do? Go home and have a cup of coffee? Twenty fucking years is what I'd have got. Anyway, c'mon, what's on the table, Jerry?"

"All in good time, kid. Relax. What's been happening with you? Any heat about after the trial?"

"No, to be perfectly honest with you, I've not been active. Well, nothing serious. I had one little touch—some bearer bonds—just passed them on, decent bit of commission though. Listen, Jerry, what's happening with the box? That stuff's been in there long enough now, eh?"

"Yeah, I thought maybe, whilst I was here, we could bring a few bits out and turn them into money. I've had one or two issues lately that may have cost me a nice few quid."

"I did move one piece, Jerry—a necklace, the one we left with Nick the Peg on Hatton Garden. He decided he didn't want it—not a problem, I drew more money for it anyway. Is this why you're here, Jerry? To sell some tom-fucking-foolery?" he asked with a short laugh.

"No, no, Mart, I have something happening. A diamond gaff in Belgium and a cash-in-transit in Gibraltar."

"A cash-in-transit? That sounds interesting, Jerry, but Gibraltar, that's an island, isn't it?"

"Yeah, I have something very daring in mind. It's just a thought at this stage, Mart, but it could well work."

Martin could see his friend was thinking; he didn't want to push. The drinks and entrées were delivered to the table, this time by a lovely girl dressed in the usual floral Chinese silk, pushing a trolley. Once the food and drink were placed delicately in front of the two customers, the pretty waitress smiled and left them to speak.

"You been up in a chopper recently?" asked Jerry, taking a business card from his pocket and handing it across the table.

"Flying, you mean?" asked Martin, looking at the card.

"I hope so. Yes," smiled Jerry.

"No," laughed McNess.

"Your licence still valid?"

"I don't know. I think you have to do so many hours—too long a break requires a refresher course." McNess now looked enquiringly at his friend and back to the card. "I think so anyway. Come on, Jerry, the suspense is killing me now—what is it?"

"It's a big one, Mart—thirty mil minimum, and we might have to take it at the airport."

"Fucking hell, Jerry, you said it was daring!"

"It is, but this could work." Again, Jerry looked distant. "I don't know." There was slight frustration in the last phrase. "Everything seems to be falling into place without me even trying, Mart, like it's meant to be, if you know what I mean?" He looked at his friend across the table, who had started to eat a barbecued rib without taking his eyes off Jerry. Jerry laughed,

"Here," he said, throwing him a napkin, "wipe your fucking mouth."

"We need to talk," said McNess.

"I know. I want you to head to Madrid, hire one of those choppers," he said, indicating the card which Martin had placed beside his wet wipes. Jerry retrieved it, washed the grease from it in the finger bowl, and passed it back to his friend. "Head to the races, Longchamp or somewhere like that, and take note."

"Take note?"

"Yeah, the procedure—pilots, self-drive, you know, make some enquiries, keep an open mind. We may need one of these for the job, and we may have to divert it..." he trailed off. "I'm only thinking aloud here, Martin. I've been sleeping on it for a day or two—you will be able to feed me more once you've completed the first step. Put that in your pocket before it gets soiled again," he said, looking at the card.

"You want to tell me anything else? Expand?"

"Not yet. Too complicated—it'll come to you in time."

"I'm with you," said McNess, realising there was, no doubt, method in the madness.

"I know. Let's get drunk," said Jerry, finishing off his drink and holding his glass up for attention.

"OK," said McNess, doing the same. "Where you staying? You want to stay with me?"

"No, thanks. I've booked a suite in the Metropole. I thought maybe we'd finish off here and get in the Met bar for a nightcap."

"Lovely. Listen, let me tell you about the last job—it's a fucking beauty."

Jerry moved closer, smiling, and asked if it was. Martin laughed and said, "Was it fuck." He was stuck in the office until the two finished with the foreplay and got into it, at which point he walked slowly from his hiding spot and made his exit—but not before he held back his shock and amazement at the old cunt getting to work with the vibrator up the young bird's cunt. Only this old pervert was dressed as a baby, complete with a fucking dummy. Now the two of them broke out in laughter, and the other customers looked over at them, breaking into uncontrollable outbursts.

Jerry asked him what happened next. Martin went on to tell how, by the time he made his way back down the stairs, the brass was talking to a couple who looked relatively normal, so to speak. Again, to cut a long story even shorter, the four of them headed upstairs to a room that was vacant because, by now, the majority of the twelve higher rooms were all occupied. Martin was a little embarrassed to tell Jerry that, for some reason, he couldn't get a hard-on. Every time he went to kiss the pleasant man's wife, he would look over to see how the brass was getting on, and the geezer would be looking over at him with his wife, as though he wanted to kill them. Jerry laughed again, and food spurted from his mouth. He grabbed his napkin quickly to catch the debris and stifled another outburst.

"Fucking hell, Mart, these people—where do they come from?"

"I know. Turns out he was something to do with the Lord Chief Justice—his son, I think—and she was related to some bigwig from the Commons. Anyway, the brass told me on the way home that he just wanted to bite her toes and suck her arse."

"Bite her toes and suck her fucking arse!"

"Yeah, and lick her arsehole, stick his tongue right up it. Oh, and have her shove a bar of Palmolive up his ring-piece."

"No! Up his jeer? Fuck off! The other, that's allowed—I've heard of that before."

"You cunt," laughed McNess. "Licking the arse?"

"Yeah, up it with the tongue."

"You dirty cunt, Jerry, you've been there."

"Have I fuck," said Jerry defensively. "But it is fashion—everybody's arsehole mad nowadays. Anyway, did you get the peter?"

"Not that night, I didn't. The month after, now that it's winter, I get there before the party. I'm in—up on the conservatory roof and in through the window. I see, firstly, there's nobody downstairs at the back of the house, and I throw the little cunt out onto the rear lawn—100 weight. It makes a deep crater; I nearly have to dig the fucker out. Anyway, I'm away with it, get it into the motor, change clothes, and I'm back in the gaff, apologising and making excuses why *Felicity* can't join us this evening. I hang about, wait till the party gets going, pole Lady So-and-So while her husband's tied to the bed, and fuck off."

"Fuck me, Mart, and these are the people who run the country."

"And the bleeding legal system."

"When's the next party?" asked Jerry before the two of them again laughed out loud and disturbed all the tables surrounding theirs.

"Why, you wanna come? You got your dummy?" McNess howled with laughter. The strong Chinese beer was making the two friends quite giddy, and the management were now getting one or two complaints.

"C'mon, let's get the fuck out of here, see what's in that Metropole bar."

"I have another tale to tell you about that," said McNess.

"Leave it out, I don't think I could take much more."

"No, seriously, I'll tell you in the cab. You know that newsreader? The famous one? A fucking darling. What's her name, you know, off the BBC?"

"Fuck knows."

"Yeah, her and her sister—me and a friend of mine had them on the Charlie in there…"

"Fuck the newsreader! What was in the peter?"

"The safe?" Martin blushed.

"Yeah, the fucking safe. What was in it?"

"Let me tell you about the TV bird."

"You cunt," laughed Jerry, now standing to put on his jacket. "You had it off, didn't you? Was it a good touch?"

"Two black dildos, three vibrators, and a bag of Viagra," he replied sheepishly.

"Get the fuck out of here!" roared Jerry with a gigantic burst of laughter. The sudden outburst had other customers at the next table leaving the restaurant in protest at the hullabaloo. Jerry walked away to pay the bill, laughing as he did, leaving Martin, embarrassingly putting on his suit jacket before he, too, saw the funny side and laughed as well.

Chapter Eighty-Five

Day Six

Demitra had stayed with Kath; she didn't want to be alone. David was on his way back from Madrid, where his father had sent him to look at a disused church. It was to be his first project in the property game; his dad was going to give him some advice and guidance. The plan was to demolish the church and build a small block of apartments. *What now?* Demitra asked Kath. *What time is it?* For the fiftieth time, Kath told her it was 1:45 a.m. and held her patience for obvious reasons. Demitra thanked her. She wanted David here with her now. Kath made the two of them yet another black coffee, only this time, she put a little brandy in the hot drink. David was due in one hour.

It hadn't been easy. In fact, it was probably one of the hardest things Kath had ever had to witness or do. As soon as she stopped the Range Rover at the doors of the police station in Estepona and the two officers approached the vehicle, Demitra knew that something terrible had happened. As the two uniformed officers neared, she broke down uncontrollably, inconsolable even before they spoke. When Kath asked her later how she knew so quickly, Demitra said it was the look on their faces, the way they were cap in hand, and the fact that one of the officers was female. It made sense. They were politely asked to come into the station and were taken into an office. The words were spoken in Spanish, but it could have been Punjabi—it was all too obvious to Kath: the seriousness, the apologies, the way Demitra looked from the police to Kath, a pleading look in her eyes. Kath stood to move closer to her friend. Demitra stood to join her, and they did just that—they joined in an embrace that was so heartfelt, no words were needed to tell each other that they were there for one another. Kath somehow got the split-second, heart-wrenching feeling that her husband, too, was gone.

The identification process was just like in the movies. Demitra didn't want to do it at first and had to be coached by Kath, who told her she might regret it one day if she didn't. She wanted to tell her there could be a mistake, but deep down, she knew there was little chance of that. She knew because Demitra had told her that Jezzie had never, in all the time they had been together, stayed out. And the car, and everything else. Kath was seething with Jerry; she knew that this had something to do with what he had told her. Jez had taken his life, and her husband was partly to blame, if not solely to blame. These dreaded feelings she had been experiencing lately were all too real. She felt sick.

The way it was done could have been a little more sympathetic. It was so surreal, like a dream almost, very clinical, with little thought to the delicacy of the mental state of the relative. The room at the town mortuary was all stainless steel and white marble. Kath was expecting a candlelit room with some religious theme, like back home in the chapel of rest. But this was more like the ones you see in those American detective movies. Across one wall directly facing the entrance, there was no table in the centre with a sheeted corpse. Instead, there were three rows of doors, each with a number from 1 to 36. Kath noted that drawer number 2 was the one pulled open by a third person who was wearing a white apron. The female officer held Demitra firmly by the arm as Kath stood directly behind her friend with her hands placed on each shoulder. She could feel the resistance from Demitra and the shake in her body as she inched closer to look at the inevitable. The noise that came from her friend's stomach and released through her mouth was a noise Kath had heard before from the children of her friend Jane at the cremation of their father, Barry. For a brief moment, she imagined the sound coming from her own children. Then other unrelated thoughts came: *How many bodies a week must they have through here?* And hauntingly again: *When will she be coming to a place like this to identify Jerry?* She looked at the body that once carried the soul of Jezzie. Slowly now, she eased her friend, without force, away from her dead husband. Her mind was made up at that point.

Chapter Eighty-Six

Detective Bill Wheeler opened his eyes to look up at the ceiling that had been the cause of his sleepless night. Never in his sixty years had he heard so much racket caused by something that was supposed to be so sweet. The act of lovemaking was just that—making love, not fucking war! He looked at the roof and thought for one second that if he could reach it without breaking his neck, he would give them a piece of his mind—or fist, in this case. There had been none of this in the Grande Palace, and if they hadn't asked him to pay for last evening, he'd still be there now. As it was, he had no intention of paying the €130. Instead, he had packed his bag in the same drunken slumber he had left Peralta's office in and made his way back to the previous shithole. He reckoned last night would be the last night he could claim expenses, especially after Smithy told him he had to return, so he would charge the €130 and keep the difference from the €40 it had actually cost.

He had told himself he would travel down to Gibraltar today, before lunch. As far as he was concerned, there was very little for him to do now up here in Malaga. He had to find out from Stone where this robbery was going to take place—it could be anywhere, he knew this, but the likelihood was Spain.

How had Stone convinced Divine he had nothing to do with the entrapment at South Mimms? And if Stone was staying in Gibraltar, what was he doing hanging around Torremolinos?

Wheeler checked his watch: 5:30. *In the morning? It can't be—the sun was blaring through the dirty lace curtains.* He looked again and noticed the second hand wasn't ticking. *Damn!* He needed a battery. He rolled out of bed and pressed the switch to turn on the battered coffee maker. Topping it up with water, he turned the dial on the radio attached to it—nothing. He looked for the remote to switch on the TV—nothing. He reached up to turn it on manually—nothing. *Fucking place.* He couldn't fit in the small shower cubicle, which had been retrofitted into the corner of the room, but he reached in and turned the water on anyway. Grabbing a flat, off-white towel, he soaked it under the running water and proceeded to wet-wipe his fat, sweat-smelling body. Once he was satisfied he wouldn't offend anyone, he put on the new suit—even he was getting sick of looking at it. He decided then and there that he would say his goodbyes, promise to be back soon, and once he had seen Stone today, he was out of here—home. Never before could he remember wanting to get back home to Maud so badly.

Chapter Eighty-Seven

Barry Stone actually thought it was too good to be true. How could he expect to get back with Jerry, convince him that everything was hunky-dory, forget about South Mimms, and get back to work? Call up the boys, and let's pull this one off? Who was he kidding? Life didn't come that easy, not for him. There had to be traumas—there always were. This time, in the form of that fat bastard Bill Wheeler. Where the fuck had he come from? Things were looking so good. He had done it; he had convinced Jerry. *What now? Does he run?* He could; he was free to run, but the job! How could he walk away from this? This was a once-in-a-lifetime crime opportunity. He had to devise a plan to sucker Wheeler, the way he had suckered him. He had to think of a way to lead him on, feed him some shit, plenty of it, and hope some of it sticks. *Fuck! His life was a trauma, a disaster.* He would like to sit down for a year or two and tell someone about it—tell them about all the devils, all the pain, the beasts that made him what he was and who they were. He wasn't born this way. He was born in the same place as Jerry, at the same time, in the same area—as far as he was aware—grew up with the same people, ate the same food, attended the same school, sat next to him in class, breathed the same fucking air. *Where did he get so wise?* There was only the one, relatively short, separation: the time he had been taken away from home and the time Jerry had gone to stay with relatives down south. How was it, then, that his life was fucked and Jerry Divine was the one who always came out smelling of fucking roses? Why wasn't Jerry the one who was taken away from home at such an early age—battered and abused, tortured and raped, molested by those who were paid to protect him, taken into the care of the local authority? That's how he remembered it; that's how they phrased it. Those white-collared cunts who knew everything. What the bastards did know was how to make him—and other desperate cases like him—suck cock.

The experts say that one in four victims of child abuse, sexual or otherwise, will grow up to be the aggressor. *Do unto them as they did unto you!* He had read this someplace, a long time ago—borstal or some other institution maybe, the Bible, in the block. That's the only time he read the Holy Book, when he was in solitary confinement—and there was plenty of that, too much. That was another thing—locked away for days on end, sometimes weeks in those times, it was allowed; they could get away with it. The time spent in chokey was mind-bending, mental torture—nothing, absolutely nothing to do, no furniture—the bed was taken from the cell throughout the daylight hours—leaving Barry and others like him to sit on a chair made from compressed cardboard and look at the four walls. Food was passed through a hatch in the door, and this became the highlight of a very long day, which crept into weeks and sometimes even months. It was too much time to reflect on what the beasts in suits did to him in the approved schools. Too much time for him to want it back. To want to be back there as opposed to sitting on the compressed chair, looking at the walls. Then he started to believe it was a good place to be, to be wanted—they wanted him, and he wanted them. This was a comfort. It wasn't a bad thing to want it back; he could suck the cocks if they let him, could let Mr Reynolds enter him again. If only he could be back there.

He didn't wake Beatrice; he was careful to slip his arm under her head and gently pull her closer to him. She opened her eyes, looked at him, and smiled as he kissed her forehead, the tears from his eyes running down his cheeks to drop onto her face. She wrapped her arms around him and buried her head in his chest. Barry looked down at her dark hair and wondered how he could hurt such a loving, defenceless person. What did she ever do wrong but try to please him? Would she be better off without him? If this Gib job didn't come off, what good would he be to anyone? Will it ever happen now that Wheeler, the fat, horrible bastard, is back on the scene? If he had never stolen the money back from Wheeler, he knows that the detective wouldn't be so determined to bring Jerry down.

For it was Jerry whom Wheeler truly believed had stolen the money. Jerry, to this day, still had no idea that the £300,000 was robbed back. It was him. Stone! This was another thing Jerry could never discover. Everyone within the team had been happy to pay the money for the documents—the papers would certainly have sunk the ship and drowned the crew. For them to disappear the way they had had been a godsend, and it was amazing that Jerry had convinced Wheeler to do the deal in the first place. But Barry couldn't do it; he couldn't see a copper walk away with so much money. He didn't give a fuck what Wheeler did to earn it in the first place—he wasn't having it, and he made sure of that. It was he who had placed the tracker in the lining of the case containing the money, and it was he who robbed it back from the house of Wheeler's elderly parents. He didn't intend to hurt them in the process, but if the victim wanted to be a hero, then they got what was coming. Even Jerry would have at least agreed with this.

Chapter Eighty-Eight

Jerry woke at 7:30 a.m. with a terrible hangover. He didn't remember much about the remainder of the previous evening, only that it was great to see his old friend and partner in crime. What he did recall, and what was paramount, was telling Martin to take the flight refresher course. Other than that, the activities of the night were a blur. The only thing that told him he must have had some female company in his suite was the lipstick marks that covered his upper body and the cream lace panties at the bottom of the bed. He made himself a black coffee, checked himself in the mirror, collected the empty champagne bottles—four in total—cleaned up the cocaine residue, picked up the scribbled message left by the girl, threw it in the wastebasket without reading it, and stood under a cold shower. The water was cool, and he imagined the longer he stayed under it, the better he would feel. Again, he checked the time—8:15 a.m., 7:15 in Spain. *Give it another hour, and I'll call Kath,* he thought. In fact, he decided to use the health spa; a good run on the treadmill should blow the cobwebs away. *I'll phone her at lunchtime instead.* Now fully dried and semi-naked, he rummaged through his case until he came across his sports gear. Pulling it from the case, he discovered the notes left by the girls, one from Jasmine and the other from Julie. The one from little Julie was signed off with the words *I love you, Daddy* from *Julie and Bonito xxx*—there was a paw print of the little dog carefully placed beside his daughter's crude signature. Jerry sat on the bedside and felt a terrible pang of guilt. He would try to make it up to them, buy them something nice at the duty-free. As he returned the notes, he recognised a large brown envelope and remembered Martin giving it to him. It contained £18,000 in new fifty-pound notes—his share from the necklace sale to the madam. *That was some story,* Jerry laughed as he secured the money in the complimentary safe, closed the room door behind him, and made his way down to the health spa.

The room was small, claustrophobic really, but the air-conditioning was nice; it helped to relieve the banging in his head, and it was clean in here. The equipment was state-of-the-art—no heavy weights, which was nice, no one banging around. In fact, he was the only one using the facility. The music was nice too, soul music, nice easy listening. He set the treadmill at a modest 12 kilometres per hour and ran at this speed for 45 minutes. This was a steady pace, and the solitude gave Jerry time to contemplate, time to reflect on the last few days. The meetings with the boys couldn't have gone much better—each one of them was in a position to go to work, and none of them had any outstanding issues that could endanger the security of the operation. The only thing Jerry could see as the obvious quandary was how to explain the Barry issue, especially to Hutchin O'Brien. Could he convince Barry to stay offside? And to supply the information? Act as an intermediary, an advisor, the source? Sometimes the source of the information is kept secret by the receiver so as not to jeopardise security. Everyone knew the source was the weak link in any investigation, so for this reason, the team preferred there to be anonymity from both sides. The boys wouldn't question Jerry—after all, there were always others in the background who needed paying. This was the norm. The only difference in this case was that the payment to the source in this instance would equate to more than an even cut because there was the fat Jew to account for too. *Fuck it, it will come to me.* The next time the crew would be together would be in two weeks' time, in Amsterdam. There was nothing unusual in a boys' weekend away to the Red Light District. Jerry had instructed each member to meet at the central station at a certain date and time to commence preliminaries.

Once back in his room, Jerry showered again. He looked in the mirror and decided to let the two-day stubble shadow his face. He dressed casually, still not quite adapted to the cooler temperature, and slipped a light woollen v-neck jumper over his open-neck shirt. At 10 o'clock, he dialled room service and ordered smoked salmon on toast with scrambled eggs. He would make his own coffee—oh, and *The Times* newspaper.

There wasn't much for Jerry to do now; his business was over in the UK. He considered travelling up north to see his mother. She was housed in one of those elderly residential communities in Huddersfield, just off the M62. He could carry on the extra few miles to Leeds and see his brother, Victor, maybe stay up there overnight and get a flight back to Málaga from Leeds/Bradford airport tomorrow. Yes, he agreed with himself, he would relax a little for a change. After finishing breakfast, he dialled reception and asked them to arrange a hire car—a small one, one he could leave at the airport in Leeds tomorrow. This was confirmed shortly afterwards, so Jerry looked around the room before leaving with his luggage.

After settling the bill at reception, he made one quick inspection of the immediate area before accepting the keys for the compact and heading up the M1. The traffic was relatively quiet for late morning, which was unusual as he remembered; the roads in the UK were a nightmare as far as he and many others were concerned, but today was fine. Radio 2 was playing some nice sounds, the weather was good, and he felt relaxed. He had told himself that after 12 o'clock, he would stop at the first services and call Kath and the girls. This he did as he pulled into Watford Gap at three minutes past the hour. At six minutes past, he was not so composed as he told Kath to calm down and that he would call her back straight away on Demitra's mobile.

The call was answered immediately by Demitra.

"Jerry, why did he do it?" she sobbed.

"I'm sorry, Demitra, please put Kath on the phone." He knew instinctively why he was apologising.

"Hello."

"Kath, darling, what happened?"

Kath didn't respond; he guessed she was looking at her friend. A moment went by. Jerry didn't push, he waited. He knew what was coming.

"Hello."

"Yes, love, I'm here. You alone now?"

"Yes, I'm in the garden."

"The girls?"

"They're upstairs, in Jasmine's room."

"OK, love, please don't cry, Kath."

"*Don't cry*, Jerry? *Don't cry!* Jezzie's dead, Jerry, Demitra's distraught, our girls are beside themselves over the dog—not to mention I've been locked in a fucking piss hole—and you've got the audacity to tell me *not* to cry! Where the bleeding hell are you, Jerry?"

"I'm sorry, love, I truly am. I'm away, I…"

"When are you coming home, Jerry? We need to talk," she said quietly.

Jerry could detect something in his wife's tone he hadn't heard before—resignation, deflation, like a part of her was gone. He wanted to be there so much, wanted to be with the people who mattered more to him than anything in this world, to hold them and comfort them. He was the one who was supposed to protect them; he always had, and now he couldn't. He needed time. He tried to talk, but the words were locked in the back of his throat. Selfishly, he hadn't thought twice about the death of his friend and business partner—the sixth sense was correct. Eventually, what seemed like a long time but in reality was only less than a minute, he told her he was sorry and that he would call back in one hour on Jasmine's phone. He held the receiver of the payphone in his hand, the dial tone still audible in his ear, as he let his hand drop to his side. He looked down as though what he had just heard could not have actually been said, but it had, and he had to compose himself. He looked toward the service entrance—the general public were coming and going, some talking, some laughing, some rushing, and some alone. He was alone. He lifted his hand holding the receiver and replaced it in its cradle. He used his other hand to wipe away a tear from his eye that hadn't watered in such a long time, other than to laugh. Who were the tears for? Himself? Relief? Jez? A small boy, holding his father's hand and dragging a teddy along the shiny floor, looked into Jerry's face as his dad tugged at his arm to carry on.

"But I don't think it will be tonight, or tomorrow. I have to go to Portugal... I will be gone only for a day or two. What about you? Where will you go?" Jerry could hear it now—the last conversation.

"I don't know, Jerry. This is not my kind of life. I don't know how to run."

"Maybe you should have thought about that before you entered into this conspiracy."

"I didn't see it as a conspiracy, Jerry. Just a way of getting rich quick. Not unlike you, Jerry." He should have done more!

"None of us had the remotest idea it would come to this."

"You're on your own, Jez. You're on your own, Jez. You're on your own, Jez. You're on your own, Jez..." *I'm so sorry, Jez.*

He couldn't leave the conversation the way it had ended with Kath—an hour was unfair. So, he lifted the receiver once more and dialled Demitra's number again. This time it was answered by Kath.

"Kath, please, I'm so sorry, love. Things are spiralling out of control, pet—things I can't discuss on the phone. Bear with me, love. I'm working on it."

"You're always working on it, Jerry."

"I know, Kath, I know," he said quietly.

"Aren't you going to ask what happened to Jez?"

"Yeah, sure, of course, love. What happened?"

"He committed suicide."

"Jesus, Kath, how?"

"In his car..." she said between weeps. "He gassed himself, Jerry. He was crying out for help, and you told me to avoid him."

"I'm so sorry, Kath. The money—I couldn't give him the money. Make sure Demitra stays with you. I'll be home soon, love. I just have to sort one or two things out, and I'll be home, OK?"

She didn't answer.

"Kath," he said in a low tone.

"Harold called," she said reluctantly.

"What did he say?"

"He wants you to call him, that's all." Again, Jerry could detect something very unusual in Kath's voice.

"What is it, Kath? Is there something else?"

"No, nothing, Jerry."

"Kath, there is. What is it, pet?"

"That policeman, Jerry, back home. What's his name?"

"Who, Kath? Which copper? Wheeler?" Jerry knew the answer and was dreading the confirmation. He felt sick, dizzy, weak—he could feel the bile rise to his throat. He swallowed before he spoke again.

"Jasmine's phone, love—have it by you. I love you, Kath."

"Goodbye, Jerry." The goodbye sounded so final to Jerry—it was a goodbye that was heartfelt, both by the giver and the recipient. He had to take heed. Quickly, he dialled Harold's number.

"Is that you?" asked Harold before Jerry had time to talk.

"Yes, what's wrong?"

"Nothing. Everything OK with you?"

"I don't know. Did you hear?"

"Hear what?"

"My friend Jez!" There was a pause. Harold was waiting. There was silence.

"What, man? Spit it out."

"He's dead."

"Dead? How?"

"Suicide."

"Fuck! I'll call Francis Cordeso."

"Who's Francis Cor-fucking-deso?"

"He's the abogado who got your wife released."

"I see," said Jerry, his mind working overtime. "You think it will be safe to come home?"

"If you get off the phone, son, I can find out."

"Please, thanks."

"What are friends for?"

"I love you, mate." Jerry hung up and realised this was the first time he had ever told his old pal—or any other male, for that matter—that he loved him.

Chapter Eighty-Nine

Harold took a note of the incoming number and made the call immediately to the lawyer, who, typically, was unavailable. He dialled a second number and got the answerphone message from Francis Cordeso's mobile. He didn't leave a message; instead, he swapped the landline for a mobile of his own and texted a message. He was proud to have recently got the knack of doing so.

Call Harold - Gib - ASAP

The call was returned within the hour.

"Harold, my friend! How can I help you?"

"Can you see me today?"

"I am in court in one hour and I will be for the remainder of the day," he stated before offering, "Tonight?"

"This evening."

"As you wish!"

"It's on me. Where would you like to eat?"

"Toni Dali's, this one is good, it is on the Golden Mile. Do you know the one? Six o'clock?"

"You like to eat well. I'll be there at 5:30." It wasn't the desired result—he would have preferred to see the *Abogado* sooner and in a tapas bar—but it was a result. He took the scrap of paper with the number Jerry had called him from and dialled it. The phone was answered after the second ring.

"I'm seeing him this evening, 5:30. Call me one hour after that. I should have something for you then, OK?"

"Yeah, sure, thanks again."

Chapter Ninety

Bill Wheeler had packed his belongings into the battered suitcase and secured it with the belt from his trousers. A bus taking a number of holidaymakers on a full-day excursion was leaving for Gibraltar in forty minutes. He had assured the driver he could make his own way back and managed to secure half of that day, with lunch, for half the price. There was nothing left for him to do here in Malaga other than to say his goodbyes, which he did by phone, and assure Angelo Perelta that he would make a report once he had the details of the Divine conspiracy and email it to the Spanish detective once he had returned to the UK. Perelta asked that he do so even if the intended victim was other than the Spanish authorities. He had to remember that Divine was still a target in Spain as far as the two jewel robberies on the mainland, and any information he could pass on to the recently formed Eurojust may, one day, benefit the two detectives.

The coach had seen better days and plenty of miles; it was full of excited passengers, most of them with screaming brats. The heat was unbearable, and the rubber protection on the seats drew the moisture from his bulk, which took up two of them. Directly behind him, the baby crying on its mother's lap told Wheeler he wished he had not opted for the cheap run.

From international crime detection, staying in a 5* hotel, chasing Europol's elite—to this. Sitting in a cramped sauna on wheels with the smell of diesel and baby crap, travelling approximately 100 kilometres at half the speed, over two hours! With a load of cheap budget holidaymakers. And the powers that be want him back! If they only knew.

Almost two hours later—there was an increase in speed downhill—the bus joined the traffic waiting to enter Gibraltar. Wheeler took one look at the length of the queue and estimated the time of one hour before they cleared customs. He stood to retrieve his luggage from the overhead compartment and made his way, with it, to the front of the coach. The driver reluctantly let him disembark, and Wheeler stepped down from the torment into the welcome open space. The piss stain from his trousers would dry quickly in the heat of the sun. Passport control was complete within thirty minutes and, as tired as he was, he was pleased he made the right decision. The next one was a little more complicated:

Should he hail a taxi and make his way to the hotel without giving notice, or should he call Barry Stone first?

He decided on the former, giving himself the benefit of surprise.

"Mr Maine?" he asked at the reception. "I've come to see a Mr Maine," he declared with authority he didn't feel.

"Momento," said the girl, lifting the receiver to call the room.

"No, Madam, I would like to surprise him. What room number is he staying in, please?"

"Oh, I am very sorry, sir, I cannot give this information."

"Very well, the bar," he tried. "Does he use the bar?" Wheeler looked at his watch before he remembered he required a battery.

"Yes, he does."

Wheeler looked at the clock behind the counter.

"What time, do you know?"

"The time, Señor, it is 6:45, of course."

"Yes, yes, I mean, what time does Mr Maine use the bar? Do you have any idea?"

"Please excuse me, sir, usually now, anytime now."

"Thank you, I will wait in there. Could you take my luggage, please?"

"Are you a guest, Señor?"

"No," answered Wheeler, getting annoyed, "but I may be. I haven't made my mind up yet. In fact, could you have someone check flight availability for this evening? Stansted, UK. Stansted, please."

Wheeler couldn't remember the last time he needed a beer so much. Forcing himself up onto the high stool, he ordered one from the dew-drenched stainless steel pump by tapping it with his fingers and smacking his dry lips.

"Large one, please."

"Grande," said the barman, placing the pint glass on a mat in front of him. Wheeler looked at the glass, which was half-filled with white froth. He scooped some of it and rubbed it around his crotch area where the urine had left a salt stain before giving the barman a look that told the youth he was not impressed with the lack of liquid. The young man took the glass and held it under the tap until the froth flowed over the brim, and it was completely full of golden-brown, gas-bubbled beer. Wheeler was finishing his second when he spotted Stone and Bressla through the polished mirrored glass behind the bar. He couldn't be certain, but he was sure Stone tried to double back before it was too late, and Wheeler had spotted the two of them. They walked over, one of them reluctantly, and sat down beside the detective.

"You're just in time, Barry. I was just about to order another one of these," he said, holding up his empty glass. "Now you can get them in."

"No problem, Mr Wheeler. Leave us be, Stuli. Take a seat," he said, looking over to an empty table by the doors leading out to the pool. Stuli was glad to take the instruction. He had only just recognised the detective and hurriedly made his exit.

"My friend, Stuli, he told me you spoke with him in Torremolinos."

"Yes, that's correct, Barry." He looked at the departing Jew and wondered briefly who was heavier, him or Stuli. "A timid man."

"He knows nothing about nothing, Mr Wheeler. I am trying to get an investment for an expansion project. He is a hotelier—nothing more, nothing less."

"Relax, Barry. I am not interested in him, or you for that matter. It is Divine. It always has been, Barry, you know that." He picked up the beer his guest had readily agreed to pay for, took a large mouthful, then turned away from the mirror to look directly at Stone. "Now, let's cut to the fucking chase, son. I don't want to be here any more than you want me to be here, so I suggest you open your mouth and every word that comes out of those paid-for lips of yours is something that will help me secure a conviction against Divine. Now, I don't give two grannies' fucks about you and your Yiddish friend over there. You could be fucking all the seedy little batty boys from here to Torremolinos for all I care, but unless you want to spend the rest of your sorry-ass life behind bars, you'd better start taking me very seriously, kid. Now, what the fuck is Divine planning?" Stone was slightly taken aback. The detective was almost frothing at the mouth.

"OK, Mr Wheeler! Calm down, calm down," said Stone. He could see Wheeler meant business. He had to give him something, and quickly, but wasn't sure what or how much. Wheeler was far from stupid; Stone knew he had to be very cunning here.

"There's a diamond cutter's in Belgium." What was he saying? "It's not a big job. Jerry's been having a few problems lately; I don't know what he's been up to." Wheeler twitched—Stone had hit a nerve. "Honestly, Bill, there's something happening which I know nothing about. He needs money, and he needs it quick. Like I said, it's not a big job, but enough to pull him out of the shit. I don't know, maybe he's been gambling too much this time, but there's something on his mind. I didn't come over for that; I came over for investment."

"How did you get back in? I mean, how did you come back to life? Not for fucking investment, I'm sure."

Wheeler was quick. Stone had to think quicker; this was already a slip. One more and it was over.

"No, you don't understand, Mr Wheeler. Divine has someone close to you on the payroll, someone very close. I don't know who, but he contacted me—Divine, I mean. He heard that my partner, Stuli, over there"—he looked quickly in the direction of the fat Jew, who smiled back nervously—"he heard that his brother owns a diamond-cutting factory in Antwerp which was ripe for the taking. He needed some inside knowledge, that's all."

"And?"

"We gave it to him—Stuli, I mean. He gave him the details."

"Such as?"

"The usual: amounts, value, times, employees, etc. You know, Bill, the norm." Wheeler looked at Stone intently. Stone could see the beads of sweat gathering on the detective's forehead. Even with the air-con on full blast, it had little effect on the overweight Wheeler.

"Is he up for it?" he asked. "Is he going to do it?"

"I think so."

"Armed?"

"I don't know yet."

"When will you know?"

"Soon. But there may be something else, Mr Wheeler, something bigger, much bigger." Barry Stone was thinking ahead now. He was beginning to regain his composure, his confidence was returning, and he began to see the detective for what he was: a cheap, bitter, greedy scumbag.

"I know, Bill, I know why you hate Jerry. For what you did for us, if it wasn't for the fact that you destroyed the evidence, we would still be doing the first half of a very long sentence now. There was no need to steal the money back. And your parents, well, that was disgusting, what can I say? You have every right to want revenge. I told you before how sorry I am. I can help you, Mr Wheeler, and I will, I promise. But you will have to bear with me. I'll be seeing Jerry in a day or two, after which time I will be travelling back to Africa. I'll know more in a month or two. This Antwerp job will not be sufficient for what you want, Bill, I know that. But this big one—maybe this is what you've been waiting for. He's going to be armed, I'm sure he will be. If it's a big one, he'll be armed. If, for any reason, he isn't, I'll make sure he is. I'll do this for you, Mr Wheeler, trust me. You can take him out, Bill." He could see Wheeler was thinking hard. Wheeler was thinking *very* hard. He was considering his options. Stone was right: a blag in Antwerp, with inside knowledge, the possibility of no weapons. What was that? 7-8 years in a cushy jail. It had to be this big one. Where was the big one? Wheeler had little choice but to go with Stone this time.

"You say you are seeing him in a day or so?"

"Yes."

"I need to know, Stone. I need to know about this big one—where it is, what it is, what it entails, value—the business, Barry! I want it all."

"I know, Mr Wheeler. Don't worry, you'll have it."

"Get me another beer."

"What about a top shelf?" asked Stone.

"A large whisky."

Chapter Ninety-One

The retirement village was ideal—ideal for Jerry's mother, ideal for him to know that she wasn't alone. These complexes were a great idea, the brainchild of some builder who saw a niche in the market. *Let's take them out of their homes, where the elderly feel vulnerable. We can do a deal with their existing property and place them in a community where they all have something in common—their age. A communal environment that will cater to their every need. On-site assistance, doctor, chemist, library, mini—very mini—supermarket, a bus complete with a chair lift. Make life so much easier. Oh! And we put it in the contract that we get the first option to buy back should anything happen to the resident, like they die, for instance—at a reduced rate, of course.*

Jerry wasn't stupid, but it was worth the money to know she wasn't alone. He couldn't live with himself should anything happen to her, even half as bad as what had happened to Bill Wheeler's parents. How some evil bastard could torture and mutilate two frail pensioners the way they had done to the detective's old dears was beyond him. The old woman had died shortly after—obviously as a result of the ordeal. Fuck knows what happened to the old man; it was truly awful. Copper or not, Jerry hoped the evil cunts were captured and left defenseless in a cell for half an hour with Wheeler. But what the fuck was Bill Wheeler doing in Spain, raiding his house?

The conservatory had recently been fitted to the rear of the Yorkshire stone property. It was adjacent to the lounge of the two-bedroom apartment, which overlooked the moorlands and the unobstructed view across to Emily Moor. It was the place where Hilda Divine liked to spend almost all the hours of the long days. The elements of the weather were a picture, especially the snow. She loved to watch the snow—so pure, so white, the soft, cold snow. But the chair, the wheelchair needed changing, Jerry. It was too hard to manhandle, especially now with the arthritis setting in. And the cold up here in the winter, it brings it on with a vengeance. One of those electric things would be better—those new ones. You know? Battery-operated! Victor doesn't help. She couldn't remember the last time she'd seen him. And the grandchildren, what were their names? There you go! It's been that long, I've forgotten what they're called. And that wife of his—all she does is sit in the hairdresser's all day. Those nails cost a fortune, you know! She fully understood why it was difficult for him—Jerry, that is—living in another country and whatnot. But him, Victor, he's only down the blinking road, just like his dad, that one—very selfish. Not like yours; he was a real man. There she goes again—senile dementia, Jerry was sure. He would have to get someone to check her. The private health was worth taking out; they were usually very efficient. Get Victor to call them. *Put the kettle on, Son. There's some shortbread in the tin, and bring me that crocheted blanket from the bedroom. Shake the cat hairs off, Son, there's a good boy!*

Jerry walked back through the lounge, glimpsing briefly at the school photos mounted above the Queen Anne dresser, and smiled. He noted there was a snap of his brother and his perfect family but none of him with his. He could only imagine the slating he would get from his mother to Victor when it was Victor's turn to visit.

Jerry called Harold back at 5:30 p.m. English time. The information retrieved from Cordeso's contact in Marbella was positive. Now that both potential prosecution witnesses were dead, there was very little evidence against Jerry Divine. There was one guy who was interviewed, released, and re-interviewed—unofficially—in a café in Mijas, high up in the mountains, very much out of the way. From what could be gathered, this guy seemed to be cooperating with the *Policía*. The name? The contact was unsure. Probably cost a few quid, thought Jerry. Could be a bluff.

The advice to Jerry was not to return for at least another day or two. This would give Cordeso more time to ensure there was no hidden agenda. Jerry thanked his friend and let the relief flow from him into the embrace as he said goodbye to his mother.

One hour later, he was seated in the conservatory attached to his brother Victor's semi-detached house situated on a cul-de-sac in a suburb on the outskirts of Leeds. Jerry wondered if Victor had got two for the price of one—there was little difference in the PVC and glass structure. Victor was a bit cute. Good luck to him, but he could have asked; Jerry would have given it anyway.

"You like more tea?" asked Heather, Victor's wife.

"Yes, please."

"Not for me," said Jerry. "I must be off."

"You going already?" Victor said, disappointed. Heather said nothing; Jerry could see she was relieved. Even Victor was unaware, after all this time, that Jerry had once given her a good seeing-to. Jerry regretted betraying his brother. He didn't think that Heather had the same feeling of guilt about the affair; in fact, Jerry knew he could do it all again. What was it about these women? They can have it all, everything they want—the perfect life: husband, children, pretty little house, garden with a picket fence, nine to five, a good man bringing home the bacon—and they risk it all for a bit of rough. Jerry could never get his head around it.

"Yeah, I'm sorry, Vic. Next time I'll stop a little longer. I'm flying out to Barcelona tonight," he lied. He wasn't sure why. He just had to get out of here. "Listen, why don't you lot come out to see us?"

"That would be great," said Victor. "When?"

"I don't know, whenever suits you."

"Heather?"

"Yeah, sure."

"Don't look so enthusiastic! I don't know, Jerry. This school holiday, maybe."

"August. What about August? Kath has one of her charity do's in August."

"We'll see, Jerry. I'll let you know," said Victor, standing to embrace his brother, who hadn't been in the house more than thirty minutes. The two siblings embraced warmly. Jerry kissed his sister-in-law on the cheek and gave the two children a hug and a £20 note each.

"Call and see Mum, eh?"

"I do, every week, Jerry. Has she been telling you things?" he asked suspiciously.

"No, not at all." *The old cunt!* he smiled.

Outside in the little hire car, he didn't start the engine immediately but sat there for a moment to reflect on the recent journey. What had been more important than anything else was the fact that he had seen his mother. He realised that every time he did see her, it could be the last—not like most, where age or health could be a factor. In Jerry's case, it was his liberty—or life, for that matter. What a way to live. He looked at the neat little house and the family smiling back at him standing in the doorway, and he thought for a split second, *Who was doing this thing called life the right way?* He often wondered. Starting the engine, he smiled back, gave a wave, and did a U-turn. Destination: Leeds Bradford Airport.

Chapter Ninety-Two

Jerry was lucky; there was a flight to Madrid leaving in less than two hours. He called Martin McNess and told him to forget the helicopter mission. He gave no reason but confirmed the rendezvous was still on in the flatlands, and he would see him—and the others—there in a fortnight's time. He was a bit apprehensive about taking the money McNess had given him through customs, but he had little choice. So, he slipped the ten thousand pounds—having deposited eight thousand in the floor safe built into his mother's bedroom floor—into the waistband at the small of his back.

He arrived in Madrid at 9:15 p.m. and was through arrivals without a hitch. He hailed a taxi and was checked in at the La Grande Hotel thirty minutes later. After showering and shaving, he checked the time and decided the night was young enough to make the call. Victoria was in town and would be more than happy to meet James at the Hard Rock Café adjacent to the hotel. He took a table for two by the window with a bottle of Laurent-Perrier pink champagne and watched the people, both inside and out, going about their business. He relaxed and realised for the first time since leaving Malaga that this was the only time he felt unburdened, at ease. There were still issues to resolve, things happening, things over which he had no control, so tonight he would forget. Enjoy the moment.

He saw her stop and watched as she reversed the small Peugeot sports convertible into a tight spot. She stepped from the car gracefully, her white shorts showing the perfectly formed curvature of her long, tanned legs. A blouse beneath a smart black jacket, which stopped above the waist, gave her an almost businesswoman flavour. She was every man's dream, and tonight she was Jerry's. She stood between parked cars until there was a gap in the busy traffic. She held her hair in place with one hand, while the other held her keys and secured the strap of her bag over her shoulder. She skipped leisurely across the road. She was, as he remembered, confident, strikingly beautiful, and a real head-turner—or in this case, a horn-blower. She smiled at the noisy compliment and looked up to see Jerry watching her from the window. She blushed slightly and shook her head at the embarrassment of the car horn. Jerry held up the champagne bottle and beckoned her in with his head. She nodded and smiled broadly. He stood to greet her as she entered the busy bar. A few heads turned, both male and female, and one or two elbows were nudged. He welcomed her with a kiss to each cheek and pulled a chair from under the table, holding it until she sat down.

"What a lovely surprise," she said, making herself comfortable.

"The pleasure is all mine," he smiled, filling her glass.

"We'll see about that."

"Slow down, tiger," he laughed. She smiled.

"What brings you to Madrid?"

"You."

"Me? Only me?"

"I think so."

"Why didn't you call first?"

"I did, I left a message. Didn't you get it?"

"Yes, I did," she said, looking stern as if to reprimand, "two days ago!"

Only two days! It sounded so quick when spoken, but it seemed so much had happened in such a short period of time. Jerry couldn't get his head around the fact that it had only been two days since he'd called and left the message. He had been in Morocco at the time, in the convenience store. He had certainly covered some ground.

"What are you thinking, James?" He was brought back to the moment and apologised.

"I've had such a hectic few days."

"Do you want to talk about it?" she asked. He felt like he could. He had no way of explaining it—he barely knew the girl, but he felt totally at ease. She made him feel this way, and he had to admit, it was nice.

"I'd bore you to tears. Have you eaten?" he asked, changing the subject.

"No, I haven't actually. I've started a diet today."

"You! A diet? I've seen more meat on a butcher's apron."

"A woman is never happy with her weight, James. You should know this."

"Why?" he laughed. "Why should I know this?"

"You're a man of the world, James. You know how a lady's mind works," she teased, holding her glass with two hands and circling the rim with one finger, the same twinkle in her eyes that had excited Jerry not so long ago.

"I can read yours now," he dared.

"And what do you see?"

"That you are inquisitive. Your mind is calculating. You are weighing up the odds."

"Odds? Are you a betting man, James?"

"Only on sure things, until they prove me wrong."

"What kind of things would you consider a good bet? A sure thing."

"Suckaterri!" he blurted out loud. "Damn. Sorry, I must make a call." He dialled a number frantically. Victoria sat staring at him. There was no reply.

"Answerphone!"

"What is it, James? What's the matter?"

"Nothing. I'm sorry. Where were we?" he checked himself.

"You were about to tell me what you considered a sure bet."

"Oh yeah, what I considered a sure bet." He studied her for a second or two. "That this is going to be one hell of a night." He took a drink and inspected the amount left in the bottle. "Shall we participate?" he asked, holding up the transparent bottle.

"Where are you staying tonight?"

"You answer a question with a question! In the La Grande."

"I'd rather we go there. It's a bit noisy in here," she said, looking around. "Don't you think?"

"Let's go," he said, standing and moving around the table to take hold of her chair. "They do a lovely club sandwich in the Grande. If I ask nicely, they may rustle up a bit of cos lettuce for you."

Chapter Ninety-Three

Wheeler had left Stone hanging onto the bar in a drunken stupor. He, too, was in such a state that he barely managed to board the plane. The small airport in Gibraltar did not have those convenient tunnels where one could walk directly into the aircraft. Instead, he walked with the other passengers across the tarmac to the aluminium steps, which were positioned and locked into place by two men in yellow, luminous body wraps. It wasn't so much the effort of climbing the steps as the embarrassment caused to the passenger who had to follow him. Twice in one day now, he had released his bladder without control, and to add insult to injury, this time his sphincter had let loose and soiled his trousers. To make matters worse, he was stopped at the top of the ladder and questioned by the stewardess about his alcohol-induced condition. He apologised and explained he was taking medication, fumbling in each pocket until he found his identification card. This, along with the complaint from the passenger directly behind him, had him quietly ushered into position, which, to make matters worse, was at the very rear of the plane.

He was oblivious, as he slept, to the utter devastation relayed from the other passengers in his immediate vicinity, who were disgusted by the stench. He became aware of the situation only when he was gently shaken by the shoulder, steered from his slumber, and politely asked to use the bathroom.

He used his key silently to gain entry, but the slight noise was detected by Judy, the abandoned race track greyhound. Wheeler was in no mood for fondness and greetings as the dog lapped around his legs excitedly. He slapped the long snout, making the bitch yelp and cower against further smacks from her absent master.

"Is that you, William?"

"Yes, go back to sleep, Maud," he replied, leaving his luggage as it dropped in the hallway.

"Go back to sleep! With that bloody racket! What time is it?"

"Twenty minutes past midnight, go back to sleep, woman."

"You want a cuppa tea?"

"No, I need to take a shower, I'm ready for bed." *Nosy cow.*

"Use the spare room, William, my lower back's playing up again."

Bill Wheeler had no problem with Maud's order. In fact, it was nothing new, something he had grown accustomed to. He now preferred the solitude. He could think without her nagging. He had a lot to think about, for although he got drunk with Stone, he remembered everything that was discussed and agreed. He would call him in a few days, and his superiors. He would have to win them over. If need be, he would travel to Gambia to take the details— only if Stone assured him he had them in full. They had to go with it.

The water was cold as it dribbled from the shower; he had forgotten to switch the timer onto manual before stepping in. He moved his hands quickly over his mass and looked down to see the discolouration as the residue from his body splashed against the glass cubicle. He dropped the soap bar and bent at the knees to retrieve it—impossible. He looked down instead and pushed the slippery object into a corner. *Red?* The water was red. He leaned sideways and took hold of the chrome pipe. At the same time, he reached around to his backside with his free hand. Bringing it back to view, he looked—*the water rinsed the blood from it.*

Chapter Ninety-Four

"That was beautiful," she said, licking her lips and taking the starched napkin from her lap, using it to delicately dab her mouth. "I didn't realise how hungry I was."

He smiled back at her.

"I'm glad you liked it. Dessert?"

She looked at her watch, then into the eyes of Jerry, who was smiling back at her.

"James, you trying to ruin me?" she rubbed her tummy.

"I would never do that." He looked at his. "You have somewhere to go? It's twelve twenty; the night's still young."

"No, just curious. The cheese board—I may have a look at the cheese board."

"I was thinking more like another bottle of this," he said, taking the empty bottle from the bucket beside the table.

"Shall we?" she giggled.

"With strawberries, of course, in the room."

"James, you are cheeky," she said, lifting her bag from under the table. "You'll have to excuse me."

"You haven't?"

"Just a little. Would you like some?"

"You go ahead, I'll take some upstairs."

"I didn't say I would join you."

"You will," he smiled confidently as she left the table, and he watched her form admiringly.

Victoria noted that all the other cubicles were unattended before entering the one furthest from the entrance. She put the lid down and sat on the chamber, placing her handbag between her knees. She looked through it, took the cocaine, and deposited a small amount onto the stainless steel roll holder, then began to chop the flakes into a line using a credit card. Before she snorted the drug, she fished from the same bag one of two mobile phones and speed dialled the only number stored in it. The call was answered after ninety seconds of constant ringing.

"I told you not to call but to text," said the Eastern European voice.

"I'm sorry, I forgot."

"Is he with you now?"

"Yes."

"Where?"

"Madrid."

"OK. You know what to do. Find out as much as you can."

"I will, Kristos." She pressed the end button and replaced the phone. She took a straw from the bag and snorted the cocaine. As she opened the door, Jerry moved in silently, taking her by the waist and kissing her hard on the mouth. He closed the cubicle door with his heel and reached around, without breaking the kiss, to secure the lock. Victoria was more than surprised to see James and did well to disguise her shock by responding to the kiss with passion and want. She was the first to explore the moist, wet concave of his mouth with her tongue, at the same time, reaching down with the hand not holding the bag to the front of his trousers and rubbing his already erect penis.

He, too, was eagerly searching with his hands for flesh, releasing his mouth from hers but staying just a breath away as he moved down to kiss her neck. He released the buttons of her blouse, exposing her topless, full breasts as they heaved from the sensation that his kiss produced. She moaned deeply as he took an erect nipple in his mouth, gently teasing the sensitive spot with his tongue.

"Not here, James." This was said half-heartedly as she dropped the bag and placed her hands on the top of his head. She pushed back to look him in the eyes, which were smiling mischievously. Her resistance was short-lived. Running her fingers through his dark hair, she exerted just enough pressure for his body to oblige. He lowered himself to his knees, kissing her stomach as he released each button of the flimsy blouse. She rotated her hips slightly to move with slow rhythm, now wanting him to delve further. His hands circled her lower abdomen and came to rest, one on each buttock. He could smell the scent of her wet pussy through the cotton and began to kiss around this area through the cloth. Slowly now, he moved his hands down behind the back of each long leg and up again to cup each cheek of her backside, putting on just enough pressure to pull her lower body closer to him. Her legs parted voluntarily as he brought each of his hands from behind to spread the flesh of her upper thighs and lower bum cheeks. She moaned with pleasure as his fingers slipped under the cotton shorts and helped to part the moist area of her slit. She took her hands from his sweat-damp hair and released the button holding up the shorts, which were the only barrier from delight. As the shorts were lowered by him from behind, he eased them over the roundness of her pantyless bottom, kissing the flesh of her pubic region as it was revealed.

"Yes!" she said huskily. He kissed the top end of her pussy, his tongue teasing the mound concealing the oversensitive clitoris. She pushed harder against his face, rising up on her toes slightly to meet him as he pulled against her rump, his fingers forcing her lower body into his mouth.

"Oh, that's good—yes, that's real good, James."

Slowly now, he brought his two hands from behind and used the thumb of each to gently part the wet gap of her cunt. Her knees buckled slightly from the touch of his fingers as one from each hand slowly entered her. Jerry was looking for the sensitive spot. She could feel the breath from his mouth. She moved forward, wanting him—wanting his tongue to prod, to lick, to enter her.

"James... Oh yes, James! That feels so good," she moaned as her hands left his head and began to explore her own semi-naked torso. She took one breast in each hand, squeezing hard, then lowered her head to take the nipple of her left breast into her mouth, sucking fiercely. Jerry had located the spot that elicited an anxious response of sound and movement from her and focused his attention there.

Victoria's moans of passion grew louder, a little too loud for comfort, and Jerry was intent on bringing her to climax before another patron entered the latrines. His tongue worked frantically—licking, prodding like a lizard—darting and licking, darting and licking. His fingers explored deeply into her now-saturated sex. He could feel the throb from within her, the sensitive nodes, the love potion flowing freely from her fanny and down her inner thighs. Her movements became frantic as she ground her hips forward to meet his lips, now sucking hard. His tongue, protruding from his lips, expertly hit the target.

Jerry, too, was excited. He needed to release. He was tempted to stand and enter her there and then, pin her up against the wall, or bend her over the basin and take her roughly from behind. But this was her moment, solely for her benefit. His time would come later, upstairs in the room. She must have been thinking the same thing because, without notice, she lowered her upper body to grasp him under each arm. Jerry resisted, continuing to lick and suck hard around and inside her hot, wet cunt. She relented, kissing the top of his head, again holding the back of it, gripping his hair and pulling him into her.

Her legs began to tremble as the first wave of internal ecstasy rose from her toes, rushing up to meet the cocaine coursing through her brain. The orgasm hit fast, and the heat of the confined space gave Victoria a rush of adrenaline. A flood of cum almost drowned Jerry—he wasn't expecting such a release, or the scream of pleasure that accompanied it. Vicki's legs buckled under the euphoria. She exhaled loudly as Jerry inhaled deeply, taking the weight of her body in his arms.

The two of them stayed in that position on the floor of the cubicle for some time, regaining their breath and composure. The heat and sweat from their overexcited bodies cooled with every passing minute. Eventually, Jerry spoke first.

"C'mon, I'm sure they'll be wondering where we are."

"Who?" she asked suspiciously.

"The restaurant manager, for one."

Victoria laughed, relieved.

"Of course," she said, rising. He stood to join her, and they both rearranged their clothing. He brushed her hair back from her red face and kissed her nose affectionately, surprising even himself.

"I bet you think I'm easy, don't you, James?"

"Don't be silly. We both like the same things, that's all."

"But I don't do this kind of thing all the time, honestly." She looked at him earnestly, and Jerry could see in her eyes that she wanted him to believe her. It didn't matter to him, but he assured her he did.

Leaving the confines of the cubicle was like a breath of fresh air; it had become quite claustrophobic. He heard the voices before the door opened and laughed out loud as two old dears reversed in shock upon seeing the two of them looking flustered. The leader of the pair looked up at the picture on the door depicting a female and shot Jerry a look of disgust. Victoria tried to hide behind him. The two of them scurried from the toilets like schoolchildren caught skiving by a teacher, laughing and pushing each other past the pensioners, who cowered back as if the lovers were lepers.

Jerry couldn't remember much of the ridiculously flirtatious remainder of the night or what transpired into the early hours of the morning. His last clear recollection before they entered the room was in the elevator—another daring escapade, even more ambitious than in the toilets, except this time, he was the beneficiary of the oral sex.

Two more bottles of champagne at dinner had put them in a mischievous mood. The constant giggling and childish behaviour had prompted the restaurant manager to have the waiter hint, in no uncertain terms, that the place was closing. When that didn't work, one of the staff began vacuuming around the late-night frolickers. The hint was eventually taken, and Jerry ordered two more bottles for the room. The late-night reception manager shot them a disapproving look as "Mr Vine" and his guest made their way to the lift.

No one else joined them on the elevator ride, which suited Victoria just fine. She wasted no time relieving Jerry of his trousers, squatting down and unzipping his slacks. She took out his cock and immediately started to suck his soft member all the way down to the base, then expertly sucked it back into her mouth, drawing back the foreskin as she did. Jerry winced slightly but continued to push his now semi-hard cock into her mouth and down her throat.

He looked up at his reflection in the mirrored walls of the mahogany elevator and almost burst into laughter. He remembered the last time she'd sucked his cock and how he'd laughed then. He didn't want to spoil the moment, so he suppressed the urge to laugh but let out a contained snigger. Standing there with his back against the wall, the lift moving smoothly, she was on all fours, taking his now-solid cock in long, deep strokes. The sensation was beautiful. Jerry, with arms splayed wide, each hand still clutching a bottle of champagne, was in bliss.

Then, inevitably, it happened: first, the bell, then the motion stopped, which was the only indication they had been moving in the first place, and finally, the release of the doors. They were back on the ground floor—the lift must have returned to pick someone up, the doors having opened and shut at the 18th floor, but Jerry and Victoria had been too absorbed in their passion to notice. The scream was one of fright, followed by a second scream of shock from—again—the two old dears.

Jerry dropped one of the bottles, which exploded on impact as he fumbled for the buttons. He managed to press one, and the lift dropped, taking the two of them into the basement. They fell out of the lift in fits of laughter as the doors closed behind them.

It was a long climb up the fire escape to the 18th floor, broken only once as the two of them sat on the marble steps to snort a line of cocaine. The boost gave them new energy, but they were still exhausted by the time they reached the 18th floor and slipped into room 18-01.

Jerry opened the remaining bottle while Victoria used the bathroom and chopped a line for him. Jerry snorted the line and collapsed on the bed, falling into a deep sleep.

Chapter Ninety-Five

Day Seven

The next time Jerry opened his eyes, the room was bright. He glanced at his watch before looking down to see Victoria sucking his cock again. It was midday. He reached down to stroke her head gently.

"Come here, Vic," he said quietly. "You don't have to do this."

"I want to," she replied between breaths, continuing to suck him gently. This time, she turned to look back into his face.

"What happened? I remember nothing after we entered the room," he asked. She stopped sucking.

"You were tired, James, and we had drunk too much champagne."

"I suppose," he said, though he wasn't convinced. He had drunk champagne on many occasions, often consuming much more than the previous night. The coke was supposed to heighten his senses, not put him into a stupor. He looked up at the ceiling, then back down at the nape of her neck as her beautiful head worked slowly, so professionally. He wondered. Was he being paranoid? He reminded himself that *he* had approached her on the road. His gaze shifted over to his luggage, sitting on the stand beside the wardrobe. It looked untouched, just as he had left it. His trousers were draped over the settee at the foot of the bed—nothing incriminating there.

"Come here," he said, easing his knees up and gently pulling her towards him. She reluctantly stopped and moved up the bed to rest her head on his chest. He kissed the top of her head and stroked her neck.

"Do you have plans?"

"Not today, James."

"Do you want to go somewhere? To the Picasso exhibition, maybe?"

She raised herself slightly, looking up from the comfort of his chest.

"I'd love to, James."

"I have to make some calls. How about you go home and change, and we meet again at three?"

She smiled, kissed him softly on the lips, and rose gracefully. He watched her move with elegance as she went to use the bathroom. As soon as the door closed behind her, he checked the safe concealed in the wardrobe. It was open, but the money was intact. He checked his suit jacket, finding his wallet exactly as he'd left it. He examined its contents, and everything seemed in order. Dialling room service, he ordered burnt toast with fresh orange juice and more unopened champagne. Yet, despite everything being in place, something was still niggling at him. He didn't like the feeling. Something wasn't right. Maybe a Bucks Fizz would help take the edge off.

Chapter Ninety-Six

Kristos Koiduste wanted to ensure the job was done the way it should be: slow, meticulous, with extreme violence, and—most importantly—witnessed. He knew people would talk, and that was the point. It was how he'd built his fearsome reputation. Koiduste was not someone to fuck with. There was only ever one loser, and today, that loser was the man chained to the chair in a disused warehouse on an industrial estate outside Cadiz.

He had assured the French Algerians that they would be reimbursed by him for the drugs lost in the sting.

The man clinging to life was the third to suffer this fate in as many days. The two before him had been tortured and killed in much the same way: a live electric cable placed on sensitive parts of the body, expertly judged to cause maximum pain before the victim lost consciousness. Pliers to wrench off ears and eyelids, hand drills to extract teeth from the gums, secateurs to sever fingers at the first knuckle. The screams of agony were drowned out by the noise of the commercial generator. The sound of the machine only added to the victim's desperate position.

Death came slowly, and the young man, who had merely insulted Kristos in a club, never found out why something so trivial had led to his own death. Koiduste, on the other hand, had saved himself a small fortune. By killing the three people, he had eliminated the need to pay for the drugs and satisfied his Arab partners by punishing the culprits of the staged sting.

"OK, do it," he said, as he took his vibrating mobile phone from his pocket. He walked to the far corner of the warehouse while the blade cut through the victim's jugular. Casually, Kristos glanced at the time on his expensive watch. 2:40 p.m.

"Yes, talk to me," he answered.

"It's me, Kristos," said a female voice quietly.

"Speak up. Do you have something for me?"

"I'm not sure. He doesn't open up much," she answered nervously.

The Russian crime boss spun around abruptly on his heels, snapping his fingers. One of his men stopped working on the chained corpse and switched off the generator. Kristos ripped off the protective jumpsuit and discarded it.

"This is not what I want to hear," he spat. "Tell me something I *do* want to hear."

Victoria was struggling. Her instructions had been plain: get anything on Jerry Divine. Anything incriminating. The honey trap had worked like a charm, but she needed more time to gain his trust.

"I managed to get a look at his passport," she said.

"Very good. Give me the name."

"Vine. Daniel Vine."

"This is good. What else?"

"I found three numbers. They're not in his mobile; he keeps them separate, scribbled on the back of a business card."

"And?"

"I'm not sure, but I have a feeling those numbers are important. Why would he keep them written down like that if they weren't? They could be nothing, but I wrote them down just in case. Do you want them now?"

Kristos glanced at the French Algerians, who were leaving through a small door cut into the steel shutter. He waved, but they ignored him—a lack of respect he stored in his memory.

"Yes," he spat.

Once she had given him the numbers, he hung up, took off his elasticised paper shoes, and instructed his men to wrap the body in tarpaulin and dump it at sea.

Chapter Ninety-Seven

Jerry was impatient. He checked his watch again, knowing full well only two minutes had passed since the last time. Standing on the stone steps leading up to the grand entrance of the Museo Nacional Centro de Arte Reina Sofía, he tried to blend in, not wanting to draw attention to himself. With an open-neck shirt and faded jeans, he could have stepped out of any walk of life. He combed back his hair with the palm of his hand and tapped the brochure against his thigh, looking like any other tourist visiting the capital's most prestigious attraction. He dressed casually, preferring to blend in, especially when he wasn't sure how hot things were for him at the moment. He certainly felt the heat from the sun and glanced at his watch once more before deciding to escape the heat and head into the cool building.

"James!" He turned and raised his designer sunglasses. Victoria was skipping between the four lanes of slow-moving traffic, waving. He brushed back his hair and waved back with the brochure. He smiled broadly as car horns blared in appreciation.

"I'm sorry, James! I didn't know what to wear."

"So you chose *that*?" he scoffed, eyeing her light, ankle-length cotton dress. She hit him playfully with her envelope bag, and the two of them laughed as they entered the exhibition.

"Do you know much about this guy?" she asked.

"I know his work is very expensive."

"Yes, I know, James, but do you *understand* it?"

"No, but I like it."

"It does have a certain fascination for the untrained eye."

"Untrained?"

"Yes," she laughed. "You said you didn't know anything about him."

"The man, yes. The paintings, I have some knowledge."

"I'm impressed."

"This one, for example—*Guernica*, circa 1937, painted when Picasso was in his 50s. It has become a universal symbol of the pain and anguish of war. It's a mural influenced by the Spanish Civil War, when much of Picasso's work became antifascist." He surveyed the large piece, while

Victoria surveyed him. "Picasso was commissioned to paint this by the Spanish government for the 1937 *Exposition Universelle* in Paris. It was inspired by the bombing of the Basque town of its namesake by the Nazis that year, which killed over a thousand people." He pointed with his brochure to a particular portion of the work. "See the agonized faces of the people? The arm holding the sword, the woman clutching her dead child?"

"You certainly know your stuff, Jerry!" she said, looking bewildered. He smiled.

"These were statements against the fascists," he continued, tapping his chin with the program. "Led by Generalissimo Francisco Franco. The piece was only returned to Spain in 1981, after Franco's death, because Picasso had stipulated it should only return when Spain was a democracy."

"Well! I'll be..."

He lifted his dark glasses and smiled. She hit him playfully again with her bag, giving Jerry the opportunity to glance up at the high glass roof and scrutinize the sensor detectors below it. Even now, he couldn't help himself—his mind never stopped working.

"Tell me more."

"*Woman in Blue*, 1901," he said, moving on. "Part of his Blue Period, painted in France. Has a Henri feel to it. Don't you think?"

Victoria looked at him, still bewildered. He stood there, all handsome and knowledgeable, arms folded, looking up at the painting. She smiled.

"And *I'm* the teacher, Jerry. Henri? Who's Henry?"

"Toulouse-Lautrec," he said seriously, tapping the glossy brochure against his lips. Bending to fasten a loose shoelace, he cast a quick glance toward the fire escape. None of his movements seemed out of the ordinary to either Victoria or the security guard standing by the entrance to the hall.

Forty minutes later, they were seated in the museum restaurant, finishing a bottle of fine wine. They talked about the artwork, the weather, and each other. Jerry made his excuses and went to the public telephone, dialing a number anxiously. He spoke to Harold. His mood was somber when he returned to join Victoria.

"What's wrong?" she asked.

"Harold's not happy I came back to Spain. He thinks it's risky."

"So, when will you leave, James?"

"I'm not sure. A day or two—it depends."

"Depends on what?"

"I don't know," he said, bemused. "On how much you please me. I'd like to get to know you better, see what you're about."

"What I'm *about*?" she laughed. "How odd!"

"We all have skeletons."

"Where are yours?"

"In here," he answered, tapping his temple.

"I bet there's enough to fill several cupboards. Excuse me, I need to use the ladies' room." Jerry stood and drew back the chair for her. As he did, he noticed two men sitting nearby—casually but smartly dressed, with that unmistakable look about them. There's a certain look some men have—call them what you will: rogue, villain, gangster. It's unmistakable to those of the same species, like Jerry Divine.

The men asked for a table in the far corner, the one furthest from the entrance but next to the fire escape and near the ladies' room. Jerry wasn't overly concerned—they could be there for any number of reasons. The important thing was that they weren't police. The waiter brought more wine, giving Jerry another chance to glance at them. As Victoria walked out of the ladies' room, one of the men said something to the other. They both looked at her, which was nothing unusual—she was beautiful, after all. Victoria glanced back for a split second and blushed, also not unusual. But then her blush turned to a pale shade of pearl—almost white. She stumbled slightly, quickly regaining her composure.

Jerry smiled, his senses on high alert.

"Can we leave, *Daniel*?" Daniel? She called him Daniel?

He smiled again, though it took extreme effort to hide his unease.

"What is it, darling? You look like you've seen a ghost," he asked, forcing a calm tone.

"I'm fine, Jerry," she replied, not sitting down. "I just remembered I have a dental appointment. I need to go home and freshen up."

Jerry glanced at his watch—5:15.

"What time is your appointment?"

She looked at her own watch. "Six. I really should be leaving."

He knew she was lying and had a pretty good idea why, though not the exact reason. His mind raced. She hadn't realised her mistake. Who was she? What did she want? He hadn't given anything away—no mention of contacts, no meetings. Then there was last night, how he had fallen into a deep sleep so quickly. The line of coke, the last one he'd taken in the room—*she had drugged him*. And Daniel! She'd scrutinised his passport. Was she a cop? No, the sex didn't fit that theory. There was more going on. Was she connected to those two men? Customers? A high-class escort? Her father—was that a lie, too?

"James, please, can we leave?"

"Yeah, sure," he said, as casually as he could manage. He took another glance toward the two men. The shorter one was speaking into a mobile phone; the taller one caught Jerry's eye and awkwardly looked away. There was no immediate danger, but Victoria didn't see it that way. Jerry tossed some euros on the table, covering them with an ashtray, and took her by the elbow. He felt her trembling.

Stepping out into the harsh sunlight was almost as terrifying for Victoria as the confines of the restaurant had been. She was desperate to get away.

"I'm sorry, James. I must rush." She kissed his cheek. "Goodbye."

"I'll call you," he said to the air as she hurried down the steps, weaving through the slow-moving traffic. Jerry watched her hail a taxi before turning and walking back into the museum. The table by the toilets was now empty, and the exit door was open. Throwing caution to the wind, he called Victoria from his personal phone.

"Please, Jerry, don't call me again," she said before he had a chance to speak.

"What is it, Victoria? Who were those guys?"

"It's better you don't ask, Jerry, please."

"That's not good enough, Victoria. Let me help you."

"It's better this way, Jerry, believe me."

"Where are you now?"

"On my way home."

"Can I see you? One last time?"

There was silence. Jerry pictured her in the back of the taxi, torn and struggling with her emotions. He sensed she was in immediate danger or, at the very least, deeply afraid of it. Then, he heard the sound of another phone ringing—she answered it. *Two phones?* Silence again. He thought back to when he'd taken her elbow as they left the restaurant, how he had felt her body trembling.

"I can help, Victoria. Whatever it is, I can help. Let me try. Please."

Still silence. He could hear traffic through the phone, then voices—her driver's, then hers. She was paying the fare. He checked his watch—six minutes since she had left. A car door slammed.

"Victoria… I know you checked my passport… Victoria…" he pressed.

"Come now, James… Jerry."

"Who are you? How do you know my name?"

"Apartment 011, Santa Ana, on the Plaza Mayor, near the Old Town. Come now, James."

"Jerry," he corrected. "I'm on my way."

The dark Vectra with Malaga plates idled across the road, watching as the taxi dropped off its fare.

Victoria fumbled with her keys, dropping them once she found them. As she bent to pick them up, her phone rang again. The two men in the car watched as she checked the number and declined the call. The car phone rang.

"Kristos."

"Are you with her?"

"No, but we see her."

"And the Englishman?"

"The last time we saw him, he was outside the museum."

"I just called her."

"Yes, she declined the call. We saw it."

"Does he know?"

"I think so."

"Did she tell him?"

"She left in a hurry. I'd say yes."

"Kill her." The line went dead.

"Step on it!" Jerry urged the taxi driver.

"No comprehendie."

"Pronto!"

"Ah! Sí." But the car still crawled along cautiously.

Jerry noticed the Vauxhall Vectra drive away quickly just as his taxi pulled up. He didn't see the occupants, but his fears were confirmed as he rushed through the open door and up the steps to the first floor. The door to apartment 011 was slightly ajar. Jerry paused, looking around for something to defend himself with. He knew that in her current state, Victoria wouldn't have left the door open. Spotting a fire extinguisher on the wall, he grabbed it and edged slowly toward the door, pressing his back against the wall.

He listened. Nothing.

He turned partially and nudged the door open with his foot, inch by inch, peeking through the gap. Victoria was lying face down in the hallway. Still, he moved cautiously. He crouched down and wedged the fire extinguisher between the door and its frame. Like a cat, he rolled into the passage and stayed still, listening intently.

Nothing.

Without taking his eyes off the hallway, Jerry reached for the side of Victoria's neck to feel for a pulse.

Nothing.

He brought his hand up to look at the sticky blood on his fingers. It was still warm. He glanced down at the dark stain spreading across the carpet as her blood soaked through. The killers could still be inside. *The Vectra!*

Realisation hit him.

Jerry stood and walked quickly but quietly down the hall, stepping over Victoria's body. He kicked the keys that had fallen beyond her. Four rooms led off the hallway: two bedrooms, a lounge-dining area, and a small kitchen. The squeal of the only witness—a frightened cat—gave Jerry the fright of his life as it darted from one room into another. He remained cautious, the only sound now being the tinkling of the cat's bell as it found a safe hiding spot.

Jerry walked back toward the still figure and squatted down beside what he knew to be the body of this once beautiful dead girl. He turned her over and bit his bottom lip hard to prevent an outcry at the sight. Her tender neck, so thin and delicate, so slender to the touch, was severed to almost decapitation. He used his other hand to support her head and helped to turn it with the body so that both parts were still intact, her head resting on his thigh now, facing upward. Her eyes were open, staring, lifeless, bloodshot. He drew his free hand across her eyes, like they did in the movies. He was surprised—it worked—they remained shut, shut forever. Again, he looked down and got an immense feeling of guilt. He reached down to rearrange her cotton dress, which had crept up above her long legs; he could only attempt to give her dignity in death. Again, he was overwhelmed with guilt and grief, even though, to him, she had brought this, whatever it was, upon herself. Who? Why? He knew not. He did know he shouldn't be here.

Again, he looked up and along the corridor. There, on the floor, two metres ahead lay her small bag, the one she had playfully hit him with just a few short hours before. He looked first to the entrance and moved sharply to close the door. Quickly now, he moved silently into the bathroom and washed any trace of blood from his hands before using the towel, as protection, to retrieve the small bag and empty its contents onto a narrow table holding a vase with fresh flowers. He picked up the two mobile telephones and checked the list on one for incoming calls: *Missed x 2 DAD*. He quickly did the same with the other: *Missed x 3 Kristos, Kristos! Answered call, Last call received. Kristos*. What the fuck? The guy in the restaurant, the tall one, he was with Kristos, the Russian, outside the club, when he had entertained Abdul and Memhet.

He scrolled down to K and located the number stored in the memory. He pocketed the phones. He looked quickly through a small black book, which held no contact to him. He wiped it of prints and walked briskly, stepping over the body and out of the apartment.

"Damn!" He retraced the few steps and retrieved the fire extinguisher, replacing it on its holder.

Outside, out into the open space. Does he turn left, or right? Even that, something so simple, seemed a difficult decision. It was broad daylight. The sun was obscured by the high buildings, but it was still bright—bright enough for any potential witnesses, who may be looking down from an array of windows, to give a detailed description. He was moving right, in the right direction, he hoped. He had little protection—no trench coat, hat, or collar to obscure any view. He had never felt so vulnerable. He had to make distance, distance between him and the murder. He walked briskly, but not too fast as to draw too much attention. As he regained his confidence, he took one of the mobile phones from his pocket, removed the SIM card and secured it in his shoe, broke the handset in two, and deposited the fragments down the next flood drain. One hundred metres and thirty seconds later, he did the same with the second unit.

Chapter Ninety-Eight

Perelta took the call from Koiduste with little enthusiasm. The Russian could detect the lack of appreciation and zero respect in the tone of voice.

"This is good, Mr Perelta, no?"

"Si, si, this is good. I think maybe we need to talk, Mr Koiduste. Where are you now? Can you come to see me in Malaga?"

"This is not possible. I am too far away, maybe tomorrow. Is this good?"

"I will let you know. Can I reach you on this number?"

"Yes." Angelo Perelta held the receiver, after the Russian had hung up, to his temple and pushed back from the table to enable him to raise his heavy legs and place his feet on the desk.

"That was Kristos Koiduste," he said, sliding a piece of paper containing the telephone numbers Koiduste had given him.

"I gathered," replied Angelica as she took the paper. "The Spanish mobile, the top one, this is the one he called you from?" Her father nodded. "The other three?" He shrugged his shoulders. "I'll give them to Index. I'm not sure about this one, Papa."

"Koiduste?"

"Yes."

"We do need our *agents provocateurs*, my darling, and already he is working."

"I know, Papa, but this one could be far worse than the one we are detecting. I mean, what do we really know about either one?"

"I'm sure that Koiduste is a bad man. We know he is involved in arms and people trafficking, drugs no doubt." He shrugged his broad shoulders and crossed one foot over the other with some difficulty.

"You need to lose a little weight, Papa. Did he tell you anything else?"

"Divine is travelling under the pseudonym of Vine, Daniel Vine." The weight," he said, rubbing his stomach. "I know, my sweet." He leaned over to reach the box containing his Cuban cigars. His stomach wouldn't allow. His daughter stood from her desk with resignation and walked around hers to slide the box within his grasp.

"Gracias." He wet the tip of the thick brown cancer stick by dipping it in a brandy glass. "You see, my dear, they will all fall. It is just a matter of time, but what we are doing is using the one most likely to assist. This Divine, who is now travelling under the *nom de plume* Vine, from what our intelligence tells us," he indicated the phone with a wry smile, "will be very much reluctant to 'play the ball,' as they say. Kristos was our safest option, and it proved correct because he is cooperating. No?"

"Yes, but which one is the immediate danger?"

"Divine. Definitely Divine!"

"Even with the death of Gonzalez and the other witness, accomplice, Jezard…"

"Dupree, you struggle for a name, my dear?"

"Yes, I know. Things have moved at such a pace. This Koiduste, I'm really not that sure, Papa. I think maybe we are giving him too much rope."

"Time, my sweet tulip, time, we have time on our side."

"Did he say where Divine is?"

"Yes, Madrid."

"The job?"

"I'm not sure, but he knows we are on to him. My guess is he knew before the raid at his *casa*, otherwise why would he be travelling on false documents?"

"Why do they ever? Do you want me to get someone on him?"

"No, let him fly for now, albeit on a broken wing. Let him be free because it will not be for too much longer, my dear."

Chapter Ninety-Nine

Wheeler had to fight *tooth and nail* to get his superiors to see sense. Was it not in everybody's interest to arrest and convict Divine and others of his calibre? And now that *Eurojust* had an interest, would it not be beneficial to the Met to have a role in their downfall? Who knew when they might have to call on *Eurojust* themselves one day?

Eurojust was established as a result of a decision taken by the European Council of Tampere, held throughout the latter months of "99. The European Council held a special meeting dedicated to the creation of an area of freedom, security, and justice in the European Union. One of its primary functions was to reinforce the fight against cross-border crime by consolidating cooperation among authorities. To bolster the fight against serious organised crime, the European Council, in its *Conclusion 46*, agreed that a unit (*Eurojust*) should be set up, composed of national prosecutors, magistrates, or police officers of equivalent competence, seconded from each Member State according to their own legal systems.

There was talk amongst the hierarchy to set up a provisional judicial cooperation unit under the name *Pro-Eurojust*, which would operate from the Council building in Brussels. Its purpose would be to act as a roundtable for prosecutors from all Member States, where *Eurojust* concepts could be tested and refined. The Swedes, Iceland, Romania, Norway, the USA, Croatia, Switzerland—liaison prosecutors from Norway, the USA, and Croatia were expected to be permanently based at *Eurojust*.

"We ought to be seen to offer our services and resources," *tried Wheeler*.

It was the resources that were vital to him, not to mention the finance. Without backing from the Met, it would be impossible to traipse halfway around the world in pursuit of Divine. Of course, it was in the interest of European crime detection—or at the very least, prevention—to arrest and convict someone like Divine. The evidence was there. A major robbery was planned, arms were going to be used during the raid. Lives could be lost—innocent victims.

Commander Phelps could see the benefits of assisting *Eurojust*; his mind was working overtime. In fact, he had only recently been invited to attend a seminar in The Hague to discuss the issue of where best to spend the many millions of euros recovered and confiscated by Europol. He knew full well how Europol enjoyed excellent cooperation with law enforcement partners in Europe and beyond. Yes, this could only help his personal kudos. And Divine... Phelps conceded that Divine was a serious criminal who, up until now, had evaded capture for anything of real consequence. He struggled with the fact that the inevitable was not likely to take place in the UK.

Wheeler argued that this could not be confirmed. When Phelps asked for the source of the information, Wheeler opted for informant confidentiality. Unsurprisingly, this didn't help his case. It was only when the curtain was about to fall that Wheeler told his superior about Barry Stone. The change in attitude was apparent to all present. Phelps asked that the room be cleared, except for him and Wheeler.

"Stone has gone off the radar. He's opted to go it alone, totally disregarding the witness protection privilege."

"I know, Sir. Which may account for his actions—you know? Divine? Work? He's in Gibraltar, which, may I remind you, is still part of the United Kingdom." It was only as he said it that Wheeler realised this fact could help his request for backing in the enquiry.

"Did you see him?"

"Yes, of course, Sir! This is what I am trying to tell you. This is our opportunity to get these guys."

"Yes, yes. Does anyone else know about this?"

"Only the detective in Spain."

"His name?"

"Perelta. Angelo Perelta. Oh, and his daughter Angelica," he added.

"His daughter?"

"Yes, she's a detective too, and a bloody good one at that!" Wheeler finished, shifting uncomfortably from side to side. His boss noticed how pale he looked.

"Take a seat, Bill. Are you alright?"

"Yes, the travelling, you know. I get cramp in my leg."

"Get it checked. That DVT is no joke nowadays."

"I know. I'm seeing the doctor this aft—" The large detective didn't finish the sentence. He went down heavily onto one knee, leaning forward to reach for the desk and break his fall. Phelps was up from his chair within seconds, swiftly moving around the furniture to kneel beside him.

"I'm alright," Wheeler breathed frantically.

"You're far from it, Bill. Look at the colour of you."

"I didn't sleep, Chief. A drop of water and I'll be fine."

"C'mon," said Phelps as he put his arms under Wheeler's armpits. "After three. One, two, three, up!" He heaved and lifted Wheeler, who fell back into the visitor's chair. Wheeler winced with the pain from his rectum.

"I'll get someone to take you home, Bill."

"I'll be fine, Sir!"

"Bill, you've done a good job. I'll make some calls this afternoon.

I'll be speaking to *Eurojust*, have one of theirs come in to see us. I think that will be the best option. You go see the doctor before you do anything—you look terrible. Don't worry, I know how much this means to you. I'll keep you updated."

Chapter One Hundred

Harold was getting too old for this, this type of thing—seeing lawyers, giving them bungs. This had been his life *a lifetime ago*. He could have been sitting in the plush waiting room for any number of reasons: to sign a deed, a will, a prenuptial agreement—anything. Anyone looking, as a few were, would never have guessed he was a seasoned, semi-retired criminal. *Vintage* was the word, like a fine wine, a complicated watch, an early Bugatti.

He looked at the others sitting in the room: two men, a mother and child, and an old dear. *Business*, no doubt. He brought the stick, resting against the arm of his chair, between his legs and moved forward to rest both hands on the silver fox head. The yew wood buckled slightly under the weight, so he leaned back and tapped his highly polished Loake brogues with the copper tip. This seemed to irritate the old woman and amuse the kid, so he did it all the more. To her relief—and a smile from the youth—the door leading from the room into an office opened. Harold stood, pulled a face at the miserable old dear, and winked at the kid, who laughed before being checked by his mother, who was not amused.

"Please, Mr Harold, come this way." Harold was fishing the brown envelope from the inside pocket of his Highland tweed suit before he entered the spacious office. Without a word, he dropped it on the partner's desk and took a seat on the guest side.

"I am sorry for the change of venue. I am so busy lately."

"Don't worry, it suits me—it's cheaper." The lawyer ignored the attempt at humour.

"I have been doing a lot of work for our Mr Divine."

"Who gave you the envelope?"

"You did, Mr Harold, just then." He looked at it lying on the desk.

"Tell me."

"I see. I am sorry, I have been doing a lot of work for you."

"What are the implications?"

"Implications?"

"You should never ask a question with a question," advised Harold, taking off his Panama for the first time and concealing the envelope resting on the large desk. *"It's an indication to us who know better that you are unsure of the answer."*

"On the contrary, Mr Harold, I have all the information, but unless the envelope"—he indicated it with a shifty eye—*"contains five hundreds, I wouldn't think you've brought enough to pay the bill. It looks relatively slim."*

"There's plenty more where that came from, Mr Cordeso—now cut the bullshit!" He swiped the ball-and-claw foot of the desk with his cane.

"I have it here, relax, señor." He took a file from his desk and slid it over to Harold. Harold felt its slimness and took it as a good sign. He decided against making a comment.

"I suggest your Mr Divine stays absent for the immediate future," advised Cordeso. He looked for a response but got none, so he continued. *"The case, as far as he is concerned, collapsed with the deaths of both Gonzalez and Dupree. The problem we have is that he is implicated in the murder of Gonzalez."* Again, he waited for a response. Again, he got none. *"Of course, there is no evidence. He would say it bears only a coincidence; they would like to differ. I presume there is no connection from Divine to, let me see..."* He looked down at some scribbled notes and read the prisoners' names deliberately: *"Sanchez, Linares, and Ricardo Montezerelli?"*

"No."

"Good."

"When do you suggest it is safe for him to come back?"

"Oh! It is safe now. It is only a suggestion. If the police want to be awkward—which, in my opinion, they can be, and I must add at times are quite entitled to be—he could be placed on remand for quite some time."

"Bail?"

"That depends."

"Ok, I get the message. His wife, Kathleen—what about her? I will be seeing her shortly. She could do with some good news. What can I tell her?"

"The firearm is certificated. There is a copy of the application here. It seems it was granted after a court application. There is a report here suggesting a break-in during the latter part of last year. During the same period, there were a number of reported break-ins along the coast and up into the affluent estates in the valleys. The method used was the same in all:

gas was filtered in through the air-conditioning units and breathed in by the occupants through the vents. The victims were completely oblivious to it—they knew nothing until the morning, when they would discover their homes had been totally ransacked. There was an influx of applications for firearm certificates; most were denied. It seems Kathleen Divine went one step further, no doubt on the instructions of her beloved. She is a member of the gun club in Mijas, although she doesn't seem to have attended any practice sessions since enrolling. The firearm should, really, be kept at the club—not an issue, legally anyway. She may get a membership suspension, a small fine maybe."

"Ok, ok, move on."

Cordeso ignored the instruction—or the way in which it was delivered.

"It seems Mr Divine has covered all his tracks. The money is a little more complicated. There is no suggestion that it's drug money; most of it is still bank-wrapped, but it will have to be explained."

"Didn't she give an explanation?"

"She refused to answer any questions."

Harold smiled.

"Yes, Jerry Divine has her well trained."

"Will a statement do? Backed up with a witness?"

"So long as it is with substance, and of course, the witness is credible."

"You know Jerry is a professional gambler?"

"Yes, there is something here," said Cordeso, opening a different file.

"Leave it with me, I'll fax you the information tomorrow, from an internet café. You'll have it at 3 o'clock sharp. There will be no connection to me, of course."

"Perfect." The lawyer stood to show the meeting was over. Harold saw him glance at the envelope. *Another greedy cunt.*

Directly outside the *Abogado* office, which was positioned on the busy main road running through the centre of Marbella, there was a taxi rank. Bruno's Restaurant and Pizza House was less than a mile away, but still too far for Harold to walk, especially in this heat. He took the pocket watch from his waistcoat and checked the time. He had arranged to meet Kath at 7 pm. He shook the watch gently to wind up the spring—it was 6.15 pm.

On the opposite side of the road, three horse and carriages stood in the shade, waiting for their fares—preferably holidaymakers, as they paid more.

Harold waited for a break in the traffic before holding up his stick and trotting over, quite agile for a man of his age. He told the driver, in Spanish, to drop him at Bruno's but to travel up and down the high street for 30 minutes first.

Kath was looking at some paintings through the window of an interior design shop next door to the eatery when Harold rolled up in the horse and carriage. She laughed.

"Only you could turn up to take a lady to dinner on one of those." He gave the driver a note and told him to keep the change before stepping down, embracing Kath, and kissing her on each cheek.

"Why didn't you go into the restaurant? Get a drink or something?"

"You know me, Harold. I won't go into a place by myself."

"I'm sorry, Kath. I'm not late, am I?" He made to grab his watch.

"No, no, I'm early. C'mon, let's eat, I could eat a horse."

"You wouldn't if you'd heard the noise coming out of that one for the last half hour."

"What do you mean?"

"*Eat a horse!*"

She laughed half-heartedly and slapped him playfully. "You do have a way with words, Harold."

"A good appetite!" He looked at her with genuine concern. *"It tells me a lot."*

"I'm holding up, Harold. I have to."

There was an awkward silence until the drinks were served, and the order of two pizzas *with the works* was placed. Harold was never any good at making small talk, but he tried.

"How are the girls?"

"They're fine... What's going on, Harold?"

"Jerry came to see me…" Harold's mobile rang. "Sorry, Kath, I have to take this—it's Jerry... Hello… Jerry… Yes, could you call me back in one hour, please? Tomorrow? Yes... a.m.? 7 a.m., you said. I'm sorry... Yes... I'm with Kath now... I will... Ok, son... will do. Who? What's the name again? Ok, bye... yes, bye for now."

"He didn't ask to speak to me?"

"No, pet, I'm sorry. Things have been a little complicated for him these last few days."

"*Tell me about it!*"

Harold looked at her for a sign, but there was no clue in her expression.

"You mean that as in *ditto? Likewise?* Or do you literally want to know?"

"You will only tell me what is in Jerry's best interest to tell me, Harold, I know that."

"I've never seen you like this, Kathleen. I've never heard you talk this way."

"I am at the end of a very long tether, Harold, having untied a hell of a lot of knots along the way."

"Drinks. Tinto de Verano for two."

"Thank you."

"*Gracias.*"

"The food, soon?" asked the waiter.

"No," answered Harold. "Give us thirty minutes."

"Certainly, Señor."

"You know how to keep a girl waiting."

"I'm sorry, Kathleen, you're hungry—I forgot."

"It's fine, Harold," she smiled, holding up her hand.

"Tell me what's on your mind, dear, but you know I will have to repeat anything you say, should Jerry ask me to." Kathleen knew this was his way of saying *tread carefully*.

"I know, I know, you two are *as thick as thieves*. I wouldn't ask you to deceive him, Harold."

"Only tell me what you want him to hear, but before you do, and before I forget, he's asked me to ask you about a detective—Wheeler, is it?"

"Yes, he was with the Spanish police when they raided the house."

"Is that it? I should tell him just that?"

"Yes."

"Now, tell me, dear."

Kath looked at the old man facing her. There were tears in his eyes—there always were—but this time they were dancing like little diamonds, looking for release. He knew this too. Kath got the impression he knew what was coming—he usually did. He was so *worldly wise*, a shrewd old man.

"I want a divorce."

"A separation, you mean," he replied too quickly. *"A divorce is so final, Kathleen, the next thing to death, my dear. Are you sure? Have you thought about this?"*

"Long and hard, Harold."

"But you two are so happy... You do still love him?"

"I will always love Jerry Divine, Harold—till the day I am laid in the ground, and even after that."

"Then why? The girls, Kathleen. What about the girls?"

It was a race of tears. Kath had the benefit of a handkerchief to hold hers at bay, while Harold used the back of his hand.

"I'm sorry, Kathleen. Look at me, crying like a baby," he said, now opting for the serviette. *"I usually do this in private."*

"Me too."

There was silence now, only the sound from a world that was without their concern. The table was conveniently situated in a quiet corner, and the couple seated at it could have been mistaken for an old gentleman with his grand-daughter, or a father who had produced late in life, but whichever it was, the bond was unmistakable—it was so apparent. Harold was the first to speak.

"Is there anything I can say or do that will make you change your mind?"

"You could listen to what I have to say first. Maybe you'll see it from my point of view and agree?"

"I don't know about that, Kathleen, but I'm all ears."

"Shall we wait for the pizza?"

Harold didn't answer but beckoned the waiter and asked that they be served now.

"I seem to have lost my appetite," she said, sliding the plate away.

"Me too. It looks lovely though. I'll ask him to put it in a doggy bag. You too?"

"Please." She laughed.

Once the food was taken away and there were to be no more interruptions, Kath spoke in her own time.

"I would never ask you your business, Harold, and Jerry would never discuss it either, but I know how the two of you met, and I'm not naïve enough to think you were in Pentonville for a bit of shoplifting."

He smiled politely.

"I would never bring your wife into a conversation like this—not usually anyway. But I want you to imagine how it would have been for her, had she been alive today. Is that ok, Harold? Do you mind?"

"No, sweet pea, carry on."

"Where do I begin? I could start at the beginning, but this place shuts at midnight," she tried a light-hearted joke. Again, Harold smiled. He was a good listener.

"Oh, Jerry, Jerry. Do you know he was my first love? At school, he was *all* the girls' first love! Him and Barry Stone." Harold shifted slightly at the mention of Jerry's sidekick, but Kath didn't notice. "Barry married my best friend Jane. The four of us courted together; we were inseparable. Anyway, that's as far back as we go—schoolchildren. Children, that's all we were, and sometimes I still feel the same, like I'm still there, a child. I've always had Jerry to protect me, always." Harold didn't interrupt; she paused because he fidgeted uneasily at the mention of Barry Stone. Maybe this was his opportunity to get a little in-depth history on the man, without Jerry's biased view. He decided to leave it for now.

"Are you ok, Harold?"

"Yes, my sweetness, carry on."

"Was it the same for you? Were you and…"

"Vera."

"Sorry, Harold. You never really speak about her. Vera—nice name. Were you and Vera together from such an early age?" He nodded to indicate yes. "And, you don't have to answer this, Harold, but were you in prison more than once?"

"No, but for argument's sake, we'll assume I was. You want me to step into Jerry's shoes here, correct?" She nodded and continued as she spoke.

"Were you living constantly by the gun? And was it only the fact that you were good at it that you didn't spend more time in jail?"

This time, Harold looked around at the other diners; there was no one within earshot.

"I have a good idea where this is leading, so again, we'll assume I did—and that I wasn't very good in the early days."

"Thanks, Harold."

"I can imagine how it was, Kathleen, and I would have hated to know how difficult it must have been for my Vera, so I can see where you're coming from."

"Thank you, Harold. You are so quick, and you are one hundred percent correct—it hasn't been easy. We seem to be going backwards. I don't know, just these last few days—last few months, really—I've been getting these terrible feelings of dread." She looked vacantly at nothing in particular, drifting for a few seconds as her memory activated. "These last six years, we've more or less been constantly based here. The girls are settled and doing fine at school, my charity work is going well—it keeps me busy anyway. And now, all of a sudden, Jerry has had to up sticks and dash. One minute he's here, then he's gone," she clicked her fingers, "as quick as that, Harold—gone, just like the old days. And here am I, holding the fort, only this time I'm in the thick of it."

"That can be taken care of, Kathleen," interrupted Harold, who was listening intently, scrutinising every word and its meaning. Kath carried on as though she hadn't heard what the old man said. Harold knew she had, but his words made little difference.

"Jerry could have been anything or anyone he wanted to be. He was so much more advanced as a youth than his friends, so beyond his years. And I, well, I was just *following my leader*. At first, it was to the detriment of my parents, and then, as time went by, I suppose for my commitment, I inherited the burden—because that is what it is, Harold, a burden. To be married to a villain is a *constant burden*. Then the children, they come along, and it's secured—the bond is complete, tighter than any ring of gold. There is no way out but for the strong; only the cowards stay, the ones without strength." She took her glass and sipped a small amount of the red wine with Sprite. "Oh, it's had its benefits! If one likes the diamond rings, the fur coats, and the open-top cars in the sun. The big houses, and fancy restaurants, the exotic holidays, and fists full of high denomination. But I haven't slept, Harold. I haven't had *one* night without fear since Jerry got serious into this business, whichever department he chose at the time—since the late eighties! That's a lifetime, Harold." She stopped and waited for Harold to speak. He didn't, so she continued. "I saw my friend Demitra's husband Jezzie, dead on a slab, two days ago. For what? Money? More money? How much do we need, Harold? Is it worth the death of a good man? A hard-

Divine Intervention

working, loving man, a father, husband?" Tears began to roll down her face. Harold felt guilty that his had dried; this was now becoming part and parcel of the life they had chosen. This was his life now. Here, his heart stopped beating for others, and it was only the hardened criminal who could possibly understand this. But he did give respect and nodded in agreement. He waited.

There was that awkward silence again. He moved his hand across the table and gently squeezed hers. He was surprised how cold it was.

"He called me, you know?" she said quietly, looking down at his hands, still holding hers.

"Jerry?"

"Jez. Many times. He must have been contemplating it at the time. I ignored his calls, Harold—totally blanked him on the instructions of his best friend and business partner."

He could see she was getting angry.

"I could have helped him, Harold." She looked up from the table. She was delicate again, the change so swift. "And then, to cap it off, I was rude and abrupt towards him when I *did* see him. He was in my house—he'd been waiting there all the time, waiting for me. I was making excuses, excuses not to see him in his hour of need." She broke again, sobbing uncontrollably.

"The girls, Harold. Little Julie, anyway—she still asks, *'When is Daddy coming home?'* Jasmine has given up. Like me, she knows the answer. The gun! I'm arrested for a gun—a *real* gun, Harold. Me! What would I be doing with a gun? Whose husband goes away and tells their wife where the bleeding gun is? And just for good measure, just in case you need to pay the milkman, there's a quarter of a million euros in the garage." Harold smiled, but not through his eyes. There was pity and understanding in those.

"That's sorted, pet."

"*Sorted*? It's always sorted, Harold. Sorted when it's too late. I still have to sleep, Harold. *That's the whole point*. And the floosies, Harold. Does he honestly think I don't know about his womanising? I ain't stupid, Harold—I have eyes, I have ears." She was having difficulty holding it together now. Some of the other customers were looking over. "I have a heart, Harold, and it's been broken a million times by the man I still love with each fragment. I'm torn, Harold. I don't deserve it, and I've had enough. I have everything and everybody, and I'm so alone—I'm so alone, Harold."

"I'm with you, Kathleen. Try and hold it together, come on, girl, take a breather. That's it, babe. I know, I know."

"I'm sorry, Harold."

"Hey! There's no need to be sorry, petal, I understand, I do," he said, reaching over and placing his withered hand on hers tenderly.

"Please, Harold, tell him to stay away. I need space, I need to breathe."

"I'll try," he said tenderly. "I'll try."

"Is he calling back? I thought I heard you say, 'call back in one hour.'"

"I did, pet, yes."

"I'll be leaving then, Harold. It's nearly been an hour now, and I wouldn't ask you to say I've already gone." She made to take her purse from her bag.

"Please, Kathleen, that's an insult."

"You men!" She stopped short and stood, leaving her salvation still seated. She moved round the table and kissed him lightly on the cheek. He tapped the hand she placed on his shoulder.

"Don't worry, Kathleen, I'll break it to him gently."

"I'm happy it's you, Harold."

"Me too," he lied.

No sooner had she left the restaurant than Harold's mobile began to ring.

"What's happening? What did she say?"

"It's not good, my friend."

"I guessed as much. The lawyer?"

"A little better."

"Should I stay away?"

"For now, yes."

"Can you come to me?"

"I'm seventy-two years of age!"

"Yes, I know, I'm sorry, I forget you're an OAP at times."

"OAP! You'll be getting a solicitor's letter if you carry on with that. I'm not so old I can't take care of you, but you're right, I do forget it too. But it remains a fact, I'm afraid."

"So what's the story? I call you from a box, you ring me back?"

Divine Intervention

"Yes, give me thirty minutes." There was a box outside; Harold had noted it on arrival, twenty metres before the restaurant. He paid the bill and refused the food in a bag. Instead, he sat in his own company and finished his drink, contemplating his predicament.

He could understand where Kath Divine was coming from, and yes, he could sympathise a little, but he didn't put her in the right. How could he? Jerry was a younger version of himself, and it was hard to self-criticise. He took a slim cigar from a singular tube and lit it from a gold Dunhill. He kissed the present from Vera and returned it to his top pocket. He blew the smoke out slowly and again studied the situation.

She was young when the two had tied the knot. It was obviously exciting at the time, a young Jerry Divine, spreading his wings. No doubt the world was his oyster, and so it was *theirs*. She had to be given support because of that fact—her naivety. She was loyal; nothing else would do, of course.

He would advise Jerry to move away for a while, give her some space. But then that would be difficult with everything that was happening. There was still the property business to sort out—that would be a nightmare in itself—and who'd want to be around Jerry while all that was taking place? For one, it was going to cost an absolute fortune in legal fees. And with everything else going on in his life, those *jobs* he mentioned, he would have to pull in the reins. Things like that needed total commitment. Jerry couldn't concentrate on matters of such importance, with a *bleeding divorce* getting in the way.

Harold decided there and then that he would go to Jerry. This wasn't something that could be discussed on a payphone—things like this could only be talked about *face-to-face*.

That's it. He would call Jerry, head home, pack an overnight bag, jump on the fast train from Malaga, and head for Madrid. *How he wished he was thirty years younger!*

Chapter One Hundred and One

On reflection, there was no need for Harold to trek back to Gib. For some reason, which now became apparent, he had slipped his passport into his pocket as he left his home. He had a cash card, which he carried everywhere but rarely used, and €900 in notes. He decided against the fast train and instead took a taxi to the airport to board a quicker plane. He purchased a travel bag from duty-free and filled it with some toiletries and a change of clothing for one night only.

Jerry was waiting for him in Terminal Three arrivals. He smiled warmly as his friend walked through the sliding glass doors. The two embraced warmly and looked, to anyone who may have shown an interest, like father and son.

"Look at the time. You should be in bed at this hour," said Jerry.

"I know, tell me about it. The things I do for you. Here, take this," replied the old man, who had lost some of his zest for life during the journey.

"Earn your keep, and be grateful I travel light, bearing the spoken word as my only gift."

"You certainly have a way with those words," laughed Jerry. *"You tired?"*

"I'm shattered, my friend."

"I've booked you a nice room."

"Lovely. Take me there. I need to shower. We can talk over breakfast."

"Not tonight?"

"Correct."

The car was parked directly outside the arrivals entrance. There was a traffic cop writing out a ticket. Jerry opened the passenger door for his guest and threw his bag over the seat and into the rear. Harold stepped into the car as Jerry took the ticket, closed the door behind him, then slipped the fine into his back pocket and walked around to the driver's side. As he did, he looked at the line of cars queuing to collect passengers, and for a moment, without letting the occupants know he had noticed, he was sure he recognised a dark-coloured Vauxhall Vectra.

"I'm going to make haste, Harold. I think we may have a tail."

When he didn't get a response, he looked over to see the old man sleeping. Instead of making haste, he moved slowly out into the three lines of traffic flow, which were all moving in the same direction. Thirty metres ahead, before the three lanes of vehicles joined the mainstream, there were a set of lights controlling the traffic into a single lane. Jerry stopped at the lights, even though they were showing green. He waited, to the annoyance of the tailback and the sound of impatient car horns, until the lights turned red before slowly moving into the oncoming traffic. If he was correct in his observations, the Vectra had no chance of catching him. And if he was right, then who were they, and what did they want?

Day Eight

"You said something last night, about making haste? What was it? I slept like a baby, there was no haste."

"Do you want to sit down first, Harold? Maybe have a coffee at least? Before breakfast?" asked Jerry incredulously. *"You never cease to amaze me, Harold, really you don't."*

"Yeah, I suppose." Jerry stood and pulled the only other chair at the table out for Harold.

"How do you want it?" he asked, retaking his own seat and holding his hand over the plunger of the glass coffee cafetière.

"Strong and black."

"Like your women?"

Harold laughed out loud. *"I wish."*

"It can be arranged."

"You trying to kill me off?"

"What a way to go though."

"I could think of better ways."

"You hungry?"

"Not really, toast will do." Jerry drew the attention of the waiter and asked for four rounds of toast, two of them burnt. He didn't wait for the food; this was too important and needed a little privacy.

"Kath, Harold. Is it serious?"

"Kath, Jerry. It is, I'm afraid. Very."

"What the fuck has brought this on, Harold? She was fine." He knew as soon as he said it that it was a stupid question and an even dafter statement. Harold looked across the table, and the look on his face told Jerry to check himself.

"I know, I know, but I never thought she would go as far as this, Harold, especially with no warning. Like I said, she was fine."

"It seems that she wasn't. From what I can gather, things have built up over a period of time—could have been years—just simmering and building, simmering and building."

Harold placed both his hands flat down on the table, slowly, showing the first signs of awkwardness as he began to iron out the already neat tablecloth. Jerry couldn't help but notice the veins protruding from the frail hands, almost skin and bone, stretching through the stiff cuffs of the new shirt. He didn't want to make his friend feel so uncomfortable.

"I can live with it, Harold."

"I know, son."

"What did she say? Is it final?"

"I think so, Jerry. This Jezzie thing has tipped her over the edge. She feels somewhat responsible."

"Responsible? How? That's a bit dramatic, isn't it?"

"You told her to avoid him, she feels, in his hour of need."

"I didn't want to give him the money," Jerry tried.

"She doesn't see it that way, my friend."

"To be honest with you, Harold, I don't give a fuck how she sees it."

"Jerry, Jerry, take it easy, my son."

"I'm sorry, Harold, but she doesn't know half of what the fuck has been going on these last few days."

"I know."

"Fuck!" he slammed the table.

"One more outburst like that, Jerry, I'm out of here as fast as a rat up a drainpipe," he glared at his young protégé. "Think of it from her point of view, try and see it from a different angle. She went with her friend to identify the body, for God's sake!"

Jerry put his head down on hearing this detail. When he lifted it up again, there were tears in his eyes. He too had both hands on the table, only his were clenched into tight fists.

"The gunman, the money—think of the pressure she was under in the police station. Albeit, these are taken care of."

"Thank fuck. The money?"

"That has to be explained, but the gun is covered. The licence held up."

"That's something at least."

"She's scared, Jerry. I think it was you she saw on the slab."

Jerry didn't want to hear this.

"The girls, do they know?" he asked.

"I'm not sure."

"Well, I'm sure. I'm sure they'll have something to say."

"Jerry." Harold looked directly into Jerry's face. "Can we talk about Kath later? You really do have more pressing matters to sort out."

"What can be more pressing, Harold? Kath and the girls are everything to me."

"I know. I didn't mean it like that, son. What I mean is, if you fuck up on any one of these projects, you won't be seeing Kath or the girls for a very long time."

"I'm sorry, Harold. I know what you mean, but what is it all for if it's not for them?"

"I'm sure they'd beg to differ, given the choice, Jerry. It's you they want. And if I'm being honest, it's really the money and the lifestyle that you hanker after."

"What are we without it, Harold? You know me! You were me! I was never a nine-to-five. For fuck's sake, Harold, they could shoot me now, lock me up and throw away the key."

His fists had now clenched into the tablecloth. Harold's cup and saucer moved with the pull.

"What you trying to be, a magician? Relax, you'll have the cutlery on the floor."

Jerry released his grip.

"Now take a breather, kid. Sit back, enjoy your toast. Thank you, pet," he added, looking up at the nervous waiter, who placed the warm toast and left in a hurry. "Do you know, before I had these porcelain fuckers implanted, I could eat anything. Now, a slice of toast is sensitive to the touch—€30,000, how do you work that one out, Jerry?"

This was a feeble attempt to lighten the mood by Harold, and the laugh that followed only brought a half-hearted smile from Jerry.

"They do look the bollocks though."

"Jerry."

"Go on, Harold."

"Tell me, tell me what you're going to do."

"I'm not sure, mate."

"You have to be sure, son. Consider your options and decide what you're going to do—and do it."

"I met this girl, Harold."

"Fuck, Jerry, this is going to complicate matters even more so."

"She's dead."

"Dead?"

"Yeah, someone killed her, and I think I know who."

"Did she mean anything to you?"

"What have we become, Harold?" He looked up from his empty coffee cup. The old man didn't answer the question; he didn't understand it. *"Did she mean anything to you?"* he repeated, *"like it only matters if she did. What really matters is that she was murdered, Harold, and that I am connected. As funny as it seems, she did mean something. Out of all the girls I've seen—and there's been a few—and I only met her on two occasions, she was beginning to mean something. She was different, intelligent, beautiful—she was that for sure—and she was fun, Harold, fun to be around. You would've liked her."*

"Why was she killed?"

"That's just it, Harold. I don't know. I am completely baffled. The only thing I know is that she had a connection to somebody I know from a distance."

"Who?"

"Kristos Koiduste. You wouldn't know him. A flash cunt, Russian Mafia—they all are, aren't they? All these Eastern Europeans, flash bastards. They all use the same umbrella—Russian Mafia." This time the term was spoken with distaste. Jerry was angry, and Harold could sense the best thing to do was remain silent for now. "He called her. She had an unanswered call from him just prior to her death. The killers—one of them anyway—I saw with Koiduste a few nights ago at a club in Marbella."

"Do you have any more on this Koiduste?"

"He had an investment with some land in Casares. We were the major shareholders—me and Jez, God rest his soul. Anyway, he offered his shares to us—his architect did, anyway. I remember he was looking over, didn't have the balls to walk over and make the offer himself. It was in the Don Carlos hotel, looking over the top of his champagne glass, the cunt, a magnum of Krug, the sparklers, applause—what a fucking farce. His eyes—mocking. I remember them still, deep blue fucker, staring, almost laughing."

"Is that it? Nothing else?"

"Not that I know of."

"What's the name of his company, the one that paid into the Casares project?"

"I don't know, I'll have to check when I get back. We can't ask Jez anymore, can we? Maybe you could drop round and have a look in his office. I can get word to his wife, Demitra."

"OK, don't forget, Jerry. I'll need that and anything else you have on him. Eat your toast, you haven't touched it."

"I'll wait for lunch. You staying for lunch, Harold?"

"I'd rather not. The quicker I get on to this, the better. Do you think your life is in danger, Jerry?"

"With this Victoria thing?"

"Was that her name?"

"Yes, Victoria Devany." Jerry thought for a second whether or not to mention her famous father.

"As in Steve Devany, the movie star?"

"That's right, it was his daughter."

"Fucking hell, Jerry!"

"I know."

"Back to my question."

"I'm not sure. I suppose we have to assume it is."

"Yes, that makes sense. Do you have help?"

"No."

"I have a friend who owns a sporting shop on the Ronda de Toledo. I won't send you to his place, but he will meet you in the Parque del Retiro this afternoon if you want me to arrange it. I would strongly advise you to carry something with you at all times."

"You never cease to amaze me, you old fox."

"Contacts, my son. Contacts and a good name—they are the be-all and end-all, especially in this life we've chosen."

Jerry thought about this for a moment before deciding to decline the offer. Harold was watching him the whole time.

"There's no need, Harold, thanks, but I might be heading back to Morocco. I got a call first thing—my friend over there has something very urgent to discuss. I asked him if it could wait, and it won't, so I have to be there." He checked the time. "I'll know before lunch. This other job, Harold, with Barry..."

"This is what you have to decide, Jerry. You've got too much going on, and now, with this added pressure, you really do need to pull in the reins."

"*I know. I have decided—even as we've been talking, I've been thinking. I can't afford to let this big one go.*"

"*This Barry thing?*"

"*Yeah.*"

"*You want to tell me about it?*"

"*It may take some time.*"

"*Liberty is paramount, my friend.*"

After Jerry had finished talking, it was time to order lunch. By now, the two were starving and bloated on black coffee. Harold had spoken very little, letting Jerry do most of the talking, butting in only occasionally to verify a certain detail here and there.

"*The diamond job could be a little more than financing the hit in Gibraltar.*"

"*Yes, I know.*"

"*A lot of these cutters, especially with the number of experts working at this particular one, do a lot of work for all the major names.*"

"*It could be big, yes, but even still—the one in Gib—fuck, Harold, it's what we dream of!*"

"*It's this Barry fella, I'm not too sure about him, Jerry. He scares me.*"

"*I believe him, Harold—his story. I don't agree, but I can accept it. He's like a brother to me, Harold, as close as you are to me.*"

"*I would have let you know, Jerry, about this police thing. And you would I.*"

Jerry didn't respond; he knew Harold was right. The old man knew he had hit a nerve and quickly moved on.

"*Why don't you let me get my ear to the ground? Maybe I can make some discreet enquiries, see if I can get some inside info on this September convention. It's a major event, really big—the authorities have been preparing for it for almost a year now. I know enough people in banking.*"

"*You mean we could look at it without Barry?*" asked Jerry.

"*I don't know, I'm just thinking aloud.*"

The two men were drained from the intensity of the meeting. They finished their lunch in virtual silence.

The Vectra was swapped for a light-coloured Ford Focus with slightly tinted windows. The driver was a little more cautious, having lost the target the previous night. The passenger assumed, based on the route they were travelling, that they were heading for the airport. He used his mobile phone to report his suspicions and was instructed to identify which flight Mr Vine and the mystery man took and report back immediately.

Jerry had called Franz Schwineshtieger from his hotel room. He had been correct in his assumption that taking the business card might come in handy one day. Franz was more than accommodating, but only after Jerry had put him in *promise land*—he had assured the German that he would be interested in leasing one of the newer versions long-term. Franz would meet him at his own convenience to do a deal on a six-month period for a new Bell Jet Ranger being delivered at the end of next month. In the meantime, he would ring through to Madrid airport and check if the demonstration model was available to take Mr Vine to Morocco today.

"I'll see you to check-in, Harold, then I'll have to leave you there. I have a few calls to make before I leave for Morocco."

"Why don't you drop me on your way, Jerry? You go right past Gib—I'm sure the pilot can land at the airport there without much inconvenience?"

"It's better I don't, Harold—too complicated to explain, but trust me, it's better you have no connection to the helicopter."

"Say no more."

"We're a bit early, Harold, but I'll get you through. You can have a coffee or something, and I can get on with my job."

"OK, Jerry, I only have this one piece of hand luggage anyway."

The two walked over to the Malaga check-in desk. The girl smiled, took the reference number from Harold, weighed his bag, and passed him his boarding card.

"I'll call you tomorrow lunch, Harold. Keep your phone on and speak to the lawyer, OK?"

"I will, Jerry. You take care, my son. I'm sorry to be the bearer of bad news, kid."

"What can we do, Harold? You take care—come here and give us a hug."

He moved closer to the old man and gently put his arms around him. As he did, he scanned the surrounding area and faces. He didn't notice the man speaking into a mobile phone, standing over by the entrance with his back to him. The guy, on the other hand, could see the two saying their goodbyes through the reflection in the glass.

"You have a description?" asked Kristos. The man described Harold to a tee. He was sure there would be only one like him coming through arrivals at Malaga from Madrid on flight Iberia 223 at 14:12.

Chapter One Hundred and Two

Harold was really old for this. Flying here, there, and everywhere was alright for young blood.

"Thank you, madam," he said to the flight attendant who helped him retrieve his luggage from the overhead compartment.

"You're welcome, señor. Did you have a nice flight?"

"What is a nice flight?"

"Excuse me?"

"It was without turbulence anyway."

"Buenos días."

"Thank you," said Harold as he stepped from the plane into the aerodynamic grey plastic tunnel, almost like an extension of the plane itself.

His legs were not the support they had been recently, and he was not looking forward to the long walk to passport control and baggage reclaim. Just then, a golf cart with a seat for two at the rear *bleeped* past him as he exited the tunnel. He was quick to signal the driver and drew attention to his exaggerated limp. The cart stopped, and he hopped on the rear seat for the ride.

He chuckled to himself as the cart, *bleeping* away, bypassed the queue from a previous arrival and sped along the highly polished walkway, with aquamarine and coral reef murals displayed along the route. He thanked the young man who, having received €10 for his compassion, decided to look for the next victim of a new enterprise. Harold, on the other hand, was happy to walk out into the mid-afternoon sun.

The car stopped sharply, directly in front of him. If he had stepped off the kerb to cross the road, it would have hit him head-on. The rear doors on each side opened, and two men stepped out in a hurry. Harold was about to complain about their impatience but was surprised when the men stopped on either side of him. He expected them to speak, but neither of them did. Instead, each man took hold of a frail elbow. Harold dropped his bag, which was left lying on the pavement, as the two brutes easily bundled him into the rear of the car. He had little time to object and decided against even trying when he realised it was too late. The car moved away at speed. It was so slick and professional that he doubted—though he could only hope—

whether anyone had even noticed an abduction taking place. His only hope was a witness and the bag to back it up.

"You no want to ask the question?" The smart-looking man, who Harold guessed was the source of the expensive aftershave, asked from the front passenger seat without turning to look at a composed Harold. When Harold didn't answer, the same man put down the sun visor and looked at him through the reflection in the vanity mirror. *"Who are you?"* Again, Harold didn't answer. *"You will talk,"* said the obvious boss, confidently. Harold drew no comfort from the manner in which he was spoken to; he was wise enough to know that these men, whoever they were, meant business.

The car was heading in the direction of Torremolinos, moving south along the N-340 coast road for just a short time before it changed direction inland, past Churriana, and further toward Alhaurín de la Torre, and the remoter still Coín. After a little over fifteen minutes into the ride, Harold was pushed down into the footwell of the car and told to remain motionless. A bag was placed over his head. He began to count and got to two thousand and one, at a slow pace, before the car turned right and moved slowly and uncomfortably over some rough terrain. He could hear dogs barking in the distance—something that some music could have disguised. They weren't as professional as he had first presumed. He was falling back against the base of the rear seat and the legs of his abductors, which told him they were climbing uphill quite steeply. Now going downhill, he rolled into the back of the front seats, and then the car levelled off, still rough for another count of four hundred and seventy-six. The car stopped. The rear door to his left opened. He could hear some chains, some gates being swung open. The car edged forward again, over rough ground, the wheels noisily crushing the dry bracken. It stopped again. The gates closed, and the car dipped as the man regained his seat, the door closing hard. It was a secluded place.

He was strapped to a wooden chair placed in the centre of a spacious garage. The floor beneath him and halfway up the walls was lined with thick PVC sheeting. If this was for maximum effect, it certainly worked, as the hood was taken from his head. Without a word, the four kidnappers left the garage through a side door, which led to what Harold assumed was a rustic *finca*.

Kristos Koiduste made a call to his men in Madrid. He was told that the main target had left by helicopter, destination unknown. Almost two hours had passed since the old man had been secured, during which time Koiduste had reported Divine's travel arrangements to Perelta. The Estonian and the Spanish detective had done a deal: for the information received by Perelta from Koiduste, the gangster, Perelta would ensure that Koiduste would be first in line to purchase the confiscated sites at a reduced market price and, of course, be immune from prosecution.

The agreement was a *double whammy* for Koiduste. Bringing Jerry Divine down would not only secure the real prize—the contract from Abdul—but also restore his standing. He had been a leading contender for the enterprise before the large drug consignment went astray. He had recouped some credibility by eliminating the supposed culprits, three in total, and in a dramatic and visual way. He was certain that the French Algerians would report back to Abdul and his people about how efficient he was. But what else was Jerry Divine up to? There was something else, something so important to Divine. What was it, and what was it worth?

It was in Koiduste's nature—*his greedy being*—to want it all. If it was available and could be his, he would seize the opportunity, no matter who had to fall in the process.

"What is your name?" Harold detected the strong Eastern European accent.

"We will start easy, and the questions will get a little harder. Same for the treatment, I should add. It will start moderate and become *excruciating*. The choice is yours, old man."

Kristos liked the man chained to the chair. He liked him already. He knew he would break him, but it was not going to be easy. The hood had been replaced on Harold's head, so he had only seen the back of the speaker's blonde head—and the eyes, of course. *Those steely blue eyes. Those eyes.* Wait a minute! What had Jerry said?

"His eyes, mocking, I remember them still. Deep blue fucker, staring, almost laughing."

This was Koiduste! Without a doubt, this was him.

He drew comfort from the fact that the leader wished to remain anonymous. *The hood.* Why would he not want Harold to identify him if he was going to kill him?

Divine Intervention

The first blow came from his left-hand side and knocked the wind from his lungs as the thud connected with his lower ribs and rocked him sharply to the right. The chair remained intact, which indicated that it was secured to the floor. Harold let his head drop forward, which eased the pain slightly. A leather strap was pulled sharply under his chin and tightened, forcing the nape of his neck against the upper back support of the chair. The rush of air escaped his lungs, hissing from his throat.

"What the fuck! I know nothing," he forced through gritted implants.

"You know something, old man. You must tell. Where has your friend gone?"

"How the fuck would I know?"

Wrong answer. The grip on the garrotte tightened slightly, reminding Harold never to reply to a question with a question.

"Mr Jerry is planning something, and I want to know what it is. You will tell me, yes?"

His feet were lifted as much as the binding would allow, his shoes and socks were removed, and his bare feet were placed in a shallow bucket with an inch of cold water. Harold guessed what was coming next.

"How is your heart, old man?"

"Wait a fucking minute, you Cossack cu—" He didn't finish before a blunt instrument struck him hard on the bridge of his nose. He felt the pain and heard the crack as the break drew immediate blood, rushing from his nostrils into his mouth. He coughed it back and spat it out as far as the material of the hood would allow. It was hot under the cloth now, and Harold felt fear rising from his feet to his head, which was perspiring, claustrophobic, and more than flushed.

"No! Stop! You don't have to do this."

"So tell us what we want to know."

"What are you going to do to him?"

"We want to know what he is planning."

"I don't know."

The bolt of amps hit like a shattering of his bones as it travelled through his entire body, jerking him rigid in the chair. It transformed his body into a bolt upright position as much as the bindings would allow. The pain reeled around his head, and the shock was expertly delivered—just enough to nearly knock him out. Whoever was at the controls had done this before.

Harold *wanted* to pass out. He wasn't sure how much more he could take, but he knew he could never forgive himself for revealing what he knew about Jerry's plans.

What he did know for sure was that these guys were professionals. After this, he would almost certainly be killed—or worse still, left in a vegetative state. A drastically reduced Harold assumed to be the leader spoke, saying something rapidly in his own tongue before a door was opened and shut. There were still people in the garage; Harold could hear them behind him, whispering quietly, then the sound of two car doors slamming, then the engine starting and departing. The two remaining were nearer now; he could feel the breath of one behind his ear.

Harold tightened his defences. He could imagine what was coming next and could almost feel the pain already. He was right, but it wasn't quite what he expected. The hood was removed from his head, and a few drops of liquid were dripped onto his ear with precision. It was cool, then warm, and by the time it became hot and *excruciatingly* scalding, Harold guessed it could only be acid. He could almost feel his ear melting. The pain was unbearable, a hundred times more intense than the shock. Harold screamed out loud, his lungs almost bursting with the cry. The Cossack furthest from him laughed, which only made the whole escapade more absurd.

Harold, as a victim, so quickly, without any warning, was now delirious. He was very confused, *bamboozled* as to the urgency these scumbags felt about Jerry's antics. *So, he was about to pull off a blag! So-fucking-what. No big deal. Why doesn't he just tell these cunts? Let them have the information. Who gives a fuck? Let them have it. Jerry would want him to tell. Liberty is paramount. Maybe they would let him live. Who wants to live? With no fucking left ear? His good one at that!*

He could hear the guy closest to him move to his right. The one furthest away sniggered, which only angered Harold more and gave him the determination to see this out. He could feel the unmistakable cold steel of the blade; the scumbag was scraping the debris of what was left of Harold's ear. By the grace of God, there was absolutely no pain. Harold winced at the touch, but he wasn't about to let these scumbags know he was numb to it.

The blade moved slowly down the side of his frail shoulder and round to meet his collarbone. It brought with it one of the cunts from the airport.

He was looking down at Harold with an unnerving coolness in his eyes. *Yes,* thought Harold, *this bastard had been here many times.*

"Our boss, my friend…"

"I'm not your fucking friend, you slime ball cunt!"

"…old man, has given us the privilege of extracting the information we require from you using any means we see fit." He put enough pressure on the handle to cut the loose skin, protecting Harold's frail bones. The bone that used to hold his nose in line was shattered from the previous blow. There was swelling now, giving the usually pristine character a severely deformed look. The blood still flowed from his nose and ran like a small stream through the cake, which had already dried.

Harold knew he was dying. He was helpless—helpless to himself, useless—and to these two cunts, he would have wiped the floor with them thirty years ago, when he was Jerry's age. *Jerry!* He hoped with all his heart he would get the cowardly bastard with the blue eyes.

The grip on the leather bind securing his neck had relaxed, and his head fell forward. He could see the knife travelling down from his upper chest to the sternum, the wafer-thin skin slicing open just enough to show him that the cut was not deep. He looked up into the grey eyes of his torturer. They were not smiling. They were worried—worried that they could be losing the prize.

"Talk, old man, tell us what you know. Tell us about Abdul."

Abdul? Jerry's contact in Morocco? There were a hundred million fucking Abduls—Mohamed, Abdul—thousands of Arab cunts. *Abdul? I thought you wanted information about Jerry, you bastard. Am I hearing things?*

Harold lifted his head to look directly into the grey eyes—the last eyes he would see on this earth. *Vera, the boys, I'm coming, Vera, I'm coming home.* The murderer moved forward and bent to hear what the old man was about to say.

"Fuck you! Kill me, you slimy bastard," he hissed back at him through the implants, now stained red. The brute straightened to his full height. Harold's head dropped again. He was ready to meet his maker.

"Believe me, old man, we will kill you, but first, you will experience something which will be a shame you will not be able to share."

Harold lifted his head in defiance. He saw the other guy hand over the eardrops capsule, for want of a better word, to his accomplice doing the dirty work. It contained so little liquid that it almost beggared belief that the contents could cause so much pain and desecration. The torturer held the small bottle by the rubber suction between his gloved hand and showed it to Harold.

"First, I do the other ear, and then we take away the eyes."

Harold was scared. Please, God, not my eyes!

"Wait! Fucking wait, you fuck-faced cunt!" He tried to tear his arms from the wooden chair, the veins on his hands almost bursting through the skin. "I'll tell you something, just wait."

The guy straightened up and looked at his accomplice with satisfaction. Harold heard, through his remaining ear, the rotation of the blades from the low-flying chopper.

"Your mother will suck Afghan dick in her grave," he screamed.

The torturer was confused. He was about to ask a question when the other spoke frantically. There were cars stopping outside, many of them in quick succession. Harold's head lifted to the roof, as if to thank God and curse Jerry at the same time. There was commotion on a grand scale outside the tin door. A loudspeaker could be heard demanding that the occupants leave with their hands held high.

The police! Never in all his years had Harold been more pleased to hear them shout their orders, albeit through one ear. He coughed hard to release more clotted blood, spat it out onto the wet sheeting, and called out for help.

Chapter One Hundred and Three

Kristos Koiduste had no intention of making things any worse than they already were for himself. When his car was stopped shortly after leaving the farm with the old man and his soldiers, he immediately told the officer in charge where the trio had been deployed. This cooperation had little effect on his arrest, and he was taken directly to the Central Policia Station in Málaga. Of course, in his version of events, he had merely dropped the three off at the secluded *finca* and knew nothing of what happened thereafter.

Angelo Perelta, on the other hand, was too old in the tooth to take this explanation seriously. What he had to decipher was, who was the victim, and why was he kidnapped? Angelica was annoyed that her father could even begin to contemplate releasing Koiduste—she was convinced he was the devil incarnate.

"Have patience, my dear, and please, do not question my judgement."

"Papa, from what our officers tell us, the old man is lucky to be alive. They were going to kill him for sure!"

"And we will get to the bottom of it, this is for sure."

"I am sorry, Papa."

"Accepted, my dear. Now, do you want to interview Koiduste with me?"

"No, but I will watch."

"Why don't you want to come inside?"

"He sends shivers down my spine, Papa. Out of all the cases we've looked at, he is the one who really scares me. Be careful, Papa."

Perelta looked at his daughter; he had never heard her speak this way. He tapped his pencil rapidly on his desk, then looked over to his daughter sitting at hers. She was so much like her mother—she would have been very proud of her. He asked her not to worry. She smiled back at him reassuringly.

Chapter One Hundred and Four

Across the Atlantic Ocean, William Wheeler was also worried, and scared—more scared than he could ever remember being in his whole sorry life. If it was to end as a result of this, that's what it had been—*sorry*, a *farce*. And the worst thing was, if he had it all to do again, he had absolutely no idea how he would do it any differently. He had lived and worked the easy way, by the book. The only brief spell of excitement had been taking the money for the job of destroying the evidence against Divine and his gang, and look what happened there—his parents were almost battered to death, and the money was gone, back to the coffers of Jerry Divine, the man who had it all.

The look on his doctor's face had convinced Wheeler of what he had guessed anyway, what he knew in his heart. A person knows his own body; he lives with his intestines. We never see them, but they are with us always—we are their protector, and they are the giver of life. The skin and bone we carry secures them, we feed and water our internal organs, we energise for them, and they reward us with days, months and, if you're fortunate, years—many of them. But at the same time, when something is seriously wrong, when the balance of the blood cells goes into disarray, or a certain intake of sugar, or whatever, is not being processed as normal, we know. We don't necessarily need any training—we feel it, and we know. So when the blood was flowing from his backend, he knew. And the look on Dr Reardon's face, now, in his surgery, didn't need words to convince Wheeler that there was something very seriously amiss.

"I am going to admit you today and refer you to see a consultant at the earliest opportunity."

"Not today, doctor, I have some pressing matters which need my full attention."

"The only matter which needs your full attention today, Bill, is the matter of getting this mess looked at and keeping you alive."

"It's that bad, is it, Doc?"

"I think so, Bill. But let's not jump to any foregone conclusions," he tried.

"Why not?"

"Come now, Bill, I never had you down as a defeatist."

"You're right. You gonna get me in today then?"

"Now, Bill. Right now. I'm going to have an ambulance pick you up here at the surgery."

"My car's outside."

The doctor didn't hear him. He lifted the phone and made arrangements for his patient to be collected, while Bill Wheeler looked on silently, thinking about his worst fears—not the real fear of dying, but Divine slipping the net, yet again, before he does.

Chapter One Hundred and Five

Stuli was relieved to see the back of Vincent. He couldn't grasp how someone could live in such disarray—nearly everything Vincent did or said resulted in a drama of the highest extent. Even Demitra, who Stuli hadn't seen for days before he left the island of Gibraltar and was so sweet, seemed to live her life *on tenterhooks* and in fear of her man. So, it was music to Stuli's ears when Vincent advised him to travel back to Gambia and take care of business there.

Stone almost fell off the bed as he grabbed for the phone. It couldn't be anyone else. It had only been four days, but they had been long, almost unbearable. He hadn't dared leave the room for fear of missing Jerry's call. There's only so much sex one can have in the confines of a one-bedroom suite, and to be perfectly honest, if he abused Demitra any more than he had in the last few days, she would either die or leave him, run away—possibly to the law.

"Hello, is that you, Jerry?" The line went dead. *Fuck!* It rang again. "Hello."

"It's me."

"Yes, I realise that, sorry." He could imagine Jerry at the other end, angry at the fact he had called him by name. There was absolutely no indication that the caller was upset in any way, but Barry knew that he would be.

"I'm not going to get back for some time. It may be that I won't make it before the first project."

"It's still on, though?"

"Still?"

"I know you didn't confirm, but you *are* going to see it through?"

"I think so. I have enough on the first. If I need more, there will be an email address in reception for you to collect. Send me a clean one in return. Then, if you have nothing else to talk about, you should head back home. I'll be in touch."

"So, you don't want me up the road?" Stone asked, deflated.

Jerry knew Barry wanted a more active part in the robberies, but it was impossible, especially where Hutchin was concerned. As far as the second job went, Jerry wouldn't entertain it without Hutchin O'Brien.

"Stay away from the first one. I'll bring you back in for the big one," he lied.

He liked what Harold had said about looking into it himself. Harold was thorough. The information would be just as good, if not better, from him than from Barry, and the detail of any robbery thereafter would be done with precision. Barry would be upset once he heard about it happening without him, but it would be too late for him to do anything about it. Jerry would make sure he was looked after financially.

The helicopter was brand new—he could almost smell the fumes from the engine burning. The blue and white paintwork gleamed in the sunlight as he approached with his head lowered. The two pilots turned to smile as he climbed aboard and slid the door shut behind him. The seats were still encased in plastic, and the smell of leather and new walnut was intense in the compact space.

"Hi! You must be Mr Vine."

"Call me Daniel. You'll be seeing quite a bit of me over the next six months," he said, holding out his hand.

"Pleased to meet you, Daniel. My name is Captain Jason Furness, and my friend here is First Officer José Cruz Ruiz." Jerry shook the hands of both men warmly.

"You're English?"

"And proud of it," the captain said all too seriously.

His friend smiled warmly, telling Jerry this was a topic of ridicule. Jerry liked him.

"Business in Morocco?"

Jerry ignored the question. The machine lifted smoothly and gathered pace too quickly for Jerry's nervous liking.

He had changed into a Christian Dior suit, bought off the peg from a boutique situated in the foyer of the hotel. The convenience was worth the exorbitant price, and with the silk shirt bearing the same motif and a contrasting tie, he looked like a businessman benefiting from his success.

He was content with the fact that he had called Barry before leaving the city and omitted him from any further involvement in the Antwerp robbery.

Something was telling him to tread carefully around his old friend, and now, with the fact that Harold had offered his services, Jerry Divine was feeling good for the first time. He asked for music to be played through his earphones, requested sixties Motown, and slept.

"Mr Vine, Mr Vine." Jerry jerked awake.

"Sorry, Mr Vine, we're dropping into Córdoba to refuel. Would you like to stretch your legs?"

"Yeah, sure." He looked out and down, surprised to see how close to the ground they were. He checked his watch. He had time on his hands—Abdul was due to pick him up at 7 pm, which gave him almost two and a half hours to play with. "Do you have to radio in to refuel?"

"Yes."

He looked at his watch again. "I'm a little early for my meeting. Can we grab a bite to eat?"

"Certainly, Mr Vine. There's a nice cafeteria here. A meal or a snack?"

"A snack and a little walk will be fine."

"I'll take care of it, sir."

"Thank you."

He left the two pilots to finish their food and opted to take a stroll outside. *His plan could work—he could actually pull this off.* Looking at the helicopter, he got a shiver through his entire body. There it was, standing in its glory. He imagined how many sacks of cash he could load into it in quick succession. The feeling of giddiness was almost childish, and he had to check himself from laughing out loud.

The time it took to fly from Gibraltar to Morocco in this modern machine would be a matter of minutes. This time, he decided to give a little more information to Abdul—maybe even look for a landing point. *The only things that could stop him were a bullet on the day or the pursuit of a Policia helicopter.* The first was final, but the second he could prevent. Jerry had already decided to find out where the Policia helicopters were stationed and sabotage them the night before the robbery.

It seemed to Jerry, as he looked across the shallow runway of the small domestic heliport, that the *big one* in Gib could well be the easiest of the two. Just then, as if to cool him from the exhilaration, a smaller chopper lowered itself within twenty metres of where he stood. The wind from the blades swept his hair back and blew his jacket open. He didn't shield himself from the sudden gust; instead, he lifted his head to the breeze, feeling that things were about to change for the better.

Kath and the girls were a million miles from his thoughts at this precious moment in time. He walked slowly back into the service area and made a call to Abdul.

Chapter One Hundred and Six

"This will save so much time, my brother," called the little Arab over the noise of the rotor. His tall sibling was behind him, ushering him into the helicopter. Jerry leaned over and took his friend by the hand, pulling him forward, causing Memhet to stumble into the helicopter behind his brother.

"I'm sorry, I am very sorry," blushed Memhet.

Jerry laughed.

"It's fine, c'mon, let me help you." He held his hand out to the tall man and pulled hard. Again, the awkward figure stumbled into the aircraft. Abdul turned and slapped his offspring for being so lackadaisical.

"Did you tell the pilot?"

"Marrakech, yes?"

"Yes, my friend, Marrakech. How long will it take?"

"One hour forty minutes."

"Amazing, almost five hours by road. Our roads are not like Europe."

"I know," Jerry remembered the last time he was in Morocco.

"This machine, it belongs to you?"

"No. I was advised by an old friend of mine, that if it flies, floats, or fucks—rent it." Jerry smiled as he noticed Abdul elbowing his brother, as if to take heed of the advice being passed on. "I have a lot of travelling to do in the next few months, and although this form of transport is expensive, it could well work out cheaper in the long run."

"I see. Oh! Away we go, we are going up. How fast it rises!" The two new passengers looked nervous. Jerry smiled, noticing the two Arabs weren't used to this form of transport.

"Here, put these on," he said, passing earphones to each. "We can talk during the flight." The hands of Abdul were shaking as he took the padded muffs from Jerry and placed them on his head. Jerry fine-tuned the dial for him and asked if it was okay. Abdul confirmed with a thumbs-up and a weak smile. Memhet said nothing, looking straight ahead and remaining expressionless. Jerry indicated to the captain that they required privacy and watched as the pilot switched a control to mute.

"What's so important?" he asked when he was sure they couldn't be heard.

"I have little to say until we reach our destination."

"I've come a long way, Abdul, at great expense and with some inconvenience, I might add."

"Okay, Jerry, I'm sorry. I have been told to say very little so as not to jeopardise the rendezvous. It is assumed that if I say too much, you may decide to avoid the meeting."

"This is not good enough, Abdul. Are you telling me that this has nothing to do with what we were looking into last time?"

"This is correct."

"I will turn this helicopter around right now, Abdul, unless you tell me where the fuck we are going, and who and why we are going there." Jerry glared at the little man. The Arab said nothing, looking back at Jerry as if to assess the situation. He was weighing up his options. He had none, so he decided to give a little.

"Did you ever meet Alba Venga?"

"Alba Venga? Riat Venga's brother?"

"Yes."

"No."

"We are going to see Alba Venga."

"Why?"

"He has something to ask you." He looked for a reaction, and there was one from Jerry—confusion. "Maybe *ask* is the wrong word, Jerry. He has something to *tell* you."

"What?" said Jerry sceptically. "What the fuck does he have to tell me that I don't already know?"

"I am not sure, my friend, he only asked that I bring you."

"*You* bring me? He beckons, and I come? And you weren't to tell me? Who the fuck does this cunt think I am? Some fucking lap dog?"

"Please, Jerry, calm down, it is in your interest, I can assure you."

"Well, do it and do it quick, Abdul, because these things cost a few quid to run, and I don't want to waste your time or my money."

"Do what?"

"A-fucking-sure me."

"But I don't know the facts of the case."

"Case?"

"Not case, maybe this is not the word. My language, you know, it is not the best."

"Am I in any danger?"

"I have been given the word of Allah, not one hair on your head will suffer damage."

"Can you guarantee this?"

"I can, my friend," he said, placing his hand on his heart.

"A lot of good that will do," muttered Jerry. "His brother died in front of me, you know? Shot like a fucking stray dog, right through the head."

"No, I did not know this. Of course, I knew that he was killed, but I did not know that you were there."

"Does it make a difference to the guarantee you've just given me?"

"No, there will be no harm to you on this occasion. Alba will know the consequences—you have my protection, and in these parts, this is solid."

"Okay, but it would be nice to have some idea what the fuck he wants with me."

"Let us wait and see."

Jerry leaned forward and tapped the second-in-command on his shoulder. He indicated the side of his earpiece and gave a thumbs-up. Once the switch was reactivated, he asked how long before landing and was told twenty-two minutes. He looked at his watch—it was 8:26. He looked out at the sun, which was totally red and dropping behind the horizon. He thought about Kath and the girls before quickly putting them to the back of his mind—he was at work and needed no distractions.

As the chopper landed on the hot tarmac under the floodlights of a moonless sky, Jerry Divine and the two Arabs stepped from the aircraft and stretched their legs. Jerry was called by Captain Furness and handed a mobile phone.

"Mr Schwineshtieger."

"Thank you. Hello... hello, Mr Schwineshtieger... Yes, I'm sorry... No, I had no idea... Yes, of course, if I stay I will... of course, Mr Schwineshtieger... yes, of course, the best... on account, yes... Perfect, Mr Schwineshtieger... yes, thank you. Oh, your mother, how is she?... lovely, please send her my sincere best wishes... yes, goodbye."

He handed the phone back to Furness, who, Jerry noted, had been listening to every word.

"I take it we may be stopping over?"

"I'm not sure. I believe we will be taking a car from here. Can you bear with me? I will let you know shortly."

Chapter One Hundred and Seven

Perelta had made some enquiries and discovered that the law enforcement representative from Estonia, Iccholas Meras, was still in Spain. *Eurojust* were tying up a few loose ends in Madrid before the operation moved onto the next stage. Perelta knew that at some point, he would have to declare the fact that Koiduste was working for him. He had promised Kristos that he would give him the opportunity to purchase some of the confiscated sites in return for assisting the police. Angelo Perelta was a man of his word, and although he felt no obligation to Kristos Koiduste, it was no skin off his nose. He would give the Russian—Estonian, whatever he was—the opportunity to purchase. Whether he was in a position to buy was another matter. The chances were, he wouldn't be, and Perelta hoped that he would be locked up like Divine and the others.

Kristos Koiduste was power-hungry and money-greedy. All Perelta could do was put in a word for him. He had assisted in the operation and would have to be given at least a little credit for that. *Operation Escatura* would have progressed without Koiduste—he was only one cog in the works—but every little bit helped. The numbers he had supplied could lead to yet another operation. They had been researched and were looking promising. Cell site data had placed Divine's phone in the same area as two of the sites recently. This, in itself, Perelta imagined, would be interesting. He might even involve the British detective in his new findings. He asked Angelica to make a note of this, then he decided to meet Mr Meras.

The information the Estonian detective had offered during the conference was a little vague. Having said that, and to be fair to the officer, Peralta had not given the details his full attention.

It wasn't difficult to arrange. Meras was prepared to travel from Madrid to Málaga, especially if it concerned Kristos Koiduste. *As a matter of fact*, he was about to contact Mr Peralta himself, with a view to discussing the possibility of an extradition option. The meeting was arranged for the following morning.

Chapter One Hundred and Eight

Kathleen Divine was never one to avoid saying it as it was, especially when the subject related to her girls. So, as the matter directly involved them, she felt it was her solemn duty to tell them about the sudden change in family circumstances before they heard it from someone else. Little Julie didn't want to hear that Daddy would be staying away for a long time this time, and that when he did come back, it would not be for long—*a day or so at the most*. This was enough to have her scurrying in a temper to her room.

"She'll come round, Mum."

"I hope so, Jas. Ask her to come down, love."

"I would leave her for now. Let's you and me talk, and I'll ease it to her gently."

"You're so mature for your years, love—like a sister to me at times."

"Is it for real, Mum? You and Dad. Is it final?"

"I'm afraid so, pet." Kath was trembling.

"Let's go inside—you're shaking."

"I'm fine, baby. Pour me another glass of wine, please."

"I'd rather not. This is too important an issue to be discussing under the influence, Mum," she said, lifting the bottle and taking it into the bar. Kathleen watched her daughter. She was growing up to be a beautiful, sensible, intelligent young woman, definitely different to how she was when she was sixteen.

Kathleen hadn't had to grow up, really. Jerry had always watched over her, provided for her, and shielded her from the outside world. She hadn't had to do anything for herself. The charity was Kathleen's first independent project, and if she was being honest with herself, it was really Debra who laid the foundations and did most of the structural work. Her commitment was truly awesome, and Kathleen was happy to hang on to her petticoat, receive some of the credit, and gain a lot of self-worth.

Of course, Debs didn't see it this way. Without Kath and her husband's contacts, she would never have been able to get the charity past the idea stage. Without Jerry, the events would probably be a 24-hour pool tournament in some Irish pub, or a fun run stretching to a half-marathon around a remote village in the sticks—*undeniably a million miles away from the glitzy events which had taken place previously.* Kath suddenly realised that this year's occasion was approaching soon and was wondering whether Jerry, having been given the news, would still involve himself and his friends.

"What you thinking, Mum?"

"I was just thinking about the realisation of it all, the impact it was going to have on our lives. To be honest with you, pet, I don't think I've given it enough thought."

"Dad will be there for us, Mum. He will always support us."

"I know he will, Jas. Your dad is a good man—he has a heart of gold."

"Why do you think it is, Mum? Why do you think Dad does what he does?"

"What do you mean?"

"Mum, I'm not stupid. He's so different from my friends' fathers. The police, his friends back home, Barry's and Kitty's dad, Dad's best friend, killed by the police—Dad going missing soon after. I don't know, Mum, it's like he ran away from something. And now this. Mum…"

"You seem to have it all worked out, Jas," she laughed weakly before asking, "What is it, love? What's on your mind?"

"Is Dad a gangster?"

Kath looked at her daughter. Jasmine was looking down; she didn't look up when she asked again, "*Is he*, Mum?" Kath had already decided to tell her the truth. She knew Jerry would disapprove, but she was the one who had to make decisions around the home now. There could be repercussions, but she refused to lie.

"Your father has lived on the edge of the law all his life, Jasmine. I won't lie. I'm not sure what he does, baby—you have to believe and understand that—but whatever he has done in the past doesn't make him a bad man," she added quickly, as a form of defence. Jasmine looked up and into her mother's eyes. They were crying, the tears already running down her cheeks. Her daughter stood and embraced her.

"It's alright, Mum," she said, wrapping her arms tightly around her.

"You remind me so much of him, Jas. You make me feel safe."

"I'm here for you, Mum, always."

"We need to be here for each other—for little Julie, Jas. Both of us."

"We are. We will always be together, Mum."

Chapter One Hundred and Nine

The car stopped at the *over-extravagant* entrance to the casino, and the rear doors were opened immediately by an elegant and colourfully clad attendant. Without speaking, the trio were escorted up the red carpet by the same man into the grandiose surroundings of the grand reception. They were led through some large, carved, ornate double doors and greeted by a tall man who Jerry assumed, by his demeanour, to be either the owner or someone with equivalent authority.

"Please, come this way."

They walked through a boardroom which Jerry imagined was capable of accommodating at least twenty people around the large oak table situated in the middle of the room. The high-backed chairs were elaborately carved from trees to represent *exquisite splendour*. Abdul looked up at the fine paintings mounted high on the walls and asked Jerry if he liked them. Jerry didn't answer; his mind was elsewhere, but he appreciated the fact that Abdul was making an effort to put him at ease. Memhet remained silent, bringing up the rear.

The door at the other end of the large room led into a corridor with a deep, pile, green and gold-coloured carpet and full-length, tinted glass windows on one side. Jerry looked through the glass and was impressed by the size of the gaming area down below. It seemed more like a casino one would see in Vegas, as opposed to Morocco. The air was cool, and the sound of water trickling down the polished chrome, which ran the entire length of the opposite wall, was refreshing after the humid heat outside.

The matching doors at the other end opened before they reached them. Jerry looked up as he walked and noticed the small surveillance camera. The leader didn't enter but stood to one side, still holding the brass handle, and let the three guests in. He closed the door behind them. The three men already seated in the office stood to greet their guests. Jerry immediately noted which one was Alba Venga. He stood from behind the large, polished, kidney-shaped desk and walked around to embrace Abdul. All the kissing and body hugs were complete within a few moments, and then the younger sibling of the man Jerry had seen murdered almost seven years previously by the British police, secret service, or whoever, walked up and stood

Divine Intervention

directly in front of Jerry Divine. Jerry stood stiff and looked directly into his eyes for a clue. The dark brown eyes gave nothing away; they were cold and dry, almost as though they were blind.

"Mr Divine," he said, holding out his hand.

"No hug or kiss? I thought it was custom."

"You like to kiss? I kiss," he said, smiling. He placed one hand on each of Jerry's shoulders and kissed him lightly on each cheek. "It is nice to *eventually* meet you, Mr Divine." Jerry didn't appreciate the garlic.

"I have heard so much about you."

"I wish I felt the same," he replied honestly.

"Heard about me, or pleased to see me?"

"Both."

"You may, when I have finished."

"I hope so," responded a slightly relieved Jerry.

"Please, please," he said, holding out his hand in the direction of a chair, "take a seat."

One of the others pulled a chair from against the wall and positioned it by the desk. Abdul and his brother sat in two of the remaining dozen or so seats positioned beside the door they had just entered.

"You have me completely intrigued, Mr Venga," said Jerry, taking his pew. The other two, who were already present when they had entered the room, sat down. Alba Venga looked at each one in turn before he, too, eventually walked around the desk and sat down to face all who were present.

"You like to drink, Mr Divine? What you like? Champagne, Cristal, Krug, Laurent Perrier pink—we have it all."

"Very good, Alba. You mind if I call you Alba?"

"Not at all! This is good. We are friends, after all." Jerry ignored the annoying over-familiarity.

"Your awareness of what I prefer to drink shows commitment to detail. I like that. *I'm impressed.*"

"Abdul, what about you? I hear you also like to drink Champagne." Jerry looked to Abdul, who was blushing.

"And water for you, Memhet? Memhet is a good Muslim."

Abdul didn't respond, which told Jerry he was inferior to Venga *so much for the guarantee.* Jerry was already beginning to dislike this man, who bore no resemblance to his brother in body shape but shared all the hallmarks of his facial features, without the puffiness of excess weight.

"We have so much to talk about, Jerry. You mind? You mind I call you Jerry?"

"Not at all."

"Good." He lit a cigarette and inhaled deeply. He held the smoke in his lungs for some time, as though he wouldn't release it until he had made his mind up which way to go. "Ok, Jerry. The death of my brother," he looked to the heavens, "was a great loss to us, a gift to Allah, and an achievement for the British police, who, may I add, gained much credit from various geographical neighbours that benefited, as they all had, in their belief, the same interest." He looked hard into Jerry's eyes. "Riat died in vain. *You were there, Jerry*, you saw him killed, *murdered like a dog*. Is that how it was, Jerry? Is it fair to say my brother was slaughtered like a rabid dog?" His voice rose with the question. "He died in vain because there were others who stepped into his shoes—there will always be others, no?"

Jerry knew this was a question. He chose not to answer.

"Of course, there will, Jerry." Again, he took a large drag of the cigarette, almost burning it down to the stub. He inhaled sharply and exhaled almost immediately. "So long as the poppy grows in Afghanistan, the coca leaf in South America, and the marijuana here in Morocco, and there is a flame to burn, a vein to inject, or a nose to snort, there will be someone to deal. *These are commodities, Jerry*, like this," he said, holding up his cigarette, "*it will never cease to exist*. Plants, Jerry—they grow from the earth's crust. But we know this," he said dismissively. "This is not an agricultural seminar. *The point*—the point is that the British police killed my brother, and the point is, they were assisted. They had help. Riat was lured into a trap." Jerry was beginning to feel a little apprehensive.

"If he was…"

"*He was!*" His fist hit the desk.

"Then we all were."

"Not all, Jerry—this is not quite true."

"What are you saying?"

"One of you knew that my brother would be killed that day."

"I don't understand."

"And I believe you. I truly believe that you do not understand."

"But you are going to enlighten me," Jerry relayed as a fact.

"*I think maybe you already know.*"

"You just said you believe me."

"I said I believe that you do not understand."

"Why don't we cut out the bullshit, Mr Venga, and get to the point here!" Jerry stood up.

"Please, Mr Jerry, remain seated. There is no need to raise your voice." Jerry sat. Venga stood, snubbed out his cigarette, looked at the guy seated to Jerry's left, who removed a large brown envelope from a briefcase and slid it across the desk to Alba Venga.

"My brother was weak. He had weaknesses like us all. *You gamble, Jerry*, you like fast cars, girls, and other vices. *Me!* I smoke too much, I miss my prayers occasionally." He shrugged his shoulders and sat back down, taking something from the envelope. He studied it.

"Who could it be, Jerry? Who could it be that knew there was going to be an ambush? Because we make no bones about it—it was an ambush, and you yourself were a target. *You were lucky, Jerry*—you were agile, not like my brother." Again, he looked to the ceiling. "Even today, we see no coroner's report. As far as we know, there was no autopsy. My brother was cremated without us having the benefit of saying our last goodbyes. *He was gone from this earth, just as though he never existed at all.*" Again, his voice was raised and cracked under the strain of talking about his hero.

"So when you tell me to cut the bullshit out and we must get to the point," he regained his composure and looked across the desk, directly into Jerry's eyes, "I ask you again, Mr Divine. *Who could it be?*"

Jerry knew the answer, but his face gave nothing away. *There could be someone else*. He didn't want to believe that he had been totally taken in by his oldest and closest friend.

"There was a time when we thought it could be you. *We had you in our sights for a long time*. You have Abdul here to thank for fighting your corner. We have more, of course. We have people inside. But no one knew, no one guessed the extent the authorities would go to disguise their actions. And then, in a remote place, on a dark night in The Gambia—West Africa, of all places—it all became clear."

Jerry knew what was coming. He thought it better to intervene at this point. He cleared his throat. Alba lit another cigarette.

"Are you telling me that Barry Stone is the one? That is, of course, *if* you have the proof."

"Oh, Mr Divine, don't you worry, we *have* the proof," he said, placing his hand on the documents taken from the envelope. "But why do you ask?" Jerry didn't answer the question.

"Do you have something to show me?" he asked, looking in the direction of the contents.

"In good time. First, I want to hear what *you* have to say."

"I have nothing to say."

"You must have *something* to say, Jerry. You see, let me tell you this—before we look at our next project, the one you discussed last week with Abdul, we have to be one hundred per cent sure that you are the right man for the job. And to assure us of this, we have to assess your reaction to such a statement as this. And before I tell you more, I have to be sure that you agree."

Jerry was confused; he wasn't sure if he was seeing the whole picture. He had to tread carefully.

"Barry Stone and I have been friends for a lifetime. You have to understand, this is very difficult for me to accept. To think that Barry was—or *is*—a snake, and that he would see me killed, is very hard for me to accept."

"I see." He picked up an onyx telephone from the desk and spoke into it rapidly in Arabic. "I just ordered mint tea."

"Thank you."

"This dirty dog is somewhere—we believe he is in Spain. Have you seen him, Jerry?" The question was asked quickly. Jerry wasn't expecting it.

"No." This was a little too quick; he would have to add to this. "Barry was killed on the same day as your brother." Alba didn't answer. He smiled at Jerry. "Didn't he?" added Jerry quietly.

"Did you see the body?"

"No, he was cremated. I did attend the cremation."

"Is it not customary in the UK to see the body? To pay respects, one last time?"

"We were advised not to. The reason they gave to the family was that he was too shot up—disfigured, you know?"

"Why did you ask me if Barry Stone was the one, if indeed you thought he was dead?"

"I heard through the grapevine... something. There was a connection to Gambia, that's all."

"Very clever. Let me tell you—Stone is alive and well. There are others looking for him. I believe they too are looking to kill him, to let the deed of his actions die with him. We nearly had him in Africa and had to make do with second best."

"What do you mean?"

"We killed two men who work for a secret agency in the UK. Before they died, they told us everything they knew about their intended target—Stone. It seems your best friend did a deal with MI6 to save his own hide, and the deal," he said, holding his arms out wide, "was that he set you and my brother up to be executed."

"But why?"

"This is something we would all like to know. *Me?* So that I can look into his eyes as I inflict the most torturous pain. *You?*" he said, bringing his hands together and pointing his two forefingers in Jerry's direction before answering his own question, "because you want to know *why*. What I am afraid of is that you will get to him first. You may kill him, you may not—I don't know. You tell me you don't know where he is; I have to accept this. It is important that we have trust. Maybe we can kill him together—who knows what will happen?" His eyes were smiling. *This man was a complicated fucker*, thought Jerry.

"What is it exactly that you want from me, Alba?"

"Let me tell you, Jerry. What I want from you—No!" he stopped and thought for just a few moments. "What I want *for* you is for us," he pointed toward Jerry and back to himself before sweeping his arm wide to include the others present, "to work together. As you know, we have been working to get our hashish into Spain by road, and then into various European countries. You have been singled out to join our group. Abdul here has worked with us for a long time now. He and Memhet had to assess who, on the Costa del Sol, was our best option. We looked at Dermot McAvoy, Robert Rauschenberg, you, Kristos Koiduste, and others. *You*, of course, were the one with the political connections, which is always an advantage. What I do not want is for there to be anything which could jeopardise the work we have done so far. And I want you to report to me if and when Stone makes contact."

Jerry understood the importance of doing the right thing here. If Alba was correct in his assertion, and Barry was guilty of setting the trap, he would have to pay with his life. As for Jerry being the best choice for the cannabis project—he wouldn't have been chosen if they had known about the recent goings-on and the demise of his political contacts. But, for now, they weren't aware, which suited him.

"I can't help but notice, that the documents on the desk, may have some relevance."

"This is true. These are photographs." he slid the pictures over to Jerry. "They are quite distressing. They show a boy, a child, being abused in a despicable manner. I said before, that my brother had his demons, he was sexually depraved and had a preference for the same sex, usually the minor." *Jerry looked at the photos and showed his distaste with a grimace.*

"You see in the background, there—someplace," Alba leaned over the desk, sits Stone, next to my brother. These pictures were taken from a case belonging to the two agents before they were killed. They also told my people that they were to kill Stone so as to avoid embarrassing this man.

He pushed a large, leather-bound, open book over to Jerry. Jerry kept his fingers as a marker and looked at the title on the front cover. Who's Who! He opened the book to the marked page and saw a highlighted area. He read the small inscription and studied the picture of the old man.

"Why would the death of Barry embarrass this man?"

"Because Stone is the only one, apart from other officers from MI6 and a detective with the British Police, who can prove that this man ordered the death of my brother—and you."

There was a knock on the door. Alba called, and the tea was brought in by the same man Jerry had assumed was the casino proprietor. He placed the tray, looked at his watch, and spoke to Alba in his own tongue. Once he had left the room, Alba checked his watch and spoke to Abdul. Abdul came forward, poured the tea, and asked Jerry if he would like to gamble.

Jerry was still looking at the photograph, hatred etched on his face. He put it down and said he would have to make a call, then asked if Alba could arrange two rooms—one for him and one for the pilots.

"I'm afraid my friend reminds me I have another meeting scheduled for eleven forty-five. I have made arrangements for chips, for you, to the value and equivalent of ten thousand euros, please," he said, standing. He drained his cup and beckoned with his palm upright. "Rojani here will take you down in the lift. Good luck at the table. I will take care of the rooms and will see you for breakfast at seven a.m. tomorrow."

Jerry stood and shook the hand of the man, who he had quickly gained respect for, changing his first impression of him.

The roulette wheel was not lucky for Jerry, and the drink tasted bitter in his mouth. He asked Rojani, who spoke very little English, if he could arrange for the pilots to be picked up from the heliport and housed in their rooms. Once this was done, and the chips were wasted, he was glad to be in his room. His mind was in complete turmoil as he flopped onto the bed without undressing. A night of unrest followed, with patches of sleep disturbed by uncomfortable dreams.

A detective from the British police? The British police. British police.

The dreams continued. He was relieved to open his eyes after the last one, which depicted Stone being skinned alive by Alba and his henchmen while Jerry watched.

The sound of traders wailing from the rooftop souk, selling the multicoloured rugs and carpets as they had for over a thousand years, was heard and seen as Jerry drew open the curtains, lifted the net, and opened the window, which magnified the call to prayer. The large dome of a mosque, the hustle and bustle of the people—the whole biblical scene— would have been a sight to behold for anyone who had paid to see it. But Jerry was paying little attention. He had the same thing on his mind as he had had all night.

How could Barry have done such a thing? What was he doing in the room with the boy? How could he, Jerry, hold himself together the next time the two met? Could he keep his composure or would he lose control?

"A detective from the British police…"

Chapter One Hundred and Ten

Day Nine

Breakfast was a two-tier affair. Alba sent a message that he would be late and to expect him at eight. This gave Jerry the opportunity to make a few calls, which turned out to be a complete waste of time, as all the calls he made went unanswered. He called Harold for the third time and received no reply, which was unusual, as Harold was an early riser. Jerry called Kath but hit the cradle to disconnect before the phone even rang once.

This Wheeler thing was playing on his mind. He couldn't, for the life of him, understand how and why Bill Wheeler had raided his home with the Spanish Policía. Wheeler had been well paid for what he'd done for the team. What he should have done—and he always regretted not doing—was to pay Wheeler a visit after the South Mimms affair. That was another thing he couldn't understand: why had Wheeler been present at the shoot-out? The evidence had gone astray, and Wheeler had received his payment. Did he think for one minute that that information couldn't get into the wrong hands? Why hadn't he warned him? Why hadn't he got word to Jerry that the raid was imminent?

This lawyer Harold had employed—could he contact Wheeler? Maybe find out a little more?

He tried Harold again. No reply!

The British detective Alba had mentioned, the one who knew that Barry had agreed to the unthinkable. Was the British detective Wheeler?

"You are very busy on the phone, Mr Vine. Is everything alright?" asked Captain Jason Furness.

Jerry sat down and asked how the breakfast was. He usually found that the best way to tell someone to mind their own business was simply not to answer their question.

"It's good, yes, but then when is a continental breakfast not?"

"I truly believe that when in a country that doesn't fully understand, especially the food, one should opt for the good old continental. You can never go far wrong with croissants, black coffee, and a bowl of mixed fruit."

"I have to agree. What are our flight plans for today, Mr Vine?"

"Please! Daniel, call me Daniel. Today I think maybe we will drop into Gibraltar."

"And from there?"

"I'm not sure."

"Do you have a time?"

"No, sorry, but it will be a.m." Jerry noticed Abdul was trying to draw his attention. "Excuse me," he said, standing and making his way over to the two brothers.

"Good morning, Jerry. Can we sit separately?"

"Of course."

"Come, let us sit by the window. I have a message from Alba. He cannot make it at eight o'clock, apologises, and he has advised that we carry on with our schedule. He will see us in a day or two. He asked that you keep your eyes and ears alert. He feels sure that your friend is in Spain somewhere, and that he is likely to contact you."

"I see." Jerry looked disappointed but felt the complete opposite. He didn't want to have to lie to Alba again. He had done more than enough of that the previous night and felt uncomfortable doing so. He was unsure if he had covered himself sufficiently when he brushed aside the Barry/Gambia thing.

What was now important was that there seemed to be a good possibility that they would be working together, which, with each passing minute, seemed more and more likely. He would have to think very carefully if he was to continue investigating the two robberies, especially after what he had just discovered.

He was tempted to go ahead—*this big one* was definitely a temptation; those types of opportunities didn't come about often. He had already decided to do the diamond robbery. Most of the work on this score had been taken care of, and he knew that Winston would have already started his part. He had got a message to O'Rourke with instructions to contact some building suppliers in Antwerp, and the rest were all on standby.

The details given by the *fat Jew* looked to be in order, and these could be double-checked. He liked the idea of Antwerp because he had looked at a job in *the flat land* before. The waterway escape route always appealed to him—they would have to be very unlucky to get caught. If Barry was at the double shuffle, he wouldn't bring him down on the first job. There were to be no firearms on this one, and why would he bring him down anyway? Was he out to double-cross for the money?

If that was the case, the diamond job would go ahead without any implications. Jerry's recent mishaps demanded that he take action in one form or another, and he was never one to sit back. Yes, the diamond job was going ahead.

"You look like you are not hungry?"

"No, no, I'm not. I had a bite over there," he explained, looking over to the table he had just left. "I'm sorry, Abdul, I was miles away."

"We are ready to leave when you are."

"Yes, yes. One minute. I'll let the crew know, and we can be on our way." He stopped short of standing up. "Before I do, is there someplace I can ask the pilot to drop you near your home?"

"Yes, that would be better. We have some land in the village which is big enough. We may attract some attention from the locals, but it will be fine."

"Attention?"

"Yes! The children, of course! A helicopter in our remote village is not an everyday occurrence. No doubt the children will want to get close."

Jerry smiled.

The same children were running toward the open space before the chopper was below three hundred feet. The debris from the dry earth swirled under the blades, causing a mini dust storm. Scores of smiling faces, with rags for clothes and no toys, thought *all their Christmases had come at once* when the shiny machine, one they hadn't even seen in the movies, landed on their patch.

Jerry, on the other hand, didn't even notice. He was looking further afield, literally. There was nothing—nothing for miles around. No cars, only dry, barren land, farmers at work, and muck tracks. There was no way anyone could even come close to capturing the chopper full of cash.

But could he still do it?

Chapter One Hundred and Eleven

Landing at Gibraltar was just as easy as landing in the field in Morocco. Jerry listened as Furness made the call to air control. It was complicated to him but would be *a piece of piss* for McNess. Jerry relieved the Captain of his duties, said his goodbyes, and told the two pilots he would deal directly with Mr Schwineshtieger. He shook hands warmly with both Furness and Jose Ruiz and quickly jumped into a taxi to The Rock Hotel.

The receptionist was sorry to tell Jerry that Mr Maine and his guest had checked out thirty minutes ago, but he had left an envelope for someone matching his description, inscribed with the letter "J." She handed it to him, and he checked that it was an email address before he made further enquiries, which revealed that Maine had taken a taxi to Malaga airport. Jerry checked his watch and made a quick call to Irish Tom. Forty-five minutes later, he stepped out of the taxi in a service area above Marbella and sat beside Tom in his Mercedes.

"How da fuck are ya? Do I still get paid for doing fuck all?"

"I'm good. Yes. Malaga airport—step on it."

"Have I got something to tell you!"

"Faster. Tell me later."

"We're touching two hundred clicks an hour!"

"Keep it up." Jerry turned up the music. He didn't want to talk about what had happened with the arrests, about Kath, the girls, the properties, gambling—*anything*. He was totally focused on what he wanted to do, and more importantly, what he *had* to do.

"Here! Stop here."

"We'll get a ticket! This is for loading only."

"Fuck the ticket!"

"You're the boss." Tom stopped the car sharply, directly outside the doors leading into departures. Jerry was out of the car before Tom had even activated the park brake.

"Shall I hold here?" he called. Jerry didn't answer. Tom tried to look through the doors, which were opening and closing automatically. He remained seated, in situ.

Jerry looked frantically at the digital information boards showing the destination and times of departing flights. There was no direct flight to Gambia. He scanned the travellers—there were too many. Again, he checked the boards, this time looking for Madrid; the chances were that long haul would fly from there. *Madrid, Gate 21, next flight leaves in one hour forty-five.* He checked his watch and made for Gate 21.

The queue was fifty or sixty people long—he would have to be lucky. *Guest,* he thought. *He left with his guest.* Stuli! *He would be easy to spot—who could miss that fat cunt?* But no, he could not see him, or Barry. Then, just as he was about to walk toward check-in to ask about Maine, he spotted them: Barry with a black girl, long hair—*the motorbike!* She was the rider of the bike!

He walked toward the two travellers. Barry looked, unsure. He looked again. Jerry smiled and raised his two arms. Barry smiled nervously and looked at the girl beside him. Jerry looked too—her face was swollen, the dark glasses hid bruised eyes, and her jaw looked dislocated. Barry noticed that Jerry was giving Demitra a little too much attention.

"Jerry! What are you doing here? You told me to leave. We're on the six-fifteen from Madrid to Banjul. Do you want me to cancel?" He moved forward to take the embrace. Jerry looked over Barry's shoulder at the girl, who bowed her head to the floor. She didn't look at Jerry.

"Let's get a coffee, Barry. You have time."

"Yeah, sure, Jerry. Let me tell my girl to keep our position in the queue." When Barry had done this, the two walked over to a coffee and snack takeaway stand situated back towards the entrance. As they did, the electric sliding doors opened, and Jerry looked out to see Tom sitting with the roof down, looking back into the building. *He could plug Barry now and be away in seconds.* This was stupid thinking, he knew. *What, with the CCTV and the abundance of credible witnesses, he'd be lucky to get within a mile of the airport before being arrested—and besides, he didn't have a gun.*

"What brings you here, Jerry? Something wrong?"

"No, no, not at all. I completely forgot to leave the email address, and I didn't get one from you."

"There wasn't one for me, but I did leave one for you at reception."

"I didn't get it," he lied.

Divine Intervention

"Right, let's exchange now," said Barry, taking a pen from his breast pocket. He wrote something on a scrap of paper, and as he did so, Jerry looked at the back of his head. *Again, for the second time in as many minutes, he thought about putting a bullet in Barry's skull.* He was only glad he didn't have a gun. *If he had, he was sure he wouldn't be able to resist.*

Barry offered him the pen. Jerry took his own Cartier from the top pocket of his Dior, which now looked like it had been through the mill, and wrote a fictitious email address. Handing it to Barry, he said, "Keep in touch," but thought, *Give that to whoever you're working with, you cunt.*

He looked into Barry's eyes, and memories of yesteryear and yesterday flashed by—from the days when they were kids, growing up on the streets, doing their thing to earn a shilling. Barry looked at Jerry, who seemed to be staring into thin air.

"Is something wrong, Jerry?"

"No. No, mate, I was just reminiscing for a moment. It's been a long road, hasn't it, Barry?"

"It sure has, pal, it has that. I'm sure there's a few miles left in the tank."

"Do you want me to do anything for you?"

"You do enough, Jerry. I know about Jane and the kids, the money and that. I appreciate it." Jerry wanted to ask him *how*—how he knew about the money.

"You'd do the same."

"You know that, Jerry."

"C'mon, I'll walk you back. Who's your friend?" The question was sprung on Barry without notice.

"She's my partner. Her name's Beatrice. Come on, say hello."

"Beatrice!" Jerry laughed. "What happened to her face? It looks swollen."

"You know what these women are like, Jerry—fucking cosmetic surgery. I've signed her in to Madame Tussauds when she croaks it." He laughed half-heartedly.

Jerry looked closely at the girl as the two joined her. She averted any eye contact with him. He could see the bruises behind her shades, her lips were swollen, and her neck was puffed, but not enough to disguise the prominent Adam's apple.

"Thank you, Jerry. Thank you for accepting me back, the way you have," Barry tried.

Jerry didn't answer. He looked down at Beatrice's feet—the leather sandals made it easy to assess the size ten feet. *It was a man!* Jerry had to cough and sputter to disguise his surprise, shock, and distaste, mixed with some odd form of humour. *It was a farce, Barry was a joke—he wasn't a threat. How could this degenerate get the better of Jerry Divine?*

Jerry would play Barry's little game. Although the stakes were high, the odds were certainly in his favour, and the prize would be achieved. *This was a gamble he was prepared to take and relish. The bet was on.*

"Well, it is a pleasure to meet you, Beatrice," he said, holding out his hand and smiling. She took it and shook it slightly without saying a word. Jerry felt sympathy towards her—*or him*—and squeezed her hand, in an almost useless attempt to let her know.

"So!" he said, again turning to his lifelong friend and newfound enemy. "Have a nice flight, and we'll be in touch shortly." He held his arms open, and Barry came between them. Jerry wanted to whisper something into the ear that was so close to his mouth he could almost taste it between his teeth. He was proud of the way he held it together.

"Wish me luck," he said quietly.

"Good luck, my friend," said Barry, so quietly it was almost inaudible.

Jerry stood back and held him at arm's length. He wasn't sure if this would be the last time the two ever met. He did know that if they ever did, it would almost certainly be the last time—and it would end in one of their deaths. He wanted to say something. *It could stop here! Here and now!* He could give him the opportunity to come clean. But he was kidding himself.

This man, the man looking at him now, was the lowest of the low. In their world, he was dirt—scum of the earth. Jerry had to fight to control the bile rising within him.

"I'll be in touch," he said sharply, and released his grip for the last time. He walked to the exit without looking back.

In the car, he asked Tom not to speak. Irish Tom looked at his boss and took the instruction as a threat. Without asking where to, he drove south through the coastal towns, with the sea glistening in the sun to their left. During the ride, Jerry's mind was in complete turmoil, even more so when he tried to call and got no response from Harold—*yet again*—and worse still, here he was in the Malaga region, going against all his usual security measures, after having been advised to stay away.

This lawyer, Cordeso—he was based in Marbella. Should he gate-crash his office? No, that would be too intrusive. Wheeler, Kristos, Barry, Victoria. This fucking Alba, who the fuck did he think he was? Riat Venga. *Wheeler— what was Wheeler doing at South Mimms? The raid on his home! Wheeler! What was he doing there? Wheeler got the money, wasn't that enough? Barry, Wheeler. Spain, together, a British detective!*

"Pull up!" he suddenly commanded.

"What?"

"Stop the car."

"What's wrong?"

"Stop the fucking car!"

"Allrighsh! Allrighsh."

The screech of tyres and the sudden smell of burning rubber, the tinkering of the hot engine, and the blaring of a car horn from behind had little effect on Jerry as he opened the door and made for the beach. Tom looked on, expecting Jerry to keel over and vomit. *What could be so important?* He watched as Jerry looked out to sea, his hands raised above his head, then lowered them to run his fingers through his hair. Tom started the engine and slowly drove the car to the kerb, to allow the tailback to drive by.

Jerry had so many questions. He needed answers before he could go ahead with the first robbery. And in that split moment, he realised that those answers might lie with Wheeler. There were things going on, things he knew nothing about. He was in the dark about something, and he decided to do something about it. He tried Harold's number again. No reply. *Fuck! Kath.* He tried Kath. Jasmine answered the call.

"Hello... hello! Who's calling, please?" The same question was asked in Spanish. Jerry listened, but he didn't respond.

"Who is it, pet?" he heard Kath ask in the background.

"I don't know, Mum. I think there is someone there, but they can't hear me."

Jerry heard Kath tell his daughter to put the phone down. The line went dead.

He looked at the calmness of the sea. There were people playing on the beach. He watched as they went about their lives without a care: a father chasing two children, a mother resting on a sun-bed, the sand so hot beneath the feet of an older man treading back with two melting ice creams, his wife of fifty years watching him, laughing, struggling to get up and help. A family securing their patch, the mother laying out the picnic, the father erecting the sunshield while the children started to build the first sandcastle of a very long day.

Jerry wished he could swap lives. He smiled. *Victors—the Victors of this world.*

Chapter One Hundred and Twelve

Detective Inspector William Wheeler, Bill to his wife Maud and a handful of friends, was told that things were not looking good and to expect the worse. The specialist was on duty when the patient was admitted and agreed to see him as an urgent case. The report from the GP and initial examination by the Senior nurse left little doubt to the Consultant that, in all probability, the Inspector had all the symptoms of advanced cancer of the colon. Maud was beside herself and was unable to hold back the tears. Wheeler, on the other hand, was determined from the outset to *beat this*. The consultant reminded them, that at this stage, there is nothing to beat and to wait until the results of the test were returned, but still, to expect the worse. In the meantime Wheeler would remain in the hospital.

Chapter One Hundred and Thirteen

Iccholas Meras was a slight man, casually dressed with dirty fingernails. Perelta smiled; he had him down—*more like one of these computer nerds*, as opposed to a seasoned detective—almost timid for someone with such responsibility. He arrived at Malaga Policia headquarters looking tired and older than the fifty years Angelica guessed. As she placed the coffee on her father's desk for the two detectives, she wondered if the cold air of Eastern Europe had the same ageing effect on the female population, and was thankful she had been born in warmer climates as she returned to her desk to listen.

"Of course, we have things we would like to talk to Kristos Koiduste about back in Estonia. Having said that, we are not stupid. We understand that we are on Spanish soil and have to abide by Spanish law. Koiduste is involved in a large criminal investigation here in Spain." He lifted the coffee cup, blew some cool air into it, and slurped some of the hot liquid into his mouth, which barely had lips—they were so thin.

Angelica took this opportunity to smile at her father, who did not return the smile until the smaller man took his eyes off him to take a biscuit from the tray.

"You see, Mr Peretta—"

"Perelta."

"Perella." The Spanish detective shrugged his shoulders; he accepted the second attempt as being closer. "Koiduste has a history back in our homeland. In his case, we do have evidence of various crimes—some of which are despicable. Like I said in the conference, he is involved in selling arms, albeit as a middleman in his case. We have passed the information relating to this to the various countries involved. What I, myself, and my comrades are concerned about is the people trafficking. Koiduste was not only paid for supplying the passports to these people—hundreds, I may add—but was also arranging employment throughout Europe for them.

"In the case of the females—though not always, in some cases boys, some as young as fourteen—he would promise them academic work, clerical work, looking after children, anything. But once they arrived at their destination, Spain being one of them, they would be forced into *prostitution*."

"This is a major problem in Spain, Mr Meras," said Angelica, who looked to her father as she spoke to their guest. Perelta nodded in agreement and chose the moment to defend himself for the benefit of his daughter.

"I have to declare, at this point, Mr Meras, that Kristos Koiduste is acting as an *agent provocateur*. He is helping us with our inquiries."

"In return for what?"

"Immunity, financial gain, the norm."

"Immunity? This hurts."

"He may not get it."

"Financial gain?"

"He wants to buy back some of the confiscated land."

"At a reduced price," Angelica added.

"Yes, yes, this is he. This is what he will do. But there will be more, Mr Perelta, I can assure you of this."

"Can you expand?" Again, the question was asked by Angelica, who was relishing the fact that she might have been correct all along.

"Can I expand? I can tell you many things about Koiduste, but I have no evidence to back up my claims. What I do know about this man is that he will double-deal his way out of anything. He will work with both sides so long as it suits him. Once he has finished reaping the benefits and you are no longer required, he will eliminate you—discard you like the muck from his shoe. He is greedy with a capital *G*. He has no morals, and really, what more do we need to say when he is bringing children into your country, and many others, for the sole purpose of selling their innocence to line his silk pockets?"

"Yes," said Perelta. "I understand."

"And you would like us to assist in your efforts to extradite him?"

"Yes, Miss, I would."

"But don't you think that first we should take all the help he has to offer us?" Angelica asked.

"But what has he given us?" she added, refusing to call her father *Papa* in professional company. "Some false detail on a passport of another suspect and a list of telephone numbers!"

"I know, my sweet, but who knows what this may lead to!"

"And in the meantime, Koiduste is let loose to do as he pleases?"

"That is not quite true, Angelica."

"But if we listen to our guest," she said, referring to Meras with a gesture of her hand, "Koiduste will be seeing it this way."

"So, what do you suggest, my dear?"

"We give Mr Meras our full cooperation, support his application, and let the Estonian authorities take responsibility. These criminals are draining enough of our resources as it is. Let them have him! What does it matter who has him, so long as the result is the same?"

Iccholas Meras remained silent. *This girl, barely out of her teens, was doing a wonderful job for him.* He was amazed at her mature outlook; she was so much more advanced for her years than any girl of her age he had met before.

"My daughter!" said Perelta, smiling apologetically at the Estonian. "She gets something in her head, and she becomes ten men!"

"You should be very proud of her."

"OK!" said Perelta, quickly returning to the matter at hand.

"I think I've made up my mind, but it is not my mind which holds the final decision. I will speak with my superiors, and of course, Europol will have to be informed. In the meantime, it would help if you could give us more information about Koiduste and his people-trafficking operation into Spain, and anything else about the prostitution side of it."

"As it happens, I have something with me," he said, taking a file from his case. "His base for this side of his criminality is in Madrid. These pictures here show some of his lieutenants. There is some background information on most of these people. This one here in particular," he said, sliding over a five-by-four photo, "was closer to Koiduste, for some time, than the rest. There was talk at one stage of the two being engaged to be married. Something happened to change all that, but he did keep her on the payroll. Her name is Victoria Devany."

"She is very beautiful."

"Yes, of course, very wealthy too. She was from a privileged background. Her father was the British movie star."

"Steven Devany. He lives here, on the coast."

"Yes, we know this. Koiduste met her in Switzerland some years back, she was fifteen, attending a finishing school there, he took her away, abused her like all the others. Her father was beyond himself. We spoke to him, this is confidential, of course, he hasn't spoke to her since, broke his heart."

"I can understand," said Angelo Perelta as he looked towards the love of his life.

"We had had our own people over here for some time. Are you aware of this?"

"No."

"Yes, we have, conducting our own surveillance. These are some other recent stills. Would you look at them, please?" He handed the pictures over the desk to Perelta. Angelica walked from behind her own desk to stand behind her father and view the photographs from over his shoulder. As the two Spanish detectives studied the frames, Iccholas admitted the people featured meant nothing to them; they had no idea who they were. Angelica was the first to recognise Barry Stone. "This man here has recently come to our attention."

"Which one?" asked Meras, walking around the desk.

"This one. He has a connection to Divine."

"Divine?"

"Yes. Very good, Angelica. Divine, Mr Meras, is a subject of Operation Escatura. You don't recall? Please, Angelica, get a picture." Once Meras looked at the photo of Divine, he remembered immediately.

"Yes, yes," he said, holding it up to the light. "The armed robber turned property dealer, I remember, yes." He replaced the still on the desk.

"What do you think?" he asked. "Have you any idea why he would be sitting on a bar terrace with Koiduste?"

"People trafficking," murmured Perelta.

"Children, prostitution," said Angelica.

"Africa."

"Yes."

"What is it?" asked the Estonian detective.

"We have reason to believe that this man," said Perelta, tapping the picture depicting Stone with Koiduste, "is a paedophile—young boys being his preference."

"You mentioned Africa."

"Yes," said Angelica. "West Africa, The Gambia."

"We have The Gambia as a place of origin!" explained Meras.

"You think there may be a connection?" asked Perelta. Angelica looked at her father as she moved back to her desk. Perelta blushed. It was more than obvious.

"What else? What else could these two be discussing? His name—do we have a name?"

"We have a few."

"I have them here," said Angelica. "He was questioned recently by us in relation to a suspicious death. Viceroy, Maine, and the one we believe to be his correct name is Stone—Barry Stone. Would you like me to get this across to Bill Wheeler, Papa?" Her father looked across at his daughter. It was the first time she had called him *Papa* at work, with another detective present. Just unusual, that was all.

"Yes, I think so. Is this okay with you, Mr Meras? Mr Wheeler has been assisting us in reference to Jerry Divine, just as you are with Koiduste."

"I have no objection."

"Send a copy of the picture too and anything else you feel is relevant my dear."

Chapter One Hundred and Fourteen

The information, which came through marked *URGENT*, meant nothing to Detective Sergeant Steven Smith. Smithy to his friends and colleagues, he had served as an officer in the Met for just over ten years, eight of them as the undergraduate and sidekick of Bill Wheeler. Some of his fellow officers envied his pairing, others felt sympathy. Steven Smith regretted it terribly in the beginning, but now he wouldn't have it any other way. He had gotten used to the unorthodox methods his senior partner employed and was impressed with the results the two had achieved over the years. He hadn't relished being his own boss for the last six—or eight—days, if you took into account the two since Wheeler had returned. He preferred the guidance of the more senior and experienced detective; it would take many more years in the field to be able to go it alone with the same confidence he felt with Bill Wheeler by his side.

The call had come from Maud. She had told him that her husband, his boss, was unwell and had been admitted to hospital. He was asked to stay away, at least until the results of the tests were received. That was fine—Smithy had no problem with that. But this was before he received the email from Spain, complete with the picture of Barry Stone! There could be no delay; this had to be taken to Wheeler immediately.

Smithy parked his car in the hospital car park and placed the *exempt from payment* ticket on the dashboard. He snatched the brown envelope from the passenger seat and, without his jacket, sleeves rolled up to the elbow, he fast-walked through the large double doors—almost getting run over by a bed on wheels in the process—and up the wide staircase. Ward Eight was on the first floor. The smell of disinfectant and warm food from a trolley left the young detective feeling both sick and hungry at the same time.

"I'm sorry, Sir, visiting is over. It's lunchtime now, the visits start again at two," said the staff nurse.

Smithy didn't lose pace, nor did he respond, assuming the badge would be sufficient to resolve the matter and grant him access.

"I'm very sorry, Sir, you can't go in there!"

"I'm a police officer, Ma'am, and this is police business," he called, without losing pace or looking back.

"Sir! I really must insist—"

"Piss off, Miss! This is a matter of life and death." He turned on her. She took one look at his face and retreated back to her clerical duties.

Bill Wheeler heard Smithy before he saw him. He was already propped up on one elbow by the time his young protégé reached the bed and sat upright before Smithy did.

"Fucking hell, Bill, you look awful!"

"Thanks. I needed to hear that."

"Sorry."

"What do I owe the department?"

"You don't, Bill, but I thought you should see this." He took some flowers from the only chair behind the curtain, pulled it beside the bed, and flopped the documents on his boss's chest. Wheeler winced; even the weight of the flimsy file caused him pain.

"Pour yourself a drink, and one for me too," instructed Wheeler as he propped himself up comfortably on the mound of pillows.

"What the fuck! This is Stone. I recognise this other guy, too, from somewhere. Who is it?"

"Some Eastern European gangster. The Russian mafia, no doubt," said Smithy, passing the drink and glancing over toward the matron.

"Kristos Koiduste. The name rings a bell too."

"I've read the literature. He's part of a big operation over there—Escatora, is it? The same operation as Divine by all accounts."

"Of course! I remember him now. He was featured in the slideshow. I haven't had time to tell you, Ste, but these are some heavy-duty criminals. It seems our own Jerry Divine has climbed steeply within the criminal fraternity over there on the Costa del Crime."

"Fucking hell, Boss! And Stone, too? Those two are back together?"

"So it seems, my son." Wheeler let out a croaking cough from somewhere deep within. He sucked in air and banged his upper chest to prompt another rapturous outburst, this time holding a white handkerchief to his mouth to catch the dark, reddish phlegm. He held out his free hand, and Smithy passed him the water. Wheeler took it and sipped cautiously, never taking his eyes off the picture. He passed the cup to a worried-looking

Smith, straightened himself upright—pain etched on his face—and looked up again before speaking. "There's something big going down, Ste. Other than this Operation Escatora. Something else. Something *really* big."

"What is it, Bill?"

"I'm not one hundred percent sure. The information came from Stone."

"A robbery?"

"What else, with those two involved."

"The crew?"

"I'm not sure if the original team is involved. We may have to put tabs on one or two of them. Nothing major or expensive, just a little surveillance. See if we can pinpoint some of the old team. O'Rourke shouldn't be too difficult; he's up to his neck in it lately. I heard somewhere McNess was to stand trial. See what happened there. What's this?" he asked, holding up another photograph.

"I'm not sure who that is. I've done a little background, but I'll do more later. I don't think they know either, which is why they've sent it, I presume—see if he means anything to us. I believe they have this Kristos in custody now, for kidnapping and torture. There's a copy of the victim's passport somewhere in there." He flipped a page in his little black notebook.

"Harold Rawson, a Gibraltarian. Like I said, I did some checks. We had him over here in the nineties—spent some time on remand in Pentonville. It was a big duty evasion, cigarette coup."

"Kidnap and torture? So he's alive?"

"By the skin of his teeth. There's another picture someplace," he said, leaning over to assist. "He's alive, but a bleeding mess. If this Koiduste is responsible, he's one evil bastard."

"Fucking hell," said Wheeler, looking at another photograph depicting the injuries. "It's a wonder he survived this. How old is this poor cunt?"

"Late seventies."

"In his seventies," Wheeler repeated. "My parents were in their late eighties," he said quietly, almost to himself. Smith knew this was a sore point.

"Where is this going?" Smith didn't hear the question. "There must be more of a connection. Dig deep, Smithy."

"I've got it, everything," said his protégé, completing a list of to-dos in his small notebook.

"You might have to go to Spain. I'm too sick to travel at the moment. I'll know more in a day or two about my condition. And these?" he asked, looking at some telephone numbers. "What do these mean?"

"I'm not sure. There's some phone traffic on the sheet behind—very little, and some wide gaps in time between calls. Fucking months in some cases. There's been some recent activity though—a call made from a Spanish number to two of them. The Spanish aren't as advanced as us when it comes to dealing with telephone evidence. Either that, or I don't understand what they've sent. We'll have to get our own cell site forensics on them. Do you want me to pass them on to our people?"

Wheeler coughed again and nodded in agreement. Smithy handed him the water. Once Wheeler had regained his composure, he looked up at Smith.

"That trip has knocked me for six."

"You're as strong as an oxo, Bill. You'll be fine."

"*Ox*, you cunt, strong as an *ox*. Don't make me laugh—ah!" He doubled over in pain. "Don't forget, you may have to leave at short notice. I'll notify the Spanish detective to expect you. Oh, and stay away from his daughter—she's a cracker and a better detective than you'll ever be," he joked.

Smithy didn't see the funny side.

"I'm all for that, Bill. Whatever you say. You just rest, mate. I'll take care of things. More water?"

"No, fuck off, son. I need to sleep."

Chapter One Hundred and Fifteen

"Jump over, I'll drive. I'll drop you home," Jerry instructed.
"As you wish. You don't need me for anything?"
"No."
"How much do you have on Suckaterri?"
"Fuck all."
"Fuck all?"
"I forgot."
"You forgot?"
"Stop fucking repeating. What price did it come in at?"
"Do you really wanna know?"
"Not really."
"Thirty-three to one."
"Thirty-three to fucking one?"

"Who's repeating now? What's with the rush, Jerry? Slow down, you'll have us nicked by the Guardia." Jerry looked at the speedometer; they were touching seventy in a thirty-five zone, travelling between coastal towns, thirty kilometres towards Marbella. He eased off the gas and asked about the Indian.

"He spread it about a bit, up and down the coast, small bets here and there. The biggest was with the footballer in the port; he took ten grand at twenty-eights. A bookie in Jersey took five at thirty-threes."

"Fucking hell. Good luck to him. Get him on the phone." Tom made the connection, and Jerry lifted the handset from the glove box. Once he had finished speaking to his friend, he stopped the car beside a *Cambio de Change*, which housed a bank of telephone kiosks. He told Tom he would call him within the hour and expected to drop him back at the airport.

He got the number of the police station from the international directory. It took three attempts to dial the number before committing himself on the fourth. It required some gentle persuasion for the admin clerk to divulge that Inspector Wheeler was off sick. With further coaching, and explaining that a long-lost relative in Australia had died and bequeathed a small fortune to William, the clerk—who accepted that, due to his recent ill health, the inspector could do with some good news—gave the inspector's home telephone number to the caller.

Jerry dialled the number and prepared himself, adopting his best English accent with a Spanish overtone. He explained to Maud Wheeler that her husband had left some important documents in Spain, and the email address he had given was not receiving them. Could she please give him an address so that the literature could be sent by post? When she told him the home address, he thanked her and was about to hang up when she volunteered the information that her husband had been taken ill suddenly and was in hospital.

Jerry, still attempting to maintain the Spanish accent, apologised and asked which hospital he was in so that he could arrange for flowers to be sent. Once he had the details, he hung up and remained seated in the kiosk.

Harold! He punched in the number by heart. No reply. He took a business card containing a list of numbers and called one, but again, no response. A dreaded feeling crept over him. Maybe it would be better to fly out of Gib and call in to see Harold along the way?

Chapter One Hundred and Sixteen

Day Ten

The flight from Gibraltar had landed on schedule at Luton. Jerry had finished travelling on the Daniel Vine papers and was now using the new documents in the name of Stephan DuPont. A business card described him as a personal trainer to the rich and famous, and he was similarly dressed in a tracksuit and trainers, with his sleeves pulled up above the forearm to show a sweatband on one wrist and a thick rubber watch on the other. He glanced at the watch as he reclaimed his luggage from the carousel; it showed 7:15 a.m. His hair was tied back with an elastic band, and his sports bag contained nothing more than two rackets, some training gear, jeans, and sports shirts. It was for this reason, and his appearance alone, that customs randomly stopped him.

He was in no mood for their formalities and showed this in his abruptness as he answered the trivial questions. Yes, he was travelling alone. Yes, the purpose was business. Yes, for the second time, he had packed the bag himself. No, he was not a resident of the UK, preferring the warmer climate. All the time, he was thinking of Harold, his whereabouts, and whether he was in danger. Yes, he would be staying in the capital and moving up north. Yes, two clients. No, he was not at liberty to name them.

"Listen," he eventually said, with restrained patience, "I've had a bad trip, I have girlfriend trouble, I'm really not in the mood, so unless there is something in particular you want from me, I'd really like to make tracks and be on my way."

"We're only doing our job, sir," replied the customs man. "I just have to scan the passport, and you can be on your way, sir."

Jerry watched as the passport was put through the machine. It came out the other side and was handed back to him with a strained smile.

"Thank you, Mr DuPont, sorry to trouble you. You are free to go. Enjoy the remainder of your day, sir."

You are a diamond, Harold! "Thank you! And sorry."

"That's fine."

The small two-door Nissan Micra hire car was waiting for him at the collection point. The youth with the clipboard and keys assured him the car had recently been valeted, serviced, and checked. The tank was full, and he could leave it at almost any airport or train station once he was finished with it—but *check first*! Jerry thanked him with a five-pound note and blew a sigh of relief as he hit the M1 North.

Two hours later, he stood beside the bed of Inspector Bill Wheeler. He had used his charm on the staff nurse, assuring her that he would not take more than ten minutes to say what could be his last goodbyes to his uncle before travelling to Canada. He pulled the privacy curtain around the bed and placed a chair beside the sleeping detective. Gently, he flicked some water from the jug into the sick man's face. Wheeler grunted, then started upright as far as he could before realising where he was and that he was in pain.

Jerry put one finger over his lips and placed the other hand over Wheeler's dry mouth. Wheeler's head remained in the same position, resting on the raised pillow. Only his eyes moved, the irises shifting to the extreme left, while his right hand raised as far as the tubes would allow.

Divine moved closer, placing his head beside the sick man's ear. "It's okay," he whispered. *"We need to talk."*

"I don't have to talk to you," replied the detective. He tried once more to raise his body weight.

"Relax, Wheeler, you'll do yourself an injury."

"What the fuck do you want, Divine? What are you doing here?" Jerry didn't answer. Instead, he pushed a monitor sticky pad back

onto the patient's chest, where it had come undone, tangled in the grey hairs.

"I want some answers, detective," he eventually said, with a hint of sarcasm.

"Some answers? You want some answers?" Wheeler said through gritted teeth.

"South Mimms for one, Spain for two, and my home, Wheeler. What the fuck were you doing in my home?"

Wheeler was alert now, his senses fully returned. He looked at Jerry. For a moment, Jerry could detect and feel the compulsion coming from the detective; he was clearly confused.

Divine Intervention

"What the fuck is it with you, Wheeler? Why all the animosity?"

"You know full well, you cunt!"

"I know fuck all! What the fuck is it?"

"Get the fu—" Wheeler reached for the bell pull, but Divine grabbed his arm and easily secured it by his side. He was amazed at how simple it was to restrain the big man; there was no strength left. Jerry felt a flicker of sympathy.

"Talk to me, Wheeler! What is it?"

"What is it? You know damn well what it is!"

"Here, have some water," Jerry said, pouring some into a plastic cup. He could see the policeman was dehydrated; white foam was gathering at the corners of his mouth, and his tongue darted out, swollen. Wheeler was reluctant but took the cup anyway and emptied it in one gulp.

"I know you're up to your old tricks, Divine," he said between gasps of breath. "We're onto you, son, every step of the way. I'll have you, if it's the last thing I do, I'll have you."

"I don't know what the fuck has got into you, Wheeler. You know I know things about you. Are you prepared to put that on the line?"

"God damn you!"

"He did, many years ago."

"Then why are you still here?"

"Did I not fulfil my half of the bargain?"

"Oh yes, very clever. You are very clever, Divine. But some of us are just as clever."

"So, you're prepared for me to disclose? You're really willing to jeopardise your whole career? Put everything on the line?"

"Put what on the line? I've got fuck all, you stole it back!"

"Stole it back? What the fuck are you talking about?"

"The money. What do you think I'm talking about?" Wheeler said, raising himself onto his left elbow to face Jerry defiantly. A brief look of realisation, or perhaps confusion, flickered across Divine's face, and now it came across Wheeler's.

"What is it?" asked Jerry.

"You stole the money back—the money from my elderly parents. You stole it back." Wheeler's words came out as both a statement and a question.

Jerry leaned closer to Wheeler, his face sincere, and looked into the detective's eyes.

"I stole nothing back."

"You did!" Wheeler coughed. He coughed again, and Jerry passed him some more water. Wheeler's cough was croaky and coarse. He drank a little and passed the mug back to Divine. Jerry propped the pillows up behind the sick detective just as the nurse popped her head around the curtain.

"Is the patient alright?" she asked.

Jerry assured her he was and that he wouldn't be much longer. Wheeler nodded to indicate he was fine with that.

The two men stayed silent for a brief moment before Wheeler spoke.

"Did you take the money, Divine?" He remained staring at the ceiling.

"No," answered Jerry.

Bill Wheeler turned to look at him. "How do I know?"

"I didn't know it was stolen. I know nothing of this. This is the first I've heard of it! When? How?"

"Not only was the money taken, my parents were physically abused in the process—within days, days of it being given to me. I put it there, at my parents' house."

"Steal the money back? Why would I? Elderly people abused? You know that's not my style, Bill."

Wheeler was taken aback by the use of his first name. He hadn't heard Divine call him by his Christian name before. The two men looked at each other without saying a word, each silently assessing the situation, quickly working out alternatives and answers. Wheeler was the first to speak.

"How can you convince me, kid, that you had nothing to do with it? How can you make me believe you? I've been convinced of this for so long."

"I can't. Why should I, anyway?"

"Because I still have something on you, that's why."

"Is what you have on me anything to do with a long-lost friend?"

"I think you know this."

"Who gave you the money, Bill?"

"Don't call me Bill, it makes me feel uncomfortable."

"I wouldn't want to make you feel uncomfortable now, would I?"

"Not in this condition." Wheeler coughed and laughed at the same time.

"Seriously, Mr Wheeler, I had absolutely no reason to take the money back, and even less reason to hurt your parents. Where are they now?" Wheeler was taken aback by the question, and even more so by the sincerity of the tone.

"My parents? They're dead. Dad died shortly after; Mum stuck around for seven or eight months later." His eyes glazed over for a brief moment, not long enough for Jerry to notice. "Dad did say that the main aggressor was hooded. He got the impression he was white. The other two, his accomplices, were black."

"Black? You should know I don't associate with blacks, never did." He didn't say it, but he knew who *did* call on the Negroes when violence was required. He also knew that Wheeler was aware of this—and *who*. It was true and well-documented in the mounds of police intelligence that Jerry Divine did indeed run a tight ship and kept his criminal activities in-house.

Again, the two fell into silence for a few seconds before Jerry spoke.

"Did you see anyone, Mr Wheeler, when you were in Spain? Anyone from a time gone by?"

Bill Wheeler was expecting the question, but what he wasn't expecting was the answer he gave.

"I think you know I did." He was being open, honest, with Divine.

"Not until this moment, I didn't."

"Are you thinking the same as me?"

"What are you thinking?"

"You first," said the detective.

"That low-life piece of shit." Jerry stood up abruptly, his chair scraping on the tiled floor. He lifted the jug and drank directly from it.

"Have a banana."

"I've lost my appetite."

"I've regained mine," said Wheeler. "An appetite for revenge."

"Revenge? I'll kill the fucking scum."

"I'm still an acting member here. My card's in the drawer there."

"You wanna stand up and give evidence?"

"I don't think I can stand, let alone give evidence."

Jerry suddenly realised how inconsiderate he had been. He looked down at the detective—his adversary, and then foe, for as long as he could remember. The man who made him tremble with fear as a youth now lay before him, a complete shadow of his former self. The weight from the bulk of the man seemed to shed before his very eyes, the colour of life actually draining from his skin by the second.

"How bad is it, Bill? Mr Wheeler."

"It's bad, Jerry. I'm waiting for test results, but I don't really need them. I know it's bad—I can feel it."

"Cancer, is it?"

"I don't know of anything else that can have such a devastating effect in such a short time. For Christ's sake, I was alright last week—over there, living the life, jet-setting, like you!"

"Can you give me something, Mr Wheeler? Give me some insight into what the fuck is going on over there?"

"Why the fuck should I?"

"Do you believe me?"

"I'm not sure."

"Well, I'm certainly not about to beg."

"You never did."

"Did Barry?"

"Did Barry what?"

"Ever beg?"

"What do you think?"

"Sir! You really will have to leave," said the nurse, drawing back the curtain. Jerry moved closer to the bed and leaned over the detective.

"I will promise you revenge," he whispered.

"Take the envelope," said Wheeler, glancing sideways at the locker and indicating the brown envelope Smithy had delivered.

Jerry picked it up, slid out the contents, and did a double take. He first looked at the passport details, then at the mutilated disfigurement of what used to be Harold Rawson's face. Jerry rocked slightly on the balls of his feet, nearly collapsing. Reaching out, he grabbed the back of the wooden chair and quickly sat down before he fell. Once more, he forced himself to take a longer look at the picture of Harold's mutilated face. He didn't speak.

Wheeler watched as the stark realisation hit, seeing Divine's expression change from shock to fear, then to raging anger.

"Where did you get these pictures?"

"They were wired through from Spain last night."

Jerry looked at the ones of Kristos Koiduste, and then realised that Barry Stone was in one of them—Barry, an associate of the Russian. It seemed to Jerry that one too many people close to him had fallen at the hands of this Cossack bastard. Wheeler was trying to piece it together, taking a guess that the old man in the pictures was a friend of Jerry's. He answered the next question before it came.

"The victim is still alive."

"He is?" The relief was obvious on Jerry's face.

"Yes, these are very recent, so he'll be having treatment somewhere. If you want, I can find out where."

"Sir! You mus—"

"Fuck off!"

"It's okay," Wheeler said, holding up his hand to calm the nurse.

"I'm sorry," said the matron, who had come to join the nurse. "I will not have my staff spoken to in that manner."

"You can fuck off too! Find out, Wheeler. I'll be back in one hour."

Jerry stormed out, securing the envelope down the front of his loose tracksuit bottoms. He didn't look back to see the detective making some excuse for his visitor's sudden outburst. Wheeler watched as Jerry Divine disappeared through the double doors at the far end of the long ward. Wheeler believed this villain was anything but a beater of the elderly. Barry Stone, on the other hand, was the guilty one.

He coughed, this time catching the phlegm in a tissue, and saw it was tinged with red.

Jerry's second visit to the hospital came later in the day. He joined the other visitors queuing by the entrance at the allotted time, now dressed in casual slacks with an open-neck T-shirt, carrying flowers, fruit, and a bottle of Lucozade.

The matron eyed him suspiciously as he approached the ward desk. She reached for the phone without taking her eyes off him. Jerry smiled warmly and held out the flowers as a peace offering, explaining with a grin that a policeman's life could get stressful at times.

Wheeler was awake, propped up against a mountain of fluffy white pillows. Jerry could see Wheeler was assessing his mood. When he realised Jerry was calm, he smiled. Jerry smiled back, placing the fruit in an empty bowl and pouring himself a drink.

"From the smile, I take it you've given our little chat this morning some thought?" Wheeler asked.

"I have, Jerry. I've done nothing else."

"I thought South Mimms might have been a coincidence. I got away, so I let it go—it went completely out of my mind."

"I was there for you, Jerry, to bring you down. You were supposed to die that day."

"Fucking hell!"

"I know."

"My house in Spain, Bill. Do you mind? Bill?"

"No, no, what difference does it make? This might be the last time you see me alive."

"Don't say that. These people can do wonders with that stuff nowadays. They have cures for even the most severe cases."

"Treatment, maybe. Cures? I doubt it. Not for this, kid. I can feel it moving through my body." He shifted uncomfortably, showing pain in his face. "Two days ago, I was a fat cunt. Now I can feel myself wasting away, so let's get on with it, Jerry."

"I take it you're going to tell me what I want to hear?"

"I'll tell you things—whether it's what you want to hear is a different matter."

"Let's start with the shootout at South Mimms."

"That 'shootout,' as you call it, should have been a shoot-to-kill." Wheeler went on to recount his version of events, which aligned somewhat with what Barry had told Jerry, except for the bike being a plant and the getaway arrangement. When Wheeler finished, almost an hour later, Jerry was emotionally drained. How could he have been so stupid as to give Barry's version any credibility? Wheeler's account felt much more viable and sincere.

Wheeler, too, was exhausted. But Jerry wanted it all—he wanted to hear about the Spanish chapter and pushed the detective to carry on. Wheeler refused, unless Jerry made one or two concessions. The first was a promise to take care of Barry Stone, but not before he had admitted his role in the assault and robbery at Wheeler's parents' home. This was easy—Jerry agreed with relish. The second concession was not compulsory, merely a request. When Jerry asked what it was, the detective asked him to consider looking after Maud financially if Wheeler didn't make it through this. Jerry said he would decide after he was given the information.

Wheeler agreed and told him everything. He started with the initial meeting with Peralta and Angelica, whom he said with a wicked smile, he was sure Jerry would appreciate. He recounted the trip in the helicopter, which brought a wry smile to Jerry's face. They discussed the conference, the two operations—Canary and Escatura—the Russian, and others. Wheeler explained how the evidence against Jerry had collapsed with the deaths of the two main witnesses. He also advised Jerry not to trust his driver. Wheeler told him everything he could remember.

Jerry's mind was racing. He suddenly realised how close he had come to losing his liberty on top of everything else. He was repulsed to hear about the young boy in Torremolinos and even more so when Wheeler opened up about the robbery in Antwerp. Jerry asked if Wheeler had reported the intended robbery, and Wheeler explained that he was about to, but he collapsed in front of his superior. Besides, he had very little to go on and had made arrangements with Barry Stone to meet again before any moves were made.

Finally, Jerry wanted to know about the contents of the brown envelope—the pictures. He explained to Wheeler that Harold was an old and trusted friend whom he had first met in Pentonville Prison and had kept in contact with. He knew nothing about the abduction and torture. Jerry considered telling Wheeler about Victoria but decided against it—after all, Wheeler was still the enemy.

"The telephone numbers—what were they? They meant nothing to me," Jerry said, frustrated. He couldn't believe he hadn't connected the numbers to his accomplices. It was only because he didn't call them regularly, and the list didn't include Hutchins, that they weren't imprinted in his mind.

Wheeler could offer very little more, other than what they already knew. He

explained that he had authorised his partner, Smith, to look into the numbers, and no doubt the Spanish authorities were continuing their own investigations. Anything more, Wheeler said he could let Jerry know later. As for the old man, Wheeler knew as much as Jerry—probably less. Harold had been bundled into a car at the airport and taken to a remote farm.

Everything Wheeler had was in the minimal notes provided. However, he did tell Jerry that Harold had been taken by *Heli-Sanitarios* to a specialist hospital unit in Madrid and was responding well to treatment.

That's all he knew.

When Jerry left the hospital, three things were certain in his mind. First and second, he had never been more sure about anything in his life: the deliberate deaths of Barry Stone and Kristos Koiduste. Third, the diamond robbery in Antwerp would go ahead.

Stone was about to double-cross Jerry—he knew this—but correctly assumed it would be after the big robbery in Gibraltar. It was becoming clear now that the scumbag would be after more than just the diamonds. Stone had sold him out, but why? That question might never be answered. Jerry could only guess: liberty, money, jealousy—probably a mixture of all three, and more. Who knows?

What was certain was that Stone would be after his life and the thirty big ones. The robbery in Antwerp had to be successful for Stone just as much as it did for Jerry and his team. There was no danger of this one being a set-up. Jerry and the team could be confident that it was relatively free from entrapment.

As for Wheeler? Jerry doubted very much whether he would see him alive again. And if he was truthful with himself, he was sorry—in a funny kind of way. It was ironic that he had begun to like and respect the man at the very end.

Chapter One Hundred and Seventeen

Day Fourteen

Jerry stayed in the UK for two days. He managed to see McNess and got messages to the others, except for Winston, whom the landlady said had gone away. He confirmed that the arrangements to meet at the agreed location would be brought forward, and for the team to congregate in seven days' time. The job was being brought forward.

It was impossible to see Harold; the security was too intense. Jerry walked through the front of the hospital and straight out the back entrance, his sixth sense triggering an alert. He did consider dressing as a doctor—there were plenty of white coats and masks available—but it didn't feel right. The language was another issue. He couldn't take the risk; nothing could jeopardise Antwerp.

The best he could do was make a phone call and ask the nurse to pass a message to Uncle Harold that his nephew, Daniel Vine, was looking after things. Hopefully, that would give the old man a little comfort and, with a bit of luck, even more strength.

He sent an email to Barry Stone, assuring him that everything was on track and the number one assignment would go ahead as scheduled. There were no delays, and the project would be complete in twenty-eight days' time. If there was anything that would assist, Stone could return to the provided email address.

Jerry reverted back to the Vine details for this sole purpose and was pleasantly surprised when he collected a wealth of useful information at his hotel reception the next day.

Chapter One Hundred and Eighteen

Seven Days Later…
Day Twenty-One

The Amsterdam meeting had been brought forward to the earliest possible date. The only complication was the pressure it put on Winston to get the accessories in place. This was completed, not without duress, in nine days from the initial meeting with Jerry on the boat. A unit was rented on the outskirts of Rotterdam, conveniently located by the docks. The vehicles had been purchased online, and the money transferred by Western Union. All that remained was to take delivery once the short-term lease on the property had been finalised, and Winston, the artist, had collected the keys.

Winston stayed tight up the rear end of the truck in front as he slowly edged down the ramp of the monster ferry. He often wondered how these mega-ships stayed afloat with all the trucks and cars adding to their weight, but he was thankful for the camouflage they provided. The sheer number of vehicles allowed him to blend in without difficulty. Passport control and customs were a toddle—he could have been carrying anything, but even so, he felt a little nervous as he drove through.

Jerry had asked him not to call until the morning after he arrived and to "have a walk, buy a paper or something, look around for any tails before you do." The unit was beneath a loft conversion apartment, which was included in the lease. There wasn't much to it: a large open-plan area with a high, visible roof, obstructed only by crude oak beams, from which hung a professional punch bag. The rest of the space comprised a kitchenette, dining area, a large table, some scattered chairs, and a king-size bed—all in one room, with a floor bare to the wooden structure.

Two doors led from the large room: one to the toilet, and the other to the fire escape, which descended into an enclosed yard via crudely constructed iron steps. The place was ideal—no prying eyes could see who or what was in the van as it pulled into the yard. For anyone observing, there would be no indication that the sole occupant would, on his next appearance, be accompanied by his four conspirators.

Using his gloved hands, Winston deposited some personal effects in the apartment and turned on the small gas heater to air out the dampness. He looked around one final time before leaving and securing the yard.

He had parked the van by the dock and took a shuttle train into Amsterdam's central station. He liked Holland, particularly the capital. The place was liberal, with a sense of indifference—*live and let live*. That was exactly how he liked it. His height, here, was nothing; he was just another tourist, another artist.

Intentionally arriving a little early, he took a leisurely stroll around the various street acts in front of Central Station. He watched in amazement as a young boy kept a football in the air using his head, feet, and shoulders while climbing a street lamp. A band of Incas from Peru played wind flutes made of bamboo. Winston was more intrigued by the vibrant colours and intricate designs of the handmade hats and woollen shawls they wore. As he examined the craftsmanship of a bronze statue, it suddenly moved, giving him a start. He couldn't believe that the work of art was, in fact, a naked, hand-painted human being.

"Amazing, aren't they?" A voice startled him again. This time, he let out a small scream.

"My God, Jerry! You scared me."

Jerry laughed. "You're early."

"So are you."

"I like to be one step ahead."

"And the others?" Winston asked, glancing around.

"They'll be here shortly. It wouldn't surprise me if Hutchins isn't already here," said Jerry, scrutinising the area. The sheer number of people made it almost impossible to keep track of anyone. It was a perfect meeting spot, but Jerry wasn't naive—he knew most of the villains and drug dealers in town probably felt the same.

"C'mon, Winston, let's get a drink. You can give me a progress report," Jerry said, putting his arm over Winston's shoulder.

Winston smiled. "I need one after that—at least a sit-down." Jerry laughed again.

Once they were seated at a street café, outside and watching the world go by, Winston looked across the table at Jerry.

"This is like old times, eh?"

Jerry didn't look at him, still observing the people passing by. "It is, my friend. Just like old times." He then turned to meet Winston's gaze. "Tell me."

Winston took some papers from his shirt pocket, unfolding them and securing them on the table with a glass ashtray. Taking them one at a time, he explained the contents.

"I've found an ideal apartment. It includes a small enclosed yard and a storage facility. It's gated and private." He looked up from the paper, which contained an address in code and a small layout plan. "Here I have..." He replaced the first paperback in his pocket and flattened the second one on the table. "A list of the vehicles at our disposal. The Jet Skis are Seadoo 1500s, each with less than thirty hours of use. I serviced them myself. Didn't have to steal them—a friend agreed to let me take them if they disappeared. He's going to claim on his insurance and didn't report them missing until I was over the water. I have the costs here..." He handed Jerry a separate piece of paper.

Jerry took it without looking at it and placed it in his shirt pocket. "The cars?" he asked.

"They're here. I'll get to them in a second. I've got rubber masks—they're with the wetsuits under the seats of the skis. Perfect cover. I wasn't stopped anyway. I've got waterproof tape and enough plastic hand ties."

"Good work, Winston."

"It's the place, Jerry. Wait till you see it—it's perfect, central as well."

"The cars."

"Yes, sorry. Two of them, small Renaults. We can collect them tomorrow. I bought them online, a small family-run painter and decorator business. The father's died—I got the full life story. Anyway, they're in Rotterdam, which is convenient, and like I said, we can collect or they'll deliver tomorrow."

"Well done, Winston. You were saying, about the property?"

"Yeah! It's by the dock in Rotterdam, midway between the two—Antwerp's a little further than Amsterdam, but nothing really, give or take a click. Wait till you see it, Jerry. It's perfect. I've got four monkey bikes in the van too. They've reinvented them—you may not remember them. They were out in the seventies, like a little chubby, miniature motorbike, strong enough to take an adult. They were built for adults—fucking amazing but"

"Slow down, Winston." Jerry laughed.

"Sorry, mate, I'm a little excited."

"So, these monkey bikes—you rate them better than the scooters?"

"Much better, Jerry. Smaller, more compact, and more power, actually."

"Good. Do they have gears?"

"No, which is a good thing. Automatic—off the accelerator."

"This yard with the apartment—is it big enough to have a little spin around?"

"Yeah, we can get used to them there. That's a good idea, Jerry."

"Anything else?"

"No. I've covered everything you asked me to do, and more."

"Well done."

"How the devil are you, old chaps!" called Hutchin O'Brien in his best English accent, walking over to them, pulling a case on wheels behind him. Jerry stood up to greet his friend, and Winston followed suit.

No further discussion was made regarding the job at hand. Hutchin asked the question, "When?" and was told that all discussions would take place tonight in the lodgings. Forty minutes later, the team was complete, and two hours after that, they were all seated in the converted loft, having emptied the van of its contents.

"Alright, gentlemen! Listen in here," called Jerry. "All the preliminaries are taken care of. It's nice to see you all again, but this is not a school reunion. We're back together as a team—a team with a mission, a job to do. We've been here before, many times. We know the score."

He looked at each one of them in turn, giving them the feeling that they were the only one in the room. Jerry had a knack for making each of them feel important. They *were* important, but they had to *feel* it.

"We all have a part to play, our own agenda. Winston, as you've seen, has supplied us with the tools—this place," he gestured around, "and the things we've just unloaded from the van. They are all tools. Well done, Winston."

Each one turned to look at the man standing silently against the wall and congratulated him. Winston smiled and blushed slightly. Jerry continued.

"Jamie. The scaffolding?"

"Done. I've got a merchant delivering tomorrow. I didn't have the full address and directions, but now I've got those, I'll chase it up tomorrow. The company's expecting my call."

"Yes, here they are," said Jerry, handing Jamie O'Rourke a map.

"There are some disused buildings opposite our target. A search tells us this property is owned by a Norwegian company that went into liquidation last year. We are assuming the bank has title, and it is very unlikely anyone would have anything to say about some scaffolding going up around it. It's a slight gamble, I know, but we can blag it. It's a perfect surveillance point.

"We have a layout of the diamond factory interior." He moved over to a large wooden, farm-like table. The others joined him, and he flattened the architectural drawing out with the palms of his gloved hands. "It's really straightforward, no more than we expect. There are two doors to gain entry to a reception area, one other to an office, and another into the workshop. There is a display area and a small showroom for sales purposes. This area here is a room for conferences—table for twelve, projector, etc., etc.

"We're gonna make a bit of a racket on the day. Jamie here has organised some Kango guns to blow holes into the building opposite, so, should any of the employees hit the panic alarm, it will make no difference to the general public. They're direct, though, so we will have to be out of there within a few minutes. I'd say three at the most before the cozzers arrive. We have Jamie outside, and Winston will have a good indication before we do. He notifies Jamie, who is our eyes and ears.

"Now then!" he said, spreading a larger piece of paper—this one almost covered the entire table. "The getaway." He looked at the faces of the team, all gazing down at the Ordnance Survey map. "You will see here"—he stabbed the pencil and drew a circle—"is where we will be. This is the actual building. You notice here, directly behind—see? colour brown? —this is the canal." He let each of them have a good look. "You'll also notice that it's everywhere, everywhere you look, but we are only interested in this section here." He moved the pencil in the direction of the railway sign, along the paper, away from the target, past two bridges, and stopped at a third. "This is where we jump ship. It's exactly three kilometres from the Eurotrack and station and almost two away from the devastation we leave. Our timing is very important, gentlemen. It is vital that we reach this point at three-forty-five at the very latest. This will give us less than twelve minutes to blow the

Jetskis out of the water, hit the monkey bikes—which will be dropped by the bridge—and reach the van and Winston, who will be waiting here." He stabbed at the map with the pencil and scribbled a circle.

"We change in the rear—two of us, Hutchin and Jamie, will be dropped here." He pointed to a small supermarket. "One of the Renaults will be in the car park with the key on the sun visor. Martin, you and I stay in the van. We then get out here, at the station. If we have no one up our arse, all good and well—we board the train. If, however, we have a tail, we hit the second Renault, which will be parked here." Again, he drew a circle around the train station, focusing on a small section showing a car park.

"The train leaves for Rotterdam at four-oh-two."

"Winston, and the van?" asked Martin McNess.

Jerry had to think. He wasn't a hundred per cent sure he wanted Winston to be any more involved than he had been and had even thought twice about him driving the van in the first place. He was thinking ahead— he had plans for Winston and his boat and didn't want to jeopardise the value that could bring to his Morocco operation. He knew he was being selfish, but it was business at the end of the day.

"We will have fuel in cans. This will be used by us in the rear should we have unwanted guests. We'll bail out and spark it. Should we, however, have a clear run, Winston will drive it back to Rotterdam, and we can delete any evidence at our own leisure."

"We're only days away. Do we have a specific day?" asked Hutchin.

"Not yet. Things are moving ahead of schedule, so it may be sooner rather than later—could even be the day after tomorrow." No one spoke. "Leave that in abeyance. Where were we? OK, we have here the address of the owner. He opens the gaff, both he and his son, and he leaves his wife and daughter at home. I don't want to make this a time-consuming or complicated operation. I did consider putting someone with his wife and dealing with it like we used to, but with the excellent getaway plan, the fact that we have the layout and other information—employees' entry time and all—I opted for the quick in-and-out approach." He stopped here to give the others the opportunity to vent any opinion. No one did, so he continued. "The diamonds are cut and uncut, they—"

"Value?" asked O'Rourke.

"I'm not sure."

"How many cutters?" asked Martin McNess.

"Approximately thirty."

Hutchin let out a singular whistle to show his approval.

"I know," said Jerry. "The cutting process is slow though, so I wouldn't get too excited. These stones are not turned out like pasties—it's precision work. But thirty is good; a small place would usually have one or two and a couple of apprentices."

"Weapons?" Jerry looked up from the documents; he didn't have to—it could only be Hutchin.

"Not necessary."

"Says who?"

"Hutchin, this is a room full of timid Jews, concentrating to the max. We will have the benefit of surprise. The owner will probably shit last night's kosher out. We're in a foreign country, Hutch—it's one less complication. Think about it. Do we really need them?"

"I'm going to declare now," said Hutchin. "I have one."

"You have one?"

"Yeah, I had a friend drop me one in the Dam."

"As a last resort, Hutchin," warned Jerry.

"Sure ting."

"What is it?"

"A Sig/Sauer P226," he said, producing it from under his jacket at the small of his back. "Fifteen-shot, 9 millimetre."

"Is everyone happy with that?" asked Jerry. Hutchin scanned the faces. No one spoke. He smiled and began to rub the weapon with a rag.

The rest of the evening was spent discussing who was to play which role in the robbery and going over every detail. Winston would drive the van, with radio connection to O'Rourke. O'Rourke would stay outside the building, on the opposite side of the road with his walkie-talkie, to let Jerry and the team know if there was any unwelcome attention. The racket would be so loud as to disallow any conversation, but a code was devised to give sufficient warning to abort. Jerry would be suited and booted, with as much disguise as possible to avoid drawing suspicion and to gain entry, leaving Hutchin and McNess for muscle and impact. If all went according to plan, the team would drop the diamonds to a contact of *the Indian*, then spend a couple of days enjoying the sights and sounds—some of them loud and red—in the capital.

Chapter One Hundred and Nineteen

Harold was delirious for almost a week. He wasn't aware that he had been airlifted from Malaga hospital to a special burn unit in Madrid. The doctors could do nothing to save the hearing in what was left of his damaged ear. What was more distressing was that some of the acid had seeped through his Eustachian tube and done severe damage to his vocal cords. Only Harold knew he could actually manage a coarse whisper, and he wasn't about to declare this as the police tried to talk to him at his bedside.

He looked up pleadingly to the doctors, who in turn advised the police to leave their questioning for another day. Thirteen days had passed in total—almost seven of those, he was comatose. The other six, he wished he still was. He could not feel any pain, though he was well aware that, without the constant supply of drugs, it was there. He had lost weight; his food was delivered via plastic—same as everything else. The medicine, food, drink, waste—everything was given and taken away by either a tube or bag.

Harold decided there and then that, if things didn't get any better, he would end it all as soon as he was fit enough to leave.

The visitors filed through quietly. Harold closed his eyes. There were some seriously ill people in this ward, some of whom had been wheeled out through the day and night and did not return. The visitors weren't for him. For all he knew, other than Jerry, nobody knew where he was. He did wonder, though, how on earth Jerry had found out. *How did he?* He hadn't spoken to a soul. Just then, from a distance, from another dimension, he thought he could hear someone calling his name. It was nice to hear his name, to have someone say it. He remained with his eyes shut.

"Harold. Harold." He felt a hand on his frail shoulder. It unnerved him. *Was this his calling?* He opened his eyes. Kathleen Divine looked down from above. She removed her hand from his shoulder and placed it on his cheek. He didn't move, still wondering if this was real. *Was he dreaming?*

"Kathleen?"

"Yes, it's me, Harold. How are you, darling?"

"I've been better," he whispered, smiling weakly.

"The doctor said there's been a marked improvement, and you can leave for home in a day or two." She removed her hand from his head and wiped the tear from his eye.

"Jerry?"

"I don't know, Harold, I haven't seen him."

"Is he alright?"

"I'm not sure. I suppose he's committed to his half of the bargain; he doesn't call."

"Oh, Kath! I was hoping you two would be back together by now. How long have I been here? The doctors say almost two weeks. The girls, Kath, how are the girls?"

"Yeah, they're fine, Harold. Little Julie's missing her dad, of course. Jasmine is studying hard. Would you like a drink?" she asked, pulling a chair up beside the bed and sitting down for the first time. "I'll speak with the nurse before I leave. Does Jerry know, Harold?"

Just the mention of Jerry's name seemed to bring a surge of life to the eyes of the old man. He looked up at Kath before he answered. She passed him a small plastic glass with an inch of water, and he sipped it slowly. She could see he was weighing up how much to declare.

"Yes. I got a message from a nephew of mine," he said hoarsely. "I know it was Jerry, Kath. He's taking care of things."

Kath remained silent. She felt sick, scared. She was waiting for more. She wanted to know more. But there was nothing else coming.

"Has he been to see you?"

"I'm not sure. He could have looked in when I was out of it. You know Jerry, Kath, he could be anywhere."

"Ask him to call me, Harold, if he contacts you again. The girls want to speak with him."

"I will, pet."

"Enough about Jerry. What about you, Harold? How do you feel?"

"Like shit!"

"You must come and stay with us. You can't go home alone until you have your strength back."

"We'll see, Kathleen," he tapped her hand, which was now resting on his chest.

Kath wanted to cry. She could feel his breastbone and upper ribcage through the sheet—there was practically nothing left of the old man. Harold wanted to tell her that he hadn't given anything away, that he hadn't spoken to his torturers, that he hadn't denied Jerry. He looked at her and realised that saying anything would only make matters worse for both of them. She obviously knew this had something to do with her husband. As much as Harold wanted to confide in her, he knew she would be just as reluctant to ask the question. Harold decided it was better to *let sleeping dogs lie. Let Jerry do what he has to do.*

Kathleen, on the other hand, was worried—worried about what Jerry would do to whoever had done such a despicable thing to his friend.

Chapter One Hundred and Twenty

Maud Wheeler was beside herself. She couldn't bear the thought of living her life without Bill. As much as the two argued and bickered—and had done for almost half a century—she never stopped loving him. It was with this thought in mind when she was ushered into the consultant's office two days ago. She tried to downplay the enormity of her responsibility and ease her tormented nerves by commenting on how busy this particular hospital was.

Professor Price looked over the desk and the top of his glasses as though she hadn't spoken at all.

"Please take a seat, Mrs Wheeler."

He could see, like all next of kin, that she was more scared than nervous. The signs were all there—the make-up applied liberally and with haste, the bag held with both hands to still the shaking. It was better to act quickly, to get it out. He sat bolt upright.

"I'll get straight to the point, Mrs Wheeler. Your husband, William Wheeler"—he looked up from some papers, over the top of his glasses for confirmation. Maud nodded—"has lost a lot of blood. We need to operate. The results of his biopsy have come back, and they show that he has advanced cancer of the colon."

Maud took in a sharp breath. Professor Price continued quickly.

"This does not necessarily mean the end, Mrs Wheeler. We at Leeds General have a good track record of curing a reasonably large percentage of our cancer patients. We have Cookridge Hospital less than eight miles away, and they will take care of his aftercare, specifically the radiation treatment. But first, we need your permission to operate. Mr Wheeler is in no fit state to give the go-ahead, as you know. For the past seven days, he has been in and out of consciousness, delirious, and not of his own mind."

"Yes, doctor, but why do I need to give permission?"

"We note from his personal effects that he is a Jehovah's Witness."

"Jehovah's Witness?"

"We have it here," said the professor, detecting this was news to Mrs Wheeler. He slid a small card across the desk. Maud picked it up and scrutinised it.

"I know nothing of this!" she said, turning it to look at the signature on the back. "There's a date here." She squinted. "It looks like 1978!"

"It's still valid, Mrs Wheeler, and it's all we have. We have nothing to the contrary."

"I understand, Mr Price. But why do you need my permission? Of course, you have it anyway, but..."

"A Jehovah's Witness, if one were to follow the letter of the faith, will not have a blood transfusion, but—"

"Take absolutely no notice of it. If this is all that's stopping the progress of my husband's treatment, then dispose of it," she said, throwing the aged card back across the table.

"Very well. You must sign this disclaimer then, please." He pushed an official form towards Maud, who already had a pen in hand.

"Thank you. Now! About the diagnosis and the proposed treatment plan." He stood up and moved across to a wall chart that displayed the human anatomy and what lies beneath. He pulled a cord which illuminated the diagram. "This is the colon, which extends from the cecum—an enlarged area at the end of the small intestine—up the right side of the abdomen (ascending colon), across to the left side (transverse colon), and down the left side (descending colon), and then loops—at the sigmoid flexure, or sigmoid colon—to join the rectum."

He turned from the chart to face Maud, who was none the wiser. She had signed the disclaimer, and that was all she was interested in. Professor Price was in his element, but as far as Maud was concerned, this seminar was a complete waste of time.

The professor continued, "The purpose of the colon is to lubricate the waste products, absorb remaining fluids and salts, and store waste products until they are ready to be passed from the body. Most absorption occurs in the ascending and transverse regions..."

If this was about bodily waste, as in crap, Maud was not the slightest bit interested. She had to restrain herself from letting the expert know.

"...where the liquid material received from the small intestine is dehydrated to form a faecal mass. The inner wall of the colon consists of a mucous membrane that absorbs the fluids and secretes mucus to lubricate the waste materials. The deeper—"

"I'm sorry, Mr Price, but this is way beyond my vocabulary. I did a little human biology at school, but that was nigh on fifty years ago, and to be honest with you, I wasn't interested then."

"Your husband is gravely ill, Mrs Wheeler. I was merely giving you some insight into his condition. If you hadn't interrupted, I was going to give you some specifics and lead on to the treatment."

"I am sorry, Doctor, I really am, but—"

"Professor."

"Professor, Doctor, see what I mean? It all means nothing to me, and I would have thought that the longer we sit here and talk about things I know nothing about, the less time you can spend working on my husband to make him right!"

"I can see you are getting irate, madam. I have the signature, and I assure you we will do everything in our power to help your husband." He stood, signalling the meeting was over.

"Thank you, Professor," she said, standing and holding out her hand.

Bill Wheeler opened his eyes, and the first thing he saw was Maud's face smiling back at him. He never thought he would admit to being happy to see his wife, but he was, and he held out his hand to her.

"What's happened, Maud?"

"The doctor says the operation was a success, Bill. They think they got it all. You will have to undergo an intense course of chemotherapy, and they say that will be unpleasant, but it's required as a precaution against it returning, Bill. How do you feel, my love?"

"Awful, pet."

"You will get a lot worse before you get better—they've told me that."

"I'm ready for the fight."

"Do you need anything? Fruit, drink? There's a bouquet of flowers from the boys at work. Look, I put them in a vase."

"I need something."

"What is it, my love?"

"Smithy."

Chapter One Hundred and Twenty-One

The Diamond Robbery in Antwerp
Day Twenty-Five

Jerry needed to ask Barry one question before the final stages of the plan could be considered. He contacted him through an email set up in the name of Daniel Divine and used an internet café to send it. There was a dual purpose for his request. First, he asked Barry to inquire with his Jewish friend if it was viable for a representative of a South African diamond mine to contact a cutting agent based in Belgium or Holland directly.

He told Stone, in the same email, that the operation had been put back a further three weeks due to a dispute over start-up costs. Jerry felt more at ease knowing that Stone would be less aware the robbery was imminent.

The reply was positive and formed the second reason Jerry had for making contact this way: *this could happen*, was the response—it was not out of the norm. *Perfect*, thought Jerry. He would contact the company as an agent for Bulgari, based in Italy. The time delay was an additional decoy, as much as possible, as far as the scumbag Stone was concerned.

The next day, Jerry left the safe house early. The others were still asleep in the apartment, except for Hutchin, who always slept with one eye open. Jerry told him over black coffee, without question, that he would be absent for the day. Then, he left and caught the train into Amsterdam.

He made his way into the area, housing the trading houses and jewellers, gathering as much literature on diamonds and Bulgari jewellery as possible. There was an exhibition and a film offering the general public and potential buyers some history on diamonds—how they were cut, what to look for in the *four Cs*, etc. The general information provided was intended to assure the public that investing in gemstones was a safe bet. Essentially, it was a clever sales tactic, and one Jerry knew he could benefit from. He, like some others (and many more who would eventually discover), understood that gemstones—diamonds in particular—are valued according to the *four Cs*: Colour, Clarity, Cut, and Carat.

In the case of colourless diamonds, the total lack of colour represents the highest grade. For coloured stones, such as rubies or sapphires, it's the purity and intensity of the colour that matters. Jerry wasn't interested in those. He was only interested in diamonds. He looked at the faces of the tourists surrounding the speaker; they looked nervous. He almost laughed at the thought of these vulnerable people paying over the odds for their retirement fund.

Talk soon returned to the matter of interest. *Clarity* refers to the lack of visible or invisible foreign matter within the stone. *Cut* is graded based on technical perfection and the brilliance it produces. The *carat* is a unit of measurement for weight, equivalent to one-fifth of a gram; the finished weight also affects the stone's value. When all these criteria are met, one other factor determines the final price: rarity and size. In general—and as though this needed to be explained—some stones, diamonds in particular, increase in value as the stone's size increases. But what the expert was really telling the people was that an increase in weight is associated with a disproportionately large increase in price. So, when a diamond doubles in weight, its price may rise by four or five times.

Jerry was patient. It could be that, for a few minutes before the robbery, he may have to spend some time alone with Stuli's brother. Therefore, there was a good possibility he might have a conversation that would include the obvious. Some in-depth knowledge of what the two might discuss wouldn't go amiss. It may only be a few seconds, but those seconds could be the difference between advancement or all-out chaos.

Jerry was knowledgeable enough about exquisite jewellery, but nobody knew everything, and it did no harm to look and listen. Besides, it gave him some time alone to contemplate his future.

The seminar moved on to the topic of cutting, polishing, and faceting. This was another area Jerry found interesting. He suddenly realised this knowledge could benefit him when the time came to sell.

After spending almost an hour in the exhibition and asking more questions than any other tourist, it was time to leave. He made his way up the stairs and out into the early evening sun. Taking a seat outside a bar in a large communal square, he ordered a glass of beer and watched the world go by.

He thought about Kath and the girls, Harold, Wheeler, before his heartbeat rose at the thought of Stone and Koiduste. *He would kill both of those scumbags*, he thought. *Even better, he would leave Stone to the mercy of Alba Venga.*

Alba was bang on, right on the nail. Jerry had no idea how he himself would react to seeing Barry tortured and mutilated. He tried to imagine it, but he couldn't. *Koiduste, yes. Barry, no.* Maybe it would be different if he were there. A bullet to the back of the head would be too quick. For what Barry had done, and for what his intentions were, he deserved more. *He had to suffer.*

Jerry took a drink and tried to eliminate these thoughts from his mind. There were far more important things to consider. Too much at stake to jeopardise it all for the sake of lacking concentration. Like a heavyweight contender before a title fight, there could be no distractions. He refused to be drawn in by the opposition. That would only lead to miscalculation and failure.

He meticulously ran through the project so far, and the upcoming events, in his mind.

Chapter One Hundred and Twenty-Two

"Papa!" called Angelica. "Look here."

She was reading the report as it spilled from the machine.

"There's news from Interpol. It's the numbers, Papa—the list of telephone numbers given to us by Koiduste. It seems we're on to something."

Angelo Perelta walked from behind his desk to join his daughter at hers. He leant over her shoulder and read the contents of the notification sent directly from Interpol headquarters in Lyon, France.

"I didn't know you had sent them to Interpol, dearest."

"Do I have to tell you everything?" she smiled, not taking her eyes off the two-page report.

Strictly Confidential

For the attention of Detective Angelica Perelta

Mr Divine has proved to be a complicated figure, and, without him being a fugitive at this moment in time, our resources have been limited. As you know, we are not a detecting agency but rather a force that compiles data and shares it with law enforcement agencies in relevant countries, as we did at the recent seminar in the Grand Hotel Malaga.

We ran the telephone numbers through our mechanics and received some feedback which you may find interesting. First of all, there is no direct connection to Jerry Divine (12.12.1966) that can be confidently attributed to him; we only have associated connections. This information would not have come to light if we had not been looking at a target level one in the first place, so it is a total coincidence, though not unusual in our enquiries.

Hutchin O'Brien (15.11.61)

A longstanding member of the Provisional IRA before its disbandment.

Convictions: None.

The son of the notorious Gerard Devlin, who was killed in Limerick, Ireland, in 1981. Hutchin O'Brien has been of interest to police in both the UK and Ireland as a suspect in several murders and an even larger number of daring armed robberies. There is no direct connection between any of the numbers and Hutchin O'Brien. However, where the connection is made is from a public telephone in Manchester, England, situated outside the Lowry Hotel. The phone was used to call a number attributed to O'Brien. The same phone box was used within seconds to call two of the numbers on the list. Surveillance cameras, both inside and outside the hotel, at the time of the calls, show O'Brien meeting Divine and one other individual. We do not yet have the name of the third person, but we do have the registration of his vehicle. We expect more information shortly.

One other number, the third on the list, was used recently in Antwerp, Belgium. Forensic Telecommunications are currently looking into cell-site data as you read this document. The second number on the list was used two nights ago at Liverpool Airport. We checked the flight schedule for three hours either side of the call, and there was only one flight to Antwerp. This phone was deactivated and then reactivated in Belgium. It seems we have a congregation. A list of all passengers will follow shortly. I suggest you forward this information to the British Detective and include him in the investigation, if, of course, you have not already done so.

I hope this information assists your enquiry. Please do not hesitate to contact us if you require further assistance. A pleasure, and thank you once again for the hospitality.
Pierre Le-Blanque

Chapter One Hundred and Twenty-Three

Jamie O'Rourke had broken into the building opposite the diamond cutter and installed new locks. He had begun erecting scaffolding and positioned monitors to observe the comings and goings of all and sundry entering and leaving the building opposite over the past few days. He set off early this morning and returned with the laptop and camera he had secured in the newly acquired building.

The team gathered around the screen. The footage was invaluable: it showed the owner, Stuli's brother, with who could only be his son, opening up the business at eight o'clock sharp. Less than two minutes later, two heavily built, weary-looking men were seen leaving the property.

"Security," commented Hutchin. They all agreed in silence.

Less than five minutes passed before what appeared to be the security replacement arrived—two men, matching in stature, the pair who had left when the owner arrived.

"Less than a three-minute window," said McNess.

"Not enough," responded O'Rourke. None of them took their eyes from the screen for a second, except Jerry, who was darting his gaze from one to the other, from the screen and back again to his accomplices.

A sound indicating a message received on a mobile phone broke the silence.

"Who the fuck has a phone switched on?" screeched Hutchin O'Brien. Jerry was about to ask the same question.

"Sorry," said Jamie O'Rourke, fumbling in his pockets. "I called my mother this morning, she isn't well."

"Turn the fucker off!" snapped Jerry. "And remove the battery."

O'Rourke did as he was told, but not before he read the message. The others continued to scrutinise the screen.

There was no one, other than the postman, either coming or leaving for the next forty-five minutes. The postman rang the bell; a flap within the structure of the fortified door opened, followed by the door itself. There was some discussion with the taller of the two security men. The door was closed, then opened again within thirty seconds. Jerry counted to twenty-eight. Hutchin checked his watch and made a note on a pad.

"That's our way in!" said Jamie O'Rourke.

"Shush!" snapped Hutchin O'Brien.

Nobody spoke for the next thirty-eight minutes. Jerry made tea, Martin McNess did some light exercise and stretching, while Winston La Bat, O'Rourke, and Hutchin took turns monitoring the film. At eight forty-five, Hutchin began to scribble notes in the pad. For the next seven or eight minutes, the diamond cutters and other employees arrived at the premises. It wasn't difficult to decipher which ones were the cutters; they all looked and dressed the same. They were all male and varied in age from their early twenties to their late eighties.

"How the fuck do they see the things at that age?" asked O'Rourke to nobody in particular, though he did receive a reply from Hutchin, which McNess liked.

"They take care of the big ones," said the Irishman.

"They have magnifying glasses that would show a pinhead the size of an egg, you daft cunt," laughed O'Rourke as he playfully dug Jamie in the ribs with his elbow.

"That hurt, la, you cunt ya!"

"Stop fucking around, you two!" barked Jerry. "And watch the screen."

There was very little to watch. No movement from the factory was observed, either in or out, until lunchtime, when there was a delivery of food from a van clearly marked as *Kosher*. Two men exited the van, walked to the rear, took out two large boxes, and did the same routine as the postman. This time, however, the two security men took the food from them at the door. After that, the son, aged around his early twenties, came out to the van and signed a book through the driver's side open window.

At three-fifteen, there was one more delivery, this time from DHL. One man delivered a brown box the size of a shoebox.

"Wouldn't you like to know what's in that?" asked O'Rourke.

"I'd say it's obvious," answered Hutchin.

"I'd say it's very interesting," said Jerry.

"I could sign one of those up in a morning," offered Winston, guessing what Jerry was thinking.

He was bang on. "Did you get the make?" asked Jerry.

"Mercedes Sprinter."

"It's an option."

"We have another day to watch, don't we?" asked Hutchin.

"Another two, actually," corrected O'Rourke.

Day two, and up until 3 p.m. on the third day, showed nothing of any significance. The film was fast-forwarded through the second day and half of the third, until some movement was observed. The arrival of the staff and cutters—thirty-eight people in total—the food deliveries, and the DHL drop-offs were the same, give or take a few minutes. The security changed over just before the owner shut up shop at seven-thirty.

"Shall I tail them tonight?" asked McNess.

"No, we have their address. We'll stick to the short, sharp, shock—*in and out,* gentlemen," said Jerry, closing the lid on the computer. "Any comments?"

"Whatever you decide, Jerry, I'm with you," said O'Rourke.

"Me too," added McNess.

"Always," said Winston.

"That's good, thank you. And you, Hutchin."

All four were looking at the Irishman, who was standing against the wall, cleaning his gun by the exit. He walked over to join the others, who were now standing around the breakfast bar, leading off the kitchenette.

"I don't agree," he said, not taking his eyes off the gun. He released the chamber and looked through the barrel. "I prefer the old method, it never let us down before."

"The language alone could be a problem, Hutchin," said Jerry.

"I'm not saying I'm out, Jerry. I'm saying I like some guarantee. We take the wife, he does the business. This Jew would play ball."

"I don't know..." said McNess, "these Jew cunts hate parting."

O'Rourke laughed. Jerry walked to stand facing the team.

"We do it my way. The DHL is the way. Winston, you get on the internet, buy a Sprinter van. You say you can have it written up in a few hours?"

Winston nodded.

"Perfect. We do it the day after tomorrow—Friday."

"Friday. Does that mean we drop the Jetskis in the water tomorrow?"

"No. The morning of, Friday. You take a look tomorrow, Martin, find a good location to drop them in. Get the map out, Jamie. What time did the DHL arrive, Hutchin? We'll have to look at the train times again. May even have to move up a station or two. If nobody sees the switch from ski to monkey bike, we're home and dry."

"Three fifteen."

"Three fifteen's good, Hutchin. I need you with me here, mate—*one hundred percent,* you hear me?"

"I'm with you, Jerry."

"Good man."

He patted the Irishman on the shoulder, and all parties now leaned over the waterways and station map.

Thursday
Day Twenty-Six

The remainder of the previous day was spent by the crew discussing each role they were to play. Winston, it was agreed, would drop the four monkey bikes on the bridge and secure a rope ladder for Jerry, Hutchin, Martin, and Jamie. Jamie would be the only one of the four who would not enter the diamond factory. As agreed, he would be on the opposite side of the canal, making as much noise as the kango hammers would allow to draw attention away from the ongoing robbery. He had an alarm of his own to activate, causing even more confusion for any prying eyes and ears.

Jerry had made the call, introducing himself as Anton Cotzia, a top executive from Kimberly Diamond Mining Corporation. He had intentionally decided against using Bulgari, after relaying another red herring to Barry Stone. He explained, as Cotzia, that he was looking for a new factory in Antwerp to cut stones on a regular basis in large amounts. He arranged to meet Abi Mayer at 2:45, deliberately intending to arrive thirty minutes before the estimated legitimate DHL delivery. Hutchin would drive and deliver the parcel, while Martin, who could speak a little Flemish, would be his mate—new to the job—and would stand beside him. O'Rourke would leave his post to place extra safety cordons on both sides of the canal, preventing any other vehicular or pedestrian traffic. This was only necessary at the bridge end because the road was only wide enough for one-way traffic. If—and there was a good chance this would happen—the legitimate delivery van arrived ahead of schedule, it would have to make an eight-minute detour. The actual robbery was estimated to take only two to three minutes.

Once everyone was happy, satisfied that they knew the responsibilities placed on them and that each could rely on the others, a toast was raised.

"May we all come out of this fit, well, healthy, and rich," said Jerry.

"Hear! Hear!"

"Jerry," said Jamie, "when are you going to fill us in on this other one in Gibraltar?"

Jerry didn't relish this question or the answer he was about to give. He didn't want to lie to his team—he knew they wouldn't appreciate that, either now or later. He replaced his glass of wine on the breakfast bar and stepped back from the others, who were all watching him. He thought carefully for a few moments before speaking, unsure where his words would lead him.

"I have to be perfectly honest with you guys. I've encountered a stumbling block—that's not to say we won't be pulling the big one-off," he added quickly, raising his hand. "On the contrary, I'm more determined than ever to see it through. The information," he said carefully, "came via someone who is not, how can I put this, as transparent as I would have liked him to be. I've discovered a flaw. But, before you start thinking about pulling out, especially you, Hutchin," he looked across the room to O'Brien, "the problem will be taken care of, I can assure you. I have another source who can give us the rundown. He's unavailable at the moment—he's recovering from an illness—but rest assured, the information will come, and the robbery *will* go ahead."

"Can you expand? Enlighten us a little more about the mishap? The original source—*is* he likely to kiss and tell?" asked Hutchin.

"The original source will be quietened permanently. Need I say more? Besides!" he chirped, trying to raise morale, "I have a sneaky, suspicious feeling that the job at hand is, by no means, a walk in the park without its benefits, so I suggest we concentrate on that. But you're right to ask, Jamie. After all, this started out as a job to finance the big one—a means to an end. As time's gone on, I think we all realise that this is a job standing on its own merits. Thirty cutters will churn out a lot of stones. I am sure, gentlemen, that when it is all over and we are celebrating in the red-light district on Friday evening, in the brass capital of the world," he paused with a smile, "we will be very happy bunnies."

He raised his glass, which was clinked by each, individually—except for Hutchin, who remained with his back to the wall. Jerry looked over the top of his glass at the Irishman, who smiled briefly at his close friend.

Jerry didn't sleep, which wasn't good. A duvet on the wooden floor didn't help. He *must* sleep tonight, especially as it was the day of the robbery tomorrow. The noise of Martin doing his exercise training disturbed him from his slumber.

"What time you got, Mart?"

"Five-thirty."

"Fucking hell! I was just nodding off. I haven't slept all night. You?"

"Me too, it's the adrenaline. I love it."

"You need to sleep, Martin. Make sure you get some tonight, or grab an hour or two today."

Martin McNess didn't answer. Instead, he stood from his sit-up position and gave the heavy punch bag a quick succession of jabs, followed by a sharp right hook and a few stirring complaints from the others.

Chapter One Hundred and Twenty-Four

It was seven o'clock on the morning of the day before, just over an hour since the last of the team was rudely awakened by the sound of Martin's early morning routine. Jamie had eaten his breakfast cereal half-asleep and without gloves, before Hutchin had to beckon Jerry to reproach him. This done, and gloves replaced, the crew—except for Winston—were gathered in the yard below and behind the loft, which had been their home for the last four days. The slight drizzle was unwelcome, but they hoped it would reappear tomorrow.

Jerry opened the large, green-painted wooden doors that led into the workshop. He stepped to one side as the engine of the van started from within. Winston La Bat drove the DHL van out slowly, an approving smile showing the pride he felt after completing his handiwork. The crew clapped their approval, as if admiring a fine racehorse being led from the winner's enclosure. Winston's smile grew wider as he stepped out of the van. Jerry smiled too; it was important that each and every one of them felt they were pivotal to the project. As the smiles grew broader, confidence was raised higher.

Martin and Hutchin, wearing grey overalls with the black DHL motif sewn into the back, moved forward and stood beside the van like proud, stable hands. Winston walked back into the unit and re-emerged, driving slowly and carefully the original van, which contained the four monkey bikes. He stepped out of the van, lifting a holdall from the seat beside him. He handed the bag to Jerry, who emptied its contents onto a decorator's trestle set up in the open yard. The crew gathered around the makeshift table under a crudely built canopy.

"We take one each of these," Jerry said, handing a black object the size of a mobile phone to each of them. "These beauties will floor a bull—fifty thousand volts. We use these if, and only if, we have to."

"Fifty thousand volts to reach one? Should be a walk in the park."

"That's quick, Jamie, but not quite true. This will be, by no means, a walk in the park, boys," said Jerry seriously. "We have to be in and out within the three-minute time limit. We know the vault is open during working hours, we know our positions and the parts we have to play. We watch out for each other. We have to have eyes in the back of our fucking heads. The ties," he said, lifting a fistful of plastic cable ties, "the two meatheads—they have to be wrapped..."

"Do we stun them first?" asked Martin.

"We have to," answered Hutchin.

"Yes, between the two doors, immediately. As soon as the first one shuts and the second is released. Hutchin, you and Martin are directly behind me. Martin, you complain about the noise across the water, make out you can't hear a thing. I'll do the same—they're going to let me in anyway. Jamie, you trigger the alarm. I want noise, and plenty of it."

"I'll bring the fucking building down if I have to, Jerry."

"I know. We have to rely on each other, boys. We've been through the escape route, and we all know what we have to do. This place..." he said, looking around, "this place has served its purpose. It was ideal, Winston—well done. Hutchin, you and Martin, head back here and acid the life out of it. There's very little to do—we've all worn protection at all times, yes?" He looked around; nobody spoke. "But we need to do it right. Winston," he looked at the tall black man. Winston nodded—he knew what he had to do with the bikes and cars.

"Relax today, boys. Just wind down before the storm."

Chapter One Hundred and Twenty-Five

"There's definitely something going down, Boss. This arrived less than an hour ago," said Steven Smith, placing the email that had come through from Spain.

Wheeler sat up in his bed, which he had settled into less than an hour ago. The specialist was more than pleased with his recovery, and even Wheeler was beginning to feel he actually *was* as strong as an ox.

"Pass me those glasses, Smithy." He read the report. "I told you about this Angelica—she leaves no stone unturned."

"What do you make of it?"

"I'd say it's obvious. Belgium, Antwerp, Stone, Liverpool airport… there's a connection there to O'Rourke, Hutchin. Telephone contact. I wouldn't be surprised if these other two numbers relate to McNess and La-Bat."

"Martin McNess got a not guilty," offered Smithy, as if to confirm this. "O'Rourke did fly to Antwerp—I've checked the flight list. He's used the same phone three times over there, twice in Rotterdam, once in Antwerp. He's received two messages—they're printed on sheet three. Interpol have isolated the districts. The Antwerp one is an affluent diamond spot…"

"Predominantly Jewish, no doubt," added Wheeler.

"What makes you say this, Bill?"

"Antwerp! Diamonds! Come on, Smithy, wake up and smell the coffee." He neglected to add what he already knew and what Barry Stone had told him.

He leaned over to take his drink from the bedside cabinet and grimaced with the pain. Smithy took over and held the cup to Wheeler's mouth. When he had drunk, Smithy finished what was left in the cup. By this time, Bill Wheeler had decided to confide in him.

"I know there's going to be a robbery in Antwerp."

"You *know*?"

"Yes, I was told by Stone."

"Wait a minute! You were told by Stone that he and Divine were going to commit a robbery in Antwerp?"

"Divine. I was told that Divine was going to commit a robbery, but to let it ride because a bigger, more audacious one was to follow—with arms."

"And?"

"I was going to let it go ahead, in the hope that Divine would be killed."

"You can't, Bill. You can't stand back and let this happen!"

"I know, Son."

"So we act?"

"Yes."

"Why the change of heart?"

"It's a long story."

"What do I do?"

"Contact Phelps. We need to act quickly. Ask him to come and see me. Let the Spanish know what we're doing, let Interpol know, and speak with this La-Blanque fella—see if he can connect us with someone in Antwerp. We need to act fast, Steve. We have to let them know it's Antwerp—there's no point in them wasting time with Rotterdam. And what's more important to us is that I don't want Divine to do the big one, whatever or whenever that may be. I still feel somewhat obliged."

The warrants were issued and enforced within one hour and the following hour, respectively. It was unusual to use battering rams at midday, but the officer in charge agreed that any element of surprise was better than none. The doors of Jamie O'Rourke's mother's house and the luxury apartment by the Thames belonging to Martin McNess went through with a crash at exactly the same time—11:45 a.m. in the UK—as did the door at the modest log cabin and residence of Hutchin O'Brien at Manor Heath Stud Farm, Galway.

Margaret O'Rourke said nothing. She let the search party go about their business, as they had on numerous occasions. She didn't move from the settee and knew all too well to say nothing that could later be used against her in a court of law. The other two properties were empty of occupants, which only strengthened the consensus among the relevant detective agencies, in the relevant countries, that what had been passed on by the British detective Wheeler was correct: the targets were together and ready to strike.

When the results of the raids reached Commander Phelps' desk, he immediately informed Europol, who, in turn, gave the green light—code red—for Operation Gamble to commence. A meeting was arranged in Belgium at 8 p.m. Detective Sergeant Steve Smith would attend in place of Inspector William Wheeler.

Wheeler told Smithy how he had been informed by Stone that no weapons were to be used by the robbers in Antwerp. The younger detective reminded his boss about South Mimms, which left a bitter taste in Wheeler's ulcerated mouth, though he had to agree. He instructed Smith not to mention it at the meeting and, in fact, to say very little and listen only.

The dilemma Wheeler had felt earlier hadn't subsided. He owed Jerry Divine *nothing*. Yes, he had fulfilled his part of the agreement and disposed of the evidence—Divine had paid, but that was it. Service provided; fee paid. There was no further commitment or obligation. Wheeler was a detective first and foremost. But then there was the agreement they had made at what was, at the time, his deathbed. Divine had agreed to take care of Stone, but that wasn't for Wheeler's benefit—it was revenge on Divine's part. The payment to Maud? Divine was an honourable thief; no doubt he would have paid. But this was no longer required, and Wheeler had to keep reminding himself—*he was a detective first*. Besides, stopping the Antwerp robbery would surely save Divine from certain death if he were allowed to proceed with the big one, especially if Stone had anything to do with it.

Detective Sergeant Smith was collected at the airport in Belgium by two uniformed officers, neither of whom spoke a word of English, and driven to police headquarters in the city. The meeting was well underway by the time he was ushered into the room; in fact, the first recess was about to commence. He was happy with the coffee and fresh sandwiches, but less happy with how fast things seemed to be moving without him. After all, he was the Brit—wasn't he the one who knew the most about these particular criminals?

"Mr Smith! May I introduce myself? My name is Angelo Perelta." He held out a podgy hand. Smithy took it but couldn't take his eyes off the gorgeous girl beside the overweight Spanish policeman. She was truly beautiful. Smithy blushed slightly.

"And I am Angelica."

"Pleased to meet you, Sir. And you, Madam, I'm sure," he said, taking her hand and holding onto it slightly longer than was comfortable. She blushed too. Her father gave a deliberate cough.

"I have heard so much about you," said Smithy quickly.

"All good, I hope."

"Very. My boss was very impressed, especially with you, Miss?"

Angelica looked to her father first, for approval. He nodded.

"Perelta."

"I was a little late—maybe you could fill me in?"

"Please," said the father, placing a hand delicately on his daughter's elbow.

"You bring Mr Smith up to date, my dear, whilst I speak with Mr Le-Blanque."

She looked briefly scared and annoyed, but her father smiled and turned his back. She turned to Steven Smith, who was smiling broadly.

"I won't bite."

Thirty minutes later, and just as round two was about to commence, he knew everything. Luckily for him, his newfound confidante was fluent in the local language and six others, she timidly informed him. He secretly hoped the two could work together.

From what he had been told, what was whispered to him during the meeting, and the snippets he could work out for himself, it seemed the team had made little, if any, errors. It was only the fact that Hutchin O'Brien was of great interest to Europol, and the use of the mobile phone by Jamie O'Rourke to pinpoint him and hopefully the others, that there was a good chance the newly formed *Operation Gamble* could be monitored, and with a lot of luck, busted before it could act—or even better, caught in the act.

Large maps were positioned on the wall, with pins marking the spots where the mobile phone had been used. Special permissions had been granted by a judge, in a court set up solely to deal with the matter, to listen in—not to the conversations being had by a call made or received, but by using the phone as a listening device. Unfortunately for the police, until an hour ago, the phone had not been activated and the battery had been disconnected. This changed briefly for less than eight minutes, during which time Jamie O'Rourke spoke to his mother on her home telephone for one minute and twenty-two seconds. After that, some invaluable information was captured as part of the conversation could be heard for the remaining six minutes and thirty-eight seconds. This was played live to the gathered police and translated, much to the annoyance of those who could understand. After the phone went dead, the translators finished, and a complete silence came over the room. Smithy was asked to move forward and introduce himself.

He was asked by the Frenchman if he recognised any of the voices they had just heard speaking.

"If you're asking if I could identify one of the voices as being that of Divine, I'm afraid I would have to be honest and say no—not one hundred percent anyway."

"If we are talking percentages, perhaps you could put a percent on it," someone asked from behind. There were approximately twenty people present. Smithy tried to identify the speaker, but couldn't, so the Frenchman asked the same question.

"Forty, maybe even thirty percent. You see, I haven't spoken to Mr Divine for six, almost seven years now."

"So it's cost us ten percent per year?" asked the same speaker. There was laughter in the room. Smithy didn't see the funny side, and Angelica felt for him.

"Any of the others, Mr Smith?" she called.

"Yes, I can identify O'Rourke—I'd say it was definitely him. One other could have been McNess, Martin McNess. He's another of Divine's criminal associates." He coughed and covered his mouth, feeling embarrassed, thinking he was telling them something they already knew. The Frenchman stepped in and saved the day. Smithy moved back to join Angelica.

A question was asked from the back of the room. La-Blanque asked the speaker to repeat. The question was asked again, this time by someone with an Irish accent.

"Can we assume the voice with the Irish accent is Hutchin O'Brien?"

"We are the law—we can assume anything," came the response from another detective.

"I suppose you have your answer," said La-Blanque apologetically.

The meeting went on for most of the night, and arrangements were made to follow up on what had been agreed throughout the night and into the next day.

Settled in his hotel room, Smithy made a call to relay what was happening to Wheeler. He also told his superior that he was staying in the same hotel as Mr Perelta. Wheeler thanked him, wished him luck, and asked him to pass his regards to Mr Perelta and his daughter. Smithy did so over a late-night cap, and included the information that Mr Wheeler had been very ill since his return from Spain but was recovering better than expected. Both Angelo and Angelica were surprised and sorry to hear this, and the talk soon returned to the operation at hand.

Chapter One Hundred and Twenty-Six

Friday
The Day of 'The Robbery'

"I'm away, boys," said Divine as he straightened his tie. "How do I look?"

"I wouldn't recognise you, and I'm not just saying that," said O'Rourke.

"Me too," said McNess.

"You could have picked a better colour for your hair. The grey makes you look a lot older. But the fake tan suits you—a little dark though, don't you think?" asked Winston.

"The grey's good, Jerry. The beard looks good too," added Hutchin. "There's some CS gas here, take it. You're the first through the door, it's less complicated than the stun guns in a crisis."

"Thanks," said Jerry, taking it from him. He slipped the small canister, no bigger than a lipstick holder, into his suit jacket breast pocket.

"It's a little early, no?"

"I'm going to take a walk around the area, spend an hour or two looking up and down those narrow streets—get the feel, you know?" he said, inhaling deeply through his nostrils.

Hutchin smiled. "God bless." He patted him on the back.

Jerry stopped short before the door closed behind him. He looked at Hutchin—neither of them spoke; there was no need for words. Jerry smiled briefly, turned on his heels sharply, and left the building with his briefcase. The time was eight forty-five, roughly six hours before the robbery.

Two and a half hours later, Jerry was sitting in a small coffee shop opposite the entrance to a shopping mall on the outskirts of the city, less than one kilometre from the target. He drained the cup and walked through the doors and into the mall. He spent the next hour checking out the exits and the three-storey car park. This had nothing to do with the escape route, but it could well be an alternative if things went wrong with the original.

Behind the mall, through the rear fire exit—which opened without an alarm being activated—Jerry noticed there was a canal over a four-foot wall. He looked around before jumping up to look over. Less than fifty metres away, to the left, was a bridge with two signs: one indicating a footpath and the other a rail link. He had seen enough. Jerry walked back into the mall and towards the front entrance. As he approached the exit, he slipped two flint spark ignition smoke bombs from his pocket and dropped them into the base pot of some six-foot ornate rubber plants situated on either side of the doors—he might have to activate them as a decoy later—and proceeded to leave the building.

Winston checked his watch—six minutes to two. The butterflies had started; his stomach churned. He didn't want to drop the bikes yet, for fear that some youths might come across them and either steal or sabotage them, although he was happy to see that this looked like a good area with little crime. He was scared, there was no denying it. He had been quiet most of the day, and it surprised him that his major concern was that, if anything happened to him, who would look after Bess?

The Jetskis had gone into the water without a hitch. They were nicely secured under the first bridge, which was within running distance of the diamond factory. The ladder was secured and needed only cutting to release it into the water. All that was left for him to do was drop the four bikes and place the cordons by the wall for Jamie to put into place when the time was right. And that was him done—except for acid spraying the cars and burning out the van.

He didn't want to go back to the safe house. There was something about it. Jerry and the boys had been happy with it, but there was something, and the feeling became worse the longer he stayed around the place—especially this morning. As he sat now, in the van, a shiver went through his body. He was relieved when the job of cleaning up the safe house had been given to Hutchin and Martin.

O'Rourke was on site early too—eleven o'clock. He had used the kanga periodically, a high-powered drill on occasions, and a hammer and chisel to remove some of the concrete pointing from between the bricks. It was now approaching two. His hat was pulled low, and the goggles he was wearing were tinted. The collar of his overall was turned up, so there was little chance of anyone identifying him later.

This is what he loved about working with Jerry Divine—*everything* was taken into account. So fucking professional. There was no way one could come on top if he was working with Jerry, and for that reason, he loved the man. How fucking easy was this? Here he was, sitting on some scaffolding, eating a ham fucking baguette and drinking a pint of milk. There had been little movement opposite, everything was going according to plan, and how he needed this money.

A small boat went by with a glass top and sides, like the ones that took tourists around the Dam—the sightseeing ones—but this one was a smaller version, with about twelve people seated in it. He waved; some of them smiled and waved back. He was a workman taking a break, that was all. He was gone from their minds as quickly as the slow boat passed him. Two lovers stopped cycling their bike and looked over the bridge. They, too, waved at the boat. They moved slightly to let a van go slowly over the hump.

Jamie watched Winston stop the van and place the cones by the wall. He was supposed to drop and leave them so that Jamie could position them when the time was right. It made little difference to O'Rourke, and he assumed Winston just preferred to keep busy. Again, he watched him jump back into the van and reverse out of sight. He was gone for about nine minutes before he reappeared—no doubt he had dropped the bikes. Jamie watched as he drove slowly by. He was glad when Winston passed and was, again, out of sight, as he didn't want him to see him use his phone.

He had promised his mother he would call her at two o'clock, on the dot. He took his mobile from his pocket and pressed speed dial to make the call. He received the engaged signal. He left it five minutes and pressed redial. He wasn't as paranoid as the others, especially Jerry and Hutchin. How on earth could they track a phone if you weren't talking constantly into it? What difference did it make whether the battery was in or out? *Fuck them,* as much as he loved them, *fuck them.*

The call activated a signal, which in turn told the technician looking at his laptop where the call was made from. He called the number the detective had given him, and the call was answered before the first ring tone was complete.

"I have the mass and a fifty-metre radius. Do you have a map?"

"Give it to me."

Jerry checked his watch. It was time. He stood from the table, folded the foreign newspaper and placed it under his arm, threw enough change to cover the three coffees, and tipped his hat to the waitress as she hurried out to wipe the table and collect the change.

It was less than three hundred metres to the job, a five-minute walk. He had seen the DHL van, driven by Hutchin with McNess as his passenger, go by twice. The next time he saw it, if all went according to plan, would be as he approached the factory. He looked down to the drop into the canal on his left as he walked—about a metre, no more. It was a bigger drop to where the Jetskis were, but the rope ladder should be secured and waiting.

The cones were set comfortably against the wall to his right. He heard the van stop behind him as he passed, the engine left idling, the door opening, Winston with a strained whistle, the scraping of the cones, the van door slamming, the engine stalling and restarting. Jerry smiled as the van drove away.

One hundred metres now. He could see the DHL van stop outside the factory doors. He checked his watch—bang on time! Fifty metres. He slowed his pace.

Where was Winston? Jerry looked past the van to the first bridge. He didn't want another vehicle entering the narrow road—it was one-way traffic. This could be a problem. More witnesses, a brave one or two could put up a fight.

To the left, across the water, Jamie pulled on a rope, releasing some roof tiles. They crashed down onto the cobbled pavement below. The music from a radio hanging from the scaffolding had a neighbour shouting out of her shuttered window. She closed them with an angry clatter. O'Rourke smiled as he pulled on his protective gloves and started up the clatter of the Kango Hammer.

Winston had no option but to brake hard and let the school party cross the narrow road in front of him. The kids had been throwing bread into the water to feed the ducks. The teacher smiled at the black man driving the white van and ushered the children to move quickly.

Heading towards Winston, beyond the children, and with the indicator flashing to show it was turning right into the road, which ought to be blocked off by Winston, was a minibus full to the brim with what looked like half a century of OAPs. *What the fuck!* Winston gave a blast on the horn. The teacher showed her distaste, and the children laughed. Again, he pressed hard down on the steering wheel.

Jerry watched as the children hurried towards him. He was sweating. He took a handkerchief from his breast pocket and felt the small canister that he hoped he wouldn't have to use. He had used CS before—it wasn't nice; it usually affected the user too. He *saw* Winston manoeuvre the van sharply to cut off the minibus. Now, with the sound of annoyance from the horn of the other vehicle, Jerry thought this could be an advantage—the more noise and distraction, the better.

Winston jumped from the van and began positioning the cordon. He held one hand up to his face in a feeble attempt to disguise himself, and waved the minibus on, past the back of his van and away in the opposite direction. He looked towards Jamie, who held the power tool with two hands. The racket was deafening. Winston smiled nervously to himself—his part was done. He looked once more toward Hutchin and McNess, who were stepping from the van. He could see Jerry drawing nearer to the factory. The children were even closer. He jumped back into his van and was gone. He hoped, without asking God but with all his being, that the next time he *saw* Jerry and the boys would be this evening in Amsterdam.

Jerry watched as Hutchin rang the bell and rapped on the door. He slowed his pace slightly; the school party couldn't be avoided. Winston had done well to get rid of the minibus—that would surely have been a disaster. O'Rourke was doing a good job; the children were screaming rather than talking to each other. Jerry was only too happy he had decided not to use guns. Hutchin, on the other hand, had insisted, but by the time the children passed, the robbery would be taking place inside.

Jerry clipped the badge onto his lapel as he joined the two waiting by the doors. The hatch opened, and Martin spoke. The security guard looked from one to the other and then to Jerry. He said something, but the sound of an alarm from over the water had Jerry cupping his ear and moving closer. The guard asked him something which Jerry could neither hear nor understand. He pointed to the badge on his lapel and bent to open his briefcase. The case dropped to the floor, and Jerry squatted down to retrieve his documents. Whilst he was down, he heard the sliding of the lower bolt. *Thank fuck!*

The children walked around the gentleman as he picked up his case and papers. The teacher apologised for the children in her care laughing and sniggering. The concern needn't have been hers. She watched in amazement as the doors opened and the two deliverymen, along with the man in a suit, barged forward with such force and aggression that the doors were nearly broken from their hinges. They screamed orders in English as she shouted likewise in her own tongue to the children.

All mayhem broke loose at the same time as a billow of smoke was released across the waterway. She looked across to the sound of an alarm to see a man up high, dressed in work-wear, screaming into what looked like a mobile telephone.

The decision to barge was taken without any notification to the others. Hutchin knew instinctively that the language barrier would—or had—caused a problem. The second door leading into the building remained closed and probably locked; they couldn't take the risk of losing precious time. Hutchin pushed from the rear, and like a scrum in a game of rugby, the security guard, as big as he was, was no match for McNess and Divine.

"*Get the door!*" screamed Jerry as he tried the handle to the remaining one. It was locked. He pulled the stun gun from his pocket and held it up to the face of the guard, who was held tightly around the neck by McNess. Nobody was sure whether the commotion was detected by the occupiers of the building, but it had to be assumed it was. Martin McNess whispered something menacing into the ear of the bulk, who remained tight-lipped. Jerry pressed the switch, which activated the volts with a snap and an arc of light. He held it closer to the man's face, within an inch of his eyes. It made little difference. The guard strained under the pressure applied by McNess; he could hardly breathe, and his face was turning purple.

Jamie O'Rourke was panicking. The red and blue lights were not a result of the alarm or smoke—it was too soon. It had to be something else. All he knew was that they were getting closer, and he didn't like it. He pressed the agreed code to abort.

The police had connected the rented apartment and unit to the team. A search had revealed a number of clues, and certain items had been taken away for forensic examination. Much more had to be done, but at this early stage it looked like a number of people had been holed up for a few days in preparation for what seemed like a planned robbery of some kind. The maps and other pieces of vital information gave the investigating officers an inkling that someone might return to clean up. The clues in the unit gave more away—it was obvious that vehicles had been disguised, and the cuttings made from the adhesive plastic clearly showed that one of these vehicles had been disguised as a DHL delivery van.

The second call came and demanded that the team of officers move quickly to the second destination provided by the cell-site technician. It was in the Edegem district, which mainly consists of hundreds of narrow roads housing a large number of diamond houses, and surrounding the zoo in Pianckendel.

The hatch in the second, secured door opened. McNess took his cue and forced the head of the hostage into the gap. He yanked it back, knocking the wind out of the victim, but still, the big man said nothing. Hutchin decided it was time to do something even more extreme. He pulled the gun from his waistband, moved forward between McNess and Jerry, and rammed the muzzle into the cheek of the frightened guard. The other guard, in the safety of the unit, was drawn into the conflict. His eyes showed uncertainty, as though he wasn't sure if this was a bluff. Jerry could read the expression—less than thirty seconds had passed. The bleeps from the walkie-talkie could not be heard, but the vibration could be felt against his ribs. He chose to ignore it and looked again at his watch.

The commotion followed the first blast from the stun gun. Jerry could see Hutchin was about to do something they could all regret later, so he pressed it against the side of the man's neck, making sure his associate could clearly see the effect as the volts ran through the victim's body. The electrocuted man screamed out and begged his friend to open the door. What felt like a lifetime, but in reality, was less than one minute, passed without the second door being opened. There was only one thing for it, and Hutchin wasn't about to waste any more time. He lowered the gun to the back of the large man's leg and blew a hole behind the knee, a sickening pop as the gristle and bone exploded before the magnified bang.

The large man buckled under the damage and pain, and the scream that was released was almost as loud as the bang from the gun in such a confined space. The door opened immediately, and the trio barged in, making as much noise as their barks would allow. The second guard backed up against the opposite wall with his hands held high above his head. Hutchin moved toward him with the gun pointed directly at his face. The man cowered to his knees, which made the task of pistol-whipping him to the side of the temple and knocking him out easier. Once he was out cold, his hands and feet were secured with plastic cable ties.

The owner, Stuli's brother, who was cowering in his office, held his son's head tightly to his chest. Jerry moved fast. He looked from the owner's face to the phone hanging from its cradle. It made no difference now whether the connection had been made to the police or whether a panic alarm had been activated—it was all over in the last *one minute and twenty seconds*.

The last and final door was kicked open to reveal the frightened cutters huddled in the far corner of the room. Jerry had a surreal vision of being in a concentration camp; every one of the skilled workers was crying and comforting each other, which suited him as it saved time and effort. Hutchin moved fast, jumping across the long planked table, scattering machines and tools as he headed straight for the holding vaults. He pulled hard to open the seven-inch reinforced steel door to its maximum and entered the room full of stainless steel numbered drawers. Releasing the nylon bag from his waistband, he started to empty the trays behind each narrow door, pouring diamonds into the bag.

"*Fifty-five seconds!*" called Jerry.

Jerry looked again at the cutters huddled in the corner. He called out to Jamie, who was holding his stun gun in a threatening manner. The clerical staff were whimpering. The next decision wasn't part of Jerry's plan, but it was always a possibility.

"*Help Dick,*" he instructed.

McNess moved quickly, also releasing a bag as he jumped across the table. There was no danger of any obstruction from within, so Jerry now began to collect all the diamonds from the work areas. He wasn't sure of the value of half-cut stones, but with the time limit left, he saw no point in leaving anything of value.

Jamie O'Rourke turned from the flashing lights and blaring sirens. He picked up the hammer and chisel and looked at the building he had come to know every brick of over the last four days. He didn't have a clue what to do. He was nervous and scared. He had pressed the code to abort, yet the boys hadn't reappeared. He doubted very much that the two security guards were any match for his three accomplices. *Maybe Jerry had decided to carry on with the robbery. Maybe they had gone a step too far.*

But the police! *How the fuck had they got onto them?* Should he move down the ladder slowly? Should he make his way casually towards the Jet Skis below the bridge?

The guide with the school children was less than fifty metres away from the diamond factory. They had hurriedly scurried away from the action. Unbelievably, the first police car on the scene stopped at the precaution barrier. The driver saw the pedestrians and accelerated off to circle round and approach from the opposite direction. Jamie quickly assumed that the police were aware something was going down, but weren't one hundred percent sure *what* or *where*. What he was sure about was that it was time for him to make haste and disappear while he could.

The doors to the factory flew open with such force that one of them actually did leave the hinge at the top. Jamie looked back and upped his pace to a slow run with short steps as he watched the trio make their dramatic exit. He was less than seventy metres from the bridge, which concealed the getaway ski; the boys, with the proceeds, were more like one hundred and fifty. He looked beyond them, towards the second roadblock positioned by Winston. The police were talking to the children's guardian, who was pointing toward the building when the doors sprang open.

Martin McNess was the first to appear, followed by Jerry, with Hutchin holding his gun up high and bringing up the rear. McNess didn't see the police to the left and was blinkered, focusing on running to the bridge on the right. Jerry, on the other hand, looked toward where O'Rourke should have been. Seeing he was nowhere in sight, he looked to his left and saw the police cars, stationary, with the first of three officers talking to the school party. Hutchin also saw the squad cars and pushed Jerry in the small of his back to move fast.

The driver of the leading police car saw the activity and immediately left the teacher mid-speech. He reversed into the car behind as he gave himself space to turn into the narrow drive-through. Hutchin heard the crash but didn't look back as he tried to catch up with Jerry and Martin, who were the faster runners.

Jamie was squatting down beside the bridge, holding onto the rope ladder that led to an almost certain escape. He could see his friends racing towards the getaway point and held his breath at the sight of the pursuing police. It wasn't clear whether the trio were going to make it, especially Hutchin, who was lagging behind. Jamie watched as Jerry grabbed a makeshift clothes horse, positioned outside one of the narrow, three-storey houses, and pulled it and its contents into the road without losing pace. Hutchin followed and ran around the metal frame.

The first car hit it at speed, and the clothes horse got caught under the car's grille but had no effect on slowing the vehicle. However, the clothes that hit the windscreen *did* have the desired effect, and the driver must have yanked the steering wheel, as the car veered left and braked hard. The front wheel left the road and hung over the water's edge as the car behind hit its rear, pushing it into a sideways position, thus blocking the road and ending the chase by car.

The two officers from the damaged car jumped free from the wreck and continued the chase on foot. Hutchin was struggling to keep pace and looked back to see the leader of the two closing in. Worse still, they were gaining strength in numbers as the others clambered over the abandoned car bonnet to join their fellow officers.

Jamie stepped carefully from the rope ladder onto the first Jet Ski. He pressed the starter button and gave it a burst of acceleration. Then, he stepped over to the second machine and did the same. Looking up, he could see Jerry now taking the lead from Martin—Hutchin was nowhere to be seen. Suddenly, he heard a splash in the water and looked in that direction. There was nothing but ripples of water.

"*Release the ties!*" called Jerry. He was standing at the top, looking down. "*Hurry. Move it!*" he shouted at McNess before descending the rope. He positioned himself at the controls of the second Jet Ski and immediately revved up the power. McNess lowered himself down the escape and sat at the rear of Jamie.

"*Go, go, go!*" screamed Jerry as he turned the machine on a hairpin turn.

"*Where the fuck are you going?*" yelled O'Rourke.

"*Fucking move it!*" answered McNess as he dug him in the ribs. The police on foot were nearing the fugitives.

"*Where's Hutchin?*" hollered O'Rourke.

"*He's in the water! Fucking move it!*"

The noise from the engines, the smell of diesel, and the spray from Jerry's machine as he turned and headed in the totally opposite direction to the agreed plan left Jamie confused and disoriented. It wasn't until Martin McNess repeated with menace into his ear to *move* that Jamie reacted, just as the first of the Belgian police began descending the ladder. He exerted some power into the machine, spraying a mound of water up the wall and drenching the pursuing officers.

As reinforcements arrived and the confusion became clear, it soon became apparent to the officer in charge that the robbers were one step ahead of the police. He called out to the officers closest to the robbers to hold fire and gave instructions via radio to block off the waterways in each direction immediately. The problem with this instruction was the speed at which these Jet Skis could travel, and with the two going in opposite directions, was there enough manpower available?

The answer came quickly, as the Jet Ski heading back towards the scene of the robbery stopped short and made a U-turn. The robber who had jumped into the water had resurfaced and was struggling to climb onto the ski. Officers above, looking down, were unsure whether to jump into the water, use their firearms, or just stand and watch. There was dismay and confusion, with no one in particular in control.

Hutchin resurfaced and gulped for air. He still held his gun in hand but was not about to raise and use it, as at this stage, he was nothing more than a sitting duck, literally.

Jerry leaned back to pull him up onto the machine. As Hutchin was hauled from the water, the two officers above noticed the gun in his hand and pulled theirs from their holsters. Hutchin looked back as the Jet Ski surged forward and the rear dipped low into the water. He saw the two officers reaching for their weapons and aimed his gun above their heads. He pulled the trigger as they lowered themselves into a combat position and took aim. The gun clicked, but nothing happened. He shook the weapon to release the water and realised he hadn't made the gun ready—he needed two hands to hold and draw back the chamber. Jerry wasn't waiting around. The Jet Ski sped through the water, and as the first bullet hit the fibreglass machine, sending a vibration through the throttle, they were already making good their getaway.

Divine Intervention

Up above, poised on the original bridge, were the police officers who had been on the tail of McNess and Jerry. They hadn't seen and had no idea that shots had been fired. The instruction to shoot was drowned out by the noise of the alarm and machinery that O'Rourke had left switched on.

Martin McNess refused to leave without the safe arrival of Jerry and Hutchin. Jamie O'Rourke tried in vain to convince him there was little they could do to help if the other two were apprehended. The sound of the sirens drawing closer to the second point, which was the monkey bike station, led McNess to think Jamie O'Rourke was showing his true colours. O'Rourke took off without looking back. He could have saved face by waiting just another minute or so.

Martin looked down at the water as the Jet Ski came into view from under a bridge less than two hundred metres away. He smiled and waved down to the two approaching. His smile turned to horror as the first of three additional police cars and two motorbikes blocked the road at either side of the bridge. He looked down to Jerry, who was nearing the getaway point. For a second, he thought he saw him smile, but this quickly changed to realisation and fear.

Martin McNess waved frantically for Jerry to continue under the bridge and to carry on, before the first of many blows struck him beside his head. He went down, not knowing if Jerry had understood the message and only hoping that Hutchin was prepared to use the gun.

Jerry did get the message, and he did see the assault on his friend. He screamed for Martin to jump, but it was too late. This time, he called out loud with frustration as the ski passed under the bridge, putting distance between them and the police arresting his friend. He remembered that the next bridge was the one he had passed earlier in the day when he had made the emergency detour. Stopping the machine beside the water's edge and clambering ashore, he voiced his outrage at the capture.

"*Fuck!*"

"*Save it,*" said Hutchin. "*Come. This way.*"

"*Where da fuck ya takin' me?*"

"*I was here this morning, there's a—*"

The screeching of brakes and more sirens made Jerry stop in his tracks. He lowered himself behind a wall, and Hutchin followed suit. Other cars slowed, paused for a moment, then accelerated.

"Where's your bag?" asked Jerry.

"In da drink."

"Don't say that!" He looked into the eyes of his friend.

"Why da fuck do ya think it took me so long to resurface?"

"You should have drowned, you cunt. Let's move." Jerry gave a disgruntled look. Hutchin knew he didn't mean what he said. He was upset and angry—more angry, no doubt, about Martin's capture than the loss of part of the proceeds. Two parts, if you took into account the diamonds Martin was holding too. Hutchin wanted to voice his own anger; he didn't appreciate the way Jerry spoke to him just now. He wasn't used to being spoken to like that, but now wasn't the time. He would raise the subject later—*if* there was a later. By the looks of things, the two had jumped out of the pond and into the wide sea.

Jerry looked over the wall and onto the busy main road. The shopping mall was almost directly opposite, on the other side.

"When I say when, we make a run for it. Stay with me, Hutchin."

"Not a bother, I'm up your arse, Son."

"Now!" He stood up and vaulted the wall. The Irishman followed behind him, almost clicking his heels. Car horns blared, and a bus loaded with passengers braked hard to avoid hitting the two men running across the road. Two bikes with uniformed officers coming in the opposite direction didn't miss the absconders. One mounted the pavement, and the other followed onto the precincts before the entrance to the mall.

Jerry saw them first and made it through the tinted glass doors before Hutchin. Hutchin almost ran into the back of him as he slowed his pace and turned sharply to the right upon entering. There was confusion and panic from shoppers as Jerry grabbed for the smoke bombs and released the ignition. The smoke billowed with such force and density that when he threw them along the polished tiled floor, it caused enough disruption to divert all attention from the two fugitives. Jerry ran through the smoke, and Hutchin followed with silent admiration.

"Fire! Fire!" screamed Jerry.

"Get out!" called Hutchin. Within seconds, others, not intentionally involved in the plot, were inadvertently assisting the getaway.

The two chasing policemen entered the shopping centre to be met by total anarchy and chaos. Jerry caused more of this as he passed the lifts to the multi-storey car park and smashed the fire alarm as he went by. Exiting from the rear of the building, it was sheer luck that a train was slowly pulling into the station across the way. Jerry knew if the two of them kept up the pace, they would reach it. Where it would take them was another matter—the further away from here, the better.

It was part of the plan that Hutchin and McNess were to go back to the safe house and clear up. There was no way that could happen now. *Never go back to the scene of a crime, especially after a close shave like this.* If the police knew where the robbery was taking place, there was a good chance they had discovered the hideout too. *How?* That was something to decipher at a later date. What was important now was creating distance. Jerry hoped that Jamie O'Rourke had seen the police arrive on the bridge and made his escape safely.

Hutchin and Jerry were to take care of the cars. The bag containing the diamonds could be with either Martin or Jamie. If Martin had them at the time of his arrest, they were gone. If that was the case, the robbery had been a disaster. He would find out tonight.

The group had agreed to meet at Central Station in Amsterdam at ten o'clock tonight, whether everything had gone according to plan or not. As it stood, Jerry could only be sure that he and Hutchin would be there. Winston was to collect the car, which contained all the travel documents, phones, and personal effects that would enable each of the crew to travel on to various destinations from Holland. Jerry hoped Jamie O'Rourke had taken the diamonds from Martin.

Winston drove the van through the car wash and continued until he found a suitable location, within walking distance of the pre-parked car, for what he had to do. He climbed into the back of the van and donned his white protective suit and breathing apparatus. He pulled down his goggles and gathered everything that wasn't tied down into a neat pile on the floor in the middle. Once he was satisfied that he had scraped up everything but the seats into a stack—including the snack wrappers and milk bottles—he poured nitric acid over it. He held his breath and watched as the pile disintegrated before his eyes. Once he was certain the evidence was non-existent, he poured the remainder of the acid over the steering wheel, dashboard, and seats. He dropped the glass bottle onto the smouldering pile and smashed it with the car jack from beneath the seat.

He walked back to the car, which contained travel and personal documents for each of the crew, and was relieved to be heading for the red lights of Amsterdam and one step nearer to Bess.

Martin McNess was dragged from the van and roughly manhandled into the holding area of the central police station. He gave no name as he was secured by two officers in front of the prisoner processing desk. He refused to have his picture taken or his fingers placed in the machine for printing. When he was asked if he required a solicitor, he again refused to talk. He waited until he was pushed into a cell and the door was banged loudly behind him before he let out the first word since his arrest.

"*Bastard!*" he called, as he punched the graffiti- and piss-stained wall.

He could have jumped, he knew he could. He could have made it. The Jet Skis were big enough to carry three. Jerry would have picked him up from the water—he would never have left him. But Martin couldn't do it. He couldn't jeopardise or interfere with his friends' escape. If he had tried to escape and relied on Jerry, all three of them would—or could—have been captured.

He lay on the floor in the blood from his wounds and the piss of the previous resident, crossed his legs, put his hands behind his head, and resigned himself to the fact that he'd better get used to this shit.

Chapter One Hundred and Twenty-Seven

"Let's look at the facts," said Wheeler.

"There is only one fact, Bill. Confidentiality."

"I know. That goes without saying."

"So why do we need facts? We know that Jerry Divine was responsible for the diamond robbery in Antwerp, just as we know about the others: Spain, France, Italy, and Ireland. It really doesn't matter now, Bill. What matters is that when we go to Musselburgh, we keep an open mind. Whatever it is they want us to agree to, we agree."

"But—"

"No buts, Bill. I can leave you out of this; it's up to you." There was no way Phelps wanted to leave Bill Wheeler out of anything. If, at a later date, things were to go haywire, he would need someone to blame, and who better than Bill Wheeler? There was a clear motive that Wheeler would happily see the demise of Jerry Divine. He didn't know that his superior was aware of this, and Phelps wasn't about to let him know—not just yet anyway.

"This is very cloak-and-dagger, Sir."

"You've been here before, Bill," replied Phelps, stopping at the large ornate gates. "You know how these people work."

"Who exactly is this old man?"

"A need-to-know basis," he answered, touching the side of his nose as he pulled the car through the open gates. The sentry checked the identification with a torch, which Phelps showed him through the open window.

They were greeted at the door by the same man who had welcomed him and Barry Divine six years ago, and were taken by him into the same library. The old man, who had walked in the first time, was wheeled in a chair this time. He recognised Bill Wheeler immediately and smiled in his direction.

"Welcome, it is nice to see you again, Mr Wheeler."

"Thank you, Mr…?"

"Windsor," he offered, as he looked down and stroked his cat, which purred contentedly.

"Mr Windsor," said Wheeler. Phelps smiled. Wheeler continued, "It's very nice to see you too."

"I suppose it's very nice to see anyone," he said. Wheeler was confused. The old man looked up. "I understand it was touch-and-go." Realisation—and then relief—hit Wheeler. For some obscure reason, he took the statement as an initial threat.

Shortly after drinks were served, the others arrived and were introduced as Morgan and Freeman of MI6. Proceedings commenced without further ado, and it soon became apparent what all the secrecy was about.

"I'm sure that without Riat Venga, the world has been a much safer place for us all to live," said Morgan, taking a seat opposite Wheeler.

Wheeler couldn't get the thought of the actor from his mind. It was almost comical that the two should share his name combined, and the even funnier thing was the fact that Freeman looked just like him. Morgan, on the other hand, looked nothing like the actor. He was bald, with a large round face resting on broad shoulders as opposed to a neck. He was short and fat and looked nothing like a government agent.

"As you know, Mr Wheeler, one other was supposed to be eliminated that day. And one was placed in protective custody. Things deteriorated shortly after. Barry Stone absconded, which I suppose was always on the cards. We should have never agreed to his reprieve on the day, but we did, and that cost us dearly." He stopped to look at the old man. Wheeler remembered that by this time, six years ago, the old man was falling asleep. Not today. He was listening intently.

Morgan continued, "We sent two of our agents to take care of Stone. They didn't return." He took a drink and looked at Wheeler as if he was to blame. "We don't think he was responsible for their deaths, not directly anyway. But they didn't return, so we are assuming they were killed."

"Why are you telling us this?" asked Wheeler.

"Because you are—or have been—what shall we say? Almost *fanatical* in bringing Jerry Divine to justice."

"With all respect, Mr Morgan, that's my job."

"And you do it very well," said the old man. Wheeler was surprised.

"I'm going to be frank with you, Mr Wheeler, and that includes everyone in this room. Barry Stone and Jerry Divine are to be... no more."

"As in *killed*?"

"However you wish to phrase it."

"So why are you telling me?"

"Because your investigation could contaminate our mission." He looked at Wheeler, then to Phelps. Phelps took his cue.

"You see, Bill, Barry Stone was always a threat. He knew that the killing of Riat Venga and the attempt on the life of Jerry Divine were sanctioned in this very room. He knew who was involved, and without going into detail, it could have been very embarrassing for some people."

"I'm beginning to understand. But why not just do away with Stone? Why kill Divine?"

"Quite simply because Stone has made contact with Divine. He must have told him everything. How else could he explain his reincarnation?"

Chapter One Hundred and Twenty-Eight

Abdul checked himself in the mirror. He brushed his left foot behind the lower calf of his right leg and felt the bulge of the miniature Walther PPK. He had been searched before and was sure that unless he was frisked fully, it was unlikely the small gun would be detected. If it was, he was sure he would get away with it. He wasn't told *not* to carry, and he would assure Alba Venga that he always did, unless, of course, he was going through an airport. He turned on the cold water and cupped enough to soak his flushed face and greased-back hair. Again, he stood up straight, took some deep breaths, and walked as confidently as he was able from the toilet and into the bar. Rojani was waiting for him.

"Come, Alba is waiting."

"You know why I call for you, Abdul?"

"No," answered Abdul. He had had no need to worry about the gun. He wasn't searched; there was no need because it would be impossible to reach it before one, or any, of the six minders got to him before he got to the gun. Alba didn't speak. He walked from behind the large desk to a drinks cabinet and poured himself a ginger beer.

"A drink for you, Abdul?" He didn't answer. He didn't like the tone of voice; it was almost mocking. "We are looking to open another casino in Algiers. Do you think this will be good, Abdul?" Again, Abdul chose not to answer.

"Champagne?" Alba tried. The sarcasm wasn't hidden.

"Why don't you come to the point, Alba? I am going to be honest with you, you are making me a little nervous."

"Don't be nervous, my friend. You are not in any danger. I would not offer a guest Champagne and then harm them. This would be a waste, no?"

"Then tell me, Alba, these people," he said, looking around at the menacing group, "why all the muscle?"

"They are my guests, Abdul, as you are too. Where is your friend Jerry?" he asked suddenly and without warning. Abdul was taken aback. *So this was it. Jerry Divine.*

"I don't know. You know as much as I do. He will contact us shortly."

"I know more than you, Abdul. I know that your Mr Jerry Divine is a traitor." He dropped two pictures of Jerry speaking with another man.

"What is this?" Abdul asked, picking them up from the desk.

"Jerry Divine is a traitor."

"Why? Why do you say this?"

"The other man in the picture is Barry Stone. The one who helped to have my brother killed. I had Divine followed; he met him at the airport."

"Maybe he has a reason."

"What reason could he have? I asked him the question, Abdul. You were there, you heard his reply. He said he has not seen this scoundrel Stone."

"Yes, I heard him, Alba, but—"

"Ah! Ah! Ah! Abdul, no *buts*, the pictures don't lie."

"I have to agree."

"But you see, my friend, I have another problem."

"Before you ask, Alba, I knew nothing of this."

"So you will take care of it?"

"You mean kill him?"

"This is what we do to people we cannot trust. We have told him of our plans."

Abdul could see a change; it started with the raised voice and the look in Alba's eyes. Abdul had to tread carefully here. He was, after all, the one who had introduced Divine—he was responsible. It was a shame, he had grown to like Jerry Divine; there was something different about him, a real sense of loyalty.

He decided there was danger in fighting the Englishman's corner. *What difference did it make to me?* There were others who would gladly take on the work. He would take care of Divine.

Chapter One Hundred and Twenty-Nine

Jerry was nervous, agitated, and without patience. *Surely Jamie had made it. But where the fuck was he?* Once again, he checked his watch. A clown spitting fire drew rapturous applause from the crowd. Hutchin and Winston would also be feeling a little uneasy. It was 10.35, and he had left them drinking beer in a strip bar. Nobody was in the mood, but it was Friday night in Amsterdam. Three men looking miserable, huddled over coffee in some hotel, would look far more suspicious. O'Rourke was over thirty minutes late. *What could be holding him up?*

The clown was now juggling four skittles while balancing a fifth on his forehead. The crowd clapped again. *How many times do the general public have to see such an act before it no longer becomes entertaining?* The hat was passed around the diminishing crowd. Jerry threw some change in it.

"You might need that."

"Where the fuck have you been? Do you have the diamonds?"

"Slow down, Jerry, slow down. I've been getting my cock sucked, why?"

"You're late. We said ten o'clock. Did you get the bag from Martin?"

"Yeah, yes, they're safe, Jerry. Sorry, I'm here now anyway," he said, trying to make light of the awkward predicament. "Where's the boys?" he asked as casually as he could muster.

"Like you care, you cunt."

"Of course I care, Jerry! What's got into you?"

Jerry didn't answer. He walked away from the crowd, with O'Rourke stepping at his heels. The sound of a mobile ringing had Divine turning sharply on his heels. Jamie took the phone from his pocket and was about to answer it before it was snatched from his hand.

"What the fuck are you doing with that? Why wasn't it given to Winston this morning?"

Jamie didn't answer. Jerry walked into the bar and beckoned Hutchin and Winston to step outside. He handed the mobile phone to Hutchin.

"What's this?"

"His phone. He's had it with him all day."

"On the job?"

"Ask him."

"You had this with you on the job?"

"What's the fucking problem, la?"

"Da fucking problem is *you*," said Hutchin, smashing the phone to the ground and stamping on it.

"What you doing, you cun—" He didn't manage to get the last word out before O'Brien grabbed him by the neck with one hand, while the other reached for the pistol secured behind his back. Jerry jumped between the two.

"This is not the time or place," he said through gritted teeth.

"You wanna take me on, you Irish cunt?"

"Take him, Jerry, take him away from me before I plug the bastard."

"We need to talk, Hutchin. We need to see what's left—Martin. We need to talk about that poor cunt." The mention of Martin McNess seemed to calm the situation. The four were now drawing attention from the passing public. The two men were separated, but if looks could kill, both would have been dead tonight.

It was just as easy to walk the narrow streets and passages of the red-light district as it was to hole up in a hotel room and discuss the events leading up to their current position. It wasn't the best, but for security, it was ideal.

"It could be nothing else but the phone, Jerry, I'm telling you," said Hutchin.

"How the fuck do you make that out?"

"Because those cunts act as a beacon. They pinpoint you to within a metre, and you don't have to be talking into them for the police to listen in. You know this anyway."

"He's right, Jamie. There is no way you should have had that with you on the job."

"I'm sorry, Jerry."

"Fucking sorry won't get Martin out."

"Ok, ok, let me think."

"Jerry?"

"What is it, Winston?"

"I don't like all this confrontation. Can I go back to the hotel?"

"You need to be here, Winston. We need to talk about Martin, what we're going to do for him—financially. He'll have to be looked after."

"I know, Jerry. Leave my whack in for him. I'm not interested in anything out of it. Martin can have mine, he deserves it." Jerry looked at the tall, beanpole of a black man, and a wave of compassion washed over him.

"We don't know what we have yet, Winston, but that is an amazing gesture—one which I'm sure Martin will appreciate. But Jamie got the bag from him; there'll be more than enough to go around. Don't be too hasty."

"I'm not, Jerry. Please, take my share and make sure he gets the best legal team. I don't need the money. I did it for you, Jerry, like before, mate. I'll do anything for you."

Hutchin and Jamie looked on. It was loyalty of the rarest kind, and it made them slightly ashamed that they had been arguing over security before discussing Martin's predicament.

"Whatever you say, Jerry, I'll agree with. Just leave me out." He turned and walked away.

Jerry looked at the remaining two and moved sideways to let a crowd of revellers pass by.

"Let's get out of here."

Chapter One Hundred and Thirty

When Stuli broke the news that the robbery had taken place, Barry couldn't believe it. Jerry had told him it was three weeks away. He had wired through the information, and the message had come back from a Daniel Vine that nothing would be happening for at least three weeks. *What the fuck was Jerry up to?* And if he could do this on the diamond job, what could he do with the cash in Gib? He would leave it for a day or two to see if Jerry contacted him. If he didn't, he would fly back to Spain and chase it up. But he wasn't happy, that was for sure.

Three more days passed, and still no word. Things didn't get any better for his state of mind when Stuli told him that the value of the stones taken was estimated to be in the region of ten million euros. The hotel was struggling, the new development was running out of money, and Stuli was asking for money owed from the original deal. And here was Jerry Divine with ten mil's worth of diamond and no contact, or cut, for the source.

A further two days passed before he picked up the phone and made the call.

"Hello?"

"Yes, hello, who's speaking please?" asked the friendly girl.

"It's Barry Stone, miss. Could I speak with Kristos, please?"

"Barry Stone. One momen—" She didn't finish before the receiver was taken from her.

"Hello, Barry. What can I do for you?"

"I have something for you, Kristos. Something very interesting, but you must come to me."

"I am very busy, Barry. It had better be worth my while. Are you in The Gambia?"

"Yes."

"Can you give me a clue?"

"Jerry Divine."

"And I must come to you?"

"It will be worth your while, Kristos, I can assure you."

"Do you have some merchandise ready?"

"This can be arranged."

"I'm on my way. Expect me tomorrow, flights permitting."

Barry was waiting for Kristos at Banjul airport. Koiduste came through arrivals with only an overnight bag. Barry shook his hand and ushered him into the waiting car.

"So, tell me."

Forty minutes later, they arrived at the hotel. Koiduste had said nothing. Barry had done all the talking, at times without even taking a breath. He didn't stop. Koiduste was fascinated and pleasantly surprised. He had absolutely no idea that the two went back as far as childhood. The information was invaluable, and the conditions that Stone stipulated were exactly what Kristos wanted. He wanted a part, if not all, of the action that Jerry Divine was planning—and the death of him, well, that was his plan anyway.

"You may have to help me, though."

"What can I do? Jerry is very careful; he has a sixth sense. I don't want to forewarn him. That would be too dangerous—for all of us."

"He has gone on the missing list. Nobody has seen him for a while. I have some of my people watching his home. We frequent the same restaurants—nothing. It's like he's vanished."

"He'll be back soon. He won't stay away from his family for too long. That's one weakness he has—he worships his family."

Chapter One Hundred and Thirty-One

There were no truer words spoken. Jerry Divine did love and worship his family. That's why he was at his mother's bedside within four hours of getting the news that she had recently suffered a massive stroke, followed by an even bigger, life-threatening heart attack. He made it to the private clinic, breaking every traffic law during the erratic journey from the airport.

"It's ok," said Victor, coming out to meet him at reception. "She's still with us."

"Thank God for that. How bad is it, Vic?"

"The doctor says she could leave us at any minute. Then again, she could last the night."

Jerry moved quickly, walking along the corridor without stopping at each swinging fire door. He slowed down outside the room and took a few long breaths to compose himself. Victor eventually caught up with him.

"Heather's in there."

"Ask her to give us a few minutes alone, Vic."

"Sure, Jerry. Me too?"

"Please."

When Jerry was alone with his mother in the room, he sat down beside her and took her frail hand in his. It was so delicate, so pure, that as he massaged it with his two hands, he got the most peculiar feeling that he was contaminating her—that he wasn't worthy to even touch her in her final moments. She was sleeping, and even then, his selfish side wanted her to wake. As he looked at her face, he remembered times gone by, times in his youth when he had caused her so much worry and pain. He wanted to tell her he was sorry—sorry for not being there, sorry for not being like Victor. He had always loved her, and to him, that should have been enough, but...

"Jerry," she whispered.

He moved the chair closer.

"Mum. It's me, Jerry, Mum, I'm here."

"Move closer, Jerry."

Jerry couldn't. He was almost on top of her. Her mouth was dry, and there were tiny beads of sweat on her nose. The heart monitor was bleeping at an even, steady pace. Jerry dreaded the inevitable constant buzz. He would refuse those damn electrical pads—based on what he had seen in the movies, those things would break her delicate ribs. No, when she went to sleep, he would let her go.

"Do you want a drink, Mum? Here," he said, placing the straw connected to the plastic bottle into her mouth.

"Thank you, Son."

"Take it easy, Mum. You're not going anywhere just yet."

"I am, my son. My time is near. Come closer, Jerry, there is something I must tell you."

He could hardly hear her—her voice was but a dry croak.

"What is it, Mum?" he said, leaning even closer, feeling the precious breath from her mouth.

"Your father, Jerry."

"Yes. I can hear you, Mum—my dad, go on."

She was struggling now, coughing and gasping for air. Jerry glanced at the red string hanging above the bedhead.

"What is it?"

"Do you remember your trips to Ireland as a child?"

He didn't answer. He looked at her—her eyes were fixed on him, but Jerry was sure they couldn't see. There were tears in them, welling up to flood. Jerry didn't want her to cry, not now, not on her deathbed. He had made her cry enough throughout his life. He didn't want to remember her like this. He gently sponged them up with a tissue. *What did Ireland have to do with anything?* She must be delirious, that was it.

"It's alright, Mum, just relax."

"I have to tell you this, Jerry. You need to know before it's too late."

Jerry stayed silent for the next twenty-five minutes and the remainder of his mother's life as she struggled to tell him what was so important to her. He was in total shock as she died in his arms. Tears rolled down his face and dropped into the wisps of her grey hair. Even in her last, precious moments on this earth, she was a giver—even if it wasn't what Jerry had been expecting.

Chapter One Hundred and Thirty-Two

Jerry stopped the car, turned off the engine, but remained seated with the radio playing low. He looked out across the ocean from the elevated car park that the mountainside restaurant was privileged to have. He was early, but even so, this popular eatery was as busy as usual. The terrace was fully booked, as it always was on a bank holiday weekend.

He had chosen this place for two reasons: one, because it was local to a piece of land he had just acquired, and two, because it was unlikely that anyone from the criminal fraternity would be here tonight. His new lawyer, Francis Cordeso—who had done a great job getting the money released and having the charges hanging over Kath dropped—had booked thirty of the fifty tables for his wife's birthday party. Jerry had asked for a table in a secluded corner so that he could have a little privacy with his own guest. There was a lot to discuss, and he had given himself enough time since his mother's burial to fully digest and decide how and when to handle it.

The funeral had been a difficult time, more so because he had made the decision to stay away and watch it from a distance. He wasn't certain if the Belgian police and Europol were still looking for him. The message from Martin was that they weren't. The authorities knew Jerry was behind the heist, but the evidence wasn't enough for a conviction. Wheeler had visited McNess in prison and tried to get him to turn. It was a feeble attempt, Martin had said—merely a suggestion, and only half-heartedly put to him. Either Wheeler knew, before entering the prison, that he was wasting his time, or he knew something they didn't.

The diamond sale had gone through with as much precision as some of the cuts on the stones. They were collected from Amsterdam by a contact of the Indian, and the agreed €2,500,000 for the cut stones was collected three weeks later in Madrid. The uncut ones, which for some obscure reason weren't included in the valuation, were shipped to Bangladesh for cutting. Six weeks later, and just the day before yesterday, Jerry had met with the Indian, who had offered a further €4,200,000 for the finished product.

Jerry had tried to hide his excitement at the price for something he considered to be a complete bonus and was eagerly anticipating a similar response from Hutchin when he eventually turned up. He looked at his watch—it was eight-fifteen. He stepped out of the car and entered the building. He was greeted with a warm handshake and some conveyance papers from Francis. He kissed the solicitor's wife on both cheeks and wished her a happy birthday before he was shown to his table.

He was being watched as he left the car and entered the restaurant. The high-powered motorbike had stayed behind him, out of sight, as Jerry drove up the mountain. He hadn't seen or heard the bike when he pulled in to park the car off the narrow road. The two professionals on the bike had carried on up the mountain until they found a vantage point where they could look down and see Jerry leave the car and enter the restaurant.

Hutchin O'Brien entered the building and was approached by Cordeso, who was welcoming the guests. Jerry stood and smiled as his friend was pointed in his direction, sitting in the corner. He greeted him warmly and handed him a full glass of champagne.

"Not for me, Jerry. Water, I'll be grand."

"Drink it, Hutchin, you might need it."

"We have business to discuss, don't we?"

"What we have to discuss, business-wise, won't take a moment. Drink it, Hutchin."

"If you insist, it'd be rude not to."

Jerry laughed nervously. He couldn't understand why he was feeling so unsettled. He looked closely at Hutchin as he took his seat opposite, searching for any similarities. There were some, he supposed—the eyes maybe.

"What the fuck are you looking at me like that for?"

"Like what?"

"Like that! You're laughing at me without laughing."

Jerry laughed out loud.

"I've never heard that one before. *You're laughing at me without laughing,*" he chuckled. "That's a good one."

"I know what I mean. What is it?"

"I'll tell you later. Here, have another top-up," he said, lifting the bottle. "Get that down you."

The Irishman gulped the drink down and held his glass for Jerry to fill again.

"First things first," said Jerry, "and before the alcohol takes effect. Martin was sentenced to fourteen years."

"Fucking hell, Jerry, and we're drinking champagne?"

"It happens, Hutchin. You know this, I know this, and so did Martin. Us drinking champer—he wouldn't have it any other way."

"I suppose, but fucking hell, Jerry."

"I know."

"What about that scumbag O'Rourke?"

"I don't know. What do you want to do?"

"I think we should take him out."

"You really mean that? There's money to divide. I've to collect €4.2 million tomorrow, or we can have it anywhere we want for 7%."

"I'll leave that to you, Jerry. I do need some in Ireland though. Will he do it for any less?"

"I'll see."

"We can't be giving that bastard anything."

"I know, but we might have to take him out if we don't."

"You mean, you think he'll talk?"

"I don't know, Hutchin. I really don't."

"Did he get anything for the first payment?"

"Enough."

"Enough not to draw suspicion?"

"I'm not sure. I haven't heard from him; he's expecting me to contact him soon."

"Leave that to me," said the Irishman, holding his glass for Jerry to fill. Jerry checked the bottle—it was empty. He held it up to signal the waiter.

"I think we should send a message to Martin, let him decide."

"That's fair," said Hutchin, ending the conversation as far as Jamie O'Rourke was concerned.

"What kind of man was your father, Hutchin?"

"That's a funny question. Why do you ask?"

"Why do you think we do the things we do?"

"I can only answer that question for myself. We all have our own reasons, I'm sure. You tell me, Jerry, why do *you* do what you do?"

Jerry didn't answer. He looked across the table, smiled with his eyes, and let the side of his mouth curl. The room had quietened slightly, as most of the invited guests had moved into the next room for music and dancing. Francis had come over to the table periodically to check that everything was alright and to make sure Jerry and his friend were having a good time. He also asked, through the side of his mouth, if Jerry had any messages for Kath and the children. Jerry didn't take too kindly to this, especially when it was asked after a few drinks. He completely ignored the question and made a mental note to speak with him about it later.

Jerry had drunk just enough alcohol to still have his wits about him, along with the courage that was somehow required to bring up the more important personal matter. He wondered if Hutchin was aware of what he was about to say and decided to ask the question outright.

"Is there something from our past that you know, and I shouldn't?"

The Irishman looked at Jerry. He didn't answer the question, clearly reviewing the situation. It only took this brief moment for Jerry to realise that Hutchin did know. Hutchin looked into his half-empty glass.

"You do, don't you?" pressed Jerry.

"How did you find out?"

"I had no idea. None whatsoever." He paused. "My mother told me."

"Before she died?" Hutchin looked up from his glass, emptied it, and glanced toward the waiter. When the glass was refilled and they were left alone, he spoke.

"I was told when I was young that we were brothers. My father—*our* father—told me never to tell anyone. He was proud of you, Jerry. He loved your mother and respected your father." He looked up. "Arnie. Arnie Divine. A good man. Arnie was a good, hardworking, straight, domestic man. Your mother would never leave Arnie. I was only a teenager when I discovered the truth, Jerry. The old man was drunk one night, and he told me everything. Those trips you made to Ireland as a kid were arranged with your dad. He knew and had to accept it. Who the fuck would go up against Gerard Devlin?"

"When did this happen? How? Did she have an affair with your father?"

"Yes. Dad was on the run over there in the UK, staying in Liverpool. As you know, Liverpool is where your parents were before they moved to Yorkshire."

"An affair. Mum didn't go into detail. She told me his name and a few other bits and bats—you, for instance. Did she love him?"

"My Da loved her, that's the truth."

"Fucking hell."

"I know, it's crazy, isn't it?"

"You're my brother."

"I am, kid."

"Do we hug? What do we do?"

"We do as we do, Jerry. We carry on doing as we do."

"Maybe this is the answer to the question."

"The question?" asked Hutchin, puzzled.

"Why we do the things we do."

"Devlin, you mean?"

"Yes, it's in our blood."

"He was a real man's man, I'll tell ya. A villain through and through."

"I want to talk with you about him, Hutchin. I want to know what he was about. This could be a long night, are you alright with that?"

"It would be my pleasure."

"Let me arrange for my driver to come and collect the car. I don't want to leave it up here. This place gets too remote after hours. We can take a cab down to the port later."

Hutchin was another hour into the family history and tales before the waiter came over and told Jerry there was a man waiting for him at the bar. He looked over and saw Irish Tom. Excusing himself, Jerry told Hutchin he wouldn't be more than a few seconds. Fishing the security card and remote from his pocket, he handed them to Tom and asked him to collect him at the Torrocabrada Hotel in Benalmádena at lunchtime the next day. He looked at his watch and realised they were already into the next day, so he corrected himself, gave Tom a five-hundred-euro note, and walked back to Hutchin, who was seated at the only occupied table.

Tom Callaghan was happy for the work; there had been little of it lately. Jerry seemed to have distanced himself from him for some reason. Tom had had a few meetings with the police since being released after being interviewed regarding the property investigation, but he could tell them nothing—Jerry Divine told him nothing—so what could he say? He had tried to bluff his way into a few quid, but that detective with the daughter was too sharp; there were no flies on him.

He hoped that by getting this last job, Jerry was coming round, and maybe the work would pick up, allowing him to learn something—something he could sell. He knew Jerry was having family problems, which could have been another reason for his strange behaviour. *Kathleen. There's a good catch for someone.* She still lived in that big house and retained her fancy jeep and things. *Maybe I should try my luck.*

He swapped the Bin Laden note in his top pocket for the wrap of cocaine, smiling as he chopped a line on the open glove box with the ignition card. Before inserting it into the slot, he changed the music from the soul ballads of Jerry's choice to something more up-tempo, pressed the starter button, and blew himself—and the top-of-the-range Mercedes—to smithereens.

The rider and pillion smiled—it was a job well done. It was too dark to realise that the job had been a total disaster. As the bike descended the mountain and dropped gears to accommodate the hairpin bends, the rider slowed to see a crowd gathering at the side entrance of the restaurant. They were dark silhouettes against the billows of smoke and flames. There was a feeble attempt by a brave member of staff to extinguish the fire with a domestic extinguisher, but then came a second explosion.

Jerry watched from the back of the crowd, Hutchin standing silently beside him. Hutchin nudged Jerry in the ribs. Jerry looked at him and followed the direction of his gaze. He watched as the bike slowed momentarily before speeding off.

The newspaper reports suggested it was a gangland killing. There was one man dead, but the body was too incinerated to form any type of identification. The car belonged to a businessman who had recently been under investigation for property corruption as part of Operation Escatura. A name could only be given after further tests, and the family of the assumed victim were made aware.

Epilogue

Kath had recovered well. The antidepressants and the many hours of counselling seemed to have worked. The girls had returned to Spain from the UK, where they had been staying with Kath's elderly parents. They had attended their grandmother Divine's funeral with Uncle Victor and Aunty Heather and didn't realise that, throughout the ordeal, they were being watched by their father. He had been proud of the way the two had conducted themselves under such extreme sadness and felt guilty that, for the sake of security, he couldn't comfort them.

Kathleen Divine refused to believe that her husband was dead. He would have got word to her if he was in danger. He would have come back to say goodbye. She talked to Harold most nights about him—this was good therapy and had been advised by her counsellor. Harold had been a godsend. She and the girls loved having him stay with them after he had been discharged from the hospital. He hadn't ventured out much during his convalescence. Little Julie would push him in his chair around the pool, and one time Kath and Jasmine came home to find the little one pushing him down the road.

But if anything, it was the charity work that kept her sane, and the upcoming Breast-Mate event at the Don Carlos Hotel took up most of her time. Harold was back on his feet now and in good form. He had told her it would be a pleasure to escort her to the event and made her promise to save the last dance for him. What was more worrying was the fact that Jerry and his friends would not be in attendance. They had always been the major players when it came to raising funds. The charity auction was always a buzz, with each of them paying well over the odds for items worth a fraction of the price. She and Debs had made cutbacks—they had to. Of course, there had been donations, many of them, but it was far from the glitzy event that had become the norm and the highlight of the Who's Who of Marbella and the Costa del Sol.

Many had heard the rumour that Kathleen's husband, Jerry Divine, and his partner had been involved in the big investigation currently ongoing. This was why attendance numbers were down compared to the previous year. Debs tried to assure Kath that it could be for any number of reasons, the current recession for one. But Kath couldn't be convinced. Although she was deeply grateful to those who did attend, she couldn't help but feel bitter towards those who didn't—especially, she thought, the ones who were probably up to their necks in it as much as her husband had been.

Even still, she put on a brave face as the cars began to arrive, and she was joined by Debs in greeting the guests.

"What are we going to do if we don't raise as much as all this has cost?" she asked out of the corner of her mouth.

"Don't you worry, Kath. There are some bloody good spenders here."

"Not as many as last year."

"Smile, Kath, you're frightening me."

Kath laughed at her friend, who went to embrace someone she recognised from the glossy magazines.

"You look truly beautiful, Kathleen."

"Why, thank you, Francis," she said, smiling broadly at the lawyer.

"You do, Kath," said Debs. "That dress is gorgeous. Who is it?"

"Stella McCartney," she answered, smoothing the black fabric over her flat stomach.

She did feel good. She was forty years old and, for what she had gone through recently, she felt exceptionally good. *And sexy.* She was almost guilty and embarrassed to feel this way. She smiled at more guests arriving on foot and caught her reflection in the mirror. It made her look taller than her five feet five inches and a touch slimmer—or was that just her looking back? She *did* look good. And sexy.

Why not?

The simple string of pearls, which hung to meet the top of her strapless dress, was all the jewellery she wore besides her wedding ring. Her hair was put up in a bun, with a single ringlet falling from each side, purposely to give—not the *tonight Josephine* effect. Jasmine had taken time to apply her makeup, and Harold had taken photographs of each of them before they left the house.

"Your dad would be so proud of you tonight, girls. The three of you—you all look beautiful."

"Thank you, Harold," said Jasmine.

"Yes, thank you," echoed Julie.

"Come on, girls, we don't want to be late to greet the guests."

Divine Intervention

Will! Your dad would be so proud of you tonight. Will!

It had happened on more than one occasion—Harold had spoken of Jerry in the present tense. Maybe it was his age. Maybe not, because as old as Harold was, she had never met anyone as sharp. And that included Jerry.

"I think you're right, Kath," said Debs. "The numbers are low, and the first half a dozen lots have raised only half of what we were hoping for."

"I know. What are we going to do?"

"Keep smiling. Why was Harold called into the manager's office?"

"I'm not sure. You know him, he knows everyone."

"I have no idea who it was, Mr Rawson. He had no invite but managed to bypass security. I will look into that later—possibly a bribe," the manager said, pursing his lips behind the grey goatee beard. "He left this."

He handed Harold a small package. Harold looked surprised but wasn't—he knew full well what this was and who it was from. He ripped the paper from the small parcel and looked bewildered.

"Who would send me anything? And to here, of all places?"

"Let us find out." The manager wasn't going anywhere. He stood over Harold as the old man took a seat without invitation.

"There's a letter here," Harold said, reading aloud. "'Please accept this donation in the form of a diamond. I hope that it helps to reach your financial goal. The charity work you do, and the proceeds of which go on to help so many people who are living with and suffering from breast cancer, is something which deserves all recognition. You truly are an inspiration, and you should know that you make others proud.'"

"Who is it from?"

"It doesn't say. There is total anonymity."

"Our final lot, ladies and gentlemen, is a late entry. You won't see it in your catalogues, I'm afraid, but you are welcome to view it."

There was a murmur around the room, and a rumour had spread that an anonymous donation had been made by someone not in attendance.

"Mrs Divine will be coming to each table with the diamond. I can tell you, ladies and gentlemen, that it is a very generous donation from someone who knows who he or she is, and we thank them from the bottom of our hearts. We are expecting the diamond, which I can tell you," he continued as he took a description and valuation from a large envelope, "is an unusual heart-shaped diamond, measuring eight point four carats. That's nearly eight and a half carats, ladies and gentlemen. It is an F in colour, and for those of us who don't know, that is bordering on the best grade. So, please have a look and don't be afraid to get the chequebooks out. This really is an opportunity to do something worthwhile and, at the same time, invest in a quality stone."

When Kath had finished walking around the tables, she was exhausted. It had taken nearly two hours, and she hadn't let the diamond out of her sight. Debs had taken care of little Julie, while Jasmine had sat beside Harold, eagerly anticipating what the precious stone would fetch in the sale.

The bidding started at sixty thousand euros, which was ridiculous, but this was an auction—it wasn't where it started, but where it finished. Kath was surprised by the excitement and buzz the late arrival had stirred up within the room. There were over two hundred people present, down on last year but only by a few. There was a recession, but even so, some very wealthy and influential people were here tonight.

"Sixty-five!" someone called.

"Seventy!" came from another direction.

"Seventy-five!" Harold held his hand up. Little Julie pulled it down, and he laughed. Kath looked down from the stage and laughed too.

"Eighty-five!"

"Tens now, ladies and gentlemen, we're going up in tens." There was a small applause. "Do I have ninety-five?"

"Hundred!"

"One hundred thousand euros! Thank you very much, madam. Do I have one ten?"

"One ten!"

"Thank you, Sir!"

And so the bidding went on, and on, until eventually it stalled slightly at two hundred and sixty-five thousand euros.

"It's once," the auctioneer announced, pausing as silence fell over the room. "It's twice." He scanned the room. "The hammer's going down, ladies and gentlemen, make no mistake. This is truly a magnificent diamond and a great opportunity. This stone will only appreciate in value." His voice rose as he prepared to end the auction. "It's going three times." He raised the small wooden mallet above his head. The room was now completely still.

"Three hundred thousand!"

The voice came from the back of the room, spoken in a thick Irish accent. There was a collective intake of breath from all present, and everyone turned to see Hutchin O'Brien standing there. The sight brought a tear to Kathleen's eyes. She hadn't seen him in so long—a year, in fact, at the last breast cancer event. She knew instinctively that Jerry was behind the diamond and Hutchin's attendance.

She looked down at Harold, who was smiling up at her. Jasmine hugged the old man from behind, and he tapped her small, feminine hands and nodded. The hammer came down beside Kath with a clatter, making her jump. She clapped along with the rest of the crowd and glanced back towards Hutchin. The manager of the Don Carlos was threading his way through the tables toward the successful bidder.

Kath felt a tugging at her dress and looked down to see little Julie pulling at the material. She scooped her into her arms—Julie was getting too big for this, but never too old to be her baby. Once again, Kath looked toward Hutchin, who was now writing out a cheque for the diamond. It was agreed that only ten percent would be required until the stone was authenticated.

It suddenly dawned on her that Hutchin could very well be the only one in the room who already knew that the diamond was real. He finished writing the cheque and handed it to Debs, who had followed at the heels of the manager. A photographer was beckoned, but Hutchin waved off the attention, modestly refusing. He looked up and smiled at Kath before leaving the building.

Kath wasn't certain, but she thought she saw him approach a tall, handsome man with a grey beard. The man didn't resemble Jerry, but he certainly had his mannerisms. She watched as the two exited the building.

Jerry was happy with the way things had developed. Harold had told him, through Francis Cordeso acting as intermediary, that Kath and Debs were concerned about this year's event. The plan had worked, and he hoped that by introducing the diamond, and Hutchin, at the very end, he had given Kath the intended message. Now all that was left was for him to complete some unfinished business before he could come back into their lives. They were safe, and he was proud.

Terry Wilcock

The Beginning…

About the Author

Terry Wilcock was born and raised on what some would consider a large underprivileged council estate in Bradford.

From a young age, he dreamed of one day escaping the concrete jungle and seeing the world, this he did but via approved school for delinquents, detention and borstal, places which were further education to a life of crime.

More serious matters resulted in lengthy prison sentences where he buckled down and found strength in faith of the Lord Jesus Christ, working in the prison library, he taught himself to 10 key types eventually to the skill of 100wpm.

Running around the prison yard, he would reflect and visualise his life gone by and write what he had seen in his mind's eye the next day after cleaning duty.

Divine Intervention took only 6 months to complete at the back end of a 10-year prison sentence, which Terry is currently appealing against conviction.

Terry also intends to one day complete a prequel and sequel which were also started at the back end of the same prison sentence. He says hopefully some good will come from bad judgment.

He currently lives in Devon with his two daughters and two grandchildren, he says he is both Mum and Dad after losing his wife, Carol, to cancer in 2015.

Printed in Great Britain
by Amazon